Tongue in Cheek

FIONA WALKER

TONGUE IN CHEEK

HODDER &
STOUGHTON

A CIP catalogue record for this title is
available from the British Library

HB ISBN 0 340 82074 8
TPB ISBN 0 340 82075 6

Typeset in Plantin Light by Palimpsest Book Production Limited,
Polmont, Stirlingshire

Printed and bound by
Clays Ltd, St Ives plc

Hodder Headline's policy is to use papers that are natural,
renewable and recyclable products and made from wood grown
in sustainable forests. The logging and manufacturing processes are
expected to conform to the environmental regulations of the country of origin.

Hodder and Stoughton Ltd
A division of Hodder Headline
338 Euston Road
London NW1 3BH

To my lovely in-laws – the magnificent Maidenhead svigermor and svigerfar; the dressage rider, karate-kicker, X-box expert and sausage-addict who all live deep in the Woodley; and the Yorkshire Phantom-riders and Spook-walkers who took me to the Pleasure Garden. With love and thanks.

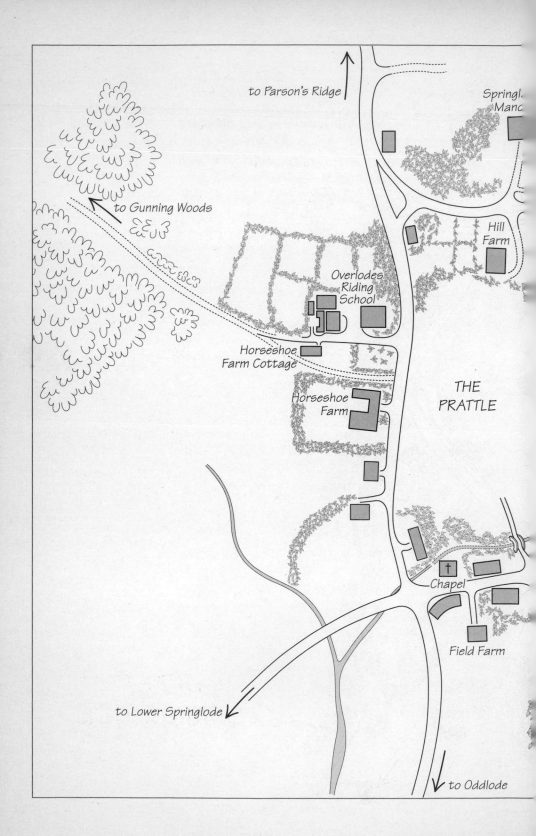

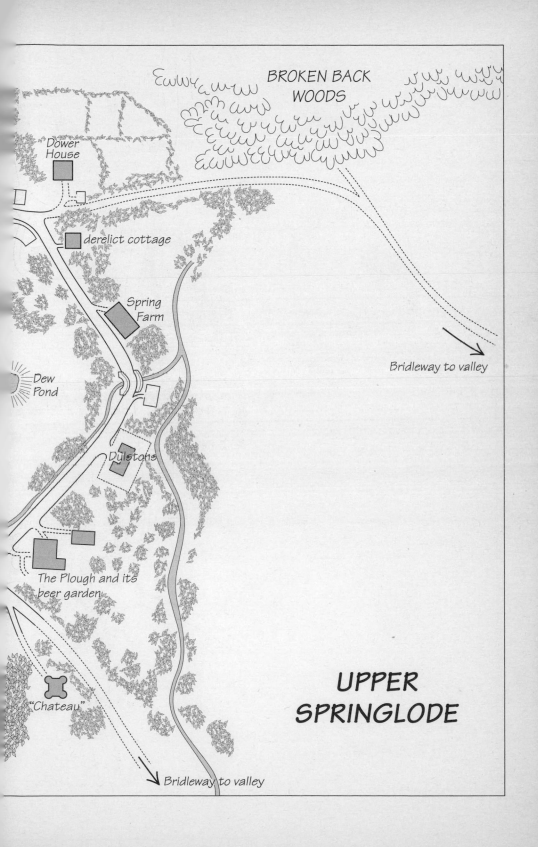

BROKEN BACK
WOODS

Dower
House

derelict cottage

Spring
Farm

Dew
Pond

Bridleway to valley

Dulstons

The Plough and its
beer garden

"Chateau"

UPPER
SPRINGLODE

Bridleway to valley

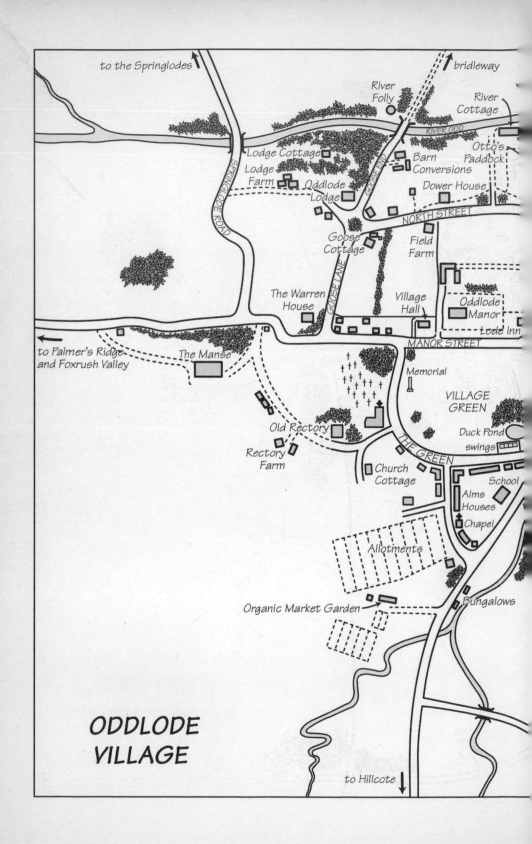

to the Springlodes

River
Folly

bridleway

River
Cottage

RIVER ODD

Otto's
Paddock

Lodge Cottage

Barn
Conversions

Lodge
Farm

Oddlode
Lodge

Dower House

GOOSE END

NORTH STREET

SPRINGLODE ROAD

Goose
Cottage

Field
Farm

GOOSE LANE

Oddlode
Manor

The Warren
House

Village
Hall

Lode Inn

MANOR STREET

to Palmer's Ridge
and Foxrush Valley

The Manse

Memorial

VILLAGE
GREEN

Duck Pond

Old Rectory

swings

Rectory
Farm

THE GREEN

Church
Cottage

School

Alms
Houses

Chapel

Allotments

Organic Market Garden

Bungalows

ODDLODE
VILLAGE

to Hillcote

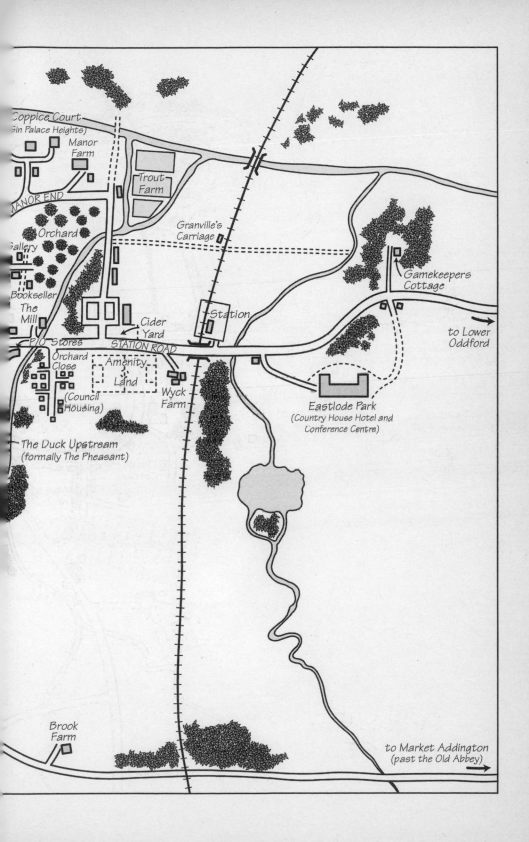

Coppice Court
(Gin Palace Heights)

Manor Farm

MANOR END

Trout Farm

Orchard

Gallery

Granville's Carriage

Bookseller
The Mill

Cider Yard

Station

Gamekeepers Cottage

to Lower Oddford

P/O Stores

STATION ROAD

Orchard Close

Amenity Land

(Council Housing)

Wyck Farm

Eastlode Park
(Country House Hotel and
Conference Centre)

The Duck Upstream
(formally The Pheasant)

Brook Farm

to Market Addington
(past the Old Abbey)

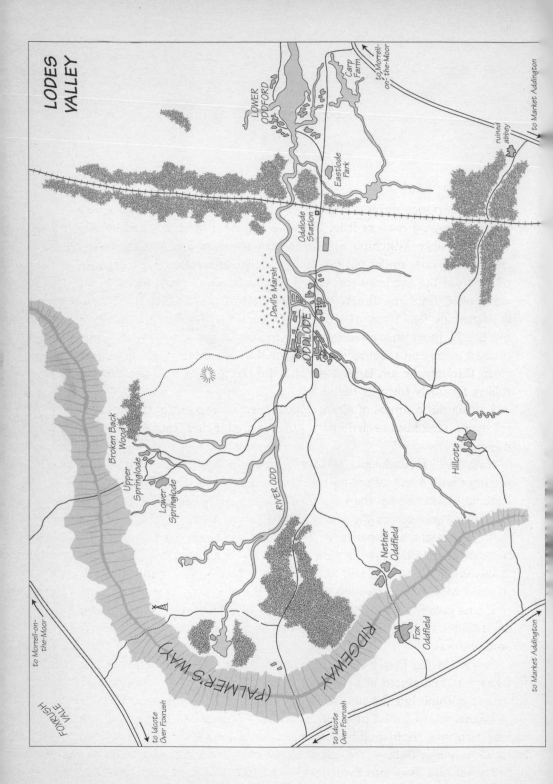

LODES VALLEY

LOWER ODDFORD

Carp Farm

to Morrell-on-the-Moor

to Market Addington

ruined abbey

Eastlode Park

Oddlode Station

Devil's Marsh

ODDLODE

Broken Back Wood

Upper Springlode

Lower Springlode

RIVER ODD

Hillcote

Nether Oddfield

Fox Oddfield

RIDGEWAY

(PALMER'S WAY)

to Morrell-on-the-Moor

FOXRUSH VALE

to Idcote Over Foxrush

to Idcote Over Foxrush

to Market Addington

Prologue

Diana Henriques threw a huge apple log onto the roaring fire in the library, stepping back as it let out a hissing haze of sparks and sweet-smelling smoke. Watching as orange tongues started to lick their way around the new tinder, she crouched down and selected the longest poker from the fire irons to prod at the firewood. Angrily, she stabbed and poked until the fire raged high above the grate and started to consume the log. Then, as she thrust the poker hard into the heart of the fire to move the apple log back and make space for another, the hooked metal end snagged on it and lifted it out of the grate. It jumped clean through the air, landed beyond the flagstone hearth and started rolling furiously towards her.

Letting out a squeal of alarm, Diana tried to leap out of the way but fell over on her high-heeled boots and sprawled inches from the burning missile.

'Silly girl!' Housekeeper Gladys Gates, who had been bustling past the door with a tray of vol-au-vents, set her salver down on the reading desk and snatched up the long tongs to put the log back into the fire. She then stamped on the singed hearthrug and helped Diana to her feet. 'You might have come of age, my girl, but you're not too old to be told off for playing with fire,' she tutted, picking up her tray again. 'Now, come along and talk to your guests in the blue drawing-room. Mr and Mrs Belling have gone to a lot of effort for you this evening.'

Diana poked her tongue out at the starched white cotton back as she trailed after Gladys. She doubted most of the guests would even know who she was.

It was Boxing Day, and Diana's eighteenth birthday. A formal drinks party was being held at her aunt's home, Oddlode Manor, where talk was of nothing but the fine day's hunting that had been enjoyed.

Diana, who loathed hunting (although would never admit that this was because it frightened her), was piqued that her aunt Isabel – known to all as Hell's Bells – had used the party as an excuse to invite the horsy set. She was also livid that her mother was taking a Caribbean Christmas cruise with her new boyfriend, James Dulston, and had abandoned her on such a seminal day. Her father, Luis, was in Buenos Aires with his new family. Younger half-brother Rory and cousin Spurs were causing havoc by feeding all the canapés to the hounds in the nearby kennels. Eccentric Aunt Til had disappeared into a hothouse with her lover, Reg Wyck, closely pursued by head gardener Granville Gates who didn't want his winter salads damaged. Only Nanny Crump was showing any degree of family pride – and she wasn't even a relation.

It was the early 1980s and Diana, who longed to look like Blondie despite her dark skin and black hair, had defied Nanny and her aunt by rejecting their choice of cocktail dress in favour of a boob tube, zipped mini skirt, fishnet tights and thigh-high boots. These were in honour of Amos, who naturally had not been invited to the party. The young bloods who had were all vying to play noughts and crosses on her cross-hatched hosiery.

Diana could only think of Amos. Her heart was thumping in time to the background music – cheesy high-gloss rock provided by local band Foxy Lady (everything had a hunting theme, she noted). It was at least to her aunt's credit that she had sought out something other than the usual Maddington chamber quartet to appeal to the 'youth'. Foxy Lady – average age forty-seven – was about as rock-on as the Lodes valley got. They were currently thrashing out a bad cover version of *Crazy Little Thing Called Love* with the aid of three lead guitars, a steel drum and a saxophone. Diana, who knew that love was far crazier than that, listened to her aunt's husband, St John Belling, making duty conversation, and smiled into the distance.

'Dancing later, eh?' St John was swaying cheerfully, blonde mane falling across his faded blue eyes.

Diana nodded vaguely. She wasn't planning to stick around for the dancing. Amos loved her; she loved Amos. What a high.

'Damn shame you didn't ride out today.' St John flicked back his hair. 'Damned fine point. We covered most of the Gunning Estate – almost worthy of the old midnight steeplechase. Full moon's on New Year's Day this year, y'know. Used to love that race. You're old enough to take part if it were still run now, eh?'

Diana couldn't be bothered to reminisce about bygone local traditions like the steeplechase, especially not with her politician uncle – a man who spoke as though he were dictating a pre-war telegram. Since being promoted to a junior post in Thatcher's defence ministry, he was becoming more and more like Richard Burton in *Where Eagles Dare*.

Foxy Lady's saxophonist let rip with the classic *Baker Street* riff and

Diana imagined Amos waiting for her in Gunning woods. She could feel her fishnets grating against her shaking knees at the prospect.

They had arranged to meet later. They were going to run away together. Gretna Green! They'd talked it through endlessly. She didn't care about her A levels. She could finish those another time. She wanted Amos for life.

'You met Tim Lampeter yet?' St John was beckoning over one of the young bloods. 'Just out of Sandhurst. Destined for great things in the Army.' He squeezed her arm as he spun her around to meet the eager, square-jawed youth.

Tim Lampeter made stilted conversation about the car that Diana had been given for her birthday by her absent mother – a Golf parked ostentatiously by the Manor's portico, covered with big ribbons and balloons.

'Got one myself. Jolly fun to drive. Passed your test long?'

Diana, who had failed her test twice already, couldn't be bothered to talk to him. She could drive well enough to get as far as the Gunning Estate woods and Amos could take it from there. Thank you, Mummy. Absent parent you might be, but you're generous in your guilt. Cinderella has her pumpkin just in time for the pantomime to begin.

Tim couldn't stop staring at her criss-crossed thighs – the olive skin glistening beneath the fishnets, the boot tops pointing their shiny leather fronts up at the zipped splits in her skirt.

'Get any other nice presents?'

'Polo pony from Daddy, diamond bracelet from Bell and St John, emerald brooch from Uncle Belvoir,' she started reeling off the list without thinking.

Tim's already red face reddened excitedly as he registered the pots to be hunted here.

Diana looked at her watch – a Cartier – another birthday gift from a godparent she barely remembered. Not long now.

'Am I boring you?'

She looked up at him, trying to remember who he was. 'A bit. Excuse me.'

She locked herself in an upstairs bathroom, heart truly hammering now. She couldn't leave until the guests were all too drunk to notice. It wouldn't be long. She must be patient.

She splashed her face with cold water and pressed her nostrils tightly together, breathing slowly and evenly through her mouth.

Life with Amos. It meant giving up all the privileges. She would never sit on her polo pony. She would only wear the jewels tonight before they would have to be sold. The Golf would have to go too, along with the fur coat and the watch.

She started to laugh. It would be such a blessed relief. Such a blessed relief.

They were dancing by the time she went back downstairs, the lights low, the bawdiness increasing. Someone was blowing a hunting horn.

They had forgotten it was her birthday. It hadn't taken long. It was safe to go. She went to collect her coat, bag and car keys from their hiding place in St John's gunroom.

'There you are!' warbled a voice.

Diana froze halfway along the back lobby. Almost safe.

Nanny Crump was still on manoeuvres. 'A nice young man was asking after you. I think he wanted to mark your dance card.'

'How lovely.' She cleared her throat, hoping that Nanny had been on the sherry and wouldn't be too hard to give the slip.

'Where *are* you going to?'

Nanny Crump was a sharp old bird.

'I have something special prepared for Aunt Bell and St John – to thank them for hosting my party,' she lied with shameful ease. 'I was just going to collect it.'

'What a generous girl you are.' Nanny's parched-earth face softened. 'I shall wait here in case there are any stray blades roaming around. Young men are so playful these days. One wouldn't want you to get frightened.'

'Bless you, Nanny,' Diana tilted her head, mind churning, 'although I would also be *terribly* grateful if you could make sure Aunt Bell and St John are close at hand for my . . . er . . . surprise? They have been so busy all night.'

'No sooner said.' Nanny pressed her palms together and tapped her fingers happily to her mouth before bustling off.

Diana raced to the darkened gunroom, twisting her heels in her haste. Two glassy eyes gleamed at her in the half-light and she crept up to the stuffed antelope, known to all the family children as Bongo. Standing as tall as a man, Bongo was a hartebeest that had been shot between the wars by her grandfather, Francis Constantine, and then shipped all the way back from Kenya to become a glorified hat stand in Oddlode Manor. She had hidden her backpack behind him, and hung her car keys from one antler, still bearing their huge gift ribbon. Diana kissed his leathery nose.

'They won't trap me, Bongo. You just wait and see.'

Her heart burning with fear, she burst out of the back door and ran past the old yew hedge and through the frost-hardened garden to the edge of the house.

Bugger, bugger, bugger!

The driveway was full of guests reeling around with mulled wine and sparklers.

Her blood was up now. She no longer cared.

'Quick!' she shouted from the darkness. 'There's a naked couple doing it in the glasshouse! This way!'

She ducked behind the laurels as guests started to pour past her, tripping their way gleefully across the lawn. As they thinned out to the most drunken of stragglers, she slipped back out of her lair and hopped into her shiny new car.

It was boxed in by two Jags and a Land Rover. No matter. She could do three-point turns – her instructor had wept bitter tears teaching her.

Crunch went her gears. Crunch went her back bumper against a Jag. Crunch went her front bumper against a Land Rover. Crunch, crunch, crunch. Perfect! Three points. She jerked her way out of the drive in a bunny hop, took out most of the gatepost and spluttered away into the night, turning on her sidelights and wondering how in hell most people drove in the dark.

Amos was sheltering in the gate folly by the Pleasure Garden entrance, his bike propped up against a gargoyle. He was shaking with cold and agitation but, when he gathered her into his arms, she could feel the heat roaring from his heart.

'I love you, I love you, I love you.'

He kissed her so hard and so fast it was as though he was compressing every three hundred and sixty-five day year of her eighteen on the planet into a second. Diana almost suffocated with pleasure.

'You look beautiful, huntress.' He pulled away, spinning around her, admiring her in the cool illumination of the Golf's sidelights.

'I dressed for you.'

'Now you can undress for me, huntress.' He held out his hand, green eyes flashing silver in the car lights, his breath pluming dragon puffs in the frost.

'Shouldn't we go?' She glanced over her shoulder.

'No one followed you, did they?'

She shook her head.

'Then we're safe.' His black hair fell wildly into his lashes, his turned-up collars formed a Dracula crest around his throat. 'We can say farewell to our secret garden.'

'Call me Mary Lennox,' she smiled. 'And I shall call you Dickon.'

He cocked his head. 'Who are calling a Dick?'

Laughing, she took his hand and followed him through the hidden entrance.

For a moment, they both stalled, mesmerised and terrified.

'The lights are on,' he breathed. 'Granville was right. It *does* all still work.'

They had never been here after dark. It was alive. Diana could barely breathe.

'They switch on automatically,' Amos explained as he studied the dim pools of multi-coloured lights around him. 'Nobody has been maintaining this place for years. It was state of the art when it was built – everything's automatic.'

'W-who pays the electricity bill?'

He put his arm around her and breathed in her ear. 'Solar-powered. Firebrand was wild on alternative energy – they say he could heat a room with his charisma alone, so why not harness the sun? If anyone could, he could.'

'And they still work?'

Amos held out his hand into a green pool of light, casting a spidery shadow over a moss-encrusted statue of a nymph. 'They're a bit dim – and some of the bulbs have gone now. But it *all* works. Listen.'

Diana strained her ears to listen beyond the rustling of dead leaves in the bitter wind and the crashing thuds of her own heart. And then she heard the water. The fountains were working.

'The pumps are powered the same way. Amos broke away from her and wandered to a leaf-clogged pool, pulling her with him. 'This one is almost frozen through so there's hardly a trickle, but it still works. Look.'

'The bald lady has hair!' Diana gasped, starting to laugh, recognising an old friend.

They had often studied the bald lady curiously, wondering at the way she stood at the centre of her near-dry pool, arms spread ready to dive, head perforated with holes like an abstract depiction of a bathing cap. Diana had once joked that she was about to have her highlights done (having herself gone through the agony of the crochet hook dragging hair through a holed skullcap in search of blondeness). Now the lady revealed her secret as water trickled from those rusty holes, lit up by red and orange and yellow lights. The lady wasn't bald. She had the wildest of flowing locks; a cascade of water in a thousand different shades of fire. At full power she would be a pre-Raphaelite siren. Even reduced to a trickle, with some of her highlights stolen by dead light-bulbs, she was a Titian sylph with a mane that flowed across her narrow bronze shoulders, over her delicate shoulder-blades, her fine little nipples, her softly curved cold metal belly and her long thighs, to the leafy pool below.

Amos and Diana threaded their bodies together again, spinning slowly around as they studied the garden over each other's shoulders, wrapping out the cold.

'I had no idea it could be so beautiful.'

'It's come out to say goodbye.' Amos smiled into her cheek.

'I'll miss it so much here.'

'We'll come back, huntress,' he promised.

She shook her head, knowing that they both understood. 'It won't be here.'

He undressed her in the courtyard of fountains, moving her between the pools of light so that she revealed a carved flank in a new colour with every turn. The boots slid off to expose one copper fishnet leg and then one in steely blue; the top slithered away so that her bare torso danced with purple light. Her skirt dropped with a rasp of zips making her buttocks gleam gold and green in their netting like glass yacht buoys and, as the fishnets slipped off, her nakedness shifted into scarlet light and then deepest claret.

Diana could no longer feel the cold. She was getting hotter with every discarded layer. She was as bright and magical as the garden that she and Amos had discovered all those months ago. She reached for his belt, freeing him with one tug at a buckle and a touch of a zip. He was bursting to get out.

They slammed together against the cool of a marble fountain-back, turning again and again so that shoulders crashed against the frost-flecked slabs and their ankles became entwined with ivy fronds. Diana climbed his legs like a monkey, arching and drawing back to cup herself around his taut, impatient erection. She pushed him inside, feeling the soft fur of his balls against her buttocks as she slid to the hilt, her bubbling passion swallowing him up and then sending him away in a rising tide.

'I love you, I love you, I love you!' he screamed as she climbed him higher, his head between her breasts. She arched and leaped, too carried away to care that her shoulders and spine thrashed against stone. He bit her nipples, making her laugh and scream. His nails dug into her flesh. She arched back and back and back, driving him deeper. Her head was amongst the leaves. She was in the pond where the wild hair streamed. Her eyes danced with red and yellow light. She was choking. She was drowning. Harder and faster. No breath. Harder and faster. No breath.

'Yes!' she screamed, leaves flying as her head reared from the water. 'Yes!'

Great gulps of air crammed in and out of her lungs as the moment came. The magic wand drew lines in and out of her body, no longer confined by the barriers of skin and flesh and bone. It delved wherever it chose, stabbing joy into her belly and groin, tickling the soles of her feet, drawing a teasing pleasure line between her buttocks, jabbing merrily at her breasts and her navel, delving and delving into her foaming depths.

She could feel Amos still discharging fire within her – shot after shot as he laughed jubilantly. Her beautiful mercenary. He'd hit his target again. She kissed his twenty years from him as fast as he had claimed her eighteen. Her lips slid to his ear.

'I love you too.'

It was the first time that she had admitted it. It was the first time that she had told anyone that she loved them in her entire life. Tears slid happily from her eyes – scarlet on one cheek, gold on the other.

And then she looked up to see two barrels of a gun pointing at their heads.

The voice behind the shotgun was deathly cool and mocking, its tones killingly upper-class. 'Now that you two have fucked – rather sweetly, it must be said – how about adding the "off" to the equation?'

Diana was not good in a crisis. Her first reaction was to scream – which she did, loudly.

Amos was not particularly good in a crisis either. Looking up, his first reaction was to be provocatively angry. 'Get that thing out of our faces or you die.'

At least it stalled the gunman, who stepped back into a neat pool of blue light to reveal a broad-shouldered, baseball-capped silhouette. The shotgun was silver-sided and very real.

Diana screamed again. Amos pressed a hand to her mouth, his breath hot against her throat. She could feel his heart pounding fiercely against her chest, but his voice was as level as a newsreader's.

'We'll leave now. We'll never come back. Okay?'

The reply was laced with mirth. 'Oh, I know that you're going. I wanted to say farewell and see you on your way. Only fair after all the entertainment your little couplings have given me.'

They both stared wide-eyed. The gun didn't move from their skulls.

The voice drawled on. 'That was a ten, by the way. Thank you for finally showing some style. Your early attempts were quite pitiful.'

Not caring that he might get shot, Amos's voice rolled with thunder. 'You fucking pervert! You've watched –'

'Every single tupping.' The gun barrels stroked Diana's hair, making her shriek. 'You really have come on in leaps and bounds. I take it you were both virgins?'

When they didn't answer, the gunman slid the barrels under Diana's chin, lifting it so that her face was in red light, now fading to a weak glow from the bulb.

'You really are a ravishing creature. Very like your mother, as I recall.'

Diana gasped, too frightened to speak, her mind whirring.

'Who are you?' Amos demanded, daring to push the barrels away, shielding Diana as best he could.

The gun jerked back, pointing at him now. 'Get dressed and leave.'

Diana raced around in the shadows, seeking out her Blondie kit in the fading puddles of coloured light.

'Oh damn, my disco is about to close.' The gunman was watching her from a black corner, only his barrel tips lit in green. He was becoming quite chatty. 'Solar energy really is a let down at this time of year. I have a generator override, but it's too damned noisy and petrol is so ruddy hard to come by. I've almost drained your Volkswagen's tank, by the way, so be sure to get to a garage soon. I should have moved to the Med when they told me to.'

To her mortification, Diana couldn't find her boob tube – an item of clothing that shrank to a wizened twist of creased nothing when not shrink-wrapped around her curves.

'On Dusty's finger,' the gunman pointed out, helpfully aiming his gun in the direction of a pink-lit nymph. 'I think you'll find your stockings on Sandy's toe and you dropped a boot somewhere near Petula's pump outlet. I did try to – agh!'

'Fucking bastard!' Unnoticed in the gloom, Amos had thrust a thick arm around their assailant's throat and now pulled him back into the darkness.

The next moment there was a brief muzzle flash and a deafening blast of gunshot, followed by a shattering thud as the bald lady lost her head. Diana was standing right in the line of fire.

'Dusty!' the gunman cried out and then was silenced as Amos brought him down.

Diana pressed her hand to her cheek and felt the hot, wet beads of pain where she'd been caught by the edge of the gunshot. For a moment euphoria blanked out all sensation. She was alive. She was alive! Then she felt pain along her shoulders and arm. Just how alive was she? With a furious bellow, she blacked out.

She awoke to the smell of Dettol and dope.

Diana wondered if she was dreaming. If so, it was a very odd dream. Amos was dabbing her wounds with great wads of cotton wool soaked in the tea-brown antiseptic while a grey-haired Grizzly Adams pulled gunshot from her arm with tweezers. The proceedings were lit by what appeared to be two paraffin lamps hanging from hooks on a branch above her and a small circle of night lights around her. The rest was darkness. It felt worryingly occult.

'Shouldn't we be in Gretna Green by now?' she asked weakly. 'Or at least a casualty department?'

Dark fringe flopping through his lashes and curtaining his green eyes, Amos dropped his cotton wool and took her hand. 'You're going to be fine, huntress. We're looking after you.'

'*We?*' Diana felt herself blink, her face fighting to find a suitable expression. 'Excuse me, but didn't he just shoot me?' She pointed at Grizzly Adams with her good hand.

'Diana,' Amos turned to the bearded man. 'I want you to meet someone who's about to change both our lives for ever. For fucking ever.'

'Happy birthday.' A calloused hand took hers. 'You've just come into a fortune.'

I

In the lanes that cats-cradled the Cotswold hills, the air was so thick with thistle blossom that it looked as though it was snowing in midsummer. The thick lion's manes of blonde grasses along the verges barely stirred in the still heat haze, and the drooping, jewelled wild flowers weaving necklaces amongst them had no scent powerful enough to battle with the reek of melting tarmac.

In a record-breaking summer, this was the hottest day to date – a squinting, sunburnt August day, one week before the Bank Holiday. The ridge around the Lodes valley was a sun-starched pelmet, its tree-line stiff, dusty net curtains compared to the usual furled, pom-pommed drapes. The checked fields on its flanks made up a true summer patch-work – some yellow and polka-dotted with huge black plastic bales, or green embroidered with white sheep; some were striped with copper corn furrows, others the faded lovage velvet of set-aside and yet more the verdigris shot silk of well-munched pasture. Several combine harvesters were out – great mechanical locusts sending up clouds of dust as they worked through the hottest hours on a shift that would take them through the balm of evening and into the black cool of night.

For once, it was too hot for all but the most foolhardy of tourists to pedal or yomp or caravan between the little clustered villages that drew thousands to admire them year after year. Village stores had sold out of ice-creams, and their chilled drink fridges were almost empty. The small accident department in Market Addington cottage hospital was doing a roaring trade in burns and heat stroke. Idcote-over-Foxrush garden centre had finally managed to shift the last of the bulk order of bad-taste flowery sun-hats ordered seven years ago. It was that hot.

In one parish in the Lodes valley, three houses awaited new occu-pants, empty spectators to summer pastimes. Beside the lush emerald pile of Oddlode village green – saved from drought-ridden dust by its shading chestnut trees – a group of young children was playing cricket, overseen by one of the small, honey-coloured cottages whose deep-set peephole windows had kept a knowing eye on many generations. A mile away, alongside the hot solder of the railway line, another honey-stone house blinked its freshly cleaned upper windows out on to the Oddlode amenity ground, where local handyman Reg Wyck was mowing the parched grass and swearing at a pair of teenagers from the nearby estate who were sunbathing their soft, reddened bodies on the football pitch penalty spot.

High on the ridge above Oddlode, the third empty house watched through cataracts of thick dust as a group of horses from one of the many local yards hacked by, their riders carefully keeping to the dappled shade of the bridleway that led into the Gunning woods. One brushed a shoulder against the rampant buddleia overhanging the track from the cottage's garden and sent out a cloud of red admiral butterflies, spooking the horses into snorting dances. The butterflies soared over the wild, untamed garden and settled on the sills of the cottage's blind, smeary eyes – unexpected mascara anointing an elderly gaze as it waited for a new guardian angel.

It wasn't a day to move house. It wasn't a day to move far from a deckchair.

At Number Four Horseshoe Cottages in Oddlode, Gladys Gates had been at work since dawn. She had already Cif-ed every surface and wrapped every one of her dear friend Rose's three hundred and twenty eight ornaments in anticipation of its new tenants, the 'Unmarried Irish Couple' as she thought of them. The fact that the couple were not Irish and were, in fact, moving from East Anglia was immaterial to her.

Number Four, like the other three Horseshoe Cottages beside the village green in Oddlode, belonged to an era when few adults grew beyond five feet five. Its ceilings were absurdly low, weighed down by vast beams dripping with horse brasses that had crowned many an unsuspecting guest – supposing the squat doorways hadn't already called seconds out upon them. So-named because the first cottage in the terraced row was attached to the old forge, each Horseshoe Cottage boasted its own iron crescent over the door. Number Four's horseshoe was the rustiest and, according to local legend, had belonged to one of the best hunters in the county – a celebrated Gunning horse called Flint. After a particularly good day's sport, the shoe had been given to Simmons, the Wolds Hunt terrier man, who had lived in the cottage in the days when the hunt kennels were based at Oddlode Manor. Gladys remembered Simmons well, particularly his passion for pickling – himself as well as his vegetables, which had been amongst the first raised in the Oddlode allotments. Some of the cupboards in the cottage still smelled of vinegar and home-made wine. Rumour had it that Simmons hadn't needed embalming.

His niece, old Rose Simmons, had until recently lived in Number Four on her own. Taken into residential care after a particularly nasty bout of shingles earlier that summer, she looked increasingly unlikely to return home. Her family had consequently decided to rent out the cottage to stop it mouldering, although Gladys suspected that the reason they were only doing so on a three-month 'cash' let was in case the old dear snuffed it and they could make merry with the investment. It was a nice little nest egg. The cottage had once belonged to the Manor, but ownership had transferred to the Simmons family at around the same time as Rose had left service at Foxrush Hall to move in with her uncle. This had always struck Gladys as strange – the Constantine family, who had always owned the Manor, were a notoriously mean lot. Gladys could smell a scandal, but had never been able to get to the bottom of it. Even today's thorough tidy-up heralded no clues.

She collected the framed photographs from above the gas mantel, admiring one of the young Rose looking like Rita Hayworth.

She had once been a very beautiful woman. Gladys had somewhat idolised her as a girl and thought it a great shame she'd never married and had children of her own. Gladys had known Rose Simmons all her life and, being kind-hearted, she was happy to keep an eye on things in Rose's absence. She'd followed the fate of Number Four with interest, reporting to Rose as prospective tenants arrived to get the guided tour.

Miss Stillitoe had come alone, parking a very tatty little car beside the village green while Gladys was standing outside the nearby post office stores. Gladys, whose network of spies was notorious in the village, quickly ascertained that she was the new teacher appointed to take over from recently-retired Miss Frappington at Oddlode primary school. Young, petite and somewhat scruffy, Mo Stillitoe (Gladys assumed the 'Mo' was short for Maureen) was moving to the Cotswolds from Newmarket. She was thought to be a Cambridge graduate (an old campus parking permit still lived on her car windscreen), a vegetarian (seen buying salad sandwich from shop), a cat lover (cat hairs spotted on skirt) and something of a dancer (the way she moved gave it away). There wasn't much that got past the Manor's housekeeper. Gladys was not known locally as Glad Tidings for her cheery hellos alone; gossip was her life.

She later learned from Netta, the school secretary, that Miss Stillitoe was one of these modern girls who referred to her boyfriend as a partner, only naming him during her job interview as 'Pod'.

'Pod and Mo,' Gladys muttered under her breath as she adjusted the lovely print of working shire-horses that lived above the fireplace. They sounded like cartoon characters.

Finding out about Pod had not been easy, and Gladys was only part of the way through enquiries. His real name – which Gladys couldn't pronounce – had appeared in the rental agreement that Rose had shown her, along with his occupation.

It was when Gladys had discovered Padhraig Shannon to be a jockey that she'd made the mistaken Irish connection – with a name like that, it seemed a safe bet that Pod was a racing import from the Emerald Isle. Her boss, Sir St John Belling, was luckily a man of the turf, but was unfortunately also a man of few words. All week Gladys had been conducting frustrating investigations into Mr Shannon whilst serving meals at the Manor. She'd thus far only gleaned a few fascinating morsels – young Pod was, it seemed, a 'bad lot' who had brought the sport of kings into disrepute. He was no longer racing for a living. Gladys was agog.

Gladys – whose own cottage almost backed on to the Horseshoe Cottages gardens – had promised Rose that she would keep a close eye on the new tenants at Number Four. She had already placed a set of binoculars by her boxroom window and made sure the cherry tree was cut back enough to afford a good view. She was looking forward to the entertainment.

At Wyck Farm on the Lower Oddford road, agent Lloyd Fenniweather was playing with the two sets of keys that he had been handed by the developer, idly spinning them around his fingers like a gunslinger. As he awaited his buyers, he admired the fifth reincarnation of the old house that he'd seen in as many years. It had certainly taken some selling – and a lot of tarting up – but the farm had made him a very healthy commission. Thank goodness the Brakespears were in so much of a hurry when they bought it. They seemed a pleasant family, although he doubted they would stay long. Nobody did. They were moving from the luxury of a modern Essex gin palace. Wyck Farm was a much darker spirit, its cold comforts barely disguised by the glow of new chrome fittings, slate worktops and beech floors.

He gave the Brakespears a year at most. He would keep the house details on file just in case. No family, apart from its original owners, had lasted at Wyck Farm for more than four seasons. It seemed cursed to destroy marriages, and Lloyd already harboured doubts about Anke and Graham Brakespear. Estate agents soon learned to read the signs – they sold enough properties for divorcing couples. The Brakespears never touched one another, and rarely stood close enough together to be able to. They talked to and through their children more than to one another. The Danish mother had been the driving force and decision-maker behind the move, the others all dragging their feet. The husband – a self-made northerner – seemed as much a child to her as the teenagers and the young son. Lloyd, who had a penchant for blondes, rather fancied Anke Brakespear, who had a Bo Derek older woman appeal, with that amazing bone structure and supercool elegance. She was far too tall to be a practical option, but he'd nevertheless allowed himself a few passing fantasies about showing her around the property very, very thoroughly – particularly the master bedroom suite and its vast whirlpool bath.

He smiled to himself now, realising that Anke's whistle-stop viewing was the very reason that he had finally shifted Wyck Farm off his books. The bath – like most other things in the house – was likely to explode the moment it was switched on. He'd had a very nasty moment with the electric gates only that morning.

Letting the sun lick a few more highlights into his treacle toffee hair and dust a few more freckles on to his bronzed cheeks as he gazed up at the gables, Lloyd pondered the old place's transformation from tatty, rundown farmhouse owned by the legendary Wyck family to desirable (or almost) country residence. It was only a shame, he reflected as yet another Intercity blasted past on one side while a loud game of football started up on another, that its location wasn't better.

At Overlodes Riding School – known to many as 'Legoverlodes' – Justine Jones was waiting forlornly in the car park, clutching her velvet riding hat. It seemed Rory Midwinter had yet again forgotten her lunch-time riding lesson. The lorry was missing from its parking space and the yard was deserted.

When The Archers came to a finish, Justine decided that it was time to give up. But, just as she was about to start the engine, she heard a rumble of tyres on gravel and leapt out of her car, heart hammering as it always did when she prepared to see Rory. Alas, the shiny metallic livery and blacked-out windows that emerged over the spruce hedges told her that this wasn't Rory's clapped out old Bedford cattle wagon. Justine watched in amazement as two vast, flashy horseboxes rolled into the drive. Each lorry had *Home Counties Horse Transport* emblazoned on its side.

★   ★   ★

Faith Brakespear was sulking furiously because she hadn't been allowed to travel from Essex with her beloved pony, Bert. She slouched angrily in the bucket seat of her brother Magnus's sports car, watching the convoy ahead of her through narrowed eyes. At its helm was her step-father, driving his pride and joy, the Lexus. Following was her mother, Anke, sharing the Mercedes off-roader with Faith's half-brother Chad, two dogs, two cats and a host of small, furry animals in perforated card-board boxes. Magnus and Faith brought up the rear, although there had until recently been another member of the cavalcade behind them. Faith cast fretful looks over her shoulder. They had lost the horsebox at traffic lights somewhere between Oxford and Witney. She was certain that there had been two *Home Counties Horse Transport* lorries following them until then. Not for the first time, she cursed her stepfather for selling the family's own horsebox when her mother retired from competition.

Faith was sweltering, her sweaty back and the clammy upholstered seat creating a hot doughy sandwich that had turned her T-shirt into a sodden filling. Magnus's 1980s Porsche was the only Brakespear car without air conditioning, but she had been loath to travel with her step-father in the leathery cool of the Lexus and her mother was being espe-cially protective of Chad today. This struck Faith as deeply unfair. After initial doubts, both the boys were now eager to move to the new farm-house, whereas Faith had been in a decline for weeks at the prospect. She might be almost twice Chad's age, but that didn't put her beyond the need to share a car with her mother on such a momentous day and perhaps allow herself a small cry. She couldn't cry in front of Magnus. He was hopeless. For almost two hours, he had alternately chatted into the Bluetooth headphone of his Nokia, selected teeth-grittingly alter-native tracks on the CD stacker, or cursed other drivers.

'Stupid bitch!' he spat as a woman in an Audi estate pulled out in front of him, butting into the Brakespear convoy. He leaned on the horn and two fingers appeared out of the sun-roof in front of him. 'Did you see that?!' He flashed his lights.

Through the Audi's tinted rear view window, two cherubic little faces poked their tongues out at the Porsche, making Faith smile for the first time that day. The smile turned into a laugh as a huge silver dog thrust its head out of a side window to stare at them, tongue lolling and ears flapping inside out. It was a Weimaraner – the rare and beautiful German gundog. It had been on the wish list that Faith had made when desperate for a puppy, but Graham, her stepfather, had insisted that, as the only child with a pony, she couldn't have her own dog, too. That honour had fallen to the spoiled Chad, now the proud owner of Bomber, the flatulent bull terrier. Faith secretly adored Bomber – certainly more than their other dog, Evig, the Japanese Akita bought for her mother as a fifth anniversary present from Graham. Weighing in at nine stone with eyes like a camp commandant, Evig – which meant forever in Danish – was cold-hearted, volatile and slavishly loyal to Faith's stepfather.

She glared irritably at the Lexus several cars ahead of them. Graham liked to flash his money around, but only very selectively, and Faith was convinced he singled her out for especially tight-fisted treatment. Not only was she not allowed a dog of her own, neither was she permitted a new horse unless she agreed to part with Bert, whom she had grown far too tall and heavy to ride. It had become a stand-off that had thus far lasted eighteen months. Apart from best friend Carly, who was now going to be over a hundred miles away, Bert was Faith's closest ally. Selling him would be like selling her soul.

She took out her mobile phone to text best friend Carly, only getting as far as '*Having a crap*' before Magnus tried a lunatic overtaking move on the Audi so that she accidentally pressed Send before she could add '*journey*'.

Diana Lampeter was running late, and she loathed running late. She also loathed emotional scenes. Her well-planned schedule was already falling to pieces.

Mim wouldn't stop crying after a tearful farewell with her father Tim (who would, after all, be seeing the children next weekend, and was being a complete heel already – insisting that he be at the London house throughout the removal process). Just as Tim had finally calmed Mim down enough to buckle her in the car and plug the portable DVD into the cigarette lighter, the removal men had dropped a Welsh dresser on their own feet. Faced with the prospect of Mim staging another tantrum, Diana had been forced to go ahead and leave Tim awaiting a replacement driver for the van. He was bound to have poked through the last of her boxes and discovered his favourite Henry Alken oil and the George III silver teapot that his grandmother had given them as a wedding present, neither of which he'd agreed to let her take.

A flat tyre on the A40 had delayed her so much that both her removal lorry and her horse transporter had sailed past as she sweated with the jack and wheel nuts in the sweltering heat while, in the back of the car, Digby stayed glued to the DVD player, Mim sobbed her heart out and Hally barked constantly. Not one kind Samaritan had stopped to help. Diana could hardly blame them. Her passengers were enough to put anybody off.

Then Digby went missing at Oxford services, having insisted on going to the loo unaccompanied, setting off a panic-stricken search. She was certain both the horse transporter and the *Kensington Quality Removals* van would have arrived by now, and bloody Rory wasn't answering the phone. To cap it all, some idiot in a Porsche had just almost driven her off the road.

'Not much further,' she promised the children through gritted teeth, glancing in the rear-view mirror. 'Digby, *stop* feeding chewing gum to Hally.' On the back seat beside her children, the big grey dog was struggling to unglue her jaws, saliva pouring from her chomping jowls on to Mim's fat little legs.

She could see the Porsche behind them, weaving in and out of an overtaking position despite the never-ending oncoming tourist traffic. Idiot. Good-looking idiot, mind you, she realised, as she took in the flop of blonde hair and the breadth of shoulders.

They slowed to a crawl as they came to a roundabout backed up with traffic.

'Someone else is on the move today.' With false jollity Diana pointed out the Pickfords vans ahead of her. Digby didn't look up from cramming chewing gum into the rear ashtray. Mim snivelled some more and said she needed the toilet.

'Lavatory,' Diana snapped. 'And you'll have to wait.'

Porsche Boy had an incredibly plain girlfriend, she noticed as he forced his way into the outside lane and alongside her, intent on overtaking on the roundabout. Compared to his symmetrical perfection, his companion had a long, thin face like a camel, round shoulders and hair the colour and texture of a dirty sisal carpet.

Diana briefly admired her own reflection in the mirror – golden skin, black hair curling around huge espresso-dark eyes set in a heart-shaped face. It had served her well, although too much crying and comfort eating towards the end of her marriage had given her bags and a double chin she was determined to shift. Tim had been particularly cruel about the weight she'd put on, calling her a fat slob and a disgrace in those tortuous final weeks. He'd told her she should get out and exercise; she'd just longed for him to be sent away on exercise to let her binge-eat in peace. But ceremonial duties had kept him in London all summer, picking over the corpse of their love with unexpected glee.

An angry beep behind her snapped her back into the here and now as she realised that the traffic had moved on, Porsche Boy long-since departed in a plume of fumes.

'Okay, okay.' She waved a hand at the impatient driver behind her. 'What *is* it with people today? Bloody white van man.'

White Van Man remained glued to her exhaust pipe all the way through Idcote-over-Foxrush and out on to the ridgeway above the Lodes valley, intimidating her with his radiator grille and his black scowl. It was only when he peeled away on to the Oddlode road and she stayed on the ridge heading for the Springlode turning that Diana realised her children had fallen unusually quiet. She glanced behind her and saw that they were both asleep at last, Hally stretched out over them both, her slobbery face pressed to Digby's chin.

Diana pulled into a lay-by, keeping the engine running and savouring the moment. Her beautiful, dark-eyed, honey-skinned children who had both inherited a streak of her South American heritage along with the Constantine freckles and curls, and their father's high-cheeked haughtiness. That he had accused her of being a bad mother had been Tim's dirtiest trick. She loved her children with a passion beyond rationality. Yes, she was impatient, probably far too liberal and shamefully fond of them when they were asleep as opposed to awake, but they were her life and the centre of her world.

Diana kissed her fingers and touched the tip of Mim's perfect, plump toe poking from her flowery flip-flops. Then she turned to look out across the valley, so coppery from drought that the black woods spreading their fingers across it looked like stripes on a tiger's back. Putting the car into gear, she set off again, driving into its jaws.

Pod arrived in Oddlode ahead of Mo, parking the van that they had hired to transport their few possessions on the tiny private lane alongside the village green. Their rented cottage was almost obscured by a huge *Kensington Quality Removals* lorry, from which two men were unloading illogically large pieces of furniture on to the grass.

'All right?' he nodded at one of them, wondering what the hell was going on. The man nodded back as he carried a stack of expensive-looking dining chairs on to the green.

Pod leaned back against his van and rolled a cigarette, watching the action thoughtfully. Either somebody was moving into one of the other Horseshoe Cottages that day, or there had been an interesting cock-up. He had no intention of getting involved straightaway. This could be fun.

Lined up nearby, Gladys and an army of locals were, for once, dumbstruck. It wasn't the ridiculous amount of furniture that silenced them, although there was enough to fill a small country house. Nor was it the sight of two sweaty removal men without tops on. It wasn't even the arrival of the white van at such speed that it had seemed destined to crash into the Fentons' Volvo. Gladys's little village army was gaping, wide-mouthed, at Pod. With his tanned forehead furrowed and dark eyebrows furled, he was as devastatingly handsome as any old-fashioned matinée idol. Nobody had warned them that the village was about to gain a stud of quite such ferocious beauty. It took them several minutes of angina-twinging excitement to recover enough to speak.

'He is a young Dirk Bogarde, and no mistake,' breathed Phyllis Tyack.

'My goodness, but he's a good-looking young man.' Kath Lacey tucked her fleshy arms beneath her waist-slung bosom, clasping her hands. 'She's a lucky girl, that teacher.'

'They're an unmarried couple,' Gladys reminded them, sniffing disapprovingly as Pod lit his cigarette. Then he caught them watching and threw out a smile of such enticing power that the village army stepped back in drill formation, taking deep breaths.

'You saying I'm in with a chance, Glad?' Kath giggled.

'Ooof.' Gladys gave her a stern look, and cast her eyes around for the young teacher. Moments later, the tatty little car came rattling along the Lower Oddford road issuing noxious fumes – mostly from the inside as Mo tried to extinguish a cigarette on several sweet wrappers in the ashtray.

'She's a pretty slip of a thing, too.' Phyllis cocked her head as the car kangaroo-hopped its way on to the gravel road beside the green and came to a halt with the aid of the Horseshoe Cottages hollyhocks.

'A bit gamine,' Gladys muttered. Having mothered a generation of well-boned, plump blondes, she found Mo Stillitoe's waifish fragility alien and unfamiliar.

'Nothing gammony about her,' Phyllis argued. 'She's just skin and bone. Reminds me of Audrey Hepburn.' She had a habit of likening newcomers to movie stars. Quite how tiny, scruffy Mo Stillitoe with her punky henna-ed hair tucked beneath a baseball cap, her stringy vest, voluminous cargo pants and stacked trainers resembled the elegant actress was a mystery to the others, although they supposed she did have the long neck and the fallow deer eyes.

'You don't think she's more like that actress with the double-barrelled name?' Kath suggested. 'What's she called? Kirsty Tompkinson-Parker? Helen Scott-Thomson? Christine Thomas-Carter? That's it, isn't it?'

'No, it's Helena Bonham-Carter,' Phyllis corrected, studying the new arrival's profile and conceding the likeness with delighted recognition. 'And you're right – it is. It's *her*.'

Beside her, Kath's bosom rose as she clasped her hands ever more tightly in mistaken excitement. 'Helena Bonham-Carter's moved to this village! You wait till I tell Vinny.'

Gladys let out an impatient huff and glared at her companions. 'She's called Miss Stillitoe. She's the new key stage two teacher at the school. I should know. My Pam is class assistant.'

'Research,' Kath breathed, determined to enjoy the new drama. 'All the top actresses do it now, don't they – submerge themselves into the role by actually living the life?'

Phyllis, who rather liked the idea of an undercover method actress in their midst – and was always happy to wind up Gladys – nodded fervently. 'We'll have to protect her, make sure the press don't find out.' She winked at Kath.

Kath beamed back, although she was not intentionally playing any part in a wind-up. She was convinced that Helena Bonham-Carter *had* moved into the village. And Kenneth Branagh's disguise was quite brilliant, too. The pile of Hello magazines in the Village Surgery were so ancient that the pensioners had yet to catch up with the actress's latest love-life.

Unaware that she was the object of such scrutiny, Mo had managed to extinguish the small ashtray fire with the last of her bottle of Coke and was making her way towards the huge removal lorry in perplexed horror at the sight of so much antique furniture being unloaded into her new front garden and across the lane on to the green.

'What in the name of . . . ?'

'Shhh – shhh.' Stepping out from behind the hired van, Pod neatly intercepted her and tugged her to his side. 'They think it's ours. Don't say a word otherwise.'

Justine Jones might be disappointed that Rory hadn't turned up for their lesson, but she'd been most impressed when three gleaming horses and three adorable ponies had been unloaded from the *Home Counties Horse Transport* lorries. When asked where the horses should be put, she'd vaguely pointed at one of the paddocks and now watched the new arrivals as they careered around, whinnying, snorting, squealing and making friends.

It was about time Rory got some new school horses. Justine eyed up a wise-looking, white-faced bay with great hope. He was the spitting image of Anke Olensen-Willis's great Olympic horse, Heigi. Things were definitely looking up.

She cast one final look around the yard and down the drive where the horse transporters had recently departed in a haze of hot dust, hoping that Rory might suddenly appear and beg her to stay on and try a new horse. But she was going to be late back to work as it was. She scribbled him a note asking him to ring her and posted it through the door of the cottage, peering in through the dusty window as she did so and smiling lovingly as she spotted the mess inside. Rory needed to be looked after. And, like so many of his adoring female clients, Justine liked to dream she might be the one to do so.

Rory and his groom, Sharon, were, in fact, miles from Upper Springlode, competing two youngsters at a novice one-day event near Cirencester. Not only had Rory forgotten Justine's lesson, he had also completely forgotten that today was the day his sister and her children were due to move into his cramped cottage.

Determined to be positive, despite some immediate causes for concern, Anke glided around Wyck Farm pointing out all the best bits.

'The light is so beautiful in this kitchen, and this conservatory will be such heaven to dine in,' she announced, her sing-song Danish voice echoing away as she moved beneath the glass roof and out into the garden.

'You could cook the food *in* it, it's so hot.' Graham fanned himself with the Aga instruction leaflet as he followed her into the conservatory, glancing up at the tens of wasps buzzing above his head before retreating hastily into the relative cool of the house to check on the removal men.

'What *was* Mum thinking of?' Magnus sighed, lighting a cigarette and resting his elbows on the kitchen peninsula, blonde hair drooping into his eyes. His enthusiasm for the move had disappeared the instant he'd seen Wyck Farm.

'We can always build you a studio, son.' Graham patted his bony shoulder as he passed. 'One of those garden office things, y'know?'

Since dropping out of university to recover from a motorcycling accident, Anke's eldest son had become increasingly determined to forge a career as a musician rather than returning to study electronics. Magnus still boasted an amazing amount of metalwork in his left leg and arm and was often in more pain than he let on. The prospect of a small recording studio at the new house had been one of the things that had lifted him out of the darkest post-accident glooms. Magnus had been certain that there would be outbuildings galore here, but Wyck Farm had nothing remotely suitable. The self-contained annexe had been earmarked for their grandfather, the small stable block was for the wretched horses, and even the garages were already being put to more important use keeping the precious Lexus and the Merc clean. He felt completely overlooked.

'I want the attic room.' Chad came running downstairs from his mission to bag the best bedroom, Bomber panting at his heels. 'And I want my own TV, PlayStation and phone up there. Oh, and we *must* have satellite.'

'Dream on,' Faith hissed from her perch on the window-seat where she had taken up residence to overlook the driveway and watch out for the horse transporter. 'Mum promised that room to me. It's the only reason I agreed to move to this flea-pit. I already hate it here.' She shuddered.

'I fink it's all right.' Chad – who had fashioned himself a strong Essex accent of late – pretended to box Bomber. 'It's pretty cool as it goes. We got loadsa space, ain't we, Bomb?'

'Not enough for a studio,' Magnus hissed, tipping his head back and glaring at the ceiling. This move had forced him to break up his band, Slackers – dubbed by some of Colchester's gig venues as the new Blur. They'd been within sniffing distance of a record contract. Now he was just within sniffing distance of a seriously bad bout of hay fever.

'Evig's going to trash that stable.' Faith was watching as the huge Akita slammed himself against the top bars of the loosebox across the courtyard where he had been confined to stop him eating the removal men. 'I can't see him lasting here. He'll get out on the railway line for a start.' She knew that would upset her stepfather.

But Graham was determined to placate.

'I think your mother's done very well.' He mustered some bravado as he watched Anke drifting between the flower-beds, no doubt already planning her sowing scheme to replace the hastily planted garden centre geraniums and petunias. 'It's a beautiful house.'

Despite Graham's words, the family – who had originally fallen in love with Goose Cottage in the heart of the village – were not convinced by the impetuous purchase of Wyck Farm on the outskirts of Oddlode. Isolated halfway along the road to Lower Oddford and trapped between the railway line, the amenity grounds and the council estate, it had a claustrophobic feel about it despite its five acres of land. The latest renovation had been a rush job, and the fresh paint and hasty finishes did little to cover the obvious faults. Beech floors laid to cover the space left by long-gone flagstones immediately started springing up or cracking under the weight of passing furniture. Light fittings gave off electric shocks, and there was no hot water.

'I wish I had a studio,' Magnus muttered.

'I want the attic room,' Chad grizzled.

'I wish we'd never left Essex,' Faith hissed.

Through the heat-haze of the conservatory, Graham watched Anke leaning dreamily against a willow archway which immediately fell over, making her laugh. He wanted nothing more than a happy wife. He'd move heaven and earth for that. Moving to the Lodes valley was a small sacrifice.

'Look, love, it says Horseshoe Cottage on the paperwork,' the removal man insisted, brushing Mo aside as he collected a huge plant stand dripping with carved oak fruit from the back of the lorry.

'Then it's a different Horseshoe Cottage.' Mo followed him. 'We're Number Four. The name is Stillitoe – and Shannon. This says Lampeter.' She read from the sheet he'd handed her.

He ignored her as he carried the plant stand on to the hydraulic ramp and started lowering himself, wiping his sweaty brow the back of his hand and inadvertently smearing the mobile telephone contact number he'd written there when leaving London.

'Surely you saw the people whose furniture this is when you collected it?' Mo persisted, talking to the top of his sunburnt head.

'Nope. It should be my day off, love, but Barney and Des dropped that ruddy great Welsh dresser on both their bleedin' feet so Mick and I had to take over the job. Hottest day of the year 'n' all – can you believe our luck? Your husband was the only one in the house when I turned up to drive the rig. I picked young Mick up from Greenford on the way out here.'

'Did you just say my "husband"?'

'Yeah. As it goes, he gave me his number in case you – oh, bollocks, I can't read it now.' He looked at the smudged number on his hand, shrugged, and picked up the plant stand again. 'No disrespect, but he told me to take none of your nonsense, love. He said you'd be trouble.'

'What?' Mo watched him carry off the plant stand. She clenched her small hands into fists and yelled. 'What do you mean by "trouble"? And I don't *have* a husband. I have Pod.'

Several more bystanders had arrived to watch the action on the village green. A couple were openly nosing their way around the ever-growing cluster of furniture, apparently looking for price tags.

Mo lowered herself from the lorry like a rock-climber and went in pursuit of the plant stand. 'Did you hear me? I don't have a husband.'

Pod looked up from a box of silverware as she passed.

'Look, love,' the removal man was trying to be tactful. 'I know these divorce cases are messy – I've had enough experience. You and the boyfriend should be happy with what you've got. There's some nice stuff here.' He nodded around him as he settled the stand beside a mahogany tallboy. 'Generous chap, your old man. I always trust an army officer.'

'I'm sorry?' Mo was bewildered.

'I quite agree, mate.' Pod snatched the paperwork from her and gave her a menacing 'say nothing' look. 'We should be *very* grateful for what we have.' He made it sound like a religious blessing.

'Are you crazy?' Mo hissed in an undertone, aware of the proximity of watching villagers. 'We can't just take someone else's possessions.'

'It's a gift from above,' Pod whispered, well aware of the quality of the furniture – even if there was a lot of weird South American stuff, he'd noted.

'It's a criminal offence.'

'Relax, baby. Just go with the flow.' Pod clicked his tongue against his cheek with a wink, reaching into a pocket for his tobacco tin. 'Have a cigarette.' He pulled out a ready-rolled fag and lit it for her.

Mo snatched it tetchily and took a deep drag before realising what he had done. Her eyes bulged as she fought to swallow the smoke and not let any tell-tale fumes waft around. 'This is spliff!' she hissed.

He started to laugh. 'Shh. *Now* who's committing the criminal offence? Don't forget we've got an audience.'

Mo looked frantically around for somewhere to stub it out.

A pink-cheeked old lady chose that moment to break ranks amongst the onlookers and proffer a basket of home-made jams.

'You're the young teacher replacing lovely Miss Frappington, aren't you? Maureen, isn't it?'

'Mo, yes – oh, thanks.' She held the spliff behind her back and took the basket with her other hand. 'That's so kind.'

'Gladys Gates.' She offered a pink hand as soft and wrinkled as a peach that has lived in the fruit bowl too long.

Mo had run out of hands. She thrust the basket at Pod, who thrust it right back and shook the pink palm instead.

'I'm Pod – hi.' He totally disarmed Gladys by kissing her on both rosy cheeks. 'Great to meet you.'

'What a lovely voice. You must be from Ireland?' She almost swooned.

'Merseyside.' He patted her soft hand, hamming up his best Roger McGough lilt, although it was obvious Gladys wouldn't know brogue from Birkenhead. 'Third generation Irish scouser escaping to the most beautiful village in the world. I really hope we'll fit in here.'

Prickling with sunburn and embarrassment, Mo winced as he laid it on with a trowel.

But Gladys was blushing delightedly. 'Oh, I'm sure you will, Patrick. I housekeep at the Manor, by the way. Rose Simmons is a dear friend of mine.'

'Rose who?'

'She's the lady who owns Number Four. Used to be a peppercorn cottage, but the Constantines gave it to her family just after the war. Lucky Rose. Shame she never had kiddies.'

'Oh, right – the old dear. Yeah. Mo said something about her. She's been ill, hasn't she?'

A jar of damson jam fell from the basket as Mo nudged him hard in the ribs, aware that only last night they had cruelly speculated whether Rose might peg out soon – enabling them to think about buying the cottage. It had been idle pillow talk, but it felt dreadful to have discussed it. Her skin burned all the more with uneasiness.

Thankfully, Gladys was too distracted by the beauty of Pod's swirling Irish coffee eyes to notice the awkwardness. He had this effect on women – always. Young or old, married, celibate or even gay. They all fell for him.

'Poor Rose is very frail these days. I said I'd keep an eye on things for her.' She cast them both a beady look.

Mo had started to realise that the hot sensation on her back wasn't just as a result of all this embarrassment. There was a distinct smell of burning. She hoped Gladys hadn't clocked the smouldering spliff.

'You have some lovely things,' Gladys was saying, looking around at the furniture. 'I hope they'll all fit in. You do know the cottage is already furnished?'

'You can never have too many lovely things.' Pod put his arm around Mo's waist and pulled her close, nuzzling his chin into the crook of her neck and whispering, 'And this is the loveliest – aren't you, queen?'

Pod's effect on women was legend. He could reduce Mo to a state of liquid-kneed debauchery quicker than anyone. Looking up at him through her lashes, she couldn't help but smile at his sheer wickedness. Then she smelled the burning again, glanced over her shoulder and let out a shriek. Her vest was on fire.

Horseshoe Farm Stables in Upper Springlode had so completely changed from the way Diana remembered it that she drove past it several times without realising. The riding school had once been run by Captain

Midwinter, Rory's uncle – she supposed that made him her step-uncle. Unmarried, fastidious, the bane of the World Hunt Pony Club, the captain had taught all Truffle's children to ride – Diana included. She remembered him and his house with affection. But the riding school was now separated from the lovely Cotswold stone farmhouse, long since sold to new owners who had renovated it, added a swimming pool and a tennis court and built a high stone wall between it and its former stables.

Now renamed Overlodes Riding School (ghastly thought Diana), the yard consisted of decrepit stabling and barns surrounded by threadbare paddocks. The only accommodation, apart from Sharon's eyesore static caravan, was the tiny, saggy-roofed Horseshoe Farm Cottage. This was to be home to Diana and her children.

Diana was overwhelmed by such a heavy, leaden feeling of disappointment that she couldn't at first even bring herself to get out of the car. Hally and the children were still sprawled across the back seats in a slumbering pack, and Diana stared despondently out of the windscreen at her dreadful new surroundings – a far cry from the Kensington house she had just been forced to leave, or the lovely village house she had originally been promised.

She cursed her mother again for changing her mind so late in the day and redirecting her daughter from the annexe of her elegant and spacious Georgian home, Grove House, to the squalor of Horseshoe Farm Cottage. Truffle had listed a plethora of justifications, but it was obvious that the truth was simpler; she didn't want the bother of a divorcing daughter and two fractious grandchildren under her slate tiles. Far better that Diana shelter beneath a leaking stone roof with her half-brother and help him reinvent his failing business.

'You are the perfect person to steer Rory in the right direction,' Truffle had pointed out in her creamy voice. 'Just think about all your experience with horses, darling. Remember what that shrink told you. He said you have a "neglected skill-base".'

Diana wished she had never mentioned the wretched therapist, who had charged her eighty pounds an hour to cry into his Kleenex as her marriage fell apart around her. 'Mummy, I was a bloodstock agent. It's hardly much help in a tin-pot riding school. Besides, I haven't worked for five years.'

'Then it's about time you started again. Tim can hardly be expected to settle a fortune on you given his army salary.' Truffle had already disloyally sided with her son-in-law.

'Tim's family is loaded, Mummy.' The house – and indeed most of

Tim's assets – was kept in the family trust, but her solicitor was confident that they could still ask for a significant sum.

'Don't be so grasping – I thought I'd brought you up better than that.' Truffle was always happy to ignore the fact that her own fortune had been made entirely by divorcing so many husbands.

'If Tim paid me a third of the money he lavished on that mistress of his, I'd be able to live in luxury,' Diana had pointed out.

'Married men have affairs, darling – it's in their nature. One should rise above it.'

'The only rise I plan is in my children's and my allowance. I'll bleed the bastard dry.'

'Oh dear, that's the Wop speaking again.' Truffle was always unremittingly vile about her Argentinian first husband and Diana's father, whom she referred to as the Wop – a nickname that made Diana almost murderous with rage.

It had been the mention of her father that had stopped Diana from begging Truffle to change her mind about the accommodation arrangements. Keeping Mim and Digby away from their grandmother's poisonous opinions was now a priority, even if it did mean slumming it. She had no great desire to help Rory – he was a hopelessly lazy dilettante as far as she was concerned, who had never deserved to inherit his uncle's farm – but Horseshoe Farm Cottage had, she was certain, some hidden potential which might insure her children's future.

It was only staring at it now, through her fly-specked car windscreen, that Diana realised the potential in Horseshoe Farm Cottage and its yard was well and truly hidden from view. It was so utterly buried, she should have brought deep bore drilling equipment with her. At the very least, she wished she had packed some protective clothing and industrial cleaning supplies.

Waking up the children, she decided she couldn't postpone exploring any longer.

'This place is horrid, Mummy.' Mim trailed sleepily after her as she looked around. 'Can we go?'

'We live here now, darling,' Diana said distractedly as she headed towards the paddocks and noted that her horses had arrived, even if her furniture was running late and her brother wasn't here to greet her.

Mim burst into noisy tears, becoming even noisier when Digby rushed at her with a pitchfork.

'Don't do that, Dig,' Diana murmured, deciding that Rory's scraggy horses looked dreadful beside her beautifully conditioned quartet. Thanks to their fiendishly expensive full London livery, her old hunter

Ensign and his new usurper Rio, along with the children's fluffy Thelwell ponies, were all looking well enough to take part in the Horse of the Year Show.

Apart from hers, the only decent types she could see were an ageing horse and pony in the same field, trying their best to avoid being beaten up by Rio. They, at least, had a bit of class about them. Perhaps Rory had started investing in some quality schoolmasters at last.

She gave her horses a cursory check over the gate, but was too frightened of Rio to do more than that. His black coat still dripping with sweat from the journey, he charged around with his nostrils flared into two red trumpets, trying to establish his superiority. He had never been turned out in company before – not wise for a stallion with such a bad temper – and he was all teeth and heels as he plunged, squealed and discharged pent-up fury and energy.

Diana knew the feeling. Leaving the children trying to murder one another by the manure pile, she stalked around in search of Rory, noting as she went what an awful state the place was in. It was a Health and Safety minefield, not fit for rat habitation, let alone equine. She tried to visualise all the changes she was going to make if Overlodes was to become the ultimate luxury riding holiday venue, with high-level instruction from Rory and guided local trail rides conducted by a band of glamorous girl grooms. Accommodation and refurbishment would be needed, a licensed bar and restaurant, permission to ride in the Gunning Estate . . .

Climbing one of the high, grassed banks behind the yard, she looked out across the ridge to the black-tipped forest surrounding the hidden Foxrush Hall. Even from this distance, it made her shudder and an icicle of chilly sweat cut a painful line from her throat to her belly button. The Gunning Estate. The last time she and Tim had entered the war zone that passed for an attempt at discussing their marriage, he had told her to go to hell. And here she was, just a couple of miles away from it. She had come back to the Lodes valley and to Gunning. What was she playing at?

At Wyck Farm, Anke had finally come back down to earth and joined her daughter's agitation at the non-arrival of their horses.

The men were of no help: Graham had taken the boys and the dogs to the village shop for cold drinks, saying he wanted to take a look at the furniture sale he'd spotted on the village green. He had little or no interest in the horses and Anke suspected that he would be quite happy if they never arrived.

'There must have been an accident,' Faith fretted, envisaging old Bert and Heigi upside down in a mangled horsebox on a country lane. 'I knew we should have kept them in sight. Bloody Magnus wouldn't slow down.'

'They'll be fine.' Anke tried the Home Counties Horse Transport office number again and, again, got an answer phone message. She glanced at her watch. 'Oh, bother – I could really do without this. I want to go and see Morfar this afternoon.'

Faith rolled her eyes at the mention of her potty grandfather. 'Can't you forget him for five minutes? The horses are missing.'

'Darling, your grandfather is the reason we've moved here in the first place.'

'And don't I know it,' Faith grizzled. 'Why can't he just go into a home or die like other old people?'

'Faith! He is your only surviving grandparent and he has dementia. Don't you *dare* speak like that!' Anke punched out the number again and was so surprised by the prompt answer this time that she didn't have time to adjust her tone. '*Where* are my horses, you silly girl? Tell me right now this minute.'

Mo had been under no illusion that Pod would mend his wicked ways somewhere between the A14 and the A40, but today he was out of control. Not only had he signed for someone else's furniture and sent the removal men on their way with a tip almost as big as their first month's rent, but he had also flirted outrageously with little old ladies, smoked a spliff openly in his new front garden, used the garden hose to extinguish Mo's smouldering vest and then lifted its sodden, burned remains at some very inappropriate moments because he found it funny.

To cap it all, he had announced that he was going to fetch beers from the Lodes Inn half an hour ago and had not yet returned. Mo didn't feel she could leave all the expensive antiquities spread across the green unguarded. Several carloads of tourists had already spilled out to admire them, thinking that this was some sort of sale. She was slightly stoned and distinctly paranoid, which made for an unsettling mix.

'Cracking bed, love. How much do you want for it?'

Mo swung around to find herself looking into two impossibly blue eyes beaming at her from a tanned, fleshy face. The man had to be a tourist. From the designer sunglasses perched in a mop of sandy hair, through the garish floral shirt, red bermudas and down the tanned, hairy legs to the Miami Vice loafers, the man was bad-taste Millionaire Row. He should have been American, but he had a distinct northern accent.

'The wife loves all this rococo stuff,' he was saying as he admired the carved walnut four-poster which had absolutely no hope of fitting into Number Four Horseshoe Cottages, even supposing it belonged to them. 'Might spice up our conjugals if you know what I mean.' He gave her a blue wink and then noticed the state of her clothes. 'You been on fire or something?'

Still sopping wet in places and clinging tightly, Mo's little cotton top was suffering from the after-effects of the garden hose.

'I just sweat a lot,' she joked.

The blue eyes widened sympathetically. 'Oh, you poor little love. You should see a doctor about that. It's all right – it won't put me off the bed. I can buy a new mattress.' He stroked the walnut cheerfully.

Not entirely sure if he was teasing her, Mo watched him swing his way around the furthest post like a pole dancer, hamming up a few moves without a trace of self-consciousness. Shooting her a come-hither pout with a winsome tilt of his head, he swayed the baggy shorts around, pressed the bad-taste shirt to the post, kicked up a hairy, tanned leg and wriggled as suggestively as his seventeen stones allowed. Something struck her as so silly about this big, beefy man doing such a thing that she burst out laughing.

'Hey, love – that's a grand laugh you've got. Prettiest thing I've heard round these parts. I can never resist a giggler. Let's hop aboard and try this baby out.' He clambered on to the bed and patted a spot beside him. 'Just don't sweat on me, eh?'

Now it was clear who was teasing whom. He reminded Mo of her loose-cannon Great Uncle Wilf, who had always been the best fun at kids' parties. Suddenly feeling very high and laughing so much she could hardly speak, she spluttered that it wasn't her bedtime and, besides, she hadn't cleaned her teeth.

'Old-fashioned type, are you?' He stretched out and crossed his hairy ankles at one end, his broad wrists behind his head at the other. The big smile (showing off very expensive dentistry) said it all. Crass, brash and undoubtedly worth a lot of brass, this man really rated himself. Yet he was surprisingly, almost magnetically, likeable.

'Graham Brakespear,' he introduced himself with another wink. 'As in Brakespear Haulage of Burnley.' He obviously expected her to recognise the name – like Eddie Stobart or Christian Salvesen.

'Mo Stillitoe – as in Stillitoe Stilettos of Suffolk,' she ad libbed, wishing the dope hadn't gone quite so much to her head. She couldn't stop giggling now.

He raised his sandy brows in *faux* amazement and looked down at her great clodhopper trainers. 'Those are more like our teenager wears. I bet you've got lovely slim ankles under all that drapery.' He pulled a Les Dawson leer. 'Call me an old goat, but I love a high heel on a slim leg.'

'You old goat,' she snorted, her sides aching.

'At least I'm not afraid to show off my shapely timbers.' He rolled a loafered foot around and shot her a simmering look.

Mo watched the laughter in those merry blue eyes and felt gloriously bucked up. She guessed it was just her luck to make her first friend in Oddlode of a middle-aged male tourist propositioning her as he lay in the sun on a stolen bed.

'I'll give you five hundred for the four-poster,' he offered.

Wiping her eyes, still laughing, Mo backed away. 'It isn't my bed. I've . . . never seen . . . it before. Sorry.'

'Bloody hell, this village is weirder than I thought.' He cast his denim gaze around, smiling and yawning at the same time. 'Who leaves a class bed like this on a village green?' He smiled at her sleepily and snuggled down into the mattress. The next moment, he had nodded off.

Mo watched him for a while, amazed that anybody could take a nap so instantly. He was curiously boyish in sleep, the long sandy lashes tipped with pale blonde, the pink nose and cheeks softening the broad ruggedness of the tanned face. If it weren't for the ghastly clothes, he wouldn't be a bad-looking man. He now reminded her of Daddy Bear in Goldilocks, only this bear didn't care who had been sleeping in his bed or indeed whose bed it was.

Remembering that she had Pod to lampoon, Mo started to skip in the direction of the pub, leaving the big, sleeping bear to guard the Lampeters' furniture, whoever the Lampeters were.

She found Pod surrounded by new friends. Pod made friends as easily as most people made tea and – like his brews – they were usually an endless procession of strong, stewed and bitter mugs. He had typically cleaved to the roughest element in the pub, a group of loutish locals who were making a lot of noise by the bar.

'Here she is!' He beckoned her over. 'Meet some great lads, queen.'

Mo found herself being introduced to a bunch of gnarled, battered and scarred men of at least three generations, all of whom seemed to belong to a family called Wyck, and all of whom appeared to be three parts cut after a long, lunch-time drinking session.

'Your man here says you likes a pint,' cackled one of the older Wycks, who had a nose like a wasp-eaten plum. 'I likes a lady who can drink like a man.'

'Thanks.' Mo watched worriedly as several pints were lined up in front of her. On balance, she preferred being told that slim ankles were pretty.

'My lads have won a lot of readies on young Pod here,' said another of the seniors, this one possessing fewer teeth than an old comb. 'It's a travesty he got suspended. Best jockey out there last year, he was.'

Pod winked at Mo, who looked away hurriedly. She hoped he hadn't said too much.

'Shame he's missed the midsummer Devil's Marsh Race,' one of the youngsters pointed out.

'What's that then?' Pod lit a roll-up.

'Local institution, mate. Big horse race over Gates's land. Reckon that's why it's called the Devil's Marsh – 'cos he's a bloody devil is Ely Gates.'

All the Wycks seemed to find this hugely funny, slapping one another on the back and roaring. The joke went completely over Pod's and Mo's heads.

'Course, Pod here is a jump jock, ain't he?' said the red-nosed elder.

'Both,' Pod reminded him boastfully, earning a sharp look from Mo. He had been one of the very few jockeys to ride both flat and jump seasons, although it was the latter that had earned him his greatest glories.

Red Nose nodded in recognition. 'When I was a lad, there was a winter race too – a point-to-point held on the first full moon in New Year, it was. Now, that was a brave man's sport – a midnight steeple-chase from the Gunning Estate chapel to Oddlode church. Crossed the hardest hunting country around here – ditches you could hide five men in and walls as high as my head.'

'Sounds my sort of race.' Pod raised his glass.

'Men got killed riding it. Hunt lost two field masters the same night in fifty-nine. Terrible year, that was.'

'That why they stopped it, Alf?' asked a youngster.

'No, Tam.' Alf shook his head. 'That was after old Firebrand topped his missus and went on the run.'

'I thought he shot himself in the woods up there?'

'Never found a body, though, did they?' Alf tapped his red nose. 'There's certainly some round here say he killed himself, and that his ghost now rides the six-mile point at full moon, horse and rider ablaze with blue flames.'

Mo, who was terrified of ghosts *and* horses, downed a pint in one and gaped at them all. 'Who, or what, was "Firebrand"?'

'You don't want to know.' The toothless one narrowed his eyes and shot a warning look at red-nosed Alf. 'It doesn't do to talk about him, especially in front of a lady.'

Alf opened his mouth to protest, but Toothless had already turned to Pod. 'You play football?'

'I'm a mean left winger. Tried out for the Reds once, but I loved the horses too much.'

'We'll have to get you to try out for the Lodes Valley Blackhearts. Best team for miles around.'

'You'll only get in if you play dirty,' one of the youngsters cackled.

'Oh, I play very dirty.' Pod grinned at Mo.

Diana slammed her mobile phone shut after speaking with Kensington Quality Removals and went in search of the children. Digby had now cornered Mim in the feed room, helped enthusiastically by Hally.

'Digby, let your sister get out of that dustbin. I want you both in the car again, *now*.'

Mim spat out a mouthful of pony nuts and suddenly smiled. 'Are we going back to London, Mummy?'

'No. We have to go to Oddlode and sort out this bloody chaos.' Diana removed two feed scoops from her son's clutches and marched back outside again, distractedly carrying them all the way to the car.

'Did you see the Audi that just passed us?' Faith swung around on the passenger seat as her mother negotiated the tight, winding bends on the lane that climbed from Oddlode to the Springlodes. 'I swear it had two feed scoops on the roof.'

Anke wasn't listening. She was trying to remember the directions the lorry driver had given her. 'I can't *believe* they'd drop our horses in entirely the wrong place. What if Heigi panics? His arthritis will flare up.'

'Are they coming back to pick up the horses?'

'They say they can do it next week. I told them we want our money back. We'll ride them home.'

Mo was having no luck extricating Pod from the Lodes Inn. More pints had been lined up. The Wycks were now drunkenly insisting that he must meet Lodes Valley Blackhearts' team manager, Tony Sixsmith, without delay.

'He'll be at the Plough up in Springlode. Always drinks there week-ends. We'll take you to meet him.'

Mo glanced worriedly out of the pub window, noticing that quite a crowd had gathered around the village green antique collection. 'We'd really better get back to the cottage.'

But one of the younger Wycks had already been dispatched to fetch the pick-up truck.

'It's only ten minutes' drive away.' The line of pints was emptied with frightening speed.

Before she knew it, Mo was bouncing out of the pub car park in the back of a pick-up, wedged between Pod, a barking dog and a pile of fencing posts. The tourist with the garish shirt was no longer napping on the four-poster, she noticed. Then she almost lost her eye to a fencing stake as the pick-up swerved dramatically.

From the cab, a hand jabbed out a V-sign at a passing Audi estate. '*Oi!* Watch where you're going, missus!'

'Piss off, you great imbecile!' screamed a hysterical voice as the woman's car mounted the verge and headed straight on to the green, parting the crowds. 'Get back from my furniture or I'll call the police!'

Pod and Mo both sank down on their bench seat and gratefully let the wind rush through their hair as the pick-up raced out of the village.

'That was close,' Pod cackled, pulling the eighth of hash from his tin ready to roll another spliff.

'I thought you were going to cut down now we're living here?' Mo reminded him gently.

For a moment he looked black-tempered and then he threw the hash over his shoulder and gathered her into a long kiss. Behind them, Fluffy the dog watched the little brown lump bounce off the bench seat and land at his paws. Sniffing it thoughtfully, he opened his great jaws and wolfed it down.

Having bribed a group of eager pensioners to guard her furniture, Diana set off once again to find Rory. She needed his horsebox to collect her beloved possessions before any more American tourists tried to buy them, mistaking the collection on the village green for an antique fair.

'I'll sue that bloody removal company,' she hissed as she drove the children back up the hill, two feed scoops still rattling on the Audi roof.

Anke and Faith were relieved to locate their horses in the deserted Overlodes Riding School, although they were less impressed to find them charging around on rock-hard pasture amid an overfed, unruly herd. There was a tatty horsebox parked at an angle across the drive and a note on the door of the cottage read '*Gone to pub. R.*'

'What a dump,' Faith sniffed.

'What a beautiful horse.' Anke was looking at Diana's stallion, Rio, who had abandoned beating up his field companions in favour of trotting stressfully up and down the rails. 'Just look at the way he moves.'

'Shall we fetch ours out?' Faith suggested, looking around for their head collars.

'Not yet.' Anke had a feeling the stallion would be a tricky customer to get past. 'We really should find whoever owns this place first. Let's look for the pub.'

When Diana finally tracked down Rory, he was holding court in the Plough's huge beer garden, drinking champagne beneath a haze of midges. On his lap sat Twitch, the Jack Russell, wearing his customary neckerchief and smug eye-patch expression.

As blonde and tousled as ever, Rory leaped up as soon as he spotted his sister, eager to introduce his companions sitting around two crowded bench tables crammed together. Guilt was written all over that high-cheeked and freckled Constantine face as he made a hasty attempt to draw her into his group and avoid any sort of confrontation. He wasn't helped by Twitch who, deeply indignant that he had been tipped off his master's lap, wouldn't stop barking.

'We're all here to welcome you home, Sis,' Rory improvised, having to shout above the yapping din. 'You'll never guess what . . .'

Too hot and bothered to listen properly, Diana cast her eyes around the motley group as Rory drunkenly drawled out their names. They included a young couple whom he introduced as Pod and Mo, along with a very tall, blonde mother and daughter combo, Anke and Faith – all of whom seemed to have moved into the area that day. With them was droopy, fat Sharon, the groom and a group of rowdy Wyck men. Diana was slightly confused as to whether Po, Mod, Annie, Faye, or whatever their stupid names were, had all moved in together, but she couldn't be bothered to ask. Everyone around the table had, it seemed, inadvertently stumbled upon a staff wake at the Plough, where long-term landlord Keith Wilmore had just announced his retirement. An impromptu get-together was well underway and all were in roaring party spirits as a result.

As Diana opened her mouth to demand her brother's help, Twitch suddenly spotted Hally at her feet and dived between her ankles, barking furiously and forcing Diana into an undignified *plié*. Bristling beneath his neckerchief, Twitch began to chase Hally around the table, starting off an even louder cacophony of barking – most of it coming from a shuddering pick-up truck in the nearby car park.

'SHUT UP, FLUFFY!' screamed several of the Wycks simultane- ously, rocking Diana back on her heels so that the unbalanced *plié* became a limbo dance and she almost fell over backwards.

'What a beautiful dog.' The tall blonde mother was watching Hally plunge into the stream ahead of Twitch. 'What breed is he?'

'Weimeranar,' daughter Faith answered long before Diana could regain her composure, snapping at Anke as though it should be perfectly obvious. 'And he's a *she*.'

As her mother watched the dog bounding around in the stream, Faith took another furtive look at Rory Midwinter and caught her breath. His eyes were the same metallic grey as a Weimaraner's coat, his sweet, lazy manner as playful and ebullient, his body as lean and muscular and his breeding as classy. Having wanted a grey gundog for years, Faith was suddenly torn.

'Beautiful dog,' Anke was saying again.

'Yes, beautiful,' Faith breathed, looking at Rory's muscular bronzed thighs poking from frayed shorts.

'She's called Hallmark Silver Spectre of Hanover,' Mim told her brightly as she clambered on to Rory's knee. 'We call her Hally. She was sick twice in the car today.'

Digby, who was trying to cram a champagne cork up each nostril, hurled himself on to his uncle's other knee, shrieking delightedly as he impersonated Hally being sick.

Rory smiled up at Diana.

'Have a glass of champagne, sis – it's free.' He shifted along his bench to make space for her, a nephew lifted on to one shoulder and a niece on the other as Digby and Mim swung delightedly from their drunken uncle. 'You'll never guess what I've just found out about Anke here. She's –'

It was too much for Diana.

'I haven't got time for bubbly!' she snapped. 'Some idiot removal men have abandoned my furniture in the wrong place. It's strewn all over Oddlode village green.'

She didn't notice Pod slipping hastily away to be introduced to Lodes Valley Blackhearts' manager, Tony Sixsmith.

'The only thing currently safeguarding everything I own is a bunch of octogenarian busybodies,' Diana raged on, 'and they're bound to bog off when the sherry hour arrives.'

'I'm sorry – that's our fault.' Mo, the elfin teacher, quickly jumped up. 'There was such a muddle, you see, and . . .'

Thankfully Diana didn't take in a word of Mo's explanation as she felt hysteria clutching at her throat. 'One of them even tried to tell me that the furniture belonged to Helena Bonham-Carter,' she interrupted in a shrill voice. 'As if that's not enough, I've almost been run off the road three times today and some idiot has turned my stallion out in company. He's having a nervous breakdown. So, for that matter, am I!' She let out a furious growling scream to release some pent-up tension.

For a moment there was a lull in the boisterous table conversation as everyone, including the Wycks, stopped talking and gazed at her. Then, just as quickly, the babble started up again as backs were turned and more champagne poured.

Only Mo carried on watching her nervously, gnawing on a finger-nail.

'Thanks for your support,' Diana muttered, turning away in despair and gazing unhappily at a hastily made banner being draped over the door: 'Don't Go, Keith!' A bearded man was welcoming another group of drinkers beneath it as he herded them in through the thatched porch.

Diana felt memories stab at her pounding heart – teenage drinking sessions in the beer garden here, the first giddy feelings of love drinking whisky macs by the fire after a winter walk. It was a beautiful, unspoilt old pub adored by locals – tiny, intimate and gingerbread cottage pretty with its black vanilla pod beams and its golden, toasted marshmallow stones. The huge garden, with its stream and willows, was still as lush as a fairy glade despite the summer drought, the syrupy reek of meadow-sweet clashing headily with the smell of hickory chips from the barbecue. Beyond the wooded stream lay an orchard and a paddock and two tumbledown cottages and barns. When she was a girl, she remembered there being plans to develop them into holiday cottages and a camp site, but the pub had been sold shortly afterwards and the new owner had chosen to keep it as it was. She supposed that owner must have been the 'Keith' of the sign.

This was when a delicious thought struck her, pouring balm on her raw nerve endings. This wonderful old thatched pub would make a dream accommodation base for high-class gourmet riding holidays.

'Did you say the landlord's retiring?' She swung back towards the table.

'After twenty-five fantastic years.' One of the Wycks raised his glass.

'Does that mean it's up for sale?' She slotted herself into the small space beside Rory, and took a swig of champagne

'S'pose it must be.' Another Wyck shrugged. 'Hope it ain't bought by one of them celebrity chefs.'

'Here's the chap to ask.' Rory waved over the bearded man. 'Are you selling up, Keith?'

'Lady here wants to know.' One of the Wycks leered at Diana's cleavage.

'All yours for three-quarters of a mill, my dear.' Landlord Keith leaned past Diana to clear away two empty champagne bottles and plant fresh ones in their place, glancing down to admire the view too. He held out his hand, jolly eyes sparkling. 'Keith Wilmore.'

She shook it, sensing – along with the customary male attraction she always drew so easily – a very real business opportunity. 'Diana Lampeter.'

The broad hand, still cool from carrying champagne, went curiously limp. 'The Constantine girl?'

Knowing the name still carried a lot of local sway, Diana nodded. 'I'm a relative, yes. Rory's my half-brother.'

But Keith's eyes now had shards of flint in them. 'You're the one who married the Guards officer?'

Diana hardly thought it was any business of his, but she determined to keep her cool. 'That's past history now. I've just moved back to the area and am looking for a project. I'd be really interested in setting up a meeting with –'

'If you want to know more about it, you'll have to ask the agents.' He became suddenly abrupt, taking a step back and wiping the hand that she had shaken on the back of his trousers. 'I have to warn you, it's already more or less sold. You don't stand a chance, to be frank.' With that, he turned and walked away.

'What a rude man.' Diana was taken aback by the hand-wiping gesture. 'I'm amazed he lasted here a quarter of a century with manners like that.'

Those who knew Keith well were gaping at his retreating back. They had never seen him so terse.

Diana glanced at her watch again and realised that it was past four. 'Rory, I need your horsebox.'

'Sure.' He nudged Sharon, who produced a set of keys from her pocket.

'And someone to drive it.' She took in the low tidemarks in the champagne glasses around her and tutted. 'On second thoughts, I'll drive the bloody thing myself. But I *must* have all the men around this table.'

'Good God.' Rory choked on his champagne.

'My furniture is in Oddlode,' she explained witheringly, looking around for her children. 'I need people who can do heavy lifting. You'll all get paid. Mim! Digby! Get out of the stream and come here at once! And what on earth are you doing to that sheep?'

'That ain't a sheep.' One of the Wycks jumped up. 'That's Fluffy.'

'Fluffy?' Diana looked at the huge, shaggy beast with alarm. On closer inspection, it *was* canine – one part wild wolfhound to three parts mutant Dulux dog, with jaws like sharp yellow mantraps. Dwarfing Hally, who was gazing respectfully from the bulrushes with Twitch hiding behind her, the enormous dog seemed to be enjoying a rabid game of hide and seek with the Lampeter children – trying to spot them through a fringe as thick as a slipping Cossack hat. It also appeared to be having some sort of fit, chasing its tail manically in the shallows of the stream, shooting up great rainbows of water and then racing up and down the banks, sending tables and chairs flying.

'How in hell did 'e get out of the pick-up?' Another Wyck leaped up to give chase. 'He was chained in there.'

'What's up with him?' Rory laughed as the giant, shaggy-coated mutt gave his pursuers the slip, flattened a few more tables and careered towards the barbecue, his eyes rolling in their sockets.

Racing to pluck her children out of danger's way, Diana found herself helped by the dark-haired man – Po or Mod or whatever he was called.

'Thanks.' She clutched a giggling and very wet Mim to her chest while he carried Digby back to the safety of the table.

Fluffy was now guarding the barbecue as though his life depended on it, refusing to let his owners anywhere near. Hackles drawn, he was an intimidating sight – drool dripping from the long stained teeth, curls of pink flesh rolling back to reveal vein-streaked gums, great powerful shoulders close to the ground as he prowled around, sniffing the food containers between roars. A moment later and he weighed in with a great crash, teeth tearing through plastic boxes, claws ripping at foil as he wolfed the uncooked meats.

'My God, that dog is dangerous.' Diana took Digby's hand from his rescuer, steering both children behind the table to watch. 'He should be destroyed.'

Settling back into his seat, Pod opened up a tobacco tin and peered into it thoughtfully. 'He could be stoned.'

Faith Brakespear let out a howl of outrage. 'You can't stone a dog to death. That's barbaric.'

Pod opened his mouth to explain and then shut it as Mo kicked him under the table. He glanced up at Diana, who knew exactly what he had meant and frowned thoughtfully.

With a jolt of surprised recognition, she noticed his beauty for the first time. Brooding shamelessly beneath those bass-clef brows were eyes of such bittersweet wickedness and lips of such curling sensuality that he should be masked for his own safety. Just for a moment, as his dissolute black gaze caught hers, she felt another memory crack her ribs into two broken ladders. Then he looked idly away, hardly seeming to notice her presence. He reminded her far too vividly of those long winter walks and hot whisky macs. Today was turning out to be one, long emotional wrestling match.

A cry came from the rear of the pub garden as Fluffy was finally cornered in the dilapidated skittle alley, several steaks clamped in his foaming jaws. 'He's collapsed! Fluffy's down!'

'Is he dead?' Faith whimpered, covering her mouth in horror.

'It's okay!' came another shout. 'He's still breathing.'

'Is it some sort of heart attack, do you think?' Anke was craning around to see where Fluffy had fallen.

'He's asleep,' Pod announced confidently, not looking up from rolling a cigarette.

'I think we should call a vet.' Faith snatched a mobile from the table, but Pod put his hand over hers to stop her dialling.

'Really, love, you don't need to worry. He's just sleeping it off.'

'Who are you to say?' She wrestled her hand free.

'Pod.' He gave her the Shannon look that never failed. 'My name's Pod. And don't you forget it.'

Faith suddenly knew what it felt like for one's heart to stop. With breath-taking speed, something close to an epiphany took place. For the first time in sixteen years, she fell in love with a being with two legs instead of four. It was a beautiful moment.

And then Faith looked up as Rory bounded back to the table, slotting himself in beside her with a big smile, and her heart raced faster as she realised that she did, in fact, adore something four-legged. Pod Shannon *and* Rory Midwinter. Two crushes in one day. Perhaps the Lodes valley wasn't such a bad place after all.

Under the table, Mo had kicked Pod again and he gave her a lazy smile before going to check on the dog.

Fluffy had indeed passed out in the skittles alley, suffering from nothing more than a serious case of doped-out afternoon lethargy. With a steak welded in his jaws, snoring voraciously, he was as benign as anyone had ever seen him. It took five Wycks to lift him into the back of the pick-up truck and, afterwards, it was generally agreed that the huge dog weighed more than any single piece of Diana's weighty furniture collection. Of course, Mim and Digby never did admit to unchaining him, and nor did they tell their mother what they had seen the huge, shaggy beast do before he plunged into the stream. It was only nine weeks later that anyone would find that out.

2

Sitting in one of Lower Oddford nursing home's high-backed chairs, Truffle Hopkinson-Dacre was having tea with Nanny Crump and heartily defending her decision not to allow her daughter Diana to move into Grove House. The children would upset the papillons, she pointed out, and her new *affaire* with local art dealer Vere Peplow was currently enjoying a healthy *frisson* that would be quite ruined by interruptions. She had deliberately just moved the Cotman above the chaise longue in the drawing-room to spice things up.

Nanny listened wisely, accustomed to her former charge's racy life. She had heard far too many tales of love and romance to bother to inject any words of caution these days. She was also having quite a lot of difficulty with her false teeth – currently crammed with granary seeds and cucumber pips from the sandwiches – so listening was a great deal easier than talking.

'Of course, I'll get Diana to bring the children along to see you this week – I know you'll like that,' Truffle said, helping herself to another slice of the toffee cake she'd brought from Mrs Beehive's Bakery in Lower Oddford because she knew it was Nanny's favourite.

'Mmm.' Nanny's teeth – now glued together with Mrs Beehive's famously sticky sponge – allowed no response. She eyed her little knick-knacks worriedly, remembering what had happened last Christmas when Digby and Mim had been let loose in her room. It had taken an entire tube of superglue to repair the damage, and poor Matron had stuck her chin to the Minton milkmaid's stool. She still had a small scar.

'And I suppose you'd like to know what Bell and Til are up to?' Truffle offered. 'I'm sure they haven't deigned to call or visit lately.'

Nanny had received telephone calls from both Truffle's sisters that week, but couldn't hope to fight through Mrs B's cake in time to say so. Besides which, she was always happy to listen to Truffle chatter cattily about her elder sisters, Isabel and Matilda. She had such a wonderful eye for detail that she painted entirely new angles to the girls (even in their sixties, Nanny thought of all three sisters as the girls). Since childhood, pretty Truffle had been the exuberant dramatist to her handsome sisters' pragmatic reticence. She had been known throughout her life as Truffle, a luxurious sweet fancy, and had been so-called for so long that there were few who remembered her real name. Isabel 'Hell's Bells' Belling and Matilda Constantine, who were known to Truffle as 'For Whom the Bell Tolls' and 'Till Death Us Do Part', would be appalled if they ever learned of their sister's lifelong indiscretion.

'I thought not.' Truffle licked her fingers and eyed up a third slice of cake. Best not. Vere was dropping hints about stalking in Scotland that autumn and her plus-fours were already plus-sized. 'Well, let me tell you that neither is behaving as you brought us up to. Bell is being very conspicuous with her money. It's quite obscene.'

Truffle was only too happy to expound on the subject of Hell's Bells and her new-found riches (rumoured to be from husband St John's gambling). Lady Isabel Belling had recently undertaken a lavish restoration project for Oddlode Manor and her beloved River Folly. Bell was also enchanted with the prospect of becoming a grandmother, as son Jasper and girlfriend Ellen were expecting their first baby.

Of course Nanny already knew all this, but she also knew that Truffle was indiscreet enough to be far more forthcoming than Isabel.

'Bell is trying jolly hard to marry them off before the bump shows – you know how Ellen likes to parade around with her belly-button hanging out, although I gather the doctor has told her she *must* remove the navel piercing (in case it pings off and injures the midwife, one assumes),' she explained salaciously. 'Bell's absolutely *set* on an autumn village wedding. But strictly *entre nous*, Nanny, I'm not certain Spurs and Ellen are entirely in agreement with her. They seem quite happy as they are.'

At last Nanny freed her teeth from chewy confectionery and let out a horrified gasp. 'But they must make the child legitimate. How else will he inherit?'

'I think the rules might have changed on that one, Nanny. But you're right, I suppose. Weddings are rather fun, and Vere would look terribly dashing in a morning suit. The trouble is that Ellen's family are –' she dropped her voice, 'a bit non-U – he's some sort of retired engineer and she was a teacher.'

Nanny's bone china cup and saucer clattered with a satisfyingly snobbish chime. 'But she is so well spoken.'

'The mother is a bit of a social climber, I gather – insisted upon elocution lessons.' Truffle sniffed. 'Listen hard and you can hear the Somerset burr. Bell is terrified the parents will want to hire the village hall and do their own catering.'

'They will marry in the village church and have the reception at the Manor,' Nanny warbled dismissively, her false teeth slipping. 'All you girls did.'

'Apart from Til,' Truffle reminded her. 'She didn't go through with it.'

'Oh yes.' Nanny sucked her teeth back into place. 'I must say, I was always secretly rather relieved about that. He was a ghastly man.'

'I married him.'

'Yes, duckling, but you married lots of people. You could cope.'

'I suppose so.' Truffle had the grace to smile. 'And he did give me the most beautiful –' she was about to say 'son', but decided to veto mention of Rory. Things were not so good there, and she had no wish for Nanny to start complaining that Rory seldom visited. That was a subject best kept closed. 'He gave me wonderful horses,' she improvised. 'He really did have an eye. Like Til, I suppose.'

'And what of Til?' Nanny knew the Rory subject was close at hand and was equally reluctant to touch upon it.

'Still buried in her wilderness, dressed like a tramp.' Truffle wrinkled her freckled button nose conspiratorially.

On the subject of Til – the black sheep of the family – Truffle always delighted Nanny by showing what she took to be disapproval of her middle sister's strange, hermitic lifestyle. Nanny had long despaired of the tomboy she'd never tamed.

'I think she's getting battier, to be honest.' Truffle straightened her already straight pearls and studied her manicured nails. 'I ask her to kitchen sups so many times and she never returns the gesture. She is inevitably late, rolling up with some gammy game that I am quite convinced she's bagged illegally on the estate. Vere almost lost his gold caps on shot the last time Til gave me venison, the pheasant have tyre marks all over them and are still warm – she always was a dreadful driver. Her own victuals are even more lethal. Bell should never have given her that Hugh Fearnley-Whittingstall book for Christmas. I wouldn't dare touch her wild mushroom pâté or hedgerow preserve, would you?'

Nanny glanced at the crumbs on the plate where there had recently been a pile of cucumber sandwiches, all wolfed by Truffle, and hid a wry smile.

But as soon as Truffle was sitting in her Mini Moke in the nursing home car park, she took out her mobile phone and rang Til to ask her to get hold of some of 'that delicious wild trout for me to cook for Vere this evening . . . yes – I plan to have it *poached* . . .'

'I'll get some out of the freezer, dear – no time for fresh. But aren't you seeing Diana and the children tonight?'

'Lord, no – she needs to settle in.' Truffle dismissed the idea with a shudder. 'She and Rory are bound to have lots of catching up to do. They won't want the wrinklies around.'

'Surely it's very cramped for them all at Horseshoe Farm Cottage? I thought they were going to be living with you?'

'Oh, you know Diana – she steers her own course,' Truffle said breezily, eager to change subjects. 'You're lucky she hasn't landed on your doorstep . . . although I gather it may not *be* your doorstep for much longer.'

'What do you mean, dear?'

'One hears that Foxrush Hall is up for sale at last. As your cottage is a part of the estate, I can't imagine the new owners will want to take on sitting tenants.'

'What nonsense!' Her sister laughed. 'I seldom occupy any chair here long enough to be called a sitting tenant. Besides, my dear, the Gunning Estate is *not* up for sale – the land is all set-aside and nobody wants a haunted old mausoleum like Foxrush.'

Truffle sensed an edge. 'I have it on very good authority that movie stars and media moguls are queuing up for the old place.'

'Oh, goodie!'

'*Do* take this seriously, Til. You might be homeless soon, darling.'

'Diana and I both.' Til remained indefatigable. 'Tell her to come and see me, by the way. We have history.'

'I am not her social secretary, darling,' Truffle muttered, starting the engine. 'And don't forget the trout.'

'Trout,' Til carried on laughing, 'I'm writing it down – Truffle's trout. It has quite a ring.'

Truffle threw her mobile phone on to the passenger seat and took her frustration out on first gear, exiting the nursing home car park in a cloud of dust and gravel.

Watching from her window, Nanny shook her head sadly. Diana should never have returned home. No good would come of this.

3

'Faith's watching them settle into their new field,' Anke told Graham as she tottered into the house, tripping over several packing boxes. 'Wasn't it kind of Diana to bring the horses down here? Her own move has been a nightmare. It *is* a shame you didn't get to meet her, but she was in a terrible hurry to collect her furniture. Such a lovely woman – she's invited us to supper next Friday.'

'Right now, I'm more interested in tonight's meal.' Graham was sulking. 'Do we *have* any food in the house?'

'Somewhere,' Anke said airily, 'although I have eaten so many sandwiches and sausage rolls at the pub, I don't feel hungry. We must go there this week. It's very pretty. Maybe we can take Morfar? Oh! I must call him!' She looked around for a telephone, realised that they were all still packed, and dug her mobile out of her handbag. A moment later she was chattering away in Danish.

Graham watched her angrily. He normally enjoyed getting his wife tipsy, but when she chose to do it under her own steam – on a day like today – it infuriated him. And it seemed that the only time she got on well with her father these days was when she was drunk. Ingmar's dementia frustrated her quick mind and saddened her when she was sober, but when she was silly and relaxed like now, they seemed to understand one another. The gales of laughter interrupting the cheerful Danish flow bore this out.

Graham helped himself to another beer bought from the village shop – the sole contents of the fridge besides Chad's half-drunk Friji and a Pepperami.

Chad was the only one in the family to have bothered to start unpacking, spreading all his clutter around the attic room, which would no doubt lead to furious rows later when Faith tried to reclaim it. Already bored and edgy, Magnus had taken himself off to watch some live music in the Lodes Inn, leaving Graham to stew and simmer alone in the food-free kitchen until his wife returned. She'd been missing for hours, cheerfully announcing her progress with various text messages – starting with *found horses in a field*, then *found field-owner in pub*, then *found a horsebox*

and, finally, *found a lovely new friend*. Despite Graham texting her back
to ask where all these discoveries were taking place, she hadn't actually
told him and he'd felt stranded and surplus. Anke was not usually this
irresponsible.

Now that she had finally rolled up, this looked unlikely to be the
cheerful, family-camping first night that Graham had anticipated. Anke
was already yawning between the laughter. He knew her well enough
to predict that too much champagne would quickly lead to all-out
exhaustion, particularly after such a long day. His stomach let out an
angry bear growl and he hastily claimed the Pepperami, chomping it
quickly in case any of the children came in and caught him devouring
the only provisions. He supposed he'd have to get a takeaway, but
where on earth you found a chippy in this backwater was anyone's
guess.

Ingmar must be telling a particularly good joke, he realised grouchily,
as Anke almost fell over hooting, trying to get a word in edgeways but
laughing too much to make sense. Not that any of it made sense to
Graham, who was always shut out of this half of her life. It had been
a concern he'd harboured about moving so close to her father, but he
knew that Anke was worried about him. At least she hadn't suggested
moving the old man back to Denmark and taking the family too. Graham
had always loved this part of England, with its beauty and its old-
fashioned class. It appealed to his aspirational side.

Most of all, he had needed a change. Selling the haulage firm had
been a surprising relief after all those back-breaking years, particularly
the last decade of commuting between Essex and Lancashire, pushing
paper rather than pulling goods. He didn't miss it at all yet, although
he was dying to get his hands dirty on the agricultural machinery business he'd bought here as an early retirement hobby. Most of all, he
hoped that the change would breathe life into his marriage. So far, Anke
looked as though she'd been hogging the oxygen tent, and Graham was
gasping for air. He missed the expensive air-con system he'd had installed
in the Essex bungalow. It was oppressively hot.

He let out a gassy, Pepperami burp just as Anke moved behind him
and distractedly stroked his hair, still chatting away in Danish.

Graham perked up. There was one thing that occasionally happened
when Anke was drunk. And, with it being such a rare event, he had to
be vigilant or he would miss it. Grasping her hand over his shoulder,
he planted a kiss on her long, elegant fingers.

Anke pressed her hand against his cheek, dropped a kiss into his hair
and moved away, fingers pulling from his grip as she drifted out into

the steamy conservatory, her strange words and laughter becoming all the more sing-song in its vaulted space.

Graham licked his lips excitedly and dashed upstairs.

When Anke followed him some minutes later, Graham was making up the bed – an unheard of domestic chore for him. He had opened a box marked 'Linen' and was clumsily attempting to fit a damask table-cloth on the mattress.

'You must be really hungry.' Anke laughed delightedly, wondering if he would put napkins on the pillows.

'Only for you,' he growled happily, moving across the room to grasp her waist.

With well-practised grace, Anke moved smoothly away and peered into the en suite. 'I think I might have a bath.'

'We've no hot water,' he reminded her. 'I've called the developer – he's sending a plumber around tomorrow. Come here.' He made another lunge, but she had already predicted it with a neat side-step.

'In that case, I can use the electric shower in the attic.' She was searching for the suitcase containing the towels.

'Come here first,' Graham purred, managing to clasp her bottom in his hands and draw it towards him.

Unbalanced, Anke head-butted a pile of packing cases and lurched sideways, landing in a sprawl on the floor. Graham hastily hopped on top.

Anke could feel him slurping and sucking at her neck and shoulders as he levered open the collar of her shirt. For a moment, she felt the heavy weight of resignation pressing her down along with Graham's bulk. She was too tired and drunk to care. But then the familiar frost-bitten fingers of anaesthetised aversion started buttoning up her clothes as fast as Graham was trying to remove them.

'The children might come in.' She tried to roll him off her.

'They're fine. This house is huge.'

'We can't risk it.'

'I'll lock the door.'

'No!'

Graham jerked away and sat back on the towel suitcase, blue eyes tormented. 'Am I that bloody repulsive?'

'No – no. I'm tired, *kaereste*, and I have to wash and fix some food and unpack. It's been a long day.'

He nodded silently, glancing across at the mattress with its creased tablecloth. 'I saw a beautiful bed today. Antique. I tried to buy it for you.'

'I like our bed,' Anke said pragmatically as she did her shirt buttons up in the wrong holes, trying to pretend that nothing had happened and that she was not drunk. 'It's good for my bad back.'

Graham glared at the big zip that formed the demarcation between her hard-mattressed side and his soft one. Even their bed was chalk and cheese.

'It was a bloody beautiful bed,' he sighed again, remembering the pretty, doe-eyed girl who had been standing beside it in her wet T-shirt. He wished Anke would wear wet T-shirts and flirt with him.

'I'll have that shower.' She nudged him off the suitcase and removed two fluffy yellow towels.

When she had gone, Graham slumped on to his soft side of the tablecloth-covered bed and stared at the beamed ceiling. 'No sex please, we're Danish,' he muttered to himself, slamming a fist down on the zip.

As soon as she was standing beneath the scalding pinpricks of a hot shower, Anke hugged herself tightly and let the self-loathing and the guilt wash away the last of her champagne high. It was supposed to be so different here. She had promised herself that she would break the habit, that she would try harder to stop punishing Graham for being more like another son to her than a lover. Her great big teddy bear, who desired her despite her wilting beauty and her grey hairs. He wanted to make her feel twenty again, instead he made her feel pensionable. She was forty-seven; Graham was forty-two. That half a decade differ-ence was half a lifetime on days like today.

He had disappeared when she finally made her way downstairs, refreshed enough to face the long evening's unpacking. Chad and Faith were having a furious row on the landing.

'I wanted the attic! It was promised to me!'

'Too late; my stuff's already in there.'

'You can just move it right out again.'

'Will not!'

Normally, Anke would mediate, but her head ached too much.

'Have you seen your father?'

'You mean Graham?' Faith made her point with a sneer. 'Maybe he's gone to the pub to join Mags?'

'He said something about a takeaway . . .' Chad suggested hopefully before turning back to resume screaming with his sister.

But the cars were all still in the drive. The courtyard was strangely quiet. Anke went to check on Evig, who had still been far too worked up to be let out of the stable earlier. And that was where she found him, moping in a corner with his beloved dog – his big man's body slumped down on a straw bale and his little boy face turned to the wall. She settled beside him, taking his hand. 'It will get better.'

'Will it?'

'We'll be happy here.'

'If you say so.'

'Can I have a hug?'

'Can *I*?'

Evig watched with them his cool, cruel eyes, his huge head on one side, ears darting around suspiciously, guarding a rare moment of connection between his alphas.

As Anke wrapped her arms around Graham's huge shoulders and pressed her chin to his head, she longed for a set of strong arms around her too.

Graham shifted hopefully. 'Don't suppose there's any chance of a quick . . . ?'

Anke hugged tighter, willing herself to say yes. But the moment dragged on. She felt her whole body rebel. She simply couldn't. She closed her hands into a fist and clamped her eyes shut against his crown, breathing in the smell of his hair that had once made her think of honey and now just reminded her of the ongoing battle she had washing Chad's tufty blond crew cut.

Pod and Mo were making love amongst the crumpled newspapers that had protected their possessions during the journey from East Anglia. The Classified section of the *Newmarket Journal* rustled and ripped as Pod pulled Mo on top of him and plugged her in. 'Your turn to ride for the finishing post, queen.'

'I'm sitting on the finish post right now,' she laughed, gasping as he filled her right up.

The property section soon shredded beneath her knees and the What's On pages became scrunched into tight balls in her fists as she rode him home.

Sitting disapprovingly on the back of the sofa, Bechers, the ginger cat, turned his head to the wall and lashed his tail angrily against Rose Simmons' lace chair-back protectors.

Later, Pod rolled a cigarette and tapped his tobacco tin against Mo's naked buttocks. 'I could use some spliff.'

Propped up on her elbows, Mo cast him an old-fashioned look over her shoulder.

Pod grimaced. 'Yeah, yeah. New leaf and all that.' He lit the roll-up and sighed theatrically. 'No grass for Pod, no scaboo.'

'No drinking binges.'

'Eh? Me?' He held out his hands innocently.

'No sleeping around.'

The hands went wider, the expression more innocent.

'A few honest days' work.'

'Now you *are* getting demanding.' He bent down and kissed her bare buttock. 'Will you meet me behind the bike sheds when you start school?'

'I might.'

He pressed his chin into the dimpled hollow of her back and blew lightly on her spine. 'You just wait, queen. I am going to turn over more new leaves than a caterpillar on the rampage.'

A balled-up page of the *Newmarket Journal* flew up in a perfect arc over Mo's back and hit him on the forehead. 'You've already tried to steal that poor woman's furniture,' she reminded him, laughing despite herself.

'So I was turning over a new tealeaf.' He handed her the cigarette to share.

Mo revolved around so that she could look at him, their eyes playing that familiar game of hide and seek – hiding smiles and seeking souls. 'You'll never leaf me, will you?'

He shook his head, stretching forward to take one of her small, pink nipples in his mouth. 'I'll never leaf you.'

Diana gave up her search for her bath bag amongst the suitcases and boxes scattered around Horseshoe Farm Cottage's landing, and settled for splashing her face in cool water and borrowing Rory's toothbrush, which had suspiciously flattened bristles. The bathroom was encrusted with dirt, she noticed, and had no curtain. She was forced to take a wee in the dark in case Sharon was doing the last check of the stables.

She was absolutely exhausted after supervising the late-evening relocation of horses and furniture. As the only sober person amongst her party, she had been forced to take sole charge and drive the death-trap horsebox from Upper Springlode to Oddlode and back. She'd also played taxi service to the other newcomers to the area – the Brakespear mother and daughter duo, their wretched horses, and Mo and Pod.

At least meeting Mo meant that she might stand a chance of getting Digby and Mim into Oddlode primary. The little school was celebrated in the area, and it was considered perfectly acceptable amongst old money to choose it above the preps of Market Addington or Morrel-on-the Moor, although some said it now took rather a lot of new money to buy one's child's entry into the over-subscribed little school. But Mo had seemed incredibly eager to please, and Diana held high hopes that her children could be redirected from the shabby gentility of Woldcote House preparatory. The headmaster there had reeked of smoky betting shop, and the fees were outrageous.

Diana switched on the light and studied her face in the rusted mirror above the basin, pressing her hands to her cheeks to pull back the skin and cheer herself up with a daydream face-lift. She could imagine Tim's glee at the prospect of state school economy, quickly wiped out when she put in her settlement demand. Her Ex-pence claim, she thought murderously, which she planned to Ex-pound upon to add several zeros. Even the drawn-back skin couldn't stop her face frowning, the forehead carved with anger. She turned away, determined not to think about Tim tonight. It had been too full a day to think about Tim. There were far more lovely distractions to dwell upon . . .

Mo's boyfriend, Pod, was really rather delicious, she reminded herself as she made her way to her room. He had wonderfully naughty eyes that made no secret of their admiration for her supple, olive-skinned curves. Pressed up against her in the packed cab during the drive to Oddlode, his body had felt as whip-hard and agile as a boxer's.

She hugged herself happily at the memory and tried to hang on to it long enough to let it blot out the depressing sight of her new sleeping quarters – a tatty futon crammed into a boxroom, with an old cardboard box acting as a bedside table.

She was surprised by how agreeably the evening had turned out, and was excited to have learned that, before becoming a Brakespear, Anke had been no less than the one-time Olympic dressage legend Anke Olesen-Willis. That was certainly a friend to cultivate, despite the somewhat starchy attitude and the drippy daughter. Rory was obviously quite overawed that Anke – whom he had fancied like mad as a teenager – was now living close by. She could hear him now, rattling around downstairs in search of the video of Anke's gold-winning Grand Prix Dressage Kur that he'd promised to show Sharon.

As networking went, it has not been a bad day's work, Diana mused, and she was pleased that she'd cleverly issued a spontaneous invitation to sups at the end of the week. 'Just give me enough time to unpack my Delias.'

Settling on the futon and looking at the cobwebby walls around her, she determinedly stayed positive, certain that she could transform the little cottage into a reasonable entertainment space in no time. She had battled with enough dreadful army accommodation in her early marriage, after all – becoming something of a legend amongst the officers' wives for her ability to metamorphose a badly decorated modern box into an elegant home in just days. As soon as she got rid of Rory's tatty furniture and moved her own in from the barn, things would improve no end. True, it was cramped, and the children weren't best pleased to find themselves in bunk beds in a shared room only fractionally bigger than their mother's cell. But Diana had plans.

Seeing Rory again had made her realise that living with her half-brother could only be a very temporary arrangement. She had no idea that he'd let things – including himself – slip so much. He certainly couldn't be trusted for the hours of uncle child-care she had hoped to foist upon him, although Sharon seemed reasonably trustworthy for babysitting and was keen to earn some extra cash. As far as Diana could tell, Rory rarely, if ever, paid his only member of staff, and she simply stayed because she was so besotted with him.

Diana breathed in the smell of damp and dust and knew that she couldn't live like this for very long. The cottage was sweet – picture postcard from the outside, with its bolero jacket of Virginia creeper and its sleepy-lidded dormer windows. It would make a very cosy little home when it was spruced up. She just needed to get rid of the dirt, the terrible clutter – and Rory.

She settled back against a lumpy feather pillow and flexed her toes as she plotted. When setting out from London that morning, she had determined to seek out her mother before the day was over and give her very short shrift for changing her mind about the living arrangements at such short notice. Diana disliked putting things off or changing her plans – especially those that involved disciplining her wilful mother. She knew that she should, at the very least, telephone. But it was too late and she was too tired. It had been a totally draining day, and she had something very important to think about, something exquisite and thatched and vastly under-utilised.

The Plough was hers in all but name, she'd decided – and she wasn't terribly keen on the name anyway. Something in the back of her mind told her that a local myth proclaimed the name unlucky. Why not change it to the Horseshoe Inn? That had a lovely ring to it. And she had a ready-made landlord; Rory practically lived there by day, so why not move him in for the overnight shifts, too? He would be much better suited to running a bar than a riding school. He could be her cook and accommodation caretaker while she handled the riding holidays.

She was far too busy trying to cheer herself up to dwell upon the fact that putting a drunk who couldn't boil an egg in charge of a hotel and restaurant would be foolish. Diana had always been an optimistic fantasist, and her ability to ignore glaringly obvious obstacles had proved to be a lifelong ally, especially in the years when her aunt had finally persuaded her to hunt and she had survived by simply ignoring the fact that she was galloping straight towards enormous Cotswold dry-stone walls. Right now she was galloping towards an insurmountable wall. She had no money. Finding the asking price for the Plough was out of the question, but it didn't stop her planning for one moment. Right now, in Diana's head, anything was possible.

All she needed to do was to make an offer for the pub – a shoot them out of the water figure that even the cranky Keith Wilmore couldn't refuse. A million, maybe? She'd find the money somewhere, even if it meant squeezing Tim dry. The thought made her chest twinge guiltily and she saw his familiar, square face giving her reproachful looks from every wall.

She tried to make it go away, but now it taunted her. She thought murderously about his betrayal, his bloody mistress and the other affairs he had confessed to over the years. Yet his face was kind tonight. She had seen how desperately upset he was to watch the children leave, and she'd been unable to comfort him. The bad blood between them was too contaminated. Only for a moment, amongst the tears and hugs and chaos had she caught him looking at her and seen through to his raw wounds. She wasn't the only betrayed one here, his face had told her. They both knew that for all his infidelity, he had once loved her with all his heart. She, meanwhile, had been in love with someone else throughout their marriage. Which was the greater sin?

Unable to bear the dreadful, stained and peeling wallpaper a moment longer, she switched off the dusty lamp on the cardboard box and blinked tiredly into the gloom. The room looked much prettier in the half-light – warmer somehow. And Tim had vanished.

'So far so good,' she whispered to herself. The children had conked out without the tears and nightmares she had anticipated, the horses and dog had settled surprisingly well . . . and she already had an action plan.

Yes, the Plough was the answer, she decided sleepily. The Horseshoe Inn. She could see a campsite in the orchard, the cottages renovated into holiday lets, the paddocks full of ponies, and the profits going through the thatched roof.

She'd been silly to envisage hell and brimstone upon her return. She had no reason to be frightened. After all, she had been little more than a child when she'd left, and she hadn't had the power or understanding to change the things that had happened then. Nobody could blame her now. It was history. She had a future to look forward to. At last, she could put something back.

Diana started to drift to a happier place, too accustomed to the orange glow of London's street-lights to realise that the glow outside was coming from an entirely different source in the normally coal-black Lodes valley night.

4

The fire burned through the night. The summer drought had dried the dusty thatch to perfection so that within two hours its blaze illuminated the ridgeway for miles. By three in the morning, the old timbers were already crashing down on three hundred years of history. Blue lights spun in the orange glow, sirens wailed above the crackling roar of burning, water pumped at a rate of a thousand litres a minute and yet the fire raged on. When the tanks emptied in the fire engines, they pumped water from the stream. It made little difference. This fire claimed everything it could.

Anke saw the smoke as they climbed the winding Springlodes lane from Oddlode, a big black thumbprint on the pale blue of the morning horizon. It was bigger than a bonfire, too dense to be illegal stubble burning.

Her hangover was pinching at her temples too much to bother commenting on it. Graham was back in cheerful mode, listening to his favourite Bruce Springsteen CD on the stereo and howling along with it as he looked forward to admiring his new 'toy', agricultural supplier Dulston's. He'd thoroughly enjoyed teasing her over breakfast about the fact that she needed a lift to the pub car park to fetch the Mercedes, abandoned there during her drunken afternoon the day before.

But when they arrived, they found no car and no pub. The smouldering remains of both were being overseen by three fire engines and a huge crowd of local onlookers.

'Bloody hell!' Graham whistled as he parked the Lexus at a safe distance.

Anke was out of the car in a flash, dashing up to the crowd to stare in horror at what little was left of the beautiful village pub. 'What happened?'

'Rather obvious, I would have thought,' drawled a voice. 'It burned down.'

It was Rory Midwinter, his handsome face hidden by huge blue-tinted dark glasses and a droopy straw sun-hat that lent him a curiously camp air. He looked horribly hung-over.

'Oh no, my car!' Anke clamped her hand to her mouth as she saw the burned-out carcasses left in the car park. She had packed her Olympic medal in the glove compartment so that it would be safe.

'Certainly lends a whole new meaning to burning rubber.' Rory squinted through the smoke. 'Keith's old Alvis was parked there too. I think he's more upset by that going up than the pub.'

Graham joined them, not noticing the tears leaking out from beneath his wife's dark glasses. 'Bloody tragic when these things happen. I lost a goods yard in the late eighties – almost wiped me out. Everyone get out safely?'

'Nobody was home,' Rory told him, dark glasses dropping down his nose as he spotted the Hawaiian shirt Graham was sporting. 'Keith was playing poker with the Sixsmiths. Only realised what was going on when one of Tony's girls came back from clubbing with her boyfriend and spotted it.' He held out his hand. 'Rory Midwinter.'

'Graham Brakespear. This is the wife, Anke.'

'We've met.' Rory blushed at Anke as he shook Graham's hand, too shy to notice her frozen face. She was the only woman who could make him feel fifteen again. He eyed Graham jealously, noticing the expensive watch, Barbados tan and designer dark glasses. 'You've bought Dulston's, I hear?'

'That's right. Good job this fire didn't spread.' The machinery yard was just a hundred yards along the road, separated from the pub by several derelict barns and a coppice. He whistled and shook his head at what might have been. 'Still haven't agreed terms with my insurers. Got the broker trying to renegotiate.'

'Don't even mention insurance,' Rory muttered in an undertone. 'The rumours will spread like . . . well,' he looked at the smouldering pub and laughed sadly, 'wildfire, I guess.' It had been one hell of a blaze, he told Graham. Such a shame. The pub was one of the prettiest in the Cotswolds. Everything pointed to it being deliberate.

'You're kidding?' Graham whistled again.

Rory shook his head. 'So Duncan says. He's one of the retained fire team from Morrell, farms the land just behind the woods there. He says the investigators are gagging to get in there – looks like arson.'

'Bloody hell.'

Graham thrived on situations like this. Introducing himself to everyone, he was soon in the thick of the talk and action – even giving quotes to the local press.

Anke moved away, trying not to think about her medal. It was weak-willed to cry. Her loss was nothing compared to the other losses here. A whole lifetime of memories and community spirit had been wiped out; hers was just a victory trinket. Her father would tell her as much.

She couldn't take in the frantic hubbub around her as the fire was discussed and dissected in minute detail. Many of the villagers knew the retained fire-fighters and could swap theories and details while the site of the fire was made safe enough for the investigators to go in. Anke had no interest; her mind was too unsettled by the loss of her medal and the dreadful start it made to life here. First, she had allowed herself to get ridiculously drunk last night, then she had rejected Graham and neglected her children. Now this.

As she waited forlornly a safe distance from her smouldering Mercedes, she spotted Diana Lampeter, who'd walked Hally to the scene of the fire to gawp with the rest of her village. She looked surprisingly chipper in her flowery lime-green sun-dress and flip-flops, giving Anke a cheery wave as she spotted her in return. 'Good job I didn't buy it last night. I wonder how much it'll be worth now?'

Anke took a couple of blinks to register what she was saying.

'D'you know I slept though the whole thing? Amazing.' Diana linked her arm through Anke's and towed her a little closer to the action. 'Rory brought the kids down here to watch at dawn; Sharon was settling the horses who were in a bit of a state over the sirens and smoke. And I just snored on!'

She seemed thrilled by all the excitement, her huge dark eyes sparkling with glee. 'What an extraordinary project this will make now, don't you think? One of my stepfathers had a house that was gutted by fire and he rebuilt it with the most wonderful additions – an indoor pool and a central atrium. It was listed, and he would never have got planning permission before the fire.' She dropped her voice. 'Clever move, tossing that half-smoked cigar into the waste-paper bin, we all thought . . .'

'You're not saying the landlord here . . . ?'

'Lord, no! I'm sure this is just a ghastly accident.'

'But they *are* saying it was started deliberately.' Anke looked across at her shell of a car.

'Reeeeeally?' Diana's eyebrows shot up. 'Who would do such a thing?' Anke shrugged.

'Kids,' Diana said resolutely. 'Bound to be. Always was fearsomely dull growing up in a village. I should know . . .' A smile twitched at her lips as her eyes darted around the scene. 'Not a great start for us newbies, eh? I do hope it doesn't affect business at Overlodes. I'm sure my brother's clients all end their lessons in need of a stiff drink.' Almost in the same breath, she offered Anke a job teaching riding. 'I was thinking about it last night. The yard needs fresh input and you really are *so* beautifully qualified. It would be fun for you.'

Anke was completely taken aback. 'Teaching children to ride?'

'Most of my brother's clients are adults, but I do think we should try to broaden the spec. I've promised to make some changes and drum up more business, although Rory is being boringly resistant. You would make *such* a difference to the profile. I had been thinking along purely riding holiday lines but, with you as a part of the team, the yard could be a top-class training centre.'

Diana, the optimistic fantasist, was completely unabashed at asking a former Olympic rider and coach to 'help out' somewhere as modest and slipshod as Overlodes. She saw no harm in trying, but Anke was totally gob smacked.

'I really don't think so.' She smiled frostily. 'I rarely ride at all these days, and I coach even less. Just Faith, when she has a horse to compete.' A thought struck her. 'But she may be able to help you . . .'

'Your daughter?' Diana remembered the drab little frizz-haired blonde without enthusiasm.

'She is a super jockey. Of course, she would need some help and would have to fit it around her education commitments, but I think the idea of working in your yard would really appeal to her. Would you like me to have a word?'

'Can she teach?'

'She's only sixteen, but I suppose she could help with novices – and she can bring on horses. Even if you just want her to muck out for a bit of pocket money, I think it would do her good.'

Diana tutted in disappointment. 'Overlodes has no shortage of teenage girls hanging around during the holidays who work for free, all with crushes on Rory. I really can't persuade *you* to put in some hours?'

Anke shook her head. 'We moved here because of my father. He has dementia and I must spend all my spare time caring for him.'

'My mother just drives *me* demented,' Diana laughed bitterly, but Anke's chilly smile told her it wasn't a good joke.

'I wish poor *Fader* was not stricken like this, but it is good to be able to give something back after all the years they have cared for us. You mother lives close by, yes?'

'Unfortunately so.' The subject of parents was anathema to Diana, especially the prospect of any parent becoming dependent. On balance, she preferred the idea of giving the drippy daughter a job. 'Well, I'll certainly think about finding some work for Faye. Where is she going to school?'

'Faith,' Anke corrected kindly, equally grateful for the change of topic. 'The local sixth-form college in Market Addington. I hear it's very good.'

Diana looked as though she knew otherwise, but smiled graciously. 'And your youngest boy? Have you managed to get him into Oddlode primary?'

'We're still working on that.' Anke sighed, glancing across at Graham who was supposed to be pulling in a few old contacts but had yet to make the calls. 'He has a place at Lower Oddford but I really wanted to get him into Oddlode. I had no idea it was so hard. My father says it is quite the best school around.'

'Ah, well I have a *very* good idea on that front . . .' Diana promised to try to get Chad into the famously cliquey primary school with Mo Stillitoe's help. '*Such* a sweet girl,' she sighed, although she secretly thought Mo almost as drippy as Anke's daughter.

'I agree.' Anke realised she was guilty of misjudging Diana. She, too, had noticed a special quality in Mo. 'She is one of life's nurturers with a very gentle psyche. I think maybe she has been quite damaged once.'

'Yes. Quite.' Diana had no idea what Anke was talking about and no great desire to find out. 'And her chap is frightfully dishy, don't you think? Paddy, is it?'

'Pod.' Anke was far too self-controlled to forget names, even if she had been somewhat spiced the night before. 'He seemed charming.'

'Charming?' Diana giggled, linking arms again so that she could be conspiratorial. 'My dear, he is obviously as feral as they come. He and Molly hardly strike me as compatible. I can't see it lasting around here – far too many predatory women. I'm after him for a start.'

When Anke looked shocked at this, she nudged her hard and laughed. 'On the job front, silly! I think he'd be great for business. If I can't get an Olympian to work for Overlodes, then I might as well go for the wild card.' She dropped her voice. 'You know that he is – or was – amongst the UK's top jockeys? I heard tell that he was expelled by the Jockey Club for gross misconduct, which not only shows great spirit, but would make for a super marketing spin if handled right, don't you think? I can just see the *Daily Mail* running with a "Where Are They Now?" feature showing Paddy as a dashing, and totally reformed, trail leader.'

'I think you are either pulling my leg, or you are completely insane.' Anke snatched her arm away.

It was Diana's turn to be taken aback. 'I'm sorry?'

As well as being famously polite, civil and kind, Anke was known for her bluntness. It was one of the reasons she rarely coached riders any more. She had been appalled by how many she could unintentionally reduce to tears.

She tried to spell it out as light-heartedly as she could. 'Taking on a jump jockey – however talented – makes absolutely no sense in a little yard like yours. Supposing he would want to work for you in the first place, which I doubt, he would hardly suit the sort of job you would want to offer him, would he?'

Anke's sincerity was no match for Diana's flippancy.

'How do you know what sort of job I was going to offer him?' She giggled.

Anke, who found the conversation baffling and a little distasteful, noticed Graham approaching.

'Oh, here's my husband,' she announced gratefully, introducing them.

'Aren't you lovely and colourful?' Diana said condescendingly as she dropped back on to her flip-flops after planting kisses on his cheeks. 'I hear you are quite the Yorkie man.'

Graham immediately branded her a raging snob. He liked his women sleek and modest, and found Diana Lampeter's busty confidence too much from the start, although he was careful to hide this for his wife's sake. It was great that she was making friends so soon – it had taken her a long time in Essex.

'Anke's already decided you two will be great mates,' he told her cheerfully, not noticing Anke's look of horror.

'I'm sure we will,' Diana said emphatically, also starting to doubt this. She'd now decided that Anke Brakespear had no sense of humour and was irritatingly pious. She regretted issuing her impromptu supper invitation the night before, especially now that she had met Graham. Anke's husband – a great, beefy northerner – was surprisingly uncouth. Her first husband, the famously divine Kurt Willis, was utterly beautiful if undeniably gay. This was a very shoddy second choice.

Pod Shannon was a different matter. The more she thought about him, the more attracted Diana became to the idea of drawing him into her inner circle – or the inner circle she planned to create. She knew potential when she saw it, and Pod's charisma was certain to make him a local mover and shaker. The thought of being moved and shaken by him herself was deeply appealing. It was high time she started following in the family tradition. Living dangerously had never done her mother any harm, after all.

Graham was asking her about her plans now that she had moved back to the area. 'Your brother was just telling me that you used to be in the racing business?'

'Bloodstock, yes – years ago.' Diana gave him a delicious smile. 'Totally different game to Overlodes, of course, but it taught me a lot about presentation. And God knows this little backwater could do with smartening up. Too many bad-taste *nouveaux* and impoverished old-timers trying to rub along. Place needs some class.'

'And how do you plan to inject "class"?' Graham asked pointedly.

'Oh, I'm spoiled for choice.' She turned to look at the smouldering pub, breathing in the smell of burning timber and thatch. 'My original idea was to make Upper Springlode a base for gourmet riding holidays, or possibly to turn the yard into a training and competition centre. Who knows? I might even dabble with racing again – point to point rather than under rules.'

Anke sucked in a tight breath.

'Secret with business is to stick with one simple idea,' Graham was telling Diana helpfully. 'Don't get all muddled up with options and diversification. Set your goal and stick to it, love.'

Diana thought about Pod. 'How very helpful. I'll do just that.'

'Don't tell me she's the new mate you were banging on about when you came home last night?' Graham muttered as they walked the hundred yards to Dulston's.

'I was drunk,' Anke said weakly. 'And at least she's got chutzpah.'

'She's a toffee-nosed egomaniac, if you ask me.'

'We're going to supper there on Friday,' she reminded him.

'Oh, how I love the taste of peasant entrails served up on a bed of freshly slaughtered farm-hands,' he teased. When Anke didn't laugh, he gathered her into a hug. 'Sorry, love. I'm glad you've found a mate. I'll dust the working-class chips off my shoulders next Friday, I promise.'

'It's not that.' She pulled away from his grip, rubbing her arms as though he'd left a residue.

Undeflated, Graham tried again, wrapping an arm around her shoulders this time. 'Don't worry about the medal, pet. We can get a replica.'

She shrugged off the arm, embarrassed that people were looking. 'It's fine. It's only a piece of metal.'

Graham missed a couple of beats as he watched her and then nodded curtly. 'Whatever you say. Talking of bits of metal, come and see my new tractors.'

Dulston's consisted of a large concrete yard with a trio of cavernous green-painted metal barns on three sides, one containing offices, another housing a workshop and a third providing secure storage for equipment. While Graham picked his way through the huge collection of keys he had been given to find the one to the yard gates, Anke gazed blankly at the investment. She had seen enough haulage yards in her time to know that she really couldn't whip up any interest, although the small collection of John Deeres and Massey Fergusons appealed to her more than Ivecos and Scanias. Tractors were a favourite of Chad. She couldn't wait for her son to come along and see where his father now worked.

'Aha!' Graham found keys for the impressive-looking padlocks that decorated the chains lacing the high gates.

'Look at this! New Holland. Ordered in for a customer who promptly went bust before it could be delivered.' He started clambering aboard the huge combine harvester that dominated the yard. 'This was the straw that broke the camel's back for James Dulston, I reckon.' He laughed cheerfully at his own joke because he knew Anke was unlikely to get it. English humour often passed her by, however hard she tried.

'Surely it separates straw from wheat?' Anke asked earnestly, but Graham was already out of the cab and playing with the green tractor parked next to it.

Knowing that it would be a good half-hour before he got around to unlocking the offices and actually collecting the books and back orders that he had come here for, Anke let him enjoy his new toys as she wandered back to the gate to look out across the village.

Dulston's sat on the elbow of a road that looped out from the narrow hilly lane leading up to the ridge road and back to it again like a cocked arm. The pub was at the wrist, where the hand cupped the rounded hip of the village proper and one of the two bridleways to the valley dropped away like a bowed leg. The overgrown village green – known as the Prattle – made up the torso, with a dew-pond at its navel. At the shoulder there was a bleak-looking epaulette of a cottage half-hidden in the woods, besides which the second bridleway track ran from Upper Springlode all the way down the valley to Oddlode.

Upper Springlode was a tiny village compared to Oddlode – probably no more than twenty houses, containing a remarkable number of farms. Anke had counted a Field Farm, Hill Farm, Spring Farm and Horseshoe Farm, already – although none of them appeared to be working farms. It felt peaceful and forgotten compared to the bustle of Oddlode – secretive and sleepy, conservative and perhaps even a little unfriendly.

To prove her point, a stone-faced man in a Land Rover drove through the gates at speed, almost mowing her over with the trailer he was towing, and propelling the collie hanging out of the back into a hedge as he braked to a halt.

'You the one who's bought this place?' he demanded as he jumped out, his local accent so strong that Anke had difficulty deciphering. She noticed that he had two shotguns attached to brackets above the cab with a wire-haired terrier snarling between them.

'Er . . . my husband . . .' She looked around for Graham, wondering if this was a disgruntled member of staff. James Dulston had apparently failed to pay anyone for months before selling.

But Graham had disappeared. She couldn't see him in any of the tractor cabs, and all the green hangars were still locked.

'Can I help at all?' She stooped to pat the collie, who seemed none the worse for his hedge dive.

'Name's Gates,' he muttered.

Anke had spoken fluent English for years, but she had to admit she was struggling. He made no sense. What did he mean about naming gates?

'Gates?' she repeated, slyly studying the tag on the dog's collar which had 'Gunning Farm' written on it, along with a telephone number.

'That's right. You got two of my quad bikes here. Name's Gates. I want them back.'

Anke looked up at him enquiringly. The accent was heavenly, but extremely tricky to follow. He was an imposing figure too – well over six feet tall with a shorn head, shoulders as wide as a rower's and eyes so dark that they were impossible to interpret, seeming both vacant and frighteningly intense at the same time.

'I'm afraid you really need to speak with my husband.'

He took a cigarette from the battered softpack in his chest pocket and lit it with a blast from a Zippo that almost took off his curling black eyebrows. Anke stepped back from the sparks of tobacco.

'I don't care who I speak to, I want those quads back.'

'Graham!' She couldn't keep the shake from her voice as she tried to summon him. There was no answer.

'He'll be along in a minute.' She smiled nervously.

'You not from around these parts?'

Somebody had to say it. She wanted to laugh, but was feeling far too unsettled by the encounter to muster more than a nervous smile. 'Denmark.'

'Long way to come.'

She was just about getting to grips with his accent. 'My husband's English. We've moved here from Essex.'

He nodded and looked around tetchily, puffing on his cigarette, saying nothing. The dark eyes, blackening by the second, made Anke even edgier. On close inspection they were the deepest of greens, like a dense forest. His face was weather-beaten and hollow-cheeked, but she guessed he had to be younger than her – maybe only late thirties. His body was certainly that of a young man. She tried not to notice the bulging thigh muscles on those long, denim legs, the flat belly above narrow hips, or the breadth of those brown forearms where his checked shirtsleeves were rolled back. There was no denying that the men around here were a fearsomely good-looking squad. He was all earthy brawn and restless brutality. He also seemed more than capable of turning violent, and that made her want to run and hide.

'Terrible news about the fire, isn't it?' She tried to be chatty.

'Think so?' He flicked ash on to his boot and glanced across at the pub.

She balked. 'You don't?'

'Depends who you ask. Place has always been unlucky since the old Baron took against it. Best torched, some say.' He turned to look at her, his expression unfathomable. 'Perhaps it was cursed after all?'

His accent was beating her again. Anke hummed awkwardly and shouted for Graham. There was no answer.

'I can't hang around.' He blew on his cigarette tip and squinted at her through the smoke. The dark green gaze was boring into Anke's face now, so that she felt he was examining the skull beneath her skin.

Anke wanted to point out that she would be very happy for him not to hang around, but she was far too well-mannered – and scared.

He threw the cigarette at her feet and turned away. 'I'll fetch the quad bikes. I've spare keys with me – you can get someone to drop off the originals when you're more sorted.'

'I really don't think I can authorise that.'

'Tough.' He started to walk towards the storage hangar.

She cut off his path by his Land Rover and barred his way. 'Whatever deal you had with the previous owner of this company no longer stands. We have to go through the paperwork properly.'

'It was cash in hand. There *is* no paperwork.' His face was thunderous. 'Fucking James! He promised me he'd service them by the time he pissed off.'

Anke stood her ground, heart hammering. 'I really know nothing about this. My husband –'

He punched the side of his Land Rover. 'I *knew* I should have taken them to Lodes Agri. This place has always been crap. Whoever torched the pub should have lobbed a match over here last night and saved us all the hassle of a jumped-up car salesman trying to wreck farmers' livelihoods.'

Anke stepped back nervously. 'I'm afraid you'll have to speak more slowly. I don't really understand what you're saying.'

A great laugh whooped in his throat as he turned to look at her over his shoulder, green gaze stagnant with that impenetrable darkness. 'You don't understand me?'

Anke stepped back further, suddenly terrified. Those eyes really were disturbing. He had something about him, a ferocious turbulence that could back anyone on their heels. He was almost wild.

'The wife says she doesn't understand *me* either,' said a cheery voice as the reflection of Graham's Hawaiian shirt lit up the black shadows in Quad Man's eyes. 'What can we do for you?'

The ensuing conversation made no sense to Anke. The men spoke in testosterone-fuelled shorthand. All she could do was stare at those frightening dark green eyes, seeing the flames in them, and hope he didn't hit her husband.

'Quad bikes – two Yamaha Kodiaks. Brought them in for service just before Dulston sold this place. Want them back.'

'No can do. I've got to go through the books before we open up again.'

'They weren't in the books.'

'Then they're not here.'

'Things don't work like that around here.'

'They do now.'

'I need those bikes. We're stuck without them.'

'Give me two days.'

'You have one. I'll be back tomorrow.'

'I doubt I'll be on site.'

'You'll be here.' The man got back into his Land Rover and whistled for the collie.

'I didn't catch your –' The engine started with a roar, and Graham emptied his lungs in order to be heard. 'NAME?'

'GATES – NAME'S GATES!' The Land Rover and its trailer rattled around the New Holland combine harvester at indecent speed, shaving its corners with millimetres to spare. Flattened to the floor of the trailer, the collie gave Anke a wise look as they roared away.

'So, he names gates,' she sighed, grateful that he was gone. 'What an awful man.'

'Not the first awkward customer I'll have to deal with, I reckon.'

Graham rubbed his forehead. 'Dulston's left this place in one hell of a state.'

'Where *did* you get to? I was calling.'

'Sorry, love.' He glanced across at her, blue eyes wary as he swung an arm around her shoulders. 'I think you'd better come and take a look at this.'

For once, Anke didn't shrug the arm away as they made their way around the side of the storage hangar. She was grateful for its weight. She was almost tempted to mention her fears that their recent visitor was connected to the fire at the pub – in fact, she was ready to believe he'd started it – but Graham seemed too edgy to need to hear that. She soon found out why.

'Bloody hell!' Anke used her husband's favourite exclamation for want of another.

There was a six-feet ditch running behind the barns, separating them from the high chain-link perimeter fencing. Mostly overgrown with brambles, elder and blackthorn, the few gaps housed stacks of old pallets, creosote containers and empty cable reels. The biggest clearing was in the far corner and it housed something far more disturbing. The far corner was a shrine.

'Bloody hell,' Anke whispered again as they scrambled closer.

'Bloody, bloody hell,' Graham agreed.

The makeshift green tarpaulin tepee was strung from two tall holly trees and a spruce that hid it completely from the fields behind. Double-layered and lashed to the ground with ropes attached to thick wooden stakes, it was erected to stay put whatever the weather. Inside, a soggy, dog-eared armchair and folding table looked curiously mundane – an R and R pit stop for passing tramps. The ground beneath them was liberally carpeted with cigarette butts and grubby white filters where the brown paper had disintegrated. To either side were piles of empty beer cans – it was impossible to guess how many, but they had to number several hundreds. On the table was a small collection of items: a faded first place rosette, a damp book of love poems, a Beanie toy of a dog, a box of matches and something that made Anke cry out in relief and alarm.

'It's my medal!' She rushed forward to claim it.

Beneath the green glow of the plastic shelter, the smell of stale tobacco and beer was overpoweringly laced with petrol. Anke fought nausea.

Graham stooped beneath the awning. 'Whoever's behind this must've broken into the car last night – before the fire.'

'Have you called the police?'

'Not yet.'

'Graham, this is freaky.'

'Let's just hold our horses a bit. It's probably travellers or teenagers. Give me a bit of time, love. I've got to think about this.'

Anke was too relieved to be reunited with her medal to question him. Right now, she just wanted to get as far away from Dulston's as she could.

While she made her way back to the Lexus to wait and watch the fire-fighters packing away their equipment, Graham collected the paperwork he needed as quickly as he could from the offices. As he did so, he glanced up through the grimy window and spotted a police car coming from the direction of the fire and cruising past the open yard gates, slowing to take a look at Dulston's now that it was under new ownership. It was almost beckoning at him to leap out and wave it in to take a look at the 'camp'.

And yet, something stopped him. He was taking over a very shaky business with an already poor reputation in a deeply mistrustful area. He had already been labelled a 'Yorkie man', a 'nouveau' and a 'jumped-up car salesman'. He couldn't risk any exposure right now. He had to find out more about both his business and his trespasser before he shouted for attention. If the police found out that half his stock wasn't officially in the books and that he and Dulston hadn't strictly adhered to every letter of the law when cutting their deal, they might be interested in a lot more than just a teenage traunt's camp.

As the disagreeable Gates had said, 'Things don't work like that around here'. Until Graham found out how they *did* work, he had no intention of stirring things up.

5

Compared to the rustic isolation of Norfolk, Cotswold village life was a culture shock to Pod and Mo. Every time they tried to make love, somebody knocked on the door to introduce themselves. The postman stayed to chat for ten minutes each morning; the staff in the village shop kept a tight hold of the couple's change until they had shared a few morsels of news; it was impossible to cross the green without being cross-examined. Having expected Pod to be under more scrutiny because of his racing fame, Mo found herself the greater object of attention as eyes followed her everywhere.

'You're their new teacher, queen,' Pod laughed when she complained. 'That makes you much more important.'

'If I'm so important, why do people keep getting my name wrong? I got called Helena four times today,' she grumbled.

But if Mo had a band of bashful, star-struck admirers who had heard that she was a famous actress, Pod had a Number One Fan. Gladys Gates was a daily feature on their doorstep, bearing cake and jams, and telling Mo that she needed to eat more and stop starving that 'lovely young man'.

'This is such a friendly village, I know you'll be happy,' she promised them from the start. 'Everyone is so welcoming.'

And they were. Within hours of arriving, Oddlode's bustle and rumour-mongering hit them full-on as they were 'volunteered' for everything from the five-a-side cricket to the village hall re-roofing team. Pod tried out for the Lodes Valley Blackhearts but was found to play too dirty for even that rough rural team with its fearsome reputation. Putting two defenders in hospital before a key league match hardly helped his case. The Wycks adored him all the more slavishly for it, and lined up the pints throughout his first week.

Talk in the Lodes Inn was all of the fire in Upper Springlode and the belief that it had been arson. Fingers were pointing at landlord Keith, with the implication that the Plough was insured for far more than he could sell it for in a rapidly slowing market. With the fire investigators still on site, the derelict pub was again being offered on the open market at a knock-down price, fuelling the rumour.

The Wycks told another story, lavishly embellished with talk of ghosts and feuds that linked the episode to the grand and secretive Gunning Estate. At its centre was Foxrush Hall, high on the Parsons Ridge above Springlode, supposedly the most haunted house in the Cotswolds, and now in near-ruin. Amongst the Hall's many dark secrets were tales of bloody medieval battles, Civil War swordfights, infanticide, witchcraft, murderous sibling rivalry and more modern rumours that it had been the centre of an aristocratic nationalist faction in the 1930s. Its most recent high-profile incumbent had been the fifteenth Baron Sarsden, William Delamere, who had inherited the estate as a teenager in the late 1950s. Throughout the next two decades, still a young man, he had run riot with increasingly wild partying and decadence.

'*He* was Firebrand,' Pod told Mo delightedly when he returned after a long, daytime drinking binge to find her repainting the spare bedroom. 'You remember his name came up the first day we were here? The Wycks wouldn't talk about him in front of a "lady".'

'Oh, yes.' Mo rollered a wall with pale green paint. 'The headless ghost that gallops around at full moon?'

'I don't think he's headless.' Pod picked up a brush and started edging the fresh paintwork up to the low ceiling eaves beside her. 'In flames more like.'

'Flames?'

'Yeah – he was renowned for his love of pyrotechnics, apparently. He went missing in the late seventies, Lucan-style, after his beautiful, wayward wife and her lover were burned to death in one of the estate cottages.' He recited the tale as though reading hammily from a Mills and Boon jacket. 'Hence the "galloping ghost" is on fire.'

'Ugh! How awful.' Mo shuddered, trying not to picture the burning cottage and its inhabitants. 'So, there really *is* a ghost?'

He pressed out his lower lip with his tongue and pulled a cross-eyed loon face at her. 'Yeah, queen – like there really is a Father Christmas, and leprechauns and little pointy-eared elves that try to steal your teeth in the night.'

'Okay, okay.' She flipped him with specks of paint from her roller. 'So why tell the story?'

'Nobody found his body.' He looked at her through his lashes.

'You mean he could still be *alive*?'

'Yougoddit, queen.' He laughed at her boggling face.

Mo swallowed hard and adopted a cynical expression, knowing that Pod was winding her up. 'Even assuming this Firebrand guy is still flesh and blood, what has he got to do with the pub?'

'One of the places that the wife and her lover used to meet was the Plough – it's famous for adulterous liaisons. *And* it was already cursed by the Delamere family by all accounts. Something to do with a peasant revolt and a gambling debt. I forget the details.' He hiccupped.

'And so now, the Wycks are saying . . . what?' Mo couldn't help sneering. 'William Delamere's popped back thirty years later to burn it down?'

'They argued a good case.' He was too beery to care about chronology. 'They say he burns down all sorts of things when the mood takes him.'

'Are we talking about the flaming ghost or the ageing fugitive?'

'Who knows? Like I say, they never found a body. It was all over the news, apparently. They had a huge man hunt, but Firebrand had vanished – assumed to have fled the country or topped himself *very* discreetly. The police even dragged the lake up there. It sounds an amazing place. The house is *seriously* haunted. They had to board it up to stop ghoulish Marilyn Manson types holding illegal raves there.'

'And it's now a ruin?'

'The house is empty, yeah, but the estate is still worked – although nobody seems to know who owns it these days. It's a paper mountain of trustees and solicitors, as far as I can tell. I think I'll pop up there and take a look this week.'

'Oh, please don't.' Mo thought the place best left well alone. 'You're supposed to be looking for work, not ghosts.'

But Pod was entranced, and had already decided to take a snoop at the estate, although the Wycks had warned him that the estate manager was far from friendly, pointing out that even poachers steered well clear of Gunning land.

'*Have* you done anything about finding a job yet, by the way?' Mo persisted.

'I have my feelers out, queen, never fear . . .' he said reassuringly, switching subjects. 'Why are you decorating this room first? I thought you were going to paint over that minging flowered wallpaper in our bedroom?'

'*Gladys is watching,*' Mo mouthed, hardly daring to say the name aloud in case it worked as a beckoning call. 'She's been spying from her cottage all day.'

Pod crept on to the landing and peeked into their bedroom to check, giving a mock shriek of horror as he leaped back behind the door and rejoined Mo.

'Still dusting her upstairs sills?' she asked flatly.

He nodded, laughing delightedly. 'How long's she been doing that?'

'About two hours. She's bloody well glued there. You know, I think we might have forgotten to shut the curtains last night when we . . .' She drew a quick depiction in the wet paint before wiping it out.

'Maybe she's hoping for a repeat performance?' He removed the roller from her hand and started to kiss her. 'Dirty old Glad. She must think we're at it all the time. Which, come to think of it, we are.'

Mo laughed between his kisses, loving the way he could cheer her up. 'I couldn't face painting in there with her spying – especially as I'm not sure we're really supposed to be redecorating at all. So I thought I'd paint in here.'

'And very nice it looks too.' Pod started sliding off her overalls.

She hastily ducked down below window height so that they couldn't be seen by the kids playing on the green. 'I want somewhere peaceful to do my yoga. The candy stripes were just too much.'

'Too, too much.' He pulled her T-shirt over her head.

'And this pale green is very soothing, I thought.'

'Totally soothing. I feel completely soothed.'

He lay her down on a dust-sheet and pulled the overalls over her feet, sweeping off her flip-flops, shorts and panties with them. Just as he buried his face between her thighs, the horseshoe door-knocker clanked against its frame downstairs.

'Ignore it,' Mo insisted, sliding her hands down to his head to stop it shooting back up.

'Coooece!' came the call through the open window. 'Patrick! Helena – oops! I mean *Maureen*. Shall I let myself in? I've got my keys.'

'Oh, fuck.' Mo sagged back in defeat.

'You mean no fuck,' Pod laughed, hastily throwing Mo's clothes at her and legging it downstairs just in time to intercept Gladys in the hallway.

'Hello, dear – thought I saw you coming home. I've brought you a homemade cake. Let's put the kettle on. Can I smell paint?'

'Tea! What a good idea. Come through to the kitchen, Gladys. That cake looks delicious. Mo! Lovely surprise, queen!' he called upstairs. 'Gladys has brought cake.'

'Hoo-bloody-ray,' Mo muttered, listening to Pod making welcome below. Gladys must have moved like lightning to drop her duster and grab her cake. The old bat had turbo boost when it came to Pod.

He was always utterly charming to her, she realised, as she crabbily pulled on her shorts and T-shirt again. Perhaps that was why Gladys came round at least three times a day? The old busybody probably had a crush on him, especially now that she'd seen him in action. Mo couldn't remember exactly what they'd got up to in the bedroom the evening before, but she seemed to recall that it had involved quite a lot of activity up against the wall, and one of the longest nipple-sucking sessions she had ever enjoyed. She didn't want to go downstairs.

Gladys reminded her of her grandmother, cheerfully disguising her prying visits with home baking. When she and Pod had first moved into Newmarket together – sharing a tiny room at the racing yard he'd then worked at – Granny Stillitoe had turned out more tarts and fancies than Mr Kipling as an excuse to pop around and check up on them. She'd interrupted them *in flagrante* quite often, too.

'Easily done.' Pod would just laugh when Mo complained – then, as now. 'We're seldom unplugged, queen.'

He was a sucker for home cooking. Mo couldn't bake a bean, let alone a three-tier chocolate torte with ripple top. And now that they had moved hundreds of miles across the country to shag in peace, they'd inherited another baking powder pensioner. Mo hated to admit it but, only three days in, she was already developing a pathological loathing for Gladys Gates.

'I had a lovely cup of coffee with Ingmar's daughter this morning,' Gladys was telling Pod when Mo finally joined them in the garden, forced to perch on the edge of the walled flower-bed because they only had two folding picnic chairs. 'Nice woman, she is – so sophisticated. She says you've already made friends?' She tried to draw Mo in.

'Have we?' Mo asked vaguely, pouring herself a milky tea.

'Yeah, I remember Anke.' Pod nodded. 'Her father runs that second-hand bookshop by the gallery, doesn't he?'

Mo – who didn't even know there *was* a bookshop in Oddlode – wondered how Pod found out all these things. All those hours in the pub, she supposed.

'"Antiquarian", it's called,' Gladys corrected. 'Caused a bit of fuss when he first moved in because a few locals got the wrong end of the stick and thought he was starting a fish shop – aquarium, you see?'

'More likely to be a fish haters' shop if it's *anti*quarium, surely?' Mo suggested.

This was lost on Gladys, who forged on. 'Poor Ingmar was a bit taken aback when he found himself asked about koi carp and butterfly fish when he first moved in. Reg Wyck even tried to order cod and chips.' She chortled happily.

Pod joined in with raucous aplomb, even reaching across to nudge her elbow as they shared the joke. Mo scowled, feeling her temper blacken by the second. She could still feel the skin on her thighs tingling where Pod's lips had been just a minute or two earlier.

'I think running that little shop is more of a hobby for old Ingmar, these days,' Gladys was telling him. 'The poor man is very *forgetful*,' she whispered with a nervous glance over each shoulder. 'That's why his daughter's moved close by, wanting to keep an eye on him, bless her. So polite and elegant, she is – quite a lady.' She cut Mo a huge slice of cake. 'Nice family. Bit of a rascal, her husband, but very charming with it. I've said I'll help find them a cleaner, but they'll have to make do with one of the Wycks. I don't think I'd trust him around any of my own girls. Terrible flirt, he is. Here – eat this up, Maureen. You're all skin and bone.'

'I'm not hungry, thanks,' Mo muttered. 'And please call me Mo, Gladys. My name isn't Maureen.'

'It's short for Maureen, though?'

'No, it's not.'

'Oh. What is it short for?'

'Mo.' She gave Pod a steely look to ensure he didn't say otherwise.

'What an unusual name.'

Mo couldn't be bothered to explain, standing up and wandering out from beneath the shady canopy of the apple trees and into the sunlight, leaving her cake behind as she slurped her tea and let the heat soothe her frosty edges. She had a suspicion that Pod only pretended to find Glad Tidings so captivating in order to wind her up. And it worked.

He was asking her about Firebrand and Foxrush Hall.

'Oh, there's so much nonsense talked about him in this village.' Gladys patted his arm. 'You don't want to believe a word of all those ghost stories. The Delameres were always a rotten lot. That boy was quite out of control – he took a lot of *drugs*, you know.' She tucked back her several chins and exchanged a look of horror with Pod.

'So there isn't a ghost?'

'Lawks, no. His car was long gone when they found the bodies of that poor little wife of his and her . . . gentleman friend. Dreadful business, it was. My husband was one of the locals the police got to help organise the search – out night and day, he was, even after they found the car at Folkestone. Young Lord Sarsden had obviously left the country, but the police kept Granville scouring around that wretched park for weeks. And he wasn't paid a penny for his efforts. Always was a soft touch.' She gave an affectionate smile, tinged with sadness.

'Have you been a widow long?' Pod laid on the compassion with a flirty edge that only he could get away with.

'Oh, he's not dead, dear.'

'But . . . I thought you lived alone?'

'I do. Granville is a little eccentric these days. He lives . . . independently. I take him his supper and do his laundry. He's as fit as a fiddle, I can assure you.'

Mo caught Pod's gaze over the top of Glady's blue rinse and they both widened their eyes.

'He's here in the village?'

'Nearby.' She wiped cake crumbs daintily from her mouth, preferring to dwell on the past. 'When we met, Granville was head gardener at Foxrush Hall, which was why he knows the estate so well. We lived in the sweetest little cottage beside the big kitchen garden up there as newlyweds; it was such a pretty place, then. But then that tearaway William Delamere inherited the house, and I didn't want to bring my girls up anywhere near him.

'I'd been in service with the Constantines before we married, and they were very kind in helping us out – giving me the housekeeper's job here at the Manor and taking Granville on as groundsman; we worked together at the big house here in Oddlode for nearly twenty years. Poor Granville always missed the Foxrush gardens, though. He still talks of them in his more . . . lucid moments. Of course, young Lord Sarsden quite ruined them. You don't want to know what he got up to there.'

'Firebrand?' Pod had an almost hypnotised expression on his face.

'Some still call him that.' She helped herself to Mo's unwanted slice of cake. 'Just a boy when his father died – at boarding school, he was, but that didn't stop him trying to change the place from day one. Granville was furious. Old Lord S had been a difficult so-and-so, especially after all the unfortunate business with the nationalists making him a bit of a recluse, but at least he understood how to keep a good garden. When young William inherited, he had all sorts of silly ideas. Granville wouldn't entertain them. The fireworks gave him tinnitus for a start, and those parties . . .' She winced. 'Capability Brown landscaped part of those gardens, you know. Within two years, they were all but destroyed. Broke Granville's heart.'

'How awful.' Mo started clearing away the tea, not liking the look of excitement in Pod's eyes. But Gladys laid a soft peach-skin hand on hers. As ever, she was saving a juicy piece of gossip for emergencies.

'It's not as though William Delamere was even a true heir to that estate.'

Pod whistled. 'What do you mean?'

Gladys wrestled the teapot from Mo and poured herself half a cup of brick red dregs. 'His mother was forty-eight when he appeared – her first child, and never a bump to show for it in the nine months beforehand. She was riding to hounds the day before the birth, they say.' She delighted in retelling a well-worn local rumour. 'The old Baron was in his fifties then and known to be – well – a little bit effete, shall we say? Everyone said that they bought the baby. Young William was no more a Delamere than I am. How else could a pair of blonde parents create a black-haired child?'

'Maybe he dyed in his sleep?' Mo said idly, spiking up her own hennaed crop cut and kicking at a flower-bed as she wandered back out into the sun. But its warmth didn't improve her temper. She found this rumour-mongering and ghost story telling maddening – and Pod's interest in it even more so.

'No dear, old Lord Sarsden had a heart attack,' Gladys was explaining, the sarcasm flying over her blue rinse. 'The boy was thirteen or fourteen then. He knew that everybody doubted his parentage. When he came home for the funeral, he couldn't have missed the talk – all the staff were waiting for the will to be challenged, although it never was. Some say that's why the young lord turned so bad, but it could just have been in his blood. Who knows where he sprang from? Some silly young floozy getting herself banged up and then selling the child to that old couple to continue the family line. Any mother who deserts her child will leave it with an unhappy life.'

'Rubbish!' Mo exploded back into the shadows. 'There are plenty of happy children who haven't been fortunate enough to know their biological parents.'

Gladys almost fell off her chair.

'Parenting isn't about swapping semen and ovum,' she raged on. 'It's about raising children with love and care.'

'Steady on, queen.' Pod loped over to her and stroked her sinew-lined neck. 'I don't think Gladys would argue with that.'

'A child needs a father and a mother,' Gladys insisted.

'And you need to bugger . . . right . . . off, you spying old cake-baker!'

'I have no idea why the school employed her,' Gladys reported to her chums beside the shuttered post office counter in the shop a few minutes later. 'She used such bad language. *And* she's one of these dreadful modern bohemian types who thinks we should breed children in test tubes.'

'Well, the school does want to modernise,' Phyllis Tyack pointed out.

'It's probably all for the part,' whispered Kath Lacey with a huge wink. 'She'll acknowledge you on Parky one day, Glad. I loved her in *A Room With A View.*'

Gladys gave her a withering look.

'You over-reacted a bit, queen.' Pod rubbed oil into Mo's shoulders as she sat in the bath half an hour later.

'I know, I know – I'm sorry.' She pulled at her wet, spiky hair. 'Christ. I must apologise to her. She'll be telling everyone I'm bonkers.'

'No doubt,' he agreed. 'But not as bonkers as her Granville.'

'The one who lives . . . independently?' She tried to giggle, but was still too uptight.

'Mad as a hatter – lives in a railway carriage somewhere beyond Manor Farm. The Wycks told me already.'

'Seriously? So why did you pretend to think she was a widow?'

'I like to see people unravel.'

'You see me unravel all the time.'

'You are my naked truth.' He dipped his hands beneath the bubbles and slipped an oily finger inside her. 'I never tire of unravelling you.'

'Like an Egyptian mummy?'

'A Mummy without a mummy.' He stretched down to kiss her, knowing that when she laughed and cried at the same time, Mo was a sexual explosion counting down. 'I am your mummy, and your daddy, and your brother and your lover.'

'I've heard incest is big around these parts, but this is ridiculous.'

'Ah, but we come from Norfolk, remember?'

Gladys panted back up her stairs, duster in hand, just in time to see a large splash of foam and bathwater appear through the obscured bath-room window of Number Four Horseshoe Cottages. She could hear screaming and cackling and groaning. Oh dear. The girl was quite mad. She felt an even greater affinity with the lovely young Patrick with his big, sad eyes and wide, warm smile. Dealing with mental imbalance was such a trial.

She tried to angle herself to see if she could get a better view through the small opened top window, but a large pigeon on a telegraph wire was in her way.

'Shoo!' She waved her duster at it. If the girl was having some sort of fit, she'd have to call the police. Young Pod might be in danger after all. Or the girl might drown herself.

The pigeon stayed put. Gladys watched another splash of water hit the window, and a few large flecks of foam floated out above the gardens, finally sending the alarmed pigeon on its way.

'Oh, dear.' Gladys saw frantic thrashing behind the obscured window. A moment later she let out a small squeak as the unmistakeable shape of a naked bottom was pressed up against the glass. To either side of it were – somebody's knees. Two small hands splatted against the glass higher up, and – oh my goodness! She hoped that was a loofah.

Pod smoked an illicit spliff out of the kitchen door while he watched Mo napping on the sofa in shorts and a bikini top – his little seraphic scruff with her delicate face, loo-brush hair and androgynous body. She was beautiful, incomprehensible and fiery. It was that fire he needed most of all – it burned great holes of love into his skin. But lately, the fire had been more angry than fun. Her wicked sense of humour had slipped beneath the hot coals. He missed her dragon laughter. He needed to throw fresh tinder on to make her burn brighter.

He cooked – as he always did – but this time he made a real effort, forgoing the usual cheese on toast and creating a feast with tinned kidney beans, canned tomatoes, supermarket value peppers, chilli powder and rice. For Pod, it was haute cuisine – and hot enough to put a dash of smoke into any baby dragon's nostrils.

Woken from a paint-induced, headachy bad dream, Mo ate reluctantly and dopily until her eyes suddenly streamed in recognition and she threw her head under the kitchen cold tap to douse her mouth.

'That's *so* bloody hot!' She glared at him for a moment before bursting out laughing.

He smiled, watching her burn.

Tears streamed from her eyes and she gobbled as much water as she could.

'Not *too* hot for you, is it, queen?'

'Of course not!' she spluttered between gulps.

Early in their relationship, they had discovered a mutual passion for very hot food – leading to something of a death-match competition. Each had tried to out-chilli and out-vindaloo the other to the point where the food had almost made them ill. It had been years since Pod had cooked anything this hot.

'Reminds me of the good old days,' he said now, forking up another mouthful. 'Mmm – I'm a fantastic cook, even if I say so myself. C'mon, queen – don't let it go cold.'

'Not much chance of that.' Mo finally turned off the tap and straightened up. 'What's this in aid of, Pod?'

'I'm going to Foxrush tomorrow.' He spoke with his mouth full, deliberately ultra-casual. 'Care to join me?'

There was a long pause while she pressed a Churches of Norfolk tea towel to her lips – a farewell gift from her grandparents. He was testing a lot more than her taste buds here, and she knew it. Suddenly the whole Gunning Estate had taken on a new significance. Pod was prone to these obsessions and, for whatever reason, he wanted to make her a part of it.

'Let's go and find Firebrand,' he breathed.

Mo's silence stretched on. She could feel the sweat on her forehead and beneath her clammy clothes as the hot chilli and muggy evening conspired to boil the blood in her veins, yet her skin prickled with icy discomfort. She was suddenly reminded of the holiday that they had taken in southern France, stopping the car on a hillside to watch a forest fire. They had drunk wine together and watched the fire get closer and closer, sharing a strange reckless challenge not to be the first to suggest leaving. Ash and sparks had surrounded them, the heat had become unbearable, the air unbreathable, the day turning to night because the air was so black. A helicopter, buzzing overhead to drop water, had spotted them and desperately signalled for them to get out, but finally it had been forced to fly away from the heat. Pod had been the first to crack, dragging Mo back to the car, which had a coat of thick ash and melted tyres. He had never really forgiven her for being even more out of control than he was that day. He'd long looked for a way to stand too close to the fire together again.

This was it. It was a make or break moment.

She broke more than the silence when she answered 'no'. Somewhere deep in Pod's chest, another heart-string snapped.

He tapped his fork against the rim of his plate, not looking at her. 'Why not?'

'Too many ghosts in my life already.'

Tilting his head to one side, he looked up at her, showing great white crescents beneath the black irises of his eyes as he adopted a Sloaney drawl. 'Yah, this marriage *is* a bit crowded.'

'This isn't a marriage,' she pointed out.

Pod kept his eyes on her, the remaining heart-strings tightening as he saw the ghosts haunting her eyes. He wanted to slay them once and for all.

'Come to Foxrush with me tomorrow.' He drew his tongue slowly across his teeth. 'And I might even propose.' There! He'd said it. He meant it.

Chuckling, she shook her head and settled back at the table to drain half a glass of red wine. 'You'll never propose, Pod. That's what keeps us together.'

Snap. Snap. Snap. The strings broke one by one.

She was right not to trust him. He had taught her not to trust him, and that was the curious secret of their success. Mo liked to live life as though she had nothing to lose, and Pod was already a lost cause. But with their fresh start in Oddlode, he had hoped for some sort of redemption. Something about Gunning was drawing him and he wanted his little dragon at his side. He wanted her there so much that he had visions of himself on one knee amongst the haunted woods. It was a crazy image, but he couldn't shake it from his head. He was ready to offer his hand along with his bitter, twisted and forsaken heart – but she didn't want it. She needed the Pod who would never propose, just as she would never accept.

He forked up some more chilli, shovelled it back angrily and watched her as she picked out her kidney beans and wiped away the sauce before popping them in her mouth.

'See?' She grinned at him. 'Even *your* eyes are watering.'

'Yeah. Even my eyes are watering.' He got up to open more wine and wiped the tears with the back of his arm.

Later, they made love defiantly with the curtains open – hours of nearly-there pleasure and pain that drove them both to the limit before finally succumbing to two angry climaxes that clashed rather than coming together. It was both unsatisfactory and yet, absurdly, amongst the best sex they had ever had.

Sweaty, dishevelled, more beautiful than ever, Pod laid his sinewy length on Mo, weighing himself down like stones as he breathed in her ear. 'If you took a lover I'd set light to this cottage with you both in it.'

Mo jerked away from the hot blast of his breath and pressed her cheek against the pillow, looking out to the blood-red sky above the apple trees. 'Good.'

He puffed disbelieving laughter into her hair. '*Good*?'

'The décor and furniture are so bad, I think torching is the only cure.'

He started to laugh. 'God, you're dark sometimes, queen. To think you're going to influence young minds around here.'

'They only see my flip side.'

'I see your flipped side.'

'It's the side that loves you.'

'All my sides love you. Even my insides. Come to Foxrush with me, queen. Come and explore.'

She turned to face him and laid her cheek against his, still debating whether to say yes or no when she fell asleep, safe at last, the request unanswered.

The next morning, he left without her.

6

Diana tried to look beyond the squalor of Horseshoe Farm Cottage as she planned her dinner party for her fellow new arrivals, primarily with the intention of getting a little closer to Pod Shannon.

She spotted him as she took an early morning drive into Oddlode to place a postcard in the post office stores window, advertising for a cleaner. There he was, setting out from his little cottage by mountain bike, a floppy, faded pink sun-hat drooping to his dark glasses. On anyone else it would look camp, but on Pod it just set off his undomesticated beauty. Diana almost crashed into a lamppost as she swung into a parking space in front of the stores, eyes glued to Pod's tanned legs and carved shoulders. Thank heavens for heat waves, she thought happily, as he passed dressed in nothing but shorts and scuffed trainers. She beeped her horn to attract his attention, but he didn't even look around.

The horn beep did, however, draw the attention of the pensioner collective gathering under the village shop's new green awning, and they all started muttering furiously behind their hands when Diana got out of her car, leaving it parked at a jaunty angle, half-on and half-off the pavement.

'Pod!' She hopped after him, leaving her children wrestling with the child-locked back doors. 'Pod!' She waved the piece of card she was carrying to attract his attention.

He slalomed his way through the chestnut trees along the edge of the green and came to a rakish halt beside her. 'Can I help?'

It was obvious he didn't remember who on earth she was, or was at least pretending not to.

Close up, he looked even better – the bitter chocolate eyes flecked with mint, the butterscotch skin glistening warmly. She felt her mouth water.

'I hear you might be looking for some work?' Diana fanned herself with her postcard.

He cocked his head, the Shannon smile almost knocking her out. 'My gigolo rates are pretty high, flower.'

Diana fanned harder, for once lost for words. He was lethal.

'Joke?' He grinned. 'Here – let me.' He took the card and waved it in front of her face. 'My mother had hot flushes for years,' he teased. 'She got patches in the end.'

'I am not menopausal!' she spluttered, trying to snatch the card back, but he was reading it now, the dark brows frowning.

'Is this the "work" you had in mind?' He started pedalling in a big circle around her, still reading.

'No! Not at all! I was thinking you might want to –'

'Forget it.' He threw the card back at her and pedalled away, calling over his shoulder. 'I always say if you're too proud to clean your own bog, you're too proud to shit.'

Diana reeled. Sexy, rude, lethal *and* volatile. He was fabulous.

In the badly parked Audi, Mim and Digby were drawing obscenities on the steamed-up windows. Hally, had made it out of the sun-roof and was chasing a cat along the pavement.

Diana gathered her troops and marched past the pensioner collective.

No doubt they were whispering to one another that she was the 'Constantine Girl'. Diana shot them a dirty look as she passed. It wasn't as though she even *was* a Constantine. She had been born Henriques.

The bleached blonde shopkeeper was amused when Diana handed her the card, saying in a strange transatlantic accent, 'You'll be lucky, honey.'

'What?'

'Everyone's looking for a cleaner round these parts.'

She took Diana's payment and posted the card in the window. When Diana went back outside, she noticed that her simple request for 'Home help in Springlode, hours to suit' was now nestling amid twenty other home-made adverts seeking cleaners, far more smartly presented than hers, offering perks such as lunch, state of the art Dysons, no need for lavatory cleaning, and pet-free, child-free homes.

As she marched back into the shop to return the sweets that Digby had feloniously crammed into his pockets and to gather Mim out of her head-first dive into the ice-cream cabinet, Diana felt a familiar, painful twinge pull at her belly. No wonder she was so on edge. She bought a packet of tampons and slid them hastily into her handbag, knowing the countdown had begun. She had been too distracted by the move to check dates. Today was PMS meltdown. Hosting a supper party was suicide. She should be renting one of the DVDs lined up above the blonde shopkeeper's head – a nice weepie like *Sea Biscuit* – and preparing for a night howling on the sofa.

'And a bottle of gin,' she added casually as she took a twenty pound note from her purse. 'Just a cheapie – for sloes, you understand.'

Handing over the bottle, Lily Lubowski caught the eyes of the pensioner collective and they all shared a moment of delicious speculation as Diana and her children marched outside to collect her howling dog from the hook beneath the postcards.

One of the 'Cleaner Wanted' postcards was from Anke Brakespear, along with a telephone number that Diana now fed into her mobile. Knowing that PMS was about to take grip, she was determined to fight it off by keeping busy. She should confirm their supper date, after all and, while she was in the village, it would be lovely to pop by and admire the changes at Wyck Farm – not that she had ever crossed the threshold during her childhood when it had been in possession of the Wyck family, but she had hacked ponies past enough times to peer over the garden walls and see the chaos beyond. Despite its family reputation and dreadful position, she'd always thought the farm incredibly pretty. It would be interesting to see what these country property developers did. She might get some inspiration for Overlodes and the Horseshoe Inn.

It wasn't yet nine o'clock and she wanted to kill some more time before returning to the stables – mostly to avoid becoming embroiled in the ghastly morning mucking-out routine. Rory had already dropped heavy hints that her help would be appreciated, especially given that she had brought two horses and two ponies with her – for whom she had not lifted a finger since arriving. He and Sharon were due to set off for a competition later that morning and she planned to stay away until they had gone. Accustomed to having her horses' every needs catered for on expensive London livery, Diana was terrified at the prospect of actually having to work around them. Even the children's ponies frightened her these days.

As she dialled the number, she also vaguely hoped that she could persuade Anke to express an interest in riding stallion Rio, whom she was still too frightened to fetch in from the field, lying to Rory and Sharon that he would benefit from a week's field rest to settle in. Rio had already settled into a little rape and pillage, covering most of the Overlodes mares and breaking into the hay barn.

But an answer machine greeted her call, explaining that Graham and Anke couldn't come to the phone. Diana left a suitably ingratiating message, reminding them about her kitchen sups. She then contemplated her options. She had already bought all the necessary groceries, including fresh flowers, for her evening's entertainment. The last of the cleaning and tidying could wait until the coast was clear. She really should pay one of the house visits that she had been putting off.

'Mummy, Til or Nanny?' None was tempting. Her mother seemed to be actively avoiding her. Visiting her aunt meant driving on to Gunning land and she wasn't brave enough for that yet. Which left . . .

'Is Miss Crump expecting you?' Matron watched in alarm as Digby and Mim crashed gleefully around the reception hall at Lower Oddford nursing home.

'Oh yes – I said I'd call in as soon as I could.' Diana leaped forwards to catch a flying vase. 'Can we have some coffee brought through to the garden, please? It's such a heavenly morning that I think we'll sit out there.'

Matron's eyebrows shot up even more. 'And are you planning to communicate with Miss Crump through her window?'

'What?'

'She has been bedridden since the fall. Old bones take a long time to heal, you know.'

As ever when caught left-footed, Diana kicked out with her right. 'Are you saying that she has broken something whilst under your care?'

'I'm afraid that Miss Crump was under your mother's care when she took a tumble at Cheltenham races back in March, breaking her pelvis. She received the best possible medical attention both from the Cotswold hospital and from ourselves.'

'Honestly – I told her not to ride the Foxhunter Chase this year,' Diana joked to cover the gaffe, referring to the big amateurs' cavalry charge over the Gold Cup course.

But Matron looked flummoxed.

As soon as she saw her, Diana took both Nanny's liver-spotted hands and kissed her crumpled cheek. 'Nanny! I had no idea about the fall. Mummy didn't breathe a word. I'm so sorry.'

'Quite all right, dear – I told her not to bother you with it. You were going through a bad time of your own.' Nanny's mealy gaze looked her up and down.

'But I could have sent you some flowers or a card, Nanny. Digby! Stop that at once!'

'My! Haven't these two grown?' Nanny peered at the youngsters. 'Pretty little things. You can tell they're Constantines.'

'Only a quarter Constantine.' Diana removed the remote control from Mim's hot little clutches and apologetically turned from the cartoons back to *Trisha* with the sound muted as Nanny liked.

Nanny was more shrunken and hunched than ever. It was almost two years since Diana had seen her at a family party, and she was torn between amazement that she still kept on trucking and aversion to such a manifest example of superannuated old age. Her white hair was threadbare, her skin puckered and discoloured, her frail old frame draped in a frilly nightie and a daintily knitted bedjacket. No longer the indomitable force Diana remembered, with ramrod back, starched dresses and patent leather bun, Nanny appeared like an old dictator years after his regime has been overthrown.

'I gather your mother told you to visit me?' Nanny tried not to wince as Diana's children roamed loose in her room threatening her knick-knacks. She would have asked one of the staff to remove her precious possessions for safekeeping had Diana preceded her visit with a call, but she always had been an impetuous girl.

'No, I haven't spoken with Mummy yet.' Diana settled on a leather wing chair and looked around impatiently for coffee.

'But surely you moved here almost a week ago?' Nanny recalled the visit from Truffle that very day.

'One's been very busy – unpacking and such,' Diana said breezily. 'And Mummy always has a very full calendar.'

Nanny gave her a wise look, 'Do I take it you don't entirely approve of her new *beau*?'

'Insincere Vere?' Diana sneered. 'Well, he's definitely gay for a start. He's probably after her money. Not the first – and I'm sure Mummy's voracious sexual appetite will eventually see him off.'

Nanny almost swallowed her false teeth.

'Sorry, Nanny.' Diana watched those rheumy eyes bulge and felt a stab of contrite guilt. Being depressed, divorcing and distracted made one terribly harsh sometimes. 'I didn't mean to shock you.' She took the wrinkled hand again. 'I'm still a "selfish little flibbertigibbet", you see.'

Nanny stopped spluttering and her eyes softened as she recalled the words – words she had uttered herself twenty years earlier.

'No. Diana.' She pressed the fingers in her frail grip. 'You are quite right. Ingmar said much the same thing.'

'Ingmar?'

'Mr Olesen – he runs the little antiquarian bookshop in Oddlode, and sometimes brings books to the residents here.' She pressed her lips together in wry amusement. 'When he remembers, poor man. I rather think he should be living here himself. He is finding it terribly hard to cope. He arrived this week with fourteen copies of *A Guide to Rough*

Shooting and half a dozen of *Practical Bee-Keeping*. But he does like to have a chat – and he *did* remember that I am terribly fond of Mary Webb. He brought me some short stories from a very old volume – on the shelf there. Terribly rare. I can only read a little at a time because my eyes are so bad, but it gives me great pleasure. No doubt Ingmar was hoping to find your mother here. He is another of Truffle's admirers.'

Diana snorted, staggered at the notion. 'Hence he thinks Vere's gay?'

'He wouldn't use quite such base language, my dear. He simply hinted that Mr Peplow has bought an unseemly selection of art books from his shop over the years, many of which featured rather disproportionate young men.'

Diana, who thought this a hugely fun conversation, was distracted by the children taking an unhealthy interest in Nanny's oxygen cylinder. She hastily diverted their attention with the magical pens and paper from her handbag.

When she turned back to Nanny, the pale gaze was locked on target. 'You've put on weight.'

'Only a little bit . . . misery eating.'

'There's no excuse for gluttony,' Nanny tutted, straightening her eider-down with gnarled old fingers. 'And have you seen Amos yet?'

Diana started, no longer finding the conversation entertaining. 'No, why should I?'

'I'd have thought it inevitable now that you have moved back to the area. He and his young family are a part of the community.'

'Oh, really?' Diana feigned insouciance. 'I'd heard he was still an anti-social misanthrope.'

Nanny looked at her sharply, making Diana blanch.

'You damaged that boy so badly, it's no wonder he mistrusts people.'

Diana glanced nervously at the children. 'We damaged one another.'

'You should never have come back to live here.' Nanny suddenly showed a flash of the old fire and brimstone Crump temper. 'You've stirred the Gunning ghost. No good will come of it.'

'Rubbish,' Diana scoffed, but inwardly she blenched. Since arriving in Springlode, she had barely allowed herself to think about Amos. Now she couldn't shake his face from her mind. She wondered how much he had changed over the years.

'He has a family now, you say?'

'Amos and Jacqui have two daughters, I believe.'

'*Jacqui*?' Diana couldn't keep the sneer from her voice. 'How old?'

'Let me think – the oldest one was born just after I moved in here, which would make her five. The younger one must be two or three.'

Diana had actually wanted to know Jacqui Gates' age. She looked to her own children now. Mim was drawing a picture of her father – she was no great artist and the face was more like a potato than a human visage, but Diana could tell it was Tim from the military hat. Digby was drawing a car – an orange car, naturally, with two misshapen wheels and what appeared to be a propeller.

So they both had children, she and Amos. The thought drew an uncomfortable claw across Diana's gut. Amos Gates, now in his forties, a husband and father. Her image of him badly needed updating, but she still saw her childhood sweetheart, turned lifelong enemy, with his tousled raven mane and his greyhound-lean body. And now, as well as a family man, he was the Gunning Estate manager, defending and main-taining the ancient, shielded parkland on which they had once fallen in love. She wondered how well he guarded the Pleasure Garden and its long-buried riddles. She suddenly fought a desperate urge to revisit it, to see whether it was still there.

'You will see him soon, you do know that,' Nanny warned. 'You must prepare yourself. He is a very bitter man. He changed after you left. He has a terrible temper.'

'He always did,' Diana sighed, watching as Digby added an orange driver to his orange car. 'If you ask me, there is no Gunning ghost – just Amos spitting his own personal fire.' She tried to cheer herself up with an image of Amos as a Scooby Doo baddy dressing up in an assort-ment of ridiculous monster suits to frighten away visitors. 'He and Til are probably in cahoots, trying to keep prying eyes away from Foxrush. It's such a waste. The Estate is so glorious. It's high time it was opened up again.'

'Don't you ever exploit that beautiful place!' Nanny warned.

'I have no intention of exploiting anything.' Diana tried not to think about Rory and her plans for Overlodes. 'I just think that it's about time people around here stopped being too frightened to go there. The place would be heaven to walk and ride in – there are rights of way all over it that nobody has used in years because they are so terrified by all the stupid stories that are told.'

'The ghosts will never rest.'

Diana snorted. 'Aunt Til is the only one who would never rest if tourists find out about the stunning secret on her cottage doorstep.'

Nanny eyed her curiously. 'You do know about the sale, don't you?'

'What sale?'

'The Gunning Estate. Your mother says that it is being discreetly "marketed" – I think that's the term she used.'

Diana's eyes widened as Nanny broke the news that the Gunning Estate was rumoured to be on the market for the first time since the land was given to the first Baron Sarsden as a love token by James I. It had been held in trust since the early 1980s, although various legitimate and illegitimate offspring of the missing Firebrand had sought to claim it.

'And what of Aunt Til? Will she still be able to carry on living there?'

'I have no idea. She refuses to accept it's up for sale. Silly girl just says they can't sell because they don't own it.'

'Well, I hope she doesn't expect Mummy to give her house room,' Diana muttered bitterly, glancing at her watch. Rory and Sharon would be long gone by now, making it safe for her to return to Horseshoe Farm Cottage and attempt a Mary Poppins transformation.

Nanny clamped a bony hand to her arm. 'Amos and his family will lose their home too.'

'Good. Maybe they'll move away. It's his turn to go into exile. I've spent long enough in the wilderness. This is my home now, and I won't hide from him.'

'Oh, Diana.' Nanny tightened her grip as Diana attempted to stand up. 'Think very, very carefully about what you are doing here, child.'

'Come on, Mim, Digby – we've got to go.' She pulled away, not looking into that pleading old gaze.

At that moment, a cheery care worker bustled in through the door with a tray of coffee and biscuits. Taking a child's hand in each of hers, Diana breezed past her without acknowledgement.

'Always was a crosspatch,' Nanny confided as she and Kelly shared the coffee between them moments later. She sucked thoughtfully on a Rich Tea to soften it.

'She's got her mother's looks.' Kelly, who had always thought Truffle very like a young Elizabeth Taylor, sighed dreamily.

'Yes, and has broken as many hearts.' Nanny took a dainty sip of coffee to see the biscuit on its way. 'My, but she was wild when she was younger. She knew no fear and no guilt. I'm rather afraid she hasn't changed.'

7

When Anke picked up Diana Lampeter's message, she let out a small sigh of relief that she hadn't been in to receive the call. Going to supper tonight was quite enough daily contact with her ambitious new friend – which reminded her to make a networking call of her own. Blushing at her hypocrisy, she looked up a number on her mobile and dialled it from the landline.

'Mo? Hi – Anke Brakespear. Tell me, would you and Pod like a lift to Springlode tonight? No, no trouble at all – we have plenty of room in the car. Good. Shall we say seven o'clock? My pleasure. See you then!'

She ticked that off on her list and cast her eyes further down, her pen nib hovering unhappily over the word *Fader*.

She hadn't visited him that day, although she had wanted to. She knew he needed proof that she trusted him. Her interference was already undermining their relationship.

Far from being grateful that his daughter had moved nearby, Ingmar was outraged by the implication that he couldn't cope. He absolutely refused to move to Wyck Farm from the flat above his bookshop (which he rarely remembered to open). Now suffering from progressive Alzheimer's, he was becoming less and less predictable and Anke found him a constant source of worry. Whenever she had visited that week, he'd made it clear that she was really just getting in the way – he didn't eat the food that she prepared and told her that his cleaning lady, Dot Wyck, made a far better job of vacuuming his flat and doing his laundry. Anke, who had seen no signs of Dot doing any of the chores for which her father paid her, doubted this very much, but knew better than to question Dot direct and risk her wrath. Securing a cleaning lady in the Lodes valley – even one who didn't clean – appeared to be a quest second only to finding the Holy Grail. Her own search was proving fruitless.

In their last acerbic, confusing conversation her father had made it loudly and abundantly clear that he was perfectly capable of looking after himself – and indeed looking after her.

'You are the child, Anke, and I am the father,' he had boomed in Danish, terrifying his only customers of the day. 'Do not try to undermine me with your mollycoddling. I thought that you moved here because you needed *me* and not vice versa. You are the one who married an idiot who does not know your heart as I do. *I* am fully responsible. I will prove it. Now leave me alone.'

Anke still reeled from the confrontation. She hated arguing with her father, especially about Graham, although, in hindsight, she wasn't certain that the 'idiot' he'd referred to wasn't her first husband, Kurt.

But today she had determinedly not mollycoddled and had avoided her usual visit to his shop on her way back from helping Graham at Dulston's. Instead, she went straight back to Wyck Farm and found Faith in her usual spot sitting on the rails of the paddock texting Carly.

'Go away, mum.'

Chad was in his attic slaying virtual monsters on the television.

'Go away, mum.'

Magnus, who was supposed to be looking after them all, was still asleep in bed, a blonde mane poking from one end of a striped duvet, a dirty heel from the other.

'Go away, mum.'

'I brought your car back.'

'Thanks. Now go away.'

Anke trailed downstairs. At least it wasn't just her father who was rejecting her attentions. She had a clean sweep apart from poor Graham, whose attentions she always rejected.

The children had settled into the village with varying degrees of success. Magnus had been an instant hit with the local girls. He had already joined a band – Road Kill – and was happily loafing about with no clear intention of getting a job. Chad played football on the amenity field with local ruffians. Anke was concerned by the number of cuts and bruises he'd acquired, plus the rumours that the boys from Orchard Grove sniffed glue there. But she was more worried about Faith, who had become increasingly withdrawn and sulky, only talking to her pony Bert and to the dogs. She showed no interest in Anke's suggestion that she do some work at Overlodes, which would at least involve some riding. Of the two horses they had at home, Heigi was too old and arthritic and Bert was hopelessly outgrown. But Faith had barely left the confines of Wyck Farm, showing no interest in exploring her new environs and only agreeing to take a look around the sixth-form college at Market Addington under great duress. There, she had scuffed around the corridors staring at her feet, saying nothing. She spent most of her days sunbathing and texting her old friends from Essex, shut out from the world by a personal stereo.

Deleting the messages on the answer phone, Anke tapped a pen on the block pad in front of her with its long To Do list and realised that she hadn't reminded Graham about tonight.

He took ages to answer the Dulston's phone. When he did, she could hear Evig barking furiously in the background.

'Is everything okay?'

'Course it is – I was just moving things around in the forecourt. The big guy can't stop barking at the combine. Jesus, that thing takes some moving!'

He was happy with his toys.

Anke battled irritation. 'Don't forget we're going out to supper tonight.'

'Romantic meal?' he suggested hopefully.

'Diana Lampeter invited us to eat at Overlodes.'

There was a long pause. 'Do we have to go?'

He sounded like one of the children.

Irritation won.

'Yes, we must. Faith is very kindly babysitting Chad because Mags is out.'

'Like she goes anywhere, love.' He laughed, sounding even more like one of the kids. 'Personally, I'd rather listen to that godawful noise Magnus makes than hear Mrs Ladida-Lampeter telling me what "class" is.'

'Don't be facet- factu- silly.' Anke cleared her throat. 'And talking of Magnus, I am really not happy using his car. Can you speak to the insurance people again about replacing the Merc?'

'No point. It wasn't covered.'

Anke bristled.

Occasionally Graham got a bee in his bonnet about something and decided to 'make a stand'. This usually involved a series of rude telephone calls to managing directors claiming their customer care was diabolical or their products were rubbish or that their staff were imbecilic. Over the years these stands had ranged from the trivial – a washing machine that kept breaking or even biscuits with bad packaging – to the career-threateningly petty, like the fleet of Scanias that he had sent back because they had the wrong upholstery finish, resulting in a huge loss of revenue for his company. However small the issue, Graham liked to make his random stand. This month, the stand was with his insurance broker.

As a company asset, the Mercedes had been covered – or rather, not covered – by the company insurance policy that he thought over-priced and, because Graham was refusing to pay instalments as a part of his latest stand, the car was a loss.

'So what am I supposed to drive now?' she demanded.

'Try driving me wild instead of mad, love.' He hung up.

Anke blinked at the phone in disbelief. In ten years of marriage Graham had never hung up on her. She wondered how much this had to do with last night when she had yet again avoided his advances, lying in the bath until she wrinkled like a raisin in order to ensure that he was asleep. Even then he'd tried a sleepy coupling, but she'd managed to feign unconsciousness until he gave up.

A moment later, he rang to apologise.

'Bit stressed, love. Forgive me. Want me to pick anything up for tonight?'

'Just don't be late, okay? I said we'd give Mo and Pod a lift.'

'Who?'

'Just don't be late.' She determinedly didn't snap, instead trying her hardest to be sympathetic. 'I'm sorry you're stressed. Tonight should be fun. Honestly.'

'I can't wait,' he joked thinly and blew her a kiss.

She laughed to try to cheer him up.

Anke hugged the handset guiltily – doubly guilty because it was so much easier to hug a phone than to hug her husband these days.

Graham was too busy to be as supportive as he'd like with the family, despite his best efforts. He was working long hours at Dulston's and under increasing stress. He hadn't anticipated that the business would be in such an appalling state – although he had known from the price he'd paid that it wasn't a healthy turnover. He'd inherited huge outstanding bills, half his stock appeared to be missing and the prom-ised workforce of three had all found employment elsewhere, leaving him without a knowledgeable salesman, mechanic or office adminis-trator. While Graham took on the two former roles himself, Anke had agreed to help him out in the office for two hours each morning, although her heart was set upon finally taking the OU degree she had long prom-ised herself.

Unlike her busy husband and withdrawn daughter, Anke had already made a start at involving herself with local groups. She'd joined the local Lodes Literature Society, taking part in her first reading discussion group the previous evening.

'I'm afraid I haven't had time to read the book,' she had confessed to her hostess – a deliciously bohemian brunette who was wearing a tie-dyed sarong and a 'Yes, I'm Pregnant!' T-shirt.

'Hardly anyone ever does,' she reassured Anke. 'They all just come to get pissed and complain about their crappy novellas and worthy poetry being rejected. We usually rely upon your father to tell us the plot. Ophelia Gently,' she introduced herself.

'I'm afraid Fad–, I mean my father, isn't coming tonight. He sends his apologies.' He had done no such thing. Having forgotten about the meeting, Ingmar had refused to come along when Anke had called in to offer him a lift, launching into a tirade of abuse about those 'stupid ignorant women and their dreadful taste in puerile suburban literature!' She'd left him watching EastEnders.

Anke thought the women rather lovely, especially Ophelia – 'call me Pheely' – and her best chum Pixie, whom she sat beside on the sunny terrace surrounded by amazing sculptures, half-listening to an earnest pensioner giving her take on George Eliot. Blue-haired Pixie was more interested in gossip, asking Anke whom she had met in the village and what she thought of them. In turn, Pixie gave succinct character summaries under her breath as *Middlemarch* was dissected.

'Gladys Gates. She seems a sweet old thing.'

'Pure poison!' Pixie breathed. 'She'll already have a file on you and your family.'

'Joel and Lily Lubowski from the shop are very good fun.'

'Devil worshippers,' Pixie said confidently.

'Prudence Hornton who owns the gallery opposite my father's shop is very bright.'

'Witch! And a raging alcoholic.'

Both Pixie and Ophelia relished warning her off Diana Lampeter the moment they heard of the acquaintance.

'We are going to dinner there tomorrow night,' Anke had confessed worriedly.

'Take a long spoon, darling.'

8

When Pod returned from his 'recce' of the Gunning Estate in a Land Rover decked with gun cases, Mo feared the worst. At the Land Rover's wheel was a square-jawed, broken-nosed thundercloud in a Tattersall checked shirt, fourteen stones of tense muscle with balding buzz-cut charcoal hair and shoulders as wide as a rhino's. Mo felt a familiar thread of fear sneak up her back as she predicted another of Pod's regular misdemeanours. But instead, he leaped from the passenger seat grinning broadly.

'Come here, queen! Meet the new boss.' He waved her out of the front garden as the male thundercloud emerged from the driver's door and glowered at his surroundings.

'Amos Gates, this is my girlfriend Mo Stillitoe,' Pod introduced them gleefully. 'Amos here needs some help up at the estate. I told you I'd get a job.'

'Clearing undergrowth ready for autumn forestry work,' Amos mumbled, not looking at either of them.

'That's great news.' Mo thrust out her hand. 'It's lovely to meet you.'

Amos – part-Heathcliff, part-Orc, almost totally silent and wholly undomesticated – was an intimidating prospect. As he took her hand in his, she could feel rough calluses grating against her fingers.

'Good to meet you,' he managed to grunt, flicking his eyes briefly in her direction. Dark bottle green with shards of flint running through them, they were far from friendly. Yet there was a curious, almost sad, nobility about him. He reminded her of an old, battle-scarred cattle dog.

'I said I'd introduce you, queen – Amos's little girl is going to be starting at Oddlode primary next term.'

'Maisy's a quiet girl.' Amos stared at his feet, making it clear that the trait was inherited. 'My wife Jacqui's worried about her starting school. Thought it would reassure her if I met you.'

'I'm sure she'll be fine.' Mo smiled nervously. 'Actually, I don't teach the really little ones, but I'll make sure I look out for her.'

'Thanks.' Amos moved his weight edgily from foot to foot as he glanced across the green.

'We're going for a pint, queen,' Pod said cheerily. 'I insisted I had to buy the boss a drink, and it turns out his local has just burned down. Care to join us?'

'No – no, you're fine. I have stuff to do.' She watched them turn away, calling after Pod, 'Don't forget we're going out to supper tonight.'

True to form, he glanced over his shoulder looking baffled. 'Are we? Don't tell me Gladys has persuaded you to try her steak and kidney at last?'

She gave him a withering look. 'Diana Lampeter – the furniture woman.'

'Oh . . . yeah. Sure.'

'I need you back by –'

'*Diana?*'

Mo was momentarily nonplussed, realising that it was Amos Gates who had interrupted her with a furious growl.

'Diana,' he repeated. 'You said Diana . . . Lampeter.'

'That's right – she moved to the area on the same day as us. There was a bit of a muddle –'

'Where?' He marched up to her. '*Where* has she moved to?'

The thundercloud face had darkened to gale force tornado. The green gaze lashed against hers now like wild waves.

'Somewhere in Upper Lodesomething?'

'Upper Springlode.'

'That's right. I think she has something to do with horses.'

He cursed under his breath, slamming a fist against his forehead with alarming force. 'Why did no one tell me?'

Pod had his mouth open and was looking spellbound at his new boss. 'Er . . . you know this woman, yeah?'

At this, Amos cursed under his breath that 'the bitch swore she would never come back'. Eyes flashing, he suddenly looked from Mo to Pod. 'I'll give you both a lift up there. It's on my way home.'

'We've already got a lift, thanks,' Mo explained hastily.

Amos glared at his fingertips. 'In that case I'm going to get very drunk.' He marched across the village green with Pod eagerly skipping after him, anxious for a pre-dinner whisky and a whiff of local scandal.

When Mo emerged from the shower to start getting ready, she noticed that Amos Gates' Land Rover was no longer parked outside the cottage.

'Pod? You home, baby?'

He must have stayed in the pub, she realised with a worried sigh, hoping he didn't get too caned before they set off for dinner. She raked a few squirts of mousse through her short hair and left it at that – it was such a hot day that it dried in minutes. Her original choice of outfit – cropped jeans and a skinny rib T-shirt was quickly rejected for something cooler, a flimsy red slip dress that Pod always found absurdly sexy because its bootlace straps tied at each shoulder so that he could undo them and let it drop in nanoseconds. Covered with small white daisy embroidery, it was girlier than most of Mo's wardrobe, so she matched it with clumpy flip-flops and a stripy triangular headscarf to make herself feel less whimsical. Rubbing salve into her lips and applying a dash of kohl and mascara – the only make-up she possessed – she went in search of Bechers who had to be confined to the kitchen while they were out because he had taken to using the bed as a loo since moving in.

It was only when a huge flashy car with darkened windows pulled up outside, tooting its horn, that she thought to look at the clock. Bloody Pod!

Anke Brakespear lowered the passenger window as Mo dashed out of the cottage. 'Sorry we're a bit late.'

'That's – er – fine. I'm just popping to the pub. Back in a minute!' Mo pulled off her flip-flops and, clutching them in her hands, raced across the green.

'How – unexpected.' Anke turned to Graham, who was watching the waifish figure skipping away.

'Probably wants to buy a bottle to bring.'

'Surely it would be cheaper in the village shop?'

The drinkers in the Lodes Inn told Mo that Pod had left with Amos more than an hour earlier.

'You want a pint, Mo darling?' Saul Wyck offered eagerly.

'Another time.' She raced back to the Brakespears' car. 'I'm really sorry. I've lost Pod. We'll have to go on ahead. He must have got the time muddled up – I'll just try his mobile.'

As she ran inside to grab her phone, she realised that she had left her flip-flops on the bar of the Lodes Inn. Now in a raring hurry because she hated keeping people waiting, she pulled on the sneakers beside the doormat and pulled the door behind her. It was only then that she realised the sneakers belonged to Pod and were three sizes too large, her keys were on the kitchen table, her mobile was almost out of charge and Bechers was looking down at her from an upstairs window. Just for a brief moment she contemplated asking Gladys if she could borrow the spare set of keys, but another beep from the car horn beside her sent her scuttling into the back seat.

'I am *so* sorry,' she gibbered, finding herself plumped up on shiny, soft leather upholstery, 'we're not very organised.'

'Really – don't worry.' Anke shot her impatient husband a disapproving look. 'Did you get hold of your boyfriend? Shall we wait for him?'

'Oh, no – he'll catch us up,' Mo insisted nervously, studying the back of Anke's husband's neck in alarm.

'Hello, love.' He turned to grin over his shoulder.

'Oh, sorry Mo – you haven't met my husband Graham, have you?'

Before Mo had a chance to answer, Graham thrust out a big, warm hand. 'Delighted to make your acquaintance, love. You settling in okay?'

'Fine, thanks,' Mo gulped. Perhaps he didn't remember her. She certainly remembered him. It was the joker whom she had met on the village green the first day they'd moved here. He wasn't a tourist after all. Today's shirt was even more garish, its picture of sun-soaked beaches so bright and inviting that she wanted to dive straight into his broad shoulders.

As they set off, she subtly started to text Pod with her phone on silent, demanding that he get himself to Upper Springlode straight away.

Steering the Lexus effortlessly up the winding climb out of Oddlode, Graham eyed Mo delightedly in the rear-view mirror, remembering their first encounter by a four-poster bed on the village green. She was like a little elf, he decided – an Audrey Hepburn in miniature. Nothing like as glamorous as his Great Dane, but very easy on the eye and delightfully coy, staring down at her hands with great concentration. Then she suddenly looked up and, catching him watching her, blushed as red as her pretty dress.

In the seat beside Graham, the Great Dane was distractedly fretting that Faith, who was babysitting Chad, had been looking almost suicidal when they left. Magnus had already set off for a gig with Road Kill, and so nobody was keeping an eye on the volatile teenager.

On impulse, Anke called her father from her mobile. If he insisted that he was responsible, then she could ask him to pop in on the farm to check the kids on his way back from his bridge game. Faith loved her Morfar, so seeing him was bound to cheer her up.

Mo caught Graham looking at her again as his wife started chatting away in Danish on her mobile. He gave her a sexy, crease-eyed smile.

She stared out of the window, watching the valley open up beyond the hedges as the car climbed. It alarmed her that she found the big, brawny northerner so attractive. He was Anke's husband and old enough to be her father. Why, oh why, wasn't Pod here?

She stared out at the landscape sliding past the windows trying to settle her nerves and her jumpy libido, but nothing about it settled her

much at all. Muggy, hazy and threatening a storm, it was a golden-hewn
steamy evening. As they climbed into the marl hills towards the ridge,
the fields unfolding away from them seemed full of all things ripening
and rotting decadently, ready to be reaped – from copper-headed wheat
to black-eyed sunflowers, fat late lambs to burly bullocks. The Lodes
valley was at its sexy best and bestially sexy. Distant bonfires smoked
everywhere, tiny volcanoes discharging plumes of smoke into the hot
blue sky.

Mo caught Graham's equally hot blue eyes smiling at her in the rear-
view mirror again and looked hastily through her side window, only to
see two llamas in a nearby paddock copulating madly. Despite the cool
air-conditioning of the car, she was burning with a head-to-toe blush.

She almost shot into orbit when her phone vibrated in her lap, but
it was just the low battery warning signal. She glared at the little LED
screen, willing Pod to reply.

9

At Horseshoe Farm Cottage, Diana felt like a small child, tempted to run away. Everything had gone wrong. Rory and Sharon had been left strict instructions to return from their horse show in plenty of time to help out, and yet there hadn't been so much as a call and, as usual Rory's mobile was switched off. Diana was consequently one man short for her numbers and hadn't got a babysitter.

Tim had called earlier to announce that, much to his 'utter horror', he wasn't able to come and take the children for their promised night away the following day. He'd huffed a lot about hush-hush last-minute duties, but Diana knew the regiment's summer routine well enough to doubt him. She could almost smell the Pimm's and cigar smoke on his breath through the phone. He was taking a sabbatical from parenthood, Mim's tears and Digby's eccentricity too frightening to face alone. Only a tiny crack in his haw-haw voice gave him away, but Diana knew him well enough to hear it.

'They'll be so disappointed,' she had pleaded, amazed that *she* was the one begging *him* to have access. 'Speak to them at least – explain why Daddy's got important duties.'

'Better you tell them. Hearing my voice will only upset them.' He had wriggled away from the call as quickly as he could.

Hearing his voice had certainly upset Diana. It had triggered rare tears and she had shut herself in the bathroom, her PMS taking a feverish hold as she wept through a miserable half-hour of Mahler and Albinoni on Classic FM.

She knew that she couldn't bring herself to tell her children about their father's call before tonight's supper.

Outside, Rio was raping Mim's pony, Bronwyn, whose cries could be heard right across the village. Hally had absconded after stealing all the chicken fillets for that evening's supper. And Diana's frozen white chocolate bowl for the mango mousse had collapsed. When she emerged from a bath to find Mim moulding ponies from the puff pastry and Digby polishing off the last of the sliced mangoes, she lost her grip. She couldn't even whisk her guests to the pub, because it had burned down.

And she couldn't raid the freezer because she had dumped all its (admittedly meagre) contents in the bin in order to fit her failure of a frozen dessert bowl inside.

Growling through her teeth, Diana had her first stiff gin and tonic.

Half-way through it, she casually flipped up the bin lid – just to have a peek.

Rory obviously lived off frozen pizza, boil-in-the-bags and fish fingers. There was a split bag of frozen peas, already glistening as they melted, half a packet of sausages, two tubs of ice-cream oozing their foamy contents out over a large box of beef burgers.

'Hmm.' Diana took another thoughtful swig.

In London, her friends had flattered her by calling her the Nigella Lawson of Kensington. And she supposed there was a passing physical similarity as well as a sumptuous shared ability to make even the most inauspicious of old-fashioned school food seem sexy.

At least there was no shortage of potatoes, both King Edward and sweet potatoes (Digby, who would only eat orange food, accepted these). And, of course, she had no end of carrots at her disposal.

Switching on the Archers, she topped up her gin and set about carefully extracting the contents of the bin.

When they arrived, horribly punctually, her guests, it transpired, were also depleted in numbers. The whole reason for the evening – Pod – had apparently gone walkabout with his new boss.

'I'm so sorry,' Mo mumbled shyly. 'He only got the job today and they went for a drink to celebrate. I think he must have got carried away. The man did offer us a lift – he lives in this direction – so perhaps he'll bring Pod along here in a bit?' she added without conviction.

'What sort of job is it?' Diana asked, ushering them through the tiny hallway to the sitting-room. She hoped Pod hadn't said anything about the gigolo/cleaner fiasco. It was almost certainly why he was planning on rolling up late.

'Hedging, I think.' Forgetful and flustered, Mo could only recount that this boss was called something like Abel or Abraham and that he had a broken nose and a lot of guns.

'He must be a Gates,' Diana told her with a snarl, still dwelling on the cleaner mix-up. 'Big farming family. They all have ridiculous biblical names. They think it absolves them from all the sins they commit.'

Mo stared at her feet in mortification, convincing Diana even more firmly that the girl was hopelessly wet. Briefly following her gaze downwards, Diana found herself staring at Mo's feet too. They were enormous.

Graham was thinking much the same thing, although his eyes hadn't travelled down as far as the floor. Despite his dislike of plump, snobbish women, Diana Lampeter had two incredible assets that were hard to miss. Poured into a Ducati yellow dress that gave her curvaceous race farings and set off her warm toffee skin to perfection, she was very easy on the eye.

'This is a very pretty cottage.' Anke admired the inglenook fireplace, knowing full well what Graham was gawping at.

'It's in need of TLC, but I'm sure I can lick it into shape soon.'

The cottage did look rather special, Diana reassured herself. Throwing open the windows, what little cool breeze there was wafted the scent from the big jugs of lemon balm and apple mint she had placed on the deep sills, as well as that of the thick pelts of late-flowering honeysuckle and clematis overhanging the windows outside. Matched with cooking smells, it almost negated the pong of horse and dog. Unbeknown to Rory, most of his clutter had been hastily relocated to the tack room, revealing what had once been a very pretty room. About a hundred back issues of *Horse and Hound* and *Eventing*, plus piles of red bills, junk mail, single gloves, hats, thermals and horse paraphernalia welded together with dust, hay and animal hair had occupied the surfaces of some very good pieces of inherited furniture, now gleaming from a fresh application of polish. The threadbare rugs had been Hoovered raw. The drying socks and pants had been removed from the radiators (and in some cases the frames of a few rather good oil paintings) and stashed upstairs in Rory's room.

Diana's hasty makeover only extended as far as the sitting- and dining-rooms and the downstairs loo. She hadn't had time to spruce up the kitchen, and had to ensure that none of her guests took 'kitchen sups' too literally by venturing in there. They wouldn't want to touch the food if they saw the state of the oven – or, indeed the state of most of the food.

'Let me fix you all lovely, stiff drinks,' she offered, having already determined to get them all as drunk as possible to increase their appetites and decrease the power of their taste buds. Hers were already working in direct inverse proportion.

'You drink, *kaereste*,' Anke offered, touching Graham's arm. 'I'll drive us home.'

Graham bucked up even more. Three beautiful women to himself over dinner, *and* he could get drunk. It was his lucky night. Just being away from his step-daughter's sulking face was cheering enough, but this was heaven.

Diana poured a drink as well as she poured herself into a dress. Graham almost passed out at the first sip. You could tell she'd been a military wife.

Winking at Mo, who was going cross-eyed just breathing the fumes from her vodka and coke, he settled back for a fun evening, grateful that he'd come here after all.

At Wyck Farm, Faith was racking up the family phone bill whingeing away to best friend Carly.

'You wouldn't *believe* how irritating Graham's being, swaggering around like a big ape and dragging Mum up to that awful tip he's bought in Springlode, and he's *still* refusing to buy me a new horse unless Bert goes. Mum promised he'd get better when we moved here, but he's worse than ever. I hate him.'

'How's Mags?' Carly had a crush on her best friend's brother.

'Out playing with his new girlfriends.'

'He has more than one?'

'They all fancy him like mad, of course.' Faith had no intention of sparing her friend's feelings. If she was suffering, her friend could share the taste. 'The girls round here are like *so* gorgeous – not as tarty as Essex, and much classier. Magnus is like *so* in heaven. They all speak with a plum in their mouths and have real tans from Tuscany not the Tanning Shop.' No need to mention that the girls in his new band, Road Kill, were all as pale as ghouls and had thick Gloucestershire accents.

'Oh.' Carly was clearly crestfallen. 'Have you met any PBs yet?' PBs were potential boyfriends.

Faith contemplated mentioning her new four-legged love triangle, Rory and Pod, but she wanted to keep them to herself for now. Analysing them with Carly would just expose the flaws she had already written about at length in her diary. They both had girlfriends. They were both at least ten years older than she was. They were both completely out of her league.

'God, no – the men are like *so* gross,' she said instead. 'It's no wonder Mags is going down a storm. The locals even make Graham look half decent, for a gorilla,' she groaned, looking out of the window. 'In fact, I've got one particularly gross specimen coming down the drive now. What the . . . ? Hang on, Car.' She left the phone on the window seat and leaned out of the open sash to get a better look at the figure weaving his way up the drive.

It was Reg Wyck from the housing estate. Faith had never met him, but he was already a familiar figure as he walked past his old family farm daily, always stopping for a good gawp. This was the first time he had ventured down the drive. He wasn't making particularly good progress as he swayed from side to side, veering on to the grass verge and tripping over a rose bush.

'I'll call you back, Car.' Faith hung up and cautiously opened the front door.

Reg was now reeling around amongst the thirsty bedding plants that Faith had promised her mother she would water that evening. He appeared to be singing to himself.

'Oh my love, oh my darling – you are always in my heaaaaaaaaaaaaaart!'

'Hello? Can I help?'

'Eh?' Reg span around a few times, losing his sun-hat in a bush.

'It's Reg, isn't it?'

'Msssshter Wycktoyou, youngladeee – and whorrare you ding on my fraaarm?'

Speaking, it seemed, came harder to Reg Wyck than singing. His voice was so slurred and his accent so strong that Faith couldn't understand a word. Even from ten yards away she could smell pub all over him.

'Gerrofmyland!' He lurched sideways and fell over another rose bush, ripping his shirt which was already undone to the waist and hanging out of his trousers.

Faith retreated under the canopy of the porch. 'I think you'd better come back another time if you want to speak with my parents.'

'Wha-?' Reg blinked at her a few times, still struggling to loosen himself from thorns. 'Wharareyoudoing in myfarmgirl?'

Scrunching up her brow in order to decipher his speech, Faith had a sudden unpleasant realisation that Reg – hopelessly drunk as was apparently usual at weekends – thought that he still owned Wyck Farm.

'I think you'd better go.'

'Don'tyoutellmethatIshouldgofrommyownfaaaarm!' he roared.

Faith retreated behind the door, peering through its small paned arch and wondering if she would have time to slam it and dash around the house closing all the open windows. Thank goodness Chad was safely ensconced in his room with the dogs – although she could do with Evig's big bark right now. She let out a few low whistles to try to attract his attention, but just ended up sounding asthmatic.

Reg managed to rip free from the roses and turned to retrieve his hat, landing face down in the bush.

At that moment a strange-looking car sped into the drive, flattened most of the flower-beds and careered straight towards Reg.

'Morfar!' Faith gasped in shock as her grandfather's invalid car managed a handbrake turn away from the bush and came to a dusty halt on top of a potted bay tree.

She ran outside.

'Who are you?' he yelled.

Reg Wyck's head popped up amid the petals, complete with his hat which had slipped back on to his head quite by accident. His eyes crossed and uncrossed.

For a moment Faith felt flooded with relief that her tenacious, lion-hearted grandfather had come to the rescue, ready to evict Reg Wyck from his former residence.

'*Well*, who do you think you are and *what* do you think you're doing here?'

Faith realised that her grandfather was talking to her.

'Trail Blazers!' Diana announced as she burst back out of the kitchen with the gin bottle in hand. 'Now, who was for that top-up?'

'I think you were,' Graham laughed. 'Although I wouldn't say no. Now, run that past me again, love? You want to buy the little pub here and use it as a base for riding holidays?'

'Trail Blazers, yes. I was going to call it Gourmets in the Saddle, but it's not punchy enough.' She splashed gin into Graham's glass and slugged a huge measure into her own, followed by a tiny dribble of tonic in each.

'Don't you think "blaze" is an unfortunate concept, given the circumstances?' suggested Anke.

'Not at all – the pub will cost a fraction of the price now it needs restoring. I'm rather grateful to whoever torched it.'

'How about Blazing Saddles?' Graham cackled. 'Or Arson Fire?'

Anke shot him a warning look. Gin always went straight to his head.

'*Was* it arson?' Mo asked, wondering whether to mention the Wycks' ghost theories. She was feeling somewhat left out of the conversation – and the drinking. Even Anke was swigging back the white wine spritzers faster than Mo could down her toxically strong vodka and coke. Diana hadn't stretched to beer. Pod would have left by now. Furious as she was with him, Mo found herself envying his wayward absence. She also envied him his dope. She could use some right now. It was going to be a long night.

'Of course it was arson.' Anke came across as more forthright than she intended.

'How do you know?' Diana jumped on the statement, draining most of her G (& token T) and wandering back into the kitchen before Anke could answer.

'There's someone doing very odd things in this village,' Anke said to no one in particular.

It was Graham's turn to shoot the warning look. He didn't want the conversation turning to Dulston's and its curious 'camp'.

'There are people doing very odd things in villages all over this valley,' Mo agreed, still trying to get into the conversation which somehow kept spitting her out.

'Well, it is the *Odd*lode valley.' He shot her a grin.

Grateful to feel included once more, Mo shot him a grin in return and wondered whether she could sneak outside for a roll-up.

In the kitchen, Diana added another sneaky dash of gin to her gin, using the supermarket-own she kept stashed behind the microwave.

'Can I help at all?' Anke appeared politely at the door.

'No!' Diana shrieked more shrilly than she intended, having been caught red-handed with the contingency gin bottle, which she hastily thrust into the fridge. 'Sorry!' She swung back, grappling to apply composure as she dropped her voice to a purring whisper. 'But the children and the dog are just outside that door.' She nodded towards the French doors that led out on to a sunny terrace on which two children were sitting at a shabby wooden picnic table, diligently slamming crayons on to giant colouring books while a slumbering grey dog kept snoring sentry duty beneath. 'I don't want them getting over-excited by seeing strangers. I'll put them all to bed in a minute.' She tried to block the door so that Anke couldn't take in the state of the kitchen as she ushered her out.

Closing it behind her trespassing guest, Diana wiped her brow worriedly and looked back at the cooker. Accustomed to cooking on a giant, gleaming twin-oven, six-hob gas range with fresh, free-range ingredients from Harvey Nicks, she was struggling with Rory's carbon-encrusted, ancient sit up and beg electric cooker with its battered rings that either incinerated everything in the saucepan within seconds or took an hour to warm anything beyond tepid. As her key ingredients had been wolfed by Hally and Digby, improvising with frozen boil-in-the-bag meals was proving tough. She'd have to make sure Trail Blazers never suffered such a crisis.

Mustering Nigella goddess status and inner calm with another swig of gin and a hefty dose of old-fashioned Diana optimism, she reminded herself that what she had achieved tonight was close to a domestic miracle.

Her ad lib appetisers had worked a treat, she realised, as she extracted the cheese on roasted onion toast from the grill and sliced it up into minute rarebits to add to the tray of miniature pizza cubes with balsamic vinegar glaze, mini sausage and mustard mash balls and mini burgers in mini-baps, which her children had happily cut from bread crusts with pastry cutters, only dropping a few on the floor.

'What does Rory make of your ideas?' Anke asked her when she started distributing them next door to admiring 'oohs' and 'ahs'.

'Oh, I don't think he's really bothered so long as this place stops losing him money.'

'I thought he had a lot of clients?' Anke was surprised.

'It's very seasonal.' Diana wrinkled her nose. 'And if he will keep seducing the prettiest ones, he can't expect much loyalty. Besides, he can still keep teaching – perhaps. Off-season.' She had yet to mention her ideas to Rory, but he was so easy-going she was certain he'd give them a go.

'You seem to have a very firm idea of what you want to do.'

'Oh, I do,' Diana purred dreamily, thinking of Pod as she offered Mo the choice of the tray.

'Which ones are vegetarian?' Mo asked politely.

Diana shot her a worried look as she pointed out the miniature rarebits. 'You do eat fish, don't you?'

'Er . . . I'm vegetarian.'

'But vegetarians eat fish, don't they?'

'Some do, yes.'

'Well, that's all right then.' Dumping her tray of nibbles on the coffee table, Diana whisked back into her lair to give her full attention to her carrot soup starter.

Graham touched Mo's knee. 'Bad luck, love. Dinner with the shooting set, what ho. Probably have to saddle up and hunt the main course down later.' His fake posh accent was appalling, making Mo laugh despite the bad joke. 'I've got a packet of cheesy Wotsits and a bag of Haribos in the car if you're peckish,' he added quite sincerely.

'Thanks.' She grinned.

'I'm sure that stallion shouldn't be in with those poor ponies.' Anke was looking out of the window distractedly. 'And what are those children doing . . . ?'

At Wyck Farm, Ingmar's interrogation of Faith from the window of his invalid car came to an abrupt halt when he inadvertently clicked it into reverse and shuttled himself at speed into the duck pond.

As the ducks flew away in shock, Faith longed to join them.

The unexpected dip did, at least, bring a little sense into her grand-father's old, muddled head. He stopped accusing Faith of being an impostor. He simply thought that she was his daughter – her own mother, Anke. Unfortunately this meant that he was also speaking to her in Danish.

'Giv mig tusind kys, og og da hundrede til

'Da tusind til, og da hundrede igen

'Endnu tusind mere, og endnu hundrede mere.' He cupped her face in his wet hands when he waded from the reedy car park.

Faith looked around helplessly, noticing that Reg Wyck was still reeling around close to the potted bay tree, covered in rose petals.

'Why don't we speak in English?' she suggested cautiously, not wanting to confuse her grandfather further.

'Lovely language – so eccentric,' he agreed, taking his shoes off to tip the water out, as though he parked in the pond every day. 'Don't you agree?' he called out to Reg, who backed away groggily.

'Then, when we have made many thousands,' Ingmar boomed theatri-cally.

'We will mix them all up so that we don't know,

'And so that no one can be jealous of us when he finds out

'How many kisses we have shared.' He wiped a tear from his cheek. 'Catullus. Of course, a purist would only quote it in Latin, but I have never been very pure.' He chuckled. 'Your mother loved that poem, Anke.'

Faith took his arm.

'Er . . . would you like a cup of tea Mor . . . I mean, Fader?'

'No, no thank you.' He took a bracing breath of air and looked around the garden. It was hard for Faith to understand how her grandfather – once impossibly handsome and always a figure of such noble gravitas and intelligence – could be so muddled and enfeebled these days.

'I am here because,' he started certainly and then paused, head on one side. 'I just promised – ah – promised I'd . . . um . . .'

Searching for answers on his behalf Faith wondered whether her mother had asked him to pop by to check that she was okay, but decided not to risk asking. Right now, he thought she *was* her mother after all.

'I must go and check on Chad.' She realised guiltily that her little brother – upstairs in his bedroom, attached to his games console controller as usual – hadn't so much as popped his head out of the window when their grandfather had tried to ram-raid Reg Wyck and driven into the pond.

'You and your boyfriends.' Ingmar cuffed her cheek affectionately. 'I can't keep up with them. No funny business up there, understand?'

Shaking her head despondently, Faith trailed inside, wondering whether to call her mother's mobile. It seemed a shame to upset her evening, although the car in the pond was an awkward dilemma.

Chad was wearing headphones and systematically kick-boxing huge-shouldered zombies with the aid of his thumbs and a long cable attached to the television. Evig and Bomber were panting on the bed, dopey with heat exhaustion. The attic was as stuffy as an oven.

'If I lose a life while you are in this room, I'll kill you,' Chad threatened, talking in the artificially loud voice of somebody who cannot hear himself speak.

'Lucky you've got more than one life then, little cat.'

Faith shrugged and opened the window to let in some air, looking out to see her grandfather dancing around the shrubbery in the last of the evening sunlight. He made her smile, despite herself. Sometimes she preferred Morfar these days – he was softer and gentler than he had been when his mind was sharp and acerbic. He still had that legendary short temper, but he so quickly forgot what he was angry about that it was less fearsome. To Faith's mind, he had always seemed critical of her. She was less beautiful and academic than her mother had been as a girl; she wasn't as bright, blonde and bold as her brothers, either. Now that Morfar barely knew who she was, he seemed to like her more.

She watched with affectionate detachment as he chased Reg Wyck away through the shrubbery, waving his walking stick. For a man with an invalid car – admittedly a drowned invalid car – he still had a decent turn of speed, although he was no match for Reg who sprinted away, cursing drunkenly over his shoulder.

Chad paused his game and pulled one side of his headphones from his ear. 'What are you doing in here?'

'Watching Morfar chasing Reg Wyck. He came up the drive thinking he still lived here again.'

'Morfar or Reg?' Chad asked without great interest.

'Hard to tell.' She sighed, turning to look at him, but he had pinged the phones back and was giving a particularly ugly-looking zombie a side-swipe karate chop. On the bed beside him, Bomber the bull terrier let rip with a loud fart that sent Faith scuttling back downstairs and outside for fresh air.

'Interesting piece of statuary.' Ingmar was standing beside the pond staring at his car. 'Did you have it commissioned?'

Faith gaped at him.

'Anyway, I can't stay here gossiping all evening like one of those village fishwives. I have an assignation.'

'Er – how are you going to get there?'

He tapped his damp trouser leg with his walking stick. 'Very good exercise, walking. You should try it, girl. You look very pasty. Very pasty, indeed. You won't break any hearts with a complexion like that.' He marched towards the drive gates, whistling strains of Mozart.

Faith watched him go, deciding that perhaps she didn't like him so much, after all. Her mother was bound to blame her for the mess in the pond, and for letting her grandfather wander away into the last evening light without finding where he was going. What if he went missing, or got mugged or something?

She went to talk to the horses as she always did when she wanted to cry. They were nose to tail in the paddock beneath the shade of a large oak, batting flies from one another's faces with their tails, eyes half-closed and coats dusty from rolling away the itches of a sunny day.

'Oh, Bert.' She hugged his old grey head in her arms and breathed in the familiar smell of his mane. 'How come you find it so easy to settle here?'

He snorted and rubbed his cheek against her chest, covering her T-shirt in grey hairs. Beside him, Heigi pricked his ears and looked up as a train rattled past noisily on the other side of the fence, windows glittering sunset red as it streaked between the cover of trees. Faith let go of her pony's head and covered her own ears.

'God, I hate it here,' she shouted above the din. 'I hate this bloody house and this village and the people. I hate bloody Graham, I hate, hate, *hate* him! And I hate Mum for loving him!' The noise of the train faded away, but Faith carried on shouting as she marched into the centre of the paddock, kicking at divots. 'Why did Mum have to marry him? He's such a big, babyish oaf. He's so thick and self-satisfied. He loves himself! He doesn't need her to love him too. I need her to love me. I need . . .' She sank to her knees and watched the grass blurring as she started to cry, curling up like a foetus and weeping. Still beneath the shade of the oak, Heigi and Bert watched her passively.

Further away, another set of eyes was watching Faith as she wept. Eyes that barely had space to peek between the folds of old, weathered skin – green, watchful, only slightly cataract-faded eyes that had seen many things along this stretch of railway line. For years, they had logged the misdemeanours of the Wycks in between the regular London to Worcester trains. They had noted the subsequent occupants of Wyck Farm come and go, seen them fighting as the local commuter services rattled this way and that, watched them arguing as they waited for the signals to change, spotted them crying as they scanned the track for freight. But they had never seen one weep as Faith did. They had never seen such abject unhappiness – and it made them blink several times as though caught in a dust storm.

Turning over a fresh page of his notebook, Granville Gates wrote in a spidery copperplate. *Girl from Wyck Farm. Investigate.*

In the farmhouse, Chad picked up the phone as he raided the fridge for a milkshake during a break in play. 'Oh, hi Carly . . . no she's out talking to the horses as usual. Yeah, she's fine – it was just Morfar, I think. You know our Grandad? He's a bit doolally these days . . . Yeah, fine thanks. I'll get her to call you, yeah? Cool. Has she told you about her boyfriends yet, by the way? Yeah, totally – I read about them in her diary. Rory and Pod. Gross. She can't decide between them . . .'

Having gathered Diana's children from their treacherous game of 'dog-bath' in the stallion enclosure water trough, Anke left them with Mo while she tried to attract her hostess's attention. Diana now appeared to have barred the inner door to the kitchen with a chair while she applied her attention to the soup, so Anke was forced to retrace the children's steps through a gap in the hedge to the garden terrace where she stood a respectful distance from the French doors and shouted. 'Hello there! Diana? Can I have a word?'

Diana, now surfing high on gin and hormones and unaware that her behaviour was coming across in any way strangely, appeared through the doors carrying a tea towel, soup ladle and her glass. 'Yes?'

'I hope you don't think I'm interfering, but we just saw your children in with that lovely stallion and I thought perhaps they weren't supposed to be there.'

A soup ladle, glass and tea towel fell to the ground with a clatter, smash and flutter.

'It's all right – they're not in there now,' Anke added quickly. 'Mo is looking after them.'

'She is?'

'You can see what a wonderful teacher she must be. They adore her. She is so natural.'

'Oh good. Which reminds me, we *must* corner her for that chat about Oddlode primary school later, mustn't we?'

'What? Oh, yes. But the thing is –'

'Terribly hard to get into, as I said to you before.' Diana kicked the broken glass into a flower-bed. 'And I don't know about you, but the thought of Lower Oddford junior school fills me with dread – apparently there were eight exclusions last year and the Ofsted report was dreadful. Mine are down for Woldcote House, but their blasted father has gone away on army business without forwarding a cheque for the first term's fees and I certainly can't afford them. I'm sure if we chat Mo up she'll be able to get our little ones into Oddlode for next term.'

'I hope so. But the thing is, about your stallion – Rio, is he call–'

'Yes, Rio! Baron Areion, to give him his true name. Gorgeous, isn't he? Top bloodlines. His paces are phenomenal. You must have a sit on him sometime.'

'That would be lovely, but –'

'In fact, let's say next week, shall we? Come and have a play. If you like him, you can take over the ride. I simply don't have time to put into him, and Rory's heart isn't in dressage. How about Monday? Bring Faye – I mean Fran – I mean Faith up for a hack out. I take it you're here over the whole Bank Holiday?'

'Yes, that would be fine.' Anke agreed to shut her up as much as anything. 'But the thing is, I couldn't help noticing . . . er . . . that his pony companion seems a little distressed?'

'Oh, yes – she's in season and Rio keeps trying to get his end away. I should separate them, but I haven't had time and bloody Rory's not back.'

'Would you like me to help out?'

'Oh, would you?' Diana beamed, collecting the tea towel and ladle from amid shattered glass fragments and turning to go back in the cottage. 'Soup in ten minutes. That gives you enough time to fetch the pony out, doesn't it?'

Anke had to forcibly close her mouth by pressing a hand firmly to her chin. By 'help' she hadn't meant that she would single-handedly try to remove the disruptive stallion from his victim.

Left on his own inside while his wife horse-wrangled and pretty young Mo helped his hostess's children look for their missing dog, Graham slyly turned on the television to look up the Test result on Ceefax. So far, he was thoroughly enjoying Diana Lampeter's dinner party. He was not only the sole man, but he also had been left with all the appetisers and a very large glass of gin. When he spotted that England had declared at six hundred and four not out, he decided that this evening was the ultimate stress-buster. Heaven.

10

After an improvised main course of fish pie, with table entertainment courtesy of the very badly behaved Lampeter children, most of Diana's guests had shipped enough wine to cope with their hostess's increasing eccentricity.

'Delicious food, Diana love.' Graham was positively swimming in sauvignon blanc, a glass of which he raised now. 'My compliments.'

'My London friends used to call me the Domestos Goddesh.' Diana beamed.

'And you are.' Graham tapped his glass against hers and winked at Mo.

If he winked any more his eye would fall out, Mo decided, but she didn't mind. She loved it. He was so cheery and straightforward and he had lifted her spirits no end, along with the children. However badly behaved, Diana's children were divine.

'Why have you picked out the bits of fish?' Mim whispered now.

'Allergy,' Mo whispered back.

'I'm allergic to boys.' Mim nodded sympathetically.

'Do they bring you out in a rash?'

'Only when they give me Chinese burns.' She giggled and kindly switched her empty plate for Mo's fishy one. 'You can return the favour some time.'

'By eating boys?'

'Don't eat Digby. He sat in horse poo earlier. But he'd probably taste better than Mummy's cooking.'

'That's enough, Mim!' Diana had caught the last few words of this, dark gaze alighting on the plate of fish. 'And don't you dare leave that food – "wilful waste makes for woeful want" as Nanny used to say. I expect you to clear that. The same goes for you Digby. *Eat.* Nobody leaves this table until you finish.'

Mo opened her mouth to defend Mim, but a small foot kicked her ankle under the table and Mim obediently began wolfing her leftovers. At the same moment a warm hand found her opposite knee and Graham started telling her a long joke.

'There's a truck driver taking a break in a transport caff when ten Hell's Angels bikers walk in and surround him . . .'

Only Anke had suspicions about the provenance of the fish pie. Like Diana's brother Rory, she had lived on a professional rider's diet of fish fingers, boil-in-the bag cod and frozen peas long enough to recognise the familiar tastes combined beneath their creamy potato topping. She had to admire the way it was disguised, the clever addition of cayenne pepper and lemon zest, the sculpted topping marbled with sweet potato that made it look far more pleasing to the eye than Bird's Eye.

Diana's cocktail of gin and pre-menstrual tension was reaching dizzy heights. She was holding together – just – but could only concentrate on one thing at a time. In order to get the food in place, she had ignored her children. Now that she was concentrating on silencing and chastising her children – up way beyond their bedtime – she had overlooked clearing plates, serving pudding, offering coffee or suggesting that they move away from the table.

Wedged beside the linen-wrapped rectangle in a glow of guttering candlelight, Graham and Mo had no great desire to move.

'. . . and then the caff owner says "He's not much of a lorry driver either – he's just reversed his rig over ten motorbikes"!' Graham cackled, doubling up over his empty plate.

Mo shrieked delightedly.

Across the table, Anke winced. Graham was telling jokes. Always a bad sign, and something he invariably did to impress women. He liked to flirt good-naturedly, but the jokes – learned from decades of truckers' stops and working men's clubs – seldom went down well in female company. She studied his glass and tried to work out how much wine he'd shipped. The jokes would get bluer the more he drank. She hoped Diana had a stodgy pudding lined up to soak up some of it. She wished she could escape to call Faith and check everything was okay, but Diana's next explosion kept her obediently rooted to the spot.

'You *will* stay sitting at the table,' Diana was lecturing her son. 'And you will finish that fish pie, Digby.'

'I've eaten most of it,' he whined.

'Digby, how many times? You can't only eat orange-coloured food! You have picked out all the bits of sweet potato and left everything else.'

'I ate some of the crunchy fish.'

'Well, eat the rest. None of us can have pudding until you have.'

Digby sulkily picked up his fork and pushed some of the creamy contents of his plate around.

'So, Anke.' Diana abandoned concentrating upon her children to concentrate upon the table conversation, squinting as she worked to keep her train of thought and not slur her words. 'Tell me what brought you to the area?'

'We've always loved the Cotswolds – and my father has lived here for many years.'

'Oh yes, I recall you mentioning that he's recently gone demented.' Diana didn't phrase the recollection quite as she had intended.

Anke took a sharp breath and forced a smile. 'He's showing early signs of Alzheimer's disease, yes, although the diagnosis is not conclusive at present. But he is still quite cognisant. He lives a very active life.'

'And you were happy to make the move here, Graham?' Diana turned to him, interrupting a joke about a truck driver in a brothel.

'Oh, aye.' He raised his glass. 'It's very pretty. Lots of beautiful things to look at round this way.' He leered at her and then at Mo.

'The scenery is splendid, isn't it?' Diana enthused, and then immediately regretted giving herself quite so many s's to say as they hissed their way out of her mouth in a jumble. She decided quickly to switch back to questions with no sibilant tongue traps. 'Tell me how you two met?'

'*Kaereste?*' Anke waited for Graham to give the potted history, which he usually loved to recount, but he was too busy filling up the glasses and finishing telling Mo his joke.

Her own version was far less passionate than his. 'I went to Graham's haulage yard to look at trucks – my first husband and I were planning to have a new horsebox made, and Brakespears was known to be a good source of second-hand chassis. Graham . . . er . . . well, he pursued me afterwards and persuaded me to go out to lunch with him . . .'

Again she looked to Graham to pick up the story which he told so much better, but he was now telling Digby a joke about trains.

'My marriage had been quite difficult for some time. Graham was married, too, and was going through similar difficulties.'

'You mean his wife was gay as well?' Diana snorted delightedly.

Anke was far too polite to rise, but her eyes bulged in horror. It was common knowledge in equestrian circles that Kurt was gay – how could it be kept a secret when he was now living with screaming dressage queen Damian Fredericks, two poodles, a Bengal cat and a wardrobe full of Versace shirts? Yet it was never spoken about so blatantly in her company.

Thanks to a prod from Mo, at last Graham was catching up, but unfortunately, he was a lot more sozzled than Anke had anticipated and she stiffened awkwardly as he rambled on about Deirdre. Hearing him talk of his ex-wife always made her feel dreadful.

'Deirdre isn't gay, love! Christ, she wouldn't even know what it meant. She's a lovely girl – woman. We had a lot of happy years together. Met at fifteen, you see – married at eighteen, babies by twenty. But she didn't want what I wanted, as it turned out. When I started making money, she hated it – preferred it when I was away driving the trucks for a week and then back being the big man around the house for just long enough to get the jobs done. She liked her little nest, didn't want to move on. She's a very shy woman. The bigger my horizons got, the more she shut herself away.

'Then I saw Anke and – whoof – my heart stopped, you know what I mean? Fireworks. I'd never seen anyone like her. I had to get to know her. It was magic. Hell for both of us to break up two marriages, but magic nonetheless. We've never regretted it for a moment, have we, love?'

Anke nodded, still reeling from Diana outing her first husband so blithely.

'Hard on the children, though, surely?' Having hit upon a successful formula, Diana's table conversation became increasingly like a psycho-analyst's.

'Oh, aye. Mine are still very defensive of their mother. When me and Anke moved to Essex it was hard to get to see them much.' Graham happily glossed over the fact that they were no longer even on speaking terms. 'Anke's kids found it easier, living with us. I'm more of a dad to them than Kurt was, and having one of our own to be a brother to them brought the family together. Don't get me wrong, Kurt's a nice guy, but I don't think he does fatherhood. I just love it.'

Anke's bulging eyes started to twitch as Graham opened their family up for inspection, giving his own unique spin on things to make life sound easy. She hadn't expected him to be this forthcoming.

'So Kurt didn't really bond with his kids?' Diana loved gossip that revolved around the horsy set.

'Hardly surprising,' Graham laughed. 'Given that he isn't even –'

'– there much!' Anke interrupted desperately, taking a swipe at his leg with her sensible shoe. 'He's away a lot, you see, competing and training. He hardly gets to see them.'

Mo, trapped between the two children, rubbed her ankle where Anke had just mistakenly kicked her under the table. Her legs were taking quite a bashing tonight.

'Shall I draw you a pony?' Mim suggested, reaching around to grab her coloured pens from the sideboard.

'Sure,' Mo murmured, keeping half an ear on the amazing conver-sation taking place around her as she stealthily helped herself to Digby's non-fishy leftovers. Not noticing that Mim was drawing her pony on the tablecloth, she listened.

'Of course, Anke only married Kurt for the passport, didn't you love?' Graham was saying as Anke turned redder and redder. He was like an unstoppable train.

'And the free lessons, I should imagine,' Diana giggled. 'What an amazing rider. You must have learned so much.'

'I married for love,' Anke said quietly. 'I was very young, and I loved him very much. We were married for ten years.'

'We've been married ten years too.' Graham gave a mock-theatrical gasp. 'Should I be worried?'

Glaring at him, Anke started to wonder whether this was just a very bad dream. 'I don't know. Should you?'

'Only if you're fighting an irresistible urge to wear pink and dance to Village People, Graham.' Diana couldn't resist a joke, her plummy voice and bravado making it, oddly, seem socially acceptable.

Again, Graham laughed uproariously. Even Mo shrouded a smile as she helped herself to another forkful of Digby's leftovers.

Diana decided to turn her in-depth interview technique upon the young school teacher. 'And how did you meet the dashing Padraig?'

Cheeks bulging, Mo could say nothing for a moment.

'Don't be shy,' Diana coaxed, suspecting some delicious secret that would tell her even more about the absent Pod.

Throat full of peas and mash, Mo spoke with a soupy, strangled voice.

'We met in a nightclub in Newmarket.'

Three faces stared at her, anticipating more.

Mo took a sip of wine to chase down a pea that was threatening to choke her.

'I take it he wasn't there to ride a race?' Diana interrogated.

'In the nightclub? No.'

She rolled her eyes. 'In Newmarket. You don't see many jump jockeys trying out the Rowley Mile!'

'He rode flat races too. He preferred to jump, but he could make the weight for flat and he got a lot of bookings. He wasn't riding the weekend we met, though. He was at Tattersalls, helping a friend look for cheap yearlings. Tattersalls is a horse sale, you see.'

Diana snorted superciliously. She was dying to show off her expertise from her career in bloodstock, but didn't trust herself to manage more than a few words at a time. Saying Rowley Mile had almost finished her. She knew perfectly well that Pod had raced both rules and had been a rare cross-bred success at both. Admitting this observation involved too many vowels and consonants, dates and facts to knit together safely. She settled for a smug smile and a simple question.

'And what were you doing at the time you two met in this club, Mo?'

'Dancing around my handbag probably.' Mo felt she had already said too much.

Graham let out a hoot of amusement.

Diana hushed him, focused on her target. 'I mean, what brought you to Newmarket?'

'My grandparents live on the Fens, just over the Norfolk border – in Swaffham – they brought me up. I was training to be a teacher at Honiton College. Suffolk was halfway home.'

'You went to Cambridge University?' Anke was impressed.

'Yes . . . well, the teacher training college.'

'It's a Cambridge college.' Anke smiled, eager to move poor Mo on to safer ground. Having been through the gay husband routine she could see Diana hooking up the little teacher for a similar fate. 'That's wonderful.'

'I guess.'

'You don't sound very sure?'

'I wanted to be a ballerina.' Mo watched Mim drawing a swan on the tablecloth beside her pony. She was a talented little artist.

'Really?' Diana couldn't hide the surprise in her voice having clocked the size of Mo's feet.

'Yes – I was very lucky at first. I went to London to train, but I got a stress fracture in my little toe, or the "fifth metatarsal" as they liked to call it to make it sound more serious than a stubbed toe.'

'But it *was* more serious, yes?' asked Anke.

'Yes. It turned out to be something called a Jones fracture. I had to have a pin put in my foot. It finished any chances I had of dancing for a living.'

'Poor you.'

She shrugged, watching Mim's swan taking shape. 'My mother was a ballet dancer. I guess I wanted to follow in her footsteps.' She smiled at the bad joke she had told too many times.

'I take it she's dead?' Diana was on increasingly blunt form.

Mo looked at her hostess for a long time. 'I have no idea. She went to India when I was three and never came back.'

'God, I wish mine had.' Diana helped herself to more wine before offering the bottle around.

Mo ran her tongue around her teeth, her flipside in sudden and very serious danger of making a public appearance. She desperately needed Pod here. She desperately needed a cigarette. She hadn't spoken of her ballet dreams in years and it had been even longer since she had mentioned her mother. Anger and resentment were bubbling up inside her like lava. Her dragon fire, Pod called it. He loved her explosions, but that was because he could control them. Here she was liable to burn out of control and destroy everything around her.

Diana's children were her stabilisers to either side, both now sketching happily on the tablecloth, totally zoned out of the adult conversation. Mo tried to draw calm from them, but the opposite was happening. Envy burned inside her. She was so jealous that they had Diana – even drunken, rude, pushy Diana was better than no mother. In fact, Mo suspected she was really quite a fun mother to have. She was jealous that Anke and Graham's children had at least four parents between them if you counted stepfathers and gay fathers. She had nothing.

The vodka coke and wine were fermenting in her belly, stirring a bubbling cauldron.

'My grandparents brought me up. They say my mother joined a cult in India, but I think they made that up. She just disappeared. Gramps went out there for months at a time, year after year, and never found her.'

'And your father?' Anke's eyes were wide, the ice chips dangerously close to melting into tears.

'I don't know who he was. Neither do my grandparents. My mother never told them.'

'How dramatic.' Diana raised an eyebrow.

Mo fought an urge to upend the table and run but she was trapped. To either side of her, small, heavy heads were resting tired cheeks against the table as crayons moved slowly on damask and yawns sighed from sleepy mouths.

'You okay, love?' Graham asked her gently, trying to disguise the hiccups he had been attempting to swallow for the past few minutes.

She nodded, trapped against the wall between two drowsy children having just conjured up her demons for all to see. She'd felt better.

'So . . .' Diana leaned back in her chair and rewound the tape with stunning abandon. 'Young Pod was in fact looking for horseflesh when he found you willing to *pas de deux* around your handbag in Newmarket?'

Anke was appalled by her hostess's lack of tact, but to her surprise Mo's big doe eyes lit up and she suddenly smiled with relief.

'That's right.'

'And he was a big hot-shot jump jockey. Lucky you!'

Mo was on familiar ground. Everyone wanted to know about Pod –
especially women. 'He was still conditional then.'

'I had no idea you'd been together so long.' Diana guessed Pod must
be at least thirty, and jockeys finished their apprenticeship at twenty-
five, or earlier if they rode enough races for their trainer. Pod's well-
documented career had reputedly started obscenely young – he was the
youngest jockey ever to ride in a Gold Cup. She'd assumed the Pod/Mo
thing to be very recent and quite flimsy. Their relationship had certainly
been low key in turf and media circles – Pod was seen as a lone trader.
'It must have been a long-distance relationship when he raced?'

Mo shrugged. 'Not really. He was based in Yorkshire when we met,
then when he got his licence he went to ride for Guy Channing in West
Berkshire. I got my first teaching post in Wantage and we've moved
around like that ever since, mostly sticking to East Anglia if we can.'

'Remind me.' Diana smiled mischievously. 'When did he lose his
licence?'

Graham let fly with an enormous trapped hiccup of surprise.

Just for a moment, Mo's eyes flashed with brimstone. 'Six months
ago. We've been back in Norfolk since then. I took a job covering mater-
nity leave close to my grandparents and Pod rode out for trainers nearby.'

Diana was leaning across the table now. 'You can hardly have moved
here to get away from racing – especially National Hunt? You're in the
heart of it here.'

'We came here for my job. Pod didn't care where we went as long
as it wasn't back to Liverpool. He's out of racing for good now.'

'But he must miss the riding?'

'He doesn't miss the falls. Or the dieting.' Mo cocked her head as
she scrutinised Diana's sparkling eyes. 'I think he misses the lasses.'

Diana smirked happily and sank back into her chair. 'So you have
one of those relationships?'

'How do you mean?'

'Open.'

'We're pretty open with one another.' Growing irritated with the
continuing cross-examination, Mo helped herself to more wine. The
children had both fallen asleep beside her, crayons in hand. 'Should
these two go to bed?'

But Graham, who had taken over the bottle to refill his own and
Diana's glasses, spoke over her as he decided to turn the tables. 'And
now tell us about you, Diana, love. What brings you back to the place
you grew up?'

'Divorce – impending.' Diana wasn't sure how much she could say before the gin and PMS bomb imploded within her. She wasn't even sure how much she wanted to say. But she surprised herself as she went on to relate her marital break-up quietly, lucidly and without malice in front of her sleeping children, whose eyelashes brushed their slumber-pinkened cheeks as they snoozed on regardless.

'Tim and I first met as teenagers. Like you and – Deirdre, wasn't it?' She looked at Graham with her face screwed up in squiffy concentration. 'We knew each other socially a long time before the relationship kicked off, and he had never made any secret of his feelings for me. Mine for him were more ambivu– ambivre– were less passionate, although as the years passed I developed quite a crush after all. I was treading water in my career – travelling a lot, going nowhere. He was jolly eligible – a Guards officer with a huge private income and a huge . . .' She dropped her head to the table and giggled delightedly. 'Huge is the operative word with Tim, but he was always an unromantic shit. That crush of mine had already worn off when we married, but the practicality and friendship still made sense – plus he had a cock to die for.'

Graham whooped, and Anke and Mo exchanged looks of horror as the children shifted in their sleep.

'He wanted a wife and I wanted to escape this place once and for all,' Diana rambled on, eyes glazing. 'We both wanted children and I rather took to the idea of marrying into the forces – plus my family rather took to the idea of forcing me to marry before I turned into the reincarnation of my aunt Til. It was very sensible, very protocol and slightly carnal.' She took a swig of wine and her head immediately started to swim. 'Unfortunately I foundmyshelf travelling a lot angoingnowhere still. But at leashtiwash married. Made family happy, happy familish.'

Up until this point, Graham had been developing a drunken and unexpected respect for Diana Lampeter and her unusual line in dinner party conversation. He was a man who was happy to wear his heart on his sleeve and he respected honesty in others. But that final sip of wine proved too much for Diana as she lost her grip on most of her consonants.

'And I washrather good at marriage. I did him proud. It's only in the past year or sho that it sh-sh- stopped making sense. I shtopped liking life ashanarmywiff. He had affairsh youshee. Turnshout he'd never-beenpticklyfaithful. Thefuckingbashtard.'

Mo fought an urge to muffle the children's sleeping ears with her arms as Diana slurred on like an unstoppable, sibilant torrent.

'Mother shays I can't blameTim becaushialwayslovedshome-onelsheyoushe. Thatshnotshtrictlytruebecaushi lovedTiminaway. I wasbloodyfaithful. He let*me*down. Now hesh lettinghishchildrendown. Bashtard. Whoshforpud?'

She lurched towards the kitchen.

'And the translation is?' Graham muttered as she disappeared.

'I'll clear these plates.' Anke began grabbing crockery.

'I'll see these children to bed.' Mo started gathering up Digby, ready to carry him upstairs.

'I'll get my coat,' Graham joked.

'No!' Diana pirouetted perilously in the kitchen doorway. 'You all shtay right where you are. I'm fetching pudding!'With that, she lurched into the kitchen, slamming the door behind her.

'Oh, Christ.' Graham rubbed his chin.

'Don't worry,' Mim piped sleepily, rubbing her eyes as Mo woke her up. 'Mummy is just drunk. It doesn't happen very often. She was upset because Hally ate our supper and then Daddy called to say that he's not coming tomorrow. She doesn't know we know but I listened on the phone extension.'

'Oh Mim, I'm sorry.' Mo hugged her.

Mim's pretty little face remained stoic, her lower lip thrust out, crayon marks on her cheek.

'Do you and Digby want to go to bed?' Mo whispered.

'No likely.' Digby plonked himself back in his chair. 'Pudding's orange.'

Suddenly there was a strange roaring and spitting sound from the kitchen.

'Do you think she's all right?' Anke fretted, still gathering up plates and laying then on the sideboard. 'It sounds as though she's setting fire to something.'

Refreshed by a can of Rory's Red Bull, Diana had managed to gather a surprising degree of demureness when she reappeared with a large cut-glass bowl containing three different types of ice-cream swimming with chocolate buttons, toffee sauce and meringues and topped with the children's marshmallows that she had just blasted with a blowtorch to toast them. She carefully let her fringe fall over her face so that her guests couldn't see her scorched eyebrows as she set the bowl upon the table.

'Wow!' Mo was in ecstasy. Digby was right – the overall hue was gloriously, tropically orange.

'Just tuck in.' Diana sank gratefully on to her chair, not realising that she had forgotten bowls and a serving spoon.

Anke, who was in within reach of the sideboard, managed to locate a small stack of dusty glass bowls and a tarnished soup ladle to spoon out great gooey portions.

'You are a wonderful cook, Diana.' Graham raised his glass.

She smirked squiffly. 'You have no idea how hard it was to cook that ice-cream.'

Graham helped Mo to more pudding, which she was wolfing up as fast as it appeared. For someone so slight, Mo Stillitoe ate an awful lot of food, Diana observed.

For someone who proclaimed to have lost his heart to his ice maiden, Diana also noted, Graham Brakespear was a world-class flirt. Yet it was obviously just a habit for him, like laughing too loudly and showering his food with too much salt. His love for Anke was almost overpowering, and she wondered at Anke's cool distance in return. The Red Bull was starting to really kick in, fast-forwarding her thoughts and sobering her up too quickly.

Yet again, her mind turned to Tim. She couldn't shake him off tonight and, however much her social and maternal conscience screamed at her to keep schtum, she couldn't stop herself from raising the subject again.

'Sorry I got a little emotional earlier – about my husband. Still very raw, you know.'

'I'm sure.' Anke smiled, although the ice-cream was thawing faster than the frost flecks in her blue eyes.

'Of course I blame myself.' Diana coasted on her Red Bull high, grateful for clear diction once more. 'He was terribly repressed, but a lot of these army types are you know. He has such a stiff upper lip, cunnilingus left one's bikini line perfectly shaved.'

'What is cunny – cornyfingus?' asked Mim.

Anke covered her eyes, but Diana wasn't thrown for a moment. 'Like sweets, darling – something you ask for all the time but rarely ever get.' If Diana and drink did not mix, then Diana, drink and a monumental sugar and caffeine high were pure combustion. Having drunk herself almost sober, she was now on a roll.

'Tell us more about your gourmet holiday ideas, Diana,' Graham urged hastily. 'Blazing Trails, wasn't it?'

Aware that perhaps she had stepped over the mark again, Diana swiftly embraced the topic of the grand gourmet riding holidays she had planned, hamming up her ideas to giddy heights with rose-tinted fantasist optimism.

'I see the perfect fusion of classical food, classical landscape and classical riding being irresistible,' she explained, waving around a spoon of garish orange goo. 'This is one of the most beautiful valleys in England – the backdrop is so ancient and time-trapped, especially around Foxrush Hall.'

'The Gunning Estate?' Mo asked nervously, thinking about Pod.

Sugar bubbled to caramel in Diana's veins. 'The riding there is quite amazing – one can get lost for days. It's kept its secrets to itself for far too long – I used to hack my ponies all over it when I was a child and the hunt's favourite coverts were there. You can't hide a beautiful place like that away from the world with hearsay and hysteria. It has the most fantastic . . .' She almost let slip about the Pleasure Garden as the Red Bull and alcohol in her bloodstream met the ice-cream full on. '. . . secrets. Fantastic secrets. I just need a very brave trail leader.' She laughed, thinking about Pod too.

'Is it true about the ghost?' Mo was spooning pudding straight from the bowl now.

Shrieking with laughter, Diana leaned back in her chair and would have tipped backwards had she not been pinned in by the door-frame. 'Who cares? I think he sounds rather fun, and a bloody good rider.'

'Firebrand?' Mo felt the chill of the ice-cream drop an icicle along her spine.

Diana stopped laughing. 'He's not the ghost.'

'But I heard that he gallops around in flames? They even say he might not be dead.'

The dark eyes blinked. 'Oh, he's dead.'

Mo looked at her curiously, noticing the way the colour had drained from her face.

'Bound to be,' she added a fraction too late.

'Pretty hard to gallop around in flames and stay alive,' Graham agreed. 'But I suppose it could make good publicity for you – haunted riding holidays, and all that?'

'Absolutely!' Diana grasped the marketing angle gratefully. 'The Americans will lap it up. The hostess with the ghostest, that's me. I might have to rattle our horseman's curb chains a bit to really wake him up.' Her voice was full of bravado, but her face remained curiously blanched.

Anke – and Mo, who already harboured fanciful fears about the ghosts contained within the ancient thousands of acres of turf – turned even paler.

Mim and Digby, who had listened to all this, watched the adults cynically, their lips dyed bright orange. As ghost stories went, they both rated this as seriously lame. They had seen a flaming horseman only yesterday, when Rory had been cantering around the sand school with his customary cigarette on the go and it had dropped from his mouth and down the front of his shirt. He'd been so engrossed in what he was doing that Sharon had been forced to throw a bucket of water over him.

On cue, a throaty diesel engine spluttered outside and headlights swung past the windows.

'My brother's home!' Diana smiled gratefully. 'He can join us for coffee and chocs.' The effects of sugar and caffeine receding fast, she skipped out through the kitchen, flicking on the kettle, falling over the dog basket and tripping outside to reel straight into the lavender beds.

Rory and Sharon had endured a hellish breakdown on the M5. Both were ragged and had immediately to wash and bed down wobbly-legged, exhausted and claustrophobic horses, much to Diana's blistering lack of sympathy. She needed new blood. There was still no sign of Pod.

'Hurry up.' She lurched around after her brother as he unloaded horses. 'You were supposed to be here hours ago.'

'The bloody lorry packed up.'

'My guests are all waiting to meet you.'

'They all met me last week, remember?' He delivered a horse into a stall with a slap on its rump and then followed it to start unwrapping travelling bandages. 'And since when did I become guest of honour?'

'Since I realised how boring they all are.'

'Can't wait to meet them, then.' He grinned up at her from beneath a horse's belly, watching her face in the dim stable lighting. 'Christ, how much have you had to drink?'

'Not a lot.' She swayed on the spot. 'It's been a very stressful evening with the children constantly in my hair. Sharon was supposed to babysit. I feel very let down.'

'First Sharon's heard of it,' said a caustic voice as Sharon lumbered past carrying piles of tack.

Diana glared at her fat, retreating back.

'And what are your guests – and children – doing now, while you're out here?' Rory asked. 'Washing up?'

'I hope not!' shrieked Diana. 'The kitchen's a bomb-site.'

She raced back through the yard and across the garden to the French doors into the kitchen, relieved to find it empty. She could hear muffled, embarrassed conversation from within the cottage and her children brat-tishly mewling that they did not want to go to bed and listen to Mo telling them a story, they wanted to watch television. Tired beyond sleep, they were acting up appallingly.

Swaying in the middle of the chaotic kitchen, cut in half by period pain and now spiralling back down into slewed confusion, Diana suddenly felt weary and unwilling to face anyone – not even her own children.

'I really think perhaps we should go,' Anke was suggesting as she stacked up bowls and moved glasses across to the sideboard.

'We have to say goodbye, surely?' Mo whispered, helping her gather empties.

They both glanced nervously at the kitchen door, but it didn't open.

On the sofa the children were slamming scatter cushions into one another's faces while Graham tried good-naturedly to break up the fight – earning him a pom-pom in one ear and a tassel in the mouth.

Mo giggled indulgently at his look of shock. Then, spotting Anke checking her out, she quickly deflected the snigger into an affectionate chuckle. 'They're great kids.'

Nodding doubtfully, Anke studied her across the table. 'Actually there is something I was going to ask you . . .'

Diana could no longer be bothered to be the perfect hostess. Switching on Book at Bedtime loudly, she started doing the washing up in the kitchen, leaving her guests baffled and embarrassed in the dining-room, wondering if they might be offered coffee. Anke's and Mo's offers of help had already been sharply rebuffed and, to her relief, neither dared try again.

But then, during a dramatic pause on Radio 4, Diana heard Anke broaching the subject of getting Chad into Oddlode primary school.

'. . . I appreciate that it is very last minute, but if you could speak with the headmistress on my behalf at any point in the . . .'

Still brandishing the large Sabatier she had been rinsing under the tap, Diana rushed back through to get in on the act.

'Did I hear someone mention schools?' Appearing in the doorway, knife aloft, she was taken aback when Mo and Anke both screamed in terror.

Diana later realised that making a joke of the situation would probably have been her best course of action. But her head and hormones were all over the place and she felt beyond humiliated. She knew it had been a lousy night – half the guests missing, dreadful food, too much booze and confessional table talk. It had been a lousy day before that. She just wanted to be understood and admired.

And so, instead of laughing, Diana threw a massive misunderstood tantrum. 'What is *wrong* with you people? I've bent over backwards to give you a lovely evening and you don't even have the courtesy to be polite in return. You've all behaved atrociously. I've never met such an ungrateful, ill-mannered group of suburban oiks in my life!'

With this, she burst into tears and ran to her room, leaving her children happily watching violent late-night television and her guests yet again speechless with surprise.

'Certainly a character, that one.' Graham managed to recover first. Yawning widely from fatigue, he settled next to Digby on the sofa. 'Shall I put a video on instead of this, you guys?'

'Now, surely, we can leave?' Anke suggested again.

'We can't leave the children here like this,' Mo whispered. 'Why don't I try to get them into bed while you check on Diana? She must be mortified.'

'I hope she's very embarrassed indeed,' Anke said chippily. 'I've never seen anything like it.'

Mo, who had a soft heart despite finding Diana both intimidating and appallingly rude, stared at her imploringly. 'She's obviously been through a lot.'

'A lot of gin.' Graham yawned again as he pressed Play for a Postman Pat video.

Anke – whose own life had hardly been devoid of heartbreak and high drama – was less sympathetic. 'I do think it would be best all around if we simply go.'

'No way!' drawled a cheery voice from the kitchen as Rory appeared, still wearing white breeches and a competition shirt, carrying the last of the fish pie in its casserole dish. 'I had to get Truck Rescue out in order to get back in time to see you again.' He grabbed a dirty fork from the pile of washing up on the sideboard and settled in the chair beside Anke. 'I'm not letting my childhood heroine leave without at least one drink.'

'I'm driving,' Anke resisted, although Rory looked so adorable and dishevelled – and smelled so comfortingly familiar – that she almost let a small smile lift her lips.

'That's okay. Sharon's making coffee.'

From the kitchen came the sound of grumbling and muttering as Sharon put the kettle on. Outside in the garden, Hally had reappeared and was chasing a barking Twitch around the overgrown flower-beds after an evening spent raiding dustbins in the village.

Rory reeked of horse, was covered in engine oil and ate like a famished tramp, but somehow his arrival brightened the room as though the day had dawned again. Ebullient from his first win in months, despite the awful return journey, he was in celebratory mood, telling Anke that he had always been madly in love with her. 'I was going to tell you last time, but I was too shy.'

Anke felt her cool cheeks prickle with pips of colour. 'You're too kind.'

'No – just love-struck.' He blew her a kiss. Winning has given him a huge confidence high. 'You were my all-time pin-up. I lent S your Olympic Kür video last week, didn't I, S?'

Lumbering through with a tray of coffee, Sharon grunted and nodded. Side-stepping as Mo started to coax two tired little bodies from the sofa, she settled the tray heavily on the coffee table, scowling at no one in particular.

Energised by a top-ranking ride that day and a top-ranking rider in his sitting-room that evening, Rory whooped, hugging both the kids and leaping up again. 'You wait until I tell Dilly who's here – she's my girlfriend. She's away at university. I'll just give her a quick call to let her know how we got on. Don't go away.'

Leaving Sharon to pour coffee, he took himself and a bottle of scotch to the kitchen to call girlfriend Daffodil and break the good news.

Anke slumped tiredly in her chair for a moment, watching as Mo quietly slipped away to take Digby and Mim to bed, showing amazing prowess with small, tired children. Holding their hands and playing a game of 'shhh' they tiptoed upstairs.

Graham had fallen asleep in front of Postman Pat with his mouth open.

Anke knew that she should really help Mo, but she didn't want to bump into Diana Lampeter on the landing wielding a cut-throat razor or a pair of scissors. The woman was demented.

'You have had a good day, then?' she asked Sharon politely.

Sharon's unfriendly, chubby face turned to her and she grunted something which could have been yes or no, or a tip for the three fifteen at Wincanton for all Anke could tell. Short, stout and red-faced, she couldn't have looked less like the sort of girl who normally worked with horses. Her short blonde hair was spiked up and streaked with crude white highlights. Her huge bosom, bulging from a badly fitting sports bra, spilled out of a T-shirt she had slashed at the neck to give her more cleavage. She had a brash, carnal anger about her.

Anke noticed the way that her face lit up when Rory came back into the room, and the secret smirk that crossed it when he glumly announced that Dilly was obviously out on the town with her new university friends and not answering the phone.

She's in love with him, Anke realised. Poor thing. She has to compete with a pretty girlfriend and a silly pash for an ageing dressage rider.

'She's gone up to Durham for the summer.' Rory was telling Anke about Dilly as he settled adoringly beside her once more. 'She wanted to come here but I can't pay her, and her student debts are going to be diabolical, poor thing. She refuses to live in halls, so she's working bars and restaurants to get a deposit on a rented flat. She's fantastically motivated like that. She's coming back in a couple of weeks. I can't wait.'

A glass was smacked on the table in front of him and Sharon glugged out some whisky.

'Thanks, S.' Rory looked up at her and blew a kiss. Just for a brief moment, the look between them could have reignited the long-extinguished candles on the table.

Anke blinked in surprise. Perhaps Sharon did have a claim after all. This household just got odder. She wanted to go home.

Then she felt a warm hand on her thigh and something happened. Shame and lust coursed through her veins in equal measure as Rory turned his sleepy grey eyes on her and tapped her coffee-cup with his scotch glass. 'Here's to childhood crushes made real. I had your poster above my bed for years.'

Anke jumped as Graham let out a rip-roaring snore from the sofa and Sharon clumped back into the kitchen, tripping over Hally.

'Did you really?' she asked disbelievingly.

He nodded, dishevelled blonde fringe falling over his eyes as he blushed. Anke's neck coloured in sympathy.

'I used to dream of being your saddle,' he told her.

Anke swallowed what felt like a huge fur-ball.

There was a loud clatter from the kitchen as Sharon laid into the last of the melted ice-cream dessert with a serving spoon.

Upstairs, Mo had put the children to bed. Digby had donned orange pyjamas and conked out almost immediately beneath his orange duvet in the bottom bunk. Mim asked for her night-light to be put on so that carousel horses danced dimly around the room while she arranged a small menagerie of fluffy animals around her in the top bunk.

Mo was surprised by the cramped tattiness of the upstairs, with its peeling wallpaper and damp patches. It made Number Four look celestial, and she suddenly saw how desperate Diana had been all night not to let her guests see how humbly she was living. It didn't matter that they didn't care. *She* cared.

'Do you think Mummy's really upset?' Mim asked her.

'Not with you. You were fantastic.'

'You won't tell her that we didn't clean our teeth, will you?'

'Course not.'

Mim closed her eyes and sighed. 'I wish Daddy was coming tomorrow.'

'I know.' Mo stretched up and kissed her cheek. 'You must miss him a lot.'

'He was away all the time. We're used to not seeing him. But I think Mummy needs a break.' With that she fell asleep, her face pressed to a large penguin.

Mo found Diana in tears in her room – a tiny, tatty cell into which the bed barely fitted.

'I'd really rather you didn't come in,' she whimpered.

Mo ignored her and carefully closed the door so that no one down-stairs could hear. 'Are you all right?'

'Never better,' she hissed sarcastically.

'The children went out like lights. Mim was a bit worried, but I said that you would be in to kiss her later and she seemed fine with that.'

'Oh, please don't say tonight is happening.' Diana spoke into her fingers as she perched on the end of the bed, her face in her hands. 'I never normally behave like this.'

'The food was delicious.' Mo tried placating her.

'It was junk.'

'I could never have cooked that. I'm absolutely lousy.'

'I was so rude to everyone. Anke clearly hates me.'

'Not at all – you're very witty. I don't think Anke always understands because her humour isn't so British. And I would have behaved much worse if I'd tried to do something like this. Ask Pod. He's seen me at my looniest. We all have nights we want to howl at the moon.'

'It's this place, this wretched place!' Diana spat accusingly.

Mo looked around the uninviting little room trying to think of some-thing positive to say.

'It's as though I've never been away, haven't changed or grown up, become a mother, been a wife, done *anything*. This wretched valley has some sort of twisted spell that turns us all back into the children we hated being. Not happy, giggling *joie de vivre* infants, but angry, besotted teenagers full of spit and fury.'

It was clear that she wasn't talking about Horseshoe Farm Cottage or her depressing little room.

'You're an outsider, how could you understand? This place sucks you dry. I remember why I left now. I thought it would be so different coming back, but it's just as bad. My mother hasn't even tried to see me yet, Nanny and my aunt are already lecturing me and they're right – I'm misbehaving just as they predicted. It's impossible to be good here. You wait.'

Mo tried to deflect the self-loathing, 'Well, Pod's behaving badly already – I'm so sorry he didn't turn up. It's really rude. He's always so unreliable, I'm thinking of tagging him.'

'He's not screwing around already, is he?' Diana asked bitterly.

Mo took a step back. 'He's getting drunk with his new boss.'

'Of course – my apologies.' Diana held up a hand and forced a dry laugh. 'When you're married to a philanderer, you tend to assume all men are unfaithful. I'm sure he's a lovely chap.'

Mo nodded. 'He makes the sun shine brighter and the rain fall more softly.'

Diana's eyes filled with tears again.

'I didn't mean to upset you.' Mo rushed forward.

'No, no, you haven't.' She waved Mo back, terrified that she'd try to hug her or something. 'I'm just totally over the top. Oh, my poor babies. Did I say dreadful things in front of Mimsy and Digs? Were they terribly upset?'

Mo shook her head. 'I don't think it really went in,' she lied carefully. 'They were very tired.'

Diana stifled another sob. 'Oh God, I don't know how to tell them that their father's not coming tomorrow. They'll be heartbroken.'

'They already know. Mim told me that she overheard when he called.'

Diana looked up, red eyes tortured, all the alcohol in her system making her maudlin. 'And she didn't tell me?' she breathed wretchedly.

'She was worried about you. She's a good kid.'

'I know.' She covered her face again. 'They both are. I don't deserve them. I'm such a lousy mother.'

'No, you're not. They adore you, and you're there for them. It's more than my mother was.'

'Why are you being so nice to me?' Diana peeked out through her fingers.

Mo shrugged. 'I guess I'm just a nice person.'

Diana pressed her fingers to her lips and almost mustered a smile, her sodden eyes creasing with genuine respect. 'I had you all wrong.

I'm sorry. I thought you were afraid of your own shadow, but you're a tough cookie, aren't you? Much tougher than me.'

She stood up and moved to the tiny mirror on the wall, pressing her fingers into the soft, puffy bags beneath her eyes. 'God, crying makes one look such a fright after thirty.'

'You're very beautiful,' Mo said honestly. 'Crying can't hide that.'

As she said this, a text message came through on her phone and she turned away to pluck it from her pocket to read, not seeing Diana's stunned expression.

'*Sorry, queen – got lost in the woods. Wasn't hungry anyway.*' The phone let out another low battery warning.

'Pod is terribly sorry. Something to do with a blown gasket,' she improvised, turning back. 'He's really upset he couldn't make it.'

'Men.' Diana rolled her puffy eyes, warming to Mo all the more for the obvious but heartfelt lie. She liked good fibbers. 'And he missed *such* a treat, didn't he?'

Mo bit her lip and realised that Diana was smiling. Suddenly she found herself smiling too.

'Would you mind very much making excuses for me? I can't face Anke Brakespear again. Tell them I've passed out in a pool of my own vomit,' she joked. 'Or that I'm reading my children *Women who Love Too Much* in bed.'

Mo giggled. 'Of course. And don't worry – I think your brother is distracting her.'

'About time,' Diana sniffed, finding a little of the old chutzpah. 'Bloody Rory. Tonight is all his fault for blowing us out.'

'And Pod,' Mo reminded her.

'Now I remember why I always loved horses so much. They make up for men's shortfalls.'

'Horses terrify me,' Mo admitted.

'Me too,' Diana confessed. 'But men frighten me more.'

As Mo turned to go, Diana caught her arm. 'Thanks.'

'Don't mention it. I've had a lovely evening.'

When Mo emerged from the bedroom, Anke came out of the bathroom.

'Everything all right?' She raised her blonde eyebrows.

Mo nodded and, feeling a curious affinity for Diana and her passion, she collared Anke halfway down the stairs and told her a small white lie to excuse their hostess's behaviour.

'So you see, it really wasn't her fault. Silly mix-up,' she whispered afterwards. 'I think you are right, though. It is time to leave.'

'Oh, we can't possibly go yet,' Anke protested, rejuvenated by Rory's flattering crush and Sharon's equally flattering jealousy. 'Rory has only got as far as telling me about today's warm-up.'

Hooking her arm through Mo's in a rare gesture of camaraderie, she towed her downstairs. Mo was so relieved that her white lie had been swallowed, she bid a silent goodnight to Diana and her children and prayed they didn't keep them awake. There was something about Anke's firm grip that bestowed the ultimate confidence – like Mary Poppins taking one for a test flight. She had a feeling the night had only just begun. Pod would love this.

By the time they were on to their third cafetiere of coffee, Anke was not the only one of Diana's guests feeling wonderful about herself once more. After a lot of scotch and cajoling, Mo allowed herself to be persuaded to have a riding lesson with Rory.

'I have to warn you I'll be hopeless. I have a lousy head for heights.'

'You were a ballet dancer – you'll be a natural,' Anke insisted. 'It's all about rhythm and balance.'

Having been struck by Anke's rather cold disapproval all evening, Mo was touched by her enthusiasm. This was obviously her great passion and it lit her up so that her blue eyes shone and her mouth couldn't stop smiling.

Mo only wished the prospect didn't make her feel quite so sick.

'Horses really do frighten me,' she fretted.

'I'll make sure you have our sweetest pony to take care of you,' Rory promised, enjoying teaming up with Anke to enlist a new convert.

'How can you be frightened of horses when you live with a jockey?' Anke was amazed.

'You don't have to be fond of flames to live with a fire-eater,' she pointed out.

'Good point,' Rory laughed.

Mo found it impossible to explain the fact that Pod liked her fear of horses. It was a part of his life he could keep entirely separate, ensuring that their relationship – and her physical energy – stayed concentrated in the bedroom where he wanted it. This exclusion had never bothered Mo as much as it did tonight. She loved horses for their grace and beauty but, close up, they intimidated her. Tonight two things had happened. Pod had let her down big time – embarrassing her in front of her new friends. And tonight, Diana Lampeter had said she had guts. Well, it took guts to ride and it would make Pod sit up and take notice if she started. That, and a belly full of spirits, seemed as good an excuse as any.

'I've said I'll come up here on Monday,' Anke remembered uncomfortably, realising that there might be a way to make the return trip slightly less excruciating. 'I can give you a lift if it suits you and Rory to start then.'

'Sure – Monday's a quiet day,' Rory said casually, looking nervously over his shoulder to check that Sharon wasn't listening. Monday was normally the horses' day off but, as it was Sharon's day off too, she wouldn't necessarily find out that he'd taught a lesson. He desperately needed the cash.

To his relief, Sharon and Graham were both fast asleep on adjacent sofas, snoring loudly.

'So tell me,' he turned back to his companions, lazy grey eyes amused, 'what *is* my sister planning to do to my yard? She won't say a thing.'

Mo and Anke both swallowed nervously.

'As long as it's not pony trekking . . .' Rory led.

Anke stared fixedly at her coffee-cup.

'We didn't really find out.' Mo spun another lie. To her relief, her phone beeped with another text.

'That'll be Dilly.' Rory grabbed it from the table without thinking and pressed the Read button.

'*In bed naked,*' he read delightedly and then frowned. '*Hurry home. Hard on like Blackpool Tower.*' Then he remembered that his mobile – which was the same model – had run out of charge while summoning help on the M5.

'I think that's my phone.' Mo took it, read the message, and blushed crimson. On cue, her battery let out a sympathetic bleep and died.

'Your boyfriend seems to have made it back home.' Rory's eyes crinkled as he looked away in amusement.

'In that case, we must get you back,' Anke announced, taking a cue to leave while the night was young and her young knight of an admirer was still sober enough to remember her name. 'Please pass on our thanks to your sister, Rory. I'm so sorry to hear that she got ACP muddled up with aspirin. Such an easy mistake. I did a similar thing with dog steroids once and passed out cold after drinking just a small schnapps. These things are dreadful when mixed with alcohol. You really should keep human drugs in the bathroom and animal ones in an outside building, not mix such things up in a kitchen drawer.'

As Mo cleared her throat nervously, Rory gave her a curious look, and she blushed even more deeply. ACP was a mild horse tranquilliser. It was something Pod and his cronies had been cited as using to fix races. In her effort to make Diana's night from hell easier, she had allowed her white lie to get somewhat elaborate.

As Anke prodded her husband back to life with a little more ferocity than was called for, Mo gave Rory a polite kiss on the cheek.

'I think I like it round here.'

'It looks even better from horseback,' he promised. 'See you Monday.'

Waking up at the same time as Graham, Sharon glowered at Rory over a scatter cushion.

Diana was upstairs cleaning her teeth until her gums bled, convinced that she was a terrible hostess and a terrible mother. On top of that, having bragged about all her plans, persuaded Anke to bring her daughter to ride at the yard, and now having overheard Mo arranging a lesson, she had yet to confess to her brother that she'd lost her nerve with horses.

She listened to car doors banging and the engine firing up and chewed on the brush fiercely, staring at her angry face in the mirror.

You are beautiful, she remembered Mo saying.

All she saw was a hideous, twisted mask of malice staring back.

Coming back here had turned her upside down and shaken out all the goodness. It was as though several chapters of her life had been edited out and she was back to the point where she had caused the greatest hurt she could inflict, cauterising love, butchering happiness, massacring a life she had only ever wanted to share – and to save.

That was the last time she had seen this face. She had hoped never to set eyes on it again.

When Rory headed to the bathroom to clean his teeth, he at first thought that he must have drunk too much as his reflection divided and fractured like a kaleidoscope while he sought his back molars. Then he realised the mirror above the basin was shattered.

Seven years, bad luck. That was all he needed.

To start with, Sharon was waiting in bed for him.

'Not tonight, darling, eh?' He kissed her lightly on the mouth and peeled back the duvet. 'I'm shattered.'

'I just want a cuddle.'

Rory was too tired to fight. Slumping in beside her, he managed a heavy arm across her broad shoulders and a quick tweak of her nipple before his breathing deepened and he was out.

Sharon traced his fingertips with hers and wriggled contentedly around to spoon against his hard body. A moment later Twitch shot out of the duvet and slunk grumpily to the foot of the bed to glare at Sharon all night, between dreams of chasing rabbits.

Mo fell over twice trying to get undressed in the dark. She hadn't realised quite how drunk she was. She had a nasty feeling that she had rambled a lot in the Brakespears' car, possibly even bursting into song. Thankfully, Graham had remained asleep with his blonde head bumping against the passenger's door, although Anke had politely pretended to understand what Mo was trying to say.

What had she said? She couldn't even remember now. Something about having a lovely night with lovely new friends in a lovely new area. There had been a lot of lovelies. She hoped she hadn't said that Graham was lovely. She had certainly thought it. And she'd been tempted surreptitiously to touch his lovely hair in the car.

'Oof!' She fell over again trying to step out of her dress.

In bed, Pod didn't stir, his face pressed into the pillows while he slept.

Clean bedding. Had he changed it? She was too drunk to remember what covers had been on before. Had Bechers been in here? She had a vague recollection about his face looking at her from the upstairs . . . Keys! Her mind jumped drunkenly. She had locked herself out. How had she just got in? She looked at Pod again, realising he must have left the door on the latch.

Lovely night. Lovely new friends. Lovely drive home. Lovely . . . Pod.

Normally Mo would have been in raptures at his still, sleeping, moonlit body. But tonight she found it far from . . . lovely.

She clambered in beside him and gave him a prod. Nothing. She prodded harder. Nothing. She hit him quite hard.

He groaned and rolled over.

If Mo was merrily wasted, Pod was completely wrecked. Mo had to hit him several more times just to get him to crank open one eye a fraction.

'Where in hell did you get to?' she demanded.

'Shorryqueen,' he mumbled, closing the eye. 'Talkaboutitinthemorningeh?'

'No, you will explain yourself NOW!' she howled, all the scotch she had drunk putting fire in her belly.

'Later.'

'*NOW!*'

Groaning again, he scrunched up his eyes and swallowed dryly. 'Smoked too much spliff. Can't talk.'

'Shall I fetch you some water?'

'Please.'

Mo lurched out on to the landing and into the bathroom, tipping the toothbrushes from the broken-handled mug they lived in and filling it from the tap. Lurching back to Pod, she emptied it over his face.

Howling, he fell out of bed.

'Better?' she asked as he blinked up at her, sodden, bewildered and totally stoned. Even in the steely moonlight his eyes were clearly rimmed bright red.

'How come,' he said as he crawled along the skirting board and found a discarded shirt to dry his face on, 'you hardly say a thing if I screw another woman, but if I miss some posh cow's dinner party you do this?' Not waiting for her to answer, he threw down the shirt and crawled on, apparently heading for the wardrobe.

Mo watched as he calmly opened the wardrobe door and started to climb in.

He was very, very stoned. He was trying to find Narnia.

She sat down on the dry end of the bed, heart hammering.

'Met an amazing woman tonight,' came a voice from beneath the hangers. 'Til, she's called. Amos wanted me to meet her. Knows more about horses than I could ever dream.'

'Horses!' Mo snorted in despair.

'She smokes a pipe – pure grass in it. Made me look lightweight. Lost the plot after a bit. All the talk of horses and ghosts and money. I heard her and Amos talking more when I went to the bog. Something about buried treasure in a sunken garden. Like a Blue Peter time capsule,' he started to giggle, making the hangers rattle. 'Christ knows. Maybe *she's* the ghost. Maybe Amos took me to meet the ghost – like an initiation ceremony.' He roared with laughter.

Mo set her jaw angrily as she watched clothes come tumbling down, the whole wardrobe shaking.

'Christ – if that's what a forestry helper goes through I'd hate to apply for the gamekeeper's job,' he cackled.

She licked her lips. 'Do you fancy her?'

'Eh?'

'Til. The woman who smokes the pipe?'

He cackled even louder. 'She's about a hundred and ten!'

She looked up at the ceiling, tapping her teeth together, fighting an urge to lock him in the wardrobe and leave him there all night. He was impossible when he was like this. But she didn't trust her wobbly, whisky-filled legs enough to make it across the room.

In fact, the room itself was spinning so much that she didn't realise the laughter had stopped. Nor did she see Pod launch himself from the wardrobe until he was on top of her, hurling her back against the mattress.

'Is Mo jealous?' he asked, his mouth inches from her face.

Winded, Mo couldn't say anything.

'Is she?' he demanded. 'Is she jealous that I spent the night having fun instead of playing guest to Mrs Posh and the local hobnobbers?'

Still struggling for breath, Mo was almost suffocated by a brutal kiss, his teeth clashing with hers, his tongue right down her throat.

And then, with typical Pod unpredictability, he started to kiss her as tenderly as he had ever kissed her, drawing the anger out of her like venom from a snake bite until she was unable to do anything but kiss him back.

11

Over the scorching August Bank Holiday weekend, the Lodes valley swarmed with tourists. They choked up the lanes with caravans and camper vans, set up picnics in passing places on single-track lanes, pushed bicycles up the steep hills and freewheeled nervously down them. Every other car had a roof box, and a passenger holding up a map in the front seat: the footpaths and bridleways were awash with new scents for the local dogs to linger over: and picturesque Lower Oddford, with its network of streams, played host to several hundred checked blankets on which shorted bottoms rested while ice-creams were consumed in bulk.

Even the village green in less idyllic Oddlode had barely a square foot of emerald showing as bare flesh reddened on towels and children fought to make the smallest of football and rounders pitches amid the human obstacles.

Pod spent most of the weekend propping up the bar of the Lodes Inn with the Wycks, who alternated between grumbling about the crowds and trying to persuade him not to take the job on the Gunning Estate.

Aware that he would not be easily forgiven for going AWOL the night of Diana Lampeter's dinner, Pod was lying low as opposed to lying through his teeth. Mo had made several unsuccessful attempts to quiz him about his evening with Amos and old Til Constantine, but, in fact, he remembered very little of it. He had a shrewd suspicion that this had been Amos's plan in the first place. The man had been in the strangest of moods after hearing Diana's name.

'All I know is that he and Mrs Posh were some sort of item once,' he told Mo on Saturday night as they barbecued chocolate-filled bananas in the back garden.

'Don't call her that.'

'What? Mrs Posh. She is.'

'Her name's Diana.'

'And she's your bestest *fwend*,' he mocked, pulling another cold beer from the washing-up bowl that he had turned into an impromptu ice bucket.

'Piss off.' Mo picked out a beer for herself. 'I just can't see Diana being with someone like Amos. He's so . . .'

'Normal?' Pod suggested. 'Common? Human? Poor?'

'Angry.'

'Maybe she made him angry?'

'Do you know what happened between them?'

'No idea. Do I make *you* angry?'

'You did yesterday.'

''Cos I didn't want to suck up to Mrs Posh and the Danish family Robinson?'

'Don't call her that!' Mo howled.

'You shouldn't have made friends with the first people you met, queen. We have nothing in common with them – Diana and her "inner circle".'

'What "inner circle"?'

'Face it, the woman's a black widow. You're on the first rung of her web. She's just using you, little Mo fly.'

'I like her!'

'She's poison. Ask Amos.'

'So tell me what he said.'

'Can't remember.' He relished teasing her.

'Oh, piss off!'

'I love it when you're angry,' he pestered in a cliché matinée idol voice. 'You're so beautiful when you're angry. You give me wood, baby.'

Had Gladys Gates not been visiting her sister in Pershore that day, she would have witnessed her most exciting Number Four spectacle to date as Pod and Mo embarked on a furious row, beer cans and hot bananas flying.

The following morning, plagued by a disturbingly erotic dream featuring a lover not unlike Graham Brakespear, Mo hardly noticed Pod slide out of bed. Pulling a pillow over her head, she heard the ancient boiler rattle into life, and tried sleepily to remember quite how she and Pod had left things the night before. Her throat hurt – a sure sign that they had either shared a spliff or argued. Given that drugs were banned from their new life – at least *she* was keeping her end up – she suspected the latter.

But before she could start to piece anything together she slipped back into her dream and the Graham Brakespear lover began painting her very slowly in nectar from the toes up while hummingbirds helped him drink it.

Much later, she tottered downstairs in a vest and ancient pants to raid the fridge, only to find the juice carton with just a millimetre of sticky soup that slicked around her dry mouth and stung her throat. The milk carton had just enough semi-skimmed to take her strong, sweet tea from borscht-red to brick. Bechers was mewling around her ankles, but they were out of cat food. Pod had finished off the sliced bread and the cereal.

Cursing him under her breath, she settled in front of a black and white film on television and recalled their fight the night before. He had been trying to get her into bed at the time. Mo had gone for the jugular.

Somewhere in the spat that had moved from garden to sitting-room to bathroom to bedroom, she'd accused him of being a loser who had given up a great career for life as a glorified wood-chopper.

His wood – about which he had been boasting moments earlier – had been well and truly chopped down by that.

He'd stormed off to the pub.

Later, they'd slept with only their spines kissing like two crossed swords.

Mo trailed outside and found the charred remains of several chocolate-filled bananas, oozing out a sticky, sap-like gloop that wasps were dive-bombing excitedly.

She had a feeling that their relationship had just hit one of its sticky patches.

A trip to the village shop for milk and bread cheered her up as Joel Lubowski, the American owner, kept her cornered for ten minutes telling her what an asset she was going to be to the village.

'You're one helluva cute thing to see around, Helena.' He flashed his bleached teeth and gave her a hefty discount.

Then one of the younger Wycks wolf-whistled her as she crossed the green, and she found a sweet home-made welcome card and half a dozen bantam eggs on the doorstep.

'Sorry to miss you – welcome to the village. Love, Pixie Guinness.'

Mo was so perked that she didn't notice Pod had taken her car. She decided that she would not allow the sticky patch to happen.

She renewed her redecoration of Number Four Horseshoe Cottages with vigour, determined to drag the last of the argument's fish-hooks from her skin. Even Glad Tidings, spending all day dead-heading roses in order to spy on her, didn't delay her two applications of oyster to their bedroom and two loving text messages to Pod's mobile.

But she had nodded off in bed with a book spine hooked on one ear long before he reeled in that night, reeking of the Lodes Inn. Even flopping restlessly in and out of bed and stealing the duvet, he didn't wake her. It was the early hours before she sprang awake, realising that she was cold, alone, and missing the fizzing inner warmth from making love. She crawled sleepily downstairs to look for him, Bechers and the twelve-tog duvet.

He was on the sofa in front of a video of John Francome's favourite steeplechases, his eyes closed as he listened while Red Rum overtook the noble Crisp. He looked beautiful and lost. She sat on top of him to wake him up, inadvertently terrifying Bechers who'd been nestling in his armpit.

He leaped into life with that haunted, cornered look that he never explained but which always softened her heart.

She nuzzled and kissed him. 'I'm sorry we fought.'

His eyes narrowed suspiciously.

'Truce?' she offered desperately.

He nodded, but she could tell he was a long way from home.

They made love as they always did, bad patch or not – and, as always when bad patches happened, they did so in silence, like strangers. Mo lay back on the sweat-creased sheets afterwards, still feeling him inside her, wondering if he'd ever return the favour by letting her inside his head.

Perhaps he was right, she thought wearily as she drifted off to sleep amid the paint fumes, riding his hunched back with soft solitude. Perhaps she shouldn't have tried to make friends with the first people they'd met; perhaps she should have avoided Diana Lampeter's cottage and that vicious 'inner circle'.

She was dreading her first riding lesson, which she hadn't even mentioned to him.

She could almost feel the ghosts of her life pacing around outside on snorting horses, let alone the flame-swept Firebrand.

Anke was increasingly worried about Faith, whom she had to drag to Overlodes on Bank Holiday Monday. Her explanation of her grandfather's visit and the subsequent fiasco of the car in the pond had been sketchy to say the least and, naturally, Ingmar could remember nothing of it whatsoever. Graham had delighted in the weekend task of pulling the invalid car out of the reeds with his new hobby tractor, an expensive piece of machinery that should have stayed on the Dulston's forecourt as far as Anke was concerned.

'He could have drowned,' Anke fretted as they drove around Oddlode green to pick up Mo en route to the stables.

'There's only six inches of water in there,' Faith muttered defensively.
'That's all it takes to drown.'

'I'll bear it in mind next time I fill the horses' water trough. Lethal.'

'Don't be fatu- fasci – fall –'

'I think the word you're looking for is facetious.' Faith had an irritating habit of correcting her mother's English when Anke was struggling for a word.

'Your grandfather should not be driving any more. He's a danger to himself and others.'

'Genes he has clearly passed on,' Faith muttered through gritted teeth as Anke narrowly missed ploughing the Lexus into Glad Tidings who was wandering past Horseshoe Cottages carrying her shopping basket and peering into the windows.

'Go and knock on the door,' Anke insisted, making Faith grumble and slump and kick the foot well as she slid sullenly from the car.

Anke fiddled with the car seat which Graham always cranked so far forwards and dropped so low that he drove with his Adam's apple rammed into the steering-wheel. She didn't like driving the Lexus – it was like wearing her husband's clothes – but he had yet to arrange a replacement and they were still juggling one car, begging Magnus's tatty Porsche as an extra and using Dulston's forecourt tractors in an emergency. She expected Graham to turn up in the combine one of these days.

She was going to have to get on top of his paperwork this week. The insurance was a fiasco for a start. But it was Bank Holiday and, even though Graham had said that he would look in on Dulston's at some point that morning she was determined to play hookey. Faith deserved a treat. She was clearly not settling at all and seemed more dejected than ever.

Faith had already decided that she disliked Mo intensely. She was too pretty, too slim, too fey and too lucky to have the most beautiful man in the world in love with her to deserve anything less than hatred. Her animosity intensified tenfold when Mo breezily greeted her at the door wearing nothing but a bra and hot pants, a paintbrush in one hand and a hand-rolled cigarette dangling from her curly pink lips.

'I'll make my own way up later,' she told Faith airily.

'But Mum says you don't have a car.'

'I do have a car. It's just not here.'

'So how will you get to the yard?'

Mo lifted *à pointe* with the aid of the door-frame and looked down. 'If I'm going to learn to ride, I might as well warm up on Shank's pony.'

Faith was mesmerised. Her legs were beautiful – like two young twisted willow branches. 'Huh?'

'I'll walk.'

'It's miles – and all uphill,' she pointed out. 'Even if you set out now it'll take over an hour.'

'I'll walk really fast.' She shut the door.

Pique curdling her blood, Faith trailed back to the car, kicking the heads off the rock roses alongside the garden path as she did so.

'She's walking,' she announced as she slumped back into the car.

'She's what?' Anke looked up from re-tuning the radio from Sport AM to Classic FM.

'She says she's going to walk.'

'You didn't say anything to upset her, did you?'

'No!' Faith glared out of the window at the thatched cottage. She only wished she had. Mo Stillitoe was a cow.

Standing in the cool of her thick-walled, low-beamed sitting-room, Mo closed her eyes and tried to slow her heartbeat. She wasn't ready. She didn't want to do this. Whatever had possessed her to agree to get on a horse? Pod would go nuts. The atmosphere between them was already dangerously toxic.

So far, so good. All she had to do was call Overlodes in half an hour or so and make up an excuse.

'This is going to be lovely, isn't it?' Anke tried to lift Faith out of her sulk as she tackled the blind bends on the way to Upper Springlode. 'It's so kind of Diana Lampeter to offer us her horses to ride. You might even find you'd like to spend some of the autumn working there if it fits around college. Rory is great fun.'

'We have horses of our own to look after.'

'Yes, but they are little old men now – they are happy to do nothing. You need something you can ride.'

'Tell that to Graham. He should buy me something.'

'Faith!' Anke chastised, but only gently. She disliked Graham's dictum about Bert going before Faith was allowed a new horse. The pony was elderly now and cost little to keep. But she knew that Graham was making a stand – *one* of his stands – and she knew better than to question it.

'I'd like to ride the stallion,' Faith muttered. 'Baron Areion. He's incredible.' Her daughter's voice gathered a little short breath of excitement at last. 'I would love to sit on him – even just for a walk around the sand school.'

'I'm sure you can.'

Faith finally lifted her eyes from glaring at the glove compartment. 'You think so?'

'Of course. You are a very good rider – much better than your rusty mother. I told Diana so. I really don't have the time to ride him regularly if that's what she wants, and she says that she is too busy to. If he's as good as he looks, that horse needs someone to take him on.'

'He's really classy isn't he?'

'Supremely, I think.'

Faith managed a twitch of the mouth that was close to a smile and envisaged the wide-eyed admiration of all who gathered around the manège rails as she took Baron Areion into a beautiful floating canter, perhaps popping in some tempi changes – and then into piaff and passage – equine balletics that would be far more graceful and sexy than Mo Stillitoe and her failed stab at dancing *à pointe* in a silly tutu.

'So do you think they'll let me ride him today?'

'I don't see why not, although I think Diana said something about us all going for a hack. We'll see what she says.'

But when they arrived, Rory was smoking his customary cigarette all alone on the mounting block by the barn. He explained that Diana was suffering from an upset stomach and had cried off.

'She's in the cottage with Nurse Mim and Doctor Digs applying hot and cold towels when they should be exercising their fat ponies,' he said, casting an irritable look towards the honey stone house and his sister's phoney sickbed

Faith caught her breath as she studied him through her fringe. He had stubble haunting his cheeks – *stubble!* so manly! – and big dark licks of tiredness under the ghost-grey eyes. He'd pulled his hair back in a topknot with a plaiting band like Beckham. Faith had never been a big fan of football, but her best friend Carly adored Beckham and Faith could suddenly see why.

'It's Sharon's morning off so I could have done with some help in the yard,' he grumbled as he stood up and beckoned them towards the American barn ahead of him. 'The horses are already tacked up.' He glanced at his watch.

'Rio?' Faith muttered hopefully, too shy to look at him.

If she had, she would have seen that Rory's cheeks were high with streaks of colour as he admired Anke in smooth cream breeches and long black boots. His teenage pin-up was still the epitome of ice-maiden cool with her neat blonde bob, polar-blue eyes, slim body and endless wraparound legs. Seeing her dressed to ride sent his heartbeat into triple figures.

'Yeah, Rio is ready. God knows he could do with the exercise. You're taking him in the school later, too, aren't you?' He looked at Anke. 'Diana said to come and fetch her when you were ready. I'm teaching at midday so we'll work around that. I can't wait to see you on that horse. He's something else.'

Feeling Faith quiver excitedly beside her, Anke bit her lip and hung back, pretending to adjust her boot tops. Riding out on her own with a dishy young man like Rory would be good for Faith. Anything to cheer her up.

'You know, I think I might pop in and see Diana instead of coming out riding right now.' She let Rory pass and then side-skipped hastily towards the cottage path. 'I'd hate to think of her on her own if she feels poorly. You two have a hack together. I'll ride a bit later.'

'But you must come!' Rory couldn't hide his disappointment.

'Mum?' Faith squeaked nervously, terrified of being left alone with someone like Rory. She felt like a small child being abandoned on the doorstep of a stranger's birthday party.

'Faith can warm the horse up for me.' Knowing it would be good for her, Anke waved cheerfully and made her way hastily towards Horseshoe Farm Cottage.

Stomping into the barn, Rory pointed at something which looked like a cross between a camel and a cow. 'That's yours. He's called Penguin. I'll just untack Rio.'

'I could ride him,' Faith blurted. 'Rio, I mean.'

'Don't be daft.' He dismissed the suggestion, not even looking at her as he went to the far end of the barn to untack the stallion, disappearing behind the barred door.

'I'm good,' Faith called out after him.

'I'm sure you are, but this isn't some pony club schoolmaster we're talking about. Don't be fooled by the soppy stable name – Baron Areion is his real name and he's every bit the in-bred, arrogant aristo.'

'I know his name,' Faith spluttered.

Rory wasn't listening. 'He's over-fed, under-exercised and very bad-tempered. Rather like his mistress.'

'You'll let Mum ride him.' She kicked a hoof shaving across the aisle.

'She's one of the best riders in the world.' A saddle and bridle were dumped on a nearby hay bale as Rory emerged.

'She says I'm better.'

He squinted along the dusty aisle, laughing as he pulled the plaiting band from his hair, shook it out and reached for a crash hat. 'Grow up, sweetheart. My mother says I'm going to be a good boy one day but that doesn't mean I will. Now, get a move on. Whitey here needs to get fit for hunting and I don't have a lot of time.' He collected a huge grey from another stall.

Faith was so humiliated that she decided she would never talk to him again.

Not that this proved to be a necessary skill once they got out on to the sun-baked bridle-path that led down from Springlode past the burned-out pub and towards the lusher valley.

Rory spent the entire time chatting to his girlfriend on his mobile phone. He clearly thought Faith hopelessly drippy and sour-faced, she realised – feeling even shyer and incapable of losing her sucked-lemon expression. Instead, she concentrated on trying to get her huge mount to look less like a vast, hairy push-me-pull-you shambling along on great soup-plate hooves. Penguin was surprisingly supple and well-schooled. She even managed a respectable degree of flexion, leg-yielding this way and that on the track and feeling his back lift satisfyingly under her seatbones as his arthritic old legs came further and further beneath his body. But it was all lost on Rory, who laughed endlessly at his beloved's jokes and told her that he missed her like mad, not looking at Faith once.

As long and lean as a foxhound, with sinewy broad shoulders and big doleful eyes, he was a classy horseman. Louche and suntanned, he rode with the ease of a gaucho who knew he could make his horse perform any trick he liked with a flick of the heel and a tweak at the reins, if only he could be bothered.

Still sulking and applying classical aids like mad, Faith realised angrily that one half her four-legged crush was intensifying. She didn't fancy Rory as much as Pod, she told herself firmly. Pod was less arrogant and more feral – a true crossbreed of wolf and lurcher, all playful puppy eyes and wild sex appeal. Pod was a grown up. He had tons more charm and far less spoiled-brat silliness. With Pod it was love.

I hate Rory because I fancy him, and I love Pod because I do, Faith decided simply. And I hate Mo because she has Pod – and probably everyone else – lusting after her. And I hate Rory's girlfriend – whoever she is – because she can make him laugh and he just thinks I'm a pleb.

A sharp crack beside her made her jump, but it was just Rory lighting a cigarette, still chatting away with his mobile propped under his chin.

It was such a hot day that the whole of the valley appeared to be on fire, shimmering in a heat haze of burnt-orange stubble-fields and dusty dry pasture – cinders in a crucible. As they picked their way down a steep track beside an old coppice, their noses were assaulted by the smell of hot bonfires and tinder-dry land.

Faith narrowed her eyes as she stared between the twitching ears in front of her. Her mother was typically dismissive about the ghost everyone was talking about since the pub had burned down – the ghost that supposedly liked fire. She rather liked the sound of him. At least he livened up this dry old grave of a place.

Holding a gate open for her, Rory blew on the end of his cigarette, phone propped on his shoulder, laughing at yet another of his girl-friend's *bon mots*.

'Can I have one?' she asked boldly as she passed through.

Rory didn't even look at her, let alone break off from his conversation, but he tossed her a packet of Silk Cut with a lighter tucked inside and then spun his big grey around effortlessly to close the gate with a flick of his wrist.

Faith had decided it was time she took up smoking. Dropping her reins, she managed to spark up one of the lethal little paper and dried foliage sticks with a bellows suck of the cheeks.

'Thanks.' She threw back the packet which Rory caught, again without looking at her or stopping his chat. He had lightning reflexes.

Faith blew on the smouldering end of her cigarette, as she had just seen Rory do, and admired the little sparks that popped out.

Mo smoked roll-ups as far as she recalled – she'd have to get some practice in to manage one of those on horseback, but it must be possible. She could see herself rolling a cigarette on her thigh while she and Rio executed perfect pirouettes in the arena. That would be the height of cool.

She took another tentative puff, immediately feeling sick and light-headed but so determined not to cough that she held her breath until she almost fainted.

'Shall we press on a bit?' Rory had finally curtailed his call and, without checking behind him, kicked Whitey into a fast canter.

Smoking whilst ambling along at a walk might be a good nursery slope for Faith's attempts at adult vices in the saddle, but cantering was a black run. Cigarette clenched between her teeth, eyes streaming, she grabbed Penguin's reins and mane and tried to keep up, stay aboard, anything cooler than rolling around in the saddle like a toddler on a donkey ride.

'Shit!' The cigarette flew from her mouth as they turned sharply into a wood and blasted through dappled shadows, slaloming around trees and jumping fallen logs.

At last they burst back out into sunshine over a hunt jump and thundered up a steep hill, scattering sheep until they pulled up at the crest.

By now Faith was not only feeling sick and dizzy, but was coughing and spluttering like a consumptive.

Rory turned to her, his slanting grey eyes laughing. 'Next time you decide to take up smoking, bum a fag off someone who can afford it, okay?'

They rode back in silence.

Faith watched his broad-shouldered, tapering back as he loped along ahead of her and tried to burn the T-shirt from his spine with her glower, but she knew it was hopeless.

She adored him. Arrogant, mocking, dismissive – he was still front runner in her four-legged crush; Pod was now dismissed to the back of her pantomime horse. Kissing Rory would be the winner's enclosure of a lifetime.

'Mo! Over here! Need a lift, love?'

Mo pirouetted neatly in the shadows of one of the village green's big horse chestnuts as she looked around, her heart giving a bad-taste happy leap when she spotted Graham Brakespear in an ancient open-topped Porsche as kitsch as his shirt.

'Hop in! Anke said she was going to call on you to take you up to Springlode, but she must have missed you. I'm on my way to Dulston's so I can take you there.'

Mo tried to think of an excuse, but he had already leaped out and made a great show of opening the passenger door. The sunbathers on the green and the late-morning drinkers in the pub garden were watching. She didn't want to draw attention by refusing.

'It's my stepson's car,' he explained as he strapped on his rally seat belt, his rugby player shoulders far too wide for the sporty bucket seat. 'Anke's got mine while we're waiting for the insurance company to admit they're complete idiots and cough up. Useless bastards. I've been using a tractor most of the week. Unusual riding gear, by the way.'

Mo looked down at her hot pants and trainers and found herself laughing along with his infectious rumble.

'I was actually chickening out.'

'I found you on the run?'

'The chicken run.'

He gave her a supportive wink as they cruised around the crowded green. 'Hey, you don't have to do it, love. I've never fancied the idea of clambering aboard anything with less than a hundred horsepower or straddling something without a decent brain. Where d'you fancy going? We can book into a classy hotel.'

Mo grinned, loving the way he flirted so outrageously. 'I've always preferred self catering.'

'Do they hire holiday cottages by the hour round here?'

'We could pitch a tent.'

'I love a cheap date.'

'I do demand slackened guy ropes, mind you.'

'I'll slacken anything you like, love. Just call me your camp follower.'

'Nothing camp about you.' She laughed happily as they accelerated away from the village. 'Why are you working on a Bank Holiday?' she called over the engine drone, not wanting to think about where she was going.

'Just want to sit on a tractor and pretend I'm a kid again.' He laughed too and then reined back with a resigned smile. 'That's bollocks. The wife wants to look through the VAT receipts. Figure we might as well do it today while she's close at hand.' He didn't like to admit that he was bored witless and even doing paperwork with Anke was better than doing nothing without Anke.

Mo looked across at him. In profile he was an ageing Greek god, like a marble bust she had seen somewhere of Zeus or Poseidon. It had been an amazing face with a strong jaw and a straight nose that belied the lines hewn so delicately in the stone and showed a power outranking any youthful beauty. She'd stared at the bust for hours.

Graham caught her looking and she swung her head away so fast that she gave herself a crick in the neck.

'Where's that young man of yours?'

He sounded like her grandfather. Mo smiled ruefully as they slowed to overtake a group of wobbling mountain cyclists panting up the Springlode hill, the engine noise dropping to a low roar.

Mo wished she knew. She wasn't even sure whether Pod had started work yet – it was a Bank Holiday, after all. He was almost certainly in Gunning Woods today, nonetheless; nosing around, feeding his new obsession.

'He's gallivanting,' she said vaguely, hoping for a change of subject.

'Then we should definitely find that hotel.' Graham patted her smooth narrow knee with a broad palm and called out a cheery 'howdo' to the cyclists as he passed.

Mo tipped her head back, enjoying the wind whipping peaks in her hair wax. He was cheesier than a fifth course in a French restaurant, tackier than a piece of Sellotape trapped on one's finger, and older than all her vintage clothes – yet, as she stole another glance across at him, taking in the tousled blonde hair, laughter lines, faded eyes and garish shirt, she felt her heart flip. She couldn't help finding him attractive. He was the ultimate leg-up.

There was something about Anke that made Diana want to apologise over and over again. The last time she could remember feeling this humbled was when pleading with the headmistress of her boarding school not to call her mother and tell her about the bottle of Malibu stashed in her tuck trunk. It wasn't an offence worthy of expulsion – not quite – and she knew that Truffle wouldn't give a hoot. But the steel-faced lack of reaction from the headmistress had brought her to her knees.

She had now apologised to Anke for her behaviour at her supper party four times. Nodding coolly, Anke had made her two cups of peppermint tea along with a lot of very polite conversation that steered tactfully clear of any reason why Diana might be feeling 'emotional'. Yet Diana was certain she had not been forgiven for behaving badly. She was equally certain that she had been rumbled: she wasn't sick at all, just too frightened to ride.

It didn't matter that today the children and Hally were behaving impeccably and lovingly. Diana knew Anke remained disapproving. Mim and Digby were splashing in and out of the cheap paddling pool she had bought – just being happy, water-cooled children on a hot day; Hally was lying panting amid the lavender, Twitch licking her ears. Looking after them all was local girl Hope, whom Diana was trying out as a babysitter in the light of Sharon's dubious reliability. A sweet, pretty thing, she was proving as efficient as a Norland Nanny so far. They were the perfect fatherless family melting sweetly in the sun, but to Diana's frustration, Anke remained frosty cool.

Under the shade of the parasol, its green canopy dying her eyes a curious aquamarine, the Dane limited her smiles to the merest purse of her lips and studied her fingernails while Diana blustered.

'It really was quite unforgivable to accuse you all of being oiks like that,' she tried again. 'I have never behaved like that before.'

'One gets very unpredictable at times of crisis.'

'Did you behave like that when your marriage broke up?'

'No.'

Diana swigged some peppermint tea and smiled bravely, starting to get fed up with Anke's superior tone. Pretending she felt sick was tiresome when she just wanted to splat into the paddling pool with the kids. 'At least I didn't start a fire on Friday, eh?'

'I'm sorry?'

'A lot of people around here think the pub burning down might be my fault.'

'Whatever makes them think that?'

'My coming back. They think I've awoken the ghost.'

'Really? I don't believe in ghosts.'

With some satisfaction, Diana noticed Anke turning pale beneath the green awning.

'Of course not,' she agreed happily. 'I personally don't even think the pub fire was arson. It was probably one of the Wycks not stubbing out a cigarette or something.'

Anke glanced distractedly along the drive in case Faith and Rory were returning. 'I think that poor family is far too much maligned. Only this weekend, I have given Reg a job in the garden. He can't wait to get started.'

Diana shrieked with laughter. 'It's no wonder – his family used to own it. He's Reg *Wyck*. Wyck Farm.'

'I know.' Anke had partly given Reg the job out of misplaced modernism, as well as embarrassment that her father had tried to run him over. 'I do not think that is a reason not to hire him. He is a good gardener, and we should not feel ashamed that modern villages have progressed so that old farming families work the land a new way. If he is willing to evolve, I am willing to take him on.'

Diana snorted disparagingly. 'I can assure you Reg Wyck is far from evolved. He still thinks that farm is his by rights. Why do you think nobody else is allowed to tend the amenity field? It used to be his cow pasture and byre.'

'At least he can remember that,' Anke sighed, thinking about her father who had told her in no uncertain terms to leave him alone after she had quizzed him about the car in the pond – and had then asked uncertainly what she was talking about.

'Quite the local "character", old Reg,' Diana went on. 'He's been having an affair with my aunt for almost fifty years, you know.'

'Lady Belling?'

'Lord no – Aunt Til. Totally batty. Knits jumpers out of binder twine. She used to design amazing gardens, but she's gone even more peculiar in the past decade. I believe she poaches now. Lives in the Gunning Woods. She was set to marry Rory's father, you know – before Mummy snapped him up – but she stood him up at the altar. Everyone says that

Reg talked her out of it although he was already married to Dot. I think she loved someone else entirely. Probably a horse. Always was batty about them to the point of oddness.'

Anke's shocked silence was lost on Diana who moved on to the rumours that the Gunning Estate was for sale.

'The place is *enormous* – thousands of acres, and much of it park and woodland. Only two or three farms and a scattering of cottages along with the house, which is practically a ruin. The potential is off the scale if someone has the capital to invest. There are secret treasures everyone around here has forgotten about. It's quite trapped in time.'

Not for the first time, she was tempted to spill the beans about the Pleasure Garden, but stopped herself. The ghosts didn't frighten her, but Amos did.

'You knew it as a child?' Anke was asking.

'I can't remember a time I didn't know it.' Diana smiled to herself. 'It lives in here.' She touched her chest and flinched in sudden surprise as a bolt of pain shot through her. It felt as though she had just stabbed herself.

'You are feeling ill again.' Anke leaped up.

'As a matter of fact I am.' Diana tried to catch her breath, cold sweat shrinking her brow.

'I'll make more peppermint tea.' Anke rushed into the house.

Diana dropped her head to her knees and apologised for the sixth time that day – this time about something far more important than over-doing the gin at a supper.

'Keep the secrets,' she told herself angrily. 'Keep the bloody secrets.'

When Mo arrived for her riding lesson, she was appalled to find that she had an audience as Diana and the Brakespears – Graham, Anke and Faith – seated themselves on jump blocks around the manège to watch her being legged up on to a fat pony who had fallen asleep, legs locked in the sand.

'Now, there really is nothing to this – staying on is the easiest part,' Rory told her. 'Just breathe slowly and deeply and feel as though your bum is glued to that saddle and you can't go wrong. I am going to put your legs and hands in the right places and then I'll tell you how to keep them there, okay?'

Rory was surprisingly gentle – amazing his sister in particular, who was accustomed to her brother's dreadful horse-side manner when teaching his less comely clients.

'He must have had some lessons of his own,' she marvelled, as Rory gently positioned Mo's bare legs before sending her off at a steady walk at the end of a lunge line

Anke was surprised too – and not just by Rory, whose teaching was patient and clear and motivating. Overlodes might appear tatty from the outside but it was a far better yard than she had initially judged it.

It was obvious that Rory was severely strapped for cash, but any he had went on his horses. And his horses were good quality and well cared for. They might be old and a little worn, but they were well-schooled and they seemed to like their jobs. Their tack fitted and was high quality; they were fed and bedded well; and they all whickered hello when Rory or Sharon passed their stalls or went to their field. They were a big, settled, equine family group.

The grazing was only poor because of the endless, rainless hot summer. Looking across to the parched paddocks, Anke could see that the dung had been collected already and that there wasn't a sour patch of dock, thistle or nettle in sight. The fencing was a patchwork of repairs – but it was a safe patchwork and lovingly tended, like an old farmer's sweater that would see out many a winter.

This place was rather special, she realised. Rory was rather special. He wasn't a lazy drunk at all. He *was* a drunk and he *was* close to bank-ruptcy, but he had passion. Even the manège on which he was starting to lead the pony around, with Mo self-consciously blushing beside him, was as well raked as a championship golf bunker.

A lick of paint, a few renovations and some younger horses and this could be quite some business, she realised. Diana's gourmet holiday and high-school dressage plans were far too grand. She just needed to invest a little trust and capital.

But when Anke turned to tell her this, she was amazed to see Diana wiping a tear from her eye.

'I had no idea he was this good,' she muttered, tilting her head as she watched Rory teaching Mo to rise to the trot.

'Young Mo's not so bad either,' Graham pointed out.

Anke looked around sharply. 'What are you still doing here?'

'Thought I might book myself in for a lesson or two.'

'Don't be ridiculous, *kaereste*.'

By the end of half an hour, Rory proclaimed Mo a natural.

'You have a very strong body and great balance. You also have a lovely sympathy with the horse. I could have you competing within three months if you wanted to.'

Mo was addicted. She had exploded a myth and found that dreams came true as a result. It was the most amazing feeling sitting high on a horse, even the rotund and nannying pony that Rory had chosen for her. To feel such a need for mutual trust, for communication without words and servitude without question, was both humbling and invigorating. Beyond invigorating. It was a new lifeblood. No wonder Pod had kept it to himself all these years.

Enjoying one last look around from her high horse of happiness as Rory led her towards the gate to dismount, she caught Graham's true blue eyes smiling at her and she let hers smile right back, almost falling off the pony as she was knocked back by their straightforward admiration.

'At last – we all have something in common!' Diana cried delightedly, patting Mo's back like a jolly school team captain as she slithered to the ground, her knees wobbly and the insides of her thighs chafed raw. 'Horses!'

'I feel an exit coming on,' muttered Graham, who had only hung around to watch Mo's petite *derrière* bouncing in the saddle and was now concerned that he might lose control and hug her for being so brave and sexy. He missed watching Anke riding, he told himself, as he admired Mo's pink inner thighs.

'I enjoyed that.' She was beaming up at Rory.

'Me too.' He patted the horse's neck just as she did, their fingers briefly tangling together amongst the warm, coarse mane.

'Me too,' Graham joked, earning a black look from both wife and step-daughter.

'You really have got talent,' Rory told Mo again. 'Give it a go and you could even give Anke here a run for her money.'

Anke, who thought this a bit of an exaggeration, turned to Graham and noticed crossly that he was leering at Mo's bottom. He'd been spending far too much time moving his tractors around this week and far too little studying Dulston's VAT records.

'You really think so?' Mo was incredulous.

Faith – who had received no comments on her far superior riding – felt her deep hatred of Mo Stillitoe crystallise into a sharp dagger. With her stupid hippy clothes, ever-sunny disposition, boyish hair and faraway eyes, Mo was contrived and far too quixotic.

'Maybe we should look at your stallion now, Diana?' Anke suggested, spotting her scowling daughter and feeling a pang of guilt. 'I'd love to see him under saddle. As he is your baby, perhaps you could put him through his paces first and then Faith or I could sit on him?'

They all turned as they heard a spitting of tyres on gravel and a dusty 4x4, plastered with 'Slow Down For Horses' and Countryside Alliance stickers almost drove into the back of the Porsche.

'What a shame!' Diana sighed ecstatically as Rory's next lesson arrived in the nick of time. 'The manège will be spoken for. Another time. I must just see if the babysitter's coping. Hope will almost certainly have run out.' She skipped away.

'One of Tony Sixsmith's daughters,' Rory explained as he ran up the stirrup leathers and loosened the girth on Mo's pony. 'Known as the Three Disgraces in the village: Hope, Faith and Charity – or Esperanza, Fe and Caridad, depending on which parent you listen to. The mother is Cuban and the girls are both bilingual and named twice. Hope is hopeless. Diana seems intent on cultivating her as a nanny, but as soon as she's left unguarded she's as badly behaved as the kids. And that *is* bad.'

'You mean there's another Faith around here?' Faith asked, desperate to draw Rory's attention.

'If I remember my RE correctly there are many, many Faiths around – and not a lot of Hope or Charity,' he laughed, turning back to Mo. 'Well done. Same time tomorrow?'

'I think I might need a little longer to recover,' she said ruefully, looking at her raw thighs.

'Next weekend then. And buy some breeches. That was really good.' With a pat on Mo's shoulder, he ambled away.

Faith and Graham both glared at his retreating bottom. Anke and Mo both admired it.

'Bit of a stuck-up sod, that one,' Graham murmured, turning to his wife. 'You ready to do some work?'

'I have to take Faith home – and maybe run Mo back?' she suggested hopefully. Having witnessed his leering at close hand, she wanted him to cool down alone with his VAT receipts. She had a feeling paperwork was the last thing on his mind.

But Graham had a twinkle in his eye that refused to take no for an answer.

'Nonsense. Mo can take Faith back in Magnus's car. Here.' He threw the Porsche keys to her with a wink. 'Come on, Anke, love, I need you on site.'

'My stepfather is a bastard,' Faith announced flatly as Mo tried to fathom out how to start the Porsche. 'Don't sleep with him whatever you do.'

'I'm not intending to,' Mo gulped, leaping forwards as the engine fired up in gear.

'Good.' Faith selected a CD from her brother's collection. 'God knows why people fall for him, but Mum's friends are always trying to get into bed with him. Not worth the effort. He can't get it up, I hear. D'you want me to drive? Only you don't seem to be doing too well. Have you passed your test?'

'Yes. I'm fine, thanks.' Mo gritted her teeth. 'I even have a car.'

'Where is it?'

'Pod has it.'

'Have you been together long?'

'Ages.'

'So have Mum and Graham, but they are so finished.'

'Really?'

'You've stalled again. Try less clutch. Yeah, I think it's the impotence thing. My real dad might be gay, but at least he serviced her occasionally, if you know what I mean.'

'I don't think we should be having this conversation.'

'It's not a conversation. I'm warning you off.'

'By telling me your mother and stepfather's marriage is on the skids?'

'By warning you off.'

'You don't scare me.'

'I think I do.'

Thankfully, Faith chose that moment to press Play on some hard core Drum 'n' Bass and they stop-started their way towards Oddlode in mutually hostile silence.

Watching them leave from the curly-lashed cottage windows, Diana clutched her shirt collar and chewed her lips. She felt like a witch in a cave, stirring her cauldron as she magically put people and passions together without being understood or loved herself. She felt hated, ostracised and misunderstood.

'Mummy! MUMMMEEEEEEE!' came a bleat from downstairs.

Wearily, Diana followed the call.

Mim had made her a card. On the front was a hugely fat squiggly head with stick legs and arms and a loopy black curl of hair on either side with a bald monk's pate between. In the middle of the blob was a childish sad face – two pinprick eyes and a downward-turned mouth. Inside Mim had written 'I Love Mummy Even Thow She Is Sad. And Digby Doz Two.'

Diana stifled a sob as she clutched her little optimist to her belly.

'Hey, kid – d'you wanna start a revolution?'

'Does that mean we don't have to have Hope looking after us anymore?'

'Didn't you like her?'

'As soon as you went away, she smoked a lot and wouldn't let us watch the television. She had it on adult stuff and was still talking on the telephone.'

'What adult stuff?'

'Football.'

'How rotten. I'll make sure she doesn't do it again.'

'We like Sharon. She tells us stories.'

'Good. We all like Sharon.' Diana looked distractedly out of the window at a bonfire blazing in the distance. 'Long live Sharon. Do you want to ride Bronwyn now, darling?'

'No!' Mim clutched her mother's legs defiantly, having taken a violent dislike to riding lately.

To be hypocritical or to be hypocritical? Diana wondered.

'Another time.' She patted her daughter's back.

'I want to see Daddy!'

Diana gathered her up in a cuddle, knowing nothing could really console the tantrum – it was a case of sitting it out and cuddling tightly.

She looked out at the bonfire again.

He was out of the ashes. It was only a matter of time before he caught up with her.

'Paperwork – paperwork! Don't you ever loosen up?' Graham snapped as Anke spread the invoices and receipts in front of him.

'You suggested this,' she reminded him, knowing full well that he'd had something entirely different in mind.

Having made unsuccessful lunges beside the filing cabinet, on the swivel chair and over the desk, Graham had finally given up on seduction and now stared at his predecessor's debts.

'Shit. Doesn't make great reading, does it?'

Anke watched a butterfly battering against the window.

'Can we go home now?' she suggested. 'I don't think Faith enjoyed this morning as much as I hoped she would, and I'm worried about Chad playing football with those boys from Orchard Close. Magnus is bound to have forgotten to check on him. And I must –'

'Call Ingmar,' Graham finished for her, gathering the bills from the desk and casting a regretful look around his office, where in his mind he and his wife had enjoyed carnal frolics on every surface. 'Sure. Can I just move the Ferguson? It's too near the fencing.'

As Graham sat on one of his company's expensive, unsold tractors and played at moving it a few feet sideways, Anke waited by the car and pulled at the raised sinews in her neck. Watching him, she wondered if she should have given into temptation and ridden the amazing stallion that day after all. Perhaps she would have vented some of *her* frustration, too. She hugged Graham's receipts to her chest and pressed her lips to their sharp edges.

Deep within the woods in the Gunning Estate a fire blazed in a clearing, blasting hot sparks high into the air.

A stooped figure fed papers into the roaring flames as a small dog raced around the pyre, catching sparks and yapping furiously.

At a nearby gate, an old mare pricked her ears and watched the bonfire with orange-lit eyes. A new era was upon them. Change would come at last.

12

Anke grew even more worried about Faith when her daughter returned from a shopping trip to Cheltenham with her elder brother, sporting newly-bought hippy clothes and a dreadfully unflattering short haircut. Magnus couldn't stop laughing.

'We'd arranged to meet on a bench in the shopping centre after her hair appointment – I didn't recognise her. I tried to give her fifty pence for a cup of tea.'

'What do you mean?' Anke often missed the point of her son's sense of humour.

He thrust his tongue beneath his lower lip in a 'duh' gesture before explaining: 'I thought she was homeless.'

'Don't be so unkind,' Anke snapped, although secretly agreeing that Faith now off-puttingly reminded her of a New Age traveller. 'You have to try lots of different looks when you're young – goodness knows, I did. I think it's very . . . bohemian.' It was the kindest adjective she could muster.

'*Mo*-hemian, you mean.' Graham tried to give his stepdaughter's new urchin cut an affectionate ruffle but recoiled as he found his fingers sticky with wax. 'You look like our new village teacher, love.'

'I do *not*!' Faith hissed. 'This is my own look and nobody in this house has any *right* to comment on it.'

She grabbed her Boots bag from the kitchen table and stomped upstairs to play with her new make-up – lots of mascara like Mo wore, plus fake tan and crazy hair colour.

'Oh dear, I think this move has really upset her,' Anke fretted.

'She's a teenager – they all get stroppy and look awful.' Graham put his arms round her and tried to plant a kiss on her neck.

Anke swiftly moved away and glanced awkwardly at Magnus who was helping himself to a beer from the fridge.

'I thought we should have a house-warming party,' Graham suggested, indefatigable as ever. 'What d'you think, Magnus?'

'Can my band play?'

'Sure – it's a booking. Next weekend.'

'*This coming* weekend?' Anke baulked.

Graham always relished a challenge. 'Got to hold it before the kids start school. We can invite all the neighbours and our new friends from the village, and some of the Essex crowd can come down to stay.' He threw his arms wide apart and announced, 'A huge house-warming barbecue for all the family.'

'Do we really have time to organise something on that scale?' asked Anke, knowing that she would be left with all the practical details once Graham had bored of the idea.

'No worries, love – we'll keep it low key,' Graham promised.

Anke, who found entertaining tiresome, was far too worried by Faith's image crisis and her father's increased dottiness to want to arrange a social gathering. None of the spare rooms was yet suitable for housing overnight guests and they hardly knew anyone in the village to invite.

'You won't have to do a thing,' he went on. 'I'll hire caterers.'

'For a barbecue?' Anke shook her head. 'Nonsense. You and Magnus can share the cooking, Faith and I will do cold prep – and everything can be eaten from paper plates. And no more than forty guests.'

'Whatever you say, love.' Graham managed to land a quick peck on her cheek before she darted away. He was on the phone to the wine merchant within minutes ordering several cases of champagne and enough beer to float a small Bavarian town.

Within twenty-four hours, a marquee the size of a barn had been booked, a hundred champagne flutes hired and a steel band arranged.

'But you said Road Kill could play!' Magnus rounded on his step-father when he found out.

'Who?'

'My band.'

'Course you're playing. You're playing your set after the food's been served.'

'I'm not griddling a single sodding burger.'

'All under control.' Graham patted his stepson's back. 'I'm hiring caterers. Just don't tell your mother until I've had a quiet word with her about numbers'.

Anke came home short-tempered after spending a wearisome after-noon with her father trying to persuade him to employ a manager. He had opened his shop that day but had then forgotten he'd done so and taken himself off for a walk, leaving half a dozen confused tourists trapped inside as he slipped the lock behind him.

She could tell from Graham's nervous, tooth-studded smile that he had a confession to make.

'*How* many?'

It seemed he had invited almost everyone in the village, all his new corporate customers and contacts at Dulston's, most of their old friends from Essex and even a few family members from Burnley.

Anke had no choice but to agree to caterers – plus portaloos, serving staff and even a car parking official.

'You'll want to put up AA road signs next,' she sighed.

'You know, that's not such a bad idea.'

Mo had stiffened up so much after her riding lesson that bending down to tie up her shoelaces was a no-no, along with more intimate routines. Going to the lavatory took for ever because pulling her knickers up and down was agony and even wiping her bottom was a contortion. Yet she still hadn't found the right moment to tell Pod what she had done, and he was looking at her hunched old lady progress around the house and village with increasing suspicion.

'What are you doing in there, queen?' he was complaining outside the bathroom door as he waited to clean his teeth.

'Just – agh – finishing – ugh – off. Ouch!'

'Have you got thrush again?'

'No!' She used the bath brush to hook her knickers up to knee height in order to avoid bending down. 'Why are you in such a hurry?'

She let him in and he raced for the Colgate. 'Want to get to Gunning. Amos has promised to show me the old ice house and the trappers' huts if I get there early enough. He reckons there was a little community of wild woodlanders there, right up until the last war – part down-and-outs, part wild gypsies, with all sorts of funny religious ideas. They were little better than poachers, but the Delameres had always accepted them as a part of the land. As well as trapping and woodworking, they ran cock-fights, baited badgers and all sorts to earn a few pennies. They sound a pretty cool outfit to me. Firebrand threw them off the estate when he inherited – they probably cursed him, too. No wonder he ended up in such shit.'

Mo watched him stabbing the brush around his mouth excitedly. He was so entranced by the old estate, he had talked about little else all week. Not that they were talking much; the awkwardness still lingered between them. He wanted her to see it too, but what he had told her so far hardly filled her with desire to cross the threshold. He made it sound like a limitless, haunted hell-hole, and seemed to relish frightening her with tales of debauched barons and persecuted estate workers.

'Come with me today,' he offered again, toothpaste foaming from his lips. 'Amos won't mind.'

'No thanks,' she shuddered.

'Suit yourself.' He spat into the basin. 'I said I'd help him out over the weekend, by the way.'

'This weekend?'

'Yeah. Didn't think you'd mind.'

'You don't want to do something together?'

'I want to go to Gunning. You know you can come along too.'

The sticky patch glued Mo to the bathroom linoleum, reminding her of its presence. 'That's okay – I have things planned too. I'm going up to Overlodes. You see, I've started to –'

'I don't want to know.' He spat again.

'You don't even know what I was about to –'

'You can play at being friends with Mrs Posh and her brats, but I'm not interested, right?'

Mo took a step back, frowning. Now wasn't the right time to mention her riding lessons.

In Upper Springlode, Diana was furious that her offer for the old, burned-down pub had been pipped at the post by a cash offer from the Sixsmiths.

'What do you mean, it's been accepted?' she barked at the estate agents. 'I want to make a counter-offer!'

'We invited sealed bids, madam. Negotiations are over.'

Given the exceptional circumstances of the fire – which was still being investigated – the sale of the Plough had suddenly taken on a new perspective that week. Diana had found out quite by chance that the sale of the business was not being postponed, as she had imagined. Indeed, landlord Keith had instructed his agents to close the sale as quickly as possible by contacting all interested parties and, with two days' notice, offering them a sealed bid auction.

She had spent ages putting figures together, hassling her solicitors and drawing up business plans for the bank. She had even been forced to visit her mother in Lower Oddford to ask for a loan, only to be turned down flat by Truffle's declaration that all her money was tied up offshore thanks to 'my nice little man at Coutts'. It had been a brief, uncomfortable reunion toasted by a very weak Pimm's in the garden at Grove House.

More frantic calls to her solicitor had ensued, and she had even tried to contact Tim, but he wasn't answering her calls. Hours of hair-pulling and calculator-bashing later and she'd arrived at a figure which would cripple her, but was just about possible if she sold everything she owned and never ate again. Now it was all in vain.

'This is almost certainly illegal!' she screamed at the beleaguered agent. 'The pub is still smouldering. You shall be hearing from my solicitors. And quite probably the police too.'

She marched around to tackle Tony Sixsmith, who lived in one of the pretty Springlode cottages that had once belonged to the Manor. Two of his temptress daughters were sunbathing topless in the garden and the third was conducting a loud argument in Spanish with her mother in the kitchen. Dogs were running around everywhere.

Tony was taking a motorbike apart on the driveway. A tall, thin man in his forties, he had a lively face with naughty green eyes that sparkled behind wire-rimmed spectacles and unkempt, receding sandy hair threaded with silver streaks.

'You haven't returned my calls,' Diana berated him huskily.

'Because you want to buy the pub plot.' He didn't look up from his bike. 'And it's mine now.'

'I'll make you an offer you can't refuse.'

'You won't.'

'How can you be certain?' She swung a leg over his bike and draped her high-heeled mule over the peg.

'Get off, and go away.'

Tony Sixsmith was more than Diana had bargained for. Not only did he show no signs of finding her remotely attractive – even poured, as she was, into a strappy bodice and see-through linen mini-skirt. He was also no businessman. He refused to be coaxed into a partnership, despite terms more generous than a zip-bag full of cash in a dustbin.

'I don't cut deals. I've always wanted that pub. I've been drinking in that pub since I was fourteen.'

'So let's make it a successful pub. I can turn it around in six months.'

'I'll turn it around in three, without your help.'

'I'll make it worth a million.'

He finally straightened up from tinkering with his engine, wiped his hands and arms with a hunk of blue paper towel, and studied her above his wire rims.

'I'm an old friend of Amos.'

Diana jumped from the bike like a stunt rider, stumbling through a mallow bush and almost tripping over a sunbathing daughter.

'We've known each other since we were kids.' Tony rested his elbows on the bike seat and studied his oil-blackened forearms. 'You obviously don't remember me, but I remember you and I hoped I'd never see you again. I certainly don't want to be any sort of "partner" of yours. That pub is mine.' Looking up, he examined her thoughtfully through the mallow flowers. 'Although perhaps I do owe you some credit. Whoever – or whatever – burned it down made it affordable at last.' He rubbed his chin, leaving a black grease goatee.

'How do you mean?' Diana peeked back at him through the foliage.

'You wakened the ghost.'

Both sunbathing daughters looked up as Diana crashed over the mallow and two rose bushes to face him. 'There is no wretched ghost!'

'Of course there is,' he said matter-of-factly. 'And, thanks to you, he's finally burning himself out. The New Inn is coming home to Springlode.'

'The *what?*'

'You heard. The New Inn.'

'It's always been the Plough!' Diana conveniently forgot her own plans to rename it.

'Oh no,' Tony explained with icy intensity. 'One of old Firebrand's ancestors had the name changed a hundred years ago or more. There'd been an inn here for centuries, and it was the New Inn to all who knew it. All the Gunning Estate workers used to drink here – bad-mouthing the baron, no doubt. Whole village was Sarsden-owned then, apart from the pub and the church. Then one day the boss turned up with his rabble and demanded a drink. This particular baron used to gamble, and the inn was famous for its gambling. Still is.' He chewed away a wry smile. 'He was a lucky sod, according to folklore. Won the New Inn and all its land in a bet and, they say, he renamed it the Plough to piss off the villagers. Everyone knows the land here breaks ploughs. Too much rock. It was his idea of a joke. The old place deserves to get her name back.'

'A phoenix from the flames,' Diana muttered, seeing her dream slipping away. Ever the optimist who galloped at stone walls flat-out, she tried one last time to persuade Tony to join forces. 'I am proposing something that can't fail commercially and will fit into the village perfectly. You have to use your brain here. What happened with Amos was years ago.'

'They may have put out the fire here, but he's still smouldering.' He gave her a cold smile, just for a moment allowing those naughty eyes to trace the contours of her body. 'He never forgives. Like the ghosts. I wouldn't hang around long if I were you.'

Diana marched away before her nerve cracked, wondering furiously how the Sixsmiths could have raised the money. The mental challenge lasted as far as the footpath which threaded through the woods beside the wild, weedy Springlode village green. There she sank on to the one rough-wood bench seat and stared at her shaking hands.

Amos was so close. She could almost smell him – along with the burning.

'There are no blasted ghosts!' she said out loud. 'Just exes with axes and matches. Burn what you like, you'll never frighten me away again.'

13

'So this will be my classroom? Wow. Can I paint it a different colour? This would look so great in a hot pastel.' Mo span around cheerfully. 'Wow.'

'Redecoration is not a priority,' Anne Chambers said tersely.

Mo Stillitoe was smaller and younger than Anne Chambers remembered her. And scruffier, with alarming pea-green paint patches speckling her tanned forearms like verdigris on copper, and trapped in her lurid red hair like mint leaves in strong Pimm's. And she smelled of cigarette smoke.

She tried to assuage the spinning. 'How are you settling into village life, Mo?'

'Oh, fine – I mean great.' Mo smiled nervously, pretending to admire the classroom's view, which looked out over two uninspiring Portakabins and several wheelybins. 'Do you live close to the school?'

Anne Chambers was stouter than Mo remembered her, with threatening bulldog jowls and a perm as tight and white as a QC's wig.

'In Market Addington.' She sniffed. 'My husband is a town planner so it's convenient for his offices. Besides, property in Oddlode is so expensive.'

'We're just renting.'

'We?'

'My boyfriend and me.' Mo immediately wondered whether she should have said 'and I' but that sounded far too regal. Something about Anne Chambers made one want to address her as though having an audience with the queen.

'Oh.' The QC perm seemed to tighten with disapproval.

The informal meeting with the headmistress of Oddlode primary school was not going as informally as either Mo or Anne had hoped. Both felt starchy and uncomfortable. Mo recalled her interview on a balmy, breezy April day, sunshine between showers as she drove towards the prettiest village she had ever encountered, a riot of garish daffodils head-banging their welcome from the verges as she'd parked on the lane outside the school and gaped at the picturesque clock tower, arched windows and that old stone as unfamiliar and exciting and gold as muscles dancing on a lion's back.

'I've met some of the kids and mothers already.' She tried to inject warmth and animation into the sub-zero atmosphere, but she was acutely aware of her Norfolk accent carving curious corners from the conversation. She hadn't even heard it during that first heady interview, but now it seemed to flatten what little warmth there was in the room into a thin air-pocket.

'So I gather.' Anne Chambers bristled, the white perm folding down towards her nose. 'And it seems you are doing a marvellous marketing job for our little school already.'

'I am?' Mo puffed up excitedly.

'Indeed. I have received two calls only this week from mothers singing your praises, and – by chance – believing that their children will be coming to Oddlode next term, when I am unaware of *any* new pupils in Reception and Year Five. I take it that you know all about them?'

'Er . . . about who?'

'Mrs Brakespear, *who* I believe is Danish and with *whom* I understand you have spent an evening,' Anne marked the 'whom' pointedly to correct Mo's sloppy usage, 'left a message on the school office answering machine yesterday to confirm that she would be bringing her son to meet us very shortly, all being well. She cited your name and mentioned something about a generous donation to the computer fund?'

Mo cringed.

'And a *Ms* Lampeter, who called me at home, assured me that you two were *very* close personal friends. So much so that she seemed to assume that her children were already on your register.'

'She had no right!' Mo burst out without thinking.

'Exactly my thoughts.' Anne Chambers' perm softened slightly as her brow lifted. 'May I suggest that you become more alert to desperate mothers who attempt to befriend you? I have been offered many bribes by parents in recent years, attempting to secure places for their little ones – holidays in their second homes, cheap cars, vast injections of cash into school funds. We must be vigilant.'

'Of course.'

'Friendship is the most hollow and callous of bribes,' Anne Chambers went on. 'A lonely newcomer is an easy target. Believe me, I know. Women like Mrs Brakespear and Diana Constantine would never befriend a humble schoolteacher without a hidden agenda.'

'You think so?' Mo felt whitewashed.

'I know so. They are quite a different class.' Snobbish, embittered and envious of Mo Stillitoe's carefree, slender energy, Anne guiltily savoured the sight of a wilting junior teacher. 'Villages are tough places to survive. I am only telling you this to make life easier.'

If Mo hadn't been so crushed, she would have picked up on the fact that Mrs Chambers referred to Diana as a 'Constantine'.

Pod's blackened temper became darker and more devilish as he and Mo got ready to go out to the Brakespears' party.

Mo wanted to duck out of the barbecue. She daren't tell Anke or Diana – who were relying upon her – that the headmistress of Oddlode primary had flatly refused to enrol three new pupils with less than a week's notice.

For once Pod was showing an uncharacteristic degree of enthusiasm for a party.

'C'mon, queen. You've gotta be there. I hear it's going to be quite a night.'

'In what way?'

'Amos is going.' Pod spoke with almost fawning expectation.

'So, go and talk to him,' Mo suggested dispiritedly as she flipped through her limited wardrobe, still steaming and dripping foam from a shower. 'You're spending more time with him than me right now.'

'He's better than your new friends.'

'Is this what this is all about? My new friends versus yours? The Wycks and Amos against the –'

'– stuck-up bitches, yeah. He *is* better, queen. He's a real person, not a social attitude.'

With Anne Chambers' warning ringing in her ears, Mo drew her blackest widow's shrouds from the wardrobe and held them against herself as she turned to face the long mirror on the inside of the door. 'I like my new friends.'

'You hate them as much as I do, queen.'

'They're my friends.'

'Wear no knickers,' he ordered, lifting her towel and admiring her butt.

'I'm not in the mood for games, Pod.' She eyed her scraggiest and most beloved jeans, but it was too hot a night with a storm brewing, and she didn't trust herself to be able to climb into them. She was still so stiff from her riding lesson on Monday that easy-access clothes were the only realistic option. No knickers was, in fact, a tempting choice were it not for Pod's dictatorial tone. At least she wouldn't have to bend down to put them on.

'I want to be able to touch your pussy all night.' He thrust his dimpled jaw into the hollow behind her ear and pressed seven taut inches against the small of her back.

'The Brakespears have a cat – you can feel that pussy in between spare ribs.'

'I'll find pussy if you're not there.'

'I'm sure you will, Dick Whittington.' She cast the jeans to one side and held a shapeless black smock dress against her chest.

Pod's teeth sank into the bones at the nape of her neck. 'Someone else will go without knickers tonight, and you can be sure I'll find them, queen.' A broken fingernail cruelly dragged a scratch from her coccyx along the bumps of her spine to her shoulder-blades. It was a very real threat.

Mo lifted her chin defiantly, glancing across at the running rail in the wardrobe with its hanger hooks breaking their necks under the weight of her heavy camouflage. Only the heatwave and Pod's entreaties had stripped her this bare. She normally covered herself from chewed fingernail to stubbed toetip, from throat hollow to ankle bump. She longed for winter, when Pod unwrapped her like a gift. He was getting too cocky. It was time to cover up.

'Go right ahead,' she told him defiantly. 'I might not come, so you finding a knickerless woman means bo diddly squit to me.'

'Heeeaaawww,' Pod feigned a girly squeal and pinched her arse so hard that Mo felt tears sting her eyes, although she kept her face firmly buried in her High Street selection as she returned clothes to her wardrobe.

'I'm not coming.' She slammed the wardrobe door.

'In that case . . .'

Over her shoulder, Pod peeled the towel from her and, cupping her waist in his hands, held her against the closed door.

'*I'm* your only friend.' He dropped to his knees and drew a slick tongue from the hollow behind her left knee, up her thigh, across her buttocks, and back down her right leg.

'Not that, Pod.'

'Oh yes, this.' Up he went again. 'Amos's wife is coming tonight. You'll like her.'

'I'm not coming.'

'So you say.'

'I'm *not*.' Mo couldn't hear her own voice for the sound of blood pumping in her ears as she knew what was coming next – hoped was coming next – prayed was coming next.

'Of course not.' Pod didn't disappoint her. In plunged the tongue – slippery, soft, delving in and around and between with no shame, no inhibitions – just greed.

Mo was lifted – higher and higher, on to tip toes, on to foaming wave crests, on to mountain tops and above clouds. Up and up she spiralled, groaning and gasping as that tongue worked its magic. Her favourite. Her absolute, sinful, shameful favourite, and he knew it. That tongue could roam wherever it wanted. It was a rare treat and it never disappointed. For a man as free-spirited and frightening and wilful as Pod to do this to her was the ultimate thrill. It meant he loved her.

But then he did disappoint her. Big time. Deliberately.

In he dived without warning – inches of rigid expectation that exploded inside her long before she was ready, leaving her so frustrated and sexually charged that she howled with rage when he drew himself out.

'No, Pod,' she gasped. 'You can't stop.'

'All over, queen.'

'You can't just stop like that.'

'You said you weren't coming,' he laughed into her throat as he leaned against her, panting, wiping her off with the discarded towel as matter-of-factly as if he were cleaning off a newborn sheep. 'And you didn't.'

'You bastard.' She pressed her face to the wardrobe door, still fizzing all over with dissatisfaction.

'Don't forget who your friends are, Mo,' he breathed in her ear.

'And my lover? Is he my friend?'

'He's joined a rival gang.'

'What do you mean?'

'Come tonight and you'll see.'

Mo, who could already hardly walk, could now hardly even turn around and stand up straight to face Pod, her body still throbbing with unspent charge. 'And will I come?'

He lifted a corner of that cruel, beautiful mouth, which sweet-talked every man and woman it met. 'Wear no knickers and you might.'

She dropped her eyes, hating her weakness.

'Don't count on it.'

'Then don't you count on me, queen. Don't count on anything.'

'I stopped counting a long time ago,' she sighed, turning away. When his infidelities had reached ten, she'd stopped the clock.

Smelling like a spice rack, pulsing with testosterone, and dressed in the tight petrol-blue T-shirt and mocha-brown pin-cords that she'd bought him because they looked as though they'd been woven around him for seduction, Pod left Mo crouched by her wardrobe on the verge of meltdown.

'I'll see you there.'

Sometimes they were so fused together that his tears were the first to seal their cheeks as he comforted her, he seemed to hug her tighter than her own skin and breathe oxygen into her veins. On nights like tonight, he dealt body-blows with his eyes, stabbed the bayonet in with his tongue and then smothered her breathing with a chloroform kiss.

She knew that she had to give chase. He was so volatile he'd screw up big time. Since he had started working at Gunning, his mood had grown darker each day. Something about the place had cast an evil spell over him, had brought out the mad, bad Pod of old. She wasn't sure if it was the influence of Amos Gates, or the legend of the ghostly Firebrand, or perhaps just her refusal to go there and see what he was talking about, but he was at his most unpredictable and that meant he was his most dangerous.

Still faced with her wardrobe dilemma, she settled for a floaty wrap-around skirt. But she defiantly managed to drag on her biggest of baddest seductress pants beneath – wafery, satiny silk bloomers that Pod had bought her one Christmas, but had been too distracted by the two pairs of edible jockey shorts she'd bought him to remember to ask her to model.

It was a wild and windy night, a storm brewing on the far side of the ridge. The marquee in the Wyck Farm garden was almost taking off, the barbecue was threatening to set light to the overhanging trees, heavy with ripening nuts, acorns and husky conkers that rained down on the Brakespears' guests. Paper plates and napkins were flying everywhere, and Mo's knickers were on almost constant display as she headed along a driveway lit by swaying flame torches which threatened the paintwork of every car that passed. One, which sent out a short horn toot as it almost mowed Mo down, was Diana's Audi with Rory at the wheel and Diana in the passenger seat frantically applying make-up. They were quickly waved into a drive-side paddock by a youth in a fluorescent tabard.

Having only admired the Brakespears' house from her own car as she'd passed on the way to Lower Oddford, Mo was taken aback by its grandeur. She had assumed that the former home of the ne'er-do-well Wycks would be far more humble, but the farmhouse was an impressive Georgian pile with huge sash windows and pretty symmetry. It was also teeming with people, many of whom appeared to be teenage friends of Magnus.

A steel band was playing *Summertime* under a windswept pagoda and, close by, two chefs were trying to hold on to their high hats as they tossed steaks on an industrial-sized barbecue.

'Welcome!' Graham was the first to greet Mo, bounding forward in yet another bad-taste shirt and kissing her warmly on both cheeks. He smelled deliciously of expensive aftershave and barbecue smoke. 'You look gorgeous, love. And you have great pins.' His blue eyes twinkled down at her legs.

Mo tried to gather her wraparound skirt together for decency's sake as the wind gusted it right back so that she appeared to be wearing nothing but chiffon bloomers dancing with daisies.

'Mo, darling, you look like you're about to set sail!' Diana greeted her with an air-kiss at each cheek. 'Is this one of your ballet outfits? Hi, Graham.' Not giving Mo the chance to answer, she kissed their host more intimately on his cheeks, leaving a smear of red lipstick on both. 'This looks such fun – I've already seen lots of old acquaintances, and most of my blasted family. Uncle St John! Well, hello –' Drifting away, she joined a classy rabble in the barbecue queue. With her olive skin, scarlet dress and high heels she looked like an exotic bird of paradise swooping in on a pheasant coop of tweedy, khaki and beige villagers.

'Already half cut.' Rory watched his sister, dropping a kiss that reeked of Pimm's on Mo's cheek. 'I'm already banned from driving, so Di said that meant I should be designated driver. My plan is to pass out before the return journey. You look delightful. Love the silky shorts.'

He was happy to join Graham in admiring the saucy lingerie, and together they paid court as Graham made a fuss about fetching her a drink and Rory insisted that he must stick around to make some introductions. 'Daffodil won't be here for hours, so I can be your chaperone. Where's your bloke?'

'He should be here somewhere.' Mo was craning to look around for Pod. 'He came before me.'

'Always let a lady come first, that's my motto!' Graham joked happily as he returned with brimming champagne flutes.

Mo winced uncomfortably and tried to make her skirt stay still.

Diana was put to shame by Anke's efficiency. The party was a spectacular success. Yet she couldn't stay jealous for long as she saw so many old friends and family mingling around. She had expected a much cooler reception but, despite the gathering storm, moods were upbeat and forgiving. Even her second encounter with her mother was a far less frosty affair than her first – mostly, Diana suspected, because Truffle had her lover in tow and wanted to appear gracious.

'Darling, you remember Vere, don't you?'

'Of course.' Diana air-kissed the aftershave fumes around a small, dapper figure wearing a cravat and blazer. Although she wasn't particularly tall, she towered over him.

'Delighted, as always.' He made a show of puckering up and dabbing her knuckles with his damp lips. 'Are your children not with you this evening?'

'They're far too young for parties like this. Rory's groom is babysitting.' She grabbed a glass from a roving waiter's tray and sank most of it back in one, blinking as the bubbles kicked at her nose and throat.

'And how are you finding life as a stable girl?' Vere teased.

Diana gave him a tight smile. 'Actually, I have some very exciting plans for Overlodes. I –'

'Whatever you do, don't lend her any money!' Truffle interrupted with a gay laugh.

'Will you excuse me? I've just seen a very old friend.' Diana stalked away before she crowned her mother with an empty champagne flute. Quickly swapping it for a full one, she circulated amongst known allies.

She was delighted to see her cousin Spurs, with his ravishing, pregnant girlfriend.

'You are privileged, Di.' He enveloped her in a hug. 'When I first came back from exile, I was a social pariah.'

'I haven't been in exile. I've been married.'

'Same thing, isn't it?' laughed Ellen, exchanging a look with Spurs.

'Do I take it you're not quite as keen as Aunt Bell on the Oddlode wedding of the year?'

Spurs gave her a look that she remembered from childhood, when her cousin had been a tearaway five years her junior who had rarely, if ever, done as he was told.

'Diana, my dear!' Hell's Bells bore down on her like a beater intent on sending up birds from cover. 'Your mother tells me that you are going back into the horse business?'

'I hope to become involved in some way.'

'You must talk to Piers Cottrell – he's around here somewhere. Brings some lovely sorts over from Ireland every month. Saw a super four-year-old middleweight only last week. Will you be hunting with us next season?'

'*Are you* still hunting?'

Hell's Bells tapped her freckled nose. 'Every last member of the Wolds is prepared to face the consequences. We shall go to prison if necessary.'

'How refreshing,' drawled Spurs. 'I shan't be the only ex-con in the family.'

His mother shot him a withering look. 'The Constantines are the backbone of the Wold. We need your support, Diana.'

Diana gave a weak smile, unwilling to admit that her lack of nerve and excess of girth ruled out any desire to follow hounds nowadays. Nor did she want to be arrested. Since St John's knighthood, Hell's Bells had used her husband's influence in the Lords as her own personal mouthpiece to voice increasingly desperate threats to keep hunting legal. She had once famously ridden through Parliament Square naked in a show of protest, which was brave but possibly misguided for a woman in her sixties. Lady Belling was no Lady Godiva, although the tabloid photographs of her jumping the police barriers to avoid capture had shown a terrific hunting seat.

'We could ride out together, darling.' Truffle appeared at Diana's shoulder, still eager to show off in front of Vere. 'Do you remember going to the big meets when you were a little girl? I would ride side-saddle and lead you on your pony.'

'I had no idea you were *that* old, Aunt,' Spurs teased. 'Did women not ride astride then?'

'Don't be silly, Jasper. I rode side-saddle as a matter of choice. I was known as the galloping goddess,' she told Vere, her eyes misting at the memory. 'One Master used to say I was a hunting habit nobody could ever kick. You know, I do rather fancy taking it up again.'

'Are you sure that's wise at your age?' Hell's Bells muttered dismissively. 'You are a galloping granny these days, after all. It's a long time since you sat on anything as large as a horse.' She deliberately didn't look at diminutive Vere. 'And you aren't quite as agile as you were. Do you have any weight-carrying cobs at Horseshoe Farm, Diana?'

Diana smirked. It was just like the old days. Aunt Isabel was in fine form, putting down Truffle with delicious relish.

For the first time in many years, she remembered what it was like to be at the heart of a big, squabbling, loving, chaotic family.

Here, the ghosts of the Gunning Estate and her childhood love affair with Amos seemed a long way away.

She went in search of more champagne, plucking one of two glasses from a passing tray-carrier at the same time as a small, curvy blonde claimed the other.

'Cheers.' Diana raised her flute and they chinked rims.

'Great party,' said the blonde in a soft local accent, looking around at the scene.

'Isn't it?' At last, Diana caught sight of Pod entertaining a growing group of admirers while he ripped into a steak sandwich. Only someone as good-looking as he was could look utterly sexy talking with his mouth full. His audience certainly seemed to think so. Diana recognised the horribly blowsy hippy Ophelia Gently and her blue-haired friend from the garden centre, the willowy redhead who ran the gallery in Cider Court, the brash bottle-blonde American from the village shop, the snobby brunette from the Duck Upstream and their hostess, Anke, towering over them all. Oddlode wives and divorcées, she thought disparagingly and then realised, with a jolt, that she qualified for that category.

'Are you one of their Essex friends?' asked the blonde.

'What? Oh, no I'm local – at least I am now. We moved here on the same day as the Brakespears.'

The blonde's blue eyes lit up. 'You're not the new teacher from the primary school, are you?'

'No – although I do know her. I can introduce you if you like.'

'Oh, please. My eldest starts school next term and she's such a shy little thing.'

'My two start there next term too.'

'Oh, how lovely. What age?'

'Mim's nine, and Digby is five. He'll be in the same year as your daughter. We'll have to introduce them.'

'Oh, that would be so great. You live in Oddlode?'

'Upper Springlode.'

'Even better. We're just along the road from you. Maybe we can share the school run?'

'Super idea. We must swap numbers. Do you work?'

'Not at the moment but, with one little one starting at school, I'm hoping to be able to look for something part-time. My mum can't really cope with the two – she has bad asthma, see – but Plum's ever so easy.'

'Plum?'

'My youngest. She's three, and not like Maisy at all. Up till I had her, I worked at the Plough – book-keeping mostly. It kept me busy.'

'Not much chance of going back there in the short term.'

'Telling me,' she giggled. 'I've told Tony Sixsmith he has to hurry up and rebuild it so I can have my job back.'

'You know him, then?' Diana registered with interest.

'I used to babysit for his girls before I married. They're a nice family.'

'Aren't they? Hope has already looked after my two once or twice.

'Sperry you mean?'

'No, Hope.'

'Sorry – we all call her Sperry. Hope, Faith and Charity are just what their dad calls them. Everyone round here knows them by their Spanish names. Sperry is short for Esperanza, Faith is Fé and the little one is Carry. Caridad is Spanish for Charity, see.'

'I know,' Diana smiled. '*Llamer al pan, pan y al vino vino.*'

'Sorry?'

'It means call a spade a spade. My father is Spanish-speaking.'

'Oh, right. My dad was just plain speaking,' she giggled.

'So, you can do book-keeping?'

'Oh, yes – I'm pretty good at that. Keith Wilmore is hopeless with facts and figures. I used to keep the accounts and do the ordering. I originally took a job there to help out in the kitchen – I trained for a bit at catering college – but his books were in such a state I ended up doing them.'

Diana's eyes lit up. 'You cook, too?'

She nodded.

Diana studied her more closely, sensing a useful friendship about to blossom. Spilling out of a flowery cotton dress, with sunburn tingeing her pretty snubbed nose and golden throat, she was as wholesome, sweet and warm as honey on freshly baked bread. They shared more than just a taste for strappy dresses that were a size too small and kitten heels that were spiked firmly into the Brakespear's lawn as they stood talking. She had an intuitive feeling that this encounter had the makings of a true alliance.

'Do you work?' the blonde was asking.

'I'm just setting up a business – tourism, riding and good food combined.'

'Oh, how fantastic. I love horses. Maisy's desperate to learn to ride, but we can't afford lessons right now.'

'We have a Shetland pony that taught Mim to ride – he's officially Digby's now but he hardly ever gets used. You'll have to bring her over and we can take them for a little walkabout. Introduce her to Digs.'

'Oh, that is really so kind.'

Soon they were getting on like a village pub on fire and Diana grew more and more convinced that she might have just found the secret formula Blazing Trails needed. Rory was far too unreliable to run the accommodation side. A pretty young mum with catering and accounting skills, willing to work for peanuts and to orchestrate the school run, was perfect. *And* she was an old friend of the Sixsmiths.

'I must introduce you to my husband,' she was saying as she stood on tiptoes to look towards the marquee. 'He was queuing for food. Oh, there he is. Over here, love!' she turned back to Diana. 'Sorry, I didn't catch your name.'

'It's –'

'Diana Henriques, as I live and breathe!' gushed a deep, sing-song voice.

Enter stage left Ophelia Gently – something of a childhood rival – sweeping into the fold in an extraordinary floor-length coffee-coloured dress matched with beaded flip-flops and a green fringed shawl embroidered with mangoes and pineapples. With her pregnant bump protruding like a bulge in a statuesque trunk and her dark pre-Raphaelite curls pinned up on her head with brightly coloured butterfly clips, she resembled a rare jungle succulent popping up in an English orchard. Her bright green eyes glittered with mirth.

'Now, this is *not* a sight I expected to see. I heard you were back, Diana. And I see you've met Amos's lovely wife.'

'You're Jacqui Gates?' Diana gasped.

'Diana Henriques?' Jacqui said weakly.

'Lampeter,' she replied through clenched teeth. 'It's Lampeter.'

The two women immediately peeled apart.

And then Diana saw Amos in the flesh for the first time in ten years. It was like being stabbed in the chest with a knife for every year.

'Not exactly ecstatic to see one another again, are they?'

Ophelia and Pixie watched enthralled as a curious courtly dance took place in the Wyck Farm gardens. Diana had retreated to the bosom of her family in the marquee and was feigning rapturous delight as she listened to Hell's Bells' long descriptions of her renovation plans. Amos, meanwhile, was brooding behind a wall of Gates' shoulders as uncles, aunts and cousins flocked around him. Anti-social to the point of being a hermit, he was rarely seen out socially and his family all wanted to catch up.

'Do you think he came because he knew she'd be here?' breathed Pixie, watching the deliberate way that Diana and Amos ignored one another.

'God, no. He came because Jacqui begged him. The poor thing never gets out.'

'I can see that,' Pixie sniffed. 'She was obviously a dress size smaller last time she wore that frock.'

'Miaow,' Pheely laughed. Pixie had never hidden her dislike of Jacqui Gates who was just the sort of flirty, silly blonde that set her teeth on edge – largely because Pixie's husband Sexton spent hours chatting them up over pick-your-own strawberries at their market garden. Having once been very flirty and silly herself, Pixie was now far too exhausted and weathered from long, back-breaking hours in the fields to bother. Between them, she and the charming but lazy Sexton had six children from their various marriages and, caring for them, combined with running the business and taking an Open University degree, left her no time for frivolities. When she'd dyed her hair blue, she'd told Pheely that she was showing her 'female chauvinist pigment' in protest at his indolence. Sexist Sexton hated the look.

'Diana's a bit of hot stuff, isn't she? I had no idea she'd be that stunning.'

'She's worn pretty well,' Pheely admitted grudgingly.

'She looks nothing like the rest of her family.'

'Argentine father.'

'Of course.' Pixie watched entranced as Diana moved on to talk to her brother. 'And she and Amos were really the star-crossed lovers of Oddlode's century?'

'Think Verona built in Cotswold stone, with a duck pond in it.'

'Except Juliet dumped Romeo.'

'That's the thing. Nobody really knows.' Pheely could see bitter words being exchanged between Amos and Jacqui in that stiff-lipped way couples have of secretly arguing in public. He clearly wanted to leave, jerking his head towards the paddock in which the cars were parked, but she had dug her heels in – literally, as her kitten mules acted like crampons on the turf – and she swapped her empty glass for another full one.

The Brakespears' caterers were doing a roaring trade. There had to be at least two hundred people ducking falling nuts and acorns as they milled between the house and the marquee, the sides of which were billowing like a bullfrog's cheeks.

'Shall we go inside and have a perv around the house?' suggested Pheely, who loved nosing around other people's possessions. 'This storm's about to break.'

'I'm rather enjoying the sideshow.' Pixie was still fascinated by Diana Lampeter, who struck her as far too provocative for somewhere as small and insular as Oddlode. 'Tell me, is that the new teacher she's talking to? The one with her knickers showing?'

'No idea, but *he* is gorgeous.'

'Oh yes, the delicious Pod that we all long to shell.'

'You know him?'

'He and Sexton are doing some business together. She *is* the new schoolteacher. They've taken Rose Simmons' cottage. I popped around to see her and apologise in advance for our rabble but she was out. That's her chap.'

'Lucky girl,' Pheely sighed and then swung around as she heard the sewing machine drone of a 2CV rattling along the drive. 'Yippee! Dilly's here.' She raced off to greet her daughter who had driven down from Durham for the weekend.

Mo almost jumped out of her skin as two warm hands slipped around her waist, up under her top and beneath her breasts.

'Feeling chilly?' Pod breathed in her ear, his thumbs encountering nipples as hard as the acorns which were showering the marquee.

Mo hastily crossed her arms and hoped their companions hadn't clocked what was happening. But Diana and Rory were too busy greeting him, and Graham had turned away to try to appropriate a fresh tray of champagne.

'We'd been wondering where you were.' Diana transferred her red lipstick on to both of his unshaven cheeks, leaving far bigger, plumper impressions than had striped Graham's.

'Yeah, I've been circulating, y'know.' His eyes had a distant look about them as he clutched Mo proprietarily to his side, one hand still up her top. Mo crossed her arms tighter and glanced up at him. He looked wired.

With her hands no longer free to hold her skirt demurely, she was inadvertently showing her knickers to everyone at the party. Word had obviously got around that she was the new teacher and parents kept coming up to introduce themselves. An obvious mother was advancing through the crowds now, a tiny, tanned elf of a woman dressed in tie-dyed dungarees over a lacy bodice, with a pretty creased brown face and extraordinary blue hair that matched her eyes.

'Hi, Pod.' She blew him a kiss as she threaded her way across to them and held her hand out to Mo. 'I'm Pixie. I left you eggs.'

'Oh, yes, thanks – that was so kind. Sorry I missed you.' Forced to put her hand out to shake Pixie's, she exposed her strange, lumpy chest with five knuckles where one breast should be.

Pixie pretended not to notice as she shook the hand and then cackled in delight, pointing out that they were wearing identical big glass rings containing blue beads, along with almost identical rows of silver and blue bangles at their wrists. 'I know half the village is convinced you're Helena Bonham-Carter, but I really think you should start calling me Mummy, don't you?'

'Sorry?' Mo snatched her hand away, colour draining from her face.

'You are obviously my long-lost daughter.' Pixie edged in beside her to point out the physical resemblance. Both were the same height and build with the same elfin features and urchin hair. 'When were you born?'

'Seventy nine.'

'Ah – nope. Can't be. I was at finishing school. We weren't even *allowed* near boys. Shame. Sexton always pulls rank because he has the eldest child. We run the market garden, by the way. Pop in before term starts and meet the kids. They're a bit wild but very willing. Pod's already been to see us.'

Again, Mo looked up at Pod curiously, but his distant eyes were watching an explosion of blonde curls and laughter that was bounding leggily towards them like a retriever puppy.

'Dilly!' Rory burst from the group and gathered her up into a high, swinging hug that sent his girlfriend's espadrilles flying in opposite directions. 'God, I've missed you!'

'Missed you too, baby.' She sank back down as they indulged in a very long, very erotic, public kiss.

Mo felt Pod's fingers tighten so hard on her nipples that she gasped.

'My brother's girlfriend,' Diana explained dryly.

'Phew – and there was me thinking it was another sister,' Pod said equally dryly, and then he whooped with sudden, unexpected laughter, planting a long kiss on Mo's throat that made her flinch as his teeth dug in.

It was Diana's turn to eye him curiously. He had definitely taken something. She was shamed by the crucifying jealousy that gripped her when she saw Pod and Mo together. She downed another glass of champagne and wished she felt that high. On cue, Graham Brakespear returned with a tray of fresh supplies.

'Here we go. Well hello, love,' he eyed Dilly with approval as she emerged from the kiss and beamed around at them all.

'I'm Daffodil,' she said brightly.

'And I'm your host in this crowd, Daffodil.' Graham slipped straight into fifth-gear flirt as he handed her a brimming glass and started making introductions.

Daffodil was as bubbly and intoxicating as the champagne she was downing, interrupting Graham happily as he gestured around their group.

'Yes, I know Pixie . . . and Diana – hi there – you look lovely . . . Hi Mo, great to meet you.' She shook hands, again forcing Mo to expose the male fist up her shirt which released her nipple like a jump lead clamp sparked off a live terminal the moment Dilly moved to offer her hand to Pod.

Warmed by Mo's breast, Pod's fingers wrapped around Dilly's and he drew them to his lips. 'Good to meet you, flower.' The big, dark eyes studied her exquisite face over her slender wrist.

Dilly blushed crimson. The legendary Pod magic had woven its usual instant spell. From anyone else, hand-kissing gestures would look cheesy. Graham laying his flirtation on with a trowel was laughable. Pod was just lethal. Dilly cradled her hand to her chest in awe, as though he'd placed a ring on it.

Arms crossed once more to cover her throbbing nipples, Mo turned away and felt a twitch of shame at her throat as she caught Graham watching her. His expression was so kind and enquiring that she wanted to dive into his big bright shirt, jump into the red Cadillac that was parked across his midriff and drive away at speed along the palm-lined highway.

Nobody else seemed to mind or notice that Pod was soon flirting so outrageously with Daffodil, his eyes all over her body and his mind inside her knickers, that her blush threatened to melt the trendy mauve shades balanced on her nose.

Rory appeared merely flattered as he smiled lazily and downed champagne, laughing at both their jokes, unaware of the sudden sexual frisson.

Diana was too distracted to care, watching Amos out of the corner of her eye as he stalked into enemy territory to dig into the puddings. In outward appearance, he had changed enormously, yet his presence was as strong and singular as ever. She might as well have never been away. Hurt and betrayal still smouldered inside her where passion had once burned. He still swept the legs from under her, made her heart hurt because it was beating too fast and her chest crack under the boa constrictor pressure of fighting to breathe. He had thickened out – his shoulders broader, lean shanks wider, and forearms as taut as an oarsman's. The eighties wolf mane had gone, replaced by a harsh, short cut and greying temples that belied the youth in his features. His eyes burned huge and black-green from such an exposed face, his cheekbones jagged out above that cliff-face jaw, his brows as black as crow's wings. The broken nose had stripped the face of some of its erstwhile beauty, but nothing of its angular power. He was weathered but not aged, and Diana clearly saw the greatest love that she had ever possessed entombed beneath the weather-beaten fine lines and broken veins, curling inside the broad mouth and being crushed as surely as the cherries he was stealing from the top of a cheesecake and biting clean through with his teeth. She wanted to throw her glass at him.

A shriek beside her made her jump, her nerve-ends jangling, but it was just Dilly laughing at something Pod had said. Catching Diana's eyes on him, Pod tipped his chin and looked at her through his lashes for a moment, his smile radiating with such unbridled wickedness that the truth hit her with a jolt. She found him captivating because he reminded her so vividly of Amos. The Amos she had loved before all that wild energy had turned to hatred.

She turned back in time to see him stalking out of the marquee. He had cream on his lower lip. Diana closed her eyes to a sudden and unexpected urge to run after him and kiss it off. How utterly stupid.

To her side, Graham was nobly making attempts to divert attention from the flirtation double act that was hotting up beside them. 'Quite a lot of familiar faces here this evening, eh Diana, love?'

'What?' She glanced at him vaguely.

'I was just saying to Mo that you probably know more people here than we do.'

'It's your party,' she said flatly. 'I've been away for years.'

'And Pod here seems to have made a lot of friends in the village.' Graham slapped him on the shoulder. 'Everyone here knows you.'

'I make friends easily.' He looked meaningfully at Dilly. 'Just like I make love.'

She giggled.

'It's all that time you spend in the pub, mate,' Graham ribbed.

'We don't make love in the pub, do we, queen?' Pod's arm grabbed Mo by the shoulders and gave her a cursory squeeze, but his eyes didn't leave Dilly's. 'At least not any more. There was a time no cubicle was safe.'

'Ladies or Gents?' Dilly shrieked.

Mo's face flamed as she tried not to look up at the expressions around her. Pod loved shaming her like this when they were hitting the skids.

'Which do you prefer?' he asked wickedly.

'Oh, Ladies are much nicer.'

'I quite agree, flower.'

'There are some students who are at it all the time in the union bogs. You should see the queues.'

'Have you ever tried?'

'God, no.' Dilly glanced at Rory who was looking quite taken with the idea.

'You should have a go – there's quite an art to it, isn't there, queen?' He lashed her shoulders tighter in his grip. 'Mo can wrap her little legs around at the most amazing angles – all those *pliés* as a teenager, I guess.'

For a moment Mo was speechless with embarrassment, gritting her teeth to stop herself exploding. Whatever he had taken was starting to push him over the edge.

'That's enough, Pod,' she hissed in an undertone.

'I'm sorry?'

'That's enough.'

'That's not what you said earlier.'

Mo froze. Surely he wouldn't?

'You were begging for more.'

A great clout of thunder shook the marquee, although the sun still shone with hazy evening heat.

Pod smiled defiantly through the awkward silence. 'Anyway, nice as it is talking to all you guys, I'd better take my Mo somewhere we're not seen fraternising with the enemy.'

'What's that?' Graham asked, baffled.

'Didn't you know?' A cruel smile kissed his lips as he turned towards Diana. 'My new boss is your ex, love. And, boy, did you leave him mean. Not your biggest fan, is he? I'd watch your back if I were you.' He turned to leave with one final wink at the blushing, mesmerised Dilly who had quite lost her heart.

Diana had lost her heart, too, as she watched him stride away and then glanced across to Amos, glowering up at the sky from the marquee entrance. And she had a shrewd feeling she was about to lose her head and knickers to match.

Something inside Mo snapped.

It wasn't just that Pod had undermined her with very public displays of ownership and then humiliated her by flirting outrageously with Rory's girlfriend. It wasn't his rudeness to new friends and disregard for any social graces that riled her. It wasn't even the fact he had quite obviously taken something a lot stronger than a few glasses of champagne and a couple of spliffs.

What made her snap was the fact that he towed her out of the marquee and across the lawn as lightning split the black sky above the valley rim around them. There, he parked her beneath a tree, patted her arm, yawned and with a 'see you later' wandered off on his own. Now that he had got her attention, he wanted her to play hide-and-seek. Well, she wasn't going to follow him this time.

'You okay, love?' Graham had found her, frozen-faced, just where Pod had left her.

'Fine.'

'Another drink?'

'In a minute.'

'Want me to fetch you some food? You haven't eaten a thing. Puddings are great. I remember you've got a sweet tooth, love.'

'No – thanks. It's really kind of you.'

He watched her awkwardly for a while.

'I'm sorry about Pod,' she said eventually. 'He can be a bit out of control sometimes.'

'As long as you're not worried, I'm not.'

'I *am* worried.' She looked up at him.

'Ah.' Graham sensed a fatherly talk coming on. He preferred to flirt, but it was obvious Mo was in no state for that. 'You want to tell me about it?'

But to his surprise, Mo pummelled her small fists into his chest and started to laugh. 'No, I bloody don't. I want to get very drunk, behave very badly and blame it all on Helena Bonham-Carter.'

Totally oblivious of the sub-currents swirling through her party, Anke was anxiously trying to keep both eyes pointing in opposite directions – one towards her father, who appeared to have lost control of his bladder whilst reciting *Beowulf* to a small group of enthralled locals, including Diana's mother. The other eye was directed towards Faith who was drinking all the Pimm's that Magnus had spiked with extra vodka, and stalking both Pod and Rory.

'Super party, darling.' A very tanned local whom Anke vaguely recognised swept up to her and gave her a downy moustached kiss on one cheek. 'Haven't seen so many of my ex-lovers in one place since my last wedding.' Off he bounded, leaving Anke wondering if she only recognised him because he looked like Magnum P.I.

'Giles Hornton,' whispered a voice in her ear as Pheely appeared at her shoulder. 'He will try to bed you by the end of the year, guaranteed. Are you having fun?'

'Oh yes,' Anke assured her.

'Bollocks.' Pheely squinted cheerfully at the low, cloud-scudded sun, rubbing her bump affectionately. 'One never enjoys one's own parties.'

'I just hope my father's all right.' She eyed the damp trousers with concern as Ingmar launched into the section where Grendel, the warrior-eating monster, starts visiting the grand banqueting hall, Heorot, and picking off merrymakers to satisfy his appetite.

'He's still rather magnificent, isn't he?'

'He's wet himself.'

'Oh, nobody will notice. Truffle Dacre-Hopkinson seems rather taken. Come and have another drink. This really is a fabulous shindig. Well done you.'

'I must just find Faith.'

'Oh, she'll be fine. Dilly hates it when I police her. Hope this wretched storm holds off, don't you?'

Dressed in her new urban urchin raver gear, eyes watering from unaccustomed make-up, Faith sat in her bedroom staring at the mirror and trying to like what she saw. Trust bloody Mo Stillitoe to upstage her by wearing such an outrageous outfit. Faith thought Mo looked beyond beautiful.

She spiked up her hair a little more with a fresh lick of wax, but it was now so gloopy with hair products that the red peaks folded over under their weight and flattened against her scalp in stiff curly lumps. The red dye hadn't worked the way Faith wanted it to. She hadn't read the instructions properly about applying it on blonde and it had turned a garish shade of ginger as opposed to the streaky scarlet and burgundy she was trying to achieve. To her horror, it looked totally natural. And her frizzy curls refused to straighten despite the heavy wax. She looked like Ronald MacDonald.

Much as she tried to convince herself that she was almost glad that best friend Carly hadn't made it to witness her looking so – ginger – she knew that Carly's non-appearance was the main reason the evening was turning out to be so much more than a mere anti-climax. It was an all-out nuclear disaster.

She slumped on her bed and picked at the straps on her baggy 'bondo cargos', as the assistant in the funky Cheltenham shop had described them – a modern must-have fusion between cargo pants and bondage trousers that every sussed hippy chick was wearing. To Faith, they just looked like something her stepfather wore around his yard, and in his size too – the crotch was between her knees and folds of fabric wrinkled at her ankles where the trousers met the clumpiest of butch trainers. Her proudest purchase – a skinny T-shirt, proclaiming her to be 'Child Porn' – had been confiscated by her mother when she first went downstairs and she was now sporting the far less satisfactory 'Gold Digger' across her flat chest.

Faith took another peek from her window and felt sick. They were still at it. She had come up here to spy on them in the first place, but this was now pure punishment.

Rory Midwinter had been kissing Dilly behind the marquee for precisely ten minutes. His hand was up her top. Hers was down his trousers.

Faith hated Dilly more than she could have imagined possible. She'd guessed that any girlfriend of Rory's would be pretty, but not this pretty – with her perfect figure and cascade of long blonde curls. Watching them kiss was torment.

She wished she had followed Pod when the two had separated from the same little group in the marquee. But she had been lurking by the Pimm's table at the time and, in the moment it had taken her to refill her glass, Pod had disappeared whereas Rory was still in full view. Now he was in *very* full view as Dilly pulled up his T-shirt and kissed his chest, revealing a blue tattoo on his belly. Faith squinted to see what it was, wishing she had a pair of binoculars in her room.

'I hate him,' she muttered, unable to drag her eyes away as a long leg wrapped itself around Rory's body. 'I hate Rory and I love –'

She looked over her shoulder in horror as her door burst open.

'Go away!'

'Sorry, flower! I thought this was the bog.'

'Next door on the left – wait!'

It was Pod Shannon. Her true love. In her *bedroom*.

'Yeah?' He stood reluctantly in the door, those amazingly turbulent black eyes darting around the room.

Faith cringed as she realised that, for one, she could no longer say a word because this was *Pod* in *her room*. For two, she was mortified that he was now studying her posters of horses and her rosette collection on the walls when she had recently decided that this look no longer worked for her and she should really go for purples and candles and sophisticated posters advertising French films.

But Pod was transfixed.

'Shit, that's me!' He approached a poster of horses looming over Bechers at the Grand National, taken from such an amazingly low angle that it was mostly a blur of metal-shod hooves.

'Which one?' Faith was so amazed her shyness melted away as she hopped across the room to take a look.

'Here – the grey, Gopher's Quest. Made it as far as the third last, then he tipped me out, the sod. That's fantastic. I've never seen that.'

'But you can't actually see *you*.'

'I can,' he assured her, still staring at the poster. 'I can absolutely see me. What are you doing hiding in here, anyway?'

'It's my room.'

'But you *are* hiding.' He wandered over to the window at which she'd been posted. 'Fuck-*ing* hell.'

Faith peeked out again. They were still kissing. Boring. She had *Pod* in *her room*.

'Oh, they've been doing that for *ages*.'

'And you were watching them?' He seemed to notice her for the first time.

'No, I was fixing my make-up.'

Looking out at Rory and Dilly and then back at Faith, Pod very slowly lifted a finger and rubbed the smudged kohl from beneath her eyes. 'There – fixed. You should wear less. Disgusting stuff.' He looked out of the window again. 'You do know what's going on out there, don't you?'

'Yeah,' she sneered, 'they're, like, kissing.'

'Sure,' he winked, heading for the door. 'They're kissing. On the loft, you say?' With that he was gone.

Letting the feeling of having him so close and so exclusive flood over her – Faith could relive this night after night – she gazed out of the window again. Kissing. Pah. That was for kids. Adults went for sexual *frisson* in a bedroom.

They weren't even very good at it. She giggled in surprise as she watched. Dilly appeared to have her hand caught down Rory's trousers. It was thrashing around like mad as she tried to pull it out. Useless.

Faith moved away to kiss her Grand National poster. So what if she couldn't see Pod in it. He'd seen himself and that was good enough for her.

Accustomed to losing Pod at parties, Mo refused to allow herself or her imagination to follow him on his wired walkabout, although she was disconcerted by the ongoing, fatherly attentions of Graham. He had been hanging around for ages and now offered to show her around the house.

'Shouldn't you be looking after some of your other guests? I feel I've got you on an exclusive here.' All the champagne that she had downed earlier had started to kick in and her head was spinning.

'I'll go if you like, love.'

'No. Please stick around.'

He made her feel safe. But that in itself was dangerous. Mo hadn't felt safe in a long time.

As they looked through the beautifully decorated rooms (Anke was an instant 'fixer-upper'), she suddenly experienced an unexpected, irresistible attraction for beefy, straightforward Graham with his flirty hands and bright blue what-you-see-is-what-you-get eyes. She was almost overcome by a libido fix.

'I think I've drunk too much,' she breathed headily, racing through the conservatory and gulping in fresh air from the open doorway.

Almost all the guests were outside now, watching the storm shatter its way around the ridge of the valley.

'Think it'll visit us?' she asked as forked lightning lit up the tree spines on the ridge's dinosaur back.

'Not while it's plaguing my tractors up on the hill.' Graham looked down at her narrow shoulders. 'Are you really all right, love?'

'Will you stop asking that!' She batted him away and weaved her way back into the kitchen. 'This house is fantastic.'

He shrugged. 'Not a patch on the Essex house, but we were in a hurry. It has the makings of a great family home.'

'And you all make a great family.'

'You think so?' He seemed genuinely touched.

'Sure.' Mo ran her hands along the worktops. 'Anke is such an efficient mother – and wife, I'm sure. She's so organised and kind. And your kids are great – Faith is so sweet the way she's shy and brave at the same time, finding herself the way teenagers do. And Chad makes me laugh. Then, Magnus,' she whistled, ogling one of the many framed photographs of the blonde, beautiful Magnus that littered the stone walls among the family collection of Faith on ponies, Anke and Graham skiing and Chad holding up fat fish. 'Well, he's just a *dude*.'

'Not my genes, I'm afraid. Anke and I met when Magnus was ten.'

'Oh, your jeans are pretty cool.' She cocked her head as she admired his legs, helping herself to another drink courtesy of a discarded bottle of champagne lying on the slate-topped island.

'I thought you said you'd had too much.'

'Stop being such a daddy.' She raised the brim to her lips. 'I like you when you flirt with me.'

'I like flirting with you, but I'm so –'

'– married.' She finished for him.

'I was going to say "so much older than you".' He raised a bushy eyebrow. 'And married. And concerned that you are very drunk and very upset about your boyfriend's behaviour.'

Mo feigned a big, loud and somewhat camp yawn before sidling up to him.

'For your information, daddy G, my boyfriend regularly behaves this badly. As do I.'

'Is that a fact?'

'Fact. Can I drive in your Cadillac?' She traced the door of the red car on his shirt with her fingernail before slotting it between two buttons. 'The upholstery is so soft.'

Graham looked absolutely cornered. He glanced nervously at the windows – the kitchen was lit up like a starship from the bright overhead halogens for all those in the garden to see, and caterers had been running in and out all night.

Mo withdrew her finger and dipped it in her champagne before sucking it. 'Why don't you show me upstairs?'

Graham hesitated. He knew this was a bad move. Such a bad move. He was a fool. But her obvious – amazing, unexpected, adorable – desire for him was scrambling his brain.

Following him upstairs, Mo watched his broad but muscular bottom encased in slightly too tight jeans and decided it was perfect. It was a working man's bottom. It was like Graham himself – hard and swaggering and muscular at first sight, but soft as a peach when he didn't think you were looking.

'Stop staring at my arse, love,' he muttered over his shoulder.

'Nice chandelier.' She looked up.

'I brought it back from Belgium when we were first married – had a long haul there. But Anke hates it. She dislikes ostentation.'

'It's Ostende-tatious.'

He let out that great guffawing laugh, bluer than blue eyes crinkling as he turned to cuff her. 'Y'know I like that. You are such a funny little angel.'

'Why angel?'

''Cause you flew down from heaven and landed in Oddlode. Thank the lord.'

Mo felt her last traces of reserve escape.

Before she knew what she was doing, she'd slid a hand into his flies. What was springing to attention there was so magnificent it almost beggared belief. Whether Graham was more shocked or Pod was – coming out of the loo door directly beside them – was uncertain but, as Mo snatched her hand away, both men diligently pretended nothing had happened.

'Pod, mate. I'm giving your girl a tour of the house.' Graham cleared his throat.

'Lovely khazi.' Pod gestured through the door. 'I can highly recommend it.'

Mo could see the cocaine grains still dusting his nostrils. Mortified, she fled downstairs.

'In fact,' Pod went on, not acknowledging his girlfriend's departure, 'if you'll excuse me, I really must finish the Survivor's Guide to Finding Your Totty Groping a Married Man. Perfect bogside reading.' Laughing his head off, Pod headed back into the loo for another toot.

Graham walked stiffly into his bedroom, wishing he were in more of a position to apologise or to give chase to Mo. Neither was possible with a hard-on so determined to out itself that doing up his flies was impossible.

Downstairs, Mo had run straight into the lascivious arms and gaze of local solicitor and divorced lothario, Giles Hornton.

'Woah woah!' He scooped her up as she landed in a heap at the bottom of the stairs. 'Not trying a Diana, are we?'

Mo glanced behind her. To her humiliation, Pod hadn't even attempted to give chase. Not for a moment had he registered one iota of jealousy.

'Diana who? Lampeter?' she asked dizzily.

'Princess Diana. Threw herself downstairs? My little gag.' He was Terry Thomas meets Alan B'stard – all cocky, mocking, drawling flirtation and bad jokes.

'Well, it wasn't funny.' Mo preferred Graham's excited labrador flirting. It cheered her up. It felt real. Oh God, what had she done?

'I think someone might need a little drinkie, don't you?' Giles' moustache twitched eagerly as he helped her up. 'Tell me, are you this delicious new teacher everyone is talking about? The one who is, in fact, a famous actress researching a role?'

Diana was on the brink of emotional meltdown. She could not cope with Amos's steely gaze a moment longer. This game of death-stare chess had gone on long enough. He had pawns everywhere on the board, and she was a lone queen trapped in checkmate. She was appalled to find tears kicking the backs of her eyeballs and a great fist of guilt in her throat.

'Excuse me,' she interrupted Pru Hornton who was mid-way through explaining how the philistine Oddlode lowbrows had conspired to cripple her failing gallery. 'Must have a pee.'

Foregoing the toxic potential of the portaloos, she rushed inside the house, but all the lavatories and bathrooms were occupied. Waiting upstairs, where at least she was in peace and semi-darkness away from Amos, she heard a familiar snort from beyond the bathroom door.

She cocked her head and listened closely.

There it was again. Another snort. Two snorts like that meant only one thing.

She rapped insistently.

Pod Shannon reluctantly answered, still wiping his nose.

'Give me some of that or I call the police.'

Fascinated rather than frightened, Pod obliged.

Graham Brakespear emerged from his bedroom, red-faced and wretched after a humiliating tug of amour, to hear the unmistakeable sound of muted, furious, unstoppable sex coming from his family bathroom.

For a moment he was too gobsmacked to react. He had hosted hundreds of parties in Essex – the shag capital of the country, some would say – and the most exciting thing that had ever happened was some skinny-dipping in the pool. Move to the strait-laced, old-fashioned hunting and shooting Cotswolds and his jacuzzi was hosting an orgy.

He guessed it was Mo and Pod making up. He wished the thought didn't make him quite so depressed. Or quite so horny.

Sighing in frustration, he headed back into his bedroom. It had been almost a year since Anke had obliged him, and usually he showed great reserves of self-control. But tonight was different. Something – or rather, someone – had jump-started him. Tonight, the accelerator pedal on his sex drive had got stuck.

'Just one little drinkie,' Giles coaxed. 'Cheer you up.'

'I don't need cheering up, thanks.'

'You really are terribly pretty.'

'And you're not.'

He laughed uproariously. 'How refreshing. I do have to warn you that you will share my bed before long.'

'Only if my boyfriend and I break into your house and shag there.'

'I thought you were supposed to be an educator of young minds?'

'I'm off duty. Besides, I'm disillusioning an old mind. That's quite another skill. Excuse me.'

At last, Mo escaped the attentions of Giles and headed in search of Pod to tell him that she was leaving. But he was nowhere to be found.

The storm was still battering the valley ramparts but had yet to drop into Oddlode. It was the cheapest and most dramatic firework display any host could wish for. She hoped Graham was pleased. Not that she could see him either. A sudden thought struck her. They couldn't both be upstairs, could they? Surely they weren't fighting or something ghastly?

She raced up two at a time.

The bathroom door was locked.

Mo tapped it tentatively.

'Fucking occupied!' came a familiar voice.

Mo opened her mouth to speak, but someone else got in there first.

'Occupied fucking!' A woman's muffled laughter from behind the door.

Mo slumped back against the wall opposite, the whimper in her throat trapped by the great ball blocking it. She couldn't breathe.

There were footsteps on the stairs behind her. Without thinking, she escaped through the closest door and shut it tight behind her.

'Oh, shit!' There was a fumble of sheets on the vast queen-sized bed in front of her as hot action was hastily covered.

'Christ, everyone's bloody at it!' Mo wailed. 'Sorry, sorry, sorry, okay? I'm out of here.'

'Don't go, love. I can explain –'

'Graham?'

The bedside light pinged on.

'You're alone.' Mo gasped in surprise.

'Aye.' He didn't look up. 'I'm so sorry you had to see this. I really can explain. It's not that I'm some sort of dirty old man. It's just . . .'

Locking the door behind her, Mo perched at the end of the bed and reached to tweak his toes, wishing she didn't feel quite so close to crying. 'We all wank, daddy G.'

He cleared his throat, mortified by the subject matter and the circumstances, yet too amazed to stop himself asking. 'Even . . . ?'

She nodded. 'Me, even.'

'But you –'

'Not, admittedly, at my own parties, but then I avoid hosting parties as a rule. I hate them.' Starting to babble, Mo was too overwrought to care that Graham was swaddled in a duvet and blushing like a furnace.

'My boyfriend usually fucks someone else at parties.' Her voice disintegrated into a tight squeak. 'In fact he's fucking someone right now. Just through that wall.'

'That's the en suite.'

'Beyond the fucking en suite. Through the next wall.' She pressed her face into her hands.

'Sorry.'

'Sorry that Pod is fucking around or sorry that you made a fatuous remark?'

'Both.'

'Don't be. Not your fault he's the way he is. I took him on knowing that. And I like your fatuous remarks. They make me laugh. You make me laugh. You're the loveliest man I've ever met.'

She peered at him through her fingers. Then it happened. The most unexpected emotion rushed her from behind and totally mugged her.

Mortification turned to that surprising desire again as those straight-forward blue eyes fixed her with a look that said it all. The wraparound skirt was already peeled back for action by the wind. Light, agile and horny as hell, Mo jumped him.

'Christ you're hung like a bull,' she gasped.

'Talk bull long enough, everything else turns to bull. Ohhhhhh myyyyy good looooord. Is that legal?'

'You're beautiful,' she laughed. 'You're so beautiful, daddy G.'

It lasted just a few seconds, but they didn't stop looking into one another's eyes. Afterwards, Mo burst into the tears that had been waiting all night.

'You just did this to get back at your boyfriend.' Graham stroked her hair. 'That's okay. We can ride this thing out.'

'I didn't.'

He wiped the tears from her cheeks. 'Shhh. Shhh, love. It's okay. I don't mind. We all have hidden agendas.'

'I truly didn't. I've never –' She lost her voice to quiet sobs for a moment. 'I've never been unfaithful to Pod until tonight.'

'Oh, Christ.' He pulled her into a hug. 'You poor little darling. Hey.'

'I feel so awful. You've been so kind to me. I'm sorry.'

'You're gorgeous. I'm the one who should be apologising here, love. I shouldn't have let this happen.'

'I wanted it to happen. I've fancied you from the first day I met you.'

'You have?' he seemed completely amazed, self-esteem flooding back like a head rush. He started to laugh in confused disbelief. 'Christ. This is madness. My wife and kids are downstairs, along with half our friends and neighbours. I've just had sex with my son's schoolteacher. And all I want to do is dance naked around the garden with her. You are so gorgeous.'

Mo was so twisted with guilt and shame and desire that she couldn't think straight. All she knew was that he had a hidden agenda – he'd just admitted it – and she had let him down.

'I can't get Chad into my school.'

Graham sat up, stunned. 'Is that what you think this is about?'

'Isn't it?'

'Christ, no! I can get him in. I'll buy them a fucking swimming pool, a hundred complete Shakespeares, a bloody stack of computers and the latest Tomb Raiders to go with them if that's what it takes.'

'The kids are a bit young for Tomb Raider,' Mo sniffed, mustering a smile.

'You are my Lara Croft.' He cupped her face. 'You've raided my heart – and that's a fossilised old tomb if ever I knew one.'

'You're right. This should never have happened.' She shook her head. Pod might be unfaithful a hundred times over, but she knew for certain that he loved her exclusively. That's what kept the glue sticking. Now her heart was untethered and she could almost smell boats and bridges burning.

'It has happened.' Graham folded her in his arms. 'How we deal with it is up to us. I just promise I won't let you get hurt, love. Nobody gets hurt. Deal?'

'Deal.' Mo snuggled tightly to his big, warm chest listening to his big, kind heart thumping away. She had no idea why, but she felt safer than she had in months. She was lying in someone else's marital bed with someone else's husband after a two-minute drunken fumble at a party and she felt safe. Pod was up to his old tricks again and she felt safe. Graham made her feel safe and, for this sweet moment, that meant she would happily pull two pistols from her hip holsters and fight wolves, raptors, T-Rex and centaurs if he asked.

Curled up together for a few stolen seconds, pretending that they could freeze-frame life like pressing Pause on a game, they formed the first corner of a love triangle that was set to become a pyramid housing untold danger and treasure.

At an opposite corner of the triangle, two rooms away, Diana and Pod were using colour-coordinated Velvet Quilted toilet tissue to mop up the after-effects of a coke-enhanced quickie (cocaine making it far from quick – at least a forty-minute marathon that involved the bidet, shower, roll-top bath and airing cupboard). Both recognised a mutual dislike, a mutual distrust and mutual talent for fantastic, guilt-free sex.

'I'll have to set up an account with your dealer,' Diana laughed. 'Anyone who can source cocaine that good around here deserves my business.'

Pod tapped his nose. 'Why cut out the middleman when he has a cock the size of mine?'

'Your middle-manhood. You really are an uncouth lout, aren't you?' She bought a gram and took his mobile number.

'Call me, queen.' He kissed her hard on the mouth before he left.

'There are some areas of London where calling you queen could get us into serious trouble,' she murmured to herself afterwards.

It wasn't quite the working relationship Diana had hoped from Pod, but the encounter had cheered her up enormously. She'd known from the start that there was chemistry between them. With his streetwise banter and back-alley morals, Pod Shannon was no love-match, but the sexual spark could combust a small town.

She tucked her gram into her bra and thought about Amos and his glaring checkmate waiting outside.

'This queen can never be intimidated,' she told her reflection in the mirror. 'Just watch your little castle burn down, Amos Gates.'

'Carly! Carly!' Faith called down from her window as late arrivals made their way towards the house from the parking paddock, 'I didn't think you'd make it.'

'We got lost. Bloody hell. Look at you girl*friend*!'

'D'you like it?'

'Way to go.' Carly put her thumbs together in front of her and steered a hip-swinging, pirouetting dance that meant 'cool' in teen body language.

'You look great, too.' Faith dangled out of her window.

'I look the same. Mum like *so* won't let me get my nose pierced.'

'Come up to my room!'

Carly burst through the door two minutes later. 'Jeez, like all your upstairs rooms are locked – this is the only door I could get in. Are you keeping prisoners or something?'

'Like, no. That's weird.'

'You look completely cool, Faith.'

'Thanks, girlfriend.' Faith smirked, happy to take the credit and to slip companionably into the teenage temptress language she and Carly had been perfecting for the past year – part LA brat, part Chelsea trusta-farian and, as far as they were concerned, utterly sophisticated.

'I thought there was no style around here. You're like the only person who could leave Essex *un*cool and transform herself to a babe in the back of beyond. You are going to be so, like, wasted here. Chad told me the guys you dig are both about forty. Ugh!'

'Chad is, like, *such* a liar!' Faith wailed. 'They are babes – I'm talking all that and some, girlfriend.'

'As fit as Magnus?' Carly whistled.

'Like way more. Wait till you see Pod – and Rory, only he's like not as nice and has a girlfriend and stuff. Pod has a girlfriend too but she's already cracking on to my stepdad so I reckon they must be shaky, yeah.'

'Oh absolutely,' agreed Carly who hadn't taken in a word because she was busy stealing Faith's new make-up in anticipation of these love gods.

'Shall we go and see if we can find them?'

'They're here tonight?'

'Yeah – but you, like, *mustn't* let on I fancy them.'

'Sure.'

'Take a picture of me, Pod.'

'Huh?' He spun round shiftily to find Rory's girlfriend watching him. 'Well, hello.'

'That is a picture phone, isn't it?' She struck a pose. 'Go on, give it a try, Pod . . . tripod! Hee!'

Pod swiftly deleted the text message he had been about to send. Smiling, he snapped her and showed her the little image.

'Cool! I must get one of those.'

'Now if you call me, your picture will appear, yeah?'

'Only if I give you my number.'

'True.' He gave her the full Pod Shannon smile.

Dilly reeled off the digits breathlessly, reaching for her own phone. 'Now give me yours.'

'Does Rory mind you swapping numbers with strange men?'

'You're practically married.'

'Makes me even less trustworthy.'

'Oh, I do hope so.' She bit her lip elatedly and lounged back against a marquee pole. 'So how are you finding it around here?'

'Getting used to it.'

'I hear you're working at Gunning?'

'Yeah.'

'How thrilling! Have you seen any ghosts?'

'Nope.'

'Oh.' She kicked an espadrille into the matting floor, clearly disappointed. 'What about the legendary Pleasure Garden? Have you seen that yet?'

Pod gave nothing away. When in doubt, smile the smile.

Her eyes lit up. 'You *have* seen it!'

He shrugged.

'Oh. My. God. I didn't think it really existed.'

'Hard to find.'

'I'll bet it is. Mum has always said you can only find it if it wants you there. She says she went there as a girl, although I've had my doubts. She's never been able to remember the way and refuses to go back. It's supposed to be full of treasure.'

'Is that what they say?'

She stared eagerly into his face. 'You have to take me there.'

Pod watched the small pink tongue dab the luscious rosebud lips, leaving them moist and tempting.

'Maybe. One day.' He looked away, watching as Rory lurched towards them with two bowls of trifle. 'Call me, eh? I want to see that pretty face again.' He tapped the phone against his nose. Nodding at Rory as he passed, he made his way outside.

'Shall we eat these in the garden?' Rory suggested cheerfully.

'The garden,' Dilly sighed, taking a bowl and kissing his nose. 'I'd like nothing more than to go to the garden.'

Anke returned from seeing her father home to find the party swinging along merrily. Faith's greatest school chum from Essex had finally arrived, along with her parents who were old friends of the Brakespears. Anke gratefully watched her daughter start to unravel and become her old self as she and Carly ran around the garden shrieking.

She noticed that they both hid behind a tree and giggled a lot as Pod Shannon idled past, heading for the drive.

'Are you leaving us?' Anke asked as he crossed her path.

''Fraid so, flower – got an early start in the morning.'

'You are working this weekend?'

'Every weekend.' He rolled his eyes theatrically and beamed up at the friends she had been greeting. 'Shame I can't stay longer. Great party. Thanks for inviting us.'

'Has Mo left already?'

'Easy come, easy go, that's our Mo,' he rhymed mindlessly, kissing her on the cheek, dark eyes playful. 'You take care, eh?'

Anke creased her brow as he left, wondering why he always made her feel so uneasy.

'What a fantastic-looking guy,' sighed one of the Essex friends. 'You are so lucky moving here. All the men are so fantastic.'

'Anke already has the most fantastic man imaginable,' another friend sighed. Graham had always been seen as a real catch amongst them.

And so he was, Anke reminded herself, wondering where he had got to. This party was down to him and, despite her fears, it was a resounding success. He deserved to enjoy himself and take some credit.

At last she could relax and circulate, enjoying old acquaintances and new. She marvelled at the simplicity of country life – true country life, not the Essex one-upmanship, designer drugs and glitz. Here, marriages lasted and families stuck together, staying in the same area and supporting one another like the Constantine sisters and the Wycks and the Gateses and the Simmons. She suddenly felt a great surge of love for Graham, who was good and loyal and true and had loved her throughout all her angst. Her Anke Angst as he called it. Divorcing Kurt before the façade crumbled, losing her mother shortly afterwards, battling to come to terms with her father's dissolving mind, bearing him Chad through duty whereas having children for Kurt had been a gift of love. Not that she had borne Kurt's children . . .

Anke Panky had been her nickname on the international dressage circuit. If only they knew. Magnus was the beautiful result of a drunken one-night stand with a Dutch trainer; Faith a less enjoyable coupling with an Irish horse-dealer. Both were her gifts to Kurt. Both were results of her very few forays into sex. Married to Kurt for all those years, she'd become accustomed to a sexless marriage. She knew the drill.

Graham had always been a whole different ball game – big, potent balls full of big, potent, testosterone-packed desire. At first it had enthralled Anke. Now it intimidated her. She wanted her space. She wanted her desire one-way – her way. That was the beautiful thing about Kurt. Their marriage was a ten-year, unresolved crush. He'd respected that. He'd had a terminal crush on her riding, after all. It was the only time he said he thought of her as a man, kicking him straight in the solar plexus. On a horse, she could make him cry for joy just watching her. Out of the saddle she was just a woman and held no appeal for him. Their bed had just been for pillow talk and for sleep and now she was happy that way. She only wished Graham could feel the same.

'Penny for them?' Rory Midwinter waved his hand in front of Anke's glazed blue eyes, a giggling blonde on his arm. 'Or should that be Krone for them?'

'Or a Euro?' the blonde suggested.

'Anke Brakespear, meet Daffodil my girlfriend,' he introduced the blonde as Anke struggled to catch up. She had been so lost in thought, she wasn't sure quite what he had just said, but she had a nasty feeling it was something about being a crone. Compared to Daffodil, she certainly felt pretty ancient. The girl was ravishing.

'Lovely to meet you. She shook her hand politely. 'You must be Pheely's daughter?'

'We all have our crosses to bear,' Dilly sighed cheerfully, spotting her mother laying into chocolate mousse whilst shaking her hips to the steel band's final medley. 'If you'll excuse me I must give her a hug – I've been far too distracted with Rory to say hello properly. Great to meet you!'

'She's lovely.'

'Isn't she just?' Rory laughed indulgently as chocolate mousse went flying and mother, daughter and sibling bump danced around together.

Anke looked around for Graham again, but he was nowhere to be seen. Magnus's band was starting to set up on stage, nudging the steel drummers out of the way although they were valiantly trying to finish *Making Whoopee*. Several couples were dancing. She recognised predatory Pru Hornton with little Vere Peplow's face pressed into her flat chest, Spurs Belling with fiancée Ellen, and Sir St John and Lady Belling foxtrotting manfully through the *mêlée*.

'Is your sister still here?' she asked Rory.

'Pushed off, I'm afraid – leaving her designated driver behind. Good job Dilly has a car. She said something about not trusting the babysitter, but I think it must have been seeing Amos that sent her running home. And I bet she was too flustered to remember to ask you about Rio, wasn't she?'

'What about Rio?' Anke spotted Graham at last, talking to Carly's parents nearby. 'I've never been there.'

'The stallion, not the city,' he laughed. 'And I simply won't take no for an answer this time. You have to ride him this weekend.'

'I have house guests,' she apologised.

'So they can come and watch. Isn't that right, Graham!' Rory called him over. 'You can bring your guests up to Springlodes this weekend?'

'Already am,' Graham didn't look at Anke. 'Said I'd show them Dulston's tomorrow.'

Anke tried not to let her irritation show. That was why he'd been avoiding her. He'd arranged a day trip to look at tractors. It was hardly her idea of Cotswolds hospitality.

'I'm teaching Mo at lunch-time, so perhaps we should make it after that,' Rory suggested and then spotted Mo herself floating past some fruit trees, bloomers flashing. 'Talk of the devil. Mo, darling! Over here!' But she skipped away behind a rose arbour, heading for the gates. 'That's funny. I'm sure she saw us.'

'She probably wants to get home to Pod,' Anke suggested. 'He left a little while ago.'

'Strange couple.' Rory shook his head.

'What makes you say that?' asked Anke curiously, having also wondered at the chemistry between the two – so highly charged as to be luminous and yet so unstable with it.

But Graham was clapping his hands and suggesting some dancing, preventing Rory from answering. 'Steel band's about to wind up – shame to miss out and, take it from me, no one will want to dance to Magnus's ensemble. Debs, can I take you for a spin?' He offered his arm to Carly's mother and they headed towards the tent, Rory loping off happily to gather Dilly while their other friends paired off.

Trying not to feel left out because Graham had not asked her to dance Anke thought about Kurt once again and remembered the way that he had danced – so light on his feet and at one with the music. She had watched him for hours when they were married, her crush raging unabated.

Graham danced like a rugby player performing the haka. It made her smile, but it didn't quicken the heart – just the feet as one tried to avoid squashed toes. Perhaps she should be grateful that he was currently stamping on poor Debs' painted toenails.

And, as she watched Rory Midwinter dancing with his exquisite young lover, Anke saw another lovely, satisfying crush forming. He had the same passionate desire to ride better than anyone. Almost as young as her eldest son, he was as sexless as Kurt to her and therefore as infinitely desirable. She resolved to ride the stallion as soon as possible.

Giggling furiously as they abandoned pursuit of the shadowy figure of Pod beyond the gates and instead headed back to the marquee, Faith and Carly made for the Pimm's for a fuel stop.

'He is like *so* awesome, isn't he?' Faith gushed, grateful to be able to admit it out land at last.

'Kind of.' Carly spooned most of the strawberries into her glass.

'Hel-*lo*. What do you mean *kind* of?'

'I think your brother's like way more phat. Aghh!' She squealed as a sound assaulted her ears. Part wild animals trapped in tin drums, part the lunatics of Bedlam at supper-time, the noise was deafening and painful.

'What *is* that?' Carly yelled over the din.

Faith lip-read the question and mouthed back. 'Road Kill. Magnus's band. Phat-free.'

If she'd hoped her brother's music would be a passion-killer then she hadn't bargained for the enormity of Carly's crush. As the only two groupies at the party – and one of them there under duress – she and Carly stuck out all five songs in Road Kill's short set. Carly even had the nerve to call for an encore. There was nobody else left in the marquee. Outside, the party had thinned considerably.

'Where's the storm gone?' asked Faith, whose ears were still throbbing too much to discern thunder.

'It missed us.' Carly pointed out the faintest flash in the distance.

Faith let out a Pimm's hiccup. 'I wanted to dance in the rain.'

'That would have been spun. Where's your other love rival? The one with the blonde girlfriend?'

Faith gave the house and garden a quick, expert surveillance sweep. 'Think he's gone too.'

'Shame,' Carly said insincerely. 'Shall we like go back and congratulate Magnus?'

'For what? Bursting our eardrums and frightening off the only decent talent? You go. I'll catch you up. I *so* need the loo.'

Faith didn't need the loo. She needed to rush upstairs and kiss her Grand National photograph at the green spot of Bechers behind which lay Pod's face.

She met Graham coming down in the opposite direction.

'Having fun, love?'

'No,' she sneered. 'It's a rubbish party. Everyone's so *old* and Magnus's band were crap.'

Graham watched her retreating back with amusement. Things were looking up at last. Faith was answering back. She must feel better about herself.

The sight of Anke greeted him in the kitchen, wiping the smile from his face. His Great Dane. Guilt made him try to gather her straight into his arms, but she shrugged him off as usual.

'Things winding down out there?' he asked hopefully, looking out at the luminous marquee.

'Not at all,' she sighed. 'Your plan of frightening everyone off at eleven o'clock by letting Magnus and his band play has backfired, *kaereste*. They all escaped into the garden, got some fresh air, and are now dancing to clubbing tapes that someone had in their car. There must be fifty people still here. You ordered far too much drink.'

'We were warned that the locals like to party, love.'

'I am trying to allocate rooms, but I can't find our house guests to count them and calculate the sleeping arrangements.'

Graham flicked an awkward smile around his mouth. Sleeping in any sort of arranged manner was going to be impossible for him now. That he had corrupted their bed in their new house, with a party going on all around, seemed almost surreal already. Their soft-hard, zip-divided bed would never feel the same again. What had happened there would haunt his dreams. It was already haunting his waking thoughts.

'You'll love this,' Magnus cackled as he limped into the kitchen to raid the freezer for vodka. 'Two mini-vans have just turned up full of Wycks. They've come back from a family funeral wake especially. Saul Wyck has brought his decks and is setting up a trance zone.'

'Oh shit.' Graham turned to Anke desperately. 'What do we do?'

As always, his Great Dane hardly missed a beat before coming up with a solution. 'Power cut. There's a storm out there, after all – and we have no close neighbours so nobody will know that we have simply flicked the trip switch. We'll leave it half an hour so that the Wycks and their friends can have some fun and feel that coming here has been worthwhile – and then we'll cut the power. When everyone but our old friends has gone home, we'll put it on again.'

'You are magnificent.' Graham couldn't look her in the eye.

She was his rock and he had just played kiss-me-quick. Suddenly everything around him felt like castles in the sand and he was sick with nerves, certain that the tide was coming in.

'Stop that right this minute, you wicked jades!'

Pheely and Pixie, like naughty schoolgirls, had been caught sprinkling sensimilla on the last of the puddings.

They were rumbled by Til Constantine – arriving at her customary late witching hour. She confiscated their stash and sent them away, settling in a corner to smoke her new treat in a pipe and watch proceedings.

Til was a rare sight at parties, but this was one she couldn't afford to miss.

Unlike her sisters Bell and Truffle, Til's Constantine beauty had not been preserved. The tallest of the three, she had started out with the best of the blood – willowy, graceful, fine-boned and china-skinned. But years of living with the elements had cut her alabaster figurine to rough-hewn garden stonemasonry. She was as stoop-backed and angular as a heron, her eyes rheumy and watchful, her weathered skin liver-spotted and broken-veined. Her Constantine curls had succumbed to a wind-thatched mop of grey constantly flattered by the wearing of floppy hats. Tonight it was pinned up in a vague attempt at smartness. She was wearing her church best – an A-line green corduroy skirt covered with dog hairs, a creased blouse with jam stains on the cuffs, and her only pair of feminine shoes, bought for fifty pence from a charity shop twenty years earlier.

She watched the dancers as she smoked her pipe, disappointed not to see Diana amongst them. She had hoped to have a word, but her capricious niece had already left. And Til had a shrewd idea why.

Despite the dope, it unsettled her to see Amos in attendance. He stood in the shadows of the marquee, his eyes glittering angrily, unable to leave without Jacqui who refused to be dragged away from a rare social excursion.

Til beckoned him over. 'Not dancing?'

'I never dance.'

They watched together as Jacqui bopped with Sexton, Pixie, Pheely and Giles Hornton.

'Can't say I blame you. Dreadful exhibitionism these days. Whatever happened to the Gay Gordon?' She offered him her pipe.

He shook his head.

There was another long silence.

'She was here, Til.'

'I know.'

Sexton and Jacqui were doing some sort of bizarre 1970s dance that involved placing their hands on their hips and twisting their upper bodies around like animated urns. They stood out amid the thrashing bodies of Oddlode youth, mostly Wyck youth.

'You have to accept that she's back,' Til told Amos.

'Never,' he hissed. 'Never, never, never, never . . .'

The lights suddenly went out and the music stopped. Plunged into dark silence, everyone blanched as they heard the roars of thunder in the distance. The last of the huge citronella torches were lapping out a weak, fading light beyond the marquee walls. Then a great gust of wind extinguished all but one, its shadows chasing demons along the tent walls.

The ghosts were restless, Til realised. The party was over.

'You won't stir things, will you Amos?' she asked.

But he had gone.

Mo let herself into the cottage and flicked on a light, almost jumping out of her skin as Bechers shot out from behind the sofa and flew up one of the curtains, tail puffed.

Pod wasn't home.

She licked her lips nervously and went through to the kitchen to make herself some strong coffee but somewhere between filling the kettle and fetching a mug from a hook, she found herself clutching a glass of vodka which she knocked back in one.

No good. Her heart still jack-hammered.

She went upstairs to run herself a bath, but the immersion was switched off and the water was stone-cold. Instead, she rubbed herself down with a flannel and crawled into bed. Bathrooms weren't her favourite places right now, anyway. Her head was pounding.

It was the early hours before Pod came in. He smelled of pub and wet earth as he landed heavily in bed beside her, passing out before she had even lifted her head groggily from the pillow. She wondered if he had gone back to the party – or perhaps the party had moved on to the Lodes Inn for one of its legendary lock-ins? Wherever he had been, he'd got soaked through. His wet hair tickled her cheek. He'd probably fallen drunkenly in the duck pond.

Head pounding too much to care, she closed her eyes and tried to sleep.

Beside her, Pod lay awake. He had walked all the way to Gunning looking for answers. All he had found was a thunderstorm raging and a darkness so absolute that the woods had frightened him away.

Late that night, long after Anke and Graham had carefully gone to bed an hour apart and the caterers had packed up the last of the mess, the expensive marquee went up in flames.

Had it not been for the eagle eyes of local train-spotter and insomniac, Granville Gates, looking out for a rare late-night freight consignment in a nearby cutting, the house would undoubtedly have burned down while its drunken occupants slept.

The first fire-fighters on the scene could smell petrol before they had even started to quell the flames.

14

Mo and Pod woke to hung-over, half-asleep sex – uncommunicative, headachy, sweaty, laborious and yet strangely satisfying. Pod immediately fell back to sleep.

Mo found her eyes were trapped open.

She twisted and turned anxiously, thinking about Graham, thinking about Pod, thinking about Graham. She got up to shower and cry behind the noise of pump and running water. Guilt and adrenaline coursed through her, sounding louder in her ears than the rush of water around her. She knew she was in a mess. Her head was playing tricks on her. She felt guiltier that she'd had sex with Pod this morning than for seducing Graham last night. Why?

She closed her stinging eyes and saw Graham's sincere, cheeful blue gaze in her head. She just adored that direct expression, his forthright manner, his stupid jokes, and the certainty and dependability that he radiated.

Then Mo gasped in shocked recognition.

She was infatuated. She had a big, fat crush. She was falling in love.

Tears turned to besotted smiles and she hummed a few bars of *Summertime*.

She remembered the feel of him inside her, the amazed, enchanted expression on his face, the revelation, the eagerness and fervour . . . and the fear.

Suddenly Mo's eyes snapped open. She was drenched in a cold sweat of terror that numbed her happy glow and chilled the scalding water that hit her shoulders as she rubbed them angrily with soap.

What if Graham had been soft soaping her as surely as she was soaping herself now? What if all that tomb raider stuff was a total line? In the cold light of day, the deep recesses of sand-locked Egypt were hardly accessible, especially to a dreamy naiad applying creamy Crabtree and Evelyn to her foamy curves.

He was married. He had a family. He was safe – and that meant he played safe. He was almost twice her age, wealthy, a happy-go-lucky chancer and out of her league. She had just been a needy, greedy drunk who'd dropped her knickers at the perfect moment to make his party go with a bang.

She scrubbed until weals appeared on her skin, trying to clean herself of her dirty thoughts and her dirty behaviour. She had seduced a married man. However willing an accomplice he'd been, Mo had been the one to take advantage. Just because she had always lived her adult life as though she had nothing to lose, it didn't mean others could. And for all her dreamy ethics, Mo had a lot to lose. She had never really risked it before now.

She crawled back into bed, Bechers licking her ankles dry as she shook in fear, terrified of losing her tiny hold on recklessness.

For Mo, growing up had been all about responsibility. Since her mother's departure, and without a father featuring in her life, she had been responsible for her actions from early childhood. Her grandparents were kind, willing guardians but they had never assumed the role of parents. They had expected her to behave as an adult from the start – something Mo's mother had apparently never achieved. By twelve, Mo was expected to assume responsibility for her life almost as though she were a lodger – accounting for her expenses, cleaning her room and doing her own laundry, earning any 'treats' like ballet lessons or new clothes by performing chores.

Her rebellion had not been like her mother's. Mo was not a conventional rebel. For her there had been no arguing and fighting, playing truant from school, dabbling with drugs, falling pregnant as a teenager or running away to far-flung climes. She had been a model granddaughter, if a little 'offbeat' as they affectionately dubbed her. She was bright, academic, popular and appealingly whimsical. She had toed the line whilst crushing her toes *à pointe*, dreaming of the Royal Ballet. When that had fallen through, she had obediently moved to Plan B and trained to be a teacher. She wrote poetry and practised yoga. She was feminine and gentle and wonderful with children. She would, everyone said, make someone a lovely wife.

Yet, inside, her soul had roared with the need for a curious love. A love without responsibility; a love that took all responsibility from her.

It became her aim in life – consciously or unconsciously – to find a man who could take control, possess her totally and take all life's burdens on to his shoulders, was slavishly loyal and yet . . . couldn't give a damn. An irresponsible control freak.

And Pod had been it. Reckless to the point of feral, unworthy, undisciplined, deceitful, he'd sell his grandmother and gamble his last penny, but he would never leave Mo. He understood her need for undying love and total distrust. He was the ultimate mix of Irish fist and Scouse backhander. Old-fashioned, domineering and romantic as hell, he was her Blarney stone that gathered no moss. He was her rock who kept rolling. Living with him was living between a rock and a hard place, but life had never been easy for Mo – and she felt she had finally got what she wanted.

Recently, Pod had rocked her faith by taking irresponsibility too far and screwing up big time. Not content with playing around, playing the fool, playing fast and loose and playing people off against one another, he had played the ultimate joker and deliberately wrecked his career. She had been shaken by it, but she'd thought they were pulling through. Pod would never leave her, after all, and the deal swung both ways. He was keeping his head down; she was trying to be less knee-jerk. They had moved away and moved on.

Then last night – when the bad, mad Pod had come out to play in classic fashion – Mo had over-reacted. She had given into temptation. She had tried to out-bad him. Now she had to take responsibility for her own actions for the first time in years. Big time.

Graham was *her* mess. Her beautiful; lovable mess. He was a rock that never rolled. He was as still and as enticing and as calm as a rock pool – the sort every little girl longed to gaze into, clutching her net in the hope of catching something. He wasn't going to go anywhere, but he was teeming with life. Mo had wanted to sit beside him and watch him for ever, but instead she had been stupidly impetuous and dived in.

His instant ability to disarm her was unnerving. After twenty-five years on the planet without one, she suddenly wanted a father more than anything. She wanted to be taken care of by an expert, not an untrustworthy tyro. She wanted en suites and big cars and a kitchen the size of a school netball pitch. She wanted a rock the size of Gibraltar looking after her. Last night, she felt like she'd come home.

Now she was a runaway once more. A near-orphan who had been rejected by both her parents – a father who had never known her and a mother who had decided not to get to know her. She was familiar with rejection, and avoided it at all costs. Why take a lover who could never love her?

She turned to look at Pod, stubble-chinned and long-lashed, breathing deeply into the pillow beside her. The unfaithful bastard she had loved most of her adult life.

Graham was unfaithful, too. But he wasn't a bastard. She couldn't shake that thought from her head. She knew she was riding for a fall.

She had to stop plummeting right now – before she landed up to her neck in love. Then she closed her eyes and groaned as she remembered she really *was* riding that day. Falling off was pretty much guaranteed.

She had dropped back into a fitful sleep when Pod got up to get ready for work at Gunning, whistling cheerfully through the cottage, slurping tea, chatting to Bechers and gathering his jeans and work boots. But Mo snapped her eyes open as she heard him pick up her denim cut-offs from the floor and start to go through the pockets.

'What are you looking for?'

'Car keys.'

She propped herself up on one shoulder. 'You can't take it – I need it.'

'But, queen – I start work in half an hour.'

'And it's my car. Take the push bike.'

Mo would not normally make a stand like this. Both were wincing from hangovers – Mo twitchily and grumpily, Pod with ebullient denial. Both registered the moment and recognised in the same split-second that they were too weak to fight it out. The sea change in their relationship was turning tides on them so fast that they were struggling just to stay afloat.

Pod opened his mouth to argue and then closed it again, face darkening to a thundercloud. Saying nothing, he slammed out of the house.

Sitting up in bed and drawing back the curtains, Mo watched him cycling away, hunched over the handlebars as he raced towards his new play-pen with its misanthropic estate manager and its myths and mysteries.

Last night, she had let a stranger inside her. More than that, she had coaxed, teased and ultimately quick-tricked a stranger inside her – into her head, her heart, her body. Yet he had felt far more familiar to her than Pod.

Last night, Pod had let a stranger inside him. Again. Breaking her head, her heart, her body. To Pod, strangers were his common landscape.

'I love him.' She looked out – the bicycle long gone. 'I love him, whoever he is. I never want to know him. If I know him, he'll go away.'

A fire engine was driving through the village from the Lower Oddford road. Mo watched it pass and remembered Pod telling her the story of Firebrand, the hell-raising Sarsden who had burned his wife and her lover in their bed. Pod had joked that if she was ever unfaithful to him, he would burn her in the cottage.

She pulled the sheet tightly around her and whimpered.

15

Mo's second riding lesson was not as successful as her first. Still fighting demons as well as a hangover, she was so distracted and highly strung that even Rory's laziest nanny of a pony picked up on her mood and misbehaved, planting his hooves and refusing to move in the sand-school no matter how hard she banged her legs against his sides.

Storms still rumbled around in the distance and the humid air was sticky with flies and thistledown.

Rory seemed hardly to notice Mo's discomfort as he led her around, chatting about the party the night before, occasionally giving her a few words of instruction. 'That band was bloody awful – Carnage was it called?'

'Road Kill, I think.'

'Diabolical. We all ran for cover. Had you left by then?'

'Not sure.'

'You disappeared all of a sudden – heels down. Dilly wanted to talk to you some more. She thinks you're incredibly cool. She's popped down to Oddlode to see her mum this morning. Shorten your reins. Talking of which, Pheely was on good form last night. Did you see Aunt Til giving her a ticking off for trying to spike the food, or had you gone? I think you had. Didn't we see you sneaking –'

'Who's Aunt Til?'

'You'll love her. Famous local character. Straighten your back. That's better. I must say, Anke throws a fantastic party – boy, did she work hard. Graham was hardly much help. Spent all night chasing skirt.'

'W-what?'

'Something tells me he'll be giving Giles Hornton a run for his money when it comes to adultery. Wrap your legs tighter around him, atta girl.'

'Sorry?'

'Graham. He's an opportunist. Try to thrust in time with him. Yes, poor Anke's married to a total rogue if you ask me. Dilly said he was positively leering at her.'

Not as much as my boyfriend was, Mo thought murderously, grabbing hunks of mane as she tried to stay on. She was convinced that Pod had cornered Dilly in the bathroom.

'I think Graham's quite fun.'

'That's what *you* might think.' He moved her hands back into the correct position as he walked alongside. 'And you might also imagine he wouldn't stray from someone as gorgeous as Anke but, believe me, there are a lot of predatory women around here. Put your legs back a bit and close them tight or he'll try it on.'

'Are we talking about Graham or the horse here?'

He whooped with delight. 'The horse, dumbass. Although Graham tried it on with you, too – I saw him. Don't deny it just because you think it's innocent fun. Obviously you're far too young and pretty to fall for those old lines of his. You played him like a pro, darling. Rather clever commandeering your own personal champagne waiter like that. Shame about the shirt.'

Mo reddened and said nothing.

'He's a prat,' Rory said emphatically.

Because he harboured a long-term crush on Anke that had germinated in childhood, nobody could match up to his ice maiden in Rory's eyes. She embodied female perfection and Graham – as a less than perfect male – fell far short of the equivalent mark. Rory had always been envious of Kurt Willis. However famously camp and bitchy he was, he rode brilliantly and had won Anke's heart. Rory felt he could relate to him in a strange way. Despite a long line of the horse world's many homos having tried to persuade him otherwise, Rory wasn't gay, but he *was* camp and bitchy – and he longed to impress Anke. He was also a snob. Graham was, as far as he was concerned, a complete oik and thoroughly undeserving of such a goddess.

'*You* might think all that flirting he does is just funny because you'd never dream of fancying him, Mo,' he explained easily, 'but there are women I know in Oddlode who'd take all that phoney charm seriously and before he knows what's happening he'll be bedded as securely as a cheap perennial. Then word'll get around, they'll all start taking cuttings and he'll be in every bed in Oddlode. It happens every time. Graham Brakespear is just the type.'

Mo swayed in the saddle, suddenly seeing four ears pricked in front of her. 'Surely if he was the philandering type he would have strayed before?'

'Who's to say he hasn't?' Rory, who loved nothing more than gossiping with his clients, relished the thought of scandal, especially if it brought the fantasy of seducing Anke within reach. Teaching Mo was going to be a treat, he decided. 'He was unfaithful to his first wife, wasn't he? Those friends of theirs who came down from Essex were a bawdy-looking lot. I bet their idea of hors d'oeuvre is a bowl of car keys on the smoked-glass coffee-table. Perhaps that's why he and the family had to move away? Okay, I think you should take this a bit faster. If he digs his heels in, try to kick him on and keep your butt plugged in, okay? Trot on.'

'Sure,' Mo said weakly and promptly fell off.

Refusing to listen to her suggestion that she have a go another day, Rory legged her back on and started leading her around again. 'The secret is not to give up. Old Worzel here's had lots of pretty girls fall for him when they get their leg over and he tries to put on the brakes. You have to show him who's in charge.'

Mo looked at him askance. This whole lesson had been strangely cryptic. Was Rory trying to tell her something? Oh, Christ. Did he know what she had done last night?

But he was just grinning up at her with his sleepy grey eyes creased against the sun. 'C'mon. Kick on. You pay me to torture you like this, remember?'

After another twenty minutes, the hangover and her mood started to lift as she found herself bouncing along in time with Worzel at last, her legs no longer flapping against his side like ribbons in a breeze but working on the girth in a way that actually made him move forwards and listen to her.

'Terrific! You'll have this licked in no time.' Rory patted the grey pony's neck. 'Ten goal polo here you come.'

'Ha ha.' Mo slid stiffly out of the saddle and landed on the pitted sand.

'Don't let the fall put you off,' he told her. 'You're good. You could take this thing a long way. And I don't say that to many of my clients . . . any of them, in fact.'

'You really think so?' She was so rarely told that she was good at anything – apart from Pod telling her she was good at sex – that Mo felt ebullient.

He nodded. 'Does Pod know your guilty secret yet?'

'What?' she squeaked, hanging on to the stirrup strap to stay upright.

Rory tilted his head. 'That you're learning to ride?'

'Oh, no,' She felt her red face burning even more. 'Not yet.'

'Why don't you want him to know?'

'He just never wanted me to learn to ride. Probably afraid I'd get hurt,' she lied.

214 Fiona Walker

'You can tell him you're perfectly safe with me – you took your first tumble today and – see – not a mark on you!'

'Yeah, you're right.' She forced a smile. 'I'll tell him this week.'

She knew she'd just taken a far more painful fall than the ungainly topple from saddle to sand. She had just dropped out of her stupid Cloud Nine daydreams and landed on the hard, earthy truth with such a bump her head reeled.

Rory said Graham was a phoney; just the type for adultery; as opportunist as all those rich, roving Cotswolds husbands who had bored of their wives and wanted some extra-curricular fun. She must be so naïve. She hadn't seen last night like that, but then again she didn't really know Graham at all.

She knew Pod better than anyone – good Pod and bad Pod. She needed to keep her dreams pinned on her irresponsible control freak. They were rapidly coming unstuck, and she had glued her hopes to a stranger passing by. She couldn't believe she had been so stupid. She just had to pretend last night never happened. It was the only way.

'I'll tell Pod I'm learning to ride,' she repeated. She had to get some sort of reaction out of him. Knowing Pod, admitting that she had drunkenly seduced Graham Brakespear but would never do it again would cause less upset than revealing that she was learning to ride and wanted to keep on doing it until she could gallop as fast as he could.

'You do that.' Rory was running up the stirrups and loosening the pony's girth. 'I'm not letting you give this up. You're showing far too much promise.' He glanced at his watch. 'Damn. Running behind as usual. Anke will be here any minute and Rio is still turned out in High Hedge.'

'Anke's coming here?' Mo squeaked.

'Yeah – I finally talked her into trying the stallion last night. She gave me some pish about needing to stay in Oddlode today to look after her guests and clear up after the party. But then it turned out that Graham had already arranged to bring their house guests up here to look at Dulston's, so she said they'd pop by the yard.'

'With the whole family?'

'And their guests.' He pulled a face, assuming her shocked tone meant that she was sympathising with his plight. 'Much as I adore Anke, I could do without them. I hope Dilly gets back in time to be coffee monitor. Bloody Diana has buggered off as per usual. Why don't you stay on and watch?'

'No, I have to get back – sorry,' she said, hurrying bow-leggedly to fetch her bum bag so that she could pay Rory for her lesson. 'Thanks so much for that.'

'Same time next week?'

'Sure.'

'I can do a midweek lesson too if you like?' He tried not to sound too eager. Business was very bad right now.

'I start teaching at the school next week.'

'I do evenings.'

'I'll bear it in mind.' She headed hastily towards her car, but it was too late. Tyres were spitting gravel as they sped along the drive towards the yard. Mo braced herself, but it was just Diana's Audi.

'Just the person I was hoping to see!' she yelled from the window as she parked at a rakish angle, Radio Four blaring, her kids screaming at one another on the seats behind and Hally barking furiously from the hatchback boot. 'Bloody Tim still hasn't sent through the children's school fees and I am desperate. How do you rate the chances of a place for them at Oddlode?'

'Practically nil.' Mo hung her head, gripping her own car's door handle and longing to make her escape.

Diana cut her engine, silencing one of the three background noises, at least. 'Oh, come on darling – I'm sure we can do better than that. Have you explained who I am?'

'I don't think it made a lot of difference, I'm afraid,' Mo lied, remembering Anne Chambers' tight perm practically unravelling at the prospect of taking on any Lodes valley children of Constantine heritage. 'It's just too late in the day – the classes are all full, and even if more space could be found, applications for places have to go through the governors and the PTA. There's already a waiting list. I'm really sorry.'

Diana's eyes narrowed behind her dark glasses and she pulled a stitch from her leather steering wheel. 'Never mind. Thank you for trying. I knew I should have gone to the head direct.'

'You did.'

Two dark eyes studied her over the rims of the designer shades. 'Nothing gets past you, does it, Mo?' She was smiling mischievously, but there was something about Diana's tone that made Mo start.

'I'm really sorry,' she said again, wishing she wasn't such a wimp. 'They're great kids.'

Shrugging apologetically, Mo climbed into her car at the same time as Digby finally managed to pour the dog dribble he had been collecting in his empty Cornetto packaging on to his sister's head and Mim retaliated by garotting him with his seatbelt until he turned puce. As Mo reversed past it, the Audi was shuddering on its axles.

When Rory watched Anke riding Baron Areion, he came his closest to weeping since breaking his femur in a point-to-point at eighteen. It was so breathtaking that he could only snatch a few molecules of air through his nostrils and drag short, joyful gasps through his lips. He knew he could learn more about riding from watching her for five minutes than a year of saddle-sore schooling on his pupils' no-hoper mounts. Poetry in motion was prose in transit compared to this.

Talking of Transits, Graham was. The man loved the sound of his own voice, Rory realised. He was talking of all forms of transport, mechanical haulage and agricultural machinery. He hadn't stopped talking since he arrived with his unruly mob of hung-over friends and family. First he had talked about the marquee at Wyck Farm going up in flames the night before. He had talked arson and arsonists, fire investigators, incendiary devices, accelerators, retardants and extinguishers. Now he was talking about his plans for Dulston's.

'Secret of good business round here is kissing – keeping it simple,' he droned in his cheery, jokey northern monotone as they all leaned over the manège rails. 'James Dulston diversified too much – taking on contract work and machine hire, servicing wrecked old tractors for tinpot smallholders. You have to sell the shiny stuff and get the profit margins right. Raise your profile – be a big presence at the county shows. Like I say, keep it simple.'

'So you kiss a lot do you, Graham?' Rory snapped, unable to concentrate with the background distraction – rather like filling in entry forms while Sharon was watching Coronation Street.

'Eh?'

'My stepfather kissed a lot of local arse and he still lost the business.'

'Don't take this the wrong way, lad, but your stepfather Dulston had been running that yard into the ground for a long time. It needs a radical overhaul.'

'It needs torching,' Rory muttered, gazing at Anke. 'Your wife is the most amazing rider I have ever seen.'

'She's not half bad.' Graham kept his eyes on the sand at his feet. He had hardly spoken to Anke all morning. His mouth didn't work when she was around him and his heart curdled in confusion.

'No point talking to Graham about dressage,' Faith sneered from further along the manège rails. 'The only reason he and Mum married was because she said she was looking for more engagement.'

Beside her, Carly sniggered delightedly. 'Engagement – like a horse's hindquarters are engaged. I get it.'

'Yeah, yeah,' Faith tittered, dragging the joke out to its butt end. 'Mum thought she was getting engagement in a ring, not an engagement ring. She was, like *so* disappointed.'

To Faith's surprise, her stepfather didn't react as he normally would, with his pompous, resentful stepfather act thinly veiled as caring but firm parenthood. He simply stomped off to take a look at Overlodes' ancient tractor, his Essex cronies shambling noisily after him, still talking all things motorised. The wives stayed behind to pretend to watch Anke while they secretly threw admiring glances at Rory.

Faith found that, today, she could speak almost normally when Rory was in her presence – in fact she felt almost vivacious. Seeing his girl-friend with her hand trapped in his trousers last night had dampened her crush enough to allow her to feel cool around him, particularly with her best friend at her side. She and Carly had stayed up all night talking and had agreed that Pod Shannon was the sexier of the two, and that Rory – whilst admittedly looking like the lead singer from Busted – was too arrogant for Faith to devote a true love crush upon. Pod was the real deal. They had both said a prayer to the sacred Grand National poster that morning.

With Carly at her side, Faith felt her self-confidence rushing back. She watched her mother with admiration, but also with a critical eye.

Rio moved like ten horsepower in one, springing from the ground with every stride so that he powered and floated and danced around the arena in just the simplest of working trots. He was brimming with energy and talent that threatened to explode at any moment, his black coat coal-bright with sweat, his eyes lined with white new moons of temperament, his nostrils flaring as angry red as fighting jets' after-burners and his tail twitching like a dominatrix's cat'o'nine tails.

'Try more transitions,' Faith suggested as her mother passed.

'Thanks,' Anke laughed. 'It's like sitting on a volcano. Has he been ridden much since he got here?'

'Nope.' Rory grinned.

'Before that?'

'You'd have to ask Di. But, as far as I'm aware, he's only had a couple of girls sit on him briefly at his old yard in recent months. He was a bit much for them.'

'Telling me.' Anke gritted her teeth and applied the Olesen glue as Rio let out a flurry of bucks and shied away from Graham and his cronies who had started up the tractor.

'Cut that out!' Rory yelled in their direction at the same time as Anke snarled the same words to Rio. Both husband and stallion complied irritably and Rory looked up to find Anke throwing a swift smile in his direction as she sat the power trot once more.

She looked like a young girl. She was the Olympic gold medallist he had fallen in love with, the glorious Danish ice maiden whose *Horse and Hound* cover had attracted so much media interest that she had modelled for *Tatler*, received proposals from oil magnates and been fêted on television across Europe.

Diana could no longer spy from her bedroom window. She had to get a closer look. This was simply awe-inspiring. It was beyond humbling, beyond humiliating. It was almost supernatural in its beauty.

'She's so amazing, your mum,' Carly sighed at Faith's side.

'You're not wrong.' Faith felt hot tears of pride spring to her eyes. Anke had refused to sit on a horse since retiring Heigi. This moment meant so much more to the Great Dane – and to Faith – than anyone realised. She was watching her mother reborn. She hadn't seen her so happy since Kurt.

'Try walk-canter again,' she called out in a stupidly choked voice. 'Flex him to the outside more like you tried before. I think that worked better.'

'You're right, *kaereste*,' Anke called delightedly. 'He feels tight on the inside. See this?'

Off they launched, like an expert test pilot at the controls of a jump jet with three times the power. She made it look simple, Rio made it look poetic, but the dynamic was a delicate trip-wire of skill negotiating with sheer force.

'She's awesome,' Rory breathed, remembering why his teenage crush had wiped him out for fumbles with teenage pony-clubbers at barn dances.

'You have my permission to adore her.' Dilly appeared at his shoulder. 'Just promise you will never touch.'

'Can I pat her on the back?' Rory hooked his arm around her and drew Dilly into a long kiss.

'As long as you are both fully clothed and wearing gloves.'

'Agreed.'

'Wow.' Dilly was watching Anke over his shoulder.

He turned to watch too. 'Exactly.'

Unaware of the admiration she was drawing, Anke was just delighted to have accidentally stumbled upon something that reminded her of her youth.

Sitting on Rio was as re-energizing as any drug she had ever dabbled with. It was heaven.

Track left, trot. Boomph.

Falling in love with Kurt.

Circle, cross diagonal with extended strides, change rein, canter. Wham.

Falling in love with Heigi.

Circle. Back to walk. Halt. Rein back. Canter again. Whoomph.

'Fantastic!' cried an approving, husky whoop.

Falling in love with Rory.

Canter to halt to canter. Back to trot, serpentine. Perfection.

Falling in love with Baron Areion. Rio.

The horse was phenomenal, undervalued and untrained. Anke was convinced he was about to sprout wings and fly her away. He was amongst the best – if not *the* best – she had ever sat on. He must have been produced somewhere exceptional – she could only think of two or three yards on the Continent capable of breeding a horse with such talent, and she knew she would have heard of him had he come from there. She felt like a prospector discovering gold long after retiring from California to the sleepy Montana mountains. And she could smell gold. This was an International horse, possibly even an Olympic horse.

Yet when she finally walked him down to relax his muscles, steam rising from his coat, all she would say to her audience was, 'He's bloody unfit.'

Rory was crestfallen until Faith sidled up to him. 'She *must* be completely blown away. Mum *never* swears.'

He looked up at Faith as though trying to remember who she was. Then, looking from her to Anke and back again, a great white hope smile spread across his face and lit halogens in his grey eyes. 'You really think she likes him? Think she might want to ride him again?'

'Definitely.' Faith nodded. 'The horse is something else. Mum could make him worth more than a Lottery win. She was offered a million pounds for Heigi once.'

'You don't say?' He kissed her on both cheeks. 'You are gorgeous, Fay.'

'Faith,' she muttered as he bounded away, but it didn't matter.

Flip, flop, leap, bang. Faith's heart somersaulted in delight.

A night without sleep favouring Pod over Rory had just been wiped out. She was in love with Rory again. Even though she hated him – especially as he went straight on to kiss Dilly with obvious tongues in play – she couldn't count him out of the running. He had just landed ahead of Pod on the sacred Bechers poster and was already out of shot, galloping towards Foinavon.

'He is so gorgeous,' breathed Carly, meaning Rio.

'Totally,' breathed Faith, meaning Rory. It didn't even matter that her mother had forgotten to suggest she have a sit on Rio. That could wait. She was far too emotionally overwrought to ride. Right now, she was seriously and completely in love. She had to make plans, starting with a makeover. She couldn't wait to grow out the ginger frizz disaster and aim for long blonde curls just like Dilly's. That was a great look.

'About bloody time!' cried Graham as Anke slipped out of the saddle. 'Can we go and look at my toys now?' His tone was peevish and tetchy.

'Sure,' she said soothingly, only mildly concerned at his crabby, childish mood. 'I just want a word with Diana.'

Anke was dying to ask her where Rio came from, but Diana got in first as usual.

'I heard about the fire – dreadful. Glad nobody was hurt. Did it do much damage to the house?'

'Only a little smoke damage. I wanted to ask –'

'And they really think it's deliberate?'

'Well, it's too early to say, but there were some lighter fuel cans nearby and the police say it could have been teenagers from the estate, although I –'

'Little louts. Such a lovely party, too. I had a high old time. Shame to have something like that happen. Do they think it could be the same lot who set fire to the Plough?'

'I really don't know.' Anke sighed as Sharon appeared from the American barn and, hissing under her breath about leaving sweaty horses standing about to get cramp, she took the stallion from her to hose him down in the wash box.

'Now you must tell me more about that horse.' At last Anke managed to get to her point. 'Is he Hanovarian? I can't see a brand.'

'Thoroughbred,' Diana muttered, obviously reluctant to change topic.

'Surely not!' Anke, who knew her horses well, had never seen a thoroughbred like it. 'But he has so much substance – and his paces are far too elevated.'

'I should know,' Diana insisted. 'I worked in bloodstock long enough. They just don't breed them like it any more. Very old, rare blood-line.'

'What's his registered name again?'

Diana eyed her suspiciously. 'Baron Areion.'

She was agog. 'Where did you get him from?'

The answer baffled her:

'He was given to me before he was born, darling. I should never have opened him up. He was the first ghost.'

She disappeared back into the house leaving her children trying to murder one another in an abandoned poly-tunnel in the garden, armed with a dibber and a piece of broken cucumber cloche, while Hally jumped backwards and forwards over the little plastic tent trying to join in the game.

Rory found his sister's reaction highly amusing. 'That's Constantine inbreeding for you. Welcome to the family. Nice horse; shame about its birthright.'

'I'm sure Areion is the son of Poseidon,' Anke remembered.

'Never heard of him. Was he a famous racehorse?'

'He was the god of the sea in Greek mythology,' she smiled. 'Like Neptune.'

That afternoon, Anke had a good excuse to check up on her father, who was wandering around in his shop wearing pyjamas.

'I've lost my alarm clock,' he complained.

'It's not going to be down here is it, *Fader*?' She led him upstairs to his flat where Toppi, the flatulent West Highland terrier, was laying into the bag of food she had brought from home.

'Are you tired? Is that why you're going to bed early?'

'What?'

'It's four o'clock in the afternoon.'

'Is it?'

Finding him some clothes, she asked about the mythical horse, Areion.

'Ah yes! "Areion of the black mane".' His mind was on razor-sharp form with Greek legend. 'He was the result of a rather unfortunate union between Poseidon and his own sister. Randy so and so, Poseidon – lusted after the poor girl. Demeter was her name: goddess of fertility. She tried to hide herself away by turning into a mare and running with the Arcadia herd, but her brother tracked her down and transformed himself into a stallion so that he could mount her. The colt Areion was their son. He was the fastest horse in Arcadia. Heracles raced him, I believe, and then gave him to the king of Argos. Areion saved the king's life by carrying his wounded body all the way from the battlefield at Thebes to the safety of Athens. Magnificent creature.'

'He certainly is,' Anke smiled, holding out a pair of trousers.

'Why on earth should I wear those? It's bedtime.'

'If it's bedtime perhaps you would like me to run you a bath?' she suggested, seizing the opportunity to freshen him up at least. He smelled worse than Toppi.

'I had one earlier.' He waved a dismissive hand. 'What are you doing here, anyway? Are you and Kurt competing nearby?'

'I am married to Graham now, *Fader*, remember? We live in Oddlode. We had a party last night and you came along. I brought you home afterwards.' And put you in your pyjamas, she recalled; he clearly hadn't remembered to change out of them.

'I went to a dreadful party last night – nothing to do with you. The Wycks family hosted it at their farm. There was a fire.'

'No, *Fader*, the fire started after you had come home.'

'I was there. I saw it.'

Anke realised that he must be thinking about the barbecue. She decided not to fox his poor muddled mind any more. He was obviously having a bad day.

'Let's get you to bed then.'

'Demeter bore Poseidon a daughter in human form as well as the colt,' he told her as he clambered under the covers – a curious reverse-roles bedtime story that made Anke want to curl up with Toppi at the foot of his bed. 'Desponia – or some call her Despina, like the star. Goddess of horses. A friend of mine wrote a very interesting thesis about her, making a convincing link to Artemis. He was quite certain the two were in cahoots.'

'Artemis?' Anke knew enough about myths to catch her breath. 'Goddess of the hunt? As in Diana?'

'Yes – Artemis, Diana – one and the same.' He closed his eyes. 'I suppose goddesses of horses and hunting being friends makes sense in this neck of the woods – woods, ha!' He was drifting off now, enjoying his own private jokes. 'Diana, goddess of the hunt and of woods and of the moon . . . *the moon, governess of floods, pale in her anger, washes all the air . . .*' His wandering mind started to quote *A Midsummer Night's Dream*: '. . . *The seasons alter: hoary-headed frosts fall in the fresh lap of the crimson rose . . .*'

As he started to snore, Anke kissed his cheek and let herself out.

16

A letter from their father to Mim and Digby arrived by registered post on the Monday of the week that they were due to start school. There was a cheque in it for the exact amount to cover one term's fees at Woldcote House. Typical of Tim to leave it so late. Diana knew it was deliberate, as was the ghastly letter which she was forced to read aloud.

'*My sweet darlings . . . words cannot express how much I miss my little tigress and my wolf cub. You are my entire world and I think of you both as I wake, as I clean my teeth and then as I eat my breakfast, and for every minute of the busy day until I fall exhausted into bed to dream about you. Your father is on a very special secret mission which keeps him from you, but he knows that Mummy tells you every day how much he loves you . . .*'

As part of his officer training, Tim had specialised in interrogation techniques, in ways of breaking down the enemy to confess to anything, bending them to your will and manipulating their thoughts through programming. This letter was pure programming, and Diana knew it as she read it as flatly and boringly as she could. But she could not deny her children a single word that their father had given them. He had not called, let alone visited, since their departure from London. They were left in tears after the letter, bleating desperately for their father, breaking Diana's heart. She was in tears, too, but she managed to wipe them up with her cuffs before they were spotted. Tim had not spared a word for her, just employed her for his propaganda.

Diana took Hally for a walk afterwards to clear her head, leaving the children with Sharon who was happy to earn extra money on her day off by looking after them. They adored Sharon, despite her bellicose, big-bellied bullishness and the fact that she refused to let them try to kill one another or watch violent television. She even made them ride their ponies. Diana found Sharon rather intimidating, but was forever grateful to be able to call upon her services.

She cut across the Prattle and plunged into a tiny crevice between the long grasses that marked the start of the little-used footpath into the valley. Most walkers preferred to use one of the two big bridleways that were ancient cart-tracks into the valley, deeply carved from the marl and easy-going because they were wide and level. Diana loved this path for its secrecy and angry refusal to succumb to passing feet. Each year it sprang back ferociously, more densely overgrown, rutted and impassable than previous years. Ahead of her, Hally bounded through the thick growth, eyes watering as her face was lashed with sharp stalks.

As soon as the valley opened up in front of her, Diana waded off the path to a small clearing by a badger's sett and, letting Hally press her snorting nose into it, she tried to form a plan.

She pulled her mobile from her pocket and texted Pod, although she knew she shouldn't.

Running out of marching. Fresh supplies?

Then she smirked at the thought that she might be breaking into Tim's cheque to refresh her cocaine supply. Actually she wasn't running out at all. She hadn't touched any of the gram she had bought, but she needed an excuse.

A text came straight back.

Steady on. Colombia doesn't work that fast. You've some habit. Leave it with.

Diana scrolled up and down the message. No '*queen*'. She had to be queen again.

She sliced her way through the undergrowth back on to the path once more and walked to the first stream before tracing its bank back towards the easterly of the two bridleways which met her path just below the old beer garden. That was when she looked across to the scarred remains of the village pub and growled furiously.

By the time she returned to Overlodes, she was out-running Hally for once. She was on a mission. The scaffolding had already being erected around the Phoenix as she thought of it – the Plough was razed and the New Inn sounded too erroneous for such an old local Sarsden folk-tale. Tony Sixsmith certainly didn't hang around, and she was a competitive girl.

She looked up the number in Rory's address book.

'It's Diana.'

She could hear a sharp, critical breath being sucked through teeth at the other end. 'You took your time. I had hoped for at least a telephone call by now.'

'Well, here it is. I've been busy.'

'Come and see me.'

'I can't.'

'Too frightened to set foot on Gunning land?'

'It's not that,' she lied. 'Like I say, I'm very busy.'

'Well, so am I. We'd better get to the point.'

'You can have him.'

There was a long pause.

'Did you hear me? I said you can have him.'

'I heard. What do you want in return?'

'Horses. Ordinary horses.'

'I'll call Piers Cottrel. And Diana?'

'Yes.'

'You're right to keep away from Gunning land. You wouldn't be safe here.' The line went dead.

Diana chewed at a nail and closed her eyes tightly, refusing to cry. What she was doing was right. She knew it was right.

She jumped nervously as her phone bleeped with a text message.

Wanna march, queen?

She smiled with relief.

Dress uniform or battledress? she texted back before realising that she had spent far too long married into the army. He wouldn't understand.

It didn't matter. His reply made her smile even wider.

Tight dress, no knickers.

What she was doing was wrong, but she didn't care. She needed cheering up.

When? she keyed far too eagerly before pressing Send.

He took several minutes to text her back.

Sweet as the moment when the Pod went pop came the reply at last.

Diana scowled and then laughed as it was followed by: *Soon, queen. Very soon. Pod's popping.*

At Oddlode primary school, the pre-term staff briefing had been a stodgy and terse affair until the arrival of Graham Brakespear in a shirt as bright as the Year Five paintings adorning the walls. Mo very nearly let slip a shriek of excitement and alarm as he manfully strode into the room and set his big blue gaze upon Anne Chambers.

'Madam, may I have a word?' The Lancashire accent was as creamy as a purring cat's whiskers. There was something heraldic about his Viking blonde hair, broad shoulders and emblematic patterned shirt.

Anne Chambers felt a couple of curls spring loose as she beckoned him through to her office.

It took only a few minutes of private consultation for him to persuade her to take Chad in three days' time – adding Diana Lampeter's children as an afterthought just to see how far he could push it. It was a total pushover. Anne Chambers made the delighted announcement that there would be three new pupils added to the roll to her astonished staff as soon as they re-emerged, before introducing Graham as 'a certain forerunner for next year's Chairman of Governors'.

'Don't be daft, love.' He gave her one of his cheery, flirty winks. 'It's been my life's ambition to be milk monitor and I'll accept nothing less. Great to see you all,' he told the teaching staff, having lightened their day no end. 'Fantastic little school, this. I hear the teachers here are second to none.'

With barely a glance at Mo, he swept out again, leaving her hollow with anti-climax.

But the forty colourful roses delivered to her door by an agog Pixie that afternoon helped fill the gap. They were signed 'your en-suitor'. Mo hugged them tightly to her chest, inadvertently breaking the stems and cutting herself to shreds with happiness.

'You are a lucky girl.' Pixie smiled wisely.

Mo was too overawed to worry that her blue-haired florist might know who they were from.

But Pixie was as innocent as the rest of the village who had witnessed the delivery. 'We work with an internet florist,' she said. 'I do hope you appreciate how much that young chap of yours adores you. I had to cut everything we had – he asked for red, but I'm afraid we only had twenty stems.'

Glad Tidings and her army were out in force by the post office stores, taking in the scene.

'Lucky Helena,' sighed Kath Lacey. 'Do you think they're from a fan?'

'More likely from Brad Pitt,' said Phyllis Tyack, who had just watched her son's DVD of *Fight Club* and was still in deep shock.

Gladys was lost for words for once as her eyes misted over. Her admiration for Pod grew with every day. She was going to have to bake another cake. He was the most welcome addition to the village in years. If it weren't for the dreadful Irish accent that he kept telling her was from Liverpool, he could have been born here.

'Get out from behind my *Viburnum farreri* right away, you little trespasser!' Til Constantine demanded in her growling bass as Pod sneaked along her garden perimeter.

'Sorry, pet. I was a bit lost.' He emerged sheepishly, his hair full of small white flowers.

She eyed him wisely as he dusted himself down, an overweight terrier barking at her feet. 'We've met. You're Amos's new work hand. We shared a flagon or two, as I recall.'

'Yeah.' He remembered little of the first, and only, night he and Amos had spent drinking together but a mad old woman had certainly been involved and she fitted this description – tall, stooped, clever-eyed and slightly scary.

'In that case, you are very lost,' she was saying. 'Shut up, Ratbag.' She waggled a plastic overshoe at her yapping dog. 'Amos is clearing the old Furze Hollow plantation today.'

'Yeah, I know. I've been there all day. Thought I'd have a little look around on my way home and – got lost.'

'Hmm.' A sceptical eyebrow shot up. 'Were you looking for anything in particular?'

'No – just having a shufty. Fantastic old woods here.'

'You are not in the woods here, boy. You are in my garden.'

'So I am.' He smiled the Pod Shannon smile.

She seemed hardly to notice it as she marched past him and closed the open garden gate that led to a small natural meadow and on to the woods. Then she turned back and sucked in her cheeks.

'You used to be a jockey, am I right?'

'Yeah.'

'Please don't say "yeah". It is terribly common and sets my teeth on edge. If you cannot say "yes" or "no" in a civilised manner then please just shake your head.'

Pod gaped at her in amazement.

'You were rather good, weren't you?'

He shrugged, making her tut under her breath. Shrugging was clearly as bad as saying 'yeah'.

'In that case, may I offer you some nettle tea and scones with hedgerow preserve? I want to pick your brains. In return, I shall promise not to mention your homeward bound diversion to Amos.'

'Have you been thieving flowers from over Gladys's garden wall, queen?' Pod asked in surprise as he came home to find the little cottage's sitting-room cluttered with jugs and milk bottles, all crammed with roses.

'No, I was given them.'

'Are you ill?'

'Only sick with worry because you're two hours later than you said you'd be,' Mo muttered.

'I never say what time I'll be home.'

'You did this morning,' she reminded him. 'You said you needed my car from six to go to Oddingford.'

'Shit! The Aunt Sally match – I said I'd stand in for Saul.' He looked at his watch. 'Too late now. The Wycks'll forgive me. Far better to spend a cosy evening with my queen.'

Mo glowered at him, but he had turned to sniff a rose.

'So who sent you the flowers? A secret admirer?'

For a moment, Mo considered telling the truth. That she had been as bad as him for once. That, on the horrible, haunted night of the storm, she had leapt into another man's arms for the first time ever, spurred there by his usual in-your-face infidelity.

It wasn't a very tempting confession. In the cold light of day, that night had been a madness she didn't want to touch upon. A cosy evening could smooth things out and make everything right between them again.

'They were a bribe from a parent at school,' she settled for a half-lie. 'Mrs Chambers says I should expect a lot of them.'

He seemed to swallow this, saying only: 'See if you can get cash bribes in future, eh?' before heading upstairs to shower away the Gunning dirt and thorns.

On the little table beside the door where he'd just emptied the contents of his pockets, his mobile bleeped.

'You've got a text message,' Mo called up the stairs as she went to fill the kettle, feeling almost normal and domestic once again after such a weird week. 'Do you want me to –'

'No! I'll read it!' Pod practically fell back downstairs to gather his phone.

Mo looked back from the kitchen door, unable to hide her suspicions. 'I was going to say, shall I make you a cup of tea?'

'Oh – right, sure.' He retreated to the bathroom, clutching his phone to his chest, knowing he was acting far too jumpily.

The photograph that accompanied the message was not of Dilly, as he had hoped it would be, but of a bathroom basin. He looked at it curiously for a moment before remembering that he had assigned the image to Diana Lampeter. The message read: *Marching on empty.*

He laughed and texted his dealer to remind him that he'd be doing some business that week. Then he showered away the grime of leaf mulch.

He had spent all day slipping away from his forestry work and searching for the mysterious garden that Dilly had told him about, and yet had found nothing. He was longing to hear from her, not especially because she attracted him, but because he wanted more clues as to the whereabouts of the garden. He'd been a fool to make out he already knew how to find it. Typical Pod, flirting his way into a corner.

He wrapped a towel round his waist and listened as Mo padded upstairs telling Bechers to get out from under her feet or he'd be scalded. A moment later a cup of tea appeared around the door, its steam joining that from the shower.

'Come in,' he offered.

She slipped through the door, eyeing him worriedly. All it took was one smile and open arms and she melted against him, her lips pressed to his hot, wet skin.

'I've been thinking,' she breathed. 'Perhaps I should come to Gunning with you one day? See what you keep talking about.'

'You mean it?' he whooped, holding her tightly.

She nodded against his chest. 'It must be very beautiful for you to have taken it to your heart so much.'

'Oh, it is, queen – it is. And full of secrets.'

'I don't like secrets. We have too many of those already.'

'So come with me and see its secrets for yourself. We can explore it together. You can help me find –'

'I have a secret!' she blurted.

He kept his arms tightly around her and caught his reflection in the small patch of mirror from which the steam had dried, a drawn and worried face surrounded by steam.

'So tell me your secret, queen,' he said, only just stopping his voice from cracking as he closed his eyes on his reflection, unable to watch the fear.

'I'm learning to ride,' she told him.

It took a while for Pod to take in this simple fact. This wasn't the secret he had been expecting. This was totally left field and knocked him back on his heels. He snapped open his eyes and watched his own expression harden in the mirror.

'Learning to ride?' He pulled away.

'Yes. Rory Midwinter is teaching me.'

'Is that a fact?' Letting her go, he took a step back.

'Only basic stuff, but I thought perhaps one day we could – you and I could –'

'Ride together?'

'Yes. I love it. I had no idea it would be so physically demanding or so difficult and I really want to get to grips with it.'

On top of the lavatory, his mobile phone let out an untimely bleep. Mo was standing right next to it, right next to the photograph of Dilly that was flashing on the screen, but she was staring at Pod too intently to notice.

'You hate the idea, don't you?' she asked.

He nodded. Til Constantine would be proud.

'Why?'

'Horses are *my* world.' He eyed the phone as it bleeped again.

'So is Gunning, but you are willing to share that.'

'Not any longer. I don't want you to come there after all.'

'Why not?'

'It would frighten you.' He started to edge towards the phone as it let out another bleep. 'I don't want to frighten you, Mo.'

Mo was rubbing her forehead in bewilderment. 'You always said horses would frighten me, but they don't any more. Here.' She picked up his phone and thrust it at him without looking at it. 'If a bloody text message is more important than our relationship, go right ahead and read it. I'll text you next time I want to tell you I'm doing something you don't approve of.'

He swallowed, saying nothing, his expression blackening.

Mo licked her lips. This was crazy. He had locked himself in a bathroom with another woman at a party just a few days earlier, and she had seduced the host. They were both aware that the other had strayed and yet here they were arguing about the fact she was learning to *ride*. And even that seemed less important to Pod than his text life.

She wanted to scream and shout, but it wasn't her style. Confrontation on this intimate level frightened her. It was one of the reasons Pod had learned to get away with so much over the years and she had learned to live with it.

But, as she turned to walk away, he caught her arm and dragged her back. For a moment she flinched in fright until she realised that his lips were on her cheek. 'I love you with all my heart, Mo. All my fucking heart.'

'So why do you always want to shut me out of a part of it?'

'Because you shut me out of all of yours, queen.'

'That's not true. I love you.'

'Not like I love you. You've got your ghosts to love. Your demons.'

'And you have the devil in you.'

'He's the only part of me you've ever let yourself love.'

Before she could open her mouth to protest, he was kissing it. The phone fell to the floor, and pretty soon they had joined it. As they twisted and turned, enjoying that peculiar, silent, bad patch sex both had grown familiar with, the phone let out another bleep.

Mo was in the throes of passion, her hot cheek pressed to the bathmat when she opened her eyes with a delighted 'Oh yes! Yes!' to spot the phone just inches from her nose, still beeping. On its screen was the ugly, battered face of Saul Wyck, who had just found out about Pod's failure to stand in for him at the Aunt Sally match and was sending a furious, badly spelled tirade. Mo groaned and closed her eyes.

Across the neighbouring garden, Gladys Gates was giving her boxroom windows a quick polish, her cheeks even pinker than usual. Oh my. They were at it in the bathroom again. Really, these youngsters were very experimental. The roses had obviously gone down a treat. She had certainly never reacted like that on the odd occasion that Reg had brought her home a posy in the old days, although she had felt quite sprightly when they were courting and he had won her a large teddy bear on the shooting range at Maddington Fair.

Remembering the occasion with a fond smile, she distractedly tried to polish the open side of the window and almost fell out on to her rose border below.

Fed up with waiting for Pod to text her back, Diana switched off her phone and went in search of Rory, who was drunkenly teaching a middle-aged man to rise to the trot.

'*Up down, up down, up down* – oh Christ. Just bounce. If it was good enough for Surtees, it's good enough for me. Hi, sister darling.' He blew her a kiss.

'Are you sure that horse is up to weight?' she muttered as she joined him at the side of the sand school and watched the poor man bouncing about on a furious-looking, bow-legged chestnut.

'Biggest one I've got that's sound. Penguin has an abscess in his hoof.'

'What about your chaser?'

He shuddered at the thought. 'Whitey's sacred.'

'You never ride him.'

'I do. You just never see me.'

'When exactly do you ride him then?'

'When I'm sober – *up down, up down* – that's right, Nigel. Just try to rise on the saddle not on your hand. Good man.'

Diana was smirking. 'I knew you never rode him. And you accuse me of avoiding exercising mine.'

'I ride him most days,' he assured her. 'And yours *are* under-exercised. They're just eating us out of house and home and, in the case of that bloody stallion, wasting his beautiful life away terrifying all my clients. He's bitten three so far.'

'Not for much longer.' She cocked her head as Nigel ground to a halt beside them and asked if Rory had a better horse because 'this one doesn't do what I want'.

'That, Nigel, is because you can't ride very well yet. When you can, you'll find they all work – although some, admittedly, rather better than others. Shall we do some more in walk?'

'I want to learn to show-jump,' Nigel snapped impatiently. 'That *is* why I came here.'

'Certainly,' Rory nodded. 'I tell you what – give me five minutes to stick a course up and call an ambulance and we'll see how you get on. Do you have any last requests?'

Diana sighed and retreated to the house, knowing that Rio wasn't the only one who was wasting his talents and good looks by frightening Rory's clients. He did a pretty good job himself. If she was going to turn this place around, it would take more than a few decent horses. But she had to start somewhere.

Two days later, eight assorted Irish hunters and ponies arrived on a cattle wagon at Overlodes riding school and Baron Areion, aka Rio the stallion, was unceremoniously taken away.

'It's business,' Diana explained to a crestfallen Rory.

'We need new teaching horses,' Sharon pointed out, cheered by the sight of a couple of cobby weight carriers. She seldom got to ride anything on the yard because Rory told her she was too heavy.

'Exactly.' Diana rubbed her hands together.

'Have you thought how much they'll cost to feed and shoe and tack and rug?' Rory spluttered.

'Of course I have.' Diana pulled out a roll of notes, fresh from cashing her husband's school fees cheque. 'I think this will ensure everything on this yard has its oats, don't you? I certainly need some.'

'Where's Rio gone?' Rory asked warily.

'Back to live with the ghosts.'

Mo came back from her first day's teaching elated. Anne Chambers was a changed woman. Mo could do no wrong. The children were adorable and the day had raced by in a blur of sunshine streaming through windows lighting up eager faces. She loved Oddlode.

She was on such a high that she decided it was definitely time to wipe out the sticky patch once and for all. She changed the bedding in their room and prepared to start a clean sheet. She and Pod had hardly spoken since she'd told him she was learning to ride. He had behaved as unpredictably as ever, telling her he loved her and jumping her bones before swaggering off to the Lodes Inn. He had hardly been home since, just catching sleep in the few hours after Mo had conked out with a pill and then leaving before she awoke.

Tonight he made a rare appearance before sunset.

'What's happened to the funeral parlour, queen?' he murmured when he got home, face scratched from battling with brambles all day. Graham's roses were no longer languishing in their mismatched vases, jugs and metal bucket in the sitting-room.

Mo led him upstairs where the bed was carpeted with petals. She reached for her shoulders. In two swift tugs her poppy-red dress fell to the floor.

Pod eyed her briefly from beneath his brows, turned her round, dropped his jeans and mounted her like an animal – quick, angry, instinctive and far from loving.

Afterwards Mo curled into a tight ball and drew rose petals to her mouth, shaking convulsively.

'I'm going to the pub.' He stomped out, thumped halfway down the stairs and then thumped back to curl around her in bed, clutching her tightly to his belly and breathing in her ear. 'I'm sorry, queen.'

'What's happening to us?'

He didn't answer, his body hot and tense, his heart thumping its way right through her back.

There was a strange overtone to the scent of roses and sex in the room. Mo knew it instinctively. It was that familiar first-date aftershave, the smell Pod had worn for so many years.

'Are you riding again?'

'Only you, queen. I only ever ride you.'

'Are you trying to break me in like a horse?'

'Never. You can't be tamed.'

It was a brief moment of fusion, but the sticky patch still coagulated and was starting to go rancid. Their shaky hold on domesticity had been the first thing to suffer.

'Are you hungry?' he asked eventually.

She shook her head. 'I'm back on school dinners. I can do us something on toast later. Let me just have a bath and we can go for a walk or something, okay?'

He ran her a bath, but didn't stay to rub her back. The scented bubbles had barely dispersed when she heard the front door bang. He had gone to the pub after all. Mo felt her own bubble popping unhappily.

She rubbed the guilt from her body again, scrubbing harder than ever, hating herself for what she had done. The first time that she had found out about Pod being unfaithful to her – a one-night stand with one of the girls at the Yorkshire training yard, revealed to her in an embittered letter from the girl's boyfriend – she had scrubbed herself raw for weeks afterwards. She'd thought that her skin had toughened up over the years, that Pod's faithlessness could no longer affect her confidence so brutally. She knew what he was like and he made no secret of it. His inability to feel guilt didn't mean that she had to take that guilt on herself, she knew that now. Infidelity was part of the deal with Pod and always would be.

But it wasn't a part of Mo's own deal, or at least it hadn't been until now. She wondered what the hell he got out of it. It made her absolutely wretched.

She gathered all the browning petals into a bin bag. They had marked the sheets so that they now looked soiled and grubby. She stripped the bed again and put the sheets in to wash before pulling on her walking boots.

It was a beautiful evening. The recent storms had washed away the dust of the heat wave and breathed life into the parched earth. Autumn was starting to take a hold as trees rattled their leaves, letting a few early explorers float their way to the ground to line the landing for the mass exodus. The green was teeming with children playing football and rounders in their school uniforms before being called home for tea, full of chatter and bravado after the first day of term. Mo recognised faces from her form group now and waved at them as she passed, stopping off at the village stores for tobacco before her planned walk towards the ridge.

Thankfully, Glad Tidings was still on duty at the Manor and not guarding the post office counter with her pensioner army to comment on how 'peaky' poor little Mo looked. But Joel's friendly banter at the till still left her drained as she forced smiles and laughs that hurt her face and throat.

She was pulling a few strands from the new pouch on to the Rizla in her palm as she wandered back out again, not looking up. The shadow that fell across her merely made her side-step. The shadow side-stepped too.

'Sorry,' she tried to do-si-do around the figure.

He do-si-do-ed in time.

Raising her eyes as she lifted the cigarette to lick the gummed edge, she found herself looking into the most beautiful sunset imaginable. A calm, foam-lipped turquoise sea stained every shade of red and orange where the dropping sun gave a final long, warm look at that day's side of the world before rolling off to light up another. In its glow, the deserted sandy beach was a burnished copper sanctum offering up the best seats in the house – two striped deckchairs just begging to be occupied.

'Hello, love.'

Mo couldn't look at him. Her tongue was stuck to the gummed paper. She could feel the tobacco falling from one end of her little roll-up and scattering in the breeze. She gazed at that amazing sunset and longed to swim straight out to sea.

'You going for a hike?' He sounded his usual cheery self as he took in the little back-pack and her boots.

She nodded.

'I'm just taking some air myself. Mind if I tag along?'

'I don't think . . .'

'Tell you what. I've just got to go in the shop here and pick up a couple of things. Which way are you headed? I'll catch you up.'

'Past the River Folly.'

'Might see you in a bit then.'

'Maybe.'

Still not looking him in the eye, Mo dashed away. It was only when she glanced guiltily towards the Lodes Inn as she passed it that she realised she still had a Rizla dangling from her mouth. She snatched it away as she searched the faces at the tables outside. They were mostly tourists or parents keeping an eye on their kids as they played on the green. Pod must be inside occupying his usual space amid the Wycks by the bar.

Diana derived a certain amount of hedonistic pleasure from the fact that she had spent a slice of the term fees cash on champagne and was now handing out more of it to Pod.

'My kids started classes today, and I shall join in by enjoying some Class A at the same time,' she giggled.

'You have no morals, do you?' he whistled as he handed over the wrap.

'We have so much in common.' She topped up his glass.

She had driven him up to Broken Back Wood, one of her favourite spots high on the spine of the ridge. To one side the land dropped away at an acute angle towards Oddlode. On the other, where they had settled on the grassy skirt around a stubble-field, lay the more gentle slopes that folded away to form the Foxrush valley, with the Gunning Estate to their left.

Pod was reading a text message from his phone and smiling, his face exquisite in profile – dark lashes absurdly long, nose ridiculously straight, lips curling with far too much beauty above that perfect jaw line. Diana tilted her face as she watched him key out a reply, amazed that one man could possess so much symmetry.

'Another secret lover?' She caught the words *pretty face* and *moonlit picnic* flash past as his thumb skittered across the keypad with practised speed.

'My mother,' he murmured, adding *won't be able to walk in the morning, flower* before pressing Send and pocketing the phone.

'Does Mo know where you are?'

'Yeah, sure.' He started rolling himself a spliff. 'I said "Just popping out to sell Diana Lampeter some coke and probably have a quick fuck, queen." She said she'd delay tea for me but wants me back in time for EastEnders. What about your kids?'

'Same.' Diana tucked the wrap into her back pocket. She hadn't touched the one that she had bought at the Brakespears' party yet.

'You certainly have a bit of a habit there.' He lay back on his elbows and lit up.

'Dreadful, isn't it?' she said vaguely, thinking guiltily about her children whom she had hurriedly left with Sharon when Pod had finally called. She couldn't stay out long. 'I have an addictive personality.'

'Bet you're glad I came along.'

'Oh, I am.' She started to unbutton his flies. 'I truly am.'

While Pod was enjoying champagne and a blow job, high on the ridge in every sense of the word, Mo was drinking Moet on the river bank behind the Folly.

'Wasn't Joel Lubowski suspicious when you bought all this?' she asked as she watched Graham pulling smoked salmon, baguettes and paper napkins from the plastic bag, too touched to remind him that she was a vegetarian.

'Suspicious at the nouveau northener flashing his cash around as per usual? No.'

'He must have thought you were buying it as a treat for Anke.'

'He must.'

'Doesn't that make you feel bad?'

'It makes me not want to think about it.' He took her hand and pressed it to his mouth, blue eyes watching her face closely. 'I didn't set out to take you on a picnic, love. But when I saw you, you looked so sad I wanted to cheer you up.'

'I got the flowers.'

His eyes didn't leave hers as they searched further. They weren't great black holes like Pod's, sucking her into the dark place, turning her soul upside down and tormenting her with confusion. They were as blue and inviting and cheerful and tempting as the sky on his shirt.

'If you want us to forget what happened the other night, love, then I can do that. It would make life a hell of a lot easier. We both know it should never have happened.'

'I can't forget about it.'

'Me neither.'

All week, Mo had longed to have someone to talk to about what she was feeling, someone to help her make sense of it. Yet who do you confess something so awful to? She had no close friends in the village. Her grandparents would never understand. Her closest friend in the world was Pod and she could hardly tell him. And her only friendships since arriving were with Anke and Diana. The former, whom she thought so kind and understanding, she had now secretly poisoned for ever. The latter she didn't trust.

But now it suddenly occurred to her that she *did* have someone to confess to. He wanted to talk as much as she did.

'I've never been unfaithful to Pod.'

'I've never been unfaithful to my wife.' He cupped her hand in both of his and pressed it to his forehead. 'That's a lie. I was unfaithful to Deirdre, my first wife. I was a total arsehole to her. But Anke . . .'

Suddenly, to Mo's horror, he started to sob. Pressing his head into the crooks of his elbows, he sobbed quietly.

Mo wrapped her arms around him and held him for a long time, her sobbing big strong man, hidden amid the reeds and the rushes on the river-bank as dog walkers stomped past just twenty yards away, crossing the bridge and whistling their charges on up the hill.

She had no idea how long they stayed like that, but the sun dropped almost as low as the red crescent on Graham's shirt, staining the river the same oranges and crimsons, before he finally looked up.

Midges danced overhead, moorhens and water rats swam as quietly as they could from bank to bank, sending up just the slightest of ripples, and a big fat frog had clambered on to a reedy tuffet to stare at the strangers on his manor.

'I haven't cried since I was a kid.' Graham rubbed his reddened eyes and almost chuckled as he realised how ludicrous he must seem. 'Sorry.'

'Don't be.' Mo sat back on her heels and hugged herself, smiling through her own tears. 'That was the bravest thing I have ever seen a man do.'

Graham looked at her, the little imp with those huge baby fawn eyes and fragile body. He wanted to blurt out the whole truth, that his wife had found him physically repellent for years, that she would not let him touch her, not even to hug her and comfort her when she was upset – like today, when she had fretted unhappily about Chad and Faith starting at their schools, when she had gone to see her father to find that he had almost burned himself and his bookshop flat to a crisp by leaving all four electric rings on his hob with empty pans on them. Anke wouldn't even accept a hand on her arm in comfort. He loved her so much and she couldn't bear him to lay a finger on her.

Yet, as he looked at Mo, he found he couldn't say any of it. They had already said enough. They knew that this was no picnic, and yet the cloths of heaven were spread at their feet.

'I love my wife,' was all he said.

She nodded.

Beside them the frog let out a great croak, making them both start and then laugh.

'If I kiss him do you think he'll turn into a prince?' she asked.

'More likely give you lip sores. If you kiss me, I'll turn back into a frog.'

She smiled sadly, not registering the invitation.

Graham shifted awkwardly, blew his nose on a paper napkin and looked across at the darkening horizon.

'Are you cold?' he asked.

'A little.' She looked down at her bare legs which were covered with goose pimples. The sun had almost dropped out of sight.

'Will you have been missed?'

She shook her head. Pod wouldn't miss her if she moved out right now. 'You?'

'Anke's taken Chad and Faith to the cinema as a first day at school treat. They were going to have pizza afterwards. They won't be back for hours.'

'You didn't want to go?'

'I'm supposed to be fixing the plumbing again.'

'I guess you should get back then.'

'I guess.'

They started to put away the uneaten salmon and bread. Graham picked up the almost full bottle of champagne and turned to tip it into the Odd.

'Don't.' Mo stopped him. 'It might pollute it.'

'Whoever heard of champagne pollution?' he laughed, handing her the bottle.

She tapped the neck to her lips and then raised it in a toast. 'To Daddy G. The loveliest man I've met in my life.' She took a deep draught which threatened to bubble up her nose. Eyes bulging, she tried to swallow it as she handed him back the bottle.

'To my little fairy princess.' He raised it to his own lips. 'Who can make grown men cry.'

Mo lost her battle and the champagne spurted from her lips as they both dissolved into laughter.

They shared the champagne in a hurried, twilit tryst, giggling like children, knowing that it wasn't the only thing that was being unbottled.

Five minutes later, Mo lay back naked, shivering from the fizzing chill of champagne sliding over her skin and then shivering more from the amazing sensation of Graham's warm tongue chasing its progress lower and lower.

Blinking thoughtfully at them, the frog plopped back into the river.

The Indian summer burned on as Pod and Mo shared the same bed and different lusts. They still made love. They always made love. It was automatic and thoughtless sex; easier than talking, easier than arguing, and a lot easier than stopping to think about what they were doing. It was easier to look each other between the legs than in the eyes.

Gunning obsessed Pod. It took up all his time not spent drinking in the Lodes Inn. By virtue of his job, he felt he had an Access All Areas pass and he spent hours exploring out of hours, searching for the elusive garden that Dilly had told him about before freewheeling home down the hills, racing away from the ghosts as night fell. As the evenings grew shorter in the rapid autumn curtain fall, he sought alternative transport, using the wages that should have gone towards rent and bills to buy a little trail bike. It speeded things up considerably, and allowed him more free time to enjoy the several calls and messages a day that were now assailing his phone accompanied by a flashing photograph of a ravishing blonde, drunk on spiked Pimm's at a barbecue.

He had cleverly engineered it so that Dilly, as desperate for him to show her the garden as he was to find it, had finally let slip a few useful facts without knowing it. Her mother had been frightened to go there even thought it wasn't near the house. It was obviously close to the lake, because Pheely had swum there when she had visited it. And there were horses nearby, although not in the Foxrush Hall stables. He was getting closer every day. He knew where the horses were. He was one of the only people in the valley who knew that, and he had walked their fields and the perimeter of the lake so many times that he was pretty certain there was one particular corner of the area which hid his bounty. The only problem was, he couldn't get in. No matter how many times he prowled around the beech hedges and the high Cotswold stone walls, there was no entry point.

The quest took up all his time, leaving him little spare to dwell upon Mo's whereabouts as she pursued her Thelwell pastimes of ponies and children. He didn't want to think about that right now. If he found the garden, he knew he could make everything right.

Meanwhile, Mo's riding lessons provided great cover for her *affaire*, given that Graham's business was just a hundred yards from the stables. Rory was far too full of scotch by evening lessons to notice anything untoward in her behaviour. He just gossiped and bitched and whooped in admiration as she rapidly mastered rising and sitting trot, canter transitions and even a small jump – learning quickly and fearlessly because she had a far more pressing appointment with adrenaline and apprehension. She'd started to love riding. More worryingly, she'd started to love Graham.

She was feeling too guilty to notice that Pod was being even shiftier and more stop-out than usual. She didn't even notice at first that he had stopped borrowing her car to get to work and was now throttling his way around the lanes on a trail bike bought with his first week's wages.

Pod found something strangely compelling about Diana Lampeter. He was aware that she was using him for three things – sex, drugs and information about his boss. It was this last reason that fascinated him most of all. The others he was accustomed to. And, however much he told her about Amos – not that there was much to tell – she refused to divulge a single fact about their past history. Pod loved secrets, and he loved secrets that involved the Gunning Estate most of all. The place fascinated him. He was determined to get the truth.

'So Amos never mentions me? You're sure?' she asked the day they met hastily in a derelict barn on the edge of the Gunning Estate – the closest he had coaxed her to estate land. She hated crossing its boundaries.

'Not a word,' he told her. 'He doesn't say a lot, to be frank. He's not what you'd call talkative.'

'Good. Do you see much of Jacqui?'

'Not a lot. He never mentions her.'

'Really? Does he talk about his kids?'

'No. He talks most about forestry or game. If he talks at all.'

'Are they going to the Oddlode harvest supper this weekend?'

'Think so.'

'Shit.' She banged an angry fist to the ground. She could hardly get out of it, given that it was her family hosting it. She'd even arranged for one of the Sixsmith girls to babysit because Sharon claimed to be busy.

Pod had no idea whether his boss was going to the supper – in fact he very much doubted it, given how anti-social Amos was – but enjoyed her reaction. 'What happened between you two that's so bad you can't even be in the same room?'

'It's dead and buried.'

'So give me a quick obituary?'

She looked at her watch and said she had to go. 'Mim and Dig will be out of school in half an hour.'

Pod shrugged. It was always the same. She took her gram, her orgasm and her scraps of Amos information and left in a hurry. Pod was starting to be bored of it.

'Daffodil's visiting Oddlode this weekend, isn't she?' he asked to wind her up.

'How do you know?'

'Nice girl.' He grinned. 'Rory's a lucky guy.'

Diana narrowed her eyes. 'She's quite pretty. Vacuous like her mother, but she and Rory seem to suit one another.'

'Pretty vacuous relationship, then?'

She'd walked into that one, her eyes now narrowed so much that she looked oriental and strangely beautiful.

'Rory adores her.'

'And I can see why.' Pod narrowed his eyes in return, smiling like a cat.

Diana hadn't let Pod's shiftiness and manipulation pass her by. He was not easily controlled, it seemed. He still reminded her frighteningly of Amos, and she was now paranoid Amos knew all about a relationship that was already starting to leave a sour taste in her mouth and a big hole in her dwindling bank balance. Living life dangerously like her mother was all very well if you married wisely and in cold blood, but Diana's solicitors had advised her that, in light of her initial avaricious attempts to get money from her husband after their separation to buy the Plough, she now stood to gain practically nothing personally from the divorce, apart from the bitter memories. The children would be well cared for financially, if not emotionally. She had resorted to begging Tim to visit them by e-mail because he wouldn't take her calls. Her fling with Pod, which had initially brought an exciting, devil-may-care, child-free nostalgia into her life, had just complicated it horribly. She still needed the highs, but the lows were rapidly outnumbering them.

She now had a strong suspicion that Pod was after Rory's girlfriend, Dilly. She couldn't sleep for thinking about it, getting up at dawn to steal into her children's bedroom to kiss their cheeks for inspiration.

Which was when she spotted her brother through the window, riding his big grey eventer in the sand school. He was schooling White Lies over a huge grid of jumps in first light – a red glow that turned the horse pink and Rory's blonde hair titian.

'You should wear a hard hat!' she told him as she leaned over the rails in her dressing-gown five minutes later.

Pop, pop, pop, POP. They executed a perfect series of jumps while Twitch watched from his perch on top of the mounting block, neckerchief dancing as he barked support. Watching Rory lift effortlessly from the saddle with each gargantuan bound, Diana remembered feeling that confident on a horse. It seemed like a lifetime ago.

'Talented bugger, isn't he?' he laughed, turning to take the line again, not thinking to question why she was up so early.

Diana had no need to ask him the same question in return. He had already answered it himself by telling her that he only rode his beloved horse when he was sober. And now, in that rare pocket of lucidity, she had an opportunity to warn him.

'I hear Dilly's coming this weekend? For Aunt Bell's harvest supper.'

Pop, pop, pop, POP.

'Yeah – hope so. It's not definite. Who told you?'

Pop, pop, pop, POP.

'Pod Shannon.'

'Who?'

'The ex jockey working at Gunning.'

'You've been to Gunning?'

'No, I . . .'

Pop, pop, pop, POP.

'. . . bumped into him.'

'Can you put that last spread up?'

'It's already almost at the top of the wings.'

'So put it right up there.'

She dragged her feet through the sand. 'Pod seemed certain she'd be here.'

'He did?' Rory threw Polos from his pockets for Twitch to catch, suddenly smiling. 'Cool! I miss her.'

'I think Pod might have set his sights on her, Rory.'

'On Dilly? Don't be daft. She's my girlfriend.'

'Rory.' She hawked a pole on to her shoulder as she fiddled with the jump cup. 'Not everyone is as old-fashioned as you are.'

He hooked his knees over the saddle flaps, lay back on White Lie's rump and lit a cigarette. 'Anyway, Pod Shannon is living with Mo, isn't he? She's gorgeous. He'd never be unfaithful.'

Diana crashed the pole down into the cup, the jump now as high as her nose. Her happy-go-lucky brother was burying his head in his sand school again. 'Rory, get real.'

'I am real. Witness.' He touched his cigarette end against his arm. 'Ouch!'

She caught hold of the horse's reins and turned him in a swift circle so that Rory was forced to sit up to avoid falling off.

'I am trying to tell you something here, Rory.'

'I know,' he said in a small voice. 'Can you stop doing that? I feel sick.'

Diana retreated to the rails as he retook his stirrups and cantered a couple of circles ready to try the line again. She found herself next to Sharon, who had emerged from her mobile home ready for first feeds and had also stopped to watch.

Pop, pop, pop, POP.

The big horse jumped higher than Diana's out of joint nose. He seemed to jump as high as the clouds in which his rider's head perpetually lived.

Catcalling and whooping, Sharon hopped the fence and went to pat Whitey.

'That was fantastic, Roar. I'll put him away for you if you like?' she offered as the full force of the morning sun finally made its way over the cherry hedge and called time on his dawn raid, stable doors banging in the barn, demanding breakfast.

'Thanks, S.' He jumped off and, seeing Diana waiting to continue the conversation, hooked his arm around his head girl. 'I'll do morning feeds. Can you get the gate, Di?'

Holding the gate open at a safe distance from the big grey horse, Diana glowered as White Lies clattered on to the tarmac and, chattering happily, Rory and his groom headed towards the narrow cathedral arch of the tall American barn doors.

He was retreating to the reliable arms of Sharon again. What a surprise. With Dilly due to arrive in less than twenty-four hours, she hardly thought it helped his cause.

Her temper was not improved by the arrival of Anke's daughter, Faith, on a mountain bike halfway through breakfast.

'You sold the stallion!'

Not in the mood for teenage tantrums, Diana looked up from the *Telegraph*. 'And?'

'Mum promised me I could ride him,' she panted hoarsely, bright red from the exertion of pedalling up the hill. Her face clashed horribly with the orange hair that she had obviously tried to bleach blonde and which had turned a lurid shade of carrot.

'That wasn't really fair of her. He was my horse and now he is someone else's.'

'Where has he gone?'

Diana was too ratty to care for bruised young feelings. 'He'll be going hunting to teach him some bloody manners.'

'You can't mean that?' Faith yelped.

'Listen, it's no business of yours or your mother's what happened to him, quite honestly,' she snarled. 'He went a week ago and as far as I know he's settled very well into his new home.'

'He went a *week* ago?' Faith gasped.

'Didn't Anke tell you?'

'She told me last night.'

'Probably didn't want to upset you during your first few days at college. How sweet.' Diana left her, breathless and humiliated in the kitchen, and went to get dressed.

Faith, who hated her new sixth form college with a passion and had been counting the hours until the weekend when she thought she was going to see the stallion again, was devastated. She knew of only one person who had thought as highly of him as she had.

She searched the yard for Rory, but the horses were all turned out and nobody was around. She checked the paddocks and then went to look in the rusty Dutch barn which housed the huge bales of hay and straw.

There, amid the dancing dust and early morning dappled sunlight that split through the holes in the east wall, Rory was lying back on bales of freshly cut meadow hay with Sharon bouncing around on top of him, naked from the waist down. All Faith could register was how fat her thighs were and how huge the sweat marks on her T-shirt.

'Fucking hell!' Sharon cursed as she spotted the teenager and hastily clambered off her boss.

Now Faith saw only one thing. Rory's erection. It was the first she had ever seen. She had no idea that they were so – huge. Or purple.

Turning on her heels, she fled, cutting her legs on her bike chain as she struggled to leap on it at the run and then freewheeling all the way down the hill to Oddlode.

It was only when she got to the safety of Heigi's and Bert's paddock and was hugging her faithful old pony for comfort that Faith's racing heart started to lift with a surprised realisation. If Rory Midwinter and his huge purple *thing* could let Sharon do that to him, then he wasn't quite as god-like and unattainable as she had imagined. Sharon was seriously unattractive. Faith might have chronically low self-esteem, but even she could recognise that she was no plainer and certainly a lot slimmer than Sharon.

She fed Bert half a tube of Polos and tried not to think about the purple thing. She sat in the shade of one of the huge chestnuts by the railway line and caught thistledown wishes in each hand. With one she wished for Pod, with another Rory and then she looked at her clenched fists wondering which one to set free first. As she did so, a great clump of thistledown wishes floated straight down on her left hand, the Rory hand, and rested on her knuckles. She gave it a big puff and watched it skip up and catch the breeze, sailing up into the tree.

'I wish I could have Rio the stallion,' she suddenly breathed out loud.

'Ugh! Gross!' cackled a voice from behind her and Chad bounded out of the hedgerow, the front of his sweatshirt weighed down with conkers.

Faith leapt up in surprise. 'Chad! What has Mum said about going near the railway line? You are so not allowed over here.'

'You still make *fairy* wishes,' he jeered.

'Go away.'

'Faith still makes *fairy* wishes for *horses*,' Chad jeered again, his newly cultivated Cotswolds accent even more annoying to Faith than the Essex one had been. 'Faith is such a *baby*!'

'No, I'm not. Bugger off!'

'Baby!'

'I am *not*!' Faith howled, suddenly thinking about the purple thing. Seeing that had somehow made her feel very grown up. It was a rite of passage.

17

On the evening of the harvest supper at Oddlode Manor, the old hunt kennels to the rear of the house crackled with life for the first time in years. The empty stalls, where Spurs Belling and his cousin Rory had years earlier lit up illicit cigarettes, were once again the scene of a great deal of smoking. Pretty soon they were blazing as stored logs, old jerrycans of petrol, piles of newspapers and assorted surplus furniture, now tinder-dry from the long drought, quickly caught light and combusted, licking flames from the broken windows and up towards the oak roof timbers.

Separated by the huge Manor yews from the house, its gardens and all the hubbub of activity for the night's party, the fire could have taken an unstoppable hold had it not been for the twitching nose of Glad Tidings. Her accusation that Lady Belling had let the first of the many shepherd's pies burn had caused a minor industrial relations crisis in the kitchens at first. Gladys, who guarded her Aga fiercely and considered all the Bellings' cooking to be her domain, was still brooding with hostility and pique that her ladyship had yet again decided it would be 'rather entertaining' to cook that night's main course herself. The smell of burning made Gladys's eyes light up above her wrinkling nose. Then she had realised that it came from quite a different source than the vast trays of minced lamb and mashed potato in the ovens. It came from outside. She instantly feared that husband Granville was at large. He loved an autumn bonfire.

Now her eyes smarted as she sheltered behind the yews with the Belling family and the rest of their staff – mostly hired help for that night – listening to the crackling fire being doused in water.

'How much longer?' Hell's Bells demanded of the chief fire officer. 'We're entertaining two hundred in the orangery tonight. I *must* be allowed back in my house.'

'I said behind the roses!' was his terse response as he ushered them all back.

'In that case, I *shall* go behind the roses,' Hell's Bells retorted proudly. 'So far behind the roses that I am, in fact, through my boot room and back in my house.'

Insisting that the supper go ahead as planned, she resumed preparations before the fire had been quelled, despite the fire officer yapping
furiously at anyone who could be bothered to listen that what they were
doing involved a high degree of personal risk. They were all far too
afraid of Lady Belling to worry about the odd singed eyebrow or third-
degree burn.

Diana arrived early with a car boot crammed full of apple crumble
to find Glad Tidings frantically turning the tablecloths on the long tres-
tles in the orangery to try to shake out the ash that had floated in.

'Her Ladyship insists we carry on,' Gladys told her, collecting one
of the trays of cutlery from the side table. 'She's taken herself off to
fetch Nanny, and those useless girls from the village who are supposed
to be helping are all outside chatting up the firemen. Can you lay?'

'I'm not a chicken, although I *am* rather good at laying sometimes.'
Diana swanned out to attend to her crumbles, bumping straight into
her aunt who was steaming back through her house at a rate of knots.

'Diana. Blessed relief! Need your help. Know we've had a small fire?'

'Yes, Aunt B. One can't help but smell the thing.' Diana found herself
hooked up by one arm and towed back through the house towards the
main entrance.

'Bloody bad timing.' Hell's Bells marched her along. 'I'm sure that
wretched sister of mine is behind it. Til was very piqued that I refused
to accommodate her game compôte starter; St John lost two crowns last
time he tried it, and people are so litigious these days – can't risk getting
sued.' She threw open her front doors and beckoned Diana down the
steps towards her Range Rover. 'As you know, Til's always been a bane
of the Vale of the Wolds Hunt. Been sabbing for years just to spite us.
Help me get Nanny out of here, will you?' She heaved open the boot
to pluck out a wheelchair and a zimmer frame.

A frail little figure in the back turned her beady eye on her former
charges.

'Til can't have started the fire. She's in Wales, dears – has been for
the past three days, staying with a silent order of nuns. She promised
to send me a post card.'

'I had no idea she was religious these days,' Diana exclaimed.

'Oh, she's not, dear. I can't even persuade her that agnostic is a better
each-way bet than atheist. She just goes there for the goat's cheese.
Apparently, it's the best she's ever tasted.'

Diana wasn't quite sure why her aunt had summonsed her help when
she single-handedly whisked Nanny into her chair, as smoothly as she
lobbed her pet Cotswold sheep between hurdles, and then hitched the

wheelchair up her entrance steps without apparent effort. Diana was about to follow with the zimmer frame when she heard the putter of her mother's Mini Moke.

'*I* was supposed to fetch Nanny!' Truffle shrilled as she parked at the usual appalling angle. 'It was my idea to invite her. Typical bloody For Whom the Bell Tolls muscling in. Hi, darling!' She air kissed her daughter from ten yards away, espying the zimmer frame. 'Don't even *think* of waving that thing near me.'

She was dressed in a wine-coloured Chinese silk dress in which she would have looked rather seductive were it not for the clear demarcations of her 'shaper' underwear – bra-straps digging troughs where her curves should have sloped, thigh-shaper knickers creating strange kinks in her legs, and high-waisted tights cutting into her flesh so that she bore soup-bowl handles on either side of her body.

'Vere not with you?' Diana asked icily.

'No, Drear is finalising some boring details to do with shipping an Augustus John to America. He'll follow on.'

Diana perked up, detecting ill will.

'Have you got company tonight?' Truffle asked, relieved that she looked considerably better groomed than her daughter whose orange satin dress hardly flattered her figure (she could learn a lot from decent corsetry) and bore a suspicious dark stain at the neck.

'No.' Diana lifted her chin and whisked the zimmer frame inside.

Truffle smirked in her wake, knowing that a late date was better than no date. Gravel was already spitting beside her as the first of the guests arrived, intent on redeeming the ticket price in wine and gossip before the food started.

Turning at the top of the stone steps, Truffle elected to greet the arrivals in the absence of the immediate family.

'Welcome! Welcome! The food will be dreadful, but I gather the red is a rather flirtatious Merlot with a come-hither bite and a quite thrilling aftertaste. Steer clear of the white – if they'd tried to put the fire out with it, the whole house would have combusted. Quite vile. Coats to the left.'

Pretty soon, she had lost all her lipstick to the sun-burnt cheeks of the village faithful, and imparted enough gossip to make their tickets worth three times the face value before guests even crossed the Manor threshold.

'Dreadful mess tonight – half the outbuildings lost to fire. My sister tried to fight the flames with an antique tapestry before the brigade arrived. Fingers are pointing to Spurs or possibly Granville Gates. Poor

Bell is quite out of sorts. Been on the sloe gin already. Don't touch the squash soup.'

The blaze had short-circuited the electricity, but in blitz spirit, Hell's Bells summoned all the hurricane lamps in the village and prepared herself to serve acres of shepherd's pie. Thank heavens for oil-fired Agas.

Pod was in the Lodes Inn car park with Saul Wyck, who had offered to help fix the blocked fuel line on his trail bike, when he saw Mo walk past, heading in quite the wrong direction for the Oddlode Manor main entrance. She was trotting along Manor Lane and around the back of the old house.

Curious, Pod left Saul happily poking around with an old wire coat-hanger and followed her past the rear drive, where two fire engines were parked bullishly in front of the smouldering kennels, and on towards the little loop that ran around the back of the Manor's paddocks towards Goose End and Oddlode Lodge, the Gentlys' shuttered family home. Having found it too expensive to run since her father's death, Pheely now lived in the little cottage deep within the grounds and that was where Dilly stayed when she visited.

Pod paused outside the door in the high wall that led through the gardens to the Gentlys' cottage. He had taken a nose around earlier that week, admiring the amazing bronzes that had been sculpted by Dilly's grandfather, although the huge Great Dane dog that had come bounding out from behind a cluster of dancing nymphs had frightened him off before he'd really explored. It was a wonderful, jungle-like garden choked and overgrown, but it wasn't the hidden secret he sought at Gunning. It was just a pleasant diversion – much as Dilly was merely a pleasant diversion from his little dragon.

He hung back as Mo paused in the dusky light and hesitated, staring up at the sky, her small frame seeming to flutter as though caught by sharp winds.

Dilly loved the thought of exploring Gunning and its Pleasure Garden. It was the only thing she and Pod really had in common. She was also pretty and eager and keen, which made her straightforward and easy to enjoy. Mo hated and feared the place without ever having been there – just as she had once feared horses without giving them a chance. And yet, when she had offered to embrace both, Pod had shunned her. Sharing something so intimate with her frightened him; he would rather share it with a pretty stranger. Strangers like Dilly were disposable. Mo was his ephemeral dream who had stayed to haunt his waking hours. He was some-times afraid that if he closed his eyes for too long, she would disappear.

Perhaps she was right. There was always a part of his life he needed to keep dark and secret from her. Everything else was far too raw. He hurt her with his philandering, but he was addicted to the hurt he caused because it showed that she cared, that something was still alive between them. Much as he longed to be fairy-tale good, to slay the ogre, climb the mountain, save the village from floods and rescue the princess from the pack of wolves, he was miscast. He was a desperado and she was a little dragon. They had always been marginalised – mythical comrades who lived in a world where life turned upside down faster than an egg-timer, there were no ties and love was a constant game of 'dare'. Without the ability to hurt her, without that control, he didn't know her at all.

Tonight, he didn't know her. He didn't know the woman who crossed the grassy bridge over the Odd and then slipped from the path and into the River Folly. He didn't know the woman who embraced a great lion of a man with a tenderness he had never seen, a tiny sapling curling around a great tree.

He turned and ran. He ran past the Gentlys' door in the garden wall and on to the back lane to the Manor, hurdling a paddock fence and crossing towards the old gardens where guests were audibly chatting and laughing. He slipped past them in the shadows and behind a long yew hedge towards an overgrown shrubbery, crashing into the deepest of the dark arbours and slumping to the ground.

His phone rang. A pretty face smiled at him as he looked at it; a face that knew nothing of relationships which tore one's soul to shreds and blackened one's heart. In their recent chats, Dilly had talked a lot of twaddle about soul mates. She was so daft, so open-hearted and romantic – and clearly knew no more about mating souls than she did about the destructive, angry, consuming danger of love. Perhaps that was what he needed. She was no more his soul mate than he was a virgin, but she made him feel curiously unsullied and adored. It was novel. It assuaged the guilt.

'Hello, flower,' he answered at last, needing to hear a cheerful voice.

'Hi, lover. Where are you?'

'In a garden.'

'*The* garden?'

'In a manor of speaking. Where are you?'

'Some grotty services near Warwick. Shouldn't be more than an hour until I get to Oddlode. Will you really take me to the Pleasure Garden tonight?'

'Promised I would, didn't I?'

He had said he would take her there. Getting *into* the garden had never been mentioned, although getting into Dilly's knickers was high on the agenda. He needed to forget everything tonight. He needed oblivion.

'How does it look?'

'What?'

'The garden, silly!'

'Dark. Very dark.'

Enjoying a rare evening out, Nanny soon abandoned her wheelchair and, armed with her zimmer frame and a schooner of sherry, stalked Diana with a rubber squeak as far as the terrace beside the orangery, demanding to know why she hadn't calmed the ghosts. 'Look at this! Just look at the mess you have caused, you silly girl.'

Diana could see the last of the black plumes rising through the red streaks of sunset above the yews. She felt a tight tic leap in one cheek and a finger poked cruelly into her heart with every beat.

'Oh, for God's sake, Nanny. It's teenagers. All villages have their rough element. I hear even the Lodes valley has succumbed to drugs and hooliganism these days.'

'This isn't the work of a local scallywag, my child. This is touching your family. You must seek peace with Amos.'

'I can't possibly speak to him now.' Diana's eyes darted towards the drive where more cars were parking.

'Well, you must. First thing tomorrow, you find that boy and you bury the ghosts between you. Whatever it takes.'

'Why not tonight?'

'He won't be *here*, child.' Nanny chortled in mockery.

'I've heard he's coming.' Diana glanced nervously over her shoulder where guests were now milling to the orangery, eager to beat a retreat from Truffle's welcome and bag a good seat with a view of the dying fire.

'Nonsense. Do you not realise what date it is?'

'September the twenty-eighth. So?'

Nanny's rheumy eyes blinked as she turned her head away in shame. That her charge could forget such an anniversary tarnished her good regard. 'It's the day you left, Diana.'

'I left on my birthday. Boxing Day.' Diana looked away, her voice a frozen hush.

'The day you left, Diana,' she pressed.

Diana felt a talon scrape at her throat. 'I don't remember the exact day I left Gunning, but it was spring. Early spring. There were snow-drops.'

'September the twenty-eighth ten years ago,' Nanny sighed, 'was the last day you came hunting – cubbing. What do they call it now? Some ghastly alternative.'

'Murder, I think you'll find.'

'Autumn hunting! That's it. They call it autumn hunting. You came autumn hunting here. Rode out on a big young gelding of Midwinter's – same colour as your hair. Amos followed the hunt. You didn't see him. I was there too. You didn't see any of us. You'd just come back from Argentina. Brown as a berry, you were.'

'And miserable as hell.'

'Your father wouldn't come to the wedding to give you away.'

'He hardly spoke to me the entire time I was there.'

'You couldn't stand still in those days. I remember you as though it was yesterday. So beautiful. So lost. One week you were in Dubai, another Hong Kong, the next South Africa.'

'It was my job.'

'You were chasing your own tail.'

'Certainly beat coming back here to chase a fox's brush with a gaggle of drunken hoorays.'

'You hunted that day,' Nanny reminded her. 'You only came back here to hunt.'

'Because I had no choice!' she hissed. 'The family all lived and breathed hunting then.'

Nanny looked mistily towards the yews shielding the old kennels which were now smouldering, their oak shoulders in ashes.

'You hated hunting as a child. So mis-named, we all thought. Diana. Goddess of hunting, and yet too frightened to wait by a covert. Then you came back like a harpy. All you did was ride. Waiting for the kill.'

Diana watched the schooner of sherry shake, depositing most of its contents on the terrace flags.

'I didn't ever see the kill, Nanny,' she said carefully. 'I didn't ever see it.'

Nanny righted her glass with a determined jerk, leaning on her zimmer frame. 'That day in September. It was your last day here.'

She nodded, finally realising what was being said. 'I haven't hunted with the Wolds since that day. It was the week before I married Tim.'

Nanny sighed with relief as she realised she was understood. 'That girl who rode out on the black horse on a September morning never came back here. You came and went with your new husband – later a new family, but we lost the huntress. She never returned. Amos gave up hope. Now you're here and it's too late. It's too damned late, girl.'

Diana felt her cheek muscles tighten to her jaw and her eyes draw their shutters, allowing just narrow apertures to scrutinise the last of the smoke plume above the yews.

'I didn't know that he was following that day.'

'He always followed.'

'He hated the hunt.'

'He wasn't following the hunt.'

Spotting Pod standing cross-armed in front of the yews admiring the smoke, Diana beat a hasty retreat and bought enough marching powder to send an army into battle.

Trapped alone with Diana, Pod noted the leaping tic in her cheek and the whites of her eyes flashing like crescent moons between scudding black clouds. She looked fantastically dishevelled in a too-tight flame-coloured dress with her black hair wild and her lipstick smudged. It was the first time he had found her interesting in weeks.

As he handed her the last of his current supply and took the fat roll of notes she had prised from her tiny handbag, he decided he was rather fond of her.

'Who *are* you getting it from?' Diana demanded as usual.

He tapped his nose again, and then tapped his fly. She had led him out to a part of the garden she knew was completely private, far from the yew hedge and the shrubbery – a little hollow behind the disused tennis court, shrouded from view by broad-shouldered rhododendrons.

Diana was feeling too jumpy to take him up on his offer. Sex with Pod had become far too one-way lately, and knowing that Nanny was prowling the premises – albeit very slowly with a zimmer frame – was a passion killer. She had just needed him as an escape, and for the reassurance that she now had an artificial high tucked in her handbag even though she would never use it.

But Pod surprised her by snatching her in his arms and planting a long, aggressive, almost proprietorial kiss on her lips. He had a strange urgency and passion that was quite delicious.

It was such heaven to feel wanted – especially tonight of all nights – that Diana tried to forget about Nanny and her neglected crumbles. His hand was already plucking her knickers expertly from her hips. Oh hell. It was better than whipping cream.

Rory had appropriated a bottle of the Merlot and wandered on to the Manor lawns to watch the last of the smoke from the kennel's fire dying away. He'd settled on a favourite perch in the crook of the arm of the old cedar that overlooked the tennis lawns, known to generations of Constantines and their successors as 'Umpires' because it was the best place from which to judge a match. He had been facing the wrong way to identify the couple that had crossed close-by and sneaked behind the rhododendrons, but he was pretty certain he knew who they were. That Liverpool accent was unmistakeable, even at a whisper.

His sister's warnings had not entirely passed him by. He had suspected a *frisson* between Pod and Daffodil the first night the two had met. Easy-going to the point of lying down, Rory still recognised high-goal flirting. And Dilly had been strange with him on the telephone ever since. In the past fortnight, she had talked of nothing but her plans to travel and her desperation to settle far from Oddlode. Rory shared both these dreams. Unfortunately, Dilly's dreams didn't seem to include him. He was pretty certain that she was driving down from Durham tonight with the precise intention of dumping him.

He was totally paranoid that it was Dilly behind the laurels with the Liverpool louse. Much as he longed to confront them, he didn't have the bottle. Then again . . . he knew where to find bottle.

Sliding from his perch, he drained the Merlot as quickly as he could and headed back into the house for more. The search took him past the official 'bar' that his aunt and St John had set up and on to the library, where he knew that the best of the Belling spirits were kept stashed behind the leather-bound 1960s *Encyclopaedia Britannica* given to the Bellings as a wedding present by an unwitting faction of well-meaning, cap-doffing villagers. The family loathed them, but they gave good cover to the best of the malts and ports.

Rory removed a couple of volumes and selected a good Islay, testing it with a few satisfactory swigs before heading back to the gardens. He settled on a bench in the lengthening shadows by the roses where he could fasten one eye on the rustling bushes and another on the orangery, now flickering brighter in its hurricane-lamp glow as the sky overhead lost its grip on another honest day and succumbed to the secrets of darkness.

Unaware of the ebbing fire, in their secret River Folly retreat, Graham and Mo slid limbs against limbs on the carpet of wood anemones and grass seeds. The Great Bear was shining through one open arch, Orion through another, Aquila through the third arch, and the huge harvest moon gleamed through the last, marbling their sun-kissed bodies in deathly alabaster grey.

'I love you,' they breathed into each other's ears – neither trusting enough to believe it totally. The more they said it, the more they convinced themselves that it could be true and could justify their lies and guilt.

'*Dóchas*,' Mo breathed.

'Huh?'

'Irish for hope.'

'*Håbe*,' Graham sighed. 'Danish for hope.'

They were so impossibly defined by their love for others that they hadn't found a common language yet.

By the time Dilly arrived, Rory was too drunk to recognise the telltale rattle of a 2CV beyond the Manor walls and realise that she couldn't have been the one in the bushes with Pod. Dilly had driven all the way from Durham especially to see her great love. Unfortunately, she had driven all the way from Durham especially to see Pod, not Rory.

Pod was up to his elbow in orange satin when the text message bleeped to his phone announcing that Dilly had parked her car as close as she could (somewhere on the opposite side of the village green) and was coming to find him.

He dropped Diana instantly. 'Gotta leave you for a minute or two, queen. Emergency.'

'Is it Amos?' she couldn't help asking.

'Nah. I've got to go see a garden.'

'You've what?' she laughed.

'A pleasure garden.' He grinned. 'Not that it hasn't been a pleasure in *this* garden, but the Pod likes to sow his seed far and wide. And I hear *this* little plot is full of secret treats. Like I say, a pleasure garden.'

Diana's face drained of colour. 'You know, don't you?'

'Eh?'

'About Amos. You know all about it.'

'I have no idea what you're rabbiting on about, queen.' He glanced at his watch. 'But I do know that I've got to be somewhere right now. I'll catch you later, eh?'

She eyed him suspiciously. He was behaving very oddly tonight.

Without warning, he grabbed her hands and pressed them to his mouth. 'You could be quite something,' he breathed into her knuckles. 'Anyone who can operate like you do, look like you do, have two kids and run a habit the size of yours is some queen. Don't burn yourself out, eh?'

Diana bristled. 'If you're trying to end this, I have to warn you it was never anything to start with.'

'I'm not ending anything,' he said, suddenly thinking about Mo and finding the smile stripped away from his face as he dropped Diana's hands. 'I'm just putting a few things on hold.' My heart, he added silently.

His head had been so seduced by the idea of the Gunning ghosts, and later of the Pleasure Garden and of secret treasure, that he hadn't felt his heart breaking. Tonight he had let his head finally cut all ties from his heart, split them with a sword so sharp he hardly felt the pain.

'In that case, you're fired – as a dealer and a lover.' Diana lifted her chin. 'Nobody puts me on hold.'

'Not even Amos?'

To his surprise, Diana whimpered as though hit. She had more heart than he had given her credit for. While his dangled limp and truncated, hers was pumping hard enough for both of them. Which was when the truth suddenly hit him.

'You and Amos used to meet in the garden, didn't you? In the Gunning Woods? When you were lovers?'

Eyes wide, totally cornered, she nodded.

'You found the secret entrance . . . in the copper beech hedge.'

She nodded.

Bingo! 'How did you ever find out how to open it? It's so well hidden.'

She blinked in surprise. 'Amos took you there?'

He tilted his head in a gesture that could have meant anything, but to Diana – who was so desperate to know about Amos – it was an affirmation.

'Accident. We were kissing and I leaned back – Amos must have shown you how the catch is levered above the mossy quoin stone. I was standing on it to be at his height. You'd never know it was there unless someone told you what to look for, but it's pretty obvious once you spot it. We went there every day.'

'It became your garden.'

'For a while. What did he tell you when he took you there?'

'Nothing, Diana. He said nothing.'

'So why did he show it to you?'

'He didn't.'

'But you said . . . but . . .'

Unable to look her in the face any longer, he surprised her with a big hug, kissing her nose and whispering in her ear 'Talk to Sexton from the market garden. He'll get you anything from ganja to Class A. I've loved being your middleman, but now that I'm fired, it's time you two got to know one another. Just tread carefully. He already has a wife, a lover and a mistress. I think you should keep your clothes on at least the first time you ask for drugs.'

Diana pulled away from him. 'What are you up to, Pod?'

'Tonight, I'm leaving for bad, but I hope I'm staying for good.'

'What's that supposed to mean?'

He cocked his head and reached out so that his hand rested warmly on her chest. 'I'll always be in here, queen. Pod never leaves his women. He lives on in their hearts.'

'That's bullshit.'

His phone let out another beep and, as he plucked it from his pocket, Diana caught sight of the little flashing photograph.

'Oh, God, I knew it. Poor Rory.'

'They were never going to make it,' he said coldly as he read the message: *Just saying hi to Mummy & will w8 for you in a min.* Great. She was seeing her mother first. Typical bird. That's why he loved . . .

'And Mo?' Diana was asking.

'Leave her out of this. She knows I'm not on an exclusive. So, I'm showing a girl round a pretty garden. So what? Dilly is just a bit of fun.'

'Then don't take her to Gunning!' she pleaded. 'Not to the gardens. You have no idea what you're doing.'

'You know what they say,' he started sauntering away, 'you can take a whore to culture, but you can't make her think. See you around, flower.'

Leaving Diana reeling in the darkest corner of the Manor gardens, he raced towards their rendezvous at the Manor gates, ready to take Dilly to the Lodes Inn car park and the trail bike. As a final insult, he left his baseball cap balanced on the sleeping Rory's head, with the felt-penned message 'You lose, I win' on the peak.

Armed with as many champagne bottles as they could lift, he whisked Dilly away amid the confusion of departing fire-fighters and arriving party-goers. Attracted by the fire, the younger Wycks were making an unsuccessful attempt to gatecrash the harvest supper. Their rivalry with the Gates family threatened to spark into a public spat, as the latter – by far the majority of the hired staff for the night – enjoyed enforcing their strictly ticket-only instructions.

Provided with the perfect covering distraction, Pod and Dilly fled to explore the Pleasure Garden. Together, they rattled up the Springlode hill on the back of Pod's trail bike. Pressing her cheek to Pod's hard denim-jacketed back as they raced around the darkening lanes, Dilly knew that she had found her soul mate at last.

Pod just wanted to see a garden. Little did he know it would change his life for ever.

Faith was having a lousy night. Her parents had dragged her to this stupid party against her will, and she had absolutely no intention of enjoying herself. So far she had seen Pod for all of a nanosecond, and he had totally blanked her. Her new hair extensions itched and she longed to be rid of them. All her classmates at Market Addington sixth-form college had obviously found them funnier than a new Shrek movie. Faith already loathed the curly blonde rats' tails. But they had cost a fortune to have done in a trendy Oxford salon and her mother refused to pay to have them taken out again so soon. Rather horrifyingly, Anke seemed to like her daughter's new 'Heidi' bouffant, but it made Magnus cackle with laughter and yodel every time he passed her, while Chad sang *High on a Hill Lived a Lonely Goatherd.* Worst of all, Graham had told her she looked 'really pretty'. Faith wanted to puke.

Glad Tidings was trotting around banging a gong to try to lure the villagers in from the gardens, where most had been lurking by the yews trying to rubber-neck the last of the action from the fire. 'Dinner will be served in five minutes,' she warbled.

Faith had no appetite. The thought of sitting with bragging Graham and her dotty grandfather was hardly appealing. Magnus would just tease her about her hair and her mother was bound to try to drag her into conversation with strangers that would make her look an idiot because she'd become shy and tongue-tied.

She recognised Pod's baseball cap on the figure drunkenly lounging on a garden bench in the twilight. This time she *had* to pluck up the courage to say hello. He *had* been in her bedroom, after all. He had admired the sacred Grand National poster. That made them friends, didn't it?

But when she got close, she realised that it was Rory Midwinter, poetically draped across the painted ironwork in a crumpled linen suit. She didn't notice the almost empty bottle of scotch that had rolled beneath a nearby box hedge.

Faith stared at him, unable to shake from her head the image of what she had seen at the stables, most especially the Purple Thing. No wonder he was so tired, she thought sourly. All that bonking.

Feeling a bit pervy for staring at him so long, she turned back the house and promptly fell over a stone urn, yelping as her shins took a scraping.

One lazy almond-shaped eye opened and studied her woozily in the gloom, taking in the riot of curls and the floaty chiffon top sliding off narrow shoulders.

'Baby! You're here.'

Faith froze, her face turned away from him as she crouched to rub her grazed legs.

'My bloody sister's convinced you're after Sod – I mean Pod – but I told her you were mine,' he said, his voice slurred and sleepy.

Faith's heart leapt.

'He's a bastard, darling,' he yawned. 'And he's practically married. Stick with me. I'll make you happy, I promise.'

She hardly dared move. Then she heard him clamber to his feet and lurch towards her. 'C'm'ere – I'll help you up,' he growled teasingly, stooping clumsily to take her hand and almost falling over. She could feel his hot breath on her neck as he pressed his face into it and giggled. 'You smell fantastic.'

Faith had splashed on half a bottle of her mother's Chanel, and could be smelled almost half a mile away.

'Mmm . . .' He started kissing her throat.

Faith almost expired. She closed her eyes in ecstasy. She'd never experienced anything this sensational.

'I know I'm a lousy boyfriend, but I'll try to make it up to you,' he drawled between kisses, one hand sliding beneath her top.

Faith didn't want this to stop. She never wanted this to stop, but she knew she had to identify herself.

'Rory, it's Faith.'

'Huh?' He switched to the other side of her throat and almost fell over again.

'Faith.'

'Yeah, I know,' he giggled.

Just for a moment, Faith experienced a wild and wicked sense of abandon. He knew it was her. He was seducing her, Faith Brakespear, teenage temptress.

'I've got to have Faith,' he breathed.

Oh boy, oh boy, oh boy! She wanted to whoop.

'You're right. I should trust you more,' he went on, nibbling at her shoulders. 'Have faith in you, Dills.'

The bubble burst. Faith wanted to weep.

'No, no, you don't understand.' She turned so that he could see her face. But, as she did so, he slid his lips straight on to her mouth and drew her into a kiss she never knew existed.

Stuff the Addington college bitches. Stuff Graham and Magnus and the whole of wretched Oddlode village. This made it worth putting up with all the torture life threw at her. It didn't even really matter that he thought she was Dilly. She was flattered. She must kiss at least as well, for a start, because he was making all sorts of happy moaning noises.

Rory was suddenly feeling very nauseous. He stumbled back towards the bench.

Faith hung her head, convinced that she had been rumbled. She started to slink away in shame.

'Don't go,' he groaned, holding out his hand. 'I'll be all right in a minute.'

She hovered uncertainly.

Vision blurred, belly heaving, he squinted up at her through his hair, seeing about eight very distorted girlfriends in silhouette, with the Manor's flickering hurricane lamps and the rising moon casting dim light on her blonde curls.

'I love you.'

'I love you too,' she breathed, because she had never said it before and she wanted to try it out. It sounded so good she believed it straight-away.

'Even though I'm a penniless drunk?'

'Especially because you are.'

'Your voice sounds funny,' he giggled, slumping back again, his head lolling. 'Come here, baby.'

Girding her loins and holding in her stomach, Faith let her hair extensions fall across her face as she scuttled towards him. She needn't have cared as Rory had his eyes shut, his face strangely pale. She stroked his hair away from his eyes with shaking fingers, unable to resist the temptation to trace the contours of his face – those razor-sharp cheekbones and wide lips.

'Mm, that's nice,' he breathed sleepily.

His shirt was open at the neck, revealing tufts of sandy hair. She curled her fingers through it in wonder, astonished at its softness.

'You are *so* damned sexy.' His voice was barely a purr. 'Do that a little lower.'

And so Faith made her first full-on attempt at flirtatious seduction, unaware that Rory had already fallen asleep by the time her fingers reached his belly button, daring herself to find the Purple Thing.

Ingmar Olesen was once again delighting Truffle – and appalling her lover Vere Peplow – by reciting Danish poetry with theatrical aplomb as they finished their aperitifs in the Manor's cavernous reception hall, overlooked by macabre oils of wild game in their death throes.

Truffle, who had always had a soft spot for Ingmar, was especially flattered by his attentions this evening because they put Drear's retroussé nose so out of joint. Her dapper admirer had become rather lax of late. Ingmar – who towered over the little cravatted one – had a deep, mellifluous voice and charming, clever blue eyes which quite devoured one when they seared in one's direction. Who cared that he could never remember her name when he had such charisma?

Magnus was equally entranced by his grandfather's performance and started to translate the poems into English in a notepad, planning to turn them into Road Kill lyrics.

'I really must hurry you, ladies and gentlemen!' Glad Tidings sallied through with her gong once more. 'The soup will go cold if you don't take your places soon.' She neglected to mention that the soup was chilled.

'May I accompany you through to the orangery, Mrs Dacre-Hopkinson?' Ingmar offered her his arm, a rare pocket of memory finding her name.

Truffle shot a look towards Vere who was colouring to match his burgundy cravat and kerchief. She shivered delightedly.

'I'm very sorry, old chap.' Vere puffed up to his full five feet six inches as he tapped Ingmar on a lofty shoulder. 'I think you'll find that the lady is my dinner guest this evening.'

'And you are?'

'Vere Peplow!' he said indignantly, convinced this oversight was a deliberate slight given previous social introductions.

'In that case, Mr Peplow, is it not up to the lady who she would like to go through with?' Ingmar peered down at him curiously, owl to dormouse.

'Well, quite, another time perhaps. But I did buy our dinner tickets this evening.'

'Oh really, Vere,' Truffle giggled capriciously. 'They were all of fifteen pounds a head – one wouldn't get a starter at Eastlode Park for that. And you made me arrive alone.'

'Couldn't be helped, m'dear.'

'Rather a poor show, don't you think?' Ingmar mocked Vere's quacky accent in a delightful loopy, Danish impersonation.

The little art dealer glared up at him. 'Listen, old chap, I don't want to get into a confrontation here. This is jolly ungallant of you. Hands off, okay?' He offered Truffle his arm.

'I have no intention of doing anything ungallant with my hands,' Ingmar continued, offering the crook of his own arm to Truffle and giving her a wicked smile. 'At least not tonight.'

'I say!' Vere puffed up again.

'Oh, what a divided duty,' Truffle clamped her hands together in front of her mouth and looked euphorically from one to the other.

'Back orrfff,' Vere growled at Ingmar.

'No,' Ingmar smiled down at him grandly.

'I mean it.' Vere marched up to glare at his rival's shirt buttons, with which his eyes were level.

'Or what will happen?' Ingmar seemed genuinely curious. 'You will challenge me to a duel perhaps?'

'Oh heaven!' Truffle squeaked.

Vere snapped. 'Look here, you pompous old Kraut! I'm not taking any more of this. I don't know what German sewer you were dragged up in, but here in England we treat women and their consorts with a little more respect than this.'

'I am Danish, sir, and if you persist in insulting me then I will have to fight you.'

Listening in – along with a gathering crowd of harvest supper guests – Magnus snorted with laughter. Then his smile fell away as his grandfather removed his jacket, loosened his tie and started to roll up his sleeves. Oh Christ. He was serious.

'Morfar. Morfar – that's enough,' he waded in cheerfully, trying to laugh off the incident.

'And who are you?' demanded Ingmar, his great oak branch forearms appearing through the folded cuffs. 'Do you want to fight me too? Do you? Do you?'

'It's Magnus, Morfar,' he hissed in the old man's ear, anxious that Ingmar was saved further humiliation amongst his neighbours and customers. 'Your grandson.'

'Don't be ridiculous!' Ingmar snapped, glaring at him as he pulled away. 'What an earth are you talking about?'

'Stay there!' Magnus insisted, although nobody was listening to him. Ingmar was prowling around psyching himself up for the fight, punching one great fist into a broad palm. Vere Peplow was whimpering anxiously and looking around for the best escape route as he hid behind Truffle, who was bouncing up and down in a state of feverish, flattered excitement. Nobody had fought over her since the 1978 hunt ball when the Wop had found out about her affair with a ten-goal old Etonian.

Magnus went in search of his mother, loping hurriedly along the terrace towards the orangery, but he was distracted by the sight of his stepfather sneaking in through the darkened rose garden, covered in grass seed.

A moment later, the village primary school teacher – who Magnus rather lusted after – appeared through the shadowy vegetable patch, also covered in seed.

'Bloody hell.' Magnus stopped and spun around in surprise.

Then his pale eyebrows shot up even higher as, on the opposite side of the terrace, he spotted his mother creeping across the garden with two new friends, all giggling like teenagers.

Tutting beneath his breath, he headed back to rescue his grandfather. But to his relief, Ingmar appeared to have completely forgotten about his fight and was happily accompanying Truffle to supper whilst Vere escorted her on the other side. Truffle shot Magnus a smooth wink as they passed.

He lingered on the terrace for a moment, peering thoughtfully up at the sky. The stars were out in force like fans at a rock concert holding up lighters during the ballad.

Something about this valley turned people's heads, he decided. It wasn't healthy.

Furious that Pod had once again abandoned her with her knickers round her ankles, Diana was mutinous. She would settle for nothing less than castration.

She had prowled the Manor grounds for ten minutes trying to hunt him down, determined to make the cocky little upstart suffer.

'"Pod never leaves his women", my bloody arse!' she growled as she peered into the potting sheds before stalking past the vegetable garden to the secluded shrubbery with its high box hedges. 'I'm not his to leave. And he's not going anywhere. He's just taken too much of his own delusional powdered medicine.'

When she peered over the shrubbery hedge, she caught her breath. Dilly was wrapped around Pod in a clichéd clinch on a garden bench. He hadn't even bothered to take off his baseball cap, the lout.

'You gutless bastard!' she snarled from her lair. 'You really have the balls of a pathetic little schoolboy, don't you? God knows why you wear grown-up underpants – talk about two peas in a Pod.'

Springing out of the covering box hedge, she was appalled to realise that they were Anke's underage daughter and her own brother.

'What in hell's name do you think you're doing?' she demanded as she reeled back in horror.

Squeaking in terror, Faith fled.

Diana looked down at Rory in despair.

At least he appeared to have been unconsciously committing statutory rape, in the sense that he was completely and utterly unconscious.

She pressed her fingers to her throbbing forehead and let out a deep, unhappy sigh before settling beside him on the bench and patting his unconscious arm.

'What a wretched pair we make, huh? The cuckolded drunk and the spurned wife whose pretty playthings fall for each other. We really are classic members of this family.' She let out a soft laugh. 'I think it's time I dried you out, sweetness. I'm not as good at coping on my own as I thought I'd be. Nanny's right. The ghosts keep waking up.'

She tracked down Aunt Bell and discreetly apologised that Rory was not feeling too well and was better off being taken home.

'Drunk again?' Hell's Bells was no fool. Her silver bullet eyes hit both targets centrally as they bored into Diana's. 'I am so glad that you are back. That boy needs sorting out before he does something very silly.'

'We both do,' Diana murmured as she headed back to try to manhandle Rory to her car.

Anke had started to enjoy the company of Pixie and Pheely, although she was convinced they were mythical dryads. Having retreated to an old glasshouse to avoid the soup, they were happily swapping stories and gossip.

'Does anyone actually eat the supper tonight?' Anke asked, glancing at her watch. She shouldn't have had so much punch. She felt quite dizzy.

'Lord, no – the food is always vile,' Pheely assured her. 'Hell's Bells considers it a great and noble gesture to cook for her beloved villagers each harvest supper. Every year Glad Tidings tries to talk her out of it. Every year she doggedly refuses any help, gives her all to some seriously cheap minced meat, and at least half the guests spend the entire next day on the bog or receiving emergency dental treatment. She could overcook a bran mash.'

'Nothing compared to Diana's dinner party, though!' Pixie giggled, having heard talk of the boil-in-the-bag fish pie and melted ice-cream pudding. 'That sounded truly noxious.'

Anke blushed. 'Oh, it really wasn't that bad,' she muttered guiltily.

'Rubbish,' Pheely snorted. 'Di is the gremlin version of Nigella Lawson, except that instead of accidentally being splashed with water, this gremlin is steeped in gin.'

'I've *heard* she likes something a little stronger than gin,' Pixie whispered knowingly.

'No? What? Not?' Pheely shook her sensimilla pouch questioningly.

'No. Stronger.'

'Don't tell me she smokes crack in the hayloft?' Pheely was agog. 'Shoots up heroin in the tack room? Steals Ketamine from the horses' first aid box?'

During the dramatic pause that followed, which Pixie eked out by rolling her eyes around for theatrical effect, Anke considered mentioning the ACP horse sedative that Diana had accidentally knocked back with gin, but decided against it. This was too fascinating to interrupt.

'*Cocaine*,' Pixie mouthed at last.

'No!' Anke was genuinely appalled.

'Probably dates back to her bloodstock days,' Pheely nodded. 'Typical Diana. Cocaine is so eighties. They were all at it in the racing industry then.'

'Some still are.' Pixie ruffled her blue hair as she leaned forwards to share, eyes stretched wide. 'She's been cutting her – um – deals, shall we say, with a certain young jockey who moved into the area at the same time.'

'No!' Anke was almost too shocked to speak.

'Hardly surprising.' Pheely raised an eyebrow. 'That girlfriend of his – the school teacher – is always wired. Strikes me as terribly druggy. Probably prescription in her case, though.'

'No!' It was Pixie's turn to join in the cry with Anke. Both of them had children in Mo's care.

'I rather like her,' Pheely went on to confess, 'but darling Dilly says she's really quite batty. Tried to kill herself a few times, I gather.'

'God! No?' Anke was horrified.

'How does she know that?' asked Pixie.

'She's at college with someone who knew her from Newmarket or Honiton, I think.' Pheely waved a vague hand. 'But she seemed pretty convinced. Abandoned by her mother as a toddler, never knew her father, crashed and burned as a singer.'

'Ballet dancer,' Anke corrected quietly.

'So you know all this?'

'Some of it. She spoke a little that night at Diana's. I think she is very sorted out now. She doesn't strike me as unstable or druggy.'

'Nobody would compared to the Nigella gremlin,' Pixie giggled.

'The Nigremlin!' Pheely joined in the laughter. 'That's what we'll call her!'

Anke tried not to feel disloyal that both women disliked Diana so much, and that they bitched about pretty Mo, too. Diana *was* very sharp and bossy, after all – and Mo was very . . . young. At least Anke could be honest with these women. They were, after all, united in their mistrust of men, most specifically their husbands and lovers. She hadn't felt able to speak openly about her relationship with anyone for years, and yet during their few meetings she, Pixie and Pheely had shared intimacies she'd thought beyond her. She had yet to confess that she and Graham never had sex together, but she'd touched upon a more recent fear that she was amazed hadn't shocked them in the slightest. Swimming with fruit punch, she couldn't help but bring it up again tonight.

'I think my husband is sleeping with someone else,' she sighed.

'I *know* my husband is sleeping with someone else,' Pixie groaned.

'And I'm sleeping with somebody else's husband,' Pheely giggled, hastily adding, 'It's okay – neither of yours.' And then, seeing their eyes dart to her stomach, she held up her hands. 'Okay, I *was* sleeping with somebody else's husband, and now I'm up the spout. It's not all green grass on the other side. Talking of which . . .'

The home-grown sensimilla was brought out. Smoked neat with no tobacco (Pheely: 'We must think of the baby'), it made them legless within seconds.

Anke felt her suspicions brand her heart as she let euphoria mix with paranoia. Graham had made up such a phoney excuse to arrive late tonight – and under separate steam from the family – that she had to laugh. For the past fortnight, he'd looked guilty and jumpy all the time. He'd stopped pawing her incessantly in bed. He was like a naughty little boy. She giggled at the memory of him mumbling and bumbling out his line this evening about needing to pop up to Dulston's to check he'd left the alarm set and that he would see them all at the Manor. She wished she felt angrier, but she simply felt the same curious fascination and throbbing guilt that she had when, years earlier, she had discovered his porn stash. Most of all she felt jealous. Jealous that someone – anyone – could desire him when she couldn't.

It was Diana Lampeter, she suddenly decided with the certainty of the unaccustomed dope-smoker. Graham was sleeping with Diana Lampeter.

'I want to have an affair of my own!' she raged.

'I want to prune my bastard husband's balls off,' Pixie cackled.

'I want a boy. They're such fun, especially around here . . .' Pheely said dreamily, hugging her belly and adding, 'Unless one's unfortunate enough to be born a Delamere, of course. They all died young, poor bastards.'

'Delamere?' Anke questioned, head spinning.

'The family name of the Barons Sarsden,' she explained, settling back to tell the story of the Gunning Estate ghosts.

'You name it, it's haunted in that place. Every flipping tree is out to get you – try riding a horse or walking a dog in there. They won't go further than a few yards over the boundary. The whole estate is criss-crossed with overgrown paths and bridleways nobody uses apart from the odd unsuspecting rambler, and they soon run away screaming. And as for the house,' she whistled. 'Well, I've only been *in* there once and it's stolen ten years of my life. I seriously thought I'd look in a mirror and find my hair grey. You can laugh!' She pointed accusingly at her snorting companions. 'You bloody well go there. I tell you, it freaks you out, that place. Amos Gates isn't a gamekeeper. He's keeper of the undead. They'll never sell it. Even the hunt won't go there, and they're trying to keep a low profile these days.'

'So what is the story?' Anke asked, the sweet taste of dope reminding her of Kurt.

'Unrequited love,' Pheely announced dramatically. 'What else? There are a hundred different stories about what started it, but all of them basically say the same thing – one of our horny Sarsden baronets fell for the wrong girl and all hell broke loose. He might have raped her, impregnated her out of wedlock, murdered her in a jealous rage, neglected her until she died of heartbreak – it makes no difference. The ghosts started rampaging around the house. They ripped turf from the parkland, they rattled the trees in the woods, and even now they refuse to let a soul rest. They set man against man in the big house – more duels were fought on the old Elm Walk at Foxrush Hall than any other place in England, believe it or not. Brother killed brother, father killed son, child killed mentor. One story says that there is a gypsy curse that means no Sarsden son will survive beyond thirty. Quite a legacy. It's no wonder they are reluctant to claim the place.'

'Shall we go there now?' Pixie suggested eagerly.

'What?' Anke spluttered.

Pheely hugged her bump uncertainly. 'I'm not sure I wouldn't rather inflict Hell's Bells' shepherd's pie on my unborn than that.'

'Oh, go on.' Pixie's winning, chinchilla eyes gleamed in the half-light. 'Pleeeeeease. I can't face sitting next to Sexton when he hits his third bottle of red. He'll already be boring everyone rigid, rambling on about organic tubers.'

'I suppose it *would* annoy Hell's Bells rather splendidly if we don't go in at all,' Pheely mused. 'And I can't even bloody drink – or catch up with Dilly because she'll no doubt be all over Rory. She must be going home with him because she gave me her car keys – aha!' She reached in her pocket to draw them out and waggle them. 'We have transport!'

'So we can go.' Pixie clapped her hands like a seal.

'I can't.' Anke could feel that sweet, familiar nostalgia from smoking dope being replaced by the far less pleasant paranoia. 'My children are here, and my poor father . . .'

'They'll all be fine.'

'I must find Graham.' She baulked again.

'Rubbish.' Pheely took her hand. 'The Gunning ghosts hate men, so he can't come.'

'What about your baby?' Anke looked at the bump, desperate to get out of the expedition.

'With a mother like me – almost certainly gay, so technically he doesn't count. Let's go. Dilly's 2CV isn't much of an off-roader so we won't get too close. We won't go near the house. I can't risk undermining my henna tint.'

'We'll be back in time for pudding,' Pixie promised Anke as they tiptoed through the garden, passing beneath the glowing windows and clattering, murmuring noise of the orangery, before slipping out of the gates and skipping across the green with whoops of nervous laughter.

Hoping Faith was still keeping an eye on Chad, Anke clambered into the waiting 2CV, feeling light-headed and rebellious, like an insubordinate teenager. The moment Pheely set off at a kangaroo hop – 'I haven't driven a car for years – what fun!' – she ducked down in the back seat and gripped her knees for dear life.

'First casualty,' Pixie pointed out happily as they passed a large estate car into which a dark-haired woman was trying to cram a very floppy drunk. 'Is that who I think it is?' She recognised Diana Lampeter, but Pheely was too busy battling with the unfamiliar gears to notice. In the back, Anke tried and failed to lift her head high enough to see. She was going to have to ride this one out with her head between her knees, she realised, feeling like the teenager who has agreed to take the scary fairground ride because her friends have goaded her into it, only to find herself feeling far too ill to open her eyes once throughout the experience.

18

Driving a comatose Rory home to Upper Springlode, Diana came up behind a 2CV being driven very erratically and painfully slowly.

'Oh, for God's sake!' She watched her speedometer crawling at twenty.

It was weaving around so much in the narrow lane that she couldn't hope to overtake it.

Diana suddenly recognised it as the silly toy car belonging to Rory's girlfriend, and flashed her lights several times. Perhaps Dilly had seen the error of her ways and was making a lovelorn dash to the yard to see Rory? She was probably crying too much to see straight, the poor thing. Then as both cars rounded a bend so that the moon was ahead of them, she saw two silhouettes in the 2CV. The driver had long curly hair; the passenger short spiky hair. It had to be Dilly and Pod. She wasn't going to fall for that mistaken identity goof twice in one night.

Anger flashed white for a moment before the red mist descended. When the car ahead took a sharp left on to a farm track and pelted away up a steep hill towards the outskirts of the Gunning Estate, she gave chase, following the red tail-lights bobbing along the rutted track ahead of her. Aware of being followed, the little French car suddenly speeded up. Adrenaline instantly coursed through Diana's veins – both at the thrill of the chase and the prospect of finding out what the hell Pod and Dilly were playing at, but also at the ever-approaching tree-line that marked the start of Gunning land.

Rory was snoring on the back seat. Book at Bedtime was on the radio. It *would* be a gothic ghost story. Diana leaned forward to try to switch it off and almost left the track, which was barely the width of her car and skirted with deep ditches. She was forced to listen.

'The howling and screaming reached a fever pitch as the two infant children burned alive,' said a blood-chillingly calm narrator who sounded suspiciously like normally cosy, coffee-hour Anna Massey. 'Their cries were heard all night, although those who saw the scene afterwards said that the children would have died within minutes. And every night from that day on those children screamed –'

'Oh, do shut up,' Diana shouted at her radio, trying to stay on the track.

She was too intently focused on the car ahead to spot dim headlights turning on to the track far behind her as a third car joined the chase.

'There's definitely someone following us!' Pheely gasped, driving even more badly.

'Oh, yippee! How thrilling.' Pixie twisted around. 'No blue lights, so it's not the fuzz. Just shake them off.'

'I'll try, darling. Pheely pulled the gear stick backwards and forwards at random like an eager first-time gambler playing a one-armed bandit. 'But would you mind awfully putting that joint out just in case it *is* the police?'

'Oh God.' Anke tried and failed to lift her head for long enough to look out of the rear window and see where they were.

She gulped at the fresh blast of air which hit her face when Pixie flipped open the window to throw out her spliff.

'*Two* cars following us!' Pixie corrected herself as she poked her head out of the window and peered back. 'The first one gaining, the second at some distance. Step on it, sister!'

'Oh God,' Anke repeated, despite her lifetime's atheism. It was time to say a few prayers. She was trapped in a whining, rattling, rusting heap of a car with two stoned women fantasising they were Thelma and Louise.

It no longer mattered that Graham, the dunce of adulterers, had left tell-tale signs of an extra-marital all over the house for a fortnight. She longed to be with him more than anything right now. She could even forgive him an affair with Diana Lampeter – her greatest dread and her secret belief. If she was only with him now instead of here, she would forgive him anything.

Diana was still so intent on catching up with Dilly's car that she hadn't seen the headlights in her own rear-view mirror. But she was aware of Rory waking up and groaning.

'Nearly home, Rory!' she told him brightly. 'Just get your head down.'

'Ugghhhmmmmmmmouch,' he groaned as they bounced over potholes, the low car body scraping noisily on the dried mud and stones of the rutted track. Ahead the rattling, high-axled 2CV had no such problems.

The ditched verges were now replaced by high hedges as they climbed towards the ridge, the track twisting sickeningly. Diana knew the track from childhood – she had ridden along it many times. The fearsome hedges now gulfing them on either side were known as Look and Leap by the hunt because, if you jumped one, you were committed to the other with no room for a stride in between. Few had ever attempted the challenge, but on one famous occasion Hell's Bells had cleared both in one huge jump on her hunter, Osprey. Diana had once tried to replicate the heroic move and had crashed right through the second hedge, galloping away with most of it hanging from her hunt coat and a great gap in the thorn behind her.

'Bugger!' She realised that the red tail-lights had vanished ahead of her and she must have missed it turning off the track. Craning around, she hit reverse and backed up around the tight twists until she came across an open gateway with a tell-tale flattening of the long grass in its entrance.

Then she jumped as she spotted lights coming up the track behind her. Surely Dilly and Pod hadn't somehow doubled back and found themselves behind her?

Craning around once more, she realised that these weren't 2CV headlights. As the strange car came into view, the lights lined up on the roof and across the grille blazed into action, bright white halogens specifically fitted to enable gamekeepers and estate workers to spot missing game or poachers.

'Oh, shit!' Diana accelerated through the gateway.

Behind her, Rory threw up over the back seat.

Had anyone been out for a late-night stroll along the footpath that followed the little brook which trickled and gushed its way from high in the marl hills to the west of Lower Springlode down towards the Odd, they would have witnessed an unusual sight in the sloping stubble-fields beside them that evening as a 2CV, an Audi and a Land Rover raced around in ever-decreasing circles. It was uncertain who was chasing whom but, as the cars bounced and skidded around on the drought-hardened ground, they inched ever-closer to the Gunning parkland. Soon one had threaded its way through an open gateway on to the ancient grassed turf, followed by another and then the third – its searchlights beaming like a light sabre across the beautiful furling deer park towards the woods.

They were slaloming through the old park trees now, narrowly missing ancient chestnuts, oaks and cedars, all three cars perilously close together.

'I think I am going to be sick!' Anke wailed in the back of the 2CV.

*   *   *

In the back of the Audi, Rory gave no such warning as he vomited for a second time.

'Oh, this is *such* fun!' shrieked Pixie. 'Go faster! They're catching us. Head for that track in the woods over there. No left – LEFT. Watch out for the – aghhh!'

Straightening up at last, rather too fast, Anke was in time to see something vast and black and very solid seconds away from making contact with the nearside wing of the car. Then, just before the loud crunching bang and the tooth-loosening jolt reverberated through them, the car seemed to spring up in the air and crash back down again with a strange ripping sound. At that moment, Anke got a lot more fresh air than she had bargained for. She was face-to-face with a fast-approaching tree and she had no car around her head any more.

'Aghhhhhhhhh!'

Pheely hung her head as she regarded the wreckage of her daughter's beloved car wrapped around the estate's famous Thousand Year Oak high on Heaven Hill. Pixie had only sustained a small cut on the head, thank goodness, and dear Anke appeared unscathed apart from the unfortunate moment when her hair clip had shredded the rotten canvas covering of the car while careering over a particularly big pothole, causing her head to pop through the roof as they approached the tree. Delayed shock was inevitable . . .

'Now is everybody sure they are in one piece?' She checked again as they examined arms, legs and fingernails.

Anke nodded shakily, clutching her head as though amazed it was still there. 'Who are they?' She watched as one of the sets of headlights turned towards them.

'Teenage hooligans?' Pheely suggested, pressing a hand to Anke's brow to check her temperature.

'Poachers?' Pixie sounded excited.

'Master criminals?' Pheely shuddered theatrically, reassured that Anke was a normal temperature and now checking her pulse.

'Ghosts?' Pixie gasped hopefully.

'*Ghosts?!*' Anke yelped, suddenly starting to believe in them as doped terror hit her full throttle.

'Don't worry, darling – gosh your pulse *is* fast.' Pheely patted her hand. 'I don't think any of the Gunning ghosts drives – apart from a headless coachman or two. They certainly don't drive Audis. *And* ghosts don't listen to Radio Four,' she reflected as a big estate car, now caked in muddy dust, drew alongside them, booming out a late-night comedy sketch show.

The window slid down a fraction, its driver not visible. 'Are you all okay? Do you need me to call an ambulance?'

'No, we're fine!' Pixie assured her brightly, impressed that she was meeting a poacher who was a 'sister'.

'Well, I'm not,' wailed a plaintive voice from inside the car and someone almost threw himself from a rear door just as a huge diesel roar announced the arrival of the third member of their unconventional convoy with its blinding lights.

'Shit!' The driver of the estate car accelerated away, rear door still swinging.

'Definitely poachers,' Pheely said confidently as she recognised the big off-roader approaching them now as one of the Gunning cars.

While Pixie crouched over the slumped figure who had just thrown himself out of the Audi, Pheely turned brightly to the roaring Land Rover, ready apologetically to introduce herself. But it was already accelerating away in a flurry of sheep droppings and divots as it once again gave chase to the dusty estate car – into the darkened heart of the estate itself.

'Wow! How exciting. Shall we stay and watch?'

'I don't think we have much choice,' Anke said dryly, joining Pixie who was leaning over the ejected passenger. 'Is he all right?'

'Oh yes. Just very pissed.'

All three women recognised Rory Midwinter, although he was far too drunk to recognise them or to explain how he had ended up in a poacher's car. He managed to stagger upright and then hugged the huge oak for support, face pressed against its bark.

'Are you sure this has nothing to do with ghosts?' Pixie suggested breathlessly once more.

The car engines were fading now, the lights long gone as they had plunged deep into the nearby woods. They suddenly felt very isolated in the big, neglected park, the harvest moon disappearing behind a black rain cloud as the wind picked up.

Pheely shivered and hugged her bump. 'God, I'd forgotten quite how creepy it is around here.'

They all jumped as an owl screeched.

Pixie span slowly around. 'Whereabouts is the old house?'

Pheely pointed west. 'On the far side of the woods. It's got trees on three sides and acres of gardens on the fourth so that it can't be seen by a living soul unless they are on Gunning land. The Delameres were an anti-social lot.'

'Does anyone have a mobile telephone?' Anke suggested weakly. 'I can call Graham and ask him to come and pick us up, maybe?'

'We could stay a little while, surely?' Pixie entreated. 'Just in case the flaming horseman is hacking about tonight?'

Anke shuddered and looked at Pheely, but her friend had her head cocked, the whites of her eyes gleaming in alarm.

'Listen? Can you hear that?'

'Is it the cars coming back again?' Pixie suggested.

'No, it's a different sound. It sounds like . . .'

They all quailed as a motorbike burst from nearby woods and pelted past within inches of them, the pillion rider reaching out to pluck the baseball cap from Rory's head as he once again bent over to be sick.

Diana drove on in a panic, pursued by a roaring Land Rover. She knew the estate and, with the moon full, could cut her lights and still accelerate through the wooded walks, driving deeper and deeper into steel-dappled forestry as she tried to shake off her devil's tail. But his lights were still on a blinding full beam and he was closing in as she twisted and turned her way towards the house.

He wouldn't follow her to the house, surely? He would never dare.

Two hundred yards short of what had once been the formal gardens, she cut left along an almost-hidden track, past the derelict gardener's lodge and on to the legendary elm walk. She could hear pounding in her ears – horses' hooves or rushing blood?

Checking her rear-view mirror once more, she saw that the lights behind her were fading. He'd stopped chasing. He wouldn't follow her past the ghosts. Coward.

Victorious, Diana drove on through the thick pine woods and along-side the long ha-ha to the copper beech hedge, six feet taller than she remembered it. She stopped the engine and took a deep breath before getting out. The hidden gateway was still there, now almost overgrown.

She reached for the secret catch, realising that her hands were shaking crazily. Damn! She couldn't find it. Surely it was just to the left of the third stone down? No. She had remembered it wrongly. Maybe it was on the other side.

Her heart was beating faster and faster as she fumbled around trying to locate the catch. No longer protected inside her car, she felt vulner-able and aware of the thousands of acres of deserted blackness around her. Nobody could hear her scream here. She wouldn't be found for weeks.

She had to get into the Pleasure Garden. She was safe in there. She had always felt safe in the Pleasure Garden.

'Oh, come on!' she howled with frustration as she found what she knew to be the little metal catch and yet failed to make it spring. It must be broken, or rusted from neglect. She jabbed at it hard. 'Ouch!'

She'd sliced into her finger, quite deeply. In the darkness, she didn't realise how deep the cut was until she automatically pressed it between her lips and found her mouth full of blood.

Which was when the flashlight pinned her captive in its beam.

Diana stayed motionless, for a terrifying moment wondering whether it was a lamper's light – a torch set on top of the sights of a high-powered rifle, enabling the gunman to shoot into the gleaming, stunned eyes of wild animals late at night.

But, as this torch dropped its beam to check the ground over which its carrier was treading, she could see that it was held in a very shaky hand, incapable of shooting even the biggest of targets. As he walked out from beneath the canopy of trees, his short peppery black hair gleamed in the moonlight. His collar was turned up high, his shoulders hunched, and he crossed the ground with that unmistakeable seven-league stride he had always had, eyes resolutely staring at his huge dealer boots.

Amos.

Diana no longer felt the pain in her finger, nor sense the blood that trickled from it, across her lip and down her cheek. For a moment she was overcome with emotion. She could hardly breathe, the longing to embrace him was so great.

'You walked past the ghosts,' she breathed.

'There are no ghosts. We both know that.' He didn't look up.

'Why leave your car?'

'I cut through the Folly spinney.'

'You *didn't* want to pass the ghosts.'

'Will you shut up about the bloody ghosts? You're trespassing.'

'I'm trying to get into the garden.'

'It's not there any more.'

'Of course it's there. The gate is still there, but the catch won't work. I need to see it again.'

'The garden's not there. It was destroyed. The gate is nailed closed.'

'No!

'You're trespassing,' he repeated.

'You can't have destroyed his garden!'

'This is private land. You have to leave.' He flashed the light in her face and she heard his sharp intake of breath. 'What in Christ's name have you done?'

Diana touched her chin with her other hand and realised that there was blood all over her face. Her first thought was how disgusting it must look. She clutched her bleeding finger tightly in her fist and tucked it behind her, ducking her face out of the light.

'Sucked the neck of a virgin, what do you think?'

For a moment, she sensed that half-beat of uncertainty that always preceded Amos laughing – a gentle rumble of mirth that she had spent so many weeks and months enticing from his lips. People who called him humourless didn't know him. His laughter was a precious commodity that she had treasured.

But the laughter never came. Later, she wondered if she had imagined it.

'Get out of my life, Diana. There's no place for you here any more.'

'You can't drive me away, Amos. I had every right to move back.'

'You have no fucking right!'

'It's my home.'

'You almost destroyed me.'

'It was years ago.' She could taste the salty blood on her lips. 'Can't we put it behind us, move on?'

'We can never forget something like that. You know we can't forget.'

'We were just kids. Look, we're all grown up now. I know we'll never be friends, but surely . . .'

'Friends? *Friends*! I *hate*, you, Diana Henriques. I hate every cell in your body. I loathe you.'

She took a step back, her wounded finger throbbing in her clenched first.

'I have to see the garden again.'

'I've told you it's not there. Go away. Forget you ever came here tonight.'

'I'll just come back again.'

'I could have you arrested for trespassing.'

'I'll come along the footpaths, then. I can find the way in through the dodo maze.'

'There is no dodo maze anymore, Diana. It's all overgrown. The garden's gone.' His voice shook with fury. He was seconds away from total combustion. 'You as good as destroyed it when you destroyed me. It died too.'

Diana opened her mouth to snap that he looked pretty much alive and well from where she was standing, but then she closed it again.

Pressing her finger to her lips once more, she let the pain of the open wound shoot right through her. It was somehow fitting that she should be stabbed through with such agony when he said it:

'Go to hell, Diana. Go to fucking hell.'

'I've already been sent here,' she said quietly, turning away.

He'd finally said it.

Behind the steering-wheel in the sealed, air-conditioned tomb of her car, it took all Diana's reserves of self-control not to break down and weep. The Radio Four newsreader was announcing the midnight headlines in a grave tone. Diana spun the tyres through the leaf mulch and went in search of Rory and the chattering boho housewives.

Unable to watch her tail lights as they faded away, Amos pressed his face into his hands, barrelling the fleshy knuckles of his thumbs into his eye sockets as though trying to rid himself of her bloodstained face by literally rubbing it from his eyeballs. Then, checking that her car was out of the woods, he turned and clicked the hidden latch of the gate. It opened with perfect precision and well-oiled silence.

Pheely and Pixie giggled all the way home. Anke fought tears and then giggles and then tears, occasionally freezing in terror and looking out of the window as she wondered what Graham was up to. Occasionally she froze in greater fear as she realised what *she* had been up to.

In front of them, Rory was out cold in Diana's passenger seat, sleeping like a baby.

Diana drove like an automaton – back to Oddlode to drop her charges back at the Manor, then up to Springlode to manhandle Rory to bed and kiss his forehead; check on her children and kiss their foreheads; pay off Fe Sixsmith and kiss a lot of arse with a big bonus and much apologising for being so late. Finally she was alone. She stole out to the fields and sat on the High Hedges gate looking out across the moonlit Gunning woods.

She was convinced she could hear Rio snorting nearby, although only two of her new placid ponies occupied the field now, grazing nearby between curious sideways gazes at the figure wearing gumboots and an orange satin dress sitting on their gate. The stallion had lived in High Hedges during his brief spell at Overlodes, she remembered guiltily. She had never visited him, never dared to touch him. Tonight, she had been closer to him than she had in weeks.

In front of her, the great mass of shedding oaks that made up the bulk of the Gunning woods gleamed like a battered, rusty shield in the moonlight – a dark tarnished knot of impenetrable metalwork fortressed against her, the trees huddled tightly together with their moulting shoulders turned in denial.

Tonight, Amos had told her to go to hell. Well Tim had already done that. Both her life's loves had damned her – great and small. Diana dropped her chin into the cups of her hands, fingertips buried in her cheeks as she rolled her tongue around her mouth and felt her knuckles jump.

She was starting to get used to hell. It had a nostalgic feel to it. The kids were surprisingly happy and Rory needed her here. She might even feel brave enough to pat a horse soon.

She lifted her chin and pressed her little fingers into the corners of her mouth to let out a piercing whistle.

From the far distance, she was certain she heard a return call. Whether it was a whinny or another whistle was impossible to tell.

Diana smiled, pulled a blackberry from the thorny bramble beside her and meandered back to the glowing yellow pocket windows of Horseshoe Farm Cottage.

Just short of the back door, she stopped and looked up at the fat white moon.

'Nanny's wrong. I never left this bloody place that day. I've never left it. It spat me out.'

19

'Get out of my room, you little monsters!' Faith screamed at Chad and his new girlfriend when she caught them reading her diary again.

'That is so *gross*.' Chad handed it to her as they raced past, shrieking.

She slammed the door and ground her teeth, flipping open the pages and realising in horror that Chad had been reading out her latest entry, detailing the embarrassment of starting her period that week at college with no pads in her bag and no change for the machines in the loo. Rather than ask anyone for help, she had spent the entire day with loo paper stuffed into her knickers and had still had an embarrassing leakage on the bus home.

Sitting down on her bed and pulling out her mobile to text Carly, she wished more than anything that she had someone to talk to. She was finding it hard to make any real friends at college. Her mother had always been a good listener, but she was so busy at the moment helping Graham at Dulston's, checking up on Morfar and catering for a house full of children and teenagers that she never seemed to have any time for Faith.

Carly rang her straight back.

'I've got loads of credit on my mobile, so you can tell me everything that's going on, girlfriend.'

'It's like so crap here,' Faith complained. 'Mags has *three* girlfriends who are all sisters, which is like so weiring me out. Chad is going out with Mim Lampeter from his school and they're only nine. Even my *grandfather* has got a new girlfriend and he's like barking mad. Why can't I get a boyfriend?'

'Magnus has three girlfriends?' Carly said in a small voice.

'Kind of. The Sixsmith sisters – the Three Disgraces everyone calls them. I don't think Mags is serious about any of them, but they all hang around together. This house is madness – they're here smoking in the kitchen all the time, Chad's silly girlfriend comes here after school along with her little brother who screams non-stop. It's like a youth club. Mum does nothing but tidy up after everyone. The only person who doesn't suffer is bloody Graham because he's playing with his tractors till late most nights. I never thought I'd say it but I envy him. I wish I had a horse to ride. At least then I could escape.'

'Ask Rory if you can ride his horses – you said he had a load of new ones – it'd be a perfect excuse to talk to him.'

'I so can't!' she yelped. 'I tried to kiss him when he thought I was Dilly, remember?'

'Yeah, but he doesn't know that.'

'His sister does.'

'So? What does she care?'

'I shouted at her for selling Baron Areion the stallion. I don't think she's my biggest fan.'

'You want to get closer to Rory, right?'

'Right.'

'You want to ride, right?'

'Right.'

'And you want to get away from your brothers and their girlfriends, right?'

'Right.'

'Go figure.'

Faith grinned. Put like that, she had a point.

She cornered her mother in the sitting-room where Anke was balancing on a chair looking through the bookshelves.

'I am sure I had a copy of *The Small House at Allington* here some-where – the Literature Society is discussing it this week. You haven't seen it have you, *kaereste?*'

'Nope.' Faith slumped down on a sofa.

'No matter.' Anke clambered down from her chair. 'I'll look for a copy in Morfar's shop tomorrow. Is everything okay?' She settled beside her.

They could hear Chad, Mim and Digby charging around upstairs and, to their left, gales of laughter as Magnus and the Three Disgraces talked in the kitchen.

'Did you have a good day at college?' Anke sensed a confession coming.

'Fine.' Faith picked at her cuticles.

'Have you made any nice friends yet?'

Faith rolled her eyes. Her mother asked that every day.

'Millions.'

'If you want to invite anyone here, you know you only have to –'

'This house is full enough as it is.'

'I know,' Anke sighed, glancing towards the noisy kitchen. 'Magnus really must find a job – he spends all day coffee-housing.'

'Coffee-shopping,' Faith corrected.

'I think I may ask Graham to give him something to do at Dulston's.'

They both looked up as there was a loud thud above their heads and Digby Lampeter let out one of his banshee wails.

'And I really must tell Diana that I am not happy with her children coming here after school every day. We're not running a child-minding business.'

'You're too kind, Mum. People take advantage of that.'

'Well, she is a friend,' Anke said without great conviction. 'And she is very busy. I know that she is doing a lot of work to the stables. She is always meeting with architects and planners and tourist board people, and Rory is trying to run the riding school around it all.'

'Maybe I can help out up there?'

Anke's face lit up. 'Would you really like that?'

'I could do a couple of hours after college and a morning on my half day. The Maddington bus stops at the Springlodes, so I can make my own way there.'

'And Graham could bring you home when he finishes work.' Anke clasped her hands together, realising that this was just what Faith needed to lift her out of the doldrums – just as she had suggested weeks ago. 'Would you like me to speak with Diana?'

And it was as simple as that. Faith lay in bed that night happily fantasising about riding alongside Rory in the twilight, telling him all her troubles and woes, while he told her that she was wonderful and beautiful and clever. She imagined the first kiss – catching her by surprise while she was soaping a saddle in the tack room, or filling nets in the hay barn. He would kiss her and then, when she kissed him back, he would open his eyes wide and gasp, 'I love you.' She'd heard him say it before and it had sounded wonderful. How much better when he said it and meant her?

Across the landing, Graham's reaction wasn't at all as Anke had expected.

'You've *said* what?!' he asked, his mouth full of toothpaste.

Rubbing cream into her face, Anke watched his face turn red in the mirror.

'I just said that you could give her a lift home after you shut up Dulston's.'

'It's not as simple as that, love. I never know what time I'm finishing – sometimes I'm not even there, if I'm visiting a supplier or a farm somewhere.'

'Which is why I thought Magnus should help you out in the afternoons

– after I've come home. He can be there when you're not, and can bring Faith back from the stables if you aren't on site.'

A splat of toothpaste hit the mirror and Graham's eyes bulged.

'I thought you'd appreciate some help,' she persisted nervously, wondering why he looked so appalled. 'Mags is very practical. He needs a job.'

Graham rinsed his mouth under the tap and grabbed a towel, stomping out into the bedroom. She hopped after him.

'Is there some sort of problem, *kaereste*?'

'No problem,' he said carefully as he clambered into his soft side of the bed. 'I'm glad you've sorted it all out. Why not get Magnus to bring Chad and Diana's children up with him after school and then we can have the whole houseful running around Dulston's instead of here?'

Anke turned off the bathroom light and joined him. 'I'm sorry.'

He lay with his back to her, doing his sulky child routine.

'I should have discussed it with you before I said anything to Mags, shouldn't I?'

'You mean you've already told him he's coming to work with me?'

'I mentioned something about it. You were so late back and he was about to go out with his friends. I wanted to gauge his reaction.'

'I was late home because I was working hard.'

'So let Magnus do some of the work for you.' She didn't understand why he was being so resentful.

It was only after he had fallen asleep that she wondered whether this reluctance to have his work-time interrupted was something to do with infidelity. The thought made her sick with worry.

'Sounds like he has a guilty conscience,' Pixie agreed as the Literature Society gathered in Giles Hornton's conservatory the following evening.

'You think so?' Anke fretted.

'Defo. Whenever Sexton locks himself away in the office to do paper-work, I can hear him cooing into his mobile at some tart.'

'Oh God.' She felt sick.

'Any idea who it might be, yet?'

Anke hardly dared mention her fears that Graham was seeing Diana Lampeter while she stupidly acted as child-minder. He had always said that she was spoiled, snobby and blowsy, but perhaps this was just a smokescreen. He worked within yards of the stables and stayed late each evening while Diana allowed her children to trot from Oddlode primary school to Wyck Farm to await collection. In the meantime, were Diana and Graham trapped in a clinch behind the combine? She hardly dared think about it. Talking to Pixie always made her paranoid.

'I think I am just being neurotic – I have no proof he's up to anything,' she whispered, looking up and smiling as more Literature Society members started arriving, including Pheely, dressed in an alarming lime-green kaftan.

'What are you two talking about in such hush-hush voices?' she demanded, squeezing between them on the tiny bamboo settee.

'Trollopes.' Pixie held up her copy of *The Small House at Allington* with a big wink.

'Ah – say no more.' Pheely tossed her dark curls back from her face and brought her luminous green gaze to rest on Anke. 'I have a suspect.'

'Who?' Anke squeaked, her heart hammering.

Pheely smiled up at Giles who was whisking past distributing glasses of wine. 'Could I have something soft, darling?'

'Nothing of mine is ever soft around you, Ophelia,' he purred. 'But I'll see what I can do.' He disappeared towards his kitchen.

'*His* ex-wife.' Pheely hissed. 'Prudence.'

'The one who runs the gallery opposite my father's shop?' Anke remembered the prickly redhead.

She nodded. 'She popped in today to look at my latest work and we had a very enlightening conversation. She was three parts cut, of course – drinks like a fish although God knows who wouldn't if they had to bring up Giles' children? Anyway, my dear, she hinted very strongly that she has been enjoying a new and rather naughty liaison.'

'Good God – she's lethal.' Pixie took Anke's hand.

'Quite,' Pheely agreed. 'A total bunny boiler. All I could glean is that he is rich and powerful and new on the village scene.'

Anke felt cold sweat clamming her temples.

'But then – and this is interesting.' She dropped her voice to little more than a breath. 'She started asking all about you.'

'Me?'

'Classic sign,' Pixie sighed sadly. 'Sussing out the opposition.'

'She knew all about you moving here to look after your father, and wanted to know whether Ingmar was going to live with you soon. Did you know he's been going out on gallivants with Truffle Dacre-Hopkinson, by the way?'

'What?' Anke was feeling too sick to take this in properly as she pictured Graham with the red-haired, pale-skinned Prudence. It made sense. She was far more his type than Diana. Pru was cool, slim, bright and nervy. She'd come to their barbecue and drunk too much, making a bit of a scene. Perhaps something had already started between them by then?

'Your grandfather is seeing Truffle,' Diana repeated. 'Pru told me.'

'Oh, I know. I think he's trying to prove to me that he doesn't need me.'

'Maybe Graham's doing the same thing?' suggested Pixie.

But before Anke could react, Giles had reappeared with a long glass of juice for Pheely and was calling for the discussion to start.

'Everybody got a drink? Good. Now let's talk Trollope. My favourite subject.' Smoothing his moustache and giving Pheely a steamy look, he gathered his notes and started introducing the text.

Anke didn't hear a word. She was still picturing Graham with predatory Pru.

During the first refreshment break, she wandered out on to Giles' floodlit terrace that abutted the river Odd, listening as small creatures splashed away in shock. She leaned on the railings and drew deep breaths, telling herself to put this thing into perspective.

Anke had always known that Graham had been unfaithful to Deirdre many times before he had finally met someone he wanted to make wife and not just mistress. She had occasionally panicked that her non-existent sex drive would drive him into someone else's arms, but it was only since the move that she had sensed real danger. Maybe she had spent too long talking to Pixie, who knew full well that Sexton was being unfaithful. Maybe she had spent too long talking to Pheely, who loved to speculate about potential affairs and had already told her that Prudence always made a beeline for new male villagers of a certain age. Maybe she had talked too much. She remembered the potting shed at the harvest supper – stoned and confessional, she had allowed herself to be cross-examined.

'He thought you were blonde and bright and Danish and delicate and a slim-thighed beauty, which you are – and you thought . . . what?'

'That he was male. So very masculine and male. And I loved him for that.'

'And now he thinks, what?'

'That I am neurotic and conservative and opinionated and cold – which I am.'

'And you think?'

'That he is male. So very masculine and male. And I hate him for that.'

She didn't hate Graham. She was devastated that she had said such a thing. She hated herself for not loving him as much as she should.

'Phew! That's better.' Pheely joined her, stretching her swollen ankles and cooling her bump. She leaned back against the railings and tipped her head up to look at the stars starting to crowd the sky. 'You all right, darling?'

'Fine.'

'Listen, don't panic about Pru. Even if she has got her claws into your chap, she's hardly a threat. The woman's totally lousy at sex,' she giggled. 'I have it on very good authority that she insists on cleansing her chakras with a crystal dowsing first, then she does lots of Tantric humming and dancing and stuff and finally lies back like a corpse, closes her eyes and takes slurps of red wine throughout. Probably never had an orgasm in her life.'

Anke swallowed uncomfortably.

In the week that followed, while a hot, dry autumn continued burnishing the Lodes valley into October, Anke grew increasingly convinced that absolutely everyone in Oddlode was behaving badly apart from her.

Even her dotty father seemed to be enjoying a strange courtship with Truffle Dacre-Hopkinson. Anke was exasperated that she had spent so long persuading him to relinquish his car, only to find that Truffle was letting him use her Mini Moke, and the two had taken rather enthusiastically to off-roading their way between assignations. He had already killed several of the village ducks and taken out the signpost at the crossroads.

Anke, who had been struggling to get to grips with the vast king cab pick-up truck which Graham had blagged on trial from the manufacturers whilst he was doing battle with their insurance company to replace the burned Mercedes, was mortified that her father was adding to the family's growing reputation as a bane on the roads. If it wasn't Magnus careering around the village green in his Porsche with one of his girlfriends whooping in the passenger seat, it was Graham trying out one of his tractors, Faith freewheeling her bike whilst lost in a dream listening to her iPod, or Chad skateboarding his way into oncoming traffic. Of them all, Anke suspected her father to be the worst danger.

Today, Ingmar was obviously out on another jaunt because when Anke popped in to Cider Court on her way back from her morning at Dulston's, the bookshop was closed despite the 'Open' sign on the door. Above it, his flat was locked. She hoped, at least, that her father remembered to get some lunch while he was out.

She let herself in with her keys to put some more groceries in his fridge, only to find it full of the ones that she had put there at the beginning of the week, including the meals she had prepared so that he only needed to heat them through. Either Ingmar had been out on the town every night or, as Anke suspected, he was forgetting to eat again.

Toppi rattled in through the cat flap from the little kitchen balcony, getting stuck halfway and having to haul himself through with a great deal of grunting and farting. At least Ingmar was remembering to feed his dog, she realised, as he waddled fatly up to her and sneezed before lifting an arthritic leg and peeing on the washing machine.

But that was about the only thing Ingmar remembered to do around the house. He was forgetting to tidy, to clean up after himself and to change his clothes. There was no evidence of any laundry to be done, making it fairly clear that he had yet to change the outfit Anke had forced him into on Monday when determined to tackle the ancient corduroy trousers and striped shirt that he had been wearing then. Having said that she would take them home to wash them, she'd secretly burned them on Reg's bonfire at the foot of her garden. She put new shirts, trousers and underwear into his drawers and wardrobe, folded his pyjamas and made his bed, wiped his kitchen and bathroom surfaces and emptied his bin, knowing that when he arrived home he wouldn't have a clue that she had been there. That was probably for the best. He resented her interference enormously. She almost suspected that he was conducting this dalliance with Truffle as a protest, to annoy his pious daughter who had so adored her mother. Yet Anke was relieved that he had more day-to-day company. From what she had seen, Truffle was just as selfish and even more eccentric than her daughter, but at least she was entertaining company for him and enabled him to venture more than a mile or two from the village without losing his way. She was also a mean bridge player by all accounts.

It was admittedly rather awkward that her father was in the throes of a companionable romance with the mother of Diana Lampeter – from whom Anke had been trying hard to distance herself of late.

But distancing herself from Diana was not an option.

There was the Chad and Mim love story, for a start. The two were in the same class at Oddlode primary school and, after a lot of initial teasing, rubber-throwing and note-swapping, had fallen madly in love. They had been joined at the hip for the past fortnight.

Then there was Faith's change of heart about working at Oddlodes. Anke was happy for her, but it made renegotiating the childcare arrangements hard. Every day since Faith had started, Diana had breezily told her children that she would pick them up from Wyck Farm and Anke was left no choice but to look after Digby as well as Mim. They stayed for hours before Diana rolled up to collect them, bringing back Faith in return. This seemed to be the new deal – Anke looked after the Lampeter children while Faith was at the yard.

Faith had spent every spare moment at Overlodes that week, going directly there on the bus after college and whiling away so many hours on horseback that Anke guessed she was going to have to limit her so that she did some homework occasionally. She was under strict instructions to walk down to Dulston's for six-thirty, when Graham shut up the yard, but so far he hadn't brought her back once.

Graham was staying at work even later and being even more taciturn.

'You are supposed to be bringing Faith home from the stables,' she had complained to him that morning.

'I've been busy,' he muttered.

'You should let Magnus stay here until you close up.'

'He works midday until four. That suits us both.'

'Why?'

'Because every day so far he's rolled up and immediately taken an hour for lunch, used the phone non-stop, played on the Internet for a couple of hours supposedly developing my web-site, taken another hour for a tea break and then pissed off. Most of the time he has at least one admiring girlfriend in tow. It's a waste of bloody time having him here.'

Anke knew that Graham was making yet another stand. He obviously resented Magnus being on site so much that he wasn't prepared to try to make it work. Magnus had no complaints. He loved his new job.

There was no point arguing with Graham when he was like this. He had become so morose and withdrawn lately that she felt she hardly knew him. During the mornings they spent working together, he talked more to Evig than he did to her. Her head was tortured with images of him having an affair – Graham with red-haired Prudence, Graham with olive-skinned Diana, Graham with practically every bored wife or divorcée in the Lodes – all of whom could give him more than she could.

Anke was too exhausted to know how to start trying to make things better between them.

She was becoming very familiar with the road from Oddlode to Upper Springlode, as the day fell into a commuting routine between the villages. Having seen Faith on to her college bus and dropped Chad at school, she would climb that twisting lane to join Graham and his dog at the yard and help man the phones whilst tackling the mountains of paperwork. At midday she would go back to check on her father and dash home to make sure that Magnus was at least out of bed and, at best, had already left for Dulston's.

At last Anke could snatch her very few, precious hours to herself – most of which were inevitably spent tidying, cleaning, shopping or cooking – before picking up Chad and babysitting the Lampeter children until Diana appeared. Magnus and his Three Disgraces still spent most evenings at the farm before heading to the pub or to band practice. Nothing had really changed. It had been an exhausting week. And she had hardly slept a wink.

Sitting in her father's little flat, holding the photograph of her mother, Anke wished that she were still alive. Her mother had been so wise and open and strong. So Danish.

The English liked to joke about sex and gossip about other people's relationships, but talking about their own problematic love lives was considered a social gaffe. Anke had learned that it was not wise to say too much and, now that she knew how loudly the jungle drums thudded in this area, she had no intention of providing her own fodder from which idle tongues could feed. That her first marriage had already been the subject of public scrutiny appalled her because she still considered it to have been loving and, in many ways, successful. To her mind, it had functioned far better than her second did. Moving here had thus far solved none of their problems. She still couldn't bear Graham to touch her and she often stayed up hours after he had gone to bed to ensure that he was asleep when she joined him. He had been so wrapped up in Dulston's and his bad mood – and perhaps in the affair that Pheely and Pixie always made her suspect he was having – that he hadn't tried too hard in recent nights. Yet she only had to roll over in her sleep and accidentally press a limb against him to find herself wide awake again, eyes on alert as he groggily groped his way closer, still enjoying his slumber. Those big hands would find her breasts, her thighs, her belly. They would lie heavily there while she tried to extract herself from them an inch at a time. Sometimes they would cling on, even though he was still asleep.

Her revulsion to his touch made her deeply self-loathing.

She looked at her mother's long, angular face – so like Faith's. Not pretty nor even handsome – Anke had always been told that she was lucky she had inherited her father's bone structure, yet she longed to look more like her mother. It was a face of such wisdom and such strength. When she had married Kurt, her mother had cryptically told her that there was no such thing as a husband – it was a social invention. 'Men and women, sons and daughters, fathers and mothers – these are real things. Husbands and wives are just a fabrication we use to clothe our lives. Remember that. You are marrying a son or a father. If you are very lucky, you get both.' Her mother had died years before Anke truly understood what she had been trying to say.

She knew that she was being terribly unfair on Graham. Throughout their marriage, he had done nothing wrong apart from want her so much for her body when she desperately needed to be loved for her mind. And her father – the only man who had ever truly loved her for her intelligence – was losing a little more of his own clever mind every day.

'You were so lucky to have died before you had to see him fading away,' she told her mother, settling the photograph back on to the mantelpiece. 'The more I lose of him, the more I see that Graham is more son than father.'

She now knew exactly what her mother had been telling her. Kurt had been a father – yet he had fathered none of her children. Ingmar would always be a father – hers and others – even as his diseased mind grew more helpless and childlike in old age.

Anke let herself out through the shop so that she could return the Trollope she had borrowed the previous week. She felt she should buy something as a thank you to her father, who hadn't even noticed it was missing. The shelves were in total chaos, as was normal these days. On top of one of the many teetering piles clustered behind Ingmar's desk, she saw a tatty old hardback called *A Horse for Emma*.

Faith always read any fiction involving four legs. Anke tucked it under her arm, put a five pound note in the till and, breathing in one last deliciously familiar breath of old books, headed outside. As she locked the door, she realised that the sign behind the glass still read 'Open'. She was about to unlock it again to remedy this when a voice called, 'Ignore that – he's gone out. Oh, it's you. Hi.'

It was Prudence Hornton, smoking a cigarette by the entrance to her gallery. A flame-haired neurotic about whom Pheely had always been particularly poisonous, Prudence stocked her little shop with a mix of local artists' work that she hid behind large displays of her own disturbing oils and watercolours.

'He's out with Truffle.'

'I know,' Anke smiled politely, turning to walk to her giant new car. 'Thanks.'

'Settled in?'

'Oh yes, thank you.' She feigned a pressing engagement by looking at her watch.

But Prudence, bored to tears by yet another day with no passing trade, hopped after her. She'd already cracked open the red wine in her back kitchen and knocked back a double Prozac dose as a lunch-time treat. The sight of Anke was too good to pass up.

'Family still holding up to the Oddlode onslaught?'

Anke stiffened and turned back to look at her.

Prudence was a difficult woman to like. She had got very drunk at the Brakespears' barbecue and offended several of their old friends by ranting loudly about *nouveau riche* newcomers who ruined old Cotswold villages with their 'Essex taste in garden lighting' and their 'Footballers Wives' bed-hopping'. She had, amazingly, sent a thank you card after the party – but it had been addressed only to Graham. Afterwards, she had been heard loudly complaining about the awful food and the dread-fully bland company. Added to this, her badly behaved children were the bullies at Oddlode primary school. She continually referred to Anke as Swedish. Anke loathed her.

And now, in the light of what Pheely had told her about Pru's 'naughty liaison', and her interest in Anke's home life, she felt something hard and unfamiliar in her belly which was close to neat hatred.

'What "onslaught"?' she asked.

'Oh, you know what villages are like – hotbeds for scandal. I hear your gorgeous son is already attracting quite a following?'

Anke was not good at conversations that skirted around subjects. For a split second she heard the question form in her head and opened her mouth to ask it, but sanity and good manners stopped her. It was crazy to stand in front of a virtual stranger demanding to know if they were having an affair with your husband.

'Yes, Magnus is settling in very well – we all are.' She spoke quickly to stop herself making outrageous challenges. 'Excuse me, I'm in a hurry – I really must go.'

'Give my regards to that lovely husband of yours.'

Anke heard the question screaming around in her head. 'I will.'

'If you ever tire of him, you will pass him on, won't you?'

She forced out another polite smile and bit her tongue to stop the question popping out.

'My ex is very similar.' Pru lit another cigarette and took a dreamy puff. 'You know Giles? I think they look really alike.'

'Oh, I don't think so.' She started backing away before the question became a maddened full-throttle statement screamed to the rooftops.

'They do! Could be brothers. Just my type. You look after him.'

'Oh, I will.' Anke added a lethal, frosty glint to her polite smile and made her way hastily to the king cab. She knew she had to do something. Paranoia was taking over.

She raced home, her heart three car lengths ahead all the way. Reg was pottering around in one of the bigger flower-beds pretending to work and lifted his hat to her as she climbed out of the car. Normally she would stop to chat although she understood precious little of what he said – he liked to admire the borrowed king cab and could mutter his way around it for hours on end, but today Anke darted into the house before he had clambered over the first of the hebes.

She ran into the kitchen, threw *A Horse for Emma* on to the dresser and opened the fridge.

'A meal for two, a sexy meal for two,' she muttered. 'A seductive meal for two. What food is aphrodisiac?'

'Oysters?' suggested a helpful voice.

Anke screamed, slammed the fridge door and spun around.

Four faces were watching her curiously from the table as Magnus and the Three Disgraces sat enjoying their customary mugs of coffee.

Petite, pretty and hard to tell apart with their dusky skin, cat-like eyes, long streaky hair, shoulder tattoos, pierced navels and penchant for mini-skirts worn with knee-high boots and tiny bootlace crop tops, Sperry, Fe and Carry Sixsmith were delightfully bright and chatty.

'I fucking love romantic meals.' Fe was sighing dreamily.

'Asparagus is good but it's out of fucking season now.' Sperry scratched her chin thoughtfully.

'How about figs?' suggested Carry.

'I thought they were supposed to give you the runs?'

'No, that's fucking prunes, Fe.'

Anke thought they were great fun, although they all smoked like chimneys and swore like troopers. When Magnus wasn't sloping away from Dulston's to see them, they inevitably arrived at Wyck Farm on mopeds to gossip at the kitchen table before heading off to the Lodes Inn or to watch Magnus and his band. Anke had chatted to them quite a bit in the past fortnight. They were fabulously indiscreet, telling tales on everyone in Springlode, Oddlode and the valley between. They were also completely irreverent and talked to her the same way to her as they did to Magnus and one another, which she had found refreshing up until today.

'I thought you were working at Dulston's this afternoon?' she asked Magnus.

'Got the day off – bonus for being so fantastic.' He grinned. 'You planning a quiet night in then, Mum?'

The Disgraces all giggled.

Anke scratched the hot prickles that had started to sting the back of her neck, certain that she must be blushing from head to toe.

'I thought Graham deserved a nice meal,' she blustered. 'He has been working very hard.'

'Want us out of the way?'

'Please.'

'No problem.' Magnus rubbed his blonde hair and creased his brows. 'What about Chad and Faith?'

She blinked, realising that she hadn't planned this very well.

He laughed. 'I'll just make a couple of calls. Leave it with me.' He headed outside with his mobile and the address book.

Anke smiled awkwardly at the Three Disgraces, who beamed prettily in return.

'You can't go wrong with a lovely fucking steak,' Carry told her with the wisdom of a sixteen-year-old. 'Bill Hudson's got some fucking gorgeous organic beef over at the farm shop – melt in the mouth. Do you want me to pick you up a couple of fillets? I can go there now.'

'Oh, would you?' Anke reached for her bag to fish out some cash.

'D'you need anything else while I'm there? Cream? Veg?'

'Oh – yes, probably.'

Carry grinned, having never seen Magnus's mother this flustered. 'I'll just get everything you fucking need. Leave it with me.'

'And I'll get the champagne.' Fe stood up beside her younger sister and held out her palm for a cash hand-out. 'Joel Lubowski always gives me a fantastic fucking discount. Have you got candles?'

'Er – I think so.'

'Dessert?'

'I'm not sure.'

'Give me another tenner and I'll sort it. You don't want to have to slave over the oven any longer than necessary. Secret of a romantic meal is to look fucking ravishing and do as little as possible – save your energy for later.' She winked. 'Now, you sit down and have a cup of coffee while Sperry sorts out the music and we'll be back in no fucking time.'

The Three Disgraces were a part of the older teenage scene that moved between all the villages in the valley, a hardened and cheery brigade of surprisingly streetwise – or 'lane-wise' – kids who had mostly known each other since infancy. They consequently knew every nugget of local gossip which they texted one another from bedroom to pub games room to village green bench in a long game of mobile tag.

As the two girls puttered away on their bikes, Anke had no doubt that her desperation for aphrodisiac food for a romantic supper with

Graham would be crossing the teenage airwaves before she had even invited the main guest.

'Here – have a cuppa.' Sperry thrust a milky coffee under Anke's nose. 'You don't mind my sisters helping out, do you? They're bossy cows but they mean well.'

'No – no, it's fine.' Anke cleared her throat. 'It's nothing special, you understand – not our anniversary or anything. Just that I think Graham deserves a bit of a treat and as it's the end of the week . . .'

The oldest and wisest of the three sisters, Sperry gave her a kind smile and dug around in her bag. 'Here – Chill Out and Make Out II. My favourite album.' She handed over a CD. 'Bung that on, turn the lighting low and get the steak sizzling and give him the surprise of his life when he gets home.'

It hadn't occurred to Anke to make the supper a surprise.

'What are you going to wear?'

'Well, I . . . hadn't thought.'

'*The* latest look is "erogance" – as in erotic elegance, you know? It is *so* fucking sexy.'

'Is it?' Anke took a swig of coffee, feeling out of her league.

'You team a lacy bra with a floaty wraparound top and a long skirt and boots. Men love it.'

'I think I'm a little too old for that,' she laughed apologetically.

'You'd look great – you have a perfect figure,' she insisted. 'I saw Faith looking seriously ero this week.'

'Faith? My Faith?'

'She had jeans on and was riding a horse, but the look was all there – I thought it was Dilly Gently at first. Now *she's* totally erogance.'

'Oh – yes, well Faith has a bit of a crush on Rory, I think,' Anke confided, feeling disloyal but desperate to get away from the topic of romantic suppers and sexy outfits.

'More than that, mate.' Sperry Sixsmith broke the news to Anke that even her teenage daughter had seen some romantic action recently. It certainly explained Faith's sudden enthusiasm for yard work.

'Faith kissed Rory at the harvest supper?' Anke gasped afterwards.

Sperry nodded. 'I found out from Sharon. She thought it was *Fe* and Rory, you see – sometimes she gets called Faith. Sharon overheard Diana and Rory having a bit of a spat, and afterwards Diana teased him about getting drunk at the harvest supper and letting Faith try to have her wicked way with him.'

'Oh God!' Anke didn't know whether to laugh or cry. 'That's not like Faith at all.'

'Oh, don't worry – it sounds very innocent. Now if it was *our* Fe's wicked way, he'd have been in trouble. Then again, I think she had her wicked way with Rory Midwinter a couple of years ago and said he wasn't up to much if you get my drift.' She raised a slanting brown eyebrow. 'A bit of a flop, truthfully.' Her soft Cotswolds accent and nonchalant air made it sound as though she was describing an unsuccessful cake-baking attempt.

Anke tried not to blush prudishly. 'But Faith's only sixteen.'

'And Rory was totally incapable of taking advantage. All credit to the girl for having a go.'

'Oh, gosh.' Anke's eyes bulged at the thought. She felt dreadful talking behind Faith's back, but it made a lot of sense of what she had been seeing.

Faith *was* behaving oddly. Her daughter's experiments with strange new outfits, hairdos, fake tan, make-up and padded bras had occupied her for hours in her room when she wasn't riding, all to the accompaniment of boy band remakes of 1980s ballads. She spent inordinate amounts of time on the telephone to Carly whispering, giggling and saying 'you know' and 'whatever' if Anke was in earshot. She certainly had a twinkle in her eye.

'I can't believe she would do that. She's so shy, and she knows he has a girlfriend. I do hope Dilly doesn't find out.'

'Oh, Dilly's hardly the faithful type herself – like her mum. Dilly's always had this fanciful notion about finding a soul mate, and Rory knows he's not it. That's why poor old Sharon's hanging on in there, bless her, hoping she gets him in the end.'

'I thought she was just his head girl?'

'And the rest.'

'I'm not sure I can keep up with all this.' Anke was wondering if there was anybody in the area not bed-hopping.

'There's so much more I could tell you,' Sperry laughed. 'You haven't heard the half of it.'

'And I thought Pheely was a terrible gossip!'

'Know who the father of her baby is?' Sperry cocked her pretty head.

'Why? Do you?'

'Oh, *everyone* does. Surely you know?'

When Sperry told her, Anke was astonished.

Now she knew for certain that everyone in Oddlode was behaving very badly apart from herself – even her own children had succumbed to it. As Sperry told her, 'It's called the Lodes valley for a reason – everyone is getting loads!'

Magnus chose this moment to wander back in looking pleased with himself. 'Phew – I have been flirting for England, Denmark and Cuba, but I've finally twisted everyone around my lovely little finger.

'Diana Lampeter is going to have Chad on a sleepover tonight, although she grumbled about it. Something about her kids' father turning up for a visit tomorrow? She was a bit iffy about collecting them, so I called the school and spoke to the pretty one, your mate –'

'Mo Stillitoe?'

'Yeah – she says she'll tell Chad. With a bit of magic Mags charm, I persuaded her to give all three kids a lift up to Springlode after school. Diana had mentioned that Mo has a lesson with Rory at four, so she couldn't refuse my winning ways. I'll drop off an overnight bag for Chad when I collect Faith from the yard later. I've just booked tickets to see the latest Orlando Bloom movie in Cheltenham –'

'Cool!' Sperry cheered.

'– and then we'll take her out for a pizza afterwards.'

'And clubbing?' Sperry suggested hopefully.

'She's only sixteen.' Magnus saw the look on his mother's face, although he'd already decided to treat Faith to a couple of hours at his favourite dance warehouse. It was about time she loosened up. And she wasn't the only one . . . 'You don't have to worry about a thing, Mum – just have a relaxing afternoon making yourself beautiful and preparing to pamper Graham when he gets home.'

Anke was touched and grateful, but she wasn't entirely certain she liked the way her son had taken over her impulsive idea and turned it into a full-blown leave-the-parents-alone theatrical event. She was obliged to go through with it now and pull out all the stops – springing the big surprise on her unsuspecting husband.

A puttering whine heralded the return of Fe and Carry with supplies which they insisted on laying out and preparing so that all Anke had to do was turn on the hob and warm the plates.

Carry had even picked up some massage oils from Izzy the aromatherapist who ran a little treatment room from her Oddlode cottage.

'She said it's got sandal, ylang ylang and clove bud or something in it – anyway, it makes you fucking horny.' She gave it a sniff and crossed her eyes.

'Now do you want us to go through your wardrobe and find you something fucking fantastic to wear?' Fe suggested hopefully.

'No – really that's terribly kind, but I'm sure I'll be fine.'

At last they all disappeared, leaving her breathless and more than a little terrified of what she had just triggered.

She called Dulston's. Graham answered.

'I'm going to cook us a special meal later,' she plunged in with her customary directness. 'Just checking you won't be too late?'

There was a shocked silence. 'You're doing what?'

'A nice meal.'

'For who?'

'Us.'

'Oh, right. Great.' He sounded bewildered.

It wasn't quite the reaction she had hoped for. Too little too late, she told herself. He has his bags packed.

'I don't know how early I can get away.'

'Please try.'

'Sure.'

Anke settled in the bath with Chill Out and Make Out II booming through from the bedroom stereo and *A Horse For Emma* in her hands. It was a curious combination. The music – if it could be called that – seemed to consist of a throbbing drum beat and violin chords with a lot of girls panting and groaning. The book belonged to another age.

She turned it over and read the foxed flyleaf with half a smile. Faith would love this. *Based on a true story, the tale of Emma Fulbrook will touch the hearts of horse-lovers the land over . . .*

She scanned the first page. How sweet. It was just the sort of book she had relished as a child and, like Faith, had secretly enjoyed almost until adulthood.

Emma is a young orphan who had been adopted by her elderly Aunt Cecily, a spinster of some fortune and land. Aunt Cecily's dashing young huntsman, Suffolk, is mean-spirited despite his good looks. The kennel-hand, Larch, is a kind boy with no education. The scene was set.

Leaning back among the bubbles, Anke turned a few pages.

Poor Emma, after a childhood in India, finds life on the cold Lincolnshire marshes harsh. She learns to ride, taught by the impatient Suffolk whom she longs to please. Larch looks on in sympathy as she is thrown again and again by an ill-suited mount, Lady – her aunt's favourite mare, as wilful and intolerant as her dark-haired huntsman.

And then the first hunt meet arrives, at which Emma's frail aunt sits in a Bath chair and waves her on her way. Bullied by Suffolk into taking a hunt jump, Emma comes a cropper and breaks her arm. Lady runs amok amid the hounds and is finally brought down by a rabbit hole, ripping a tendon, her hunting career over. Furious as he leads the mare away, Suffolk blames Emma. She vows never to ride again.

Anke was so entranced by the melodrama, she didn't notice the bubbles popping away and the water going cold. Nor did she notice the red dye from the old binding creeping out across her wet hands and down her wrists until Bomber, the bull terrier, wandered in to remind her about his walk.

'No, Bomber – go away – aghh!' It looked as though she'd slit her wrists. Propping up the book on the loo seat to dry, she set about scrubbing away the stains.

An hour later she was as smooth and clean and perfumed as she could hope to be, apart from an unsightly red stain all over her hands and forearms which refused to budge. The bed was changed, flowers on each bedside table, and Graham's favourite Rock Love Anthems CD poised in the bedroom stereo (she decided Chill Out and Make Out II was a bit risqué for a man who loved Bonnie Tyler and Jennifer Rush). Her outfit was laid out ready on the button-backed sofa in the corner. There was the underwear that Graham had bought her for their first anniversary, dreadful red satiny stuff with frilly black lace bits that itched; the plunge-necked velvet dress he loved even though it made her shoulders look massive and her chest look flat. Her highest heels were lined up, which meant she towered over him despite his six foot one frame – but he seemed to love that. She had yet to make up her face, but that wouldn't take long and she didn't want to sweat it off too early. She still had several hours to wait.

She called Horseshoe Farm Cottage and spoke with a surprisingly upbeat Diana who had accepted her unexpected guest very graciously.

'You have been *so* good about having mine after school and Magnus really was too charming to refuse. Chad can sleep in Dig's bunk and he'll come in with me. They're all watching their teacher bouncing about on one of the new horses now. Faith is doing a lovely job trying them all for size and letting us know their talents. You're right. She's a super rider. Rory's impressed.'

Anke, who couldn't shake the image of Faith jumping on Rory at the harvest supper, let out a nervous half-laugh. 'She seems to have quite a soft spot for your brother.'

'All girls do. I think even our Miss Stillitoe might be a tad smitten.'

'You do?'

'Just a hunch. She dresses up like mad for her lessons, I've noticed, although God knows she doesn't stay long – probably just as afraid Pod is behaving badly while she's away. I think they might be heading for a break-up – I gather he is completely unreliable. Up to no good on the night of the harvest supper. Then again, we all were.'

'Yes – quite.' Anke's memory of the return trip from the Gunning Estate to Oddlode that night was shaky, but she distinctly remembered Diana tersely suggesting that she lay off Pheely's sensimilla in future, which was rich coming from someone who had got totally looped at her own supper party and was rumoured to take cocaine. She still hadn't entirely figured out what Diana had been doing in the parkland but, given that Pheely and Pixie didn't even *remember* being there and Rory had been unconscious throughout, she thought it best to forget the whole incident.

'Talking of unfaithful bastards,' Diana was chattering away. 'Bloody Tim's rolling up tomorrow.'

'Tim?'

'Husband. Soon to be ex.'

'Oh dear.' Anke picked up *A Horse For Emma* from where it had been drying on the Aga and moved it to the kitchen table to stop the pages singeing.

'If it's all right with you I thought I'd tell him Chad is my new toy boy.' She giggled.

'Sure.' She straightened the wrinkled pages and found the last of her red fingerprints at the end of Chapter Seven.

'Anke, are you all right?'

'Fine!'

'You are so lucky having a husband who totally adores you. You're right to spoil him. I don't think Tim would have known what a romantic meal was if I'd set the table placings on my naked body with a rose in my mouth and an arrow pointing downwards. Typical army. You know his bloody solicitors have totally got me over a barrel. I thought I might at least get enough in the settlement to finance converting the old Horseshoe barn into an accommodation block for my holiday guests but they say I'll be lucky to get enough to redecorate Sharon's mobile home. *I'm* the injured party here. He was the one who shagged around for thrills because I was too exhausted to do the naked dinner setting thing every night.'

Anke didn't answer, the first page of Chapter Eight blurring in front of her eyes as she suddenly remembered Pru Hornton and her chakra-cleansing Tantric dance. Was that what Graham had been enjoying every night?

'Are you really all right?' Diana asked.

'Absolutely. Thank you so much for having Chad. If he's outside, I won't drag him in to talk – just tell him I called and that I'll pick him up first thing tomorrow. Goodbye.' She hung up.

Anke wrung her red hands as she sat at the kitchen table.

I must not think about it. I must not think about the fact that everybody everywhere seems to enjoy jumping in and out of bed together for fun. I must think about my husband. Tonight is his night. Our night. Tonight is the night I jump into bed instead of creeping into it trying not to wake him. It might not be fun, but I will give it my best shot.

All will be well, Anke told herself. All will be good. You *do* want him and you need him and you love him and you must do this for him.

She started to clear the kitchen table, gathering all the Open University material that Pixie had lent her and which she had been poring over for a fortnight, dreaming of the academic life that had always passed her by. She longed to follow her father towards an understanding of that idiosyncratic English literary heritage that had drawn him to these shores and obsessed him for so long. Constant learning that had sharpened his mind before dementia dulled it, that had led him to read classics not just once – and slowly – as she did, but over and over, intricately, infinitely and with such love and regard that he spoke of them almost more passionately than he did of his family. Sometimes, on a really bad day, Ingmar could not remember who Anke was. He never, ever forgot the characters of his favourite novels.

As she cleared away the papers, she picked up *A Horse For Emma* and laughed. This was more her level. The innocent orphan, benevolent maiden aunt, sexy but evil horseman and downtrodden, kind-hearted youth. This was *her* classic because, unlike the books her father found so easy to understand and which she struggled to digest, this went straight into her bloodstream as she read. Even now her eyes were dragged along the page, greedy for a few more morsels.

She glanced at her watch and settled down in the conservatory to read a little more, skipping ahead to concentrate on the action.

Poor Emma, bored and isolated at the big house as she recovers from her broken arm, seeks distraction by befriending shy Larch, the stable boy. Realising that he cannot read or write, she sets about teaching him. The two become inseparable. One starlit April night, they watch as Lady gives birth to a colt foal, but the capricious mare rejects it and Suffolk immediately proclaims it a runt which will die before the night is out, its body to be sent to the kennels at first light. Distraught, Emma persuades her aunt to give the foal to Larch to hand rear. They call him Kindness.

Anke was so absorbed that she let Bomber share her sofa as she read on, through idyllic summers and snow-dusted winters as the youngsters and Kindness grow big and strong and self confident. In secret, Larch gives Emma riding lessons. Hunting seasons come and go and she improves so much under Larch's gentle tutelage that she finally agrees to grant her aged aunt's wish to attend another meet.

But it is brooding Suffolk at Emma's side when, mounted upon Larch's 'runt' Kindness, she rides out to hounds once more. In charge if the pack, Suffolk gallops ahead on his beloved stallion Passion and does not see how much Emma's riding has improved until she is left alone with him in the field on the last foggy point of the day, racing him for Charlie's brush.

Anke giggled along and, just when she thought it couldn't get any better, she gasped.

Hacking home, Suffolk calls Emma the best lady rider that he has ever seen. She is so elated that she tells of her secret lessons with Larch and announces that she loves the kennel-hand and will one day marry him.

'No! Silly girl!' Anke berated, as Emma begs a secret from him in return to seal their silence.

In a gruff whisper, he confesses that as a boy he ran away from his noble but embittered family, taking the mare Lady with him. Forced to sell her to Emma's aunt when both were close to starving, he begged for a job because he couldn't be parted from the horse he loved. He forsook a title and many riches to live his current life, a life 'lit up by a mare and then a girl who broke my heart.'

'Who is the girl?' Emma asks in genuine bewilderment.

Suffolk says nothing.

Bitten by the hunting bug, Emma joins him at every meet. The final dew-dusted covert of that season's closing meet gives forth the best point of the year and Suffolk leads the field across the fens for six miles of galloping, ditch-jumping joy. Then his stallion, Passion, casts a shoe as the pack chase their quarry to the weir. The young huntsman looks around desperately to requisition another horse to keep up with his pack, now in mortal danger.

Without hesitation, Emma offers him Kindness. Man and horse speed away as though possessed, but the tired little thoroughbred is almost buried by the soft and holding ground. Hounds drive the fox into the weir ahead of them and, desperately crying out his horn to stop them following, Suffolk rides on over a wide ditch. But as his fearless pack dive to their deaths the brave horse beneath him falls to his, unable to span the gap.

Tears in her eyes, Anke no longer checked her watch.

Larch's beautiful thoroughbred has been killed trying to please, and

Emma blames herself. In turn, Suffolk is maddened with grief. He has lost horse and hounds as well as his heart.

Further upset awaits at home, where Aunt Cecily has discovered that Emma and Larch intend to marry and he has been dismissed. In a letter left for Emma, he tells her that he is joining the army and asks her to look after Kindness, not knowing that the horse has died that day.

Anke wept as she read on. Poor Emma is beside herself with unhappiness and to crown her woes, her aunt's fragile health finally fails her.

At the funeral, Suffolk shocks the grief-stricken Emma by declaring his love for her and admitting that it was he who jealously told her aunt of her secret engagement to Larch. He proposes marriage. She tells him to leave and never return.

Emma has inherited Cecily's fortune. As a farewell gesture to her aunt, she puts the old broodmare Lady to the brave stallion, Passion.

Anke sobbed, hugging Bomber to her side as she read on.

'I can't stay much longer, angel,' Graham told Mo. 'Anke's got some sort of family dinner planned.'

Mo grumbled sleepily, kissing her way up his ribcage as they sprawled on a pile of cushions in their secret hideaway, moths dive-bombing the flickering citronella candles.

Being with Graham was the only time she felt sleepy – a lovely, languid luxury that melted her whole body and slowed her heartbeat to a crocodile's sluggish thud. They spoke little, always making love frenziedly as soon as they met – Graham was ever-ready and waiting. And afterwards she could sink beneath the waters, deep into the lake of guilt, her heartbeat steadying to a blissful crawl – or sometimes she basked in the sun on the river-bank, her heart swollen with guilt-free happiness. Tonight, the crocodile woke up with a snap of its jaws.

'Can't be a family meal.' She pressed her chin into his chest hair and looked up at his nose. 'I gave Chad a lift up to the yard – he's sleeping over with the Lampeters tonight. Magnus set it up.'

'Magnus?'

'Yup. He called me at the school. Sorry – I thought you must know.'

She felt Graham's breath quicken beneath her chin. 'First I've heard of it.'

'He said something about seeing a movie – I think he was taking Faith.'

'Shit!' Graham sat up and looked at his watch. It was close to eight.

Special meal. She had said she was cooking a special meal. With Anke that could mean anything – all her meals were special. She was a great cook. Distracted, still fuming guiltily that his entire family appeared to be patrolling Springlode this week, Graham hadn't really listened. He'd thought it was yet another of her attempts to play happily families, inviting Ingmar to talk him into moving into the annexe or, worse still, inviting some of her ghastly new friends – the muesli witches Pheely and Pixie or the pushy, selfish Diana Lampeter. He had been looking forward to seeing Mo – to having sex. He hated himself for it, but he had been simply looking forward to getting his end away so much that he hadn't taken in what special meal meant. Now he felt sick, binged out on fast food.

'Don't go,' Mo pleaded as he stumbled up to find his clothes. 'Pod will be in the pub for hours. He might not even come home tonight. I want to snuggle.'

'I have to go, love. I think I may have just fucked up big time.'

'You fucked beautifully, Daddy G.' She rolled over and squirmed amid the satin bolsters, desperate for the crocodile sleep.

Graham looked at her and felt his heart pull. His naked nymph. She was so utterly gorgeous, so completely available to him during their brief, snatched hours of intimacy. To Mo, sex came as naturally as breathing.

To Anke, it was suffocation and yet he still buttoned his shirt so fast he ripped it, hoping against hope that he wasn't too late. Special meal. Christ. It had been so long that he'd forgotten the last special meal.

'I have to go, love,' he repeated. 'And I have to lock up so you've got to get some kit on.'

Mo sat up and rubbed her neck, knowing that this was part of the deal and that crying was pointless. She'd fallen off her horse during her lesson with Rory that evening – unceremoniously dispatched over his long-eared head as he'd ground to a halt in front of a tiny jump. She was glad. Every time she fell off a horse, she remembered that fall from Cloud Nine the day after she and Graham had enjoyed their first sudden, guilty coupling in his marital bed. It stopped her falling in love. Falling in love with Graham would be as easy as falling off a log – falling off a horse was considerably more painful at times, but at least it stopped her going there. Graham made her feel safe. He kept the ghosts away. That was enough.

As she gathered her clothes and blew out the candles she wondered if Pod was playing with *his* ghosts tonight. He almost lived at Gunning these days. On the few nights a week that he returned to her bed, he smelled so strongly of them – of horses and fire – that she couldn't sleep.

'Hurry up, love.' Graham handed her a riding boot.

'Steady on,' she muttered. 'I know you like to rip my clothes off, but putting them back on again takes a bit longer.'

'Sorry – sorry, sorry.' He gathered her into a hug. She could feel his heart pounding through his shirt and she hugged him back tightly, drawing the last of the safety.

'*Dochas.*' She pressed her forehead against that pounding heart. 'Don't give up.'

'Irish for hope,' he remembered, his big hands knitting together behind her narrow back as he squeezed her to him so tightly she almost catapulted up into the sky to join the stars. 'I love my wife, Mo. I can't bloody help myself.'

'I know.' She reached up and cupped his face. 'I love Pod, daddy G. That's a lot harder.'

His eyes shone down from his lovely safe, wide face.

'You really are an angel.'

'Only because you make me one. You have no idea how bad I am.'

'We're both bad.'

'We're both in love with impossible people. Which is why it's impossible to try to find love anywhere else.'

'That,' he kissed her nose, 'is impossible to understand.'

'Am I still your Lara Croft?'

'Always will be my tomb raider, angel.' He kissed the top of her head.

She could feel him looking at his watch again over her shoulder and she finally let him go, stooping to pull on her boot and fighting an urge to kiss his foot.

It was the most they had said to one another since that first night. Somehow they knew it was almost over. But that didn't need saying.

He drove her to the track by Broken Back wood where she always hid her car. They both jumped nervously as they spotted two strange cars parked there – an ageing diesel estate and a small van. But the van's steamed-up windows and shuddering suspension reassured them that it was just another pair of impossible cases.

As Mo sat in her car, rolling a cigarette, Graham's Lexus raced away like a Formula One front gridder, headlights illuminating the Oddlode Organics logo on the bouncing van's sides. Mo studied it curiously and then caught her breath as the Lexus wobbled and almost went off the track to the road.

'You have a clock on the dashboard – stop looking at your watch,' she said out loud, watching Graham's tail-lights disappear around the corner and congratulating herself on not crying.

★   ★   ★

Anke hadn't looked at her watch for three hours. She hadn't noticed the sun dropping behind the tall spruces behind the stables, nor remembered the romantic meal that she had thought up in a panicked moment and that Magnus and his Disgraces had taken to their hearts. She had become completely engrossed in the lives of Emma, Larch and Suffolk.

Emma tried to track down Larch to no avail. Anke chewed off three nails worrying about her as she turned the pages – the poor bereft child left alone to look after the big house and yard, her heart broken.

The outbreak of war has taken thousands of young soldiers to their deaths. Emma guesses Larch must be one of them. She tries to keep the estate going despite her grief. When Lady bears a colt foal, Emma calls him Love. The old mare dotes on him.

Seasons pass and Emma struggles on, following the horrors of the war. Peace is declared, and the men return, but Larch is not among them. Hunting starts again and Emma rides young Love across the fields she raced and chased with Larch's Kindness. Suitors come and go but are all rejected. She is haunted with unhappiness.

Then, one frosty morning, she sees a soldier in the field with Love and the old mare. It is Larch, but he does not recognise her. He has shell-shock.

'Oh God, how much more can the poor thing take?' Anke howled, blowing her nose on her sleeve.

Emma nurses Larch, but he develops pneumonia and the doctors say there is little hope. His lungs are already riddled with shrapnel and he has no will to live. He has come home to her to die. He is delirious, talking about the war and about Suffolk.

Emma, who has not thought about Suffolk for years, listens as Larch tells of the officer who saved his life in the trenches, carrying him to safety through gunfire that had ripped the man's kneecap from his leg and shot his coat from his back. Despite a hundred entreaties from Larch to leave him and save his own skin, the man had not let him go until they were safe – the only two survivors in a trench that became known as 'The Graveyard' after that night. The officer had been Suffolk. Larch weeps deliriously as he recalls the night, not knowing if the estate's bravest, baddest horseman had lived or died.

As he lapses into unconsciousness, Emma realises that he will die if she does not summon help. Frantic, she saddles Love and rides to fetch the doctor. It is a five mile gallop across treacherous country but, guided by the full moon, she leaps every hedge and dyke in her way, racing for her life. Then, as the young colt tires beneath her, she fears her chase is in vain. Love almost falls, but the pounding of hooves and a strange, familiar 'view halloo' called through the darkness pricks his ears. Joined by another horse and rider, Emma feels Love rally and they gallop the final mile to help. Yet when she arrives at the doctor's house, she looks around to find herself alone.

When she and the doctor return, Larch is sleeping soundly. There is an army officer's hat on the chair beside the bed that was not there before. The doctor says that the worst of the fever has passed and, with God on their side, he might pull through.

When Emma goes to check the horses, Passion is missing. On his empty saddle rack lies a telegram addressed to a Lord Suffolk, telling him that his son Edward was missing in action, presumed dead.

That same night the old mare, Lady, passes away.

Anke had soaked both sleeves and was blowing her nose on a cushion when suddenly Bomber scrabbled his way across her, ripping the book in his haste to welcome returning pack members.

'Oh, no!' Anke looked at her watch in horror, recognising the bleeps ringing out as the Lexus was locked from the remote. It was Graham. It was past eight.

She was dressed in a track-suit with snotty sleeves, wearing no make-up, her eyes red from crying, and her romantic meal still housed under cling film in the fridge. There were only eight pages of *A Horse for Emma* left to read.

'Forgive me – I couldn't get away!' Graham burst in through the conservatory doors, Evig bounding behind him.

Anke stuffed the book under a cushion and jumped up.

Graham took in her tear-stained face and almost fell to his knees. 'Oh, Anke I am so sorry – I am such a thoughtless sod.'

'No, no – I should be the sorry one –'

'I didn't realise tonight was special, love. I've upset you by being late and that's unforgivable.'

Had Anke been less flustered and distracted, she would have noticed his shirt buttoned up incorrectly, his dishevelled hair and the smell of sex and guilt that radiated from him like fox scent. Graham was a lousy adulterer. But Anke was too embarrassed at her own self-indulgence to spot the signs she had never needed to look for until they had moved here. Her mind was struggling too hard to leap from Larch's deathbed to her own marital one, with its clean sheets and erotic massage oils waiting nearby, to run down the just-got-out-of-bed checklist.

'I hardly gave you much notice.' She jumped up and raced towards the kitchen, both horrified and grateful that he had mistaken her tears for Emma for tears of sadness that he had stood her up. 'And it is all very quick to prepare. Steak.'

'You sure you still want to cook for a dirty stop-out?'

'Of course! I have to just change! There's some champagne in the fridge. Why not pour out two glasses? I won't be long.'

'Don't change,' he said, heading for the fridge.

'What? I look dreadful.'

'You look beautiful. You look the way I remember you when we first met – in your training suit, no make-up.' He plucked out the champagne. 'You look beautiful like that.'

Graham's heart was somersaulting, the adrenaline fix of guilt and gratitude giving him an unexpected high. He had never seen her looking this vulnerable.

Anke hung her head in shame. This had all gone horribly wrong. She was struggling to pull herself back from a place where shaky, sexless marriages did not exist. A place where Graham would be strong and old-fashioned and never apologise for being late. A place where he would hunt hard and fight for his country. A place where Graham didn't belong. She tried not to think about *A Horse for Emma* burning a hole beneath the cushion, begging to be finished. She had let him down before she had even started. She was a terrible wife. She didn't feel remotely beautiful.

'I have a lovely dress lined up.' She struggled to get back on course.

'Wear it another time.'

'I should be wearing it now, *kaereste*.' She remembered the plan. 'I was going to run you a bath and have it ready for you so that I could cook while you soaked. I was going to make everything perfect.'

He popped the cork and poured two glasses.

'You cook perfect meals every day.' He lifted his glass. 'You wear beautiful clothes and always look immaculate. You run me baths every week, love. That's not why I can't believe how lucky I am to be here with you right now.'

'It's not?'

'We're alone. You've already made tonight special by arranging that. I don't need posh nosh and lacy fripperies to appreciate you. I just need to know that you still love me.'

'Of course I love you,' she muttered and then looked up at him incredulously. 'You don't know that?'

As his eyes softened, elsewhere he hardened impatiently. 'So show me. Let's go to bed. In fact, forget bed – let's have that bath together.'

'Now?'

'Yes, now.'

Anke started to panic. 'We haven't eaten.'

'I'm not hungry.'

She looked at him, the familiar dread clutching at her belly. To her, the preamble was an important part of the task ahead. She needed to look seductive to feel seductive. She needed the distraction of cooking and the numbing effect of alcohol. She needed to forget about Emma and Larch and Suffolk and think about Graham – to dress for Graham, cook for Graham, flirt for Graham, seduce for Graham. She needed desperately to put off the moment. But she had blown it.

He was already towing her upstairs. She'd asked for this. She had to play along.

The unpredictable Jacuzzi decided to play ball today and was soon bubbling and frothing. Graham dived in as eagerly as a setter into a river. He was already in a state of excitement. 'This feels fantastic! Get in.'

Anke fiddled around by the basins, removing her rings and cleaning her teeth, still trying to shake Emma's fate from her head as it lingered there, helpfully distracting her from the cold anaesthetic already drenching her body.

'Have you been crying?' he asked, watching her over her shoulder.

'I was reading a sad book.'

'You daft bat,' he chuckled affectionately, splashing water around.

At last, Anke could put off the moment no longer. She knocked back half a glass of champagne and climbed in.

It was a wet, hurried coupling and at one point she was convinced she was going to drown, but it was over mercifully quickly. Anke felt nothing but wretchedness. It was the first time they'd had sex in over a year and she remembered every reason why. It hurt because she was so tense that every muscle contracted. That, in turn, excited him to thrust deeper and hurt her more, mistaking her gasps for ecstasy. It hurt because her chest ached with unhappiness. It hurt because she had to think so hard about not crying she forgot to breathe. It hurt most of all because she couldn't enjoy it as he did and she couldn't tell him that. She could take love but not make love. That hurt more than a mortal injury.

'Now *that* has whetted my appetite,' Graham announced cheerfully. Wrapped in fluffy towelling gowns, they made their way downstairs. Anke looked longingly towards the conservatory where *A Horse for Emma* was waiting. She needed a happy ending tonight.

But Graham was dogging her every move in love overdrive.

Fantasising himself in the sex scene montage of a Hollywood movie – he had always been particularly taken with *9½ Weeks* – he tried to feed her grapes and lick champagne off her while she cooked.

'You'll ruin my robe.' She tried to play-fight him away with a fish slice, determined that tonight she must not completely shrug him off.

He put on one of his beloved rock anthem albums, far too loudly, making Anke wince – and he danced around the kitchen telling her that the food smelled fantastic and that he loved her and that this was the perfect end to a stressful day.

Anke cooked on autopilot, her head pounding from planning too fast, reading too fast, making love too fast and now thinking too fast.

She wanted to talk. She wanted to ask Graham if he was happy with their marriage or appalled by it, as she was. She wanted to ask whether he was being unfaithful, or had thought about being unfaithful even, because she dreamed about it more and more, fantasising about the most unlikely of characters: Rory Midwinter, almost young enough to be her son; Giles Hornton, bad enough to be her nemesis; Reg Wyck, was mad enough to be her murderer. Earlier tonight, it was Larch from *A Horse for Emma*, a fictional character for God's sake. She wanted to know if he was in the same place as she was.

Yet she said nothing, unable to admit something so gargantuan. She just listened as he sang along to Foreigner and Meatloaf and The Cars. Talking was impossible, anyway. The music was too loud.

He did notch down the volume a little as they ate, complimenting her on her food and telling her she was beautiful. He was on Graham overdrive, loving looks and touches and romantic gestures coming so fast that she couldn't dodge them. Anke could hardly bear it. She kept reminding herself that this had been her idea – however spur of the moment – and that she had to see it through. It was a crazy idea. There was no food, no drink and no talk capable of acting as an aphrodisiac for her. This was a good marriage to a good man and she couldn't find a way to enjoy it. She was a lost cause.

'You are the most beautiful woman alive,' he told her as he offered her his last sugar-sweet pepper tang mushroom on a fork, his blue eyes bursting with ebullience. 'You are beautiful and sexy and a great cook and a great mother and I love you more than the world.'

Anke ate the mushroom, grateful that it filled her mouth so that she didn't have to reply. Her head pounded with frustration. I don't care that you think I'm beautiful and sexy; I want you to love me because I am clever and talented. And I love you too. I do so love you. I just can't seem to show you physically. You are good and kind and true. You are the best of men. But you have to love my mind before I can love your body. You have to understand me. Someone has to understand me. I don't.

She wondered if she was going mad, if she had been afflicted by her father's dreadful legacy.

First, she had panicked herself into springing into action tonight with no planning. Anke always planned. She had let others take over – the Three Disgraces, who were so many worlds apart that they could never hope to understand what made her feel good. She felt out of control and negligent.

Secondly, was the thought that Graham was being unfaithful total and unjustified paranoia? Nobody who behaved as devotedly as he was tonight could be unfaithful, could they? He had told her he loved her about sixty times so far. When a friend's husband had been having an affair he had become an unpleasant, snarling monster continually criticising her – seeking some sort of justification for his actions. Diana had said that Tim had behaved in much the same way. Graham was just being lovely. She had simply starved him of love too long.

Finally, she had abandoned everything to read a book. She had read a book rather than prepare. Not even a good book; no classic of which her father would be proud. She had read a silly, forgotten melodrama set in a forgotten age. And now all she wanted to do was get the meal over with so that she could finish it. She cared more about whether Larch survived than whether Graham was happy in their marriage. What was going on?

Soon she had a sore chest and stomach from eating too fast to add to her pounding head. Graham was on thirds of sticky toffee pudding as she started to clear away.

'You go up and get an early night while I clear up,' she insisted. 'I'll join you in a minute.'

He shook his head. 'Leave the washing up till the morning. We'll take a nightcap to bed together.'

'I can't go to sleep on a full stomach.'

'Who said anything about going to sleep? We've hardly begun.'

'I can't do that on a full stomach either,' she tried to joke, her heart plummeting to her belly, punching at her solar plexus to try to get a response from below. But there was nobody home. Her libido remained in its vault.

'We will take it really, really slowly,' he promised.

Anke allowed herself to be towed upstairs again, looking longingly over her shoulder at the cushion hiding *A Horse for Emma*. Her haven.

A world where loving someone with all your life, as she did Graham, meant being torn apart by a passion that never entered a bedroom unless cold damp flannels were being applied to fevered foreheads.

This was much worse than the Jacuzzi moment. That had been over in a wet, uncomfortable instant. This took hours. The only thing that tore apart was the fragile skin inside Anke as the cold wet flannel of racing thought extinguished her sex drive. It hurt. It really hurt. Her head, her heart and her pelvis screamed with pain as she bit her lips and waited for Graham to come.

Plunge, plunge, plunge. Thrust, thrust, thrust. This way and that. Turning her, talking to her, asking her what she wanted when she just wanted it to be over.

'Relax, love. We've got all night,' he soothed as Anke tried to hurry him along, desperate for an end. 'We are going to make love good and proper this time. Earlier was just the warm-up. This is the *Kür*.' He pulled out from her hated, aching, dysfunctional pit and started to play with her body again.

Anke closed her eyes and pleaded with herself to relax and enjoy this. He loved her. She was a lucky woman. Other women would kill for a man like Graham. She tried to concentrate on stopping her skin twitching as his lips slid all over her, concentrate on holding back from those involuntary tics and shudders of revulsion.

She tried not to think of Prudence Hornton and her hungry, freckled body clamping men of a certain age to her antique bedspread during long lunch breaks and illicit after-work liaisons. She thought about Emma and Larch. She thought of their long summers of innocence together, of their mutual dependence and trust. She tried to imagine Larch recovering from his illness, growing strong and broad again, finding solace from the echoes of cannons in his head. She imagined them galloping through the fens on the stallion and his son. Riding Passion and Love. She imagined Larch taking Emma in his strong arms and . . .

Anke was Emma. She was dressed in an Edwardian riding habit, laced up with corsets beneath, boots to her knees and hair tumbling from her bowler. Larch was in his uniform – no, he was in a rough working shirt and breeches, sweaty and manly from throwing grain sacks from a cart. His black hair was tousled.

No, that wasn't right. Larch had blonde hair in the book. It was the other one who was dark. And it was a dark-haired lover who pulled her from her horse and lay her back on the soft leaf mulch. A dark-haired lover with burning eyes, a burning heart and rough manners who pulled up her skirts and loosened his belt.

'Suffolk!' Her eyes snapped open in surprise.

'What?' Graham mumbled from deep beneath the duvet where he was sucking her toes.

'Nothing. Mmm. Don't stop.' She meant it. The hellfire pit that had ached was starting to bubble and spit with longing.

Anke closed her eyes again and tried to resume the fantasy, concentrating on Larch and Emma galloping across the fens. But it was Suffolk sliding his lips across her ankles now and kissing his way up past her knees. Suffolk with his wild eyes and his mean temper. Suffolk the bully, who had asked Emma to marry him on the day of her greatest grief.

And it was Suffolk who was turning her on. This was all wrong.

But as Graham licked and kissed and tickled and stroked, Anke softened and yielded for the first time in more months than she could remember, perhaps even years.

Larch was too adoring, too meek, too kind, too devoted. She suddenly hoped he would die. The poor man should never have come back from the war. Emma should have married Suffolk, who was tough and manly and knew how to keep her in check. Emma was like Anke – she needed to be dominated and looked after, not smothered and pawed.

Graham was trying to roll her on top of him now, but she kept her back wedged into the mattress and refused to budge. She didn't want to go on top. She needed him to possess her, as Suffolk would – a big brute of a stallion, not a meek gelding.

And, as he finally obliged and thrust his way in, Anke gasped in something close to delight. She could see those angry green eyes, the black hair, the craggy face. She could feel his brute force.

'Suffolk!'

This time Graham did hear and he paused briefly, looking down at her ecstatic face and kissing her nose. 'We've only just moved to the Cotswolds, love, but if it makes you happy we can look into it.'

'Sorry?' She opened one eye.

Suddenly she was confronted with Graham's red face, the veins bulging across his temples, the greying blonde hair plastered sweatily to his forehead and the blue eyes gazing at her with such lust-drunken love they seemed to be pointing in different directions. It wasn't a pretty sight. Suffolk put on his officer's cap, tapped it down on his black locks, blew her a kiss and galloped away.

'Let's talk about it later.' He started thrusting and groaning again.

The fantasy broken, Anke gazed at the ceiling and waited for him to finish. She cranked her head around to glance at the bedside clock, hoping that the kids weren't about to arrive home. It was after eleven.

Four minutes past, five minutes past, six minutes past, the digital numbers reliably informed her. Seven minutes past, eight minutes past, nine minutes past . . . at last.

'Yeaaaaahhhhh!' he roared as he finally came, the old Brakespear victory holler that she hadn't heard in a long time. Then he slumped down beside her and reached out a warm, sweaty hand to squeeze her breast. 'That was great.'

'Mmm. Lovely.' She clamped her thighs together and reached for a tissue.

'Do you really want to move to Suffolk?'

'Ummm . . .'

'We don't have to stay here if you don't like it. Truth is, I'd be quite grateful to be shot of Dulston's. Too much like hard work. And the locals are bloody snobby round these parts.'

Anke opened and closed her mouth a few times, working out how to say what she had to say, what she had told herself to say as she'd watched the clock tick up its minutes like the years of her life sliding away.

'I don't want to move again – not physically,' she blurted, knowing it was now or never. 'I hoped moving here would change things, but it hasn't. Tonight has shown me that. I hate what I cannot feel. I really think it might be time to think about some sort of marriage therapy, *kaereste*. I love you very much, but I cannot carry on like this.'

She looked across to gauge his reaction and realised that he was already asleep.

Later, she crept downstairs and finished *A Horse for Emma*. Larch didn't die. He made a full recovery. Suffolk was never seen again, although Passion trotted back home the next day, none the worse for wear.

Emma and Larch marry and call their first-born son Edward. Occasionally, in the misty dawn, Emma thinks that she can see an officer on horseback across the fens. He seems to be waiting for her, but she never dares ride to him. She has her Larch, their son and her Love and Passion at home.

Anke had wanted a happy ending, but she found herself weeping again as she closed the book. This wasn't her happy ending. In her happy ending Emma would have married fierce, clever, passionate, misunderstood Suffolk.

Upstairs, Graham was standing in the bathroom staring into his own wet eyes – the colour of old blue jeans with that faded-with-every-wash look. Hauliers didn't cry. It was pathetic.

He splashed water on his face, hiding the evidence.

Hauliers didn't seek marriage guidance, either. They just feigned sleep and waited for their wives to leave the bed so that they could punch a pillow instead of crying.

Heading back into the bedroom, Graham plumped his dented pillow and realised that his knuckles had broken right through the Egyptian cotton.

Bloody Egypt. Bloody tombs. How could poor little Mo ever hope to raid his heart when it had been plundered already?

When Anke gave *A Horse for Emma* to Faith the following day, the reaction was more than muted. 'I don't really read stuff like this any more.'

'Try it. It's very well written.'

'It's a bit old-fashioned, isn't it?'

'It's romantic.'

'I prefer a bit of passion. They didn't write about sex and stuff in those days.'

'It *is* passionate. That's sexier than a few pages of lurid descriptions.'

'Yes, but I like the details. It's educational.' Sometimes, Faith was even blunter than her mother.

'Oh, I see. Well, I'll put it in your room anyway.'

'Thanks.'

Looking at her daughter's bookshelf, Anke realised that she couldn't have got it more wrong. She hadn't noticed that Faith's tastes had changed so dramatically. Alongside her set texts from school – those books which Anke considered to be the most passionate such as *Wuthering Heights*, *Far from the Madding Crowd* and *Jane Eyre* – were a host of bright pink and purple and lime-green jackets with titles like *Flirting with Danger*, *Hot Dates* and the alarming *Three's a Crowd, Four Play*.

Anke drew one out and read a few pages before hastily putting it back. All the pony books had gone, she noticed – as had the rosettes and horse posters and trinkets. Only one equestrian picture remained, that of a host of wild-eyed horses' heads looming up over a huge spruce Grand National fence.

Anke sat on the end of her daughter's bed clutching *A Horse for Emma*. Just as she had started to realise that she wanted to be an irresponsible, daydreaming child again, her daughter wanted to be a grown up. It wasn't fair.

20

Diana was not in the best of moods when Tim rolled up for his first weekend's child access since the marriage had shattered in two. She had slept badly, her head haunted with dreams in which she was lost in the Gunning woods with no clothes on because Pod had stolen them from her, running away and laughing, hiding behind trees like a sprite. She could hear hoof beats, faster and faster but, before she could hide, Tim was suddenly charging at her on horseback wearing full ceremonial uniform, screaming 'Go to hell!' in his best parade ground bellow. And then he turned into Amos, chasing after her on Rio, his body in flames. 'Go to hell, Diana, go to hell, GO TO HELL!' At one point she'd sat up in bed, drenched in sweat and breathless, to find Digby watching her from behind a pillow.

'Why were you shouting, Mum?'

'I'm sorry, darling. I was dreaming. Go back to sleep.'

She lay awake for hours, holding his solid little body in the crook of her arm and staring up at the shadows, not wanting to slip back into her unhappy dream-world for fear of screaming and waking him again.

As dawn was breaking, she could no longer force her eyes to stay open and had dropped down the long tunnel to unconsciousness for about five minutes before Mim bounded into her bedroom telling her that she and Chad had been awake for *hours* and were *really, really* hungry. Wearily she had thrown on the first clothes that came to hand and gone in search of cereal. She was still wearing those clothes when Tim's car rolled up, her hair and teeth unbrushed and her makeup-free face puffy from lack of sleep.

Mim and Digby, hopelessly excited at the prospect of seeing their father, had behaved appallingly all morning, totally wiping out Diana's hopes of looking radiant and organised and I-don't-miss-you cool when Tim arrived.

She had, of course, expected him to be punctual – he was a stickler for timing. But she hadn't expected him to look so tanned. She hadn't expected him to come bearing so many presents for the children that it was a hundred Christmases rolled into one. And she hadn't expected him to have the girlfriend in tow.

She wanted to scream at him for his thoughtlessness. His children needed to spend time with him alone, not share it with the stranger who had helped wreck their parents' marriage. But she said nothing as Mim and Digby crawled all over him, demanding to know where they were going and what they were going to do.

Diana drew some small satisfaction from the fact that Hally bounded up to the girlfriend just as Tim was explaining to the kids that 'Katie will be coming with us', depositing two perfect manure paw prints on her pale cream trousers.

'Sorry – she's just been on the muck heap.' Diana grabbed the dog's collar and dragged her off. 'I'm sure it'll brush off when it dries.'

'Of course – you two haven't been properly introduced, have you?' Tim gave Diana a nasty smile. 'Katie Penfold, this is Diana –' he suddenly faltered.

'Diana Henriques.' She held out her hand and shook Katie's, noting how cold and clammy it was. The kids would give her hell.

Apart from that, and checking that the children had their overnight bags, the only thing Tim said to Diana was 'The dog's put on weight.'

When they all disappeared down the drive for a jolly weekend in Somerset, Diana fled to her bedroom to cry. Yet the strangest thing happened as she threw herself on to the duvet, pursued by Hally and her horse dung paws. The catch in her throat raked its long talons through the lump that had been welling there, punched it into her stomach to grab at her guts, reached up to wrench the tears from her eyes and then paused along the way to tickle her funny bone. It tickled through the tears and jealousy and trauma.

She laughed out loud. She laughed until her ribs creaked. She pummelled her legs and feet on the bed and howled as Hally bounced above her excitedly. The tears still rolled, but she was almost overcome with the joy of anti-climax.

Seeing Tim again had been a relief. It had been a blessed, bittersweet relief. Her excessive, obsessive, agonising jealousy was entirely focused around the children. It ate her up, it tore at her heart and chest and abdomen – and yet she knew how to ride it out. She knew that it was a hatred that she could control.

Her love for her children was an absolute, as was their love for her. It was her love for Tim that she had no longer been able to quantify all these weeks.

Today had finally put him on the map. She felt sadness, anger, regret and bitterness – it ached like hell. That placed him way higher than anything she felt for Pod – off the scale as far as Pod was concerned. Yet, compared to seeing Amos again, Tim hardly registered. A decade of marriage hardly registered.

She sat up and hugged Hally to her side as she pressed the heels of her hands to her eyes to dash away the tears.

'Lord, you *are* getting fat.' She patted her dog's metallic grey paunch and then pinched her own bulges oozing above the waist of her jeans. 'As are we both. I think we need a lovely long walk or two, don't you?'

She looked out of the window as she heard tyres on the drive, her heart leaping for a moment as she wondered whether the children had demanded that their father turn around already because they missed her so desperately. But it was just Mo's tatty car arriving for her weekend riding lesson.

Mo loved the idea of an autumn nature walk for the children in her class. It was when Diana mentioned the Gunning Estate that she started to get bad vibes.

'Won't we need permission?'

'No, there are dozens of public footpaths. We'll get Anke to help us.'

Mo was even more disconcerted by this suggestion. She'd become very jumpy that Anke was on to her, so the thought of a ramble in a dark, treacherous, eerie wood with her lover's wife hardly filled her with glee.

She regretted accepting Diana's offer of a coffee. Normally as soon as her lesson ended she would dash off to see Graham, who had starting putting in a few weekend hours at Dulston's so that they could meet, especially now that his two stepchildren played sentry at the horse yard and agricultural yard on weekdays. But today he was *en famille*. Last night had changed things, although nothing had been said. They were both starting to wake up from the daydream.

'Aren't there better walks closer to Oddlode? The bridle-path past the River Folly for one?'

'*So* dull and pedestrian.' Diana shook her head kindly, knowing that Mo was going to be a pushover in the face of her determination. 'Gunning has nature like you will not believe – one can identify such rare native flora and fauna, all sorts of "bush tucker" that the children can try out . . . plus spotting red deer, muntjak, fox, badger and so on – the wildlife there see so few humans that they are as bold as brass. Children rarely ever get to learn these things first hand. I am happy to fund the entire day, and I'll try to coax Aunt Til into a guided tour or a short talk at least. Nobody knows wild Britain like Til. She's a dying breed. The children will remember her all their lives.'

Put like that, it was an outing Mo was powerless to refuse. She wanted to see the woods everyone talked about, too. She wanted to see the place that obsessed Pod and had almost stolen him from her. It sounded beautiful.

'I'm so thrilled!' Diana patted her arm. 'We'll have a wonderful time, I promise.'

'I need to ask the headmistress for permission first.'

'Leave that to me. Perhaps you could have a quiet word with Pod, make sure we won't be disturbing anybody?'

'Pod?'

'He's practically on the gamekeeping team, isn't he? He can tell you which part of the estate they're working in that day and we'll make sure we don't venture near.'

'He won't be able to help,' Mo insisted, the full implication of what she had just agreed to at last sinking in. How could she imagine that she could keep the visit a secret from Pod? He was bound to find out. 'He's only doing casual work there.'

'Looking for something more serious, is he?' Diana asked.

'Pod's never serious.'

Diana raised an eyebrow. It was an eyebrow that stayed raised for an amazing three and a half minutes. Mo spotted the time on the mantel clock as her eyes darted around nervously.

She knew that Pod was being bad. He was being very bad. This time, Mo was being bad too. She was learning all about bad and how addictive it could be. Their sticky patch had solidified. It was worse than she had ever known. He had stayed away all night twice this week. Glad Tidings was patrolling the shared garden border with her radar on alert at all times, sniffing meltdown.

Yet Mo had no doubt that they would see this out to the other side. Her faith in Pod was stronger than her faith in any religion. He had let her down a hundred times, but he had never forsaken her.

When Diana's eyebrow finally descended, she poured Mo another coffee and curled up on the sofa beside her for some girl talk.

'Do tell me if I'm intruding here, but are you and Pod going through a bit of a difficult time?'

Mo picked at a seam of her jeans and shrugged. 'A bit of a sticky patch, yes.'

'Think you'll ride it though?'

'Well, I'm getting better at riding.' Mo forced a smile. 'So who knows?'

Diana laughed. 'I think Rory has rather a soft spot for you. 'He really looks forward to your lessons.'

'That's nice.'

'He's a bit low at the moment, too. He and Dilly have grown so apart. It's pretty much over.'

'Poor Rory.' Mo was grateful that the focus had moved away from Pod. 'I guess that's understandable with her being so far away at university.'

'*Au contraire.* Dilly has been in Oddlode rather a lot this month. Something – or someone – is justifying that long drive from Durham, but I'm afraid it's no longer Rory.'

Mo pulled at the loose thread in her jeans again, suddenly realising that Pod was still the topic of conversation. Diana was trying to tell her something. It was something that, in her heart, she already knew. But she didn't want to go there. She really didn't want to go there.

'The Gunning ghosts.' She thrust out her chin, eyeing Diana closely. 'Do they do much apart from start fires and ride around at midnight?'

'What do you mean?' Diana almost dropped her coffee.

'Can they be like poltergeists or evil spirits? Do they try to wreck relationships?'

Diana looked away, burying a half-smile in a far corner. 'According to some, that's their speciality.'

Mo nodded, letting this sink in.

'And you want me to take my pupils in there to meet them?'

Diana unearthed her gaze and used it to full force, the smile widening to a supersize advertising billboard complete with a small sparkle on her believe-me white crescent of teeth. 'There are no ghosts, Mo. I would never dream of allowing my children near the place if there were, however fanciful. It's a magical place. That doesn't mean it's a haunted place. You'll see for yourself.'

Despite the dazzling smile, Mo noticed the tiny tic leaping in Diana's cheek.

'I will ask the Head, but even if she says yes I'm afraid I really don't have the time to organise transport or contact parents for permission.'

'Really – leave it to me. I'll do everything.'

And Diana was true to her word. She soon had the school dancing to her tune as she orchestrated mothers' helpers and local field guides, which, alarmingly, included Reg Wyck. She had even cleverly tied it in with the children's October Halloween project – 'Just in case the ghosts do stage an appearance,' she told Mo with a wink on the eve of the nature walk.

Organising everything had given Diana a much-needed focus to take her mind off her latest battle with the local planning authority and her bank and, more upsettingly, with Tim. The children had returned from their weekend hyperactive and full of stories, seemingly none the worse for wear, although Katie looked ragged. But Tim's face had been like a thundercloud. He had discovered about his misappropriated school fees cheque.

'My children are attending a state school!'

'If you took more interest in them you'd have known that weeks ago,' Diana had retorted. 'I got them into the best school in the county, regardless of status. The money is still benefiting them – only this week I'm funding a nature walk.'

'My solicitors will hear about this.'

It hardly made any difference. Diana already knew that she would get almost nothing. She sat up the night before the trip to Gunning with a large glass of wine, thinking about the small fortune that lay deep in those woods. She was planning to make a diversion tomorrow to search for buried treasure but, however much she needed cash, she wasn't going to be looking for the hidden riches. Her treasure was much more personal.

Mo had a dreadful feeling of foreboding that night, especially when Pod deigned to return to the cottage, crashing in at midnight full of beer and bad spirits.

'Where's your tobacco? I've run out.' He started searching through her bags on the table.

'No – it's here!' She grabbed it from the sofa arm, but it was too late. He was already studying the photocopied map that Diana had given her.

'This is Gunning.'

'I know.'

'What's this shit mean? "*Stop for talk on fungi, 11.30. Picnic lunch by spring and ghost talk, 12.00*"? What does it mean, Mo?'

'You figure it out.' She snatched the map away and stuffed it back in her bag.

It was their first conversation in days of more than a few syllables and he was incandescent with rage.

'Amos will throw you all out.'

'We're sticking to the footpaths.'

'You can't bring children on to the estate. It's dangerous.'

'Why?'

'There's shooting and stuff.'

'Not near public rights of way. And who shoots there? Hardly licensed guns. No one ever dares go near the place.'

Pod clenched his jaw. 'You can't bring kids in there, you stupid cow!'

'We are.'

'But you just fucking said it – no one dares go near the place.'

'You do.'

He glared at her.

'I want to see what obsesses you so much, Pod. Why it's got a hold over you. Whoever owns it just wants to keep the public away by spreading stupid rumours about ghosts and fugitives. Well, I don't buy it. I want to see it for myself and the kids want to see it for the wildlife. We're not going to break any laws.'

'I'll lock you in the cottage. Here and now. I'll stop you bringing them.'

'Why, Pod? What do you get up to there? Dance naked around fairy glades with Amos?'

'It's mine now. You didn't want to go there. And you can't go there.'

'I will.'

Suddenly he lunged across the room, reaching for her. Mo side-stepped and he crashed against the wall.

'It'll steal your heart away!' he roared, spinning round, shouldering the old stone and blinking at her.

Mo stepped back anxiously.

Pod's big, bruised, baby, black-hearted eyes were legend. They were great soft, peaty meres into which women fell. They had trapped Mo for years, up to her waist in his darkness, his depth and his soul.

Now, without warning, his eyes were glass. Inches thick, bulletproof, like nothing Mo had ever seen before, shutting her out.

'Has it stolen your heart, Pod?'

He said nothing, eyes blank.

'Do you love that place more than me?'

His eyes were inaccessible.

'I want to go there.'

When he finally spoke, his voice was barely a whisper. 'We can still get away from here.'

'I'm going to Gunning.'

'It'll corrupt you.'

'I'm already corrupted.'

Turning away, he walked upstairs.

Mo chased after him. 'What are you doing?'

'Ending the pain.' He was packing.

It was here at last. The sticky patch, which had congealed and then hardened to a brittle husk, had finally shattered.

'You're fucking Graham Brakespear,' he announced calmly, tossing T-shirts into his case.

Mo whimpered, darting behind the bed and pressing her face into her arms.

'I've watched you two,' he went on as he pulled trousers from the wardrobe.

'No!' Mo clamped her arms to her ears, but she couldn't blot out every word he shouted.

His mouth moved in front of her, looming inches from her face as he hurled abuse between hurling possessions into his bag. Dates, times, places, sexual positions. He knew it all.

'*You have* never *been faithful to me!*' she screamed, her own voice a dull explosion in her head as she kept her arms pressed to her ears.

'I have never stopped loving you.' He squared up to her, his arms full of socks.

'I love you,' she sobbed.

He shook his head. 'You don't.'

Mo unfurled her earmuffs and hugged herself tightly. 'I sure as hell don't love Graham.'

'I know that.' The glassy eyes watched her. 'Whenever I've slept with another woman, queen, I've known that I love you more than her. It's affirmed my love. And when you slept with Graham Brakespear, you didn't fall in love with him. You fell *out* of love with me. You killed our love.'

'No!'

'It fell from a great height.'

'No!'

'A very great height. We were as high in love as high gets. Welcome to Ground Zero, queen. You burned our love to nothing, little dragon.'

With that, he zipped up his bag and walked out on her.

Listening from her garden wall, Glad Tidings almost expired with shock.

Relying upon what had once been an inexhaustible supply of optimism and was now war rations, Mo sat awake that night reminding herself that Pod had left before. His leaving her was one of the staples that pinned their relationship together. Pod always came back to her. Unlike her mother who had never looked back, or her father, who had never cared to know, Pod always came back.

He would be back.

She started to hum a tune . . . she couldn't remember where it came from. A nursery rhyme maybe, or a childhood ditty she had clung to. Over and over in her head the melody looped as she hugged a pillow to her chest and rocked on the spot, staring at the window.

She watched the new day dawn, a grey, steely searchlight through the cottage windows, and wondered whether going to Gunning that day was suicidal. If she stayed away, he might come back sooner. She marked the clock until seven-thirty before ringing Horseshoe Farm Cottage.

The machine answered. When the beep sounded for a message to be left, Mo started gabbling: 'I am going to cancel the field trip today. I think I should have gone to the place myself before guaranteeing it was safe to take children there. We can do a village walk instead. The head-mistress had already allowed a half day for the project outing. The river is perfect for their wildlife task and much more topical given its prox-imity to the –'

'We *are* going!' Diana snatched up a handset, breathless from running downstairs. 'I have booked the minibus. I have helpers. We have maps and secret treats to hide.'

'I really don't want to go.' Mo burst into tears.

'Oh, for God's sake.' Diana was blistering in her lack of sympathy. 'This is their Halloween project. Mim and Digby have been reading up about ghosts all week, not that we'll see any. So, don't be so wet, Mo. There *are* no ghosts.'

'Yes there are.' Mo curled up in a ball, the phone dropping away from her ear.

'I don't tell many people this.' Diana pressed her own receiver tight to her mouth. 'But there is something in the Gunning Estate which is worth facing every ghost and ghoul for. There is something so beauti-ful that you will never want to leave. It makes brave souls of all who see it. If you step over the threshold you fall in love. That's the true ghost. It's a love that never leaves you. I think it may have stolen your Pod away.'

But Mo had her arms to her ears again. She didn't want to chase Pod. If she followed him, he wouldn't come home.

When, later that morning, Mo didn't turn up to take the register, her classroom assistant Pam Gates took it for her and checked that the chil-dren all had their packed lunches and their field trip kits with them. The parent helpers were already lined up in the car park along with the minibus.

'No sign of Miss Stillitoe yet?' Pam checked outside again.

'She must have overslept,' said Netta the school secretary. 'Mrs Lampeter and Mrs Brakespear have gone to knock on her door.'

'Must be a heavy sleeper if it takes two of them.' Pam giggled.

'What can have happened to her?' Anke lifted the letter-box flap and peeked in again.

'I think she had an argument with her boyfriend,' Diana sighed. 'She mentioned they were going through a rough patch.'

'Poor thing.' Anke straightened up and knocked again.

'We can always go ahead without her.'

'I'd like to know that she's all right.'

'Need any help?' asked an excited voice as Glad Tidings bustled up the path behind them, pink cheeks glowing from a hasty sprint over the green, having spotted the action outside Number Four from her usual vantage-point. 'Those two had another tiff last night? I thought I heard something.'

'You mean it's a regular thing?'

'Screams like a banshee, that girl. How poor Pod puts up with it I never know.'

'We're worried about her,' Anke explained. 'She's supposed to be leading a field trip today.'

'Oh yes, my Pam said about that.' Glady's mouth tucked up disapprovingly. 'Don't want to go poking round in them woods if you ask me.'

'We didn't ask you.' Diana turned to knock on the door again. 'Mo! Mo, darling? Are you all right?'

'I have the spare keys if that's any help?' Gladys suggested eagerly. 'Promised old Rose I'd keep an eye on the place.'

'Oh, yes – please do fetch them.'

'We can't just let ourselves in!' Anke was appalled.

'What if she's done something silly?' Diana pointed out as Gladys hurried away, euphoric at the prospect of having a poke around. She hadn't gained access for weeks despite a frenzy of cake baking.

As soon as Gladys had turned the corner towards her own cottage, the door of Number Four opened and Mo crept out. She looked dreadful, the hollows under her eyes like caverns.

'Even walking in the forbidden woods with ghosts and murderers and God knows what is better than being invaded by Gladys,' she hissed, leading the way towards the school, muttering over her shoulder. 'Sorry – I overslept. Late night.'

Astonished, Diana and Anke followed her.

21

With packed lunches bumping in duffle bags, and jam jars hanging from strings around their necks, an unlikely little band of wildlife ramblers set off along one of Gunning's seldom-used footpaths in the sharp morning sunshine.

Diana, who had planned the route carefully, put Mo and Pam in charge of map-reading so that she could keep a lower profile at the rear of the group, pretending to look after Reg Wyck, who was muttering and cursing incoherently under his breath. He seemed to be complaining that Til had talked him into this and 'the stupid bat' hadn't turned up.

'She's meeting us later,' Diana told him.

The wildlife walk started from the little lane that linked the Springlodes to the Oddfields, enabling them to park the minibus and the parents' cars away from Gunning land, using the wide grass verges that Diana had cantered along as a child. She was confident that her little circuit was well away from trouble, avoiding both the commercial conifer plantations and the old game-bird enclosures.

A wide farm track led between steep-sided fields of sheep, with breath-taking views across both the Lodes and Foxrush valleys. Then the track dropped into the ash and hazel coppices, which were great for spotting birds and flowers. Here, the path would lead them across a wooden bridge over the ha-ha that separated these coppices from the ancient beech woods, where they could look for squirrels, plus amazing fungi like puffballs, Dryad's saddle and the red-capped fly agaric, although Diana didn't entirely trust herself to know which mushrooms and toad-stools were poisonous. She had no doubt Reg would know, but didn't put it past him to lie. Mercifully, Til was due to join them at that point. The trees were in full autumn turn and shedding their leaves, so the children could admire the amazing flame-red copper beeches and the yellow of the wych elms that ran alongside one of the many park avenues that criss-crossed the woods. This neglected highway would lead them up towards the far edge of the most ancient part of the old forest – the oak woods, with their fox dens and badger setts, the wood pigeons cooing in the branches and the continual rustle of small gatherers claiming acorns for their winter stash and luring the predatory buzzards and sparrow hawks which sometimes circled over the woodland canopy. Diana knew this part of the woods best, adoring the holly trees with their hollow canopies that could shelter you from the biggest downpour if you were brave enough to climb inside. She and Amos had tried almost every one.

Finally, they would emerge from peeking into just the smallest corner of the huge woodlands and the walk would skirt the banks of one of the many little streams which fed the great park lake and then flowed on to the Lode. They would climb up against the current, still in the shadows of the woods, looking out for minnows and newts, lifting stones to find toads, until they reached the point where the little stream disappeared beneath the ground at its spring. Then it was just two stiles along the windswept ridge before they were back at the lane.

Diana planned to have left the group long before this, however. She knew a well-hidden footpath from the elm walk that would take her alongside the pine woods to the Pleasure Garden. It was a detour that should take no more than an hour and she would be back long before they had finished eating their picnics by the spring source, listening to Aunt Til telling them a tamed-down version of the stories behind the Sarsden Curse and the Gunning ghosts. They'd never know she'd been gone. At least that was the plan.

Their first obstacle was one she had predicted, although they hadn't even reached the coppices when Amos and Pod appeared in the gun-laden Land Rover, trying to turn the children back. Diana ducked down at the back of the group and guiltily let Mo take the flak, too obsessed with her own mission to realise what this meant.

'This is private property.' Amos came out with his favourite line, smouldering threateningly at the wheel.

Mo stared past him, at Pod sitting in the passenger's seat, his dark brows low as he determinedly didn't acknowledge her.

'Did you hear me?' Amos thundered. 'This is private property.'

So was her heart, but Pod had trespassed all over it for years and she had willingly let him. He had stolen in, ignoring the No Trespassers and Private Keep Out signs.

'It's too dangerous to take children in there. You must have heard the rumours.'

Her heart was a dangerous place, too – and haunted. The only people safe to go there had been children, until Pod came along. Children were always safe with her. She'd make sure they were safe.

'Are you listening to me, you silly bitch?'

The corners of Pod's mouth curled up in a small sneer on hearing his boss abuse her.

Mo's haunted, barricaded heart felt as though it was exploding, but she knew she must never show him what he had done to her. He'd spent so many years trying to set fire to her heart with his infidelity, his unreliability, his recklessness. Now that he finally had, she was going to hide the fire if it killed her.

'We'll only be walking on public paths,' she told Amos through his window, her voice shaking with effort. 'We promise not to disturb anything.'

'Hard to stick to footpaths round here.' Amos snatched the map from her, studying her plan and grunting as he realised immediately it was based upon legal rights of way. 'You'll never find your way through.'

'We'll try our hardest.'

'I don't want to be wasting my time or Pod's here by hanging about to put you and the little ones back on track. It's a dangerous place. There are old poachers' traps and all sorts. You'd be better going somewhere else. Plenty of local woods all set up for this type of thing.'

'We won't get lost.' Mo could see Pod's hands playing with his Zippo lighter, flicking the lid back and forth. He must have told Amos to come looking for them. Of course he had. She wondered whether that was where he had stayed last night, with Amos and his family, although little Maisy had said nothing about it.

'I can't let you go in there.' Amos tapped his fingers tetchily on the wheel.

'Your own daughter is here today, Mr Gates,' Mo told Amos gently. 'This is such fun for all the children and so good for them to learn about the woods in autumn. They'll come to no harm.'

'Who's damnfool idea was this, anyway?' Amos demanded, starting to lose his temper. Then he spotted Reg Wyck. 'Jesus!'

Mo had spotted something far more alarming. Anke Brakespear was making her way through the children to come and talk to Amos. Mo looked desperately at Pod, certain that he was going to cheerfully make a public announcement about her affair with Graham the moment he saw Anke's face at the Land Rover window. She felt sick and faint, her tongue suddenly huge and cumbersome in her mouth, her lungs unable to breathe.

But as Anke placed her long, strong fingers on the sill and stooped to talk to Amos in her deep, gentle voice with its curious accent, Pod looked up directly into Mo's eyes and she knew he wouldn't say a thing. Just for that brief moment, the opaque black glass marbles that had replaced the windows to his soul the night before cleared and sparkled with a curious understanding. He flicked the Zippo so that it lit, held the flame to his mouth and blew it out. As he did so, his eyes clouded again and he looked away. She was reprieved – at least for now.

Still ducking down behind a wall of small bodies and pretending to retie her shoelace, Diana pulled her hat lower over her nose, hoping that she wouldn't be recognised. Much as she longed to leap out and tackle Amos – they had every right to be here, after all – she had to keep a low profile. If he knew she was ringleader, he would guess what she was up to and police her so that escaping on her detour would be almost impossible. At the front of the group, Anke had joined Mo and was placating the enraged estate manager.

'Mr Gates, these are beautiful, old, wild woods – which is precisely why we want the children to see them. They are very special. And we do understand that this is why you want to protect them, but it is also the reason that there are footpaths here to enable the public to see something quite so remarkable. We have every right to be here and you cannot stop us. Please move aside.'

Such was Anke's cool, determined self-possession that Amos was forced to grunt a reluctant consent, warning her that he would be keeping a close eye on them and would throw them off Gunning land if they strayed so much as one small foot from the paths. 'And put those bloody dogs on leads,' he demanded, spotting Evig and Bomber panting at her heels.

He was about to reverse his Land Rover down the track towards the woods when his eyes narrowed as he spotted a vehicle approaching in his rear-view mirror and he hit the brakes with more curses.

'There really was no need to rally more troops, Mr Gates,' Anke assured him, watching the three khaki-clad figures in an open-topped vehicle bouncing towards them in a haze of dust.

'And I can assure you they have nothing to do with me,' Amos snarled. 'And they are *definitely* trespassing. Jesus!' He swung around to gape through his rear cab as the strange car veered off track for a moment, almost wiping out several sheep, before rejoining it by hurtling across a ditch and gathering a small elder bush in its grille.

'Oh no.' Anke suddenly recognised the figure at the wheel. It was her father, wearing a peaked desert hat that made him look as though he'd joined the Foreign Legion. Beside him, in an equally military, if jauntily angled, green beret and matching Husky jacket, was Truffle Dacre-Hopkinson and, sitting behind them in a headscarf, bearing an alarming resemblance to Beryl Bainbridge, was Nanny Crump.

'What in God's name?' Amos demanded, leaping from his cab.

'Hello!' Truffle called out cheerily as Ingmar parked the Moke practically on top of Bomber the bull terrier, on whom Anke was trying to put his slip lead, causing him to bound away with an alarmed yelp, pursued by Evig. 'We thought we'd come up and join in the fun – just been to see Til at the cottage. She said there was a bit of a jamboree and that she's even giving a talk later. Where's that daughter of mine? As soon as I heard Diana had planned all this, I just knew she was up to something. Diana!'

Slowly, Diana straightened up and forced a bright smile. 'Hello, Mummy.'

Amos pressed the palm of his hand to his forehead. 'I might have guessed.'

When the walk resumed, the children were the least of Amos' and Pod's worries. It was the OAPs that caused greatest concern. Amos dispatched Pod in the Land Rover to keep check on Ingmar and Nanny Crump, who had careered off in the Moke to find the one by-way track through the estate that was legally accessible by motor vehicles (thankfully, though legally accessible, it was illegally blocked by a great many logs, as far as Amos knew). He, meanwhile, glared furiously at his watch and stalked behind the little wildlife walk, eagle-eyed for a foot out of line, shooting murderous looks at Diana. He hadn't been able to bring himself to say a word to her, furious that she had brought chaos to his safe harbour. Reg Wyck, currently terrifying several small children with descriptions of badger baiting, was almost certainly on a poaching recce. And the arrival of Diana's mother had so enraged him that he had totally forgotten Anke Brakespear's dogs were on the loose.

'I have to sneak off and fetch them back,' Anke muttered to Mo at the head of the line as they tried to decipher the map. 'Is there a foot-path I can scoot along to put him off the scent?' She glanced back at Amos as Mo studied the map.

'There's something marked off to the right here.' Mo held the map in front of her and looked at the path ahead, where the coppice led into the woods proper. 'What does this line stand for?'

'I think that's a field boundary.' Anke frowned, looking at the map. 'It's this thing.' She pointed down to the ha-ha ditch, overgrown with bracken. 'It's a black line, see? Paths are marked with red dots or dashes.'

'Oh.' Mo rubbed her neck before pointing at Diana's highlighted lines. 'In that case, the next path you can take isn't until this big track thing here.'

Behind them, Pam was telling the children that the bracken was not all the same, pointing out clumps of male fern: 'You see how it doesn't turn brown in autumn?'

'Is that because it's boy bracken so it's really hard?' asked Digby Lampeter, uncapping his jam jar to add yet another captured earthworm to his booty.

'No, Digby – and stop trying to tip those worms into Mimosa's hood.'

Up ahead, Anke turned to share a smile with Mo, but her small, pale face was pinched and distracted.

'You look tired.'

'Thanks.'

'Sorry.' Anke patted her arm. 'I just worry that you are not sleeping well? You are normally so buoyant. And Diana said maybe you had argued with your boyfriend?'

'I'm fine.'

Mo wished Anke was not walking with her. They said that if you walked a mile in someone's shoes, you would always understand them. Right now, she would love to walk a mile in Anke's shoes, because that meant that there would be a mile between them, and Anke would have no shoes on to give chase. Instead, they had walked little more than a few hundred yards in step and she wanted to break down and weep.

Anke was right. She had not slept at all last night. She had hugged her pillow and hummed her tune. It was in her head now.

'Is everything all right at home?' Anke persisted gently. 'I couldn't help notice that you and Pod seemed a little frosty with one another earlier?'

Eyes glued to the leaves through which they were trudging, Mo gulped twice, squeaked like a field mouse facing a combine harvester, gulped again and said nothing.

'I know today is not a good day.' Anke glanced behind her. 'But if you ever want to talk to anyone, Mo, please do call me. You are a lovely person and it is so awful to see you sad.'

Mo gulped a few more times as she closed her left eye to cut off a tear and then repeated the process with her right eye. 'I'm fine.'

'Sure.' Anke patted her arm again and looked across at her anxiously.

Mo felt the lump in her throat cut off her airway and knew she deserved suffocation at the very least. Anke was lovely. Just as Graham was lovely. Anke and Graham were lovely people. He was her Daddy G, but Anke was such a maternal person that Mo wanted her to be her Mummy A just as much. She longed to be a part of their family. She saw herself scrapping with lazy, arrogant, talented Magnus, nurturing shy, quirky, witty Faith and play-fighting with the eternally optimistic, ever-joking Chad. They were a fantastic family. And she had done something that could break them apart. Pod was right. She wasn't in love with Graham. She was in love with the family.

'I'm really fine – honestly,' she managed to squeak around the lump in her throat. 'This is your path coming up on the right, just through those trees there.' She checked behind. 'Amos isn't looking – he's on his phone. Just go. If he asks, I'll say you're having a wee and will catch us up.'

'Thank you, *kaereste*.' Anke peeled away into the undergrowth to double back and locate her dogs.

Mo could hear Reg Wyck behind her, loudly proclaiming that they were now walking on the most haunted turf in England.

'The elm walk!' he cackled at an over-excited Chad. 'Where Sarsden ghosts gallop in flames each night screaming in agony for their lost souls.'

'Do their eyeballs burn too?' Chad asked, agog.

'Child, even their entrails burn.'

'That's enough, Reg,' snapped Diana, who was darting around between the children, looking agitated. She caught up with Mo. 'Just popping behind a tree for a quick widdle. You happy you know the way?'

Mo nodded distractedly, checking that Anke was well out of sight.

She felt a sharp tug at her trousers and looked down to find Mim Lampeter walking to heel.

'Miss Silly Toes, can ghosts really eat people?'

Mo shook her head, smiling down at her. 'They're mostly vegetarians.'

Mim grinned back, kicking up some leaves as she slipped her hand into Mo's. 'I think you're a princess.'

'Thank you.'

'My mummy told Rory that he should fall in love with you.'

Mo looked down at her curiously. 'She did?'

Mim nodded. 'She said that Silly Dilly isn't very nice, but that you are very nice. I wasn't supposed to be listening, but it still made me really happy even though I knew I was being naughty.'

'I know that feeling.' Mo squeezed her hand.

'If you married Rory you would be my aunt.'

Mo dropped down and gathered her up into a piggyback, racing her through the elm trees until she shrieked with laughter.

'You were like my pony doing gymkhana races!' Mim panted

breathlessly into her ear afterwards. 'I want you to be my aunt so much!'

Mo let her down and gave her a hug. 'Mim, I'm your friend and your teacher. That's two wonderful things to be because it means that I really get to know you. I don't need to be anything else.'

'I want you to marry Rory.'

Mo looked at her little face – the prettiest of her pupils by far, and the most troublesome because she was so bright and secretive and passionate and calculating.

'Mim, I've already got a boyfriend.' If she said it out loud, there was still hope.

'I know. He's called Pod. Mummy says he's with Silly Dilly now.'

Mo knew exactly from whom Mim had inherited her bright and secretive and passionate and calculating streaks. She didn't put it past Diana to have briefed her daughter beforehand to break the news. The news that her heart knew but her head had refused to acknowledge. Now, it was banging at her temples, clawing at her skull, ringing in her ears and punching her between the eyes. She pressed her hand to her mouth and looked away.

'What was that noise?' asked Mim.

Mo couldn't speak. She tried for a smile, forcing it into place with her fingers before removing her hand and waving at a particularly unusual-looking elm that was hunched over them with two mismatched trunks like a little old lady with a stick.

'You just squeaked.' Mim looked up her curiously. 'You sounded like a guinea pig.'

Behind them, Reg Wyck had shambled up to the two-trunked tree, thrust his arms wide, and growled.

'The Sarsden split elm. Been growing here for more than two hundred year. Planted just afore the fifth Lady Sarsden lost her twins in a fire in the nursery. Eight year old, they was – like some of you. Now they lives in this tree, and some nights they say the tree unearths his two trunks and the little 'ns exact revenge by rolling right down the elm walk and crushing everything in their wake.'

There was an unpleasant pause and three children burst into tears.

'That's enough, Reg.' Amos cut his call and looked around for Diana. Realising that she was no longer with them, he raced away, punching out a number on his mobile to alert Pod.

If Diana's plans to slip away unnoticed had gone seriously awry when Ingmar, her mother and Nanny Crump had appeared, they suffered a

catastrophic blow when she found herself tailed by Amos on her bid to
revisit the Pleasure Garden.

She had made it as far as the edge of the pine woods when he caught
her up, eyes blazing.

'Where do you think you're going?'

'You can't stop me.'

'I bloody well can.' He grabbed her arm and hauled her towards him.

'Let me go!' she wailed.

'Willingly.' He shoved her to one side and drew back the bracken she
had been wading through.

'Jesus!' Diana stared at a great jagged-toothed metal shark jaw of a
trap rearing out of the leaf bed. 'Aren't those things illegal?'

'Probably. I don't get paid enough to find all the ones that are scattered around this bloody wood. Firebrand left hundreds.'

'But it's on a public footpath!'

'Actually, it's not.' He nodded towards a line of trees about twenty
yards to the left. 'That's the footpath. You strayed. Bad luck. Game over.'
Grabbing a piece of fallen branch, he sprung the trap with several hefty
stabs and curses. Looking at the effort he had to put in, Diana suspected
she could have danced on it and it wouldn't have snapped. Amos had
sprung her far more easily.

'I'll still follow the path.'

'And I'll follow you.'

'Why?

'Because you can't get to the Pleasure Garden. The path runs short
of it. You'll be trespassing if you try to go in there.'

Diana sighed, looking up at him. 'Amos, I'm already trespassing,
look.' She jumped on the spot. 'I'm trespassing. Let me go to the garden.'

'Never.'

'Just once.'

'Never.'

Diana gazed at his face, so flooded with hatred that it threatened to
burst its high-cheeked banks. He couldn't look at her. He couldn't even
stand within two feet of her.

'I'm just trying to make sense of things.' She kicked the mulch on
which they were standing.

'Nothing you've ever done makes sense, Diana.'

She looked up at him, frowning. Age had worn a great groove between
his brows, she noticed. It had roughened his skin, thinned his hair and
broadened his jaw, but it had stolen none of his beauty and none of his
pig-headed fury.

The frown lifted from her face. She had never stopped loving that brow, that hair, that jaw, those amazing eyes. She had never stopped loving that anger. He had loved her with all that anger once, too. Now he hated her with it.

'Well, maybe,' she said carefully, 'it's time to start making sense of things?'

'Not if it means trampling around in my life again.'

'It's my life, too.'

'No, Diana.' He leaned against a tree, pulling two low branches across his shoulders like a cape. 'This place is *my* life. It always has been. You went away. You left it to me. You have no right to claim it back, or to visit, or to remember. My memories live here and they don't want disturbing. You're trespassing in *my* life now and I don't want you here.' He ducked his head, unaccustomed to saying so much, and furious with himself for admitting to anything.

Diana watched the red oak leaves clothing his face, dropping from the branches that surrounded him like feathers from a great eagle's wings. His voice was an old song in her head – the soft burr that haunted her dreams, telling her he loved her, telling her he hated her, telling her to come back, telling her to stay away. Telling her he could make life happy again, even though she had made it her own personal hell. She knew it was as hollow a chant as mermaids singing from rocks to lure sailors to their deaths. It was her own head telling her what she wanted to hear, but she still needed it – just as he needed his woods. Now that it was playing live after weeks, months, years of hearing a distorted recording, she couldn't bear the clarity.

She had no right to see the Pleasure Garden. She had no right to see him. It was making her wretched.

To Amos's surprise, she walked away – not towards the garden but towards the children. She ran, stumbled, sobbed, scrabbled and fled towards safety.

Amos let the branches spring from his grip, weeping their leaves around him.

He had kept the garden for her. Now that she was here, he wanted to wreck it.

She had almost rejoined the group by the time he caught her up and ruined her noble moment.

Cutting her off at a narrow gap between a holly tree and an oak trunk, he breeched the gap with his shoulders and glared down at her.

'Stop troublemaking, Diana. I know you're behind those fires.'

'You *what*?'

'You come back and they start. What am I supposed to think? We both know what happened here.'

'Don't you *dare* accuse me of that, Amos Gates!'

His eyes had never looked so cold or so convinced. 'You're an arsonist.'

'And you're an arsehole. A twisted, sad, disillusioned arsehole.'

They both almost jumped out of their skins as one tall figure and three small ones appeared out of the bracken beside them.

'And this is a fungus known as a Greasy Tough Shank or a Butter Cap,' Pam told her charges as she towed them past Amos and Diana, shooting them a warning look. Waggling a mushroom, she marched her three back to the main group.

Diana flounced after her, sticking a finger up at Amos over her shoulder. It was childish, but it felt good.

Amos chewed his lips and followed, casting a look over his shoulder, grateful that his secret was safe for now.

Another trespasser was far closer to Amos's secret memorial.

In search of her missing dogs, Anke had stumbled across an isolated, high-hedged paddock contained within the heart of the old forest. Grazing in it were two beautiful horses. Anke couldn't mistake the broad forehead, the thick flying buttress neck, the short-coupled perfection and black-dappled quarters of Baron Areion, as he patrolled his terri-tory in that dancing, million-dollar trot – eyes and ears flicking like radars. He was running with a black mare who watched him admiringly from a patch of emerald grazing, her eyes soft, big, black pearls set in a wise, aristocratic face. She was well past her prime, but Anke could tell she was something very special indeed.

An old woman was standing just inside the gate, her back to Anke. She held up a hand of greeting but didn't look round.

'Bred to win the Gold Cup, that mare,' she said with a rueful laugh. 'Never left her field. Always thought it was a damned waste until now.'

'She's very beautiful. They both are.'

'That's what I thought. Make a damned fine couple. More than can be said for most of the buggers around here – equine and human.' She turned around and thrust out a hand from beneath a trug weighed down with sloes and hazelnuts. 'Til Constantine. No need to introduce your-self, you're Anke Panky. Came to your party, but you turned the lights out before I could say hello. Rather impressive tactic that – must remember it when Truffle next pays a visit.'

She wasn't as old as Anke had first assumed. Bent-backed and broad-beamed like a comfortable Windsor chair, Til was easily as handsome and age-defying as her sisters, but whereas they were cultivated flowers – Truffle a rare hothouse orchid and Isabel a hardy annual – Til was a wild, rambling rose. Anke had seen her before, she was certain, but they had never met.

'I haven't been called Anke Panky in years.'

'My nephew was so in love with you when you were, I never heard the end of it. He has rather a splendid eye for fillies of both my favourite species. He's also been in love with Dolly here for both decades of her life.'

'She's twenty?' Anke admired her again.

'Not sure she'll conceive at that age.' Til closed one eye worriedly as she looked at the old mare again. 'But worth a go. She's the last of my line. She might as well go out with a bang.' She let herself out of the gate. 'I bred the stallion, too – on behalf of a very close friend of mine – and he is the last of his line, too. Something of a star-crossed pairing, and his sire liked old birds, so one never knows. Far too late in the year for much hope of a covering, of course.' She slammed the gate shut and pursed her lips, face creased in thought. 'But never too late for a cover-up. Are you lost, by the way?'

Anke heard barking and snapped back to her immediate problem. 'I'm looking for two errant dogs.'

'Bull terrier and a big beast that looks like a husky on steroids? My terrier Ratbag took them off to show them his favourite haunt. Follow me.'

'Haunt being the operative word around here, I gather.' Anke laughed nervously as she hopped after her.

'Oh, there are no ghosts. Stuff and nonsense.' Til marched through the brambles. 'Used to be a good way of keeping trespassers away, but then lots of weirdos started turning up with ghost-recording devices. And of course drunken women on a dare.' She gave a wise look as she led the way to a high hedge.

Anke was ducking her head in a gesture of embarrassment so didn't see how Til Constantine opened the secret gate. She didn't even see the secret gate. All she saw was a gap in the hedge, a steep flight of steps opening up below her and, in front of her, a huge, secret, sunken garden, filled with strange ruined follies, walkways, grottos and streams.

'You haven't seen this,' Til said, putting her little fingers in her mouth and letting out a great wolf shriek that propelled Anke on to the steps.

As the dogs came thundering towards them through the garden, Til beckoned Anke back towards her. 'Take another step and you'll wish you hadn't.'

But Anke had no choice as Evig thundered up to her, his pale eyes gleaming with excitement. Weighing as much as a man, Evig sat lovingly at Anke's feet, straight on top of the pressure pad stone that triggered one of the garden's many tricks.

On cue, a marble cupid, almost hidden in the overgrown hedge, squirted them both with water.

Anke shrieked with laughter as Evig backed away, barking indignantly.

'Ha!' Til couldn't resist a chuckle. 'Young Firebrand used to love that. Quite his favourite, as I recall.'

Anke stepped on the stone and the cupid squirted her again. She found the laughter bubbling from her throat. It was like a drug.

Til looked on in alarm, realising that she had already revealed far too much.

'Now I must insist you come out of here,' she blustered, holding Ratbag and Bomber by their collars. 'There's another pressure pad close to your feet which is far more dang – oh, dear.'

Evig had backed right on to the second pressure stone. As he did so, half the stone steps slammed down into a recess in the ground, leaving Anke and her huge dog teetering on a precipice, unable to access the garden without a suicidal leap. Both yelped and rushed so hurriedly towards safety that they got stuck side by side in the tiny gateway and had to wriggle their way free.

'Most of the mechanics are broken now,' Til explained as she closed the gate on temptation. 'And I fear that the few which still work are the most dangerous. I daren't go in there. Never do,' she lied.

Anke stared wide-eyed at the tall beech hedge concealing such an amazing secret. Looking at it, you would never know the garden was behind it.

'This was Firebrand's, you say?'

'It was in his care when I first saw it, and he certainly added his own unique touch, but he didn't build it. It was already falling apart by then. But my late aunt attended parties here in the thirties – she was rather racy, like Truffle – and the garden was in its heyday. Nanny Crump says they got up to the most nefarious antics behind these beech hedges. She was in service at the Hall at the time with old Rose Simmons. You should hear them talking when they get together for a sherry.'

Til explained that the Pleasure Garden was started in the late nineteenth century by one of the Sarsdens as a gift for his wife. Successive generations took it over and added to the three acres of trickery and riddles.

'There is a huge series of chambers underneath our feet, full of mirrors and revolving doors to baffle the mind – I was trapped in there for a whole day as a child. Frightened me witless. Some had been converted to bunkers before the war, piled high with tins of soup and the best claret. Probably still are. They're all far too dangerous to explore now, no doubt. The poor old place is almost derelict.' She turned to walk away.

'Why does no one preserve it? It's magical.' Anke lingered, wishing she could open the gate again.

Til didn't answer, reaching down to gather up her trug.

'It's kind of sexy.' Anke stood on tiptoes to try to take another look.

'So a lot of people seem to think,' Til tutted, marching off and calling over her shoulder. 'Don't forget, you haven't seen it! Mention it to anyone and I may be forced to kill you.'

Following her, smiling, Anke wondered why she had been shown and told so much if it was supposed to be a secret. She didn't care. She felt amazing.

Mo was trying to explain the purpose of the icehouse that she and the children had found, shouting to be heard over the squawks of Diana arguing with Amos.

'It is a big, cool cave where the inhabitants of Foxrush Hall would have stored ice in olden times, before they had freezers.'

'Will you stop shadowing me? Get back in that big Land Rover of yours and drive around your precious woods feeling important.'

'I don't trust you, Diana.'

'I'm not going to set light to anything. I don't even smoke any more.'

'The ice was collected from the lake when it froze over in winter and then brought here, where it would stay cold underground to be used through summer.'

'You burnt yourself out years ago.'

'Yeah, and you're such a bloody success story.'

'I have two fantastic children.'

'So do I!'

'I think the ice might melt if it were stored here now,' murmured Truffle as she looked on, thoroughly enjoying the show. She knew she was right to persuade Ingmar to bring Nanny on a day out. This was better than any of those reality television spectaculars the old dear loved.

Having parked the Moke at the junction between footpath and old by-way, she, Nanny and Ingmar were watching Amos and Diana in fascination whilst enjoying a thermos flask of coffee and a hip-flask of cherry brandy.

'Do you remember Diana's eighteenth?' Nanny asked Truffle and then shook her head. 'Of course, you weren't there. Dreadful night.'

'I remember it.' Ingmar nodded. 'Terrible.'

'You lived in Denmark then, darling,' Truffle reminded him gently, turning to Nanny. 'I know Diana ran away – much as she did every teenage birthday.'

'It was the night they say Granville Gates went mad,' Nanny reminded her darkly.

'So it was. Quite mad, bless him. Shame he never recovered.'

'Your sister Isabel was furious. He was the best gardener she ever had. Couldn't so much as dig up a turnip afterwards.' Nanny re-knotted her headscarf. 'Although the truth is he didn't go mad that night at all.'

'He didn't?' Truffle was only half-interested.

'But he *is* mad, yes?' Ingmar checked.

'Oh, yes.' Nanny nodded. 'But the night of Diana's eighteenth, when she ran away, Granville passed out in the potting shed at the Manor after too much sloe gin. I know. I found him and gave him a ticking off. Always was a cowardly man, hiding behind his wife's apron-strings.'

'*She* drove him mad then, eh?' Ingmar laughed uproariously as he took a toot of cherry brandy.

'No. He went mad the day Diana came home again.'

'But she was missing for weeks that time, wasn't she?' Truffle recollected vaguely. 'Turned out she'd been holed up with Belvoir in London. Some silly notion about going to Argentina to live with her father and raise polo ponies, silly girl. She was never a good enough rider to impress the Wop.'

'These two were going to run away to Scotland and marry.' Nanny nodded at Amos and Diana.

'Don't be ridiculous,' Truffle scoffed.

'They were lovers.'

'Good grief, Nanny, you do get some fanciful notions sometimes.' Truffle grabbed the hip-flask from Ingmar and took a long draught. 'I recall him sniffing around her a lot – God knows they all did then. She was almost as pretty as I was as a young girl – and she was rather fond of rough types, so perhaps they had a little dalliance. But I don't think for a moment she intended to *marry* him. It was just a teenage pash. She was always such a hothead.'

'They were lovers.' Nanny gritted her teeth.

'Oh, dear children.' Ingmar watched them. 'Such sweet notions. Do we know what stopped them?'

Nanny's rheumy eyes studied Diana and Amos, remembering them as children with their beauty and their love. They should never have been stopped loving one another.

'Diana came to her senses, of course.' She straightened the blanket over her knees, content that Truffle didn't know a thing. Til had clearly kept her lips buttoned. At least she could rely on one Constantine sister to be discreet.

Truffle was watching her daughter, her own lips pursed thoughtfully. What an ill-fated match. She'd always believed the Amos affair – which had been blown out of all proportion in the village, as so much was – to be no more than a silly phase Diana went through. And, as Nanny said, Diana had come to her senses and ended it. But now, looking at her daughter's passionate, angry face, she had a nasty feeling that was the only thing Nanny *hadn't* just told the truth about. Diana and sense were strangers. Everyone knew that.

'You always were the most pig-headed idiot!'

'And you were always a selfish bitch!'

'They are very much in love.' Ingmar pulled his pipe from his pocket and started going through the ritual of clearing it, even though Anke had been confiscating his tobacco and matches for weeks as a result of all the scorch marks in his flat.

'You mean they *were* very much in love?' Truffle corrected.

'Oh, no. They *are* in love.' He searched his pockets for his tobacco and then, giving up, sucked his empty pipe. 'They are very much in love.'

'How many times do I have to say it? Get the hell *out of my life.'*

'Willingly. You get out of mine.'

'You first.'

'I'm not going anywhere.'

'Me neither.'

Still reeling from the discovery of the Pleasure Garden, Anke and her dogs were walking with Til and Ratbag back in the direction of the school outing.

'That stallion is one of the best horses I have ever sat upon,' she told Til.

'Oh, you were the one who rode him? That makes sense. Rory said that when he was between the best legs, he lit up like a bonfire. The horse, that is.'

'And you bought him?'

'I traded him.'

'Who's riding him now?'

Til looked askance. 'What makes you think anyone's riding him?'

'He's as fit as a racehorse. Is it Rory?'

'Lots of sex makes one fit, I hear.'

Anke gave a sideways glance in return and Til chuckled. 'All right. I admit it. He's in training.'

'For what?'

She prodded her walking staff into the roots of a tree and rolled her tongue around her mouth before clearly deciding not to answer. 'You want to buy him from me?'

'My daughter adores him.'

'Are we still talking about the stallion?' Til gave her a wise look and then chortled. 'He might be available once he earns his keep. But who knows how long that will take? The mare was always my favourite. Gunning horses have a reputation for foaling old, but I have my doubts about her.'

Anke suddenly found herself thinking about Lady in *A Horse for Emma*, bearing young Passion his foal. She shook the thought away with a smile at her silliness. 'Old brood mares can keep going into their twenties.'

'Oh, but she's like me, dear – an ageing spinster.'

'You've never had children?'

She tapped her nose. 'Love takes you in curious directions, don't you find?'

They could hear shouting as they waded deeper into the oak wood.

'Dear lord, I do hope Reg isn't rampaging.' Til quickened her pace. 'He only agreed to do this for my sake. Ah! No. Oh, dear. It's Diana and Amos. I knew no good would come of this. Only agreed to help today to try to stop it.'

'Were Diana and Amos lovers once?' Anke couldn't resist asking.

'Lovers?' Til's clever, creased face had suddenly lost its smile. 'My dear, Amos and Diana were love. Pure and simple. They *were* love. Bloody fools.'

Anke was on a curious high. Something about Til, about the garden she had just seen, about the day she was having, had lifted her sprits unimaginably. She was feeling as receptive and starry-eyed and tender-hearted as a practical Dane could be.

What she and Til witnessed as they rejoined the group looked nothing like love, either pure or simple. It was stagnant and corrupted and complicated. Yet Anke looked upon it with misty eyes, seeing love, passion and kindness locked in noble combat. Had she known it, she and her father were in total agreement. These were two people very much in love.

Amos and Diana were at each other's throats and no longer cared that they had an audience. They no longer cared that their own children were just a hundred yards away and barely out of earshot. They no longer cared that the garden was within their reach and could put everything right.

'*You bitch!*' he raged, stooping to pick up fallen branches and hurling them into the bracken. 'You deserved to marry that stuck-up bombastic twat. I'm glad he made you miserable.'

'And I wised up enough to leave him.'

'That making you happy, is it? Now you've lost your looks and have come home to Mummy to cry.' He threw a rotten oak bough at a trunk.

'I have my freedom back and my looks aren't far behind, which is more than can be said for your hair. That's gone for ever, along with your guts.'

'And what do you do with your "freedom", Diana? You make a beeline for someone else's lover and make his life hell.'

'Don't you dare bring him into this!'

Amos picked up a long shaft of dry timber and pointed it accusingly at her. 'Pod is no match for you. He's been climbing the walls since you got your claws into him.'

'He was a perfect match, I can assure you. My Swan Vesta lover, sparking a little pleasure that burned out very fast. It was just recreation. Now it's over.'

'I know how the poor bastard feels.' He split the stave in two on his knee, hurling one half towards the ground. 'No wonder he's in such a state.'

'That has nothing to do with me.'

'Do you leave us all for dead, Diana? All your lovers? Do you like to watch us suffer?'

She caught her breath, for a moment too stunned to fight. And then, looking away, she stopped screaming and told him in a hoarse whisper:

'Pod is in a state because he's just dumped his little teacher girlfriend and thinks he's in love with Daffodil Gently. They've been meeting in the Pleasure Garden.'

'*No!*' He was so incensed that he hurled the broken stave into orbit, not caring where it landed. It ricocheted around in the branches overhead, a hollow percussion that rattled like a death-knell. Then it crashed to earth at Diana's feet. She felt it scrape against her brow and bounce off her shoulder as it passed, but she was too angry to feel pain.

She ran her tongue over her teeth, glaring at Amos.

It was his turn to stall, staring back at her at her, watching the tiny beads of blood creeping from the cut in her brow and sliding towards her cheek

'Spare your sympathy for someone who really knows what love is.' She turned away.

He stood his ground. 'We both know what love is, Diana!'

She started walking deeper into the woods, muttering under her breath. 'And you certainly feel very sorry for yourself, don't you, Amos?'

He turned, as though intending to walk away from her. But then his green eyes darkened and he gave chase with a fresh war cry, their screaming voices soon moving deeper into the woods.

They might not have cared that they could be overheard, but very few ears had caught a word. The children had hastily been ushered away by Pam and the parents to look at a fox's den; Ingmar and Truffle were so squiffy on cherry brandy that they hadn't picked up enough to understand it; Nanny Crump had nodded off after what had already been her wildest day in weeks.

Only four people made sense of the screaming death match that was taking place in the haunted, cursed woods.

Anke stood in the shadows, unable to believe her ears. Beside her, leaning heavily on her walking staff, Til closed her eyes and shook her head.

Approaching the clearing in which the argument had just taken place, like two cold stray cats drawn to a fire from opposite directions, Mo and Pod stared at one another through the trees, the betrayal absolute.

Mo was the braver. She hugged her arms tightly around her tiny frame and walked up to him.

'You're in love with Dilly?'

He nodded. 'I think so.'

'That was why you wanted me to love *him* so much, wasn't it?'

He shrugged. 'I didn't want you to stop loving me.'

'You made me feel so bad, Pod.'

'You hurt me.'

'And all those times you slept around, you thought you weren't hurting me? Hundreds of times. I've been unfaithful *once* and you take your love away.'

'I never cared about them.'

'I don't care about him.'

'You do.'

'But I don't love him.'

He looked at his feet, narrowing his eyes. 'You sleep with your ghosts. You love your ghosts.'

She pressed her fingers to her mouth, saying nothing.

'You love them more than me.'

Tears slid from her eyes. He was trespassing in her heart one last time, and this was a rampage.

'You can never love me – yourself – anyone, until you stop sleeping with your ghosts, Mo,' he said hoarsely, angrily. 'I begged you to come here, to see real fucking ghosts, to face real fears, but you wouldn't. And she wanted to come here so much. She came here looking for love, not absolution. Now you're here too late. Too fucking late. I love her. I love you. I love her. I love you. Get the picture? I will never stop loving you, but you suffocate that love, burn the oxygen around it and I have to keep loving, keep breathing. It's what keeps me alive. Your love is entombed because you love your ghosts before anything.'

He glared at the leaves at his feet. 'All the time I've known you, I've had to compete with them. A fucking bitch of a mother who abandoned you and a dad you never even knew. I was always there for you, Mo. They weren't. I was always there to love you. They weren't. But still you always loved them more than me, didn't you?'

She couldn't answer, tears streaming down her face and over her fingers as she watched him turning away.

'All I wanted was to make you happy.' His voice cracked. 'A little house of our own with a big strong door to shut them out and big warm bed to share with you. I thought we had it here, you know? I really thought we had it.'

'Me too.'

'But it was too empty, wasn't it?'

She nodded, blind with tears.

Falling leaves spiralled in a tiny whirlwind in the centre of the clearing. For a moment it was as though an embrace hung in the air between them, inviting them in. Neither Mo nor Pod saw it, their arms too tightly wrapped around their hearts and their hands pressed over their eyes. The leaves had hidden themselves amongst the wide carpet that divided them long before either spoke.

'I'm sorry I hurt you,' he said in an undertone. 'It's just sometimes you are so damned weird.'

'*Touché*,' she sobbed, a sad laugh catching unexpectedly behind the tears.

Hearing it, he looked up at her. 'It worked for a long time, didn't it?'

She rubbed the streaming, salty mess away from her cheeks. 'All sorts of things work for ages even though they should have died or killed someone years before. Look at our washing machine.'

'Your car.'

'Your cooking.'

'We've had a ball, queen. At least admit that.'

She shook her head, looking up at the spider's web of branches overhead. 'You were what I wanted and needed. You were everything. You kept me sane.'

'Don't fall apart on me, Mo.'

'I'm not yours to hold together any more, remember?'

'I care about you. You're my special girl. You always will be.'

'But I'm not your queen any more, am I?'

He shook his head. 'I was never your king.'

That was when Mo heard it again. The song that had been playing through her head every night for weeks.

'Lavender's blue, dilly dilly, lavender's green . . . when you are king, dilly dilly, I shall be queen.'

Dilly. Her heart had told her head all along.

She turned and ran. Past Anke and Til, past the pensioners in the Moke, past the big holly bush shaped like a bell where the children were taking it in turns to go into its hollow belly. She would have run on, crossing the elm walk and racing through the beech wood to the ha-ha, the spinney, daylight and freedom. But a tiny hand reached out and grabbed hers with surprising force.

Tripping to a halt, Mo looked down into the sweet face of Mim Lampeter.

'Will you marry Rory now?'

Til Constantine sighed, glancing across at her dumbstruck companion. 'The old woods are certainly having their fun today. One would almost think Falstaff was out to play.'

Anke was watching Pod turning a very slow full circle in the clearing ahead of them, handsome face tipped towards the branches as though trying to spot what Mo had just seen there. He stopped spinning and cocked his head for a moment, glanced in the direction which Mo had run, his eyes full of tears. And then he started walking the opposite way.

He walked deep into the woods, into the darkest heart of Gunning, straight towards Diana and Amos. They were still shouting, their voices hollowed and muffled by the dense forestry around them. Pod didn't acknowledge them, and they didn't even see him as he passed. But as he did so, something curious happened.

'You have no right to interfere in my life!' Diana was screaming. 'I didn't come back here to have anything to do with you!'

'So why come here?'

'This isn't your bloody estate! You just work here. You're staff. I have every right to be here.'

'You have no right at all. You're not welcome.'

'I am totally with –'

'You're not –'

They both shut up at the same time – breathless, flame-cheeked and exhausted. They looked at each other for a moment, two red deer so well matched that the long fight had drawn blood, sweat and felt from antlers but no victor. And then both turned and walked away from one another without a backward glance.

Amos walked through the black heart of the forest to the high-banked track to take the wheel of the Land Rover, in which Pod was slumped in the passenger seat with his head in his arms. Diana walked to the wildlife group where jam jars were crammed with specimens and notepads filled with drawings. Mo was telling them that the oak was the king of trees, her eyes too full of tears to see that she was pointing at a birch.

Standing beside Anke, Til pulled in her chin and tutted in amusement. 'These godforsaken woods. They play such tricks – taking love from one to give to another. I could quite happily cut the entire ruddy forest down sometimes, couldn't you?'

Anke looked around the huge old trees, still on a curious high. She loved these woods. She wanted to bring Graham here. He would love them too.

Mo had no idea how she got through the rest of the day, seeing the children home and then finding her way back to the cottage, without hurling herself to the ground and disintegrating.

That evening, alone in the cottage, she rang Graham to tell him their affair must end. He was at Dulston's awaiting her arrival; so the fact that he answered her call with the announcement 'Daddy G has the mother of all hard-ons' didn't help.

Barely able to speak, Mo sobbed her decision in a staccato morse code. 'Y-ou were . . . r-r-right. I d-did . . . want to m-m-make P-p-p-pod . . . jealous all al-al-along. It d-d-didn't work. He's . . . g-g-g-gone.'

Graham only put up half a fight. He loved Anke, not Mo. It was too obvious to deny. And the fact that he became more fatherly than ever almost finished Mo off.

'You call me if you need anything, love, you understand?'

Mo hiccoughed her assent. She wanted him to argue, to fight, to tell her he couldn't live without her. Instead, he showed gracious, fatherly concern.

'You're such a special girl. My special girl. I want you to know I'll always look out for you.'

Two relationships ending in twenty-four hours, Mo tortured herself later as she curled up in bed with a pillow over her head and Bechers draped over her feet, purring unsympathetically. Both had told her she was special. She felt about as special as a wart.

'Roses are red, dilly dilly,' she sang tunelessly into the cotton and duck down. 'Lavender's blue. You're falling apart, Miss Mo Silly. And you have no glue.'

22

Heading into the village stores, Anke was sent spinning as fourteen stones of over-excited Phyllis Tyack raced past her, panting as she joined Gladys and Kath at the counter, her eyes gleaming. 'You'll never *guess* what I just heard?'

Glad Tidings had a victorious smile waiting on her lips. 'That handsome Pod has left the young teacher for Ophelia Gently's hippy daughter?'

'He's left *Helena Bonham-Carter*, you mean,' Kath whispered.

'Oh, you already know.' Phyllis sagged disappointedly by a display of Jiffy bags.

'I always said she was a bad lot.' Gladys sniffed.

'Takes after her mother,' Phyllis agreed breathlessly. 'Ophelia was never a normal child.'

'Not her, the teacher – Miss Sillytoes, the kiddies call her,' Gladys huffed. 'You should have heard some of the goings-on in that cottage. The arguments and hysteria! She was always throwing things. I'm surprised he lasted so long, to be honest with you.'

'I had no idea.' Phyllis tutted.

Kath tilted her head thoughtfully. 'Well, these theatrical types are very complica –'

'How many times, Kath, she is *not* Helena Bonham-Carter.'

'But you *said* she was Helena Bonham-Carter! It'll probably be all over the papers now, won't it? You wait. The village will be full of those tabloid people soon.'

Leafing through the paltry selection of greetings cards, Anke found herself unable to avoid listening as Glady's little army bickered amongst themselves.

'I've said to Rose Simmons that she doesn't want that young lady living in her cottage any longer,' Gladys was saying. 'Not with all this going on. The lights have stayed on every night this week and she's been acting ever so strange. I keep hearing noises.'

'What noises?'

'Sort of wailing and moaning. And singing.'

'Goodness!'

'I took her a cake yesterday, out of the kindness of my heart – one of my lemon sponges. Baked it specially.'

'Oh, they're so good, your sponges.' Kath sighed greedily.

'Exactly. Young Pod loves them, but she wouldn't even answer the door, just shouted at me to go away. So I left it outside thinking, poor little thing, she's probably too upset for company. Five minutes later, I'm in my garden and I sees her coming outside with it to feed to the birds. All over Rose's lobelia, it is.'

'How awful.'

'Yes, well, if that's all the thanks I get, it's her own fault if she finds herself out on her ear. I wanted to warn her, but she wouldn't let me.'

'How do you mean?'

'Like I say, I went to see Rose yesterday, tell her all about the Bellings' wedding preparations. She wasn't too impressed by what's been going on in her cottage. Says she thought they had sounded such a nice young couple. She's going to give Mo notice.'

Kath was shredding a Guide to Posting Overseas. 'Poor Helena.'

'But she's only just started teaching at the school!' Phyllis had her grandchildren to consider.

'Won't be there much longer if she carries on like this. Them poor little kids are already suffering on account of her daft antics. My Pam says it's been bedlam, especially with Diana Lampeter's horrible children causing a riot.'

Anke studied a 'Get Well Soon' card, listening closely.

'I heard she took them all up to the haunted woods last week.'

'Yes, those poor kiddies. Frightened witless, they were. And she even had Reg Wyck helping out.'

'Never!'

'Poor little mites. Fancy taking them to a place like that. Irresponsible, I call it. Like I say, I wouldn't be too hasty to blame young Pod for what's gone on between them. I know he's been a bit naughty with the Gently girl, but he *has* suffered.'

'He's a lovely lad,' Kath agreed. 'Such a charmer.'

'Very good looking. Daffodil probably threw herself at him. Just like her mother, that one.'

Anke bought the card and some flowers and crossed the green, stopping to sit on a bench to write a message. She chewed the top of her pen worriedly. Chad had told her that Miss Stillitoe was off sick, but Anke knew that poor Mo was really just heartbroken. What she wanted to write didn't exactly fit with a cheery little card decorated with teddy bears wearing stethoscopes. She doubted Mo would answer the door. She had already called on her several times that week and had no answer.

The Wycks' pick-up truck was parked beneath one of the horse chestnuts and Saul was unloading broken wooden pallets to add to the already teetering pile of timber that had been mounting up in the centre of the green all week.

'Afternoon, missus,' he nodded at Anke as he passed.

'What is that for?' she asked, still chewing the top of her pen.

'Bonfire night – the Oddlode fire is always the biggest in the valley.'

'But Guy Fawkes' Night is over a week away, isn't it?'

'You wait. It'll be three times this size by then. One year it got out of control, set light to the thatch on Horseshoe Cottages over there.' As he spoke, Anke looked across and spotted Mo coming out of her front garden and heading towards her car. Seizing the opportunity, she scrawled a quick 'you're in our thoughts' into the card and licked the gummed edge as she ran. 'Mo! Hello. How are you?'

Mo's heart sank. She had only sneaked out to raid her glove compartment for Rizlas because she had rolled her last cigarette over two hours ago and was starting to twitch.

'I heard you haven't been well?' Anke caught up with Mo as she dug a packet from the folds of the passenger's seat.

'I'm a bit under the weather.'

'I brought you these.' Anke thrust the flowers and card at her.

'Thanks. That's really kind.' Mo knew she looked terrible. She had hardly eaten in three days and hadn't slept for more than an hour at a time. The old T-shirt she was wearing was covered with tea stains and cat hair.

'Oh, you poor thing. Let me come in and fix you some soup or something.'

'I'm fine.'

'I insist.'

'No, really.' Mo could feel the tears welling up. 'I d-don't h-h-have any soup.'

'Come on.' Anke steered her back into the cottage and tried hard not to look shocked at the state it was in, although Mo guessed she was revolted.

'Sorry it's a bit of a mess. I'll make you a cup of tea if you don't mind having it black? There's no milk.'

In the little kitchen, flies buzzed around several open cans of cat food, mugs were piled up in the sink reeking of sour milk, and there were rotting apples on every surface.

'I pick up the windfalls when I can't sleep, but I can't think what to do with them so they've just been building up,' Mo explained. 'The maggots have got at most of them. They've all started to go mouldy. I keep them there to remind me of Pod.'

'Your rotten apple,' Anke acknowledged as she looked through the cupboards but, apart from cat food, rice and a can of kidney beans, there was no food in the house, although there were plentiful mouse droppings.

'Bechers is scared of mice,' Mo explained.

'You must come back and eat with us tonight.'

'No!' Mo yelped, backing away. She couldn't bear Anke's sympathy, knowing that she had betrayed her so totally.

'Then I shall bring you something later.'

Mo wrapped her arms around herself and stared at the kettle she had just switched on. 'I do appreciate this – honestly – but I really need to be alone right now.'

'Oh no you don't,' Anke told her brusquely. 'You have been alone for far too long already this week. You need someone to look after you.'

Mo watched the kettle divide into two, then four, then a teardrop kaleidoscope of kettles that danced around each other. 'Please don't feel you have to be kind to me. This is all my fault.'

'Right now it doesn't bother me whose fault it is, Mo.' Anke located a pair of rubber gloves and started washing mugs. 'It *does* bother me that someone so bright and kind and joyful can be so sad. You need someone on your side, even if she's a bossy Dane who will force-feed you soup.'

Mo snorted a tearful laugh.

'That's better. Now it's half-term next week, yes?'

She nodded.

'In that case, I think your cold should last until the end of this week, and you will get a good fortnight's rest. I will tell Mrs Chambers that you are really quite poorly and that I am looking after you. She believes everything I say. I am a very good liar.'

Impressed, Mo blinked at her tearfully.

'I work with Graham in the mornings and then I go to see my father, although he is seldom there. I shall call on you after that – say about one-thirty? We can get this house clean.'

'Not much point. They're throwing me out.'

'I heard something along those lines.'

'News does travel fast,' Mo whispered glumly. 'Rose Simmons' son only phoned an hour ago. They're selling the cottage. Something about paying for her residential care.'

'All the more reason to make the place presentable.'

'I don't want them to sell the cottage. I love this cottage. I haven't finished painting the walls. Pod was going to grow vegetables in the garden.' She started to cry. 'We bought grow bags and seeds, but he said it was too late to plant anything and the drought would kill them anyway. I think he already knew he was leaving me. I think he's wanted to leave me for years, but I was so clingy and I just held on to him, I just held on to him so tightly that he couldn't go . . . he couldn't go . . .' She was babbling now, tears coursing down her face, her nose running, her throat gulping. These were ugly, angry tears, the sort impossible to stop.

Anke was not overly fond of physical contact – even hugging her own children felt awkward at times – yet she instinctively put her arms around Mo and hugged her tight. 'Shhh, shhh, you poor lamb – goodness, you're thin.'

'Extra-fattening soup then,' Mo tried to joke, sobbing and laughing and pressing her cheek tightly to the smooth, cool cotton of Anke's shirt as she breathed in the reassuring smells of soap powder, deodorant and Chanel.

That night, Anke drove the king cab back into Oddlode after supper, bearing a huge Tuppaware container of pumpkin soup and a bag of French bread. The Brakespears had followed their soup with a lamb casserole swimming with dumplings (one of Graham's favourites) and then a vast trifle (another of Graham's favourites), the latter of which she had hoped would leave a portion for Mo, but Magnus and Graham had both had thirds and then Chad had scraped the bowl with his fingers. However, Mo's shrunken stomach was already overawed at the prospect of the soup and bread.

'Don't you dare feed it to the birds,' Anke instructed kind-heartedly.

Mo stared at the Tuppaware container after Anke left, wondering how very bad it made her to accept such kindness from a woman whose husband she had seduced. Very bad.

The soup was delicious. Mo slept for almost five hours afterwards – her longest stretch in weeks.

True to her word, Anke visited every afternoon that week and helped Mo reestablish a degree of normality. She insisted that they clean and tidy, listening to Radio Two which made Mo feel pensionable. Anke asked no questions about Pod, and kept the conversation light and practical – mostly talking about what they were doing and how best to go about it, or telling Mo about her family. Mo knew that this was her kind way of waiting for the floodgates to open, but hearing about Graham drove stakes of guilt into her heart and made her clam up.

'He's been very low this past week, and I really don't know why. I am trying so hard to cheer him up. His business is finally picking up in Springlode – he had two very big orders yesterday, and even Magnus is starting to take a real interest. Anything to avoid being sent back to university this year. His love-life here is far too active. But poor Graham still seems very glum. Perhaps it's a middle-aged crisis or whatever they call it? Men have those in their forties, I think.'

Mo listened to her chattering away, her curious Danish accent easy on the ear. It was almost as though Anke was talking to herself, and Mo sometimes wondered if she was paying these lunch-time visits to make up for the increased absence of her father – both in body and mind. Anke joked about Ingmar's relationship with Truffle, but she was obviously worried about him. 'We moved here to be close to him and it is as though he is hiding from me, the old fool. He needs looking after. Truffle is very entertaining but very irresponsible. We have an annexe at Wyck Farm all ready for him to move into, but he refuses to budge from his flat.'

She worried about all her family, fussily turning each of their lives over in her head as she talked – from Faith's crush on Rory – 'I think it might be getting a little obsessive' – to Chad's unruly school friends – 'You will keep an eye on him after half-term, won't you, Mo? I think he might be in with a bit of a bad lot. I had hoped this friendship with Mim might help, but if anything she encourages him to fight.'

As she listened, Mo felt like a part of the family – a part of the world that Anke fussed over. The feeling was as much painful as pleasurable. What she had longed for all her life was being offered to her and she couldn't take it. She had already taken one of her rotten windfalls and offered the wrong person a bite. All the time she had seen Graham as a father figure, Anke was waiting in the wings as a mother figure. Her guilt almost crucified her. She cried and Anke hugged her but, although Mo's floodgates leaked like mad, she refused to let them fly open. She couldn't risk talking about Pod and what had finally destroyed her life with the irresponsible control freak. It was too closely linked to Graham.

By the third day, with the house almost spotless and the fridge bursting with soup, Anke was desperate to make Mo talk, certain that it was what she needed. She couldn't keep bottling things up.

'I heard that the estate agents came here today?' she asked, having encountered the Post Office mafia moments earlier when buying milk.

'Somebody called Lloyd waved a laser room-measuring thing around and asked me on a date. Creep. He says weekenders will snap this place up in no time.'

'Have you sorted out anywhere else to live?'

Mo shrugged, looking out of the window. 'They've given me until the end of November, but it's obvious they want me out sharpish. I may assert squatters' rights.'

'Don't be silly. Why not come and stay in the annexe? At least for a little while. My father is showing no inclination to move in.'

'No!' Mo spilled tea on her lap. 'That's really kind, but no!'

'Oh dear,' Anke laughed. 'I must have put you off us with all my talk, I am sure. Really, Graham, is not that grumpy – he's very funny and very good at flirting to cheer people up. Faith would love having you around – she needs younger female company. The boys would hardly bother you – well, Magnus will probably chat you up like mad, but he's overstretched as it is. The annexe has its own front door and little garden. You can be quite independent.'

Oh, the temptation. It was Mo's dream. She would be so happy there, a little satellite to a big, happy, boisterous family. But she had ruined her chances of that.

'No! Thanks, but no. I'll find somewhere.'

'Where's Pod staying?'

'With Dilly, I guess.'

Anke shook her head. 'Not according to Pheely. Dilly's back in Durham and Pod is still working at Gunning. I see him on his motor-bike most days on the Springlode road.'

'How does he look?' Mo couldn't resist asking.

'Like he's wearing a motorcycle helmet.'

Mo hung her head and hid a smile, although the tears kept leaking out.

'It does get better,' Anke assured her. 'When my marriage with Kurt was over in all but name, I thought I'd never laugh again. Then I met Graham and I just couldn't stop laughing.'

Mistaking the silence that greeted this for anger, Anke added quickly, 'Of course I'm not saying you should rush out and try to meet anyone new yet – of course not. It will take time. My mother used to say that life is not one rich tapestry – it's a very complicated knitting pattern and, just as you think that you have worked it out, you drop some stitches and it all unravels. It takes a long time to knit a new bit and the wool never changes. When you finally reach old age you have a sweater that is made up of all sorts of funny squares and shapes that formed your life, with the same thread running throughout. You should wear it with pride and comfort.'

'I like that,' Mo sniffed. 'Although I'm so rubbish at knitting I might make mine a scarf.'

Anke patted her arm. 'You're young. You knit whatever shape you like.'

Mo picked at the hem of her jeans. 'You and Graham are so lucky to have found one another.' There! She'd said it. It was like plunging one of life's knitting needles into her side.

Anke sighed. 'Maybe. I'm not sure he'd agree. I haven't been a very good wife.'

'You're perfect!'

Anke looked at her sharply. 'What you see on the outside is rarely the truth.'

Mo thought about Pod and his charming, easygoing, heart-lifting manner that hid such a maelstrom of anger and passion and edginess. She had lived with that dichotomy for so many years she knew him like she knew herself. He knew her dark side, too. She'd always imagined they would share those secret sides for ever. At that moment, she didn't think it possible for one human being to miss another with such fierce, angry desperation.

'I've got to get out.' She stood up suddenly. 'I can't bear being cooped up any longer. What am I doing hiding in here? I have to find Pod.'

'You want him back, don't you?' Anke said eventually, her voice cracking with compassion.

Mo shook her head furiously, nodded furiously and then fell, sobbing onto the recently shampooed carpet. 'We are so different inside from out. Nobody knows us. But he's all *I* know.'

She sat up and turned to look at Anke, the kind, calm angel sitting on her sofa. Why did she have to be the one to tell?

For a moment, it didn't matter. She'd just slit her own truth vein. 'Where we've lived before – around racing people, always on the move, as isolated as we could be in little cottages and caravans – nobody much got to see our outside. Then we moved here and I think *everyone* saw the cracks except me.' She pressed her fingers to her wet eyes. 'I just thought relationships worked that way. I thought they all worked that way.'

'What way?'

The floodgates that had been splitting were now buttressed shut.

'Our way.' Mo blanked.

They watched one another warily, aware of the fragility of their bond.

Was it do-gooder and done-badder, therapist and patient, mother and child, wife and mistress, or friend and friend? Whatever the mix, there was a mutual dependence. The cocoon they had created in just a few hours over just a few days was intimate and addictive.

Anke made her way across to where Mo was kneeling and folded herself down beside her. 'Let me tell you something – and this is something that I have told very few people in my life and that you have to promise me you will keep a complete secret.'

'Sure.' Mo was grateful for the shift of direction.

'It's common knowledge that my first husband was gay. And whilst I didn't think that was "normal" as such, it became *my* normal and I ended up justifying it as better than normal, as ethereal. I thought of it as pure love even though he couldn't ever bring himself to sleep with me.'

Mo stared at her. 'Not ever?'

She shook her head. 'My children know this, so I am not betraying them by telling you, but you must keep our secret. Kurt is not their father. In nine years of marriage, he didn't touch me in that way, and I grew to think of that as a part of the perfect, pure love.' She took Mo's hands in hers and suddenly Mo saw tears behind those cool blue eyes – as unexpected as seeing a fire burning on an iceberg.

She remembered Faith telling her a different story on the day the teenager had tried to warn Mo off her stepfather. She had claimed Kurt and Anke had made love. But she had also claimed that Graham was impotent. Feeling guiltier than ever, Mo suddenly guessed what was coming.

Anke smiled sadly. 'What I am trying to tell you, Mo, is that I, too, believed relationships "worked that way". I saw no cracks – or refused to see them – right up until I met Graham. And even then . . . even now . . .' She looked away.

Mo felt the guilty mousetrap weld her tongue in a vice. She knew that Anke and Graham didn't make love. He had said as much. She'd thought it a recent thing or a temporary setback. Knowing how much Graham loved his wife, she'd assumed it to be to do with menopause or stress or something. The truth was far more terrifying.

Anke rolled her wedding ring around her long finger. 'I believe I didn't understand what loving a man was all about until very recently, and maybe that means I have left it too late. I love my parents, I love my children and I love my friends without barriers, you understand? It is only the men in my life that I have never been able to love without constructing rules. You must be stronger than I was, than I am, Mo. I think we are very similar, you and I – I thought that the moment I saw you.'

'You did?' Mo looked down, watching guilty tears land on her fingers, her heart hammering in her throat.

'We couldn't look more different, but we share so much.' Anke clasped her wet hands.

Mo's heart seemed to be pumping the tears that poured from her eyes, faster and faster. What had she done? She understood what Anke was trying to tell her. She knew that she was in danger of losing her faith in love. Loving Pod had taught her to think of infidelity as normal. She thought all men could sleep around and still stay faithful in their hearts.

'You want to know something funny?' Anke turned to her.

'Will it make me laugh?'

'Oh, I have been laughing a lot and I hope you share it.'

'Go on then.' Mo rubbed away the last of her tears and looked up.

'I fell in love with Graham this week. Head over heels in love with him again – and he wasn't even there. I fancy him rotten, as Faith would say.'

Mo blinked at her.

'There's a garden in the Gunning estate. A magical place. I only saw it for a moment and it was as though Graham was there – holding my hand, in my heart, in my head, in my body. It was as though we were making love. I had such a rush.' She sounded like a little girl who had just seen Disneyland for the first time.

'A garden?'

'I can't explain. It's exquisite.'

Mo remembered a conversation with Diana Lampeter, that Gunning held magical secrets. All she had found there was misery.

'Pod knew about that garden.' She realised in sudden horror. 'He wanted to take me there, but I refused, so he took her instead. Oh God. It didn't make me love him like he's always wanted me to. It made *him* fall in love with Dilly.'

Anke put an arm around her shoulders and tucked her in tightly beside her. 'I can't explain it. I just know that from the moment I stood there, I have only been able to think I love him, I love him, I love him!'

Mo felt the knitting needles stabbing from all directions. 'And what did he say when you told him?'

'I haven't yet.'

'Why not?'

'I think . . .' Anke screwed up her noble face and looked at the ceiling, tilting her head this way and that as she urged herself to say it. 'I think I may be too late. I think he's having an affair.'

Mo froze. 'What makes you say that?'

'He works later and later at Dulston's – hours after Magnus has left. Yet, when I call, the machine answers. He has become tetchy, picking faults, no longer telling me that he loves me all the time. He showers as soon as he comes home from work. He goes out at strange times. He is different. I have cuddled him every night and he would normally be all over me, but he just turns away. I know I'm right.'

Mo pressed one palm to her mouth and watched Anke over her forefinger, uncertain what to say or do. A moment ago she had been close to cartwheeling for joy. Now she was back on the rocks.

'I can only blame myself.' Anke pursed her mouth sadly. 'You starve a man of love for this long and he cannot cope. There are so many predatory women here.'

'Do you know who?' Another knitting needle punctured her side.

'I have suspicions.'

'Has anyone said anything?' Needle through chest.

Anke shook her head. 'Pheely and Pixie know I have worries, but it's all a big joke with them. Pixie is equally convinced that Sexton is sowing wild oats when he hardly has enough time to sow cauliflower.' She laughed sadly. 'I just have a gut feeling. No proof. No firm suspects.'

Relief flooded Mo's tense shoulders and she tried to peel her hand from her mouth and nose so that she could breathe again. But what Anke said next made her clamp it right back on her lips.

'I suppose I should ask Glad Tidings? She knows everything. Pheely tells me that her spies are everywhere. She knew all about Pod and Dilly.'

Mo squeaked, partly in pain and partly in fear. 'She hates me.'

Anke gave her a curious look. 'How can anyone hate you?'

'Pod hates me.'

'He just no longer loves you the same way he did. Believe me, that feels like hate.'

Mo let her shoulders slump, feeling the yearning again. If homesickness was a kick in the teeth, being lovesick was a slow, painful extraction without local anaesthetic. However bad things had become, however twisted they had always been, he was her morning, noon and night. He gave her life rhythm and meaning.

Anke was on a bolstering offensive once more, her own confessions tucked neatly away. 'Tomorrow, I want you to brave coming out of this place – just for a little while. Maybe I'll take you for a drive.'

'I can't! Everyone will be looking.'

'No they won't. The Belling son is getting married – Jasper, is it? The whole village is completely fixated with it. There is a huge party at Eastlode Park.'

Mo felt as though she had been in exile for months, not days.

'Aren't you invited?'

Anke chuckled. 'Much to Faith's disgust, no. She is so desperate to go.'

Mo watched Bechers pad across the carpet towards them. Normally he hid from strangers, but he head-butted Anke's ankles and flopped on his back to pummel her toes with his white back paws.

Something welled up inside Mo that was impossible to fathom – a great rushing explosion of gratitude.

'I love you.'

'Sorry?' Anke looked up curiously.

'I was talking to the cat.'

They both knew that she was lying, but it didn't matter.

'Before I go, I brought you something.' Anke reached for her bag and pulled out a foxed old hardback.

'*A Horse for Emma.*' Mo read the title warily.

'See what you think.'

Mo flipped a few pages, smelling the must of bygone fiction. 'Thanks.'

'I stayed up all night reading it!' Mo announced the next morning, ringing Anke on her mobile. 'It is so lovely. I am completely besotted with him. You are so clever.'

'I am?' Anke was surprised.

'Larch is the perfect rebound lover – honest, kind-hearted, noble and so sexy. He has cheered me up so much and the most perfect thing is that he's not even real!'

'Larch?'

'Yes! Isn't he lush?'

Anke smiled. She supposed this reaction was better than Faith's, who had finally deigned to flip through the book only to pronounce Passion the stallion the best thing in it while the rest of it was 'tripe'. At least it had brought Mo alive again.

'Did you say something about going out today? If you're not too busy?'

Anke could hear the eagerness in her voice and knew that she had put it there. She couldn't let her down.

She was feeling very glum having yet again cuddled up to Graham and received nothing but a hard rock-face of back all night. He had left for Dulston's before eight, plonking a cup of tea on her bedside table and dropping a kiss equally randomly on her head in what she hoped had been a conciliatory gesture.

'I'm working for a few hours.'

'But it's Saturday.'

'I have paperwork to catch up on.'

He had hardly looked her in the eye all week.

Anke sat down in the conservatory and looked out at a perfect, crisp autumn morning, the sun trying to box its way out of a mist above the shedding trees.

'Of course I'll take you out,' she told Mo. 'Magnus can mind Chad. Faith will no doubt want to play with the Overlodes horses all day. I'll pick you up in twenty minutes.'

She prodded Magnus awake to tell him his duties, which he accepted with surprising grace. 'The Disgraces are coming round. Their dad wants them to help with the pub building work, but they've gone on strike until he pays them. They love playing with Chad's X-Box. That's cool.'

Faith was less obliging, refusing a lift to Overlodes.

'I'm not riding today,' she announced when Anke finally tracked her down to the family bathroom, where she was plucking her eyebrows into an even narrower line, a white towel on her head with a few suspicious red streaks around its edges.

'Have you been dyeing your hair again?'

'Nope.'

'I don't think those hair extensions will take a tint like normal hair.'

'Whatever.'

'So what have you planned today if you're not riding?'

'Stuff.'

'Well, enjoy your stuff.'

'Whatever.'

Shaking her head, Anke gratefully headed downstairs and grabbed her car keys.

'Haven't you *gone* yet?' Magnus and Chad were sitting at the kitchen table in their dressing-gowns. Both groaned when she tried to kiss them goodbye.

Mo was far more excited to have her company.

'Can we go to the magic garden?' she asked as soon as she climbed in beside her.

Dressed in her heftiest combats, hoody and clumpy trainers, with a

Kangol hat pressed down over her head and huge Aviator shades covering most of her face, Mo looked like a badly disguised terrorist.

Anke felt a brief, excited compulsion to grant her wish and find the garden again, but not only did she doubt her ability to locate it in those dark woods, she also had a far more pressing urge.

'Maybe next time. I thought we could go to the Springlodes.'

'Why?'

'I want to see Graham and he's at work.'

'No!' Mo yelped, trying to unbuckle her seatbelt as they set off.

'Why ever not?'

'I . . . hate tractors. It's like a phobia.'

Anke's sweet gullibility made Mo feel even more rotten. 'You poor thing. How strange. Shall I drop you at Overlodes to see the horses and I can collect you there?'

'Sure. Thanks.'

Overlodes was eerily quiet for a Saturday. Rory normally taught all day, but the manège was deserted and most of the horses were turned out. Mo found Sharon sweeping out the exterior boxes, listening to Radio One.

'Hi. Is Rory around?'

'Getting ready for the wedding party.' Sharon glared at her wheelbarrow. 'He made me cut his hair with horse clippers earlier.'

'Oh, right. And Diana?' she checked nervously, not wanting an encounter.

'Gone already. Her brats are bridesmaid and pageboy. You want to ride something?' She looked at her watch wearily.

'No. Thanks. Not today.'

Sharon nodded and flicked a few more lumps of droppings into the barrow with a deft twitch of her shavings fork. 'Sorry your bloke pissed off with Dilly.'

'You heard?'

'Rory's pretty cut up about it.'

'Of course.' Mo sucked her lips. 'I guess everyone knows.'

'You know Diana was banging him too?'

It was by far the chattiest Sharon had ever been to Mo, but the subject matter was far from desirable.

'I had heard.'

'Just checking. Still, you have Anke Panky's husband to comfort you, eh?'

'I beg your pardon?'

'Nothing gets past me.' Sharon smiled nastily. 'See you around then.'

Realising she was being dismissed, Mo trailed away and nuzzled one of the few horses standing in a stable – old grey Worzel, who had given her one of her first lessons. She loved his smell – so sweet and warming. Clipped out for winter, he had one apple-sized patch of hair deliberately left long on his rump, shaped into a love heart. Looking along the line of Overlodes ponies, she realised that they were all sporting tufty hearts. The sight made her manage a wobbly smile. She bet the children loved them.

She went and stood wretchedly by the manège again, remembering how much she had enjoyed her hours there, and not just because they had become so linked with seeing Graham. It had marked her independence from Pod. She would take it up again, but not here, she decided. Here, Graham was too close at hand, and Rory was obviously taking far too much pleasure from talking about her. He was a hopeless gossip – even at his own expense. Mo was livid that Sharon knew.

She jumped as a warm little body brushed her leg and looked down to see Rory's terrier, Twitch, sitting lovingly by her foot, a ball in his mouth which he immediately threw at her feet and backed away from, inviting her to pick it up.

Mo threw it a few times, realising that his usual checked red neckerchief had been replaced by a smart spotted grey silk one. He was obviously going to the wedding.

'Twitch! Here! Where are you?'

In a matching neckerchief and full morning suit, Rory rounded the end of the path from the cottage and spotted what was distracting his dog.

'Mo! Hi! Wow! You okay?'

'Fine.'

'Sorry, did you want a lesson? We're closed today.'

'So I see.' She stooped to throw Twitch's ball.

'Family wedding.'

He was his usual mildly pissed, foppish self – except that he was dressed up like an Austen hero and had the worst buzzcut Mo had ever seen – Auschwitz meets So Solid Crew. He rubbed it self-consciously as he approached her. 'You really okay?'

'Yes, despite the fact that my lover has been shafting your sister *and* your girlfriend and you have been telling everyone, I am surprisingly well.'

'Woah.' He backed away. 'Great. I mean, sorry. I mean – Christ, are you really okay?'

She shrugged. 'Mildly suicidal. You?'

'Hell. Freefall, basically. Wondering how come I fucked my life up this much.'

'*Touché.*'

He creased his eyes, but the smile only twitched at his lips. 'I honestly haven't told anyone.'

'Sharon?'

'Ah.' He had the grace to blush. 'S doesn't count. I tell her everything. Dilly used to say I treated the poor old thing like a dog – letting her sleep on my bed and telling her all my secrets when I was down, then booting her out to her kennel when I had company.'

'Do you love her?' Mo asked.

'Sharon?' He laughed incredulously. 'God, no.'

'Dilly.'

He rubbed the awful hair again and squinted across the manège. 'Not sure. Never figured love out. It certainly hurts a lot right now.'

'Love's the one where you have no control.'

'I must love everything in life then.' He grinned shyly, groping in his pocket for a cigarette.

Mo laughed and leaned back against the railings, spotting Sharon watching them, her skunk-striped spiky hairdo poking out from above a stable door.

'How come you know about Graham?' she asked.

He flicked his lighter a few times before sparking up. 'Graham who?'

Mo checked his blank expression and then glanced across at Sharon again. 'Anke's husband.'

'Oh, him. What about him?'

Mo studied his face. Not a trace of recognition.

'Nothing. Do you want me to sort that hair out before you leave? You look like Forrest Gump. I used to cut Pod's. I'm quite good.'

'Oh, could you? I did think it looked a bit odd.'

As he turned to lead the way to the cottage, Mo squeaked in surprise.

'You okay?' He looked back at her.

'Fine – just stubbed my toe.'

'Amazed you can feel anything through those boots.' He set off again. Clipped out on the back of his head, an inch longer than the rest of his hair, was a perfectly shaped love heart.

Glancing towards the yard as she headed off in pursuit, Mo saw Sharon glaring at her, pitchfork in hand.

At Dulston's, Anke watched Graham while he schmoozed on the phone. Graham was a master of persuasive telephone calls. His deep, cheery, ripe Lancashire accent worked best when he perched the receiver on his shoulder as he was now, leaning across his desk to pluck a card from a rotofile. Anke knew how his voice changed once the receiver slipped to his throat, deepening and tightening. She shivered at the thought.

Unaware of the effect he was having on her, Graham slid this way and that on the casters of his chair, finalising a deal with a weekend hobby farmer who wanted an automated poop scooper for his llamas.

Business was picking up. He had hired a decent part-time engineer to ensure reliability, he had used all his powers of persuasion to secure discounts from suppliers and increase his margins, and his low prices were attracting local farmers and landowners. The books made much better reading this month.

Anke felt a rush of pride as she watched him, mingled with a rare buzz of lust. He was no longer one of her sulking children. He was the dynamic breadwinner. He was exhausted each night, stressed each day and yet brimming with vigour. She only wished he would share it with her.

She pulled her chair a little closer and stretched out a hand to rub his big shoulders, but he distractedly mistook the gesture and handed her a pen.

Anke tapped the Biro against her teeth, waiting for the call to finish.

'Checking up on me, love?' he asked afterwards, dropping a quick kiss on her forehead as he headed across the office to fetch another file.

'No – we were just passing on the way to the yard.'

'You brought Faith up, then?'

'Mo.'

'Mo Stillitoe?' he asked, carefully flipping through a filing drawer.

'Yes. She is looking in on the horses. I hope she will start riding again. It may cheer her up.'

'You've been spending a hell of a lot of time with her this week.' He slammed the drawer shut.

'She is very upset. It must be hard for her. I like her. I thought you did, too?'

'Mmm.' He distractedly read the file as he wandered back to his chair.

'Sorry – I know you are busy.' Anke reached for her bag. 'I just brought you some sandwiches and a thermos, *kaereste*.'

'I have a kettle and a fridge full of garage Ginsters, love.'

'I know. But this is fresh coffee and bacon I cooked this morning.'

'On white?'

'The fluffiest processed white bread I could find.'

He dropped his file and put his hands on her shoulders. 'You're too good to me, love.'

Anke tried to eke out the gesture, slipping her hands around him and pressing her lips clumsily to his neck, but he was already moving away and reaching for the phone. 'Just a few more calls to make and this guy from Tewkesbury to see and I'll be home.'

Anke nodded, trying not to notice the girly calendar on the wall – October's photograph consisting of a buxom redhead draped suggestively over a huge tractor wheel in a ploughed field. She hoped he didn't look at it too often.

Leaving him to his call, Anke trailed out into the yard and kicked a few of the quad bike wheels to make herself feel better. She knew that if she were really brave, she would go for broke – stripping to her undies and draping herself seductively over a tractor wheel. But Tony Sixsmith was clambering around on his scaffolding nearby and she didn't think he would be any more taken by the sight of a blue-veined Dane in sensible Sloggis straddling a filthy off-road tread than Graham would.

Evig was prowling around checking his territory and only gave her a cursory glance as he passed en route to the back of the biggest galvanised barn.

All the men in my life are ignoring me, she thought grumpily. Father, husband, sons and dog. Her friendship with Mo was the most exciting thing she had to look forward to, and she worried that she was taking that too far. Poor Mo was so fragile and Anke was bossing her around like a worthy and slightly unhinged hospital matron. She wished she hadn't confessed so much of her own unhappiness, and yet she felt there was a curious affinity between them. She longed for friendship. Even Graham – her greatest friend in the world – was too distracted to offer her more than a few moments of his time each day.

Hearing Evig bark from the far corner, she pocketed her car keys and went to check what he had found.

In the office, Graham pressed the receiver to his forehead, not hearing the officious recorded voice telling him to replace the handset and try again.

He was certain Anke knew. This sudden friendship with Mo, the way she was fussing around him and being overly loving. It was so unlike her that Graham felt constantly sick with fear. She was waiting patiently for a confession, just as she did with the children. It was a tactic that usually worked, although occasionally even patient Anke snapped and demanded the truth. He dreaded that happening.

At that moment, Anke stormed back into the office, realising his worst nightmares.

'Graham! I am so upset. Why didn't you tell me?'

'Tell you what?' He put up a half-hearted fight, although he couldn't look her in the face.

'I can't believe you would keep this from me. You've just let it happen. You should have stopped this weeks ago!'

Graham crumbled. 'I know. I know. But I was weak and –'

'It's disgusting – and it's probably illegal!'

'Eh?'

'We must call the police.'

Graham was too bewildered to speak.

'Oh for God's sake!' Anke was infuriated by his silence. 'At least let's stop them getting back in.' She turned and stomped outside.

Following her nervously, Graham found himself back at the little 'shrine' they had discovered on the day of the pub fire.

'Holy shit!' He feigned horror.

'I thought you had destroyed it?'

'I did – at least I threw out the tarp and took the chairs to the tip.'

The camp was back, this time on a grand, reinforced scale. Just inside the chain fencing, almost buried inside one of the holly trees, was a little house built out of railway sleepers, pallets and roofing felt. Inside, on a carefully laid groundsheet, was a mound of huge cushions surrounded by a ring of hurricane lamps. Instead of the pile of beer cans and cigarette butts, there were three empty champagne bottles and a stack of plastic cups.

'Don't touch it, there might be fingerprints!' Anke snapped as Graham stooped to pick up one of the bottles. 'We must call the police.'

'We can't.' Graham hurriedly replaced the bottle and rubbed his forehead.

'Why ever not? There's an arsonist out there. This has to be where he has been hiding.'

'We don't know that. It's probably just kids.'

'How can you say that? Kids don't drink Moet. This is someone seriously twisted.'

'I can't compromise my business, love. I'm on a knife-edge here. We're just pulling through. If I start kicking up a fuss I could risk everything.'

Anke felt her cheek muscles twitch as she glared at the little lair. 'You can't just let this happen.'

'I'll deal with it.'

'You said that last time.'

He raked his hair back anxiously with his fingers, hating the sight of the little love-nest he had built. He had to destroy it. 'I will deal with it, love. Please believe me. I love you. I would do anything for you.'

Anke closed her eyes as he said those familiar words – words she had heard throughout her marriage and taken for granted until this week – a week during which she had spent hours yearning to hear him say them again. Why did it have to be now?

'Please call the police. This man tried to burn down our own house. He burned down the pub and then our marquee and then the Manor. Who knows what he's going to try next? He's dangerous.'

'We don't know that, love. The fire officer said that the profiles didn't match between the pub fire and ours, remember? One was deliberate sabotage, the other mindless vandalism, he said. And the last I heard, the Manor fire was almost certainly sparked by faulty old wiring.'

Anke looked at the strange little nest and stifled a sob. 'What sort of maniac tries to light a fire with champagne?'

The one who tried to melt your heart with a blowtorch, Graham thought sadly.

'Believe me, I will sort this out,' he said.

Anke nodded, touching his arm, shot through with regret. She had wanted to make today's visit a seductive little punctuation in his busy morning. Instead she had sparked conflict. It was supposed to be such a romantic day.

'You don't think . . .' She gasped in sudden anguish. 'You don't think he might be planning to start another fire at the wedding, do you?'

Equipped with the kitchen scissors, Mo did the best she could as Rory chain-smoked and watched the Morning Line. For one so handsome, he was completely without vanity. Mo could have given him a mohican and he wouldn't have noticed, although he was absurdly grateful for what she did, levelling off the worst of the tufts and removing the love heart so that he had a neat, army-short cut which strangely suited him.

'Don't suppose you want to come as my guest?' he asked afterwards. 'You can borrow one of Di's frocks. Dilly's not very likely to turn up now.'

Mo ruffled his improved hair and shook her head. 'I'm only on short outings. I think I'll sit out this afternoon in front of the box.'

'You can watch the racing for me and text me the results,' he suggested hopefully.

Mo winced. 'I'm not really following this season.'

'Of course – sorry.'

To her surprise, Mo found that she could just about laugh as he stood up to gather his car keys and a huge gift-wrapped box.

'Forgotten.' He shrugged when she asked what it was.

'Tell me.' He rested his chin on the box. 'Why was Pod banned from racing?'

She stooped to pat farewell to Hally who was lying by the Rayburn. 'Is she expecting puppies?'

'Phantom pregnancy, Di says.'

'Another ghost.' Mo tickled her ears and looked up at him.

'You haven't answered my question.'

She sucked her teeth and let out a little kissing sound. 'Pod fixed races. Had done for years – all his career. Riding winners was easy. It was riding losers that took the skill.'

'Was that all? I thought there was more to it?'

'He was fucking most of the trainers' wives which didn't help.'

'They wouldn't remove his licence for that though, would they? He was set to be champion jockey when it happened.'

She felt a hard edge digging into her thigh and groped towards the big pocket in the leg of her combats. It was Anke's book, *A Horse for Emma*. She pulled it out and handed it to Rory.

'What's this?'

'Something to keep you entertained between speeches.' She turned to leave.

'Will it tell me why Pod was banned?'

At the door, Mo turned to look at him again. 'Pod didn't lose his licence. He junked it in.'

'A month away from making champion?'

'He said it was the only way he could feel anything any more.'

Rory started to laugh. 'Oh, Christ. No wonder Dilly loves him.'

Mo tried to hold her face together long enough to make a graceful exit, but it crumpled into an ugly, tearful grimace and she fled.

Dropping the wedding present with a worrying smash, Rory caught her up by the gates, grabbing her shoulders to stop her.

'I'm sorry, I'm sorry, I'm sorry!' he gasped, pulling her into a tight, stiff, morning-suit hug. 'I am a bitter bastard. I know you love him. You and he had way more going on than Dilly and I ever did. Way more.'

She shook her head fiercely. 'I was too devoted to him. I can see that now. I think Dilly might understand him. I never did.'

Rory kept a tight grip on her shoulder and drew her dark glasses from her face.

'Oh, Christ. You've been crying for days.'

'Just one night. I was reading that book.'

'I'll have to give it a go.' He stepped back and tapped his breast pocket with a clunk where the novel was stashed, his sleepy, indolent face softening into a kind smile.

Still holding her shoulder, he dropped a friendly kiss on her forehead and ruffled her hair before running his knuckles along her jaw and up to the nib of her nose to tweak it – a curious, child-like caress that made her laugh.

'Thank you.' His slanting grey eyes crinkled.

'For what?'

'For making sense of it.'

Mo nodded. 'I wish it worked both ways. Enjoy the wedding.'

She was secretly watching the racing that afternoon when Rory texted her.

'Got as far as Chap 8. Blinding. Can you txt back a Best Man's Speech? Am on in 10.'

Mo found herself grinning as she replied. *'Best man?!'*

'Trade descriptions wud have field day. Do I thnk bridesmaids?'

'With big kisses.'

'Ugh! Pheely & Mim.'

'Just say they look beautiful.'

'Can I giv kisses to U? U R much more beautiful.'

Mo felt the laugh fall from her face and she switched off her phone. Anke was right. It was way too soon.

'Such a funny speech, don't you think?' Truffle was winding up Diana in the sumptuous ladies' lavatories at Eastlode Park. 'Rory is so clever. Spurs looked terribly moved.'

'It was passable.' Diana sniffed. 'Although I thought it was bloody rude of him to have his nose in a book throughout the ceremony.'

'Rory always was a big reader.'

'Hmph.' Diana teased the curls that were already dropping out and then started to reapply her lipstick.

'I see Amos and his pretty wife are here.' Truffle continued stirring. 'Yes.'

'She is a lovely little thing.'

'Hmph.'

'Such pretty children too.'

Diana was saved from throttling her by the swing of the lavatory doors as a curvaceous figure in a honey-yellow dress with matching hat sashayed in.

'Jacqui dear!' Truffle greeted her cheerfully. 'We were just talking about you.'

Close up, Jacqui didn't look so great, her eyes pouched with bags and her neck stiff with tension. The dress was, as usual a size too small. She flicked a terse smile and made straight for a cubicle.

Mouthing a little 'o' at Diana in the mirror, Truffle tipped up her head to check the state of her chins and shimmied back out for the dancing.

Diana slipped into a cubicle, extracted the 35mm film pot from her bag and unpopped it to study its powdery contents. Six weeks with Pod had left her with a magnificent stash. It could help her through the rest of the day. Seeing Amos was hell. She was livid that he had been invited.

She tapped a finger against the pot and watched the crystals jump. She couldn't bring herself to take a toot. Her children were here. They were badly behaved enough without her risking her own reputation.

She pressed the lid back and listened as Jacqui came out of her cubicle – no flush, curious – and spent a long time at the mirrors with accompanying clicks, lip-sucks, mascara wand crunches and handbag emptying indicating a lengthy reapplication.

At last, Diana heard the door open and close and let herself out from the cubicle, studying her reflection and wondering what had possessed her to wear dark silver. She looked like a fat mackerel.

Something bleeped by the basins. Diana ignored it and craned around to try to assess the size of her bum.

Another bleep.

She saw a tiny mobile phone abandoned by some scrunched-up tissues. It was bound to be her mother's. Picking it up, she saw that the LED screen was flashing 'Text message – read?'

Retreating into a cubicle, Diana pressed OK.

'Ker-ist!' She gasped as she scrolled down. She checked the saved text messages.

'Ker-ist!' She sat on the loo seat.

She checked the sent messages.

'Ker-ist!' She almost dropped the phone.

She could hear a familiar old tune striking up on the dance floor in the distance. *I'm Not in Love* by 10cc. She and Amos had kissed their way through it a hundred times once.

The lavatory door's opening increased the volume for a moment as someone swept in. Diana heard her searching breathlessly and banging in and out of the cubicles to her right, cursing in a constant whisper. 'Shit, shit, shit!'

Diana's door rattled. There was a pause and an impatient huff, and then it rattled again.

'Excuse me?' the phone forager asked eventually. 'I haven't left a mobile phone in there, have I?'

'No chuck,' Diana threw out her best Corry accent.

'Okay. Thanks.' The doors swung open again as the inquisitor left, briefly increasing the volume from the dance floor and blasting in the 10cc line that it was 'just a silly phase' he was going through.

Diana held the phone to her chest and felt sick. She couldn't think straight. The cubicle was spinning around her like a vortex – any minute now she expected to be spat out into another time spectrum. She closed her eyes tight, willing herself back in time, twenty-two years ago. She could show him the mobile in their woodland hideaway and they would marvel at such a space-age thing with its little messages from lover to lover, telling him that one day he would be betrayed. Not by Diana. She would never betray him.

But when she opened her eyes again she was still in the cubicle, in the here and now, and the betrayal wasn't something she could warn him about. It had happened. He hated her now. Telling him would make him hate her all the more.

'He has to know,' she breathed. 'He deserves to know. There are too many secrets already.'

Now she did need some of her Pod stash, and she needed it fast.

She uncapped the film pot once more and dusted a little on to her compact mirror, seeing her dark-painted eyes looking down on it. Closing her eyes, Diana blew hard and listened to twenty pounds worth of Class A sprinkling on to the marble floor.

Like a child blowing out half-lit candles on a birthday cake because she doesn't want to grow any older, it cost Diana a further hundred pounds of scattered dust before she pulled out a credit card and started chopping. Starting to cry, she said silent apologies to her children, to her family and most of all to Spurs and Ellen, but she had to do this. She had to do this right now, for Amos and for justice. And the only way to get through it was to get high. A further eighty was blown angrily to the floor before she rolled up a twenty pound note and inhaled deeply.

Fired up with courage and conviction, she stood up on the dusty debris of indecision and carried the little phone on to the dance floor.

10cc had been replaced by Nickelback, to which Ellen's surfer friends were flailing around. Diana ducked between the whirling limbs and located Amos sitting at a table with Aunt Til and Nanny. The honey monster was searching for her mobile beneath a nearby table, she noted, spotting two little spiked gold heels poking out from underneath the damask. Good.

She slid into the empty chair beside him, moving Jacqui's sparkly handbag to one side.

'Your wife left this in the loo.'

'Thanks. She's been looking for that.' He made a grab for it.

Diana clung on. 'I think you should read this.'

'No thanks.'

'Read.'

'I said no.' His face was quilted with tension, the black eyes a riot of anger.

'*Read!*'

'Just give me the phone, Diana.'

'SHALL I READ FOR YOU?' She dragged her hand from beneath his and started scrolling the messages. This had all gone wrong. The drugs had made her louder, not braver. Her hands were shaking almost too much to be able to read from the screen.

'Message sent: *Can't wait to see you again, my sexy Sexton.* Message received: *Usual place tonight?* Message sent: '*Will drop kids at Mum's and be there at eight. Have told YNW I'm at yoga.* Message received: *I'll be the one bending you over backwards.*'

When Nickelback came to a close, the first slow, quiet bars of *Ride On* – played especially for Spurs and Ellen – were drowned out by Diana screaming out text messages. She couldn't look at Amos's frozen face or the other guests' astonished expression. She knew she was cutting her own throat, and yet she couldn't stop herself.

'Here's today's – Message sent: *Bloody posh wedding with YNW sucking up to nobs.* Message received: *Wish you would suck my knob.* Message sent: *Park round the back during the reception and you never know.* Message received: *I'll be there.*'

Underneath a nearby table, Jacqui Gates had slid off her honey-coloured hat and her honey-coloured shoes and now made a run for it, grabbing the first mobile phone she could.

'Oi!' Rory looked up from the book he was reading. 'Give that back!' But he was too engrossed to give chase.

On the dance floor, Ellen and Jasper Belling didn't even glance up as they circled in one another's arms, the growing baby that they had created enfolded in white silk and grey morning suit.

*　*　*

Faith had decided to gatecrash the Belling wedding reception party to get closer to Rory. It was just two fields from Wyck Farm to Eastlode Park – crossing the railway line and Hillcote Brook being the biggest hindrances. The Lower Oddford road was too exposed and meant walking along the long drive to the hotel, through open parkland. She had to slip into the grounds unnoticed. She had already walked the route, and knew that an old farm bridge would keep her feet dry.

Crossing the railway track was more of a dare. Dressed in a flimsy yellow dress that clashed with her newly-dyed titian hair, carrying her party shoes in her hands and wearing hiking boots on her feet, Faith bounded the single track like a steeplechaser over an open water, whooping as she made it safely to the far cutting.

She danced through the park, dreaming of the moment Rory set eyes on her.

Forget Mo, forget Dilly – Faith had created a fusion of the two. Modilly, Dillymo – whatever, it was going to be Rory's Alamo. She knew she had never looked this good. It was now or never.

She skirted the boundaries of Eastlode land, finding her perfect entry point. There! Shrouded by the weeping willows until she reached the path around the lake. Then it was a quick skip across the rear driveway and she was in through the fire escape.

But as she sat at the lake's edge pulling her hiking boots from her feet and slipping on a pair of her mother's high heels, she heard a furious revving from one of the old farm tracks. Then, just as she was tiptoeing across the rear drive, she was almost mown down by an Oddlode Organics van driving at breakneck speed from the back of the hotel. The driver didn't even seem to see her, although his blonde passenger screamed. If it hadn't been for a strong hand grabbing her arm and hoicking her back into the reeds, Faith would have gone under the wheels.

A mobile phone flew out of the passenger window as the van raced past, landing neatly between the peaked points of Faith's padded bra.

It was her turn to scream as she looked up into two mad eyes the colour of a toad's back, buried in an old leather face as weatherbeaten as a wrangler's saddle.

He dangled her hiking boots in her face.

'Go home, pretty girl. It ain't safe here. The ghosts are out.'

Faith grabbed her boots, scrabbled for the stray phone, screamed again and ran like smoke.

The racing had been followed by *Breakfast at Tiffany*'s. Cried hollow, Mo hugged a reluctant Bechers to her chest and kissed his ginger head as the titles rolled. When he finally clawed his way to freedom and shot behind the sofa to hide, she switched on her phone again and to cheer herself up, re-read Rory's last text message telling her she was beautiful.

She replied. '*How did Best Man's speech go?*'

When he didn't respond in five minutes, she sent another message, realising that he would be very drunk. '*Is the Best Man capable of speech?*'

No reply.

She went to make a cup of tea. As she squeezed out the bag, her phone bleeped.

Telling herself off for being so cheered up, she dashed through to read it.

'*Get lost.*'

Mo creased her brows. Oh dear. He was obviously drunker than she'd thought.

Another message followed it with the speed of lightning from practised fingers. '*I never want 2 c u again. Pod had a lucky escape.*'

Mo yelped in alarm and threw down the phone.

Beep!

She picked it up with shaking hands. '*Where do u get ur strappy dresses from?*'

'Eh?'

She hastily switched off the phone and pulled a big cushion across her belly, chewing at her lips. Christ, she missed Pod.

The following afternoon, Pheely couldn't wait to drop in on Anke with the splendid news of the wedding party antics. Dragged up the drive by Great Dane Hamlet, she let him loose with Evig and Bomber and cornered the other Great Dane in her conservatory with a coffee.

'Poor Pixie has gone to stay with her parents after Sexton ran away with Jacqui Gates in the middle of the bride and groom's big dance – can you imagine? The market garden is being run by the Wycks of all people. Pixie must be mad.'

'I beg your pardon?' Anke yawned tiredly after a night of sleeplessly trying to entice her husband towards lovemaking. He had yet again hunched his back to her until dawn, and then headed for Springlode by eight – unheard of on a Sunday. Now he wasn't answering office or mobile lines and she was getting jumpier by the minute.

'I know!' Pheely didn't notice her distraction. 'The Wycks running the market garden? Isn't it a hoot!'

'Sorry, not that bit – Pixie's husband has run away with somebody called Jenny Fence, you say?'

'*Jacqui* GATES – Amos's wife.'

'Amos?'

'The one Diana Lampeter eloped with in the eighties only to dump him before they reached the village green let alone Gretna Green. Do keep up, Anke.'

Anke yawned again and smiled apologetically. 'It sounds very dramatic.'

'Well, I thought you might appreciate it a bit more than this. Hamlet and I walked all the way from Oddlode to tell you.'

'Sorry. What happened?'

'Diana blew the lid off the affair in the middle of the wedding reception – no doubt hoping that she would win Amos back, but he went into the blackest of all rages and damned her to hell for it. It was all wonderfully public.'

'And Jacqui was there too?'

'Not for long. Sexton had the getaway car practically parked outside. Apparently they've been planning to go public for quite some time, although one would assume that they had planned something a little more discreet – an ad in the parish rag or a postcard in the village stores, maybe? Poor Pixie is so devastated. It's been going on for years, according to Glad Tidings.'

'So lots of people knew about it?'

'Darling, you can't fart in this village without everyone knowing. Copulation is practically a spectator sport – especially when it came to Sexton and Jacqui. They were known as the easy lay-bys because they used to meet in their cars at picnic spots and car parks all over the Cotswolds. Hard to be discreet in an Oddlode Organics van, shuddering on its axles in a discreet passing place.' She giggled. 'I gather Bill Hudson the farmer has had to pull them out of the odd wet field gate when their cars have got stuck. Talk about verging on the ridiculous and being ridiculous on a verge.'

Anke didn't laugh.

'No wonder Diana lapped it up. You should have seen her face. She looked quite insane waving that telephone around. Spectacular. She and Amos were so busy hurling abuse and hired crockery at one another that Jacqui probably had time to powder her nose before she and Sexton legged it.

'To cap it all, mad Granville Gates turned up uninvited and accused Diana of unearthing the Oddlode demons. He really is quite barmy.'

'What about the couple who were getting married? Were they upset?'

'Ellen and Spurs? I think the distraction rather suited them. The wedding was very much a Hell's Bells spectacular. They're surfing in Spain now, bless them. Ellen had a wet suit made especially to cover her bump. Brave girl.' She patted her own burgeoning belly. 'I just surf the Internet these days. I'm going to start a web page of village gossip. This year has really been a vintage one. You turned up at just the right time.'

'Is everyone in Oddlode unfaithful?' Anke asked bitterly.

'Most are. Making merry beats making jam. Although I'm livid with Dilly for adding to the scandal quota. Rory is such a nice chap and this new one of hers is terribly gangland.'

'Do you dislike Pod so much, then?' Anke asked curiously.

Pheely wrinkled her nose. 'He is splendidly beautiful and certainly has the patter, but I do think he's a bit uncouth and untamed. I would probably have been madly in love with him at Dilly's age, so I can hardly blame her. They are utterly besotted with one another, which is sweet. I suppose he's quite lovable for an oik.'

'Mo seemed to love him.'

'Oh, your new best friend.' Pheely raised her eyebrows jealously. 'How is the poor mite bearing up?'

'She's devastated.' Anke muttered, not liking Pheely's tone.

'Don't be so sure. I've heard tell that she's not entirely untarnished by the brushes of our village foxes.'

'Who?' Anke gasped.

Pheely shrugged. 'One of the fathers from the school, I gather.'

On cue, Graham arrived home, looking grey and troubled.

Accustomed to him flirting with her, Pheely cocked her head enquiringly. 'Don't tell me someone's slashed your tractor tyres?'

'In a manner of speaking.' He slumped at the table and reached for the coffee pot with a shaking hand. 'I've been with the police all morning. Someone deliberately started a fire at Dulston's last night.'

'Oh God, no.' Anke leaped up to hug him, but he shrugged her off.

'Malicious damage, they reckon.' He found a bottle of Scotch in the larder and poured himself a glass with shaking hands.

'Has much been lost?' she asked, sitting down and feeling useless.

'All the paperwork. Half the stock. Rest is blistered and smoked. It's a write-off, but the bloody insurance will never pay up.'

'Why ever not?' Pheely asked, incredulously.

'Because it was so bloody expensive, I refused to pay the last instalment.'

'We weren't insured?' Anke gasped.

'You should know, sweetheart. You filed the letter telling me they were withdrawing cover.'

Anke flinched. There was no missing the accusatory tone in his voice. 'I didn't start the fire.'

Graham closed his eyes. 'Sorry, love. After coming out of Market Addington cop shop I'm ready to believe everyone is a suspect. They haven't a fucking clue.'

'Did you tell them about the shrine?' asked Anke.

'What shrine?' Pheely asked eagerly, practically taking notes.

Graham rubbed his pleated brows. 'I told them everything.'

'Do they have anyone in the frame?' Pheely's eyes gleamed at the prospect of local sedition.

'Not even a fucking ghost.'

23

Ingmar's driving was becoming legend, but Truffle still believed he was far safer than she was behind the wheel. She was probably right. With her favourite Hermès headscarf protecting her hair and a pair of fabulously dark tortoiseshell-rimmed glasses protecting her eyes, she loved to turn up her collar and whoop as Ingmar swerved caddishly around corners and took on hills like a Gumball pro hitting the Alps. He made her feel young again.

She wouldn't let him drive the Bentley, but considered him perfectly capable of ferrying her on local trips in the Moke, particularly as they could take so many short-cuts across farm tracks which avoided the tiresome business of meeting oncoming traffic – with which Ingmar was not entirely safe.

Today's jaunt took them to Upper Springlode via the Oddlode bridleway, which was a treat. Truffle hadn't seen the old path since her riding days, perhaps twenty years earlier. She had forgotten the way it sliced a laughter line up the rugged cheek of the valley, climbing on to the hazy mist of the ridge.

Ingmar seemed to know this route well enough, in contrast to his recent attempts to navigate his way to the Market Addington branch of Tesco when they had ended up somewhere near Cheltenham.

Truffle had decided it was time to pay a visit to the stables to see her children. Being with Ingmar – whose daughter doted on him – had reminded her that children could be an asset. Anke was always dropping off little parcels of food at his home. No longer able to afford a housekeeper, Truffle missed home cooking – and dining out was playing havoc with her waistline. She rather relished the idea of Diana popping by each day with a foil-wrapped tray of goodies – as long as she didn't stay too long, and left her children at home. Having one's laundry done would also be a pleasant reprieve, and there was a plethora of odd jobs around the house that Rory could undertake, saving her the cost of a handyman.

Yes, her children could be quite useful, she had decided. Ingmar's refreshing attitude to his daughter – a combination of distracted gratitude and devil-may-care rebellion – rather appealed to her. She saw that she had finally reached an age where one's children were no longer burdens and could, in fact, be cultivated into valuable resources.

The bridleway broadened into a gravel track as they climbed the final cusp of the hill, rattling beneath the tall sycamores that skirted the old pub beer garden.

'Gosh, they *have* made progress.' She marvelled at the restoration of the burned-out shell – still swathed in scaffolding and plastic, but with roof battens almost completed and glass in the windows. 'I had such fun here in the old days – always was the best place to take lovers. The garden is full of secret glades.'

'Quite agree!' Ingmar launched into one of his delightful anecdotes, but with the usual problem attached. '*Jeg huske en den gang da –*'

'English!' Truffle interrupted, patting his leg kindly. 'Please do talk in English, darling. You know how tiresome I find Danish.'

Ingmar always forgot that Truffle knew not a single word of his mother tongue.

'I was saying that I used to drink here when I first moved to the area,' he bellowed over the Moke engine. 'Shared many an hour with a very interesting fellow named Falstaff. Owned a lot of land here, I think. Used to carry a shotgun stitched into a trench coat. He took me into the woods by the stream there one night and got three rabbits and a fox with a single shot. He was only aiming at the fox, but it was still rather impressive. I took two of the rabbits home and made stew. Lost this tooth here on a piece of shot.' He pointed out one of his gold caps, almost driving into a ditch as he did so.

'Falstaff, you say? I've never heard of him. He owned land?'

'Half the Springlodes – and the Oddfields. Always struck me as anomalous because he looked like a tramp.'

'Most landowners do.' Truffle smiled. She loved Ingmar's tales – all imaginary, she had no doubt. They traded in tall stories

As they passed the burned-out Dulston's Agriculture, she peered across to survey the damage. 'Not as bad as I thought. Rather like James used to keep it. He was always dropping cigars under the machinery by mistake – whoomph! Instant bonfire.'

'So it has burned too, yes?' Ingmar hit the brakes and took in the scene.

There was red and white tape everywhere. The sides of two of the green hangars were blackened, a few windows were smashed and one perimeter fence had smelted into the razed undergrowth. The tractors closest to the office hangars had melted tyres and charred, blistered sides. But the little agricultural supplier was still looking strangely functional. Truffle half-expected James to appear from one of the hangars with a syrupy smile, cigar and brogues smoking as he called out 'Sorry, darling – dropped a match!'

Remembering him with needling affection, she explained to Ingmar that she had once been married to the owner. 'He was rather a sweet chap, although very hard on Rory who was only a tot at the time. Took to wearing my undergarments, which was rather a bind. I didn't mind the Marks and Sparks stuff going missing, but he went straight for the Rigby and Peller if he could – and they were made to measure.'

This caused some confusion because one of the few modern facts of life Ingmar had grasped was that his son-in-law now owned the company.

Truffle soothed him by pointing out a large, incongruous modern house resembling a miniature Cotswold stone French *château* that peeked out of the woods to their left.

'Do you remember that funny little pop star building it in the eighties? The one who married his first wife's daughter? They say he filled the swimming pool with champagne.'

'Oh, yes. He used to come into my shop,' Ingmar chuckled. 'Always wanting first editions for his library – as long as they were bound in red to match the décor. I sold him worthless first editions of the most dreadful fiction imaginable and he was none the wiser.'

Ingmar remembered almost everything about the part of his life that had taken place in the previous century, which was why Truffle adored him. It was only the recent past with which he struggled, which was why he failed to recognise his grand-daughter when she hacked past on a big grey horse as he steered the Moke up the Oddlodes Riding School drive.

'Hello, Morfar!' she greeted him cheerfully as he drew level with her.

Ingmar gave her a noble, if irritable, wave and carried straight on.

'I do think it so rude that children today call anyone over sixty "Grandad",' he muttered to Truffle and parked beside the horsebox. 'Why are we here again?'

'I want to see my children.' Truffle sighed indulgently.

'Ah, yes.'

Diana and Rory were a sour disappointment to Truffle. Both were in very glum spirits and showed no gratitude that she had made the gracious gesture of visiting.

Rory was teaching Mim and Digby a lesson on their over-fed and under-exercised ponies. It was Halloween, and Mim and Digby were dressed as a witch and the Incredible Hulk respectively. They had already terrified most of the horses on the yard, and their ponies were now wreaking revenge by careering around the manège, eyes rolling as they tried to rub the little monsters off on every railing.

'Steer!' Rory bellowed in between puffing on one of his endless cigarettes. 'Inside leg outside hand! Sit up! Slow down. Hold on to the mane, Mim. Stop screaming, both of you. Steer! Oh, Christ I give up. Just gallop wherever you like.'

Truffle watched indulgently from the railings.

'Reminds me of you racing around on ponies in your Prince Philip Cup days,' she told Diana. 'You were so fearless in those days. And thin.'

She was looking absolutely dreadful, Truffle observed. That served her right for behaving so badly at poor Spurs' wedding.

Diana, who had just eaten two entire value bags of the kids' packed lunch fun-sized Mars bars to cheer herself up, felt as bad as she looked – guilt-ridden, fat and, for once, totally incapable of standing up to her mother.

'You were quite pretty in those days,' Truffle recalled now. 'Such a shame you inherited your father's complexion. The Wop aged dreadfully quickly.'

'Hmph.' Diana turned to collar Sharon who was trailing past with a wheelbarrow. 'Can you rustle us up some coffee, Sharon? Thank you.'

Sharon glared at her, but didn't argue, dumping the barrow of manure within sniffing range of the visitors and sloping towards the house.

'Your children are divine!' Ingmar was laughing rapturously at the sight of Mim and Digby charging around.

'Thank you.' Diana's spirits lifted slightly until Ingmar looked at her as though she were mad and took a step back.

'I was talking to their mother,' he snapped, smiling at Truffle.

Which bucked Truffle up no end. Ingmar always made her feel young.

'Such a shame you have lost your nerve,' she told Diana. 'You used to ride so well.'

'I have not lost my nerve!' Diana snapped. 'I've just been too busy to ride since I got here.'

'Yes. Breaking up marriages takes a lot of time, doesn't it?' Truffle said lightly.

Diana opened her mouth to let rip, but at that moment Mim's pony, Bronwyn succeeded in flinging her rider through the air with a victorious buck.

Having scooped up her wailing daughter from the sandy surface, dusted her off, crammed her crumpled witch's hat back over her helmet, hugged her and plonked her back on the sweating, breathless Bronwyn, Diana rejoined her mother with no desire to scrap about the wedding party.

'Why are you here?' she asked instead.

'Can't a mother visit her children on a whim?'

'Not if she's you, she can't.' Diana watched Digby race past on Furze, the black Shetland, his saddle slipping up the pony's neck.

Truffle feigned a look of deep hurt and double-bluffed her by issuing an invitation to the Oddlode fireworks evening. 'I thought I'd gather a little party beforehand. They're trying for the biggest pyre record this year.'

'Is that an entirely wise plan, given all these fires?' Diana snapped. 'You do know Dulston's was almost razed this week?'

'Oh, this arson business has been blown out of all proportion.' Truffle watched as a small, green Hulk completed another fast circuit, now clutching on to a surprised black Shetland's ears. 'Awful coincidences, I say. You don't want to listen to Nanny rattling on about ghosts – or Bell's theory that Reg Wyck and Til are behind them all.'

'I thought it might be Pod Shannon?' Diana said idly.

'Who?' Truffle laughed. 'What a silly name.'

'There have been fires started here many times in the past century,' Ingmar announced grandly. 'I have quite a collection of material on the matter in my shop.'

'You do?' Diana and Truffle both turned to look at him, not noticing the Hulk galloping past now hanging upside down from his pony's neck.

'It is quite extraordinary how many houses have burned down in this village alone.' Ingmar nodded, removing his trilby to scratch at his downy grey hair. 'There was one year – I think it was maybe twenty years ago – when four houses were lost in six months, all to infernos.'

'Waaaaaaah!' The Hulk hit the deck nearby.

Diana dragged herself away to whisk him up, noticing that Rory was now sitting glumly on a plastic show-jump block, lighting yet another cigarette and completely lost in thought.

'I hate Furze!' Digby complained as she legged him back up, having moved the saddle back to the right spot and tightened the girth.

'You don't really.'

'I hate you too,' he yelled. 'And I hate Rory and I hate Mim!'

Diana hugged him, despite his squirming. 'You are the most consistent man I know. I love you for that.'

The squirming stopped. 'What does consistent mean?'

'You stick to your guns. You're fab. You are the *best!*'

A big, toothy grin lit up his green face. 'I made Daddy's girlfriend cry by telling her that you were prettier than she is.'

'Good for you,' said Diana – knowing it was the wrong response, but not caring. She hugged him again and then saw him on his way with a pat on Furze's fat bottom. 'Just walk him now, okay? Imagine you are carefully riding him through a treacherous bog. That goes for you too, Mim.'

Rory looked up briefly. 'Sit up, heels down, inside leg and outside rein.'

Diana hauled him off his jump block and hooked his arm through hers as she towed him towards the rails. 'You okay?'

'Think I might cry.'

'Is it seeing Mummy?'

'Has that effect, yes.'

Diana was touched by his sensitivity. 'Still feeling down about Dilly?'

'God, no. Just pissed off that Mummy's turned up with the mad Swede.'

'He's Danish.' She couldn't help laughing. 'Have a coffee. It might help.'

Sharon had lumbered out of the cottage with a tray of mugs slopping milky Nescafé over their chipped rims. Hally and Twitch trailed after her, meek from being rumbled eating their way through four defrosting pork chops.

'According to Quigley, the Lodes fires are nothing to do with the Sarsden family and their curses, but associated instead with pagan rituals . . .' Ingmar was still regaling Truffle with tales of fire-raising in the Lodes valley, but broke off as the coffee was thrust under his chin. He looked down his long nose. 'Is she pregnant?'

'It's a phantom pregnancy – she always gets them,' Diana insisted as she clambered through the rails, Hally greeting her with guilty kisses and yelps, her belly swinging low beneath her.

'I was talking about your housemaid.' Ingmar was peering at Sharon's broad girth.

A snarl escaped Sharon's narrow lips as Rory folded double, snorting with laughter. She set the tray down on an upturned bucket with a furious rattle and stalked back to her barrow to wheel it towards the midden. As soon as she had rounded the corner and was out of sight, she pulled out the pilfered sweater that was hidden beneath her sweatshirt and held it to her nose, breathing Rory in from the collar.

Oblivious that yet more of his laundry had just been stolen from the cottage, Rory was still guffawing happily at Ingmar's gaffe. 'Pregnant housemaid! She'll be so mad.'

'So hard to get decent staff these days,' Truffle murmured, reluctantly clutching the mug she had been handed which bore the slogan *Fat Old Bag*. Her eyes narrowed on Diana and she mustered a sly smile. 'So, darling, have you seen Amos since you two had words at the wedding?'

Diana stopped to gather a coffee from the tray, glancing across to check that her children were now happily hacking through their imaginary steaming bog. 'No.'

'Hardly surprising. The poor man is out of his mind with misery, I gather.'

Diana pressed her lips to the cracked rim of a mug advertising an equine supplement called *Stroppy Mare*.

'Of course it will hardly come as a surprise that he blames you for the fact that he is now fighting for his children,' Truffle said haughtily.

'His children?' She didn't feel the chipped china rim snag on her lip.

'Jacqui and Sexton have the little ones with them now. They are staying with her mother in Morrell-on-the-Moor. Amos is distraught.'

Hating herself, Diana pressed the mug to her chin. 'He needed to know.' But her voice lacked conviction.

Truffle sighed. 'Much as I am in favour of a woman scorned reaping a little revenge from time to time, I do feel it was rather excessive to do that to him more than twenty years after a teenage fling.'

'His wife was being unfaithful in front of his nose and he couldn't see it,' Diana snapped. 'The thing that hurt me most about Tim's affair was the secrets. I hated the secrets.'

'Well, you know what they say – there you go, darling.' Truffle handed *Fat Old Bag* on to Rory and collected *Best of Breed* from the tray. 'Shoot the messenger.'

'The text messenger.' Rory was still giggling about Ingmar's gaffe.

'You've broken his heart,' Truffle told Diana matter-of-factly.

Diana looked at her mother with a mixture of love and loathing as her heart hammered in her chest, finally spurred into action. She licked her lips as she set her mug down on the ground, not tasting the saltiness there until Ingmar let out a clubbed-seal wail of horror.

'Blood!' He leaped away. 'I cannot abide the sight of blood.'

Diana felt her lip, split by the cracked mug, incredulously. Every time Amos made her heart flip over with self-loathing, she bled.

She looked across at Mim and Digby, her little witch and Hulk, now bumbling side by side on their drying ponies.

'I'm going riding,' she announced suddenly.

Rory splurted his coffee in shock. 'You? Riding?'

'Yes, I'm taking Ensign out.'

'He hasn't been ridden in months. He has no shoes on.'

'He's my horse. He'll be fine.' Diana was already heading towards the tack room, mopping up blood with her wrist. 'Can you mind the children for an hour or two?'

'Sure – we'll go trick-or-treating.' Rory was too amazed to remember he had a full afternoon of lessons booked.

Mim and Digby whooped delightedly and exchanged high fives, their ponies exchanging relieved looks beneath them.

Diana marched up to Sharon who was hugging a red sweater to her cheek and stabbing a hay bale with a penknife, randomly trying to snap the binder twine.

'Can you fetch Ensign from the hawthorn field? I have to find his tack.'

'If you insist.' Sharon glared at her.

'And what are you doing with my jumper, may I ask? I've only just got Rory to wash it after his wretched dog buried a tripe stick in the arm.'

Sharon dropped the sweater and trudged away.

Twenty minutes later, having inelegantly hauled herself into the saddle from the mounting block, Diana waved farewell to her amused brother, bemused mother and a confused Ingmar. As she and Ensign weaved a cautious path along the drive, snorting all the way, Faith Brakespear came lolling along in the opposite direction, feet dangling out of the stirrups, the big grey she was riding soft-eyed and dark-sided after a long blast around the valley.

'Going for a hack?' she asked cheerfully, sublimely oblivious of the notion that sitting six feet up in the air on something significantly less intelligent than your average family dog was in any way perilous.

'I'm riding for my life,' Diana told her through gritted teeth.

'Here – have my high viz gear.' Faith pulled a fluorescent tabard from over her head and held it out it to her. 'It's getting quite misty out there – and the nights are really drawing in now. You know it'll be dark soon?'

Realising that Diana was too frightened to let go of the reins, Faith put the tabard over her head and fiddled with the straps, then hopped off her horse to wrap its reflective boots on Ensign's knobbly old legs. 'He has no shoes on.'

'We're not riding on the roads,' Diana assured her in a nervous mumble.

Now glowing radioactively, she and Ensign wobbled their way towards the bridleway, spooking at every falling leaf.

'Don't mention it,' Faith grumbled under her breath as she watched them go, piqued that Diana hadn't even thanked her. Sometimes sucking up to the in-laws was a thankless task.

She patted the grey and led him up the drive, heart leaping as she saw Rory lifting his niece and nephew from their ponies with big hugs. He was so good with kids. He'd make a fantastic father.

She had slept with his phone under her pillow all week. He had got another one already, of course, but she was still receiving text messages and voice mails, using Magnus's charger to keep it alive. Mostly horsy acquaintances wanting to chat about competitions and hunting; a few clients enquiring after lessons, and a lot of people demanding to have bills paid. She read and listened to them all. Mo Stillitoe hadn't texted again, which made Faith happy.

Rounding the turn of the drive, she suddenly spotted her grandfather standing nearby Rory's mother, and she baulked. That was way too many in-laws. Truffle terrified her.

'Anke!' Her grandfather spread his arms wide in customary confusion. 'My little angel. So beautiful!'

Faith registered the way that Rory looked up in delight when he heard the name 'Anke', only to lower his brows in disappointment and look away when he realised that it was her daughter.

Rory's flirtation with Mo Stillitoe she could cope with. Mo was a minor irritation in her plans – the far superior Dillymo Modilly fusion look that she had created would see her off in no time. But her own mother was another matter. How could she compete with that? Rory had as big a crush on her mum as Faith did on him.

Anger curdling in her stomach, she led the grey towards the washdown box.

Sharon was waiting in the shadows. 'I want a word with you.'

Faith could feel her eyes bulging in the dark. If Truffle Dacre-Hopkinson was scary, Sharon was heart-stoppingly gothic.

'About w-what?'

The answer came as a complete surprise. 'Do you want to come over to the caravan later? Share a pizza and watch a video? I've got Phar Lap and Champions. And a bottle of Lambrusco.'

Faith gaped at her. 'Okay. Cool.'

24

A For Sale sign had gone up outside Number Four Horseshoe Cottages. Mo peered up at it through the small sitting-room window every now and again as she flipped dispiritedly through the local paper looking for cheap rentals. There was nothing remotely close to Oddlode within her price range. Anke was still trying to push the idea of a short stay in her granny annexe, but Mo knew it was impossible.

The front page of the local paper ran with the story of the blaze at Dulston's, excitedly announcing 'LODES ARSONIST STRIKES AGAIN'. Graham was described as 'millionaire ex-haulier, Brakespear, 42' and quoted as denying the likelihood of a connection between the Dulston's fire and the others. This was also the official police line, although Mo knew differently.

Anke had told her that the police had interviewed Graham for hours, along with the rest of her family. The fact that there had been fires at both his home and his work put Graham firmly in the equation. The proximity of Dulston's to the first fire at the Plough added another factor, as did the fact that Graham had been at the harvest supper party on the night of the blaze at the old kennels.

Only Mo knew that he had been with her in the River Folly when that fire had started.

Mo's heart went out to him, although she hadn't dared try to contact him and, by staying inside the cottage, had avoided seeing him. She was terrified that the police would find out about their relationship and question her too. She was equally terrified that Anke would find out. The Brakespears' plans to take a holiday during half-term had been scuppered by the investigation and they were forced to stay put. This meant Anke could keep up her soup and sympathy deliveries to Horseshoe Cottages, her worries about her family, and most especially her husband, always on her mind.

Anke said that Graham was devastated. Mo found it hard to imagine him capable of devastation. She had only ever seen the positive, flirtatious, joking Graham. Even though she had seen how remorseful their short affair had made him, he had still managed to turn his guilty conscience into a self-deprecating joke. The man whom Anke talked about was a darker, sadder man filled with frustration and anger. He was someone Mo had never met.

'He hasn't even hugged me since the fire,' Anke had told Mo that day. 'There was a time I would have been grateful to be left alone, but it makes me very sad. I have left it too late to show him that I need him physically. When I try to touch him, he just thinks that I am offering sympathy. I hadn't realised how far I have pushed him away until now. He used to be so strong, so resilient, but he was hiding so much hurt from me. The fire has broken him.'

Mo prayed for her sake that Graham was too tough to break. Anke had told her that everyone had a hidden side which was only revealed in their closest relationships.

If Graham's hidden side was melancholy and Pod's hidden side was wildness, she was certain that Anke's secret self was pure passion – it was just that she had never found it. It was bursting to get out, but she couldn't find the exit.

Mo's own hidden side frightened her. Sometimes she thought it close to total madness. From early childhood she had felt moments of such blind, irrational anger and loneliness that she had lost all control and sense. Her grandparents had treated them as simple temper tantrums, not realising the agonising sadness that they left her feeling. Only Pod had seen their full intensity. Now that he wasn't around to hold her tight until they passed, she wondered how she would cope.

Her phone bleeped with a text message. Mo felt a little tic of hope in her chest and then smiled as she read it: *Larch fed up waiting for Emma to get her legover to Overlodes.*

On Monday, an unfamiliar number had pestered her phone with messages that simply said '*Mo?*' She'd finally replied to find out who it was. Rory had sent back a photograph of himself. He was standing in Carphone Warehouse, posing by a large cut-out of a mobile phone with arms and legs, having just bought a state-of-the-art new camera phone to replace his old one; Mo now knew that had been stolen, along with all his stored numbers – the thieves no doubt behind the weird wedding-day texts. When she'd asked him how he'd got her number, he'd sent two words that backed up her self esteem no end: '*Remembered it*'. Rory, who regularly forgot appointments, competition start times, dressage tests, the names of his clients and even his horses, had memorised her number.

He had been sending messages all week demanding that she come for a ride, mostly with silly photographs attached of him holding Worzel saddled and ready, and looking at his watch. She knew it was too much for her to face, but his flirtation cheered her up. She pressed the Reply button and looked at the little blank screen, wondering what trait Rory Midwinter held back from public view.

'Sobriety,' she told Bechers with a sad laugh. 'He's secretly sober.'

Rory's text messages always got more random and difficult to decipher after he started hitting the scotch in the evening. A couple of nights ago, when she had texted that she was thinking of going to Suffolk, Rory had confused the county with the character from *A Horse for Emma*, resulting in an hour of confused messages. He had really taken to the funny old book that Anke had lent Mo.

Still thinking about Suffolk, she texted him now.

She looked up at the sign again. A curious mist was settling over the village, fading everything white. It reminded her of the mists over the fens that had terrified her as a child.

Weeks ago, long before the sticky patch had stuck fast, she and Pod had talked about going back to Suffolk and then the Fens to visit her grandparents during half-term. She knew that she should have gone alone, should have told them what had happened with Pod, and sought comfort through distance, but the thought of the starchy, old-fashioned world they inhabited depressed her. They wouldn't understand for a moment how she was feeling. They would be secretly pleased that Pod had finally proved them right and deserted her. Right now, Mo needed to be close to Anke, who understood only too well the anguish of losing faith in love.

The sign was so swathed in mist that she could hardly read it.

'For Sale,' she sighed. 'Small heart in need of restoration.'

Someone had stopped outside to peer at the cottage. All day villagers and visitors who had spotted the sign had wandered over to take a good look, letting themselves into the front garden to get up close – not caring that she was sitting immediately inside. Feeling like an exhibit in a glass cage, Mo longed to poke her tongue out, jump up and down on the settee and moon at them. The first few times, she had just stayed very still in the hope that they would not notice her. It seemed to work. Then she'd got the idea of testing the theory by staying very still in an unusual pose. So far she had adopted ballet positions one and two, arms daintily aloft, with no reaction from outside. She had done a head-stand against the sofa. Nothing. She had even posed with a lampshade on her head, listening as the elderly couple staring in through the window discussed the possibility of the vendor leaving the curtains.

She heard the gate creak. Here we go . . . another window gawper heading her way.

To cheer herself up, she lay back on the carpet and played dead, adopting a twisted position with an open-mouthed, death-mask grimace. In her peripheral vision she could see the shadow moving across the window and then moving back again to take another look.

The next moment the front door opened with a crash as it swung back, sending the phone flying.

'Jesus Christ – oh, my sweet life!' Pod ran into the room and crouched down over her, frantically feeling for a pulse.

'Get off me!' Mo screamed, wriggling away.

'What the fuck do you think you're playing at?' he yelled, standing up and backing into a corner.

'I thought you were looking at the For Sale sign.' Mo struggled to her feet and brushed herself down.

'I *was* looking at the For Sale sign. Then I looked in and thought you had fucking topped yourself.'

'It's a new yoga position,' she bluffed hastily.

He snorted sarcastically and looked around, surprised by the tidiness. Apart from the abandoned paper on the floor and the up-ended table by the open door, the cottage was *Homes and Gardens* spick and span, with jugs of fresh flowers on the sills, silk throws on the furniture and all the cushions plumped up on their points.

'Did the agents do this?' he asked.

'No. I did.'

'On your own?' His faith in her domesticity was stretched to the limit.

'A friend helped.'

'Been keeping busy, then?' He looked at her thoughtfully, those soulful dark eyes almost stripping away her skin.

Seeing him again, so close, in the little nest that they had shared with such high hopes made her red-raw. He was so familiar and yet now terrifyingly aloof and strange. She fought an urge to fold to the floor again and beg him to hold her, just to let her know they had touched once, that it hadn't all been make-believe.

But she forced herself to keep her chin high and to look at him. At least she had taken a bath and changed her clothes that day. She might look thin, drained and wretched, she reflected, but at least she smelled fresh and her hair was clean. She was coming on in leaps and bounds. Anke would be proud.

Pod wasn't looking so hot himself. Unshaven, with great smudges of tiredness under his eyes, he looked as though he'd hardly slept all week. Mo wished he wasn't so beautiful. It always took her breath away. Standing in the same room as him was torture.

She took a sharp breath, pinching her heart with an extra beat to make her strong. 'What are you doing here anyway?'

'Come to pick up the rest of my stuff.'

'You could have called.'

'It was a last-minute decision. I've been having a drink in the pub. Needed Saul to take a look at the fuel pump on my bike.'

'You won't be able to carry much of your stuff on your bike.'

'Dilly's bringing her car around in a bit.'

Mo managed to give nothing away. She didn't even wince, which she considered amazing for someone being stabbed repeatedly with anger and jealousy and hatred and self-loathing.

We will part friends, she told herself over and over again in a silent mantra. We will part friends, we will part friends. I will not give him the satisfaction of making him hate me. We will part friends.

'So, you two are living together then?' Her voice wobbled, but at least she got the words out in the right order.

'Planning to. Dilly junked in her degree course this week.'

'Can't bear being apart?'

'Something like that. Her mum's not best pleased.'

'I'll bet.'

'We're going to stay with Amos. He needs looking after.'

'I know the feeling.'

He gave her that skin-stripping look again, his face chequered with emotion as every muscle clung to his skull, yet she had no idea what he was thinking. The opaque black marbles were still set into the place where his lost-soul eyes had once been.

'You could have called,' she repeated, looking away, unable to bear the glazed shutters.

'I didn't think you'd be here.'

'Where did you think I'd be?'

'I thought you were planning to be in Suffolk this weekend.'

'*We* were planning to be there. Plans change. Something to do with you leaving me for a start.'

'I didn't leave you.'

'Well I didn't throw you out.'

'Not of the house, maybe.'

'*You* walked out on *me*, Pod.'

'Now I'm walking in.'

'To collect your stuff.'

He ran his tongue over his teeth, but his indecision was lost on Mo.

'You should have bloody called,' she snapped again. 'I've hardly left this cottage in days, but I'd have kept clear if I'd known.'

The muscles leaping in his cheek tightened into his jaw. 'Yeah. Well. Anyway, I thought you rode on Saturday afternoons.'

'I've given up.'

'Guess there's no point now that you don't need it as a cover story when you're fucking Graham?' he sneered.

'I'm not doing that any more, either.' We will part friends, she repeated in her head. I will not give him the satisfaction of making me hate him. We loved one another too long.

He stared at her for a long time with those dark marble eyes before turning away from her, snorting, turning back and grabbing a cushion to hurl across the room, smashing a vase of carnations. 'How can you be so calm? How can you be so *fucking* calm!' He suddenly raged, marching up to her.

The marbles had been replaced with black coals that burned with emotion. She could see into his soul and what she saw was turmoil.

'I think the ghosts have gone, Pod. My ghosts.'

As the knife stabbed into her heart again, again, again, Mo tried to breathe, tried to stop the hurt swamping her.

'I've never been unhappier in my life than I am losing you. And that's chased them away. You were always right. You were my mother, my father, my brother, my lover . . . my friend. Losing you is the biggest bereavement imaginable, but it's also an exorcism. They can't haunt me any more. They mean nothing to me. They never gave me anything. You gave me my world. And hope.'

Pod stared at her, his mouth half-open, his eyes blazing.

'*Dochas.*' She mopped her eyes with her sleeves.

Pod's brain sent every muscle in his body a single, clear message in that split second. Hug her. Hold her. But, in the same fragment of time, Mo asked a question that stopped him.

'Do you really love her, Pod?'

Nostrils flared, breath short, eyes wide, he reached for another cushion and took out the print of the heavy horses above the fire.

'Do you?'

He slumped to the floor by her feet, head in his hands. 'She wants to start a family straightaway. She can't wait to have a big, screaming clutch of babies and toddlers. We're going to breed horses – not racers. Family horses – big, fat cobs with no brains and stabilisers that all the family can ride. Dilly is going to paint, too, and I'll renovate an old house for us to live in.'

Mo felt her heart being gently cut out and placed beside him.

Their lives had collided, fused, ignited so suddenly from the start – for years they had burned in the oxygen of love, passion and forgiveness without ever casting a light ahead. Somehow, the synthesis between them had distorted them from being lovers to Siamese twins – mutually dependent, wrestling beneath the same skin, knowing no way out that wasn't fatal. They had never realised that they wanted the same thing.

He looked up at her through damp lashes. 'I feel like I've just woken up from a bad dream and found paradise.'

Mo reached down to touch his hair with her fingers, stopping herself and pulling back as her fingertips traced the first soft strands. It wasn't hers to touch. So familiar. She had cut it for him just a few weeks ago. The last cut. The last touch.

'I feel like I've just woken up too. I'm still looking for paradise.' She laughed and sobbed. 'You know how crap I am at reading maps.'

'You'll find it.'

'Maybe.'

'I'll always love you. You know that.'

'Good luck, Whitney,' Mo whispered.

He blinked, eyes changing from thunder to kindness as he remembered. In the early days, silly with love in the heyday of the nineties rock ballad, they had flirted in cheesy song titles and lyrics. Saying farewell with a few was only fitting.

'No more I love yous.'

'Nothing compares to you.'

'So unbreak my heart.'

'I will do anything for you, but I won't do that.'

'I know.' She pulled her tears back with a laugh that only just made its way out of her throat. 'My heart will go on. Now, get your stuff and get out of here.'

She helped him pack his clothes, CDs and papers into black bags, throwing them all in, a memory at a time, trying not to cry. It was impossible. Tears kept sliding out.

To her amazement, Pod cried too. He wept as he laughed and talked, telling her his plans, trying to make the ritual appear normal when both knew it was one of the worst moments they had shared.

Neither acknowledged the tears. They just dropped to the floor as they gathered his few belongings, leaving trails across the carpets like Hansel and Gretel's breadcrumbs.

It would have only taken one song lyric pleading for a second chance to stop the packing, but they had lost the urge to sing as they separated the CD collection.

Bechers hid behind the sofa, mewing worriedly.

'Can I take him?' Pod asked as he heaved the last of his bin bags down the narrow stairs.

Mo felt a flash of fury heat up the blades that were still stabbing through her chest. *No, no no! He's been my friend. I've fed him. I love him more than you do.*

'He's your cat.' She punished herself with the truth out loud. Pod had turned up with the tiny red kitten tucked into his big leather jacket three years ago, explaining that he was a gift from a yard he had ridden out for – the unwanted result of a liaison between an under-age pedigree Burmese and a feral ginger tom. Mo had always felt a close affinity with his heritage. 'He needs to know where home is.'

'You can come and visit him,' he offered lamely, pulling the cat basket from the under-stairs cupboard, wiping his wet cheeks with his sleeve.

'As long as Dilly isn't around. I couldn't bear that.'

'You'd like her.'

'I'm sure I would. I just don't want to. Not yet.'

She watched him dragging a protesting ginger cat from behind the sofa and, feeling the thin veneer of calm about to desert her, she looked hurriedly away, glaring at the For Sale sign. The mist had turned into a thick fog. She could hardly see the sign at all now, tears and fog making it vanish. She wanted to stay here for ever, hiding in her gingerbread cottage, waiting for a happy ending.

'Where are you going to live when this place is sold?' Pod was asking as he shut the little barred door on the yawling Bechers.

The gingerbread went mouldy, the happy ending had a bitter twist.

'I might move right away.'

'I feel like I belong here, queen. I thought you did, too.'

'I did. I do.'

'We both do.' For a moment he looked as though he was going to shout something. But then he stopped himself.

'Just not together, eh?' Mo muttered, filling the pause.

He shrugged. 'So – don't move away on account of me. Stay and have fun.' He made it sound like they'd had a scrap at a party and should both stay for the buffet and disco.

Mo mopped her face with her sleeves.

He was looking around the room – at the tacky horse brasses and lace doilies, the shire print Mo had replaced above the fire and the corn dollies dancing on the mantel. 'I love this fucking cottage.'

'Me too.'

'I hope whoever buys it appreciates it. We talked about buying it, remember?'

'Buying it with what?'

He swallowed, not looking at her. 'I'd still like to buy it for you.'

She laughed bitterly. 'And would that make everything better?'

'Maybe.'

It was the ultimate leaving gift. Such a hollow promise. Pod could no more afford a Horseshoe Cottage than he could afford a single horse-shoe.

'Okay, you buy me this cottage and we'll live happily ever after. Deal?'

'Deal.' He spat on his hand and grabbed hers for a moment before she snatched it away, hating the make-believe of it all.

We will part friends. We will part friends. She turned to stand at the window, looking out at the blank white sheet of fog. She started as she heard a blood-curdling scream somewhere on the green, just yards away – and then realised from the laughter that followed that it was just children. Of course. It was Halloween.

'I can't be here when Dilly comes.'

'She said she'd text me when she sets out.'

On cue came a tinkling from behind a cushion. Pod grabbed the phone and flipped up the cover.

'Eh?' He read the message and then turned over the phone. 'Oh, it's yours. What does *u r plying hard 2 git but I walnut guv up* mean? And this looks like an upside-down photograph of the Incredible Hulk.'

Mo grabbed the phone and quickly deleted the message.

Pod perched on the edge of the sofa, clutching the cat basket to his chest and pressing his chin to it. 'I always knew that if I let you go you would float higher and higher, like a helium balloon.'

'I'm not floating anywhere, Pod,' she sobbed. 'The balloon popped.'

'You will fly high again, queen.'

'You already are. I'm so jealous.' Mo hit the brave smile button and finding that it had broken, looked out at the whiteness again. 'I'll go before Dilly gets here.'

'We'll be out of your way in half an hour tops.'

She felt her face disintegrate and struggled hard to put her features back into the right place before turning to him one last time. 'I've never loved anyone else but you. This is so bloody scary.'

'Tell me about it.'

Mo felt a great phlegmy, choking, amazed laugh burst from her chest. Trust Pod to say that.

Racing across the room she gathered him and the wicker basket into a tight hug. She'd done it. They'd done it. They'd found a tiny chink of light through the blackness, beckoning the slow start to new beginnings.

'Be good.' She pressed her lips to his wet cheek and ran to the door, pulling her sneakers on as she left.

'Queen, those are my –'

The door slammed.

'– shoes.' Pod pressed his cheek to the coarse wicker and chewed at his muscle-quilted cheek, a final tear sliding from one big, dark eye. 'Silly cow.'

He'd tried . . . 'I never loved anyone but you' . . . 'Tell me about it' . . . He had even offered to buy the cottage for her. How many more ways could a man declare love?

It was as clear as day as far as he was concerned. Tell me about it. Tell me about it. Of course he still loved her. Loving Mo meant you really couldn't ever hope to love anyone else.

His phone buzzed. Dilly was on her way. He looked at the photograph of that pretty, happy face and tried to draw strength from it.

What she lacked in Mo's fire, Dilly made up in sheer warmth. She told him she loved him all the time, and meant it. She told him that he was her soul mate. She wanted his babies. She made him feel great. With Mo, he had never known if she'd hang around from one week to the next. With Dilly, he had a lifetime guarantee and an extended warranty if he wanted it. True, there was no cash back, but he was working on that. He was planning to buy a cottage, after all. He needed some readies.

Running through the fog, Mo felt nothing but gratitude for the whiteout that hid her tear-streaked face from the village. Away from Pod she could let rip. She wept her heart to splinters. Over-sized pumps flapping around on her feet like great clown shoes, she sprinted across the green with its amassing trick-or-treaters wailing through the mist. She ran across the road towards the village stores, falling over the ice-cream sign that had been hopefully placed outside, despite the cool of late autumn. She flapped her big feet along the pavement, past the council estate and the amenity ground, lungs burning.

She ran as far as the Wyck Farm driveway and slid to a crunching halt on the gravel, spinning around in the comforting hug of the whiteness, sobbing senselessly, so out of breath that she thought her tears might suffocate her.

Legs wobbling, she slid down against a gatepost and pressed her hot, slippery face into the crooks of her arms.

Which was where she was sitting when Graham's Lexus, fog-lights blazing, ran over the rubber fronts of her over-sized plimsolls, pressing them into the gravel and missing her toes by millimetres.

'I think you just ran over a drunk, Dad,' Chad piped up excitedly from the back seat.

'What?' Graham braked and looked over his shoulder. 'Christ – don't say Reg Wyck is hanging around again?' Pulling up on the verge with a creak of hand-brake, he reached for his seat belt.

'We're going to be late for Miles's party if you go and check!' Chad whinged.

'I'll be one minute, okay?'

Graham switched on his hazards and walked back to his drive-way.

'Hello? Anyone here? You okay?' He couldn't see a thing in the fog.

There was no one there, he realised with relief, peering around in whiteness. They were all seeing ghosts tonight. Anke had wanted Chad to forget about the party in the bad weather, but the boy was desperate to go, and Graham still needed to get to Springlode where Faith was stranded at the stables. He wasn't happy leaving her there with Rory Midwinter for long. The poor boy wasn't safe.

He took one last look around, jumping as an owl shrieked overhead.

He could smell something familiar. He couldn't place it but, some-where inside, his heart steadied and the ghosts retreated.

'Okay, son – let's get you to this party.' He strapped himself back into the driver's seat.

It was getting dark. Trick-or-treaters were all over the green, looming out of the mist as they drove cautiously past.

'Dad,' Chad asked as he dragged his Scream mask over his head and pulled up his black hood, preparing to terrify his friends in the village hall, 'did ghosts really set fire to your office?'

'Who told you that?'

'It's what everyone's saying.'

'No, son.' He looked at the terrifying mask. 'It wasn't ghosts.'

'Who was it, then?'

Graham didn't answer, letting himself out to see Chad to the door.

Minutes later, driving up towards Springlode at a crawl, he saw a luminous figure riding a horse on the other side of the low hedge by Tyack's Farm.

'Jesus!'

Hitting the panic locks, he braked hard but, when he looked again, horse and rider had gone.

'There are no bloody ghosts,' he told his reflection in the rear-view mirror.

'I'm sorry. I'm so sorry,' Diana whispered to Ensign as they plodded through the woods in the all-encompassing fog and gathering gloom.

They were lost. Hopelessly, utterly lost. And she was losing her wits with fright.

The big old horse was exhausted. His snorty, ear-twitching excitement at being out and about again had long since been replaced by heavy-headed heavy breathing. The creature of flight had no fight left in him. He stumbled and shambled his way forward, obediently going where he was told.

Diana slid from the saddle to rest his back and tried to find her balance on the soft leaf mulch as she pulled his reins over his head and walked beside him.

Trusting, and grateful for the rest, Ensign followed her as she led him around trees and across paths in ever-decreasing circles for what seemed like hours. Eventually even his loyalty ran out and he planted himself on the spot, refusing to budge.

'Please move!' Diana pleaded, tugging on the reins.

But those kind, dark eyes blinking at her through the mist told her that she had pushed him too far.

She pressed her face to his hot shoulder and groaned.

Suddenly, Ensign threw up his head, let out a snort of alarm and shot off. Propelled sideways, Diana landed hard against a tree and almost knocked herself out on a stump.

'Come back here!' she howled, already unable to see him through the fog. The cut on her lip had opened up again. She could feel it stinging in the cold air. 'Oh fuck. Bugger. Bollocks. Pants.'

'I could shoot you now,' a soft voice breathed in her ear. 'But I think we should find the horse first.'

Diana felt every hair on her neck tighten, knit itself together into a silky noose and grip her throat, stopping her breathing.

He walked around to face her, twelve-bore uncocked over his shoulder, shot loaded in his eyes.

'I thought you might turn up.'

'Well, it's Halloween, isn't it?' She managed a hoarse whisper. 'Time the ghosts had a reunion.'

★   ★   ★

'I am so glad that you felt you could come here!' Anke opened a bottle of wine as Mo pulled another hunk of tissues from the box in front of her at the kitchen table and blew her nose.

'I really can't stay. I just have to wait until Pod and D-dilly have gone.'

'I understand.'

'Will Graham be long?'

'He's fetching Faith. It might take a while in this fog. Stay as long as you like.'

'No, I can't stay,' she repeated. 'I don't want to take up your time.'

'You're not. Magnus is out with his band – they are playing a Halloween gig tonight – Graham says that it's the only time their music will be fitting. I am all alone. Have a glass of wine, at least. Tell me how you feel about Pod coming today?'

'Fine,' Mo said untruthfully. 'I feel fine. Upset, jealous, murderous. You know. The usual. Fine.' Her voice shook.

Anke poured them both a glass of wine and sat down beside her.

'I wish I could make it better, *kaereste*.'

'You do. You can.' Mo ran a shaking finger around the rim of the glass. 'I want to go to the Pleasure Garden in the Gunning Estate. I have to go today. You know the way.'

'We can't go there *now*,' Anke laughed nervously.

'Why not?'

'You can't see beyond the end of your nose out there.'

'We'll find it.'

'I need to be here for Graham.'

'Leave him a note.'

'It's almost dark. Believe me, we don't want to be there after dark. That silly, drunken night with Pheely and Pixie almost finished me off.'

Mo nodded, lifting the glass shakily to her lips and spilling wine everywhere. 'Will you tell me the way, at least? From the path we took on the wildlife walk? I can find that – just tell me from there.' She blotted the spilled wine with her sleeve.

Anke looked at the wine soaking into the pale cotton, the tiny, white-knuckled fingers gripping her cuff as her arm hammered down on the table.

She had dreamed about seeing the garden again, sure that it held the secret to her absurd, hopeful, happy certainty that things would work out in her marriage. Seeing it had been the first fix of a drug she needed to taste again.

'I'm not sure I could find it again, Mo – certainly not in this weather.'

Those huge, sad green eyes took her heart away. 'The answers are there. I know they are.'

Experiencing a distinct oh-no-not-again feeling, Anke fetched her car keys.

Mo downed her wine and willed it to give her courage. She had to come clean. She had finally seen off her ghosts tonight. It was Halloween and she was frightened of nothing. It was time to admit the truth.

Amos knew how much it had cost Diana to come to Gunning, yet he was unwilling to relinquish his tight grip on her remorse. He wanted to make her suffer. He turned the screw as they searched for Ensign, reminding her of her betrayal – years ago and then again so recently.

'I spent years – *years* trying to get over you. I had you fucking right down there in the hole where you belong and then you sail back in and fuck up my life again.'

Diana's eyes darted every which way through the fog, seeing nothing but his face. Long-haired, wild-eyed, teenage Amos. Short-haired, angry-eyed, middle-aged Amos. Same broadsword cheeks, same wide lion nose – broken now by the long battle with life. Same curling mouth that she had once kissed so much she almost believed they breathed with the same lungs. Same long, wide, strong, sinewy body that had now fathered children as she had mothered them. Same desire. Same hatred.

'You had no right to break up my marriage.'

'Your marriage was already broken – like a rotten tooth that only takes a pip to rupture in two.'

'You forced her away.'

'She was already running. I just opened the gate, Amos.'

Squeals and snorts beckoned them towards the tall beech hedges, where Ensign was reacquainting himself with Rio through three feet of shedding copper foliage.

'You always put yourself before your horses,' Amos muttered as he caught hold of the reins and patted the old campaigner. 'You've broken me as surely as you broke them.'

'I haven't! I wouldn't.'

Diana's hyperbole of emotions could barely cope, but she was too desperate for redemption to back out. She let him pick over the bones they had left twenty years earlier.

'I had nothing to lose. I know that – just my heart. Take that.' He handed her his gun and led Ensign to the derelict yard beside the woodland paddock, removing his tack and rubbing the old horse's tucked quarters to loosen him up.

Diana watched his big hands moving over the horse's muscles and remembered how they had felt on her body. She closed her eyes. The cut on her lip was tiny, but it throbbed like a mortal wound.

'You had everything to lose,' he went on. 'Your family, your reputation, your wealth. I think I always knew you'd bury me alive.' He threw a musty rug over Ensign and posted him through a gate into a field of fog. 'Now you're trying to dig me up and pick over the bones.' He listened as the horse let out a shrill whinny of gratitude and thundered across the lush field to talk to the others through the hedge.

His voice dropped to a whisper. 'Who are you going to exhume next, Diana? Firebrand?'

Jumping at the mention of that name, Diana bit her lip, the little cut jagging wider open.

Amos took a step closer and, lifting a hand, pressed his thumb to her lip. It smelled of hot horse and tasted of wood bark as he stemmed the blood.

'Not blue, after all?'

'Never was.' Dropping the gun with a clatter, she covered his hand with hers to hold it there, feeling the sinews behind his knuckles lifting like steel wires as she touched it.

His dark eyes gleamed. But he pulled his hand away, making her wince as cold air stung her lip. He picked up his gun, loaded two cartridges, and cocked it.

Almost as though there was an unspoken ritual that they both had to carry out, Amos turned and marched towards the beech hedge with Diana in step, walking beside him before she knew what she was doing or where they were going, her heart thundering as her head finally fell into step too.

At last, it was time.

They had reached the high, copper-leafed fortification that screened the Pleasure Garden – now a sleeping, pink-scaled eel in the twilight gloom, curled around its secrets. Diana followed mutely as Amos unlatched the hidden gate and then swung back towards her, his great shoulders barring the way.

'This is what you wanted to see, isn't it? This is what you came here for?' His voice was accusing.

She nodded. 'I know it's ruined. I know it's almost gone. But I have to see it.'

He handed her his gun once more. 'This time it's loaded. So don't bloody drop it.'

Disappearing into the darkening fog, he strode down the steps and reached into the gap in the wall that housed the power cut-out.

Diana let out a cry of wonder, stumbling down the steps towards him.

The garden was alight and awash. It was a hundred shades of illuminated colour and dancing animation. The bald lady's hair gushed golden, titian and auburn as she stooped over her rushes. The cupids played naughty water sports in amongst the lilies, the gargoyles spat at each other, and the entrance to the dodo box maze was a glowing, enchanted blue arch in the white haze.

'You kept it! You saved it!' She sobbed, stooping to hug a cupid.

Amos watched her black hair trailing in the water and tried to hide his smile. Hurt, betrayal, anger, sorrow meant nothing when enclosed in the sunken paradise they'd shared. They were home once more. He smiled so widely, so truly, that his cheeks were ploughed with fresh furrows, his eyes folding deep new laughter lines towards his ears, his brow wiping out the vertical frown marks with horizontal ones underlining exquisite joy.

'The bald lady got her head back!' she cried, wading into the fountain to kiss the statue's nose, her own hair gaining a veil of jewelled water drops.

Amos couldn't speak. He had been waiting for this moment so long that he couldn't say a word to spoil it.

On she danced, threading through the statues, splashing through the ponds, leap-frogging the bird-baths and saddle stones, changing from red to green to gold to blue to violet as she skipped between the coloured lights.

At last she danced up to Amos, breathless and smiling. 'Why didn't you tell me?' she laughed. 'Why didn't you tell me you'd brought it back to life?'

He looked at her, the smile going nowhere despite his best efforts. 'When someone's dead, you put flowers on their grave to remember them.'

She spun around in a giddy circle. 'Meaning?'

'This is our grave, huntress. This is where our love –'

'No!' Diana pressed a hand to his mouth and then covered it with another, the whites of her eyes gleaming. 'No! It didn't! Nothing died here. Nothing ever died here. You called me huntress!' She laughed. 'You just called me huntress.'

He reached up and pulled her fingers from his mouth, enfolding them in his big hands.

'Nothing died here,' she repeated, tears in her eyes as she looked frantically from the bald lady to the stone nymphs and cupids, laughing and sobbing incredulously. 'Look at it. It's alive.'

With a hollow laugh Amos released her hands and rubbed his neck, his brows furrowed, his smile still burning deep grooves in his cheeks. 'I told you not to drop the bloody gun again.'

'What gun?'

He rubbed a calloused hand across the smile.

Whooping, she pranced away again to jump on the narrow stone wall around the cupid pond and balance on tiptoes as she walked its narrow diameter.

'When I gave you my shotgun, I was going to tell you to shoot me,' he said in barely more than a whisper as he sat down on a stone bench and pinched his brows hard to make sense of what was happening to him, the smile still ludicrously glued to his lips.

'You what?' Diana danced around the statues and fountains, a hazy, multicoloured vision of rediscovered youth and renewed vigour.

'I wanted to know if you hated me enough to shoot me.'

'Why should I hate you? I never stopped loving you.' Diana ran towards the dodo maze, eighteen again, laughing through her tears.

'You'll never find your way through,' he warned her.

Left, right, left, left, right – straight ahead, double back at the gap, almost a full circle then left – on to the blind end, through the tiny gap. Right, left – made it!

Diana let out a whoop of victory and danced for joy.

Picking up his gun from the steps where Diana had left it, Amos followed her through the maze and watched from the last turn of the box hedge as she reached the inner garden. His smile still wouldn't budge.

Diana stopped dancing and stood at the door to the underground labyrinth, breathless and excited. 'Is this still the same? Amos? Are you there? Can we go in?'

'Try it and see,' he called out.

This was where Firebrand had shown them his home – at least, now that's whom they knew him to be. On the night of Diana's eighteenth birthday, the night they had agreed to elope, he was just a wizard.

Amos's uncle Granville had tipped them off about the garden, hinting of a small fortune hidden there. Several locals knew that the secret folly existed, although none knew of its extent. In the 1980s, rumours abounded that the last Baron Sarsden haunted it. A terrier-man for the hunt had spotted someone there when the hounds ran a fox to ground in the old bohemian's playground. He'd thought it was a ghost. Granville had suspected differently, but was too fearful to go himself.

Amos and Diana knew no such fear. It became their playground. They saw no ghosts. They got lost in the maze every time. They laughed and played and stripped and danced and made love there for months.

Then the night that they had planned to run away – the first time they had been in the garden after dark – the owner had turned up and almost shot Diana's ear from her cheek. Apologising like the gentleman he was, he had led them through the maze and shown them the secret at its heart.

Falstaff. That's what he called himself. And he threw a party in their honour. Such a party. He grew his dope hydroponically. It was magical. He made chemical hallucinogens in his underground workshop. He told them that they could live for ever, however bad they were. They believed him. They believed everything he told them at first.

They should have run away, but he told such stories and made them laugh so much. He gave them gifts, promised them riches, fuelled their love with drugs and hedonism.

They stayed. They helped him reinvent himself. Diana ignored the entreaties of her aunt Til and of Nanny Crump, the only two people to know of her happy, fugitive love-nest. But the two had kept her secret. He had a hold over them, too. He was a magical, magnificent wizard. Diana knew that while Falstaff was around, she and Amos were invincible. They didn't need to be accepted or even married. They could live for ever after in this fairy-tale place.

Diana felt beneath the top of the door-frame for the secret pull. It wasn't there.

'I've changed the locks,' Amos breathed, suddenly at her shoulder. 'That's what happens when you run away.'

She looked up at him. His smile had gone. The dark eyes blazed. He was holding out his gun to her.

Taking the twelve-bore, she slipped the safety catch with practised ease and took a step back.

'NO!' Amos yelled, but he was too late.

She blew the door open, muzzle flashing in the fog. It knocked her back on to her heels and she whooped as she saw their temple once again.

'Good shot,' he muttered dryly, struggling to recover from the moment's doubt. 'You could have just asked me for the key.'

'Did you think I was going to shoot you?' she asked breathlessly.

Amos watched the light glowing on Diana's face as she stood in the entrance to the underground world they had once shared. Then he took her hand, leading her inside.

A year of hurt melted away for every step they ran down; a heart-stopping, time-concertina staircase that stripped away two decades. By the last step, Amos was crushing her up against the wall, his lips against hers.

They kissed like the lovers they had been once before it all went horribly wrong. It was a kiss that both had held just beneath their tongues for years, refusing to swallow the bitter pill that fate had pressed there.

'This is where I saw the stallion.' Anke stood at a wooden gate. 'We can't be far away. See how the fog has lifted? He must be here.' She let out a series of clicks.

But the field was empty.

Moonlight had started to knife its way through the last of the fog, revealing a deserted, silver-tipped expanse of grass that sloped away to distant rails. Just audible beyond them came the sound of splashing and muffled laughter.

Anke and Mo crossed the field.

The rails divided the field from a huge, moon-streaked lake still partly swathed in mist.

Two riders were racing through the reedy shallows, riding bareback and naked on a huge stallion and a beautiful black mare. Close to the rails, a riderless horse stood guard. He turned his big white face to Anke and Mo and tossed his head angrily, eyes glowing in the steel of the moon, warning them away.

'Are they ghosts?' Mo whispered in awe.

Anke took her hand and led Mo away.

She found the garden straightaway, drawn instinctively to the secret gate which lay open, revealing a kaleidoscope of light. Stepping down on to the trigger stone, she let the cupid drench her as she realised the true magic in front of her eyes. It worked. It worked!

Mo stood at the gate and tried to remember how to breathe.

Anke carefully steered her past the second pressure stone that would drop the steps away, and led her down into the enchanted kaleidoscope.

Together, they jumped through the water cascades, shrieked at the illuminated red eyes that glowed from the walls as they explored the sunken garden, unaware that it was only the ante-chamber to a playpen they could never dream of, one that had just recently been enjoyed more than it had in the best part of a century.

Neither could find their way through the dodo maze to see the garden's biggest secrets. They laughed and howled as again and again it spat them out in the same place.

Breathless and sated they finally collapsed on the wall around the redhead's fountain and leaned against one another.

Mo stared at her feet. She had lost her huge shoes – she couldn't remember where. Her toenail polish was chipped and growing out. She remembered applying it in a different lifetime, the evening of the harvest supper.

'I thought I was in love with your husband,' she blurted suddenly.

To her surprise, Anke took her hand. 'I know.'

'We slept together.' Mo closed her eyes, trying to wriggle her guilty fingers away.

'I know that, too.' Anke squeezed her hand reassuringly.

'You do?'

'Yes. I think I have known that from the day I found you hoarding apples in your kitchen.'

Mo gulped. 'But you came back and brought me soup and talked to me and took care of me. You have been so kind to me. You helped me. And you knew all along?'

'Mo, I have a confession to make. I am a selfish woman. I guessed you had captivated Graham. I *needed* to help you. I needed to know what I was up against. And you are so entrancing, so delicate, so layered, I thought I would lose him to you.'

'No! He never loved me. I don't think he really even fancied me much, except as a novelty. I was the one who was all over him. It was just sex. Like a reflex action. It made me feel wanted and it made him feel like a man. We didn't talk much, but when we did it was to say how much I love Pod and how much he loves you. He loves you so much.'

'I know that now.' Anke started to shiver. 'I love him too. Only I think I've left it too late to show him.'

'No!' Mo pressed the long-fingered hand to her lips before tucking it into the warmth of her collarbone. 'You *so* haven't. You *so* bloody haven't.'

'You sound like Faith.' Anke half-laughed, trying to stop her teeth chattering.

'Can you ever forgive me?' Mo felt the fingers start to warm up against the hollow of her throat.

'Of course I can.' Anke turned to her, blue eyes wide. 'I do – I *so* do. Our friendship is one of the most unexpected and precious jewels to come out of this blackness. I know that you never tried to steal his heart. You kept it safe.' She hooked her long arm around Mo's shoulders and they sat close together, looking out at the rainbows arcing from the fountains.

'I wish I'd kept Pod's heart safe.'

'Well, you know what they say, *kaereste* – make a wish in here and it comes true.'

'In that case, you wish and you wish right now.'

'I wish my husband and I could make mad passionate love as often as possible,' Anke blurted, giggling at her own daring.

'You sound like the queen,' Mo snorted.

'The Danish queen maybe. Even our royal family talk about sex a lot. I think I must have been born to the wrong nation. I am such a prude.'

'Say some rude words in Danish.'

'*Pik – fisse – pule – kusse – bunkepul*,' Anke recited with increasing hilarity.

'What does that mean?'

'Willy, lady garden, bonk, bottom, orgy.'

'You are *definitely* going to have to start having sex in Danish.'

Together they collapsed on to the flagstones in heaps of laughter, a tiny nymph and a graceful Amazon brought alive among the garden's decadent statuary.

Much later, Anke slid into bed beside a sleeping Graham and curled around him tightly. A slothful hand reached automatically for her thigh. She covered it and clutched it there.

He jolted awake.

'Where the bloody hell have you been?'

Letting go of his hand, she reached around the warm folds of his belly and slipped her hand down to the soft velvet that had repelled her for so long.

It leaped in response – velvet stretching its smooth fibres to taut silk, warming to her touch, cleaving up towards his belly in disbelieving animation.

'I'm sorry,' he mumbled, accustomed to attaching shame to his desire.

Anke pressed a finger to his lips and, peeling back the duvet, mounted her husband with delighted abandon.

'*Eg elskar dig*,' she breathed ecstatically, truly talking dirty.

Mo lay awake alone in bed, listening to the Oddlode youth trying to scare the village with late-night Halloween catcalls, shrieks and fire-crackers. She was no longer frightened.

Her childhood had frightened her more than anything. Then Pod had frightened her because she needed him too much and he abused that. Then Graham frightened her because she wanted him to be her father, not her lover. Tonight, she was no longer frightened.

Her mobile phone rang. She looked at the illuminated screen.

RORY flashed up in capitals.

'Hi.' She rolled over and hugged the phone to her ear. No longer frightened. Fearless.

'Er . . . sorry. But you're good with kids and they scare me. My sister's done a bunk and left me with the brats. Bit of a bad night. Hally has just had a litter of puppies in the laundry cupboard. Mim and Digby are like a couple of deranged midwives. I can't them to go to bed. Any tips?'

'Sleep with a teacher.' She hung up and smiled.

It was time to go in search of paradise. Pod had already found it, after all.

She pulled on her joggers and a T-shirt, shouldered her coat and fetched her car keys. Paradise by the dashboard light, she realised dizzily. Bat out of Hell was one of Pod's favourite albums; it had been released the year he was born. Tonight, Mo would be reborn. At least she'd never have to listen to Meatloaf again.

25

It was bonfire night, but the windswept Oddlode fireworks had nothing on the village newcomers' internal combustion. Glad Tidings was having a field-day.

'What is going on *there*?' she chuntered as Rory Midwinter walked past with his arm looped around Mo, each holding the mittened hand of a sparkler-waving child. They looked like an advertising executive's dream family. 'Where is the mother, I'd like to know?'

'Mrs Dacre-Hopkinson's in the beer tent with Ingmar from the book-shop,' Phyllis told her as she tried to stop her felt hat flying off. 'I just saw them talking to Lady Belling.'

'Not Truffle – Diana.' Gladys looked around at the faces of the villagers battling through the wind as they gathered on the green.

'Fancy young Rory going out with a movie star,' Kath Lacey sighed as she watched Rory and Mo stopping to chat to Spurs and Ellen. 'They make a lovely couple. I didn't know Helena had children.'

'They're Diana Lampeter's!' Gladys snapped impatiently. 'Aren't you listening to a word I'm saying?'

But her friends were too excited at the prospect of squibs, screamers and Catherine wheels to concentrate. The bonfire night firework party was an annual village highlight and, as always the turnout was high and the weather precarious. There had rarely been a bonfire night in Oddlode without gales, storms, fog, hail or, at the very least, rain. Tonight was set for gales – the favourite forecast for local thrill-seekers.

'It's awful windy, isn't it?' Kath knotted her headscarf more tightly beneath her double chin. 'I do hope them rockets don't get blown off course.'

'Remember the year Jonah Gates set off a Roman candle too close to the box of fireworks and everything went off at once?' Phyllis chuckled.

'Oh lord, yes. We all dived for cover. A rocket went right through Mrs Fenton's window. Took Seth Wyck's cap clean off as it passed. He always said it was deliberate.'

The village firework party heralded the rare and potentially dangerous coming together of the Wycks and Gates families. Traditionally, the Gates provided the firework display while the Wycks were in charge of starting the huge bonfire, complete with its macabre selection of Guys created by each class of the primary school. This year's Guys were almost all dressed in Jacqui Gates' clothes, donated to the school jumble sale by a furious Amos, just days after she had run away with Sexton.

Jacqui had screamed when she had spotted the lumpy transvestite rebels piled high on the pyre – all dressed in her summer wardrobe.

She and Sexton were conspicuously on display this evening, now settled in a rented love nest, another reason for Glad Tidings to clutch her arms disapprovingly beneath her bosom and tell anyone who was interested that the village was full of debauchery and devilment these days.

'Perhaps we should be burning a few witches, eh Glad?' Phyllis cackled delightedly, having already laid into the cherry brandy on offer in the beer tent.

Giving her a scornful look, Gladys trundled off to help Lady B with the refreshments, passing Rory and his cousin Spurs en route.

'Evening, Gladys,' they chirruped mischievously.

She paused, sensing information at hand.

'Where is your sister tonight, Rory?'

'Oh, she's frightened of fireworks.'

'Doesn't like bangs.' Spurs nodded. 'Not that sort of bang, anyway.'

Rory snorted with laughter.

Gladys assessed them shrewdly. 'I hope wherever she is, she's a long way from young Amos.'

'Not so young any more,' Rory pondered.

'You know what they say – a rolling stone gathers no Amos.' Spurs looked at him.

'And Diana is a Honky Tonk Woman,' he agreed.

'What are you boys talking about?'

They both feigned long, baffled faces straight out of Monty Python's Upper Class Twit of the Year, barely covering their repressed laughter.

Furious at being mocked, Gladys turned away. Some gossip was too treacherous to touch. She only hoped that Granville would stay away tonight. It had been many years since he'd attended a firework party on the green, but he had been behaving oddly lately, even by his standards. If he heard that Diana and Amos were together again, the madness would truly take hold.

'Now that's a first.' Rory watched her go. 'Glad snubbing news of such magnitude.'

'I can't believe how frightened people around here are of an old wife's tale.'

'What *is* the story between Diana and this guy then?' asked Ellen.

'Depends who you hear telling it.' Rory shrugged, pulling out his hip-flask. 'I was just a kid. They ran away together – Di was missing for ages. That's all I remember. Then she reappeared, went abroad for a bit, visited sporadically to hunt a lot of horses, got a job in blood-stock and married Tim.'

'And Amos?' Mo looked up from lighting more sparklers for Digby and Mim.

'Always was a loner. Became more so. Pity the poor bitch who married him.' Rory nodded towards Jacqui who was still pointing furiously at the drag act Guys.

'Some people around here say Amos and Diana woke Firebrand's ghost.' Spurs laughed disbelievingly. 'A few still won't have anything to do with Amos because they think he's cursed. Some of the Wycks even think he *is* Firebrand.'

'Or his bastard son,' Rory nodded.

'Who *are* his parents?'

'Noah Gates and his first wife, Iris.' He helped her light Mim's stubborn sparkler. 'She was a bit of a blue-blood, in fact – ran away with one of the hunting set about ten years ago. Lives in South Africa now. Caused quite a scandal at the time, particularly as Noah moved Peggy Wyck into his house less than a fortnight later – she's Reg's dimwit sister and has about a hundred children, although she'd never been married before Noah. Of course, all the rest of the Wycks were outraged because the two families hate one another. Noah and Amos had a terrible row afterwards and haven't spoken since.'

'Noah lives in the old mill, yes?' Ellen checked. 'The house with all the rusty cars outside?'

Spurs nodded. 'Never comes out. Thinks that the moment he leaves the house, a property developer will break down the door and start turning it into a B and B. Even Peggy got bored after a couple of years locked inside the mill and pushed off back to the bosom of her family. Noah's almost as crackers as his brother Granville. Pity poor Amos. Madness is clearly in the family.'

'Oh, look – they're lighting the bonfire!' Ellen gasped as a crowd of Wycks let rip with flaming torches.

'Not long until the fireworks.' Rory took Mo's hand as they hugged Digby and Mim to their sides and watched the blaze take hold. The Wycks hadn't held back on the petrol this year. Soon every face on the green was glowing orange and reddening with heat.

'I got the impression the fireworks had already started,' Mo muttered, watching the sparks fly.

She looked around again for Anke, but the Brakespears were conspicuously missing.

As a gust of wind pulled a flaming branch from the top of the pyre and spirited it straight towards Horseshoe Cottages' ancient thatch, everyone gasped – and then cheered as it landed short, crashing down in a litter bin which blazed into life.

'That's not the only thing that will go up in flames tonight,' Spurs predicted.

Standing nearby, Faith watched jealously as Rory gathered Mo into a long, loving hug. His cousin Spurs was rubbing noses and laughing with new wife Ellen just a few feet away.

Turning away, she saw Pod and Dilly standing close to the bonfire, in silhouette, lips dancing together between the flames.

Even Chad, who had just walked with her to the green from Wyck Farm, had raced straight up to girlfriend Mim to give her a Chinese burn and a sloppy kiss. Faith wondered if she should complete the romantic symmetry by whisking Digby Lampeter into her arms, but decided against it. He had snot dribbling from his nose and was waving a lit sparkler rather menacingly.

She stomped to the drinks tent to steal a bottle of cherry brandy. Her grandfather was holding court as usual. For once she was grateful. He provided a mesmerising distraction for all except a cynical granddaughter he no longer remembered.

'In my shop I have Quigley's summary of the diaries of the fifth Baron Sarsden, telling of the curse,' he told an enraptured crowd. 'This talk of fire is a modern myth based on old pagan rites and rituals from the area. The thing all Sarsden men feared above all others was – Faith!'

In a sudden lucid moment, he spotted his errant teenage granddaughter trying to steal away with a bottle of Bols.

Faith improvised hastily, unscrewing the cap and offering top-ups.

'Mum says she's sorry she's late, but sent me along to help,' she told Lady Belling as she slugged red liquid into every glass she could access.

'How considerate.' Hell's Bells smiled politely, trying to work out who on earth the girl was.

Guarding the trestle drinks table Glad Tidings was livid that she had been so engrossed in Ingmar's story that she had missed the Brakespear girl making off with a bottle. She made a mental note to warn Joel at the post office stores that the teenager was light-fingered.

To her relief, she had not been the only one gripped by the story.

'What was that about the true Sarsden curse, darling?' Truffle was asking Ingmar.

But to his audience's frustration, Ingmar had already forgotten what he had been talking about. Taking Truffle's hand in his big paw, he took her to look at the bonfire, which was raining sparks everywhere in the wind.

'I love flames,' he told her as he cupped her face with his broad, sentient fingers. 'They dance like children.'

'I never danced as a child,' Truffle said matter-of-factly.

Taking her hand and cupping her waist, Ingmar started waltzing a laughing Truffle around the fire. Earlier that evening, she had been livid that her little pre-fireworks party had been shunned by every guest except Ingmar. Ironically, her forgetful admirer was the only one to remember to come. Rotten Diana had stood her up, Rory and Spurs had forgotten, and she had no idea what had happened to the usually reliable Brakespears. Now she was grateful that she'd had Ingmar all to herself. She planned to keep him all to herself for as long as possible.

'Good God, will you look at that!' she laughed as she spotted a furtive-looking couple over her shoulder.

It was her ex, Vere Peplow, holding hands with a familiar redhead as he led her hurriedly past the dancing couple, pulling the ridiculous Russian hat he wore to make him look taller low over his eyes in a hopeless attempt to avoid being recognised. His partner, who still towered over him, shot Truffle a furtive look.

'Isn't that the silly woman who runs the gallery opposite your shop?' she asked Ingmar. 'Pru something? Has incredibly unruly children?'

'My shop?' Ingmar waltzed her towards the horse chestnuts, his mind back in the dance halls where he had courted Anke's mother in the 1950s. 'What are you talking about? It is the English who are a nation of shopkeepers, not the Danes.'

'Quite right,' Truffle laughed. '"It's always a temptation to a rich and lazy nation, To puff and look important and to say" –'

'Ah! Kipling!' He laughed, recognising the quote. '"But we've proved it again and again" . . .'

'"You never get rid of the Dane."' Truffle skipped to the finish, reaching up to kiss him on the nose. 'Oh, I do hope not.'

'We will walk along in just a few minutes, *kaereste*!' Anke hustled her son and his friends out of the back door as she and Graham started to don hats, scarves and coats from the hallway pegs.

'You'll miss the fireworks, Mum,' Magnus protested. 'Let me give you guys a lift. It takes ten minutes to walk to the green.'

'We want to walk – it's a beautiful night.'

'If you say so.' Magnus turned up his collar against the howling wind. 'Don't forget to make sure the dogs are safe.'

'Yes – I will. And the horses are tucked up inside, and the cats are shut in the dining-room. Now go – shoo! Shoo!'

Listening as he and the Three Disgraces finally set off with the usual thunder of Porsche engine and whine and splutter of over-choked mopeds, Anke hastily started ripping off her outdoor layers.

'What are you doing?' Graham laughed.

'Magnus is such an old fusspot,' she giggled, taking his hand. 'I thought they'd never go. Come up to bed.'

'Are you feeling ill, love?'

'I just want to quickly – do it.' Despite trying hard, Anke had not yet managed to master talking dirty.

'Do what?' Graham had visions of some forgotten DIY project.

'Sex. I want to do sex, *kaereste*. Now hurry up, before the children come back to check where we are.'

'Bloody hell!'

Still wearing one glove, a scarf and a woolly hat between them, they raced upstairs.

Deep within the Gunning woods, in Amos's farmhouse, two bodies were lit by flames. A log fire burned in the grate and fat church candles flickered on the mantels and window-sills, dripping wax from curling lips.

The mattress on the bed had long since lost its duvet and pillows. The fitted sheet was twisted and creased, two of its corners losing their grip on the plump rectangle and trapping an ankle and a wrist as the bed's occupants thrashed and snaked together – pinning down, rolling over, wrestling under and wriggling between their sweaty cotton bondage.

Amos and Diana made angry, noisy, self-indulgent love. Theirs was a tenuous intimacy, born of a love that both had believed so dead neither could trust its rebirth.

They hadn't slept all week. They hadn't slept together all week. Yet they had made love every night.

To Diana's frustration, she still couldn't get Amos to talk to her. She couldn't get him to agree with her. She couldn't get him to open up to her. She couldn't even get him to admit a single moment that they had ever shared together. All she could get him to do was take his clothes off, which he did willingly.

Now she no longer cared to talk. Words said little compared to this. This was souls talking.

Her first love was bedding her with more passion than an anthology of the best orgasms she had ever experienced in the years since they had parted – shared or singular. He just had to touch her for her skin to fizz, her muscles to leap beneath, her sinews to tighten as they pressed her bones around him like an exquisite cage, melding bodies in a tightly bound combustion of heat and anger.

And they were angry. They were both wildly angry. It made for mind-blowing sex. Not because they didn't care about bumps or bruises, about screams or pinches, about selfishly and greedily demanding their own pleasure. Not because they could force one another to the edges of pain and the limits of humiliation. Nor even because they were bitterly, hurriedly, making up for so many years of lost love. What made the sex mind-blowing were those rare moments of intimacy and tenderness to which neither admitted. The lips tracing the ear as the hand pinched the arm; the cheek pressed to heartbeat as the teeth bit into flesh: the fingers entwined as the thrusts became so deep and hard and furious that both yelled in wrath.

Tonight they crossed another boundary, daring one another on. Slippery with baby oil and shaking with anticipation, Diana spread her chest low and arched back at Amos, insisting that he go there. At first he resisted, bending down to grip a soft pellet of buttock between his teeth, fighting temptation.

'Why not?' she demanded.

'He's riding us.'

'Who?'

'You know.'

'He's dead. We're alive. We're here.'

'We're waking him.'

'Kiss my butt and see if he appears.'

Amos did as he was told as the candles kept up their steady, fragile glimmer. When the only thing to burst into flames was his craving, he gripped her hips in his hands, leaned back on his haunches, dug his nails deep into soft flesh and accessed the forbidden zone with an outraged lunge.

Diana tensed, yelped, and thought she would faint with guilt and pain.

'Tell me it hurts,' he ordered.

She said nothing, gritting her teeth and refusing to let the tears slide. And then suddenly that rare gentleness stopped him short as he withdrew from hilt to tip and lowered his forehead into the small of her back, not quite touching her, only his beads of perspiration touching the drops of sweat sliding along her backbone. She could feel his warm breath on her spine – beyond a kiss.

With incredible, tender care, he felt his way back in. As he did so, he breathed a whisper in a dialect only they understood – a language of savage gentleness that they had shared so many years ago and that they had both thought lost in translation. 'My huntress. My one huntress. Eating my heart.'

She gasped with amazed joy as the feeling was so far from pain as to be sweet, ecstatic bliss. It was like nothing she had ever felt before.

'I love you,' she gasped.

'Don't *ever* say that,' he hissed and then climaxed with a forlorn groan. He was out of her and off the bed in an instant. 'Get out.'

Diana pressed her face to the raw mattress where the fitted sheet had sprung away. He still hated her. They could make love all night, but they made hate immediately afterwards.

'Get out,' he repeated.

She turned to look at him, already buckling the belt on his jeans, his face in shadow.

'If you've got that gun handy, I'll shoot you now. After all, that's what you think I'm capable of, isn't it? Just like you.'

The whites of his eyes flashed in the gloom, his voice steely and seething. 'I've never shot a man.'

'Neither have I, but sometimes I wish I had.'

He left the room, slamming the door.

She waited, holding her breath, hearing him banging doors and rattling drawers. Was he looking for cartridges?

The house fell silent. For a terrifying moment, she expected him to reappear with his gun.

But as she lay frozen in the light of guttering candles and a dying fire, she realised he wasn't taking her up on her threat.

She rolled on to her back and covered her face with the crook of her arm, moaning.

They were destroying each other. Yet it was such exquisite destruction. She couldn't bear to think that it could be over because she had dared to give voice to his suspicions.

Reality bit hard. She felt cold and dirty. Her arse hurt. Her temples pounded. Her heart hurt. Her heart really hurt. It was trying to claw its way out.

Teeth chattering, she dressed hurriedly and raced to let herself out of the farmhouse. The front door was double-locked.

Whimpering, she headed through the house towards the back door.

He was sitting in darkness at the kitchen table, a bottle of whisky in front of him. Two shot glasses sat beside it, one half full. He filled the other.

'Sit down.'

'You want to talk?' she asked through chattering teeth.

'No. I want to drink.'

She looked at the shot glasses, wondering for a moment if they were some sort of bizarre silent prompt. 'I didn't mean it about shooting you.'

'You shot me down years ago.' He drained his glass and refilled it as she took her chair. 'Now shut up.'

'We have to talk about it sometime,' she whispered, sick with dread.

But he didn't say another word as they drained a brace of shots.

'Is this a double-barrelled drink?' she joked nervously.

He refilled the glasses and pushed one across the table to her.

His hands shook, his temples pumped with blood vessels like leaf venation, his dark eyes flashed crescents of white through the darkness and his breath was quick and heavy in the shadows. But he said nothing.

Diana let the whisky warm her blood but not her heart. She knew that she couldn't stay much longer. Each night this week she had come here – uninvited but without opposition, praying for a reception that involved more than just silent, exquisite, addictive sex – flesh connecting without barriers. Alone, she was tortured by the need to share what they had been through at last. Yet when she saw him, any care for confession disappeared as their bodies argued and fought and occasionally made up with incredible compassion. There seemed no need for talk. To say anything would break the spell. The fragments that escaped their lips spoke volumes.

But tonight, in just a few words, she had already said too much. She had touched the forbidden subject.

Now they drank, and she knew she was being tested. She was not to speak another word. It was a blessed relief. As the numbing, warming, comforting false fuel coursed her bloodstream, she kept her heart and her mouth closed.

His hand found hers and gripped hard.

Still she said nothing, heart hammering despite her attempts to still it, to keep it calm and cold and incapable of being hurt again.

He let out a strange half sob.

Still she said nothing, heart bursting.

With one broad arm, he swept the scotch and the glasses and the unopened mail and the ring-marked coasters and the empty fruit bowl and the litter of receipts from the table and then up-ended it.

His mouth landed a moment before his body followed through by colliding hard against hers, tipping her off her chair and on to the flag-stones.

Diana felt no pain. She simply felt heaven inching closer as his lips slid to her ear. 'I love you, too. I love you with all my heart, huntress.'

On the Oddlode village green, as fireworks exploded all around, Pixie and Ophelia were on the warpath. Having only just returned from her parents' Shropshire farm to the bungalow behind the market gardens, Pixie was extremely jumpy about Sexton's and Jacqui's whereabouts. To have them on full parade was persecution beyond her tolerance level, especially with all the children running around.

'I need revenge!' she hissed at Pheely. 'Do something!'

Pheely was at heart a gentle soul and, given that she was seven months pregnant, she was hardly in a position to threaten physical violence. But she sensed their friendship was at stake. To her relief, she spotted the newest of those few confidantes she considered to be worth cultivating. The Brakespears had turned up fashionably late, but just in time to be useful as far as Pheely was concerned.

'Anke! Psst! Over here!'

Under a barrage of squib squeals, her ears protected from the wind by a thick fur hat, Anke failed to react – her gloved hand threaded tightly though her husband's.

'Oh, shit.' Pheely went into retreat.

'What?' asked Pixie.

'Stepford wife syndrome. Can't even *go* there.'

'Ohmygod.' Pixie pulled a face. 'I tried that with my second husband. Ghastly.'

'Ever try it with Sexton?'

'Fuck off.'

'Oh look! There's Til Constantine. She'll help us out – always has a few evil herbs in her handbag that turn people itchy or mad or what-ever.' Pheely ducked as a few stray purple comets flew past at head level.

Til had brought Nanny Crump, whom she'd parked up on the safety of the little gravel lane by Horseshoe Cottages while she discreetly smoked her pipe. Not that discretion was necessary because Nanny – having seen far too much action lately – had nodded deafly off while the strobes, bombshells and girandoles exploded colourfully overhead.

'Ophelia,' Til greeted Pheely formally.

'Need your help.' Pheely turned into a nervous schoolchild, as she always did when facing Matilda Constantine, *aka* the Witch, the Sorceress, the Old Hag or the Enchantress, as Pheely had variously nicknamed her when Til had briefly conducted an affair with her late father.

'I know.' Til gave her a wise look, not spotting Pixie lurking in the shadows beside the burned-out litter bin. 'What kept you?'

Pheely licked her lips, clutching Nanny's wheelchair handle for support.

'The thing is –'

'They should marry.' Til offered her a toke from her pipe, and then snatched it away as Pheely reached for it. 'Oh sorry – I forgot you are pregnant. As I say, they should marry.'

Behind Pheely, Pixie let out a low growl.

Pheely looked at the pipe longingly. 'You surprise me. I was rather hoping you might think otherwise.'

'Why should I? The village hasn't had a love like this since Diana and Amos, but this is so innocent.'

'*Innocent*?' Pheely gagged. 'They've crushed hearts.'

'So? They haven't killed anyone.'

'I'm *sorry*?' Pheely baulked, inadvertently pushing Nanny's chair so hard that she unlocked the brake.

Til was applying her lighter to her pipe, eyes narrowed as she peered thoughtfully into the bonfire. 'Reg and his family have done a jolly good job with that this year, don't you think?'

'We need revenge, Til.'

'Nonsense, you need to open your heart and your house to them.'

'*My* house?'

'Indeed. Offer them Oddlode Lodge. You no longer live there. Once your baby arrives, your little cottage will be full of quite another love. They need a home. It will do the old house good to have a heart again. Your father would like that.'

Pheely was speechless. For years, she had acted as guardian to her father's home – the decrepit Oddlode Lodge. She could no longer afford to live there, instead inhabiting its modest cottage. The idea of offering it to the village's notorious adulterers made her clutch tighter to the wheelchair and glare accusingly at Til's pipe. Behind her, Pixie flounced away, disenchanted.

'Look at them.' Til nodded, a rare smile lifting her creased cheeks. 'Tell me that isn't a love that will change this bitter old place?'

Pheely followed her gaze to where Pod and Dilly were lighting sparklers for one another on the bench by the duck pond.

'Oh, thank God for that! I thought you meant Sexton and Jacqui you stupid old bird.' Pheely threw her arms around Til and kissed her wrinkle-pleated cheek before she was finally fought off. 'Much as I hate to admit it, Dilly and her new chap are horrifically besotted. They've already moved into the big house. I gave them the keys last week.'

'What?'

'They moved in last weekend. Amos threw them out, telling them he couldn't cope with all that bonking in his spare room.'

Til blinked in momentary bewilderment. 'But I've passed Gunning Farm each night and I've seen . . . I've heard. Oh no. Oh, lord no . . . Someone must stop her. Oh, Diana. Please, no.' Closing her eyes, Til thought about the curse on her beloved woods and her beloved estate.

Looking up, Pheely echoed her words. 'Oh, no! NO! SOMEONE *STOP HER*!'

But they weren't talking about the same thing.

Pheely had spotted the wheelchair accelerating away towards the bonfire. As it gathered speed, Nanny awoke and let out a pitiful bleat.

Pheely gave chase. 'STOP IT!!!!' she screeched at the figure which stood between the speeding bath chair and certain doom.

As his broad arms stretched wide and plucked Nanny from her conveyance, Granville Gates let out one of his maddest roars.

'Oh hell.' Til hastily tapped out her pipe against a tree stump. 'That will have finished her off.' She marched up to him.

Amazingly, Nanny was still breathing and looking quite content in Granville's fireman's hold. Til tucked her pipe in a back pocket and prized Nanny from his reluctant grip. 'Thank you, Granville. Well done.'

The moss-green eyes darted this way and that. Overhead a rocket exploded into a burst of red tear-drops. He looked up, shrieked and dropped to the ground.

'Would you like me to fetch Gladys?' Til asked as Pheely tried to extract Nanny's wheelchair from the hot embers at the base of the fire. The seat was already aflame.

Granville snarled and backed away. 'Harlot!'

'Fair enough. Thanks for your help.' Til nodded at him brusquely, turning to carry Nanny to the closest bench.

'He gave them things that warped their minds!' he yelled after her. 'And you let him. You were his lover, weren't you? Whore!'

Ignoring him, Til marched away. Suddenly, a voice inches from her ear hissed. 'Stop right there! I want to hear this.'

It was a voice Til was powerless to refuse. A voice that had been telling her what to do with wise authority since she was a small child. Til almost dropped Nanny in shock. She longed to run, but the frail old grip on her arm made her falter.

'He drugged them!' Granville was screaming. 'He trapped them there! You couldn't see that. You were a blind fool!'

Crouching in the heat of the flames amidst potatoes in foil skins and chestnuts in wire baskets, Pheely abandoned her attempt to pluck out the wheelchair and crawled closer to Granville to listen.

'Beautiful young things they was. I watched them sometimes, God forgive me. I watched him watching them too. Known he was there for years, I had. Knew them horses were there too. Used to see you visit, telling him things. Desperate to know what was going on outside he was. I heard him shouting at you. Started riding about at night, din he? Nearly giving himself away.'

'Shut up, Granville!' Til hissed. 'You're talking nonsense.'

'Be quiet, Til,' Nanny snapped, still hanging around her neck.

'Years I watched him there.' Granville was ranting, arms flailing. 'Evil bastard. Never gave away his secret, though. Waiting for the treasure. He had treasure buried. Knew that. Then them kids turned up. They din' know anything about it, poor mites. They din' know he was there.'

The fireworks had stopped. The fire still roared and the crowd gathered on its far side still babbled cheerfully, unaware of the shocking revelations nearby, but those within earshot of Granville listened in confusion and amazement.

'He trapped them easily as he trapped them hares an' rabbits an' stuff. I even saw him catch a deer once – with his own bare hands. Jumped out at it he did, like a wild cat. Them kids din' stand a chance. Moment he saw 'em he had 'em. Played with 'em like toys. Never thought I'd see 'em alive.

'They had a party one night. All naked and dancing they was in that hell pit. Bodies painted orange and black like tigers. Acted like wild animals, too. I saw stuff I never seen. I saw stuff I knew no man should see. Them poor children. Such a pretty girl. He wanted her all to himself, din he? She should never have come back here. He's back again, you know. He's walking. Lighting fires, bigger 'n him.'

Granville turned to the huge bonfire and started to howl. It was a sound so eerie that Pheely covered her ears, looking anxiously around for Pixie. This was way too scary. She needed to hold hands with a friend.

But Pixie was happily distracted a hundred yards along the lane, stabbing her folding pruning knife into Sexton's van tyres.

She was the first to hear the hooves on the lane.

At first she assumed some poor horse had broken loose from its field, terrified by the fireworks. She saw the sparks from its shoes and folded her knife into her pocket ready to brave a human barricade to turn it back. But something far more substantial beat her to it as, behind her, there was a great whoosh of noise and a sudden yellow glow made the bonfire on the green seem like a small taper burning beneath a vast medieval torch. With a loud snort, the horse turned and galloped away.

Sipping from a plastic cup of cherry brandy in front of the bonfire, Anke was tentatively slipping her hand beneath Graham's rather tight jeans waistband when she heard the explosion behind them.

She almost lost her hand as Graham turned, let out a bellow of alarm and started to run.

'It's your father's shop! It's a fucking inferno!'

Anke took a moment to take in what he was talking about. Above the roofs of the corner cottages opposite the pub and the village stores, a blaze was ripping its way high into the air as thousands of old books and frail memories burned furiously in Cider Court.

26

Ingmar was remarkably unfazed by the fact that he had lost his home and his business. He almost seemed thankful that the loss had relieved him of the memories he could no longer hold on to and the life he could no longer lead.

To Anke's surprise, he refused to move permanently into the Wyck Farm annexe, which had supplied his accommodation since his flat had burned down.

'I have made alternative arrangements,' he announced grandly just two days after the fire.

'Don't tell me you're moving in with Truffle?'

'Of course not. The woman would drive me mad and I cannot abide small, yappy dogs.' It seemed to have escaped him that he owned a small, yappy dog in the form of Toppi, spared on the night of the fire because he had been staying at Wyck Farm, far from the noise of fireworks.

'So, where *will* you live?' Anke asked fretfully, entertaining visions of her father moving into a railway carriage beside Granville Gates and starting a mad old eccentrics' colony.

'I have secured a short-term place at Lower Oddford nursing home,' he told her. 'My name has been on the waiting list for a sheltered flat there for quite some time but, given my new circumstances, they have found me a room.'

The news came as a blow to Anke. 'You would rather live in a nursing home than with your family?'

'I shall only be there until there is an opening in the sheltered accommodation wing, where I shall have my own apartment and a warden to call upon in emergencies. It is very civilised. They won't start liquidising my food or making my bed with plastic sheets just yet. I am planning to write a novel.'

'What?'

'A novel.'

Graham found the announcement hilarious. The rest of the family were equally delighted – Magnus finally got the annexe as a studio and independent quarters; Chad got Magnus's old bedroom as a study; and Faith got her own dog at last in the form of Toppi, who was not allowed to live at the nursing home although special visiting rights were granted.

'He's probably best off there, love,' Graham reassured Anke as he watched her cooking supper that evening. 'It's what he wants.'

'How could that be better than being cared for in a family? He's being a stubborn old fool.'

Graham shook his head. 'I think maybe this is one of the wisest things he has done in years. Who knows how quickly he'll go downhill? They have a specialist unit there for when he really can't look after himself.'

Anke wanted to argue that she would look after him, that she would care for him when the time came. But looking at Graham's kind, concerned face stole her words away. There was a time when she would have seen caring for an elderly relative as not having much effect on her marriage – Morfar would just add to her collection of children: a loafish student, a sullen teenager, a primary school hooligan and a forty-something boy. But she had started to see Graham with new eyes. The boy had grown up all of a sudden without doing a thing to change. She believed what he said. And, much as it pained her, she had a feeling he was right.

Maybe even dear, noble Morfar had recognised, in his muddled way, that her marriage was enjoying a second honeymoon. He didn't want to trample on her new love affair any more than he wanted her involved in his. He was looking forward and making a fresh start with typical gusto. The past seemed to mean less to him than it did to Anke.

'He'll still only be down the road,' Graham pointed out

'I know.' She tried a brave smile.

She didn't want to think about it. She wanted to think about tonight, and the food she was cooking and the fact that she had planned this evening long before the disastrous bonfire night that preceded it. She had planned it for over a week. She wouldn't let it go wrong this time. Graham deserved it. He was looking very tired and drawn.

'Where is the old guy tonight?' he asked, trying the sauce she was stirring, pressing his solid belly against her back as he leaned across to dip a finger.

'With Truffle,' she murmured, wriggling back against him.

Mistaking this for the customary shrug-off, Graham backed away obediently and went to pour her a gin and tonic. Old habits died hard. He still hadn't got used to the new, sex-mad Anke and this evening he was too distracted to read the signs right.

'What did the police say?' she asked, covering her disappointment.

'Bloody idiots still haven't a clue,' he sighed, sliding a large tumbler of gin into the ice-making slot of the freezer door. 'They even started suggesting that prat Vere might be behind it as some sort of revenge for your father nicking his bird.' He had spent most of the afternoon at the Market Addington police station making yet another statement.

'The art dealer?' Anke dropped slivers of beef into the sauce.

He put the drink down on the surface beside her and leaned back against the rail of the gas range. 'Bloody far-fetched if you ask me, especially as he's been banging Pru Hornton for weeks. The Three Disgraces told me.'

'Ah – her "naughty liaison".' Anke suddenly laughed as she remembered her early suspicion that nervy, flame-haired Pru was having an affair with her husband. 'No wonder she wanted to know all about Morfar and his plans. She thought she was stealing Vere from under Truffle's nose.'

'You what?'

'Nothing.' She took a swig from her drink and pulled a face. 'Tonic would be nice.' She handed him her glass with a kiss.

'Good point.' He headed back to the fridge. 'Sorry – long day. The bloody police kept me talking for hours.'

'Have they found any link between this fire and the others? Surely they must?'

He shrugged. 'Well, it was certainly deliberate, although this one has all the hallmarks of a pre-calculated attack. If we do have an arsonist, they reckon he's a very clever one.'

'How so?'

'Different profile each time. Yet the targets are so close geographically they can't dismiss the connections.' He returned with her drink and settled back against the range.

'Why are they targeting us?' Anke sighed, leaning against the rail beside him and pressing the glass to her chin anxiously. 'Why do they want us out of this village so badly?'

'Hey, we don't know that, love.' He hooked an arm around her shoulders and gave her a squeeze. 'The police really *do* say that there could be no connection.'

'Or it could be a ghost, after all?' she suggested nervously, leaning into his comforting bulk.

'You've been spending far too much time with the muesli witches,' he scoffed as he went to fetch himself another beer from the fridge, leaving Anke tipping sideways with no comforting bulk to support her.

She looked at her sauce, bubbling away on the hob, and sympathised.

The blood pumping through her heart felt the same way. 'On the contrary, the mueslis have decided that I am a boring housewife.'

'They what?' He laughed and uncapped a bottle.

'They say that I have become a Stepford wife'

'Like bollocks you have. Do they know you at all?' He laughed even more, leaning against the fridge door.

She looked at him for a long time, smelling her sauce burning and feeling her heart melting. He was so accustomed to her that he could not see the changes taking place. He didn't dare hope that changes could happen for the better between them. She had trained him as well as the horses she had worked with for so long – they, too, had been relaxed, settled, obsequious, accustomed to a routine and to trying hard for her, however much their subconscious dreamed of wide open spaces. Despite possessing the power to flatten her instantly, they – like Graham – had learned to control it to please her.

Turning back to the range, she hooked up the pan's long handle and carried it to the bin, tipping the contents inside.

'What are you doing?' Graham wailed. 'That smelled delicious.'

'Cutting out the foreplay.' She threw the pan in the sink. 'I smell better, and I taste delicious too.'

'Eh?' He looked at her worriedly.

'Taste me, Graham.'

She remembered to turn off the gas burners and check that the blinds were down before walking up to him and pinning him against the fridge with the longest kiss that they had shared in a decade.

'Taste me.'

Both kept their eyes open – his wide and incredulous, hers blinking away tears of relief and passion as she felt his lips respond in wonderment and with true passion at last – on and on and on. His hands gripped her and he let out a low, joyful moan.

'You taste so good,' he growled.

As she steered him towards the kitchen table, Evig, Bomber and Toppi looked up from their sprawled tangle on the conservatory sofa in bewilderment.

Anke couldn't wait. She was clumsy with impatience and excitement, having discovered a new world of pleasures she never knew existed. Tonight she was trying something else new. The kitchen table. The idea had come to her over breakfast that morning and she'd been stealing excited glances at it ever since.

Coasters and candlesticks flew from the scrubbed oak surface as she laid her husband back upon it and started to unbutton his flies.

'The kids?' he managed to gasp between kisses.

'All out – all night.' She pulled down his jeans, pressing her lips to his warm, soft stomach and butterfly-kissing the coarse hairs there. She wouldn't get it wrong this time. This was her true seduction night. She didn't want fictional love any more – not a tender classic work of literature, nor even cheesy, girlish escapism. She didn't want Darcy, Rochester or Heathcliff. She didn't want Larch or Suffolk. She wanted Graham, her big bear of a husband. And boy, did she want him. She'd wanted him all day and the frustration was killing her.

Poking joyfully from his underpants, his erection nuzzled her throat.

Anke hadn't been planning on this, but while it was so conveniently close . . .

'Now, *kaereste*, it is time for me to taste you,' she giggled, sizing it up.

'Oh, my dear life!' Graham laughed in amazed delight as her lips slid around his cock. She'd got the bit between her teeth many times during their marriage, but this bit of action was a first.

'If you could just – ah! – not bite it?' he suggested helpfully.

'Sorry. Is this better?'

'Heaven. Oh my heaven!' Graham held his wife's blonde head in wonder as it bobbed between his legs. Throughout their years together, she'd also let a lot of Danish nonsense come out of her mouth, but she had never let Graham come in it. The feeling was paradise.

Together they fumbled and stumbled their way around the kitchen, knocking the phone from its hook, Chad's homework from the dresser, drying socks from the radiators and apples from the fruit bowl. They trod in the dogs' water bowls, they fell over a discarded pair of trainers, and almost knocked themselves out on the pan rack.

'Are you *sure* the kids aren't about to come home?' Graham asked as they lay hot and naked on the cool floor, Anke's long legs wrapped around him.

She nodded. 'They're away all night. Magnus is staying with the Sixsmiths, and Faith and Chad are at Overlodes. I'm hoping they'll make it a regular Saturday thing.'

'Oh, me too.' He smiled up at her.

'Then we can do this every week.' She kissed his left nipple and then his right, 'With nobody to –'

They both looked up in horror. Somebody was unlocking the farmhouse door.

'Let me show you around my annexe!' Ingmar ushered Truffle into the hallway, mistakenly using the wrong entrance.

'Oh God, I knew I shouldn't have given him the full set of keys.' Anke yelped, trying to roll Graham under the kitchen table.

But it was too late. Turning the corner, Truffle let out a surprised little squeal of delight.

'Please do not be alarmed, my dear,' Ingmar told his consort as he appeared over her shoulder, taking in the scene with remarkable calm. 'We Danes are very open about sex. I'm afraid it takes a little getting used to.'

'Oh, that's quite all right,' Truffle gurgled as Graham frantically tried to shroud his wife with a tea towel while covering himself up with an oven glove. 'I've been caught in much the same predicament – nineteen fifty eight, with young Zack Gates in the Manor tack room. Mummy fainted and knocked herself out on a saddle rack, and Daddy just grabbed a couple of head collars and went to fetch the horses as though nothing had happened. Hell to pay afterwards, of course. Shall we take a look at your annexe now? I think the door is on the other side of the house, darling.' She took Ingmar's hand and led him away.

'He obviously didn't know who we were.' Anke tried to reassure herself.

'Definitely not. He's having a bad day.'

'The sooner he moves out the better.' She sagged back against him and started to laugh, because it was so ludicrous and so sad at the same time.

Graham hugged her tightly, kissing her shoulder. 'Truffle might find it harder to forget, of course.'

'If she tells Diana, I'll die.'

'If she tells her what? That a middle-aged, married couple still shag like rabbits when their kids are away?'

She turned to kiss his hand, suddenly smiling. 'We have only just started to . . . do it . . . like rabbits.'

'And can we keep on "doing it"?' he asked cautiously. 'At least on Saturdays?'

She felt the oven glove lift hopefully against her thigh.

'Oh, yes please.'

As winter set in, a new warmth was heating the heart of Wyck Farm. Anke and Graham had fallen in love all over again. After ten years of marriage, a sea change had taken place – melting glaciers and icebergs, turning polar caps into sunset beaches. Graham brought out his summer shirts again, with their printed palm trees and deckchairs; Anke shed her cashmere and camel layers and started wearing shocking pink T-shirts.

The central heating was always tropically high as Anke allowed herself to thaw and Graham basked in the heat. He had always loved his wife, but it was a love that had become muted by physical rejection and guilt. Now it was allowed to be as demonstrative and loud and crowing as it wished.

Graham felt ten years younger. His energy, so long directed into being a workaholic, was entirely focused upon his home life. While Anke started studying for an OU degree in literature at last – in between kissing her husband and visiting her father, now the heartthrob of Lower Oddford nursing home – Graham began patching up the fault-lines in their hastily renovated farmhouse and pondered happily on his wife's naked body every Saturday night. He had written off Dulston's as a loss and, despite tightening finances, was determined to enjoy some time with his family at last. Not that the family was around much . . .

The children weren't sure whether to be delighted or appalled at what was going on. Having one's parents behaving like lovesick teenagers was absurd. They all beat a regular path up the hill to Springlode.

Magnus sought solace in the arms of all three Sixsmith daughters, helping with the ongoing work on the New Inn. Chad and Mim continued playing doctors and nurses in the Overlodes hayloft.

Meanwhile, Faith spied jealously on Rory and Mo whilst working at the yard, exercising the Overlodes horses and babysitting for the increasingly absent Diana. She had formed a tentative friendship with Sharon. They had a lot in common, sharing a mutual love of horses and of Rory, mixed with enmity for Diana and downright hatred of Mo. Both wore Rory's stolen jumpers for comfort and warmth. It was getting bitterly cold as, with its shortening days and dwindling light, November lost the fight to December.

While deep in its valley dugout, Wyck Farm smouldered with heat and passion beneath its newly insulated roof, hard frosts had set in outside. High on the Lodes ridge, neglected Horseshoe Farm Cottage was a draughty icebox. Diana had abandoned all her renovation projects as she spent more and more time stealing away to Gunning. The planning application notices that had been pinned to the telegraph pole at the end of the drive in autumn now flapped stiffly in their plastic covering, two rusty drawing pins lost, the damp paper with its smudged print frozen to a crisp. The unopened letters from the council granting permission for conversion of the old barn to an accommodation block still lay unopened on the hall table along with Rory's mounting bills.

'Everybody is bonking around here,' Faith complained one Saturday night as she and Sharon shared a four-pack of Smirnoff Ice whilst on regular babysitting duty, both swaddled in two of Rory's fleeces that they had stolen from the coat hooks. 'My mother and Graham, Magnus and his harem, Rory and Silly Toes, Diana and the ghost man – even Chad and Mim are flashing their privates at each other in the top bunk up there.'

It was the one night that Diana could not rely upon Mo and Rory to be around to babysit because they had made a point of going out on a romantic 'date' which Faith thought loathsome.

She had taken to staying the night on the sofa in Horseshoe Farm Cottage while Chad was having his weekly sleepover with best friend Mim. It meant she could be there to help with yard duties on Sunday mornings and ride all day. And it had the added benefit of being able to play with Hally's puppies and enjoy a good bitching session with Sharon late into the night.

'Rest assured Chad is probably better in bed than Rory,' Sharon told her as she turned a puppy upside down and tickled its pink belly.

Sharon didn't say a lot, but what she did was always sweet music to Faith.

'Is he really bad then?' She tucked a puppy to each ear for warmth and then lifted them away to hear the answer.

'Pretty diabolical. But seriously well hung. All Constantine men are.'

'How d'you know that?' Faith snorted.

'Read it somewhere.'

'You *read* it?'

Mistakenly thinking Faith was doubting her literacy, Sharon snarled: 'I can read you know. Fuck all else to do round here.'

'I know that,' Faith said quickly. 'But where does it say in a book that Constantines are well hung?'

'I dunno. It was some stupid book I read about the Sarsden curse. It has a chapter on the Constantine family.'

'And the fact they were well hung?'

'It's mentioned in passing.'

'Can I borrow it?'

'Got it from the library.'

Faith nuzzled the puppies beneath her chin, thinking about Rory's Purple Thing. It had certainly been big.

'So why d'you sleep with him if he's rubbish in bed?'

'Because he's so fit. And he's my boss.'

Faith shivered, dreaming of the day that he would be fit and bossy to her. 'Do you think he's bad at it because he drinks so much?' she asked.

'Could be.'

'Maybe when he meets the right woman he'll stop drinking?'

'Could do.'

'He drinks even more now he's with Silly Toes, doesn't he?'

'Sure does.'

'She must be even worse than him in bed,' Faith sneered and then collapsed into giggles.

Sharon's cold slab of a face, which seldom changed expression, broke into a rare smile.

They each cradled a brace of puppies in their laps and watched *International Velvet* on video, laughing mockingly at Tatum O'Neal's riding and the sight of Anthony Hopkins in jodhpurs.

'So you and Rory aren't "seeing" one another at all now?' Faith asked shyly as Tatum shared a peanut butter and jam sandwich with Christopher Plummer.

'Nope.' Sharon opened a fresh bag of crisps.

'But you reckon he's on the rebound with Silly Toes?'

'Definitely.'

They watched on in silence. Then, as Nanette Newman chopped onions, awaiting news of Tatum at the Olympics, Faith couldn't resist pursuing her favourite topic.

'Think he'll dump her eventually?'

'Absolutely.'

Faith loved their friendship. It felt very grown up. They both held their breaths delightedly as the Olympic action scenes started, inter-cutting shots of Tatum and the rest of the cast wombling about on old plods with real footage of event riders.

'Have you ever met Hugo Beauchamp?' Faith asked excitedly, refer-ring to the recent British gold medallist who was a confirmed Pony Club pin-up.

'Loads of times,' Sharon swaggered, tipping crisps into her mouth.

'Is he seriously sexy?'

'To die for.'

'Sexier than Rory?'

'Loads.'

'Maybe I'll take up eventing instead of dressage,' Faith pondered, watching Tatum fall off at a brush fence. 'The men are classier. Mum used to say dressage is for gay men and stallions, eventing for straight men and geldings.'

Sharon spat out a shower of crisps as she laughed.

'I wish I knew what had happened to Diana's stallion.' Faith sighed.

'Rio?'

'Baron Areion,' Faith gave him his proper name.

'He's just down the road.'

'Seriously?'

Sharon nodded, watching Anthony Hopkins stalking about in his jodhpurs looking tense.

'Where?'

'Gunning. In a field in the woods. Life of Riley he has there.'

'Doing nothing?' Faith was appalled.

'Oh, someone's riding him all right. Looks way too fit to be idle.'

Faith felt sick with excitement. Suddenly she was Tatum, finding the neglected stallion in a field and jumping aboard to gallop across streams and beaches – in the film it had been The Pie who had won the Grand National with Velvet Brown before being retired to stud. In Faith's mind it was Rio.

'Will you show me where he is?'

'Sometime, yeah.' Sharon nodded vaguely, opening another packet of crisps and watching Tatum trotting into the show-jumping arena with her shoulder strapped.

On her lap, the tiny fluffy grey bundle let out a plaintive whimper and Hally plodded across from her basket, hoovering up the stray crisp fragments before gently plucking up her tiny youngster by the scruff of its neck and taking it back to her basket for a drink.

Hally had given birth to four puppies on Halloween night – Spook, Spectre, Ghost and Goblin – three bitches and a dog. All looked like miniature grey sheep, with vast paws and ears. Faith secretly wished that her mother had offered her one of these instead of her grandfather's disagreeable old ankle-nipper, Toppi, who had permanently grubby whiskers and bad wind.

Heart racing, Faith took the rest of the puppies back to the basket too, and carefully slotted them in by free nipples.

'These were conceived the first day I ever saw him,' she told Sharon.

'Rory?'

'The stallion.'

Watching Tatum accepting her gold medal on the podium, Sharon smirked. She had always known Faith loved the horse more than the man. She was still a kid and was good to have on side. Mo was much more dangerous.

'Will you move in with me?' Rory asked Mo that night as they looked at one another lovingly across a candlelit table at the Duck Upstream in Oddlode, both sporting cream-tipped noses from their Irish coffees.

'I'm already practically living with you,' Mo pointed out cheerfully, trying to lick her nose.

'So make it official.' Rory licked her nose for her.

Mo had been sharing his bed in the already cramped Horseshoe Farm Cottage almost nightly for weeks and had already grown accustomed to looking after Rory and his niece and nephew while Diana played at being eighteen again. They were her ready-made family.

'When do you have to leave your cottage?' He settled back in his seat and snuffed out his shirt collar which he'd just set alight with a candle flame.

'Yesterday. 'I'm waiting for them to throw me out.'

'So there's no argument.' He signalled for the waitress and ordered champagne. 'Let's celebrate.'

'Rory, you said you'd drive, remember?'

He had only got his licence back that week, although he'd largely carried on driving cars – and driving people mad – throughout the ban.

'I thought we could go to your place – I'll help you pack everything up and move in the morning.'

Mo blinked anxiously at the candle flame, wondering if her head could cope with that. The cottage was her cocoon. Before that it had been her secret cave, where she and Pod had shared their flip sides. She had yet to find Rory's flip side. He had barely been sober since they had got together. She liked him drunk. He was a happy, carefree, attentive drunk, without self-consciousness. He danced to cheesy music, laughed a lot, let her paint his toenails and draw henna tattoos on his belly, and he made love eagerly, like a teenager, although sometimes he was so drunk that he fell asleep halfway through. He couldn't be more different from Pod the passionate control freak.

Equally, he had yet to see her flip side and she was almost certain it would frighten him off. She knew moving in with him was crazy if she couldn't even face having him stay in the cottage. They didn't know one another at all. But she had nowhere else to go and she did love being with him and his family.

'Okay, let's go to the cottage tonight,' she agreed cautiously. 'Just remember, Gladys will be watching.'

He leaned across and set light to the other side of his collar as he whispered in her ear. 'She already *is*. Look.'

Mo peered around as the champagne was uncorked with a precocious pop at their table.

Her eyes bulged as she recognised the faces at a nearby table scrutinising her discreetly in return.

'Rory, your *mother* is here!' she whispered.

'Out with Nanny Crump and the Viking.' Rory nodded, raising his glass at them and then clinking it against Mo's. 'Gladys will know all about this before we even make it over your doorstep. Guaranteed. She and Mummy are thick as thieves.'

'Aren't you going to say hello to them?' Mo whispered anxiously, certain that he must be too ashamed of her to fashion the greeting.

'God, no. Mummy's sent Diana to Coventry which means I'm somewhere near Warwick – not quite on speaking terms, but possibly available for the odd fax in an emergency. They think I'm colluding with Diana.'

'In what way?'

'The Amos thing.'

Leaving her plans for her gourmet riding holidays half-done, her children to run riot and her life on hold, Diana was almost always at the Gunning Estate with Amos. Both appeared to be in denial that they were four decades into life with children and divorces to worry about.

'Mummy is *livid*,' Rory told Mo. 'Doesn't matter that she abandoned *us* every time she fell in love. This is different. Nanny has convinced her that Sodom and Gomorrah have come to Oddlode.'

'It can't last,' Nanny Crump was telling Truffle darkly. 'The ghosts won't let Diana get away with what she did. Nor Amos. He was as much to blame.'

Admiring his glass of Shiraz, Ingmar narrowed his eyes. 'The Sarsden curse was nothing to do with fire.'

'So you keep saying,' Truffle humoured him. 'It's an ancient pagan rit –'

'Infidelity,' he interrupted. 'They were cursed with infidelity.'

'Aren't we all?' Truffle mused.

But Ingmar's eyes were ablaze as he finally remembered the legend. 'No man or woman with Sarsden blood could remain faithful, however strong the love. It killed them all off. Nothing is so destructive as betrayal. Fire has nothing on it.'

'If you say so.' Truffle crunched a petit four and shelved plans to call Vere for a catch up.

Nanny was watching Rory and Mo leave, champagne in hand. 'I think they are rather becoming together. She would make a charming little wife for him.'

'She's terribly common,' Truffle sniffed, shovelling up more petits fours. 'But I suppose she is, at least, better than Ophelia's girl. Might be acceptable for a starter marriage.'

Nanny gave her a shrewd look. 'And when are *you* planning to settle down for your *final* marriage, Tallulah?'

Choking on sweet shortbread crumbs, Truffle glared at her through streaming eyes. Nobody called her by her real name. Not even her doctor. She was appalled anyone remembered it.

Checking that Ingmar hadn't heard – but thankfully he was still waffling about infidelity – she mustered a smile for Nanny.

'I'm working on it. Shall we order digestifs? I rather fancy a flaming sambucca.'

Rory and Mo sat opposite one another, tucked in the window-seat at Number Four Horseshoe Cottages, sharing champagne and watching Bechers stalk around the frost-bitten garden. He was a hopeless hunter – leaping out of dark shadows and then frightening himself into a great puffball of nerves.

'He keeps coming back,' she told Rory. 'Pod took him to the Lodge, but he visits all the time.'

'D'you ever let him in? Feed him?'

She shook her head. 'He runs away if I open the door. I like to watch him when I'm here. I think he knows that. I guess he'll give up when I go for good. I'll miss him.'

'You still miss Pod too?'

'Of course.'

'Want him back?'

She reached for his fingers. 'I'd never let him in or feed him.'

'Would he run away if you opened the door?'

'I guess I'll never know.'

'Sure about that?'

'Sure,' she lied, frantic to stop the demons rushing in.

Rory kissed her forehead and she closed her eyes in a panic, realising that the ghosts were grabbing hold of her again, turning her over, exposing the underside of the warm, sun-soaked stone to reveal the part hidden in earth that was wriggling with black insects and worms.

But to her amazement, when Mo's flip side turned up its dark face, nothing changed. She just felt deeply content and very safe. She was perched at the edge of a familiar abyss and yet she was fearless.

She watched Rory as he pressed his cheek up against the window-pane, his breath clouding his view of the comedy attack cat.

'I'd like to fall in love with you, Mo. I think we can get there, you know?'

She nodded. She so wanted it to be true.

'So you'll really move in with me? If I let you in and feed you?'

'You'll be my family?' She felt their fingers tightening together and this time she willingly let herself slide over that familiar cliff. This time she knew she would be caught.

He gripped tightly and laughed that carefree laugh. 'Happy families!'

Holding his hand tightly, Mo swung over her cliff and felt her flip side fall away. Happy Families. A card game her grandparents had kept in their sideboard, along with Lexicon, Monopoly and Scrabble. She had played with those cards endlessly, dreamily matching up the perfect little groups. Now fate had dealt her the right hand at last.

27

Diana refused to acknowledge Christmas. The usual hysteria, decked shopping malls and television schedules on overdrive passed her by. Boxing Day was her fortieth birthday. She had no desire to be forty. It highlighted the fact that she and Amos had been apart for more than half her life. Thank goodness they had found one another again.

Gradually, painfully; they were emerging from the woods side by side. They still left their secrets hidden there, unspoken and untouched for years. They were as awkward as teenagers when they were in the open, yet they could no longer keep their lives completely separate. Their children attended the same school, their families circled the same few thousand hectares of valley, and they shared a growing dependency that drew them together time and time again.

The intimacy between them had deepened, the moments of tenderness no longer always nakedly charged with silent nostalgia and sexual excess. Neither could admit that the love they shared was fit for human consumption and yet it consumed them so wholly that they couldn't hide it any longer.

They wanted to touch all the time. And fingers secretly tracing fingers at the Oddlode primary school gates while waiting for their children to appear could be as ecstatic a moment as bodies fused feverishly by firelight. They called one another just to hear breathing, or laughter, or the background babble of a family moment they longed to share. They might not be able to talk, but they couldn't bear to be out of hearing range. And although they spoke so little, and certainly never about their past, their understanding of one another intensified and strengthened every day. They lived totally separate lives in reckless synthesis.

Pressed by Amos's solicitor, Jacqui had relented to allow him access to Maisy and Plum three days a week. Diana kept her distance, but shared his happiness. He took them to the Lodes Farm park and to the Oddford Model Railway. He took them for tea and cakes and for frosty walks along the ridge. But mostly he brought them home for comfort and for reassurance. All traces of Diana were removed. Their home was sacred.

Diana's greatest shame came from her neglect of her own children. She tried her hardest to keep her preoccupation from them and to make her nightly visits to Amos something of which they were hardly aware, yet she knew they were deeply affected. Their own father's neglect added to their unease. Tim's rare visits, always with girlfriend and with gifts falling out of his sports car as he rushed up the drive, did more harm than good. These were hyperbolic, over-excited, unexpected events that inevitably ended in tears. Diana longed for continuity.

She just couldn't keep a grip on the reins. Her life was running away with her. Such was her passion and exhilaration that she no longer cared for normality. Her happiness, at least, infected the children and made their topsy-turvy world tolerable. She hugged them, she told silly stories; she lost interest in what little discipline she had once established. Their mother might be existing on four hours' sleep a night, forgetting their packed lunches, forgetting ballet and judo lessons and forgetting Christmas – but at least she was fun to be around. When she *was* around.

Continuity could wait. Diana needed Amos. And the feeling was mutual.

The Sixsmiths had rallied everyone in the village to help the builders finish work on the New Inn so that it could open in time to host a New Year party. Amos helped out two days a week, although Diana's offer of an extra set of hands was shunned by the cliquey clan. She was still being given a cold shoulder in the village.

Normally she would have marched down to give Tony Sixsmith a piece of her mind, but knowing that Amos – perhaps for the first time in his life – was willing to down tools and leave a job half done in order to meet her was satisfying enough to curb Diana's tongue.

He came to the cottage during his coffee break, his lunch break and his tea break. He warmed her cold shoulders with his lips while she found places where her extra set of hands could make tools go up, down and all around.

The pub lost a labourer again and again, the farm cottage remained cold and unrenovated, but Diana and Amos had scaffolding on their hearts and were starting to rebuild their foundations. They were discovering foundations that were stronger and deeper than either of them could have dreamed.

Like two archaeologists excavating an ancient Roman villa, they had not only unearthed the erotic mosaic they knew was lying beneath the surface – they had found a house and a home and a fortress complete with underground heating system and bath houses. They had found a way of living that made them want to keep on digging for ever.

The only thing they both wished with equal passion was that the past could stay buried.

Aunt Til refused to allow this.

She waited for Diana on the track that led to Amos's farmhouse, determined to right wrongs.

Dressed in an ancient fox fur coat, a flat cap laced with fishing flies and a college scarf dating back fifty years, she was an alarming sight on a hail-swept night as she waved her arms in front of the Audi headlights, sheepskin gloves slamming on to the bonnet as the car stopped.

'Just what the hell do you think you're playing at?' she demanded as she opened the passenger door to the heated fug and settled herself in the seat, scattering hailstones everywhere. 'Hasn't that poor idiot suffered enough?'

'He's not an idiot!' Diana raged, turning off The Archers.

'Good start,' Til muttered sarcastically, pulling the door shut so that she could light her pipe. 'Go on . . .'

The sweet smell of that hydroponic Gunning dope almost wiped Diana out. She scrabbled at the dashboard, buzzing down all the windows and opening the sunroof, mindless of the hail.

'I have to see him, Til. You can't stop me seeing him.'

'Of course I can't.' Til settled back in the seat, her melting coat starting to give off the faint reek of fox and hanging game as the Audi heaters fought to combat the open windows. 'I can simply remind you that what you both did killed this place for ever.'

'It's not dead. It's alive and beautiful.'

'The line is dead.'

Diana chewed her lips, refusing to let her aunt blow open the vault she and Amos had kept closed. 'Maybe this estate should be sold. It needs new blood.'

'It can't be sold.'

'How do you know? The trustees hold all the deeds.'

'The trustees hold nothing but an old lease that ends this year. If they think they can sell, they are fools. It belongs to the line.'

'The dead line?'

Til glared out of the windscreen as the wipers swept great mounds of hailstones around.

Diana watched them too, her voice as cold as the tiny fragments of ice. 'You don't know what happened in the garden. You just knew we were there and reported back to Nanny.'

'I told you to get out. I warned you.'

'We were half-crazed with all the things he made us take.'

Til puffed on her pipe. 'Been taking it most of my life. Never made me indulge in a naked threesome painted like a tiger, but maybe I'm too self-controlled. Never killed anybody either.'

Diana yelped as a long-buried memory was triggered, as painful as a hot brand on her side. The orange and black paint. The music. The spinning, spinning room that turned from damp, leaking cave into a rain forest.

'He gave us other things,' she groaned as she remembered the acid – the pictures it had painted, the confusion it had brought.

'Oh, I know.' Til located a half-eaten bag of Minstrels that one of the children had left in the door caddy and popped one in her mouth. 'He gave you pretty things to play with, didn't he? Jewels and ornaments from the old Hall, dresses from the attics, and wines from the cellars. And, of course, he promised you Areion. The eternal horse.'

'*You* gave me Areion,' Diana reminded her. 'I never wanted him. The past was behind me then!'

'It was his wish.'

'He's yours now.'

'I hold him in trust. I hold everything in trust, apart from you, Diana. You, I can never trust.' She threw a chocolate out of the window for Ratbag.

'I love Amos!' Diana screamed in despair. 'Whatever happened doesn't matter any more, don't you see? We love each other. We deserve to be together. Our hearts have always stayed together.'

'Oh, spare me.'

As Ratbag yapped furiously outside, Diana fought to justify herself. She argued and screamed and lectured and pleaded on deaf ears. 'I have never stopped loving Amos!'

At last she was spent, her throat raw, no longer able to repeat the mantra with more than a hoarse croak. 'I love Amos.'

'You don't know the meaning of the word,' Til hissed.

The wind had turned, driving the hail straight into the car and straight on to Diana. As it spat on her cheeks from the side and stung her eyes from above, she felt fresh fire stoking her belly, burning it away.

'And you do?' she sneered. 'You call half a century of furtive gropes with Reg Wyck in the potting shed "love"?'

Til sucked in her cheeks. It made her look curiously beautiful, an echo of the young woman who, as little more than a child, had taken to rural seclusion forsaking lovers and family life for rustic eccentricity. 'Don't be such a fool. I've never loved Reg. We have an understanding.'

'So *you've* never been in love.'

'I didn't say that. I have been in love. Very deeply in love.'

'With whom?' Diana thought about Til's brief engagement to Rory's father and dismissed it. Local rumour always had it that she had only ever agreed to marry Midwinter in order to secure his best mare as an engagement token.

'Isn't it obvious?'

Diana looked at her. Til was handsome and brave and rather sexless and, up until tonight, she had thought her somewhat splendid for it. She was frightening and indomitable and furiously independent, true. Weirdly attached to Reg Wyck, true. Yet Til had always struck her as far keener on fauna than fornication, and on horse husbandry than her own. Tonight she was weirder than usual, but no less quarrelsome and truculent. That was just her way. She had been one of the very few to know about the Pleasure Garden and its secret occupant, after all.

Then it struck home, after all these years, the astonishing truth.

Diana gasped, her feet feeling as though they were slipping beneath her on planes of hot lava. 'F-f-firebrand?'

'I called him Falstaff.'

'You were lovers with Fire–' Diana's head span. She pressed her palm to her temple. 'You were lovers?'

'I loved him,' Til said carefully.

'Oh, Christ!'

Til rubbed the tip of her pipe beneath her eye, discreetly flicking away a rare tear. 'You never knew. You selfish bitch. You never even knew.'

Meanwhile, tears were pumping from Diana's eyes as though a fire hydrant had been kicked in her head. 'I couldn't know. How could I know? We hardly even knew we were here.'

'You've found your way back well enough.'

Diana sobbed. 'I had to. I love him, I love him, I love him.'

'I loved Falstaff.' Til tapped her pipe out of the window and tucked it in her pocket. 'Falstaff. Firebrand. William.' The catch in her voice stopped her short and she took a sharp breath. 'My sweet William. The man you killed for his money.'

'But I didn't –'

'Didn't get a penny of it. Of course you didn't, despite his promises.'

'No! No, Til – I mean I didn't kill him. You must believe me.'

'Tell that to the ghosts,' Til spat, turning to clamber out of the car. 'The fires won't stop burning until you tell the truth about what you did.' She vanished with a slam of the door that rocked the car.

'Til!' Diana wrenched open her own door and rushed out into the driving hail. 'Til – I didn't kill him! I don't know who killed him and Amos won't talk about it and doesn't want to –'

But she was screaming into hail-hammered blackness. Til had long gone, a discarded Minstrel packet fluttering in the car headlights.

Diana drove the last mile through the Gunning woods like a lunatic, screeching to a halt outside Amos's farmhouse, where the windows glowed a warm welcome.

He was waiting on the doorstep, dogs at his feet, his huge coat collar turned up against the hail.

'My aunt knows!' she wept desperately. 'She knows about Firebrand and the time in the woods. She knows how he died.'

Amos held her tightly his great chest pounding, breathing life and courage into her. It was minutes before he spoke, the hail lashing down on them like gunshot.

'I forgive you. May God help me, Diana, I forgive you.'

Diana sobbed. 'You really forgive me for leaving you there?'

'I forgive you for killing him.'

She wrenched free. 'You killed him, Amos! I heard the shots.'

He shook his head.

'You must have!'

Suddenly Amos was ready to talk. He talked fast and he talked without looking at her. What he said turned her life upside down.

'Diana, I was in chains. He'd fucking chained me up. God knows what he'd given you that past week, but you were so high – so out of it. You didn't know whether you were coming or going. He took you away. Promised you everything. I was trapped there, knowing he wanted you to himself. I couldn't do anything. It almost crucified me. I thought he'd leave me there to die, that I'd never see you again. I heard the shots, but no one came.

'I waited hours. I thought you were dead. I thought he was dead. I didn't know what to fucking think. Til found me – I was pretty out of it by then. I don't know how long I'd been there. She's looked after me since. Kept me together. She was the one who told me you'd gone abroad. I came to try to find you, but kept getting sent away.

'And it was Til who told me to stop in the end. Saw it was killing me. She got me the job on the estate here. Made me stop running, stop grieving, stop trying to understand why you killed him and then didn't come back for me.'

Diana pressed her sleeves to her head, shielding herself from the hail and the horror. 'I didn't kill him!'

Silhouetted above her in his doorway, taller than a spire and holier than thou, Amos hugged his arms around himself. 'I was in chains and you didn't come back for me! You killed us both that day, Diana.'

She started to turn on the spot, disoriented and bewildered, almost as confused as she had been that awful day. 'Oh God, oh God, I didn't know! I don't know anything any more! I don't trust my own mind. You already said it – I was out of my head. I don't trust anything any more.'

'You didn't come back for me!'

'I'm here now!' she howled into the hail,

'Twenty years too fucking late!' He crashed his great fists against the door-frames. ''Til was right all along. You should never have come back, and I should never have let you anywhere near me. You wrecked my life once and now here you are, wrecking it again – my marriage, my friendships, my sanity. Go away, Diana. Go to hell – and this time I mean it!' The door slammed shut.

Diana slumped at the foot of a tree, staring up at the blackened windows of the farmhouse, drawing on her reserves as she prepared to put up the fight of her life. She would not go. She would not run away this time. He'd have to kill her this time. She wiped tears and hail furiously from her eyes.

But as she stood up, a hand slipped stealthily around her throat and held a knife there.

The voice in her ear was rasping, hot-breathed and foul-smelling.

'Leave him alone until you make peace with the ghosts.'

Even as she swallowed dry-tongued terror, she felt the sharpness of the blade snag against her skin.

'I don't know how.'

'You'll know soon enough. Tonight, you go home and you leave him alone.'

The blade moved to her back, slicing through her coat and shirt and pointing its tip against the bare knuckles of her spine. Marched to her car, Diana was driving before she was breathing. She didn't dare look back. Every hailstone bouncing from her windscreen made her jump as she slalomed and skidded away from Gunning.

Folding his trusty gutting knife back into its handle and pocketing it, Granville Gates suddenly realised that he was alone in the haunted woods after dark and let out a small, maddened squeak. Tonight, he was certain the ghosts were out. He might have seen off their tormentor, but they were still prowling the forest avenues in search of revenge.

He hammered on the door of his nephew Amos's farmhouse but,

although the dogs inside barked like the hounds of hell, nobody answered. Amos must have thought he was Diana. Granville shouted, but there was still no answer. Letting out another warbling bleat, he rushed to hide in the woodshed.

28

'*Gaedelig Jul og godt nyter!*'

How Anke ended up hosting quite such a large Christmas supper would remain legend in the family for years to come.

Traditionally, the Brakespears held two Christmas celebrations – a small family gathering late on Christmas Eve that Anke kept as tight-knit and Danish as possible, and then the British Christmas lunch on the day itself, a time of excess and indulgence, to which stray friends were always invited.

Yet this year it was their private Christmas Eve party which was invaded.

She had invited Ingmar – of course she had. But, alas, he had forgotten that the evening was always intimate. He had invited Truffle and – even more alarmingly – Nanny Crump. Taking it to be open house, Truffle had invited Rory and Mo, plus Diana and her children, much to Chad's delight as he and Mim heralded in the big day with endless X-box games. Most unexpected of all, Faith had invited Sharon. Only Magnus had reversed the trend by uninviting himself and spending Christmas Eve with the Sixsmith girls and his band members, whooping it up at the Lodes Inn. Anke had at first wailed at her elder son for deserting her, but was now secretly relieved that at least one gargantuan appetite would be feasting elsewhere that night.

Having planned duck for six, she was facing the prospect of having to creep out to the village green to snag extras from the pond when another unexpected guest came to the rescue.

It was Diana who answered the door, praying it was Amos.

'Gatecrasher!' she announced, ushering Til into the kitchen and making straight for the sherry, looking jumpy.

'I'm not staying.' Til gave her niece an arch look before offering Anke a brace of duck. 'Wild mallards – fabulously gamey. I take it you're cooking Barbary?'

Anke nodded in amazement.

'These will go with them a treat.' She shuffled up to her and said in an undertone, 'Sorry my mob has descended.'

'This is really terribly kind of you. Would you like a drink? We have Danish *glogg* – a sort of mulled wine,' Anke offered.

Til was typically gruff. 'No – thanks awfully. On my way to see a friend. Always meet up on Christmas Eve.'

'Give Reg my love,' Diana said under her breath.

Shooting her another stern look, Til marched back outside to her car to fetch a big bag of gifts, which she dumped on the table. 'Hope you don't mind me using you as a chimney – I'd save these for tomorrow, but I'm not going to the Manor this year.'

'You are not spending Christmas Day with your family?' Anke asked, studying the ducks and wondering how on earth one plucked and gutted such objects.

Til pulled her flat cap lower over her brow and rapped her knuckles on the table edge, making Diana spill sherry. 'Not this year. Looks like my last at Gunning. Thought I'd spend it there.'

Anke wiped her hands on a tea towel. 'The Estate has really been sold, they say?'

'Pheely told you, no doubt.' Til tutted. 'Such an indiscreet girl. The father of her unborn child is one of the trustees – and equally indiscreet. That poor baby will be born screaming secrets.'

Anke blushed furiously, knowing full well who the father was thanks to the Three Disgraces. 'Has someone really bought Gunning in its entirety?' Graham had told her that old estates of that size were inevitably broken up for sale because they cost too much to run.

'I believe it has a new owner.' Til looked surprisingly sanguine, helping herself to grapes from the fruit bowl. 'As do many things this year.'

Diana lingered, ears flapping but, to her frustration, Til changed the subject to the best method of plucking a duck in a hurry.

Afraid she might be roped in, Diana grabbed the sherry bottle and wandered out through the conservatory and into the garden – not noticing the relieved gasps behind her as Anke and Til changed the subject back to more pressing matters.

Diana needed some air. She couldn't stay in the same room as Til after what had been said between them. It had wrecked any chance of happiness with Amos.

Wrapping her long, heavy mohair cardigan tightly around herself she searched for the stars and saw nothing but heavy frozen fog. No wishes would be granted tonight.

Yet it was the best Christmas Eve weather the Lodes valley could come up with, short of dusting its curves and hollows with snow. Frost-whitened and misty, like a dessert dusted with icing sugar hidden under a mesh cloche, it was a magical night, all ready for Santa to swoop secretly through the air.

She double-tied her scarf around her throat and set off along the drive, pausing to look in at the sitting-room windows where the unlikely revellers were drinking *glogg*, munching on rich vanilla butter biscuits and listening to Graham's music choice – The Best Christmas Anthems Ever Five, which had been preceded by One, Two and Four (Diana wondered what the problem with Three was). A classic rock version of the Wassail Carol was belting from the speakers and rattling the windows.

Digby was sitting on Rory's lap, looking almost angelic as he watched his uncle and Mo chasing kisses around the rims of their glasses in a lover's toast.

Graham was watching them, too, a tanned and shaved modern Father Christmas whose wide cheeks creased with an indulgent smile that no longer bore a lascivious twinkle.

Faith and Sharon – a meeting of true minds, as far as Diana was concerned – were muttering between themselves as usual.

Nanny was holding court between Ingmar and Truffle, still frantically knitting her Christmas gift to Ellen of a fluffy lilac cardigan with dangly bobbles. Lucky Ellen tomorrow, Diana thought smugly. Sometimes she was grateful that because she was such an unpopular member of the family she usually only received bath salts. The Constantines and their descendants were famously mean with presents. One Christmas, Truffle hadn't spoken to any of the family until Easter because all she'd received was a gift voucher from a fishing tackle shop that, it transpired, had gone out of business three years earlier.

A big bank of sprawling dogs in front of the fire looked up at the window curiously as Diana lingered. Evig let out a warning bark.

She moved away from the light and hugged her mohair tighter to her torso as she crunched along the drive, peering up at the powdered mist sky.

Sherry ran through her veins, muddying her head, making her maudlin.

Amos had to make contact tonight. They had made their pact on Christmas Eve, agreeing to run away together. It was the night he had told her he loved her more than life. Over half her lifetime ago. So much of that life apart. She'd been certain this would be the night he'd break the ultimate silence. She stumbled on, stifled by the cold and mist.

'Where are you, Amos?'

Disoriented by the darkness, she brushed against an old rose bush, snagging her face.

'Ouch!'

She felt beads of blood eking out just below her cheek-bone.

Without warning, a tear splashed down to rinse them away.

The Classic Rock Christmas album was truly getting into its swing from the house, as Diana heard *Ave Maria* thumping its way from the windows to a discreet bass beat.

She mopped her face and sagged against one of the Wyck Farm gateposts, looking out at the lane. 'Amos, where the hell are you?'

From the opposite gatepost, a match briefly lit up a wizened face as it was held against the last taper of a rolled cigarette.

Diana held her breath.

The thin cigarette end glowed in the darkness. 'He ain't coming tonight.'

'How do you know?'

Granville Gates spat out a thread of tobacco and rubbed his lips with his knuckles.

'Ghosts are out.'

Diana snorted, hugging the sherry bottle to her chest. 'There are no ghosts.'

'Haunted me ever since you went.'

'That's your problem.'

'Always was an impudent little cow, wasn't you?'

'Yup.' Diana swigged a gulp of sherry and, gripped by sudden Christmas spirit, offered the bottle to him.

Pulling a thick sheepskin glove from his hand to reveal frayed and fingerless mittens, Granville took it and wiped the rim before draining a full three inches.

'I always liked you, mind. You're as mad as me.'

'Thanks,' she laughed.

He handed back the bottle. 'Been waiting a long time for you to come home. Make things right.'

'I don't think I can really manage that, Granville.'

'Oh, you can, girl. Only you can.'

'How?'

'Race the bastards.'

'I'm sorry?'

'Race the ghosts. In the moonlit point.'

Diana hugged herself tighter, teeth chattering with both cold and the beginnings of hysterical giggles as she imagined herself in the starting-gates with a fire-smelting horseman and a few headless cavaliers.

'Race him, Miss Constantine.' Dropping his cigarette end into the sherry bottle and handing it to her, he started shuffling away.

'I've never been a Constantine!' she snapped.

'You've never admitted it,' he muttered over his shoulder. 'Just like you never admitted what happened with that old bastard in the woods. None of us brave enough to admit that. Not even Amos. You must leave that boy alone until you face the ghosts, girl. Only a Constantine can face them ghosts . . .' His voice was retreating into the mist, babbling insanely.

Suddenly Diana realised who had held a knife to her throat in Gunning woods. It hadn't been Firebrand's ghost or Aunt Til or Amos himself, or any number of suspects that had haunted her dreams ever since. It had just been mad Granville, incapable of cutting off a corn, let alone cutting her jugular.

'Where is Amos, Granville?' she called as he slipped away.

But he just waved an arm and disappeared into the bushes.

She slammed the bottle down beside her and reached for her mobile.

'I'm sorry. We cannot connect your call. The mobile telephone that you are calling may be switched off. Please try again later.'

Diana clutched the phone to her cheek and then jerked her head away as she realised she was bleeding on the keypad.

'Race the ghosts,' she mocked in a bad Cotswold accent.

News of the Gunning Estate's sale had broken that morning. She had heard about it quite by accident when hacking Ensign past the New Inn. The Sixsmiths and their builders were still on site, wearing novelty Santa hats as they dashed around trying to finish the rebuild for their party in a week's time.

Sperry had rushed out as Diana passed, bursting with the latest.

'Is Amos okay about the sale? We were expecting him today.'

Thanks to Ensign taking exception to Sperry's flashing red hat, Diana had been saved giving herself away with a shocked expression as the old horse span around.

'Everyone's certain it's a Hollywood star. My bet's on Johnny Depp and his skinny French bird,' Sperry had gone on. 'Heat magazine said that they were house-hunting round here. Wouldn't fancy living in that creepy old house myself. I hope they keep Amos on to manage the woods. He knows them better than anyone. Will your aunt have to leave?'

'It's early days,' Diana had said vaguely. 'We're all very hopeful.' With which she had trotted away, pulling her mobile from her pocket. The well-spoken voice had told her then, as now, that the telephone she was trying to contact was switched off. Trust Amos not to have voice mail.

He was a male who used his voice very little except when groaning in ecstasy or telling her to go to hell.

Sherry swilling happily through her system, Diana smiled as she thought about Amos. She couldn't help herself. However bad things got, however much fate threw at them, she just smiled at the image of his face. Her love.

He could live with her once the new owners took over Gunning, she had decided. It didn't matter that the cottage was already bursting at the seams and that the village disapproved of them. They would find a way. He wouldn't want to work for a Hollywood star or an hotelier or Arab sheik or whoever else was rumoured to have parted with millions to buy the Estate, its ghosts, its legends and its derelict house.

She'd talk him round. As soon as she figured out what to say, she'd talk him round. She hadn't abandoned him that day in the woods. They had both been abandoned. She had only run because . . .

She went to take another bolstering swig from her bottle and gagged as Granville Gates's cigarette butt touched her lips. Retching, she spat and spluttered into the verge, rubbing her mouth furiously with her sleeve.

She knew she was kidding herself. She knew that Amos would no more live with her than he would hold her hand in public. She had run away. He hadn't even tried to contact her tonight. He had told her to go to hell.

She slumped down against the gatepost, mopping the chilled blood from her cheek.

Til's headlights picked her out five minutes later, head still in her hands.

'Buck up.' Her aunt wound down the window. 'Been looking for you. Combined birthday and Christmas present.' She handed her a fat A4 envelope from the window. 'Sorry – know you loathe them.'

Diana's chattering teeth stopped her attempts to joke that Tim had beaten her to it with the Decree Absolute which had arrived on the doormat the same day as a Christmas card written by his girlfriend, spelling Mim's name wrong and explaining that the children's Christmas presents would be waiting for them in the Somerset cottage at New Year.

She looked up at her aunt, hollow-eyed.

'Aren't you going to thank me?'

'For accusing me of murdering Firebrand?'

Til's creased eyes darted away. 'I think perhaps he loved you.'

'Oh, Christ, please no.' She sunk her head in her hands again.

'Hear me out.' Til pulled up her handbrake and leaned from the window. 'He had hated his life for a long time. He was wretched from years of hiding, from so little contact with the outside world. His first wife's death haunted him – he killed her, you know. Silly fool. A judge and jury would have sentenced him to less solitary confinement had they ever had the chance to try him.'

Elbow on the sill, chin resting on it, Til might have been passing the time of day with a neighbouring farmer in any local gateway, her cut-glass, matter-of-fact voice slicing through the cold air. Diana gaped up at her.

'I loved him desperately, of course – but it was never going to happen. We once thought . . . well, it was all rather ghastly and we remained very close. I visited him as often as I could. He had his horses and his drugs and his dying garden, but he became more and more unhappy – almost gave himself away endless times. Then you came along and – lit up his life. Pure and simple.'

'It was neither pure nor simple.'

'Agreed, all very turgid after those first happy weeks. He could see that too, I'm sure. Which is why I now think he would have been grateful for the dispatch. You had brought joy back into his life – however fleetingly – and then you brought blessed relief. He couldn't have wished to meet a prettier maker.'

'I didn't kill him.' She could feel the sherry bubbling up in her throat as the first retching gags forecast a serious stomach emptying.

'Prove it.'

With furious effort Diana swallowed down the rising bike so that she could speak. 'I can't. I can't prove it.'

'In that case, my dear, only the ghosts will haunt you.' Til shook her head with seasonal serenity in the face of such denial. 'You have nothing to fear from me, although Nanny is *very* disapproving. I think Amos may even understand why you did it one day, too.'

'Do you know where he is?'

'No idea,' she lied. 'Not at Gunning Farm, I know that. Place was all locked up when I passed – left him a bottle of his favourite tipple on the doorstep. And don't you forget to open your pressy tomorrow. Merry Christmas!' Crunching the gears and hooting the horn, she reached across to open the passenger door.

A moment later, Reg Wyck reeled out of the bus shelter along the lane and leaped in beside her.

'Prove us all wrong, Diana!' Til called as she drove away. 'Prove us all wrong!'

Diana stared blearily at the soft glow of rear-lights retreating through the fog, too upset to wonder why Til was towing a horse trailer.

'Oh bugger,' she groaned and threw up beside the Wyck Farm gatepost.

Afterwards, she spotted the envelope on the grass. Til's 'gift'. She had missed throwing up on it by inches.

Rolling the stiff envelope with some effort and tucking it into her jeans pocket, Diana wondered at the curious little routines of annual normality that accompanied each Christmas, however traumatised. Every year for as long as she could remember, Til had given Diana a combined birthday and Christmas gift of a twelve-month subscription to a worthy charity. From fostering one-eyed donkeys to sponsoring starving Africans, she had always said that it was the only way Diana would ever earn favour in heaven.

'She's probably right.' Diana hauled herself up, knowing she must rejoin the throng.

Anke was standing back in awe as Sharon plucked the ducks, one after the other, with deft skill.

'Did you grow up on a farm?'

'Council house in Orchard Close,' Sharon told her, prodding the naked carcass. 'I'll gut and truss in a minute. It's well hung.'

Chopping cabbage at the kitchen island, Faith got the giggles.

Anke did not entirely approve of the friendship, but she was grateful that it made Faith so chirpy. She just hoped Faith didn't start trying to look like Sharon as she did the other girls she idolised.

'You always have duck in Denmark, yeah?' Sharon was asking. Several *gloggs* had loosened her up and her tombstone face was high with colour.

'Or roast pork.' Anke nodded. 'It's a midnight feast. We have a special rice pudding with a lucky almond in it.' She drew a bowl of unappetising-looking gunk from the fridge and waved it at her guest. 'It's basically leftovers from last night.'

'Great.' Sharon selected a knife from the block and expertly beheaded the first duck.

'I hide the lucky almond in it,' Anke explained. 'Whoever finds it will be granted a wish.'

Sharon and Faith exchanged a look, knowing precisely what they would wish for: that Mo would drop down dead and Rory would step over her still warm body to whisk either Faith or Sharon – whoever had got the almond – away to paradise.

Sharon decapitated the second duck.

'The Danish Father Christmas is called Jule Mander,' Anke told her. 'He has the usual sleigh and presents and stuff, but his little helpers – Jul Nisse – live in the attic.'

'Cool.' Sharon hacked off the ducks' feet, looking up suspiciously as Diana wandered back in through the conservatory, her cheeks and nose bright pink from the cold.

'Is everything all right?' Anke asked as Diana made straight for the range and ladled herself a large measure of *glogg*.

'Feeling very festive.' Diana knocked back a mouthful, not noticing it scorch her throat. 'Need any help?'

'You can take a jug of that through to offer top-ups?' Anke suggested, glancing anxiously at the clock on the wall. 'We don't eat for a couple of hours yet. I hope everyone knows that. It's Danish tradition to make this a midnight feast.'

Diana reeled through the house spilling *glogg* on the immaculate floors, uncertain if she'd last the course. The others were already fading fast.

Nanny had nodded off with her knitting needles at a jaunty angle while Truffle and Ingmar still made eyes at one another across her, too in love and squiffy to speak. Mo and Rory had obviously taken themselves off for a walk to sober up and raid the hedgerows for sustenance. Chad and Mim were no doubt upstairs slaying zombies on the X-box. Digby was curled up with the dogs in front of the fire, out like a light.

Graham was lolling in a leather armchair with a fat cigar, listening to the Christmas Rock Anthems contentedly. He had put on weight, the brightly knitted decorative sweater that had replaced his garish summer shirts straining at the seams. Yet he looked good on it. Diana envied him his big lazy smile and half-closed eyes.

She offered him a top-up before setting the jug on the coffee table and gathering her son in her arms. 'Mind if I pop him in a spare bed?'

'Be my guest. Top of the stairs third left is made up.'

She paused, her chin resting on Digby's head. 'Thank you for letting us intrude.'

He looked surprised. 'Don't apologise, love – the more the merrier.'

'You really mean that?'

He cocked his head and smiled at her, blue eyes creasing benignly. 'Best Christmas I ever had, this.'

Diana remembered the flirty, lazy man who had sprawled in a similar fashion on her sofa at Horseshoe Farm Cottage the night she had hosted the dinner party from hell. He looked the same, talked the same and yet there was something about him tonight that made her smile back, warmed through by his pure self-ease. He was a better tonic than a glass of *glogg* any day.

She kissed Digby's forehead over and over again as she put him to bed, longing to be a better mother.

She checked on Mim and Chad, who were not slaying Zombies at all, but wearing one another's clothes and writing each other love poems.

'Go *away!*' Mim shouted at her, turning pink.

Diana headed for the bathroom, but the scene of her summer recklessness was locked. She could recognise only too well the muted sounds coming from inside. Rory and Mo were making merry among the rubber plants. It was one hell of a bathroom.

She perched halfway down the stairs and felt something digging into the small of her back.

Diana drew the envelope from her pocket.

Good old Aunt Til, accusing her of murdering the love of her life with one pointed finger and then signing a charitable cheque with the other. Knowing the old bat's dark sense of humour, Diana thought she would probably find herself sponsoring a rehabilitating murderer for a year.

She tapped the envelope against her lips. She would open it on her birthday. Subsidising a small child in Cuba or a starving camel in Egypt might cheer her up at being forty. It didn't look as though Amos would be around to make her smile.

'Oh God, Amos.' She dropped her head in her hands as optimistic fantasist Diana finally got kicked down the stairs like Baby Jane. He would be wretched that this was the first Christmas apart from his children – he missed them far more than bloody Tim did his. Amos would be reeling from the news of the sale of Gunning and still burning with fury that she had left him all those years ago, convinced he had killed Firebrand. She didn't remember his chains. She only remembered her own. Scales sliding from her eyes alongside more tears, she finally realised how much he must hate her.

Faith was starting to regret inviting Sharon to share their Christmas. She had thought it would be good fun to have her new friend around to share in the pleasure-pain torture of seeing Rory and Mo so close at hand, but Sharon was taking over her role.

Amazed at her efficiency, Anke had her mixing and ladling and basting over the range while Faith lurked miserably at the kitchen table chopping cabbage.

They hadn't seen Rory in almost an hour.

She decided to go on a solo recce, only to find all the old folks asleep in the drawing-room and Diana Lampeter blocking the stairs and staring into space, her jeans hems covered in mud.

'Excuse me.' She cleared her throat when Diana didn't budge.

'Oh! Hi! Shorry, Faye – mileshaway.' Her voice was tellingly slurred.

'It's Faith, and I want to get past.'

'Of course.' Diana shifted sideways, frantically trying to mop her mascara-stained face and make her stair-hogging appear normal, seasonal behaviour. 'Hoping for anything shpecial this Christmash?'

Faith looked up as Rory and Mo let themselves out of the bathroom. 'A new life. You?'

'The shame.' Diana nodded and then laughed. 'And, you know, I think I might just get it. I think I already have it. The shame.'

Wishing adults weren't all so pathetic and alcoholic, Faith brushed past her, stormed past Rory and Mo, and slammed her way into her room to text Carly.

Anke's meal was a huge success, despite the late hour. The duck was pronounced delicious, and the 'leftovers' rice pudding consumed so greedily by the children in search of the lucky almond that they all developed a sugar high and went screeching outside to look for Father Christmas.

But it was Diana who got the almond. She didn't feel particularly lucky as it cracked a filling clean out of her tooth, leaving a cleft gap that pulsed with pain. But she didn't tell anyone. Eyes watering, she accepted a hug from Anke.

'Make a wish. You will have a wonderful year now!'

'Blazing Saddles will be a huge success!' Graham lifted his third glass of port.

'Trail Blazers,' Diana corrected distractedly and then winced as the throbbing ripped through her jaw. All she wished for right now was pain-killing sleep. Wishing for Amos was hopeless. She'd done it enough times without success. Her hopes had all fallen downstairs that night and all the king's horses, men and paramedics couldn't hope to put them back together again.

The meal dragged on through coffee and cognac as Diana's tooth tried to explode in her skull and her hangover decided to join it before she had even sobered up. It was the early hours of Christmas Day. Their hosts seemed oblivious of flagging guests as Anke and Graham flirted over schnapps, laughing at one another's jokes and touching one another's faces. Eventually, when her children had fallen asleep at the table, and Rory and Mo had nodded off, leaning against one another like the knave and queen in a house of cards, Diana girded herself to commit the social gaffe Nanny had always told her was ghastly. She was going to be the first to leave a dinner party. It hardly seemed to matter, as Nanny herself had fallen asleep sometime between the duck and the rice pudding and was now snoring reedily.

'Thanks so, so, *so* much for letting us all share such a festive treat.' She stood up, tooth screaming in pain. 'We'd really better get off home.'

But as Rory and Mo groggily went in search of coats and car keys, Anke poured another tray of *glogg* and announced that she had one special Christmas present to give before the party broke up.

'Faith.' She beckoned her daughter.

Faith's heart leapt hopefully having just exchanged texts with Carly and found out that her friend was being given a video-capture mobile – the height of cool. She needed one too – desperately – so that they could keep up.

But her face fell as stepfather Graham smiled indulgently and started ushering everyone outside. It was probably a stupid moped like the Sixsmith girls drove everywhere. She would have to wait three months until her birthday to be able to ride it on the roads and the helmet would ruin her hair.

Sharon shot Faith an envious look as she lumbered outside ahead of her. Inviting her here had been a mistake, Faith realised. Their lives were so different – hers one of privilege and Sharon's of shoestring survival. A united love of Rory and horses meant nothing in the face of such dichotomy. Faith was spoiled and surrounded by a big loving family; Sharon was poor and had no one. It didn't matter that this wealth of love and riches brought Faith nothing that she wanted. It didn't matter that she could not hope for Rory, nor a horse of her own any more than Sharon could.

The little dinner group trooped out by torchlight towards the small Wyck farmyard, pensioners causing chaos at the rear as they reeled around drunkenly and sleepily, and Nanny's wheelchair rattled off in the direction of the muck heap.

Faith didn't notice. She had heard something that made her heart stop.

Snorting out great dragon-blows of steam, the stallion was pacing around in the big corner stable, dark eyes bulging.

'OMG,' Faith breathed. 'Please tell me he's mine?'

'All yours!' Anke hugged Graham and watched Faith creep incredulously to the door, the stallion leaping to the back of the stall and bobbing his head anxiously.

'Nice one,' Sharon muttered bitterly from the shadows.

At the back of the group, Diana caught her breath, tooth throbbing all the more.

Baron Areion was at Wyck Farm. What in hell was Til playing at?

Faith burst into excited, noisy, laughing tears as she hugged everyone.

'*Is* he mine? Is he really mine?' she sobbed.

As Anke and Graham hugged the ecstatic teenager, Diana backed away in despair. She had returned the stallion to Gunning, trying to link up the circle. Til had broken the link. With the estate sold, perhaps she had no choice. Yet Diana had a sneaking suspicion the old witch was up to something. The Brakespears had probably paid tens of thousands for the horse. What was Til buying with the money? A missile to launch at Horseshoe Farm Cottage, probably. Til hadn't forgiven her. Selling Rio was proof.

She found herself standing beside Sharon, whose small eyes were playing tennis ends between the snorting horse and the sight of Rory and Mo kissing, lost in their own world.

'Why d'you hide him in the woods?' Sharon muttered.

Diana looked at her sharply, holding her aching jaw.

'I saw him there.' Sharon watched jealously as Faith touched the snorting black muzzle, the shaking fingers making contact with a warmth and power that wiped out her crush on Rory in an instant. Sharon's own fingers were curled so tightly into her palms that the nails broke flesh.

'None of your business,' Diana snapped, turning away.

Ingmar and Truffle were noisily manhandling Nanny into the Moke, picking straw from her twin set.

'Merry Christmas,' Diana muttered as she marched past to gather her children.

The farewells took ages. The Brakespears were harder to leave than Tim, Diana thought wearily. Her jaw ached so much that every kiss on the cheek felt like a decapitation, but she thanked them again and again for a lovely night. It *had* been a lovely night. It wasn't their fault her heart had broken halfway through and her tooth had broken shortly afterwards.

'You don't mind about the stallion?' Anke asked quietly, taking Diana to one side as Rory and Mo strapped the children in the back seat of the Audi. 'I know he was your baby.'

'He was never my baby.' She pressed her tongue into the jagged tooth. 'Til gave him to me when he was weaned – he'd been a sort of promise from a . . . a mutual friend. She bred him. I simply returned him home.

I hope Faith loves him as much as I did – I always felt I let him down because I lost my nerve after Digby was born.'

Anke kissed her on the cheek again, almost finishing off the tooth. She whispered, 'I lost *my* nerve after having Chad.'

'You did?'

She nodded. 'Why do you think I never ride any more?'

'You rode Areion.'

Anke smiled dreamily. 'I had to. He is like the legend he was named after.'

'Til named him,' Diana told her flatly. 'I had nothing to do with it.'

'She is quite a lady, your aunt.'

'Quite.' She turned to flop into the passenger seat beside Mo – Rory had already conked out drunkenly between the kids in the back – but Anke said something that made her spin around like a marionette.

'She made us agree to the most unusual terms, we have to let her have the horse back on the first full moon of the New Year.'

Diana felt fate cut her marionette strings and she clutched the car to stop herself falling. Oh God. *That* was what Til was up to.

When they got back to Overlodes, Rory, Mo and Sharon disappeared straight into the American barn to check on the horses while Diana carried the sleeping Digby to the cottage, Mim trailing behind dragging a bin bag of presents.

There was a big grain sack on the doorstep, blocking their way.

'Father Christmas has been!' Mim shrieked, waking Digby who started to babble deliriously and try to claw his way down towards it despite being half-asleep.

Setting him down, Diana let them both pull at the string tying its top, wondering if Tim had staged some sort of fatherly appearance after all and found no one home. It served him right.

'It's just full of sawdust,' Mim grumbled a moment later as the powdery contents spilled over her best party shoes. She and Digby scrabbled inside but found nothing, simply covering themselves with wood crumbs so that they looked as though they were about to be dropped in a deep fat-fryer. Mewling tiredly, they both agreed Father Christmas would never play such a rubbish joke and that it was probably the Danish elves that lived in Anke's attic.

Diana let them inside and watched them rush up to the bathroom, desperate to clean their teeth and get to bed so that the real Santa could visit. The puppies were yawning and yelping and whimpering excitedly in the kitchen, scrabbling around on their damp newspaper which Diana would have to clear up before she started thinking about wrapping presents. It was set to be a late night. Hally waggled her way up to her mistress looking self-satisfied and guilty, having clawed her way into the fridge during their long absence and bolted a side of smoked salmon. She let out a fishy burp, dropped down on to her front legs to stretch and yawned widely.

Fondling her head, Diana yawned too as she dragged the sack to one side. Something small and dark spilled out with the sawdust.

As she picked it up, she let out a puppy-like yelp and a whimper of her own.

In a small, dusty velvet box was a gold ring bearing a tiny cluster of diamonds.

It was the ring that Amos had given her before her eighteenth birthday. Christmas Eve. Her engagement ring. It had only been on her finger for a few ecstatic seconds before it had to be hidden as they planned their escape.

She took it out with shaking hands and slid it on to her ring finger, but it stuck at the knuckle, refusing to go further.

She could hear trudging feet behind her as Rory and Mo returned. This was too special to share.

Diana ran to her room, pressing the ring to her lips. Her bed was strewn with unwrapped stocking fillers for the children. She would be up until dawn. Her tooth throbbed, but it no longer mattered. She put the ring back in its box and placed it on her bedside table, pulling Til's envelope out of her pocket as an afterthought and laying it alongside – the sublime and the ridiculous propped together. She didn't care that throughout her lifetime everyone had combined Christmas and her birthday and then forgot both. This year, all her Christmases and birthdays had come at once.

She raced to see the children to bed, kissing their toothpasty mouths and making them promise to sleep so that Santa could visit.

'Will you put out porridge for him?' Mim asked sleepily.

'Porridge?' Diana laughed. 'Not a mince pie?'

'Chad says the Danish Santa likes porridge.'

'Then I'll put out porridge,' she promised.

Downstairs, she cleared up the puppy mess and laid out fresh newspaper. Then she dumped a box of Quaker oats on the table along with a schooner of sherry and a mince pie that Hally wolfed the moment Diana had retreated to her bedroom with a roll of Sellotape, a bag of satsumas, a pair of tights that were drying on the radiator and the kitchen scissors.

Upstairs, she looked at the ring box sitting on top of the worthy envelope, and pressed her tongue into her gappy tooth, thanking her lucky almond after all.

29

As Christmas Day dawned, Santa had left Diana's children a bulging tights leg each, filled with citrus fruit and forgettable presents. Beneath the lop-sided tree at Horseshoe Farm Cottage, far more exciting wrapped shapes revealed the hugely expensive and unnecessary items that they had spent the build-up to Christmas claiming they could not live without. There were gifts from Rory and Mo to each other and to the children, but nothing for Diana.

She didn't care. She kept running upstairs to look at the ring. In the end she put it on her necklace so that she could feel it all the time and stop herself hyper-ventilating halfway up the stairs.

'We couldn't think what to get you,' Rory apologised lamely.

Nor, it seemed, had her mother or aunt found inspiration. At Oddlode Manor, while the children drowned in yet more wrapping paper, Diana opened nothing. Sir St John admired his racing tipster books, cigar cutters and brandy, and Hell's Bells trotted around her huge house cheerfully sporting new wellies, shooting waistcoat and rabbit fur hat; Rory and Mo delighted in their chocolates and bath oils; Truffle played with her manicure set and her eyelash curlers; and even Glad Tidings joyfully basted the turkey with a new set of oven mitts on her hands.

Diana curled up tightly in a dog-eared Chesterfield and turned the little ring on her necklace, thinking about Amos, thinking about Rio, thinking what Granville had said about racing the ghosts.

'How long is it since the midnight point-to-point was run on the first New Year's full moon?' she asked St John.

He looked up over the *Tipster's Almanac*, half moons propped on the end of his nose. 'Thirty years or more? You'd have to ask Spurs. He always wanted to revive it.'

Ellen and Spurs were spending Christmas in Spain with Ellen's parents. Diana thought about calling her cousin and told herself not to be so stupid. Knowing Spurs, he would take it as a challenge and jump on the next flight home to race her from the Gunning chapel to Oddlode church spire.

She scratched the diamonds of the ring against the soft skin behind her ear and counted her way through the month.

'There's a full moon this New Year, isn't there?'

'Hmm, probably.' St John was only half-listening. 'Don't tell that idiot Pod Shannon. He'll be hopping hedges before you know it.'

Diana chewed her lip and made a mental list of ten things to do before she was forty. Breaking the lock to the safe in which Amos had stowed his heart was top of it. Riding the midnight point didn't qualify, given that it would almost certainly orphan her poor children and she would have turned forty by then, anyway.

Somewhere on the list was a trip to the Manor's attics which she made that afternoon, clambering over generations of Constantine junk to locate the one legacy she had left there. Underneath a large pile of Baily's Hunting Directories going back half a century and a moth-eaten dress uniform that appeared to date back to the Crimea, Diana found her old trunk, her initials peeling in gold between the catches.

D.I.S.H.

It had seen her through ten years at boarding school – Dishy Diana: there were worse nicknames. Now it housed a lot more than school memories. It housed her purgatory. Here was where she had kept her life that had surrounded Amos all these years. Her life before death.

At Oddlode Lodge, Dilly was lovingly hosting a family Christmas for lonely hearts, complete with the promise of fat goose and flaming pudding. At least Dilly thought it was a loving gesture as she struggled to breathe life into the ancient Aga. Pod was baffled by the guest list.

Pheely – obviously – was guest of honour with her massive belly threatening to spill at any moment. She complained constantly that her child's father was enjoying his all-inclusive yuletide golfing break in Portugal while she suffered alone.

Blue-haired Pixie Guinness and several of her children didn't stop screeching and racing around the cold, damp rooms of the long-neglected house leaving doors open. Whenever she paused for breath, sagging down beside Pheely to suck up half a bottle of wine in one sitting, Pixie complained about Sexton and Jacqui enjoying 'trad turkey' in their new rented barn conversion near Morrel-on-the-Moor.

If Pod found the two women unappealing company, he was frankly disturbed by Sharon.

'Why in hell did you invite her?' he'd gasped when she rolled up with a Terry's Chocolate Orange and a face like a half-finished stone writing tablet.

'I bumped into her in Tesco buying a discount turkey meal for one,' said kind-hearted Dilly.

Having had her sullen offers of help rejected by neurotic chef Dilly, Sharon sat like a gravestone at the head of the table for the majority of Christmas Day.

Pod wished they had a television to park their guests in front of, but the old house barely had a square socket, let alone modern luxuries like heating, decent plumbing or entertainment. Abandoned by Pheely after her father's death because it was too expensive to run, the Lodge was a grand old Victorian gothic pile, but it was falling apart. Paper sagged from damp walls, dry rot clambered its way up from the cellars, tiles jumped suicidally from the roof several times a day, and rats stopped to say hello every time you opened a door. Dilly thought it romantic and was wildly excited that her mother had said she and Pod could live there. Pod thought it was a death-trap and he was starting to develop an unpleasantly consumptive cough. They more or less lived in the kitchen, the only warm room in the house. If they made love in the chilly bedroom, they had to keep their clothes on. If they tried to have a bath in the claw-footed antique upstairs, they had to have a wash at the kitchen sink afterwards to warm up and scrub the rusty residue of old copper and lead pipes from their skin.

Hosting Christmas had not been a good idea, Pod reflected, as Dilly's mother screamed that her waters had broken, causing a panic until Pixie pointed out that she'd knocked her glass of apple juice into her lap. Sharon's boulder face didn't even twitch. Wailing, Dilly thrust her head in the Aga.

'It's oil-fired, queen,' Pod pointed out. 'You can't kill yourself that way.'

'It's freezing cold,' she groaned, pulling out a raw goose. 'We've run out of fuel again. Grab the jerrycan and siphon some from Giles Hornton's tank. He's in the Med.'

'Why not take it to your Mum's house and cook it there?'

'Where's your pioneering spirit?' she grumbled, but she saw his point.

While Dilly traipsed across the garden to the Lodge cottage and its electric fan oven bearing the goose, followed by her mother bearing a tray of potatoes and Pixie weaving around with a pan of sprouts, a bottle of wine and a joint, Pod sat down at the table and rolled a spliff of his own.

As the sweet taste of Rizla gum touched his tongue, he felt that now familiar pang of pain pincer his chest. He missed Mo. Christ, he missed Mo. She might have told him to quit weed a hundred times while Dilly actively encouraged him to share spliffs with her, but the taste of gum and ganja and grass was still the taste of Mo, just as the taste of coffee was Mo, chilli was Mo, curry was Mo, beer was Mo, whisky was Mo and soft skin was Mo. Any woman's skin was Mo. He missed her with every taste bud. And that was just the start.

Scrunching up the soggy cigarette paper, he kneaded his brow angrily and rubbed his tongue around his mouth, trying to erase the taste of Mo.

'You riding the midnight chase on the stallion then?'

He jumped, having forgotten that Sharon, the one-woman monolith, was still there, creating her own chilly standing stone at the end of the table.

'Nah. Horse got sold. Owner must have changed her mind. Mad as everyone else around here, that old dear. Paid well, though.'

Sharon's small eyes alighted on the bridle hanging from the coat hooks. 'So you're racing Dilly's horse instead?'

'Who says I'm riding the chase at all?' He started glueing Rizla together again before sprinkling grass on his little paper hammock. 'No one's done it for donkey's years.'

'Everyone knows you want to do it.'

He shrugged. 'Not much point without an opponent. I can hardly see Faith Brakespear wanting to gallop her new "dressage" horse in the dark, can you?'

She slid her small, hooded eyes towards him. 'I'll make sure you've got a challenger.'

'Sorry, pet.' He laughed, rolling the spliff into a neat tube and twisting the end. 'I hate to break it to you, but you're hardly racing weight.'

He flicked his lighter tetchily as he realised the same applied to him these days. Dilly's home cooking was spreading his sides alarmingly quickly. Dilly's horse, Otto, took a lot less riding than the stallion, and Amos had more or less laid him off at Gunning with most of the winter forestry work done. He was getting stout and unfit. He wasn't sure he was up to a five-mile point.

'I'm not riding,' Sharon snarled.

'Who, then?' he humoured her. 'The fucking ghost?'

'That scare you?'

Sharon watched as he lit the spliff. Pod gave nothing away. His face was as stony as hers as he took a long drag.

His big, dark eyes studied her through the smoke. 'Where d'you get off on all this, pet?'

'Your Mo is riding pretty good these days. Jumping nearly three feet. Rory's well impressed.'

He knew he gave himself away – eyes starting, muscles leaping, lips sucked between teeth in an involuntary twitch. Grass might make him paranoid, but he had barely had a take. This paranoia had nothing to do with drugs.

'She's not my Mo,' he snapped, pulling again and holding in an exquisite drag for several seconds, glancing at the door in case Dilly was coming back, 'and she's jumping Rory.'

'She *is* your Mo.' Sharon out held her hand, waggling her fingers.

He passed her the spliff and then slapped his palm on the table and let out a great hoot as it struck him. 'You're not suggesting I race Mo, are you?'

Just for a moment, a tiny flicker of a smile crossed Sharon's lips as she lifted the joint. 'No.' She inhaled and fixed him with eyes narrowed against the smoke. 'Rory would race you.'

'For what?'

'For Mo.'

He cackled even more. 'Yeah, that would be just great! I can just see everyone loving that.'

'You want to race or not?'

He shrugged, still fighting giggles.

'You could win her back.'

He glanced at the door again, crossing his arms across his chest. 'What if I don't want to win her back?'

'You do.'

He reached for the spliff but Sharon snatched it high in the air, keeping it for herself. Giggles fizzling out, Pod slumped back in his chair and glared at her.

'Bought any nice Christmas presents this year?' she asked, hamming up the small-talk.

Pod said nothing, thinking about Number Four Horseshoe Cottages. That was the only present he longed to be able to give. If he bought it for Mo, she would know that he still loved her. He was her infidel. The man who had forsaken her for all those bodies that never compared, but made hers yield to him all the more, that stopped her disappearing into mist. Between them they had got it so wrong.

He could be faithful. She could love him back with trust and self-worth. He wanted to make her feel good and safe and adored.

'Bought Dilly something special?' Sharon persisted.

Pod glared at her.

'I'm broke.'

'Shame. Can't afford racing silks for the midnight point?'

'I'm not racing.'

Rat – rat – rat!

The final Christmas dinner guest had arrived with a clatter of the ancient door knocker. Bearing a bottle of scotch, a five o'clock shadow and the door knocker that had just fallen off in his hand, Amos Gates stepped reluctantly into the house. It was obvious he'd been in two minds about coming.

He baulked when he saw Sharon going happily cross-eyed with a spliff. Now he was single-mindedly set on leaving.

Pod hastily fetched glasses and slugged out scotch, desperate not to be left alone with Sharon.

Amos stayed, but only because he hadn't eaten in three days and the thought of a Christmas lunch was too tempting to pass up. At least Pod knew better than to say a word, and Sharon was soon too stoned to bother pursuing the conversation.

The two had almost reached the bottom of the label in a silent pact of horror and hunger by the time the catering party trooped back through the garden from the Lodge cottage bearing an under-cooked goose, charcoal roast potatoes and Brussels sprouts that looked as though they had been in a nuclear reactor.

'Jesus!' Amos spotted Pixie and realised he was being paired up with his wife's lover's ex.

'I'm sorry, mate.' Pod took the scotch a few more centimetres below the label as he refilled both their glasses. 'Dilly's idea . . .'

At the head of the table, Sharon let out a low snarl.

Beneath a canopy of fairy lights in the one warm room in the house, Dilly and Pod's ungrateful guests ate their way around the more palatable edges of the disastrous food longing to be somewhere else.

Pheely thought about the father of her unborn, kick-boxing child, currently enjoying the nineteenth hole. She suspected that his memory of their glorious hole-in-one dinner date was now marred by the fact she was about to drop the result of his shot.

Pixie thought about Sexton enjoying succulent, idiot-proof turkey and all the trimmings in the rented barn conversion near Morrell-on-the Moor, and drank so much wine she fell backwards off her chair, to her children's delight.

Sharon, still high as one of the fairy lights overhead and soon almost as drunk as Pixie, thought about horses and ghosts and races and Rory and fires in no particular order. Her occasional random, cackling laughs alarmed her fellow diners. Her sporadic growls distressed them more. When she started to mutter, Pod got the giggles.

'. . . doesn't love her . . . loves me . . . farrier coming Tuesday . . . been hurt enough . . . cursed by infidelity . . . mustn't forget Penguin's barley rings . . . ghost gallops at night . . . check the quad bike . . .'

And Amos, the drunkest of them all after so much scotch on an empty stomach, wishing more than any of them that he hadn't come, thought about Diana and the gift he had delivered. Bloody fool. Stupid bloody fool. He let his head slump down on the table and covered his ears with his arms to block out Sharon mumbling. He started to moan.

Winking at Dilly, who was now smiling benignly at her lovely table which had brought such happiness to such lonely souls, Pod manhandled Amos outside to get him some fresh air.

'Jesus – sorry – oh Jesus.' He reeled around the Lodge gardens, which were wild and overgrown, crowded with the late Norman Gently's broken statues looming from every bush and peering out from behind every tree.

'You all right there, mate?' Pod watched as Amos lurched from a life-sized bronze of a Labrador to a ballerina covered with ivy.

'Why d'you bring me here?' He fell over two boxing hares and stumbled into a large rhododendron. 'Whyd'youfuckingbring me here?'

'I hope you're not planning on driving home tonight, mate.' Pod winced in sympathy as Amos almost knocked himself out on a red deer's antlers and then lurched back into a group of naked stone nymphs dancing around an overgrown flower-bed. Clutching a breast with one hand and a buttock with the other to try to stop himself falling backwards, Amos tottered before losing his fight with balance and slumping back so that he stared up at a hazy three-quarter moon, his feet propped up on a pair of lichen-dusted thighs.

'Pleasure Garden, my fucking arse!' Amos yelled at the sky. 'Brought me nothing but misery this place.'

Pod's eyebrows shot up. The poor sod was so drunk he thought he was at Gunning.

'Pleasure Garden, treasure garden,' he was ranting. 'You knew I was after it from the start, didn't you, you old bastard? That's why you chained me up in the end. Knew I was going to try to steal your money and run away with my huntress. Taking away your treasure and your pleasure. Well, I fucking would have!'

Pod lit his spliff, eyebrows shooting higher.

'You tried to steal her from me!' Amos was screaming at the sky now, his voice cracking up. 'She didn't want it though, did she? She'd given up all that and more for me – she didn't want your bloody riches. Til thinks Diana killed you for them; thinks she's come back for the money.

Never! She doesn't want it any more than I do. You can keep it, wherever it is. I hope it burns too . . .' He started to sob and mutter.

Hopping off the step, Pod crept closer, thinking back to his first night at Gunning with the old woman when he'd been high and wasted and thoroughly over-excited by all the talk of ghosts and fires. He hastily ground out the spliff underfoot, trying to make sense of what he was hearing.

Amos was muttering to the trees overhead. 'I'd have killed you, you bastard – but not for your money. You took her away from me. She gave up everything for me. The money was your trap, wasn't it? You trapped me here with it and you knew she'd stay too. You knew I thought I could give back everything she'd sacrificed. Thought we'd live happily ever after, I did. Ended up losing everything here. Losing her here. Losing hope here.'

Pod knew there were riches hidden in the estate. The old witch Til had hinted at them; Dilly reported the local myth regularly; and the Wycks loved to talk of gold and cash buried in the woods they feared like death.

Pod had embraced the talk of buried Gunning treasure from the start. Then it had been a diverting quest – a crazy challenge to find bounty amongst those amazing, intoxicating woods. Now it was suddenly a mission. Plundering Firebrand's cache would buy Mo's cottage. Treasure could win her heart more than any horse-race could, he told himself. Her heart was in the cottage along with his broken one. If she lived there again, she could mend his heart.

'Where's the treasure, Amos?' He leaned against a nymph's cool, flat belly and it reminded him so vividly of Mo, he had to stop himself kissing it. It was covered with bird droppings for a start. Amos was not the only one with a head fat with scotch. Pod could hold his liquor better than most, but it was starting to turn the nymphs upside down and make them dance together.

Amos was rambling incoherently. He and Sharon would make a great debating pair, Pod mused, as he stooped to give his shoulders a shake. 'Hey, mate . . . What's all this about treasure in the Pleasure Garden?'

'Not in this godforsaken garden any more,' he moaned. 'Took it away that night. Tried to give it to Diana. Gave her the key. Granville saw it.'

Pod sat him up and he leaned shakily against a nymph.

'What key?'

'The key he kept around his neck on a chain.' He closed his eyes. 'I bet she keeps it in her box of treasures. I bet that's where she's put the ring. She puts all her bad memories in there. She'll never come with me this time. I'm such a bloody fool.'

No matter how much Pod shook him, he couldn't get another word out of him.

'You can't just leave him out there!' Dilly complained when he stomped back inside. She immediately put on the kettle for emergency strong black coffee rations.

'Colder in here than it is out.' He shrugged, stepping over Pixie's sleeping body and helping himself to the last of the whisky. 'Where's Miss Havisham gone?' He nodded to Sharon's empty chair.

'Oh – she said to say goodbye. I think she was a bit embarrassed. I know she's rather weird, but her heart's in the right place – she even brought us Christmas presents. Look.' She pulled on a truly hideous brown woolly hat with dangly ear-flaps that made her look like an eager basset-hound. 'Yours is here somewhere – there, behind the cracker paper. I think it's a book.'

Pod, who was desperate to take himself away somewhere to think through what he had just heard, ripped hastily into the cheap glittery paper.

'What is it?' Dilly asked.

'Some old book about Gunning.'

'That's nice – you love that place.' Dilly reached for the jar of Nescafé.

'Yeah,' he murmured, flipping through and then catching his breath as he realised it was a small treasure trove in itself, complete with plans of the Estate and house – and a chapter about the midnight steeple-chase. He let out a snort of laughter. 'You're right, queen – her heart is in the right place.'

'Can you take this out to Amos and then help me clear up?' Dilly handed him a coffee as thick as soup. 'I'll try to get Pixie upright. Mum's taken her kids back to the cottage to make up a bed for them all – they can hardly get home tonight, and our rooms are too cold. Do you think Amos will be all right on a put-you-up in here? I know the Aga's out but at least it's not damp.'

Not taking in a word, Pod carried the book and his scotch into the cold heart of the house to occupy the loo and have a think, Amos's coffee abandoned.

'Thanks a bunch!' Dilly huffed angrily, fingers drumming. He could at least have shown some gratitude for all her efforts. It was Christmas, after all. She turned sideways and looked at her reflection in the glass panels on the garden door, wondering if she'd put on weight. Oh help, no. She looked as fat as her mother!

Then she realised with relief that it *was* her heavily pregnant mother letting herself back in.

'Pixie's boys are both asleep already. I think Pod might have to carry her across, or can Amos do it?'

'Pod's in the lavatory and knowing him will be there about an hour. Amos has keeled over in the fairy glade.'

'I've just walked past that.' Pheely switched her torch back on and pointed it out of the door. 'No, he's not there any more. Drunks are like toads in gardens, I always find –' she waved her torch around, 'look away and they've hopped off. God, I hope he hasn't crawled into the shrubbery to be sick or something. He could die of hypothermia in there and we would never find him.'

'Did you enjoy my Christmas dinner, Mummy?' Dilly asked petulantly.

'I did, darling,' Pheely lied, waddling forwards to give her a kiss and thinking how much weight her daughter had put on lately. 'Now, would you mind awfully carrying Pixie to bed?'

At Lower Oddford nursing home, Ingmar and Nanny were enjoying a thoroughly jolly, confusing Christmas Day.

Brimming with Bellinis lavishly poured by Ingmar, who had a case of Taittinger stashed beneath his bed, Nanny spilled the beans on the Gunning secret to the one person guaranteed never to repeat them.

'William Delamere – fifteenth Baron Sarsden – commonly known as Firebrand, didn't take his own life as the police eventually concluded. Nor did he run away to South America or become a monk in Spain or any other of the many stories that abounded at the time. He *did* kill his poor wife, of course – dreadful trollop who slept her way through most of the gamekeeping staff, but still unforgivable of him to start a fire like that while she and her lover were sleeping. Always was inordinately fond of fire, that boy. I don't personally think he ever intended to murder them, simply scare the living daylights out of them, but she died nonetheless, as did her lover. Firebrand was forced into hiding. And he was clever enough to get away with it. Abandoning his car at the ferry port was a nice touch – always wondered how he did that. Anyway, I digress:

'He lived in the woods for years. There's a garden there – a folly quite unlike anything you could ever imagine. He was obsessed with it as a young man – made all sorts of changes, created a little underground mansion full of modern wizardry. Solar power and what-not. It was the perfect hermit's cave. He was a jolly clever chap. He lived there for years. Existed on a diet of venison, rabbit and fish with side helpings of wild herbs and lord knows what. Quite the savage, but ingenious with it.'

'Atkins diet, very unhealthy if you ask me.' Ingmar waggled a finger and dropped a clutch of cards, reassuring Nanny that he wasn't taking much of this in.

'For all his twilight hunting, he still had a very sophisticated laboratory at his disposal,' she went on, puckering her lips disapprovingly. 'He manufactured something called LSD. Dreadful poison. I'm sure that's what drove Granville Gates mad. The price the poor man paid for discovering the secret, you see. Firebrand didn't let anyone get away. He kept a fortune buried in his underground hideaway – had been squirrelling it away for years. Cash, gold – every deed and document relating to the estate. He pilfered everything from the house long before that dreadful fire business which took him into hiding. It's one of the reasons the trustees still have no real power to this day. He was a clever man, a twisted clever man. And he had an accomplice.'

'An *amoureux transi*?' Ingmar had back to front cards in his pack and was trying to sort them out, turning more the wrong way than right.

'Not trembling at all, alas – rather bold and very devoted.'

'You?' He started shuffling the cards even though most were now face up.

'Good lord no, dear. Matilda. Poor child. Remained loyal even after he went into hiding. She and young Delamere had been lovers years earlier, you know, before he married the trollop. Quite the wild children, they were. I'd tried my hardest to discourage the girl; she was already engaged to someone else – the Midwinter's eldest, rather ghastly chap but very eligible – Firebrand was dreadfully unsuitable. She fell pregnant, of course. Lost the baby. Thank goodness we kept it from the family. Never really got over it, especially when she learned the truth about Firebrand's parentage. Hated telling them, but I had to nip it in the bud. So he married his trollop and Til – well, Til didn't go through with her marriage plans. That's why she moved there, to Gunning, became such a recluse. Always my favourite, dear Matilda. I love all the Constantine girls, but she's always been extra special. Such verve and vigour, and such a waste to stay devoted to him all that time. She knew where he was hiding from the start and became his link to the outside world. I suppose you could say she became a sort of wife. They bred horses, called them their children. Such delusion. Those wretched drugs . . .'

'Far too many drugs,' Ingmar agreed, removing a card he had just dropped in his drink. 'Matron thinks I should take vitamin supplements. Know they're laced with sedatives.'

Nanny patted his arm reassuringly. 'He lost his own mind eventually.

Became dangerous. Til carried on trying to cover up for him but it was impossible. He took to riding around the valley at night, lighting fires. He dressed up in disguises and popped up all over the place. It was only a matter of time before he was discovered.

'But poor Diana and Amos had no idea he was there. They were barely more than children. And I think they provided the entertainment he was looking for. They just walked straight in and he trapped them – snap!'

'Wrong game. Please don't get distracted.' Ingmar, who had been drunkenly dealing out whist, collected up his cards and started shuffling again.

Nanny hiccupped into her Bellini. 'We all thought they had run away to Scotland – Diana left a note to that effect. Nobody thought for a moment that they could be at Gunning, so close, so confused. Not a soul went there, you see – certainly not into the woods. It had become quite a forsaken wilderness since the big searches for Firebrand had been abandoned so many years earlier. Nobody believed he could possibly still be there – except in ghost form.

'He held them prisoner for weeks, although they had no idea that they were captives at first. Lord knows how much of his mind-bending creations he fed them, but they were quite frenzied, I gather. Til found out they were there. She was beside herself. She knew some of what was going on, but said nothing. Foolish girl. She loved him so much. Told me eventually, of course – she tells me everything – but it was too late by then.

'I have never wanted to think about the wicked goings-on in that place, and I still don't, but I think it's safe to assume that it was a very unhealthy trio. Amos was the first to rebel. The poor boy ended up in chains – can you imagine?'

Ingmar, still dealing most cards the wrong way up, laid the ace of spades on the table and studied it with a frown.

'That was when Firebrand had Diana to himself at last.' Nanny touched a bony hand to her face, discreetly dabbing a small tear from a network of creases by her eye. 'I think that was what he wanted all along. Til had tried to keep an eye on things, but she wasn't there the day the last Delamere eventually met his match, the day the man who had fashioned himself a ghost for so many years finally found the myth becoming truth. Granville was there, but his mind was so tortured that he made no sense of what he saw. Only Diana knows what happened.

'Amos was still in chains when Til found him. The poor boy was close to madness. He had no idea where Firebrand and his treasure were. All he cared about was Diana.

'We decided not to tell him that she had already come home, although "home" was a euphemism. Truffle had moved in with a new lover in Stratford, the Bellings were away and Diana had no true home. She came to me. To Nanny. She looked terrible – like a Romany waif. Her hands were burned to shreds, but she refused to say why. I bathed her and bound her poor fingers and nursed her back to strength, waiting for her to tell me what had happened, but she wouldn't utter a word. In the end, Isabel and St John came back from a skiing holiday in France and took over. The family still believed that she had run away to Scotland. I knew otherwise, but before I could help her the wilful child was whisked away to Uncle Belvoir's villa in Italy to "get over it".

'Til looked after Amos. His mind was so estranged from sense by the drugs and the fear that he took months to recover. His family were no help. They simply assumed he had taken after Granville and his father Noah. That he's sane today is a miracle. He searched for Diana for months. I relented and gave him the address in Italy, but she had already gone by the time he reached the villa. He came home penniless and retreated into the woods again. Til got him the gamekeeping job – nobody else wanted it. They became quite a double act, Amos and Til. Between them, they persuaded the trustees to ban the hunt and close the last of the shoots. They hid in there with their memories.

'Meanwhile, Diana ran and ran – Argentina, America, France, Hong Kong, Dubai. She moved around, always running away from the past. She should have contacted him, but she was too terrified by guilt to face the past, I imagine. Every time she had a moment to stop and think, she moved on. The family tried to haul her back occasionally, but she only came in winter. And she hunted. Strangest thing. Always terrified of the sport as a child – still was, I think. You should have seen her in the field; more frightened than the fox – but she galloped as though her life depended on it and stopped at nothing. Only ever came home to hunt and be hunted.'

Ingmar shuffled his cards. 'She was hunted by Amos?'

'He followed the hunt, but he never hunted her,' Nanny mused thoughtfully, too absorbed by the past to realise how much forgetful Ingmar was taking in of the Christmas present. 'Foolish man. He knew she was here, but he wouldn't leave his woods for long – agoraphobic like his father – and of course the hunt was no longer allowed near Gunning. I think Diana desperately wanted him to stop her running but she never even knew he was there. She just galloped behind those wretched hounds with the devil on her back, too frightened to turn her horse and ride in the right direction. She was quite crazed. Earned a fearless reputation that still lives on today. So untrue.'

'And why did Diana the huntress stop hunting?'

'Foolish girl married the besotted army officer to escape once and for all but found herself trapped all over again. And when he heard that, Amos married the first girl who would take him. Both such cowards. Both such silly young fools.'

'And now they are in love again?'

'They never stopped. Their love was badly cauterised when it bled strongest. A hot blade stemmed their lifeblood and it's seeped through open wounds for twenty years, destroying their lives.'

Ingmar held out the cards, dealing out the queen of spades and raising an eyebrow.

'Did she kill Firebrand?'

Nanny sighed sleepily, hiccupping again. 'I do hope so.'

'For the money?'

'Til certainly suspects as much. Thinks she's back to claim it.'

Ingmar raised the other eyebrow and Nanny suddenly realised who he reminded her of. Sean Connery. Or was it Clint Eastwood? No matter. He made one's heart flutter. No wonder Truffle was so smitten. One could forgive him the odd lapse of memory and bladder.

She smiled woozily. 'Whether Diana killed Firebrand or not, he disappeared the day that she came to me. I hope he's dead. I could not bear the thought of him in those woods like a wild animal. Even the blackest souls deserve rest. Til never saw him again. Only the ghosts remain.'

'The ghost that burned down my shop?'

Nanny nodded. 'And until Amos forgives Diana, the ghosts will not rest. She must tell the truth. She must find forgiveness.'

Ingmar picked up the queen of spades and slotted it into the pack. 'What were we playing again?'

'Whist.'

He nodded, dealing out a whist hand once more.

Laying the queen of hearts face-up as trumps, he suddenly let out a gasp of realisation and trapped Nanny in a sharp blue gaze, the faded eyes radiant with a long-forgotten focus that had just bubbled up from a mislaid corner of his mind.

'Was Sarsden your lover too?'

She blinked nervously.

'Hmm.' Ingmar narrowed his eyes as he studied her face. 'Maybe not. But you loved him. You certainly loved him. I think maybe you were denied the chance to ever share that love. You blame yourself for his misery, do you not?'

Groaning, Nanny closed her eyes. He had guessed. 'Like poor, dear Til.'

'Snap!' He smiled, the sea-blue eyes floating away. 'Or did you say whist?'

Nanny let out a sigh of relief, reaching shakily for her Bellini. 'Shall we try a round or two of poker?'

In the Pleasure Garden, Til set out her small Christmas feast on a tray on her knees in the centre of the dodo maze and raised a glass of sloe gin to the fat stone Bacchus by the entrance to the underground cave.

'Merry Christmas, you old rogue,' she toasted him. 'This is your last chance to break bread with me. I've handed you over. I think it's time they made their peace, don't you?'

The Bacchus hung on to his grapes and said nothing.

Til ate her Christmas meal and polished off rather a lot of sloe gin, talking all the time.

'Of course, they may not want you,' she twittered on companionably. 'You're one hell of a liability. I'm afraid I really can't afford to keep you on now the lease is up, and I know you loved her most of all, so . . .'

She lit her pipe and hollowed one cheek as she sucked on it nostalgically.

'Had to give up your stallion, too – turned a nice profit, mind you – price I got just about covered a little croft near Wick. I shall take the old mare there and see what we get. Think she might be up the duff after all, you know. At least I'm carrying on the line, eh? Feel a bit cowardly buggering off without saying my piece to the bloody doubters around here, but at least *we* can have this chat.'

Casting her tray aside, she re-lit her tightly packed pipe and pressed her elbows into her knees.

'And you can still ride your race, my darling. I made sure I negotiated that. He's fit and ready for you, wherever you may be . . . whoever you may be. I was almost certain it was Pod Shannon . . . but now, well, I think not. Forgive me. You would never return with a scouse accent and never dilly dally with the Gently girl.' She cackled at her joke, enjoying the first thermals of a high. 'I just know you're there, my darling. Just there. Right here.'

She stretched out a hand towards the stone Bacchus and smiled as he winked back at her. All the statues winked at her when she smoked her pipe and talked to them.

'Merry Christmas, my darling. I love you.'

She reeled through the maze, her eyes closed, humming happily.

Something stamped a hoof as she span dreamily towards the steps from the fountain courtyard. Til opened her eyes.

It was the oldest of the park stags, eyes boring into her, nostrils flaring, muscles twitching.

'What are you doing in here, you silly sod?' She laughed, realising it must have jumped over the beech hedge. Lucky to be standing after such a drop. Hardly a scratch on him.

'Shoo – shoo!' She chased him up the steps. As he skittered away, one hoof slammed on the pressure pad and the lower stones fell away, leaving her stranded. She could hear the stag thundering away into the distance, the old mare setting off across her paddock in panic as he passed.

Far too stoned to remember how to reset the thing – the maze was a doddle, but the technical stuff left her baffled – Til settled on a stone bench and restuffed her pipe. The titian-haired temptress winked at her.

She would miss this place, but it was time to go. Just the race to look forward to. He would ride the stallion now that he was back. She knew he would. He couldn't resist. He hadn't ridden the midnight point in years.

30

Diana woke on her birthday with an impression of the little diamond ring firmly indented in her cheek. She had slept with it on a chain around her neck and it had crept between the pillow and her face as she dreamed disturbingly of galloping across fiery landscapes, chased by her mother and aunts riding reindeer.

She tried to rub away the deep crease, but it wouldn't budge.

'Great.' Her other cheek still bore two long scratches from the rose bush in the Brakespears' garden. At least they matched. Her broken tooth had mercifully stopped throbbing and now just hummed on the lower pain slopes.

'Happy fortieth, you old wreck.'

She could hear the radio blaring in the yard. Even though it was still dark, Rory and Sharon had already finished morning stables and were frantically shampooing horses and ponies ready for the Boxing Day meet in Market Addington.

Diana propped herself on her pillows and yawned. A smell of toast wafted up from the kitchen and she could hear the children giggling excitedly downstairs.

Suddenly she perked up at the chance of breakfast in bed.

Having a birthday on Boxing Day had never been great shakes. In addition to the combined birthday/Christmas presents and the fact that her special day clashed with a big annual day out for her hunting-mad family, there was no post and the non-hunters in the house were inevitably too hung-over to bring her croissants, tea and juice on a tray. Diana had grown accustomed to birthdays being an anti-climax.

And this one was set to be a humdinger.

Forty! Aghhh!

She pulled the duvet up to her eyes and squeaked. Her broken tooth now sent shooting pains to her temples and dragged crows' feet from her eyes, ploughed frown lines across her temples and sliced little puckers around her lips.

Forty and still no better behaved. She deserved to feel old.

Since she had arrived back in the Lodes valley she had felt herself undergoing a curious second childhood. In a peculiar way she had felt orphaned by her marriage ending, cast back to a family who didn't want her. Overnight, she had lost the intimacy she'd shared with her in-laws and with army-wife friends. Half her world had been wiped out and she had reacted with petulance and anger and self-absorption. At this rate she would grow old throwing temper tantrums and stamping her feet with her head in the sand.

Her great plans for a new career had so far got nowhere – Tim's lawyers had ensured that she took nothing for herself from the marriage and she had no money of her own. That had hardly seemed to matter when she could give it all up for Amos – she had been happy to sacrifice everything for him before and she was again – but he had yet again given her a ring and hidden his heart in Gunning.

Oh, Amos. She took the ring and slipped it to the first knuckle of her forefinger, pressing the little stones to her lips. They had both acted like children. Babes in the wood. They needed Robin Hood and his Merry Men to rescue them.

The thought made her smile. It *was* panto season, after all. Maybe today would be the day that someone would shout 'He's behind you', and she would be quick enough to spin around and see him. She knew he was close.

Just as her radio alarm clicked on with Radio Four, Mo knocked on the door and clanked in with a butler's tray heaped with a full fried breakfast, pot of tea, fresh fruit and a few bent twigs of holly in a vase. Red hair on end, eyes baggy and egg stains on her jumper, she looked adorable, if flustered.

Behind her, still dressed in their pyjamas, Mim and Digby were carrying home-made cards and presents.

'Happy birthday.' Mo settled the tray on the end of the bed and shooed away Hally, who had escaped from her demanding puppies.

'Mo says you are really old!' Digby announced, crash-landing on the bed and rattling the teapot.

'I did no such thing!' Mo blushed, steadying the tray.

'Yes you did. We asked if forty was really old and you said it was.'

'I said it was all relative.' She pulled a package out of her cargo pants pocket. 'From Rory – well, both of us. I know it doesn't seem like much, but it meant a lot to us.'

'Thanks.' Diana felt absurdly moved as she laid the parcel aside, admiring the cards that Mim and Digby were thrusting at her.

Mim had done a splodge painting of a princess complete with glitter that scattered all over the bed. Digby had drawn her an orange tractor in crayons and signed it with his full name, age and address. Between them, they had made her an egg-box jewellery casket, a butterfly bookmark and a tangle of colourful pipe-cleaners that looked like a psychedelic hedgehog.

'It's a ring tidy,' Mim explained. 'For hanging your rings on. Mo helped us make it.'

Diana felt the ring-mark on her cheek give a timely throb above her broken tooth and she laughed, hugging and kissing them both. 'Thank you so much. I feel very special.' She looked up at Mo and mouthed *Thanks*.

Mo smiled distractedly, turning to leave.

'Are you coming to hunt with us today, Mummy?' asked Mim. 'Rory says you must. Mo is riding with us.'

'She is? You are? Mo?' Diana caught her just before she slipped out of the door.

Mo shrugged, looking nervous, dragging a small hand through her red crop. 'Rory kind of talked me into it. He says all you do on Boxing Day is drink lots of whisky mac, avoid arrest and hang about. Not like a proper hunt.'

Diana knew otherwise. The Vale of the Wolds hunt liked nothing more than a good gallop on Boxing Day to shake away the hangovers and burn off an excess of turkey.

'So are you coming, Mummy?'

'Go on,' Mo urged. 'I dismount and lead if we even hack into an open field. You used to hunt like a demon, Rory told me. You were known as the galloping goddess.'

'That was my mother. I was just known as a lunatic.'

The thought of hunting made her feel sick with fear. She had only just got accustomed to taking Ensign on very slow hacks, stopping regularly for a brief panic attack. He wasn't remotely fit enough to hunt, and she had no intention of trying to cling on to one of the yard horses in his place. She had already refused point-blank several times when goaded by Rory, but now felt pathetically wimpy knowing that even Mo was taking part.

'I'd just hold you back,' she muttered nervously, imagining the obituary in *Horse and Hound* – tragic death on the hunting field on her fortieth birthday, the former bloodstock agent and daughter of 1960s polo legend. Hopeless rider. Terrible coward. Such a tragic death, leaving two young children motherless. 'I'm pretty ring-rusty when it comes to hunting and I really couldn't concentrate if I'm trying to keep an eye on the children – and you.'

'That's okay. Rory promised Sharon will look after us all, although I hope she's up to it. She spent Christmas Day with friends and looks dreadful, poor thing.'

Diana could well imagine Sharon's horror at the prospect of leading Digby on fat Furze whilst ensuring she, Mo and Mim stayed aboard their mounts in the Boxing Day *mêlée*. Of all the VW hell-raisers and hound-chasers, Sharon rode hardest and fastest. Rory called her the Big White Bottom because that was all he ever saw of her as she raced off ahead.

'I think I'd rather follow on foot,' she insisted. 'Then I can take lots of photographs and be on hand to help.'

'I'm going to wear my new jacket,' Mim announced, having been given a smart black riding jacket by Hell's Bells the day before. She raced towards the door to fetch it. 'And Mo says that I can wear mascara.'

'Honestly, Mim! I didn't say that.'

'I want to wear my spider man outfit, but Rory won't let me.' Digby was galloping after his sister, diving between Mo's legs.

'Have *you* got all the right stuff to wear?' Diana asked Mo.

'Think so.' She screwed up her face. 'Sharon's lent me her spare jacket. It's a bit big and has a button missing, but it looks okay. I've borrowed an old Oddlode primary school tie from our history display and Rory says jods and short boots are okay as long as I pretend to be under sixteen.'

'Have a look in that trunk there – the one under the box of shoes.'

Mo pulled it out and flipped the catches, running her fingers over the initials D.I.S.H. as she opened it, trying to remember where she had seen them before.

'Wow!' She tilted back on her heels.

It smelled of horse, although everything in it had been meticulously cleaned before being stored away. The sweet, musty tang of equine memories still permeated every article inside – a velvet beagling cap, three wool hunt coats, polo helmets, hunt boots, tan polo boots, breeches, spurs, rosettes, photographs and trophies.

It was a box of memories, Mo realised – a time capsule untouched for years. She picked up a photograph of a beautiful young woman on a boggle-eyed chestnut, laughing as she held up a steaming glass of mulled wine.

'You were . . .' Her voice trailed away.

'Fearless. Foolhardy.' Diana shifted beneath the bedclothes. 'I didn't care if I lived or died in those days.'

'How old were you here?'

'Mid twenties . . . maybe older. It wasn't long before I married. See the suicidal look in my eyes?'

'You look absolutely stunning.'

'And so shall you.' Diana smiled. 'That coat will fit you much better than Sharon's size eighteen. I was pretty skinny the last time I wore it. The boots might fit too – what size are your feet?'

'Four.'

'Wear thick socks.'

'Are you really sure? These things seem so precious.'

'Be my guest.' Diana settled back on her pillows. 'Don't worry – I never fell off, and God knows I should have. They're lucky. I used to come back to the Lodes three or four times a year and ride out to hounds like a mad woman. They always looked after me.'

'This was after . . . you and Amos . . . after . . .'

'Yes. After.'

'Did you ever see him?'

She shook her head. 'No one hunted Gunning then. They still don't.'

As Mo sat cross-legged on the floor gathering her day's wardrobe, Diana picked up the wrapped gift from beside her breakfast tray and studied it.

'I want to thank you.'

'It's really not a very generous present.'

'Not for this, although I'm sure it's lovely.' She looked up. 'For looking after Mim and Digby – and Rory. I know I haven't been a very good mother or sister lately. You arrived when they needed you most. You're like an angel.'

Mo fingered the hunt buttons on the coat, feeling the VH initials embossed in silver, knowing this was a heritage of which she would never really be part.

'I love being here.'

'I'm so glad you are.'

'Really?'

She nodded. 'You belong here. You're already at the heart of this family, Mo. I feel I'm getting in the way.'

'It's your home!'

Diana shook her head. 'It's Rory's home. I have no real right to be here. I should start looking for a place for the children and me.'

'But Rory and I love the children – and you too,' Mo added hastily, hugging the hunting jacket to her chest. 'It's a real family. I've always wanted to share a home with a real family. And you're a part of it.'

Mim was calling for Mo to help her with her outfit. Digby was demanding equally shrilly that Mo help him retrieve the spiderman's outfit that Mim had thrown on top of the bathroom boiler.

'I'd better sort them out.' Mo closed the trunk. 'Are you sure I can wear these?'

'Please do,' Diana smiled, although she could feel the scratches and marks on her cheeks threatening to crack and her tooth threatening to stab its way out.

As soon as she had skipped away, Diana battled the wave of jealousy that consumed her

She understood Mo's passionate need for a family, and she hadn't thought for a moment that she was trying to steal hers. She still didn't. It was there for the taking. Her children cleaved to Mo's natural maternal energy and *joie de vivre*. Diana loved her children with a passion but had never felt like a true mother. She never helped them make pipe-cleaner jewellery holders or butterfly bookmarks. She had seldom read to them when Wendy Craig's soft tones did it so much better on the CD of fairy stories she'd bought. Bedtime kisses and cuddles were lovely, as long as they conked out quickly so that she could have a much-needed G and T. Then she would steal back to watch them sleep – sometimes for hours – grateful that she knew how to cope with them then, to love them and need them.

Diana had often experienced the guilt of the self-blaming bad mother. Today it was mixed with the bittersweet realisation that there was another close by who had proved to be a worthy deputy. When they had first met, she recalled Anke Brakespear telling her that Mo was born to nurture. She finally understood what that meant. Mo was the sort of girl who collected broken-winged birds and one-legged hedgehogs to nurse back to health. She was Hayley Mills in *Whistle Down the Wind*. She would make Rory very, very happy.

She propped her chin up on her knees as she poured her tea and felt a great wave of gratitude for the unlikely friendship of Anke and Mo, fellow orphans in life – one whose only surviving parent had almost forgotten who she was, and the other whose mother had abandoned her at such an early age. She supposed that made them curious sisters. She had always longed for a sister.

Perhaps it wasn't going to be such a bad birthday after all.

Sipping on deliciously milky tea and eating succulent mushrooms from her fried breakfast, she opened the gift from Mo and her brother.

It was a book. *A Horse for Emma.*

She let out a little sob of laughter as she turned it around in her hand, immediately recognising it.

Her father had bought it for her, picking it up from a charity stall in London. She had read it many times as a girl. It had meant so much more to her than the jewellery and watches and designer clothes and polo ponies.

Setting down her tea, she opened it.

D.I.S.H.

It was her own copy, lost years ago amongst many moves and running away and chasing her own tail.

She clambered out of bed, spilling tea and toast as she made her way to her trunk and stored it safely inside, dropping down to smell the contents, the past.

Digging deep beneath the satin rosettes, wool jackets and cotton breeches, she felt her way towards the familiar tobacco tin with its rough, rusty edge.

Tucking it into her dressing-gown pocket, she slung the robe around her shoulders and took a deep breath, looking out of the window.

A weak, yellow sun was peering through the beech hedge that separated the cottage garden from the bridleway to Gunning as it struggled up through hazy cloud to burn away the hard frost. It was going to be a bad day for scent. The children and Mo might be safe from hell-for-leather gallops.

She pressed the ring to her lips again, wondering if Amos would be at the meet. Their past was getting closer. The circle was closing. Soon they would have to face the truth. There was no escaping it.

Washed and dressed, she watched Sharon and Rory load the horses and the children's ponies in the lorry.

'Shall I drive you to the meet?' she asked the children.

But they wanted to travel with Mo in the groom's compartment of the horsebox, all part of the day's excitement. Their mother's warm, sensible hatchback was no rival.

'I'll follow,' she told Rory as he clambered into the cab, Sharon proprietarily taking up the seat beside him with her customary sour glower. She definitely looked as though Christmas had disagreed with her, her face pasty grey.

'Can you do a thermos of sweet tea with a dash of brandy?' Rory remembered.

'Sure.'

'And lots of biscuits and chocolate!'

As the lorry rattled away along the drive, Diana headed back into the cottage, pulling her collar up against the chill. Her tooth ached again, twisting in her jaw.

Then she stopped dead.

Pod was sitting on the step, black fringe over his eyes, puppies crawling all over his feet. In another lifetime, it would have been the most beautiful sight in the world. Swaddled in a lovat-green moleskin puffa jacket, legs swathed in tight black jeans and shod beneath with shiny, puppy-covered dealer boots, he was the ultimate country calendar pin-up. He'd put on weight – lots of it – but it just enhanced his sex appeal, filling out the gaunt hollows, squaring his too-beautiful boyish face, fleshing youth into man. Life with Dilly clearly suited him.

He was holding the tobacco tin in his hands.

Diana let out a bleat of horror and lunged for it.

He whipped it away, standing up and tipping the puppies on to the path where they blinked bright blue eyes and poddled away to regroup in the lavender to try out their new teeth on each other's ears.

'Morning, queen.'

She said nothing, staring fixedly at the tin.

'Mind if I take a look?' He flicked it open. 'Didn't have quite as bad a habit as I thought, did you?' He picked out the cocaine he had sold her over many weeks, stashed away unused in a plastic money pouch. Beneath it, amongst dried four-leaf clovers and locks of hair, was a key.

'Amos told you,' Diana groaned.

'Well, he was very, very drunk at the time.' Pod joked the Fast Show catchphrase.

'Where is he? Is he okay?'

'He's very chipper,' he said sardonically. 'Bit wound up about you. Seems to think you killed someone.'

Diana was too anguished to register sarcasm.

'Assures me the Sarsden riches are still hidden in the Gunning Estate somewhere,' he steered her back on track.

'And you want to claim them?'

He was chewing his lip, big black eyes admiring the key. 'Hey, share and share alike, I say. Mind if I make myself a cuppa?' He walked into the cottage.

Diana thought anxiously about her children trundling their way towards the meet as she hopped after him. She had to be there.

Pod was already laying himself out two lines of coke amid the toast crumbs on the work surface.

Frozen with shock and fear, Diana automatically fetched the thermos from the cupboard, along with a chipped mug. She put on the kettle and dug the cooking brandy out from behind the microwave.

'That's better!' Pod rubbed his nose as he straightened up, pocketing the rest of the stash in his jeans. 'Good gear is hard to come by now that Sexton's done an extra-marital, and I can't take much more of the mother-in-law's home-grown. You look well, queen.'

He admired her bottom as she stretched up to a cupboard for tea bags.

'Bet it's pretty cramped in here, all of you living together?' The coke was already starting to kick in. Not waiting for an answer, he chattered on. 'Rory must be a great guy to have won our Mo's heart. My little dragon likes to walk on the wild side. Drove me demented. Guess I didn't have what it took in the end. Want to make it up to her now, though. Always longed to make her feel safe. That's what she needs. Don't we all?'

Diana glared at him as she glugged brandy into the thermos.

'Lost your purrs of spooch?' he joked.

She turned to take the milk from the fridge.

'Mo seems happy enough shacking up here.' He studied the many pictures that the children had made of Mo and Rory on horses and in tractors. 'I miss her. Crazy bitch, but one hell of a shag. You know when you have a lover you can just access all areas? You're both so in tune there's nothing you won't try? That was me and Mo. Maybe you and Amos were like that?'

Diana poured boiling water on to tea bags, first in the thermos and then the mug, her heart beating in her chest, throat, head, belly. She felt faint.

'Trouble is,' he examined the key, 'I never had one of these for her heart, you see. I guess your brother does?'

Diana said nothing.

'Early days – I know. Like me and Dilly Dilly. But she wears her heart on her sleeve, bless her. Like a tattoo. Like you.'

Diana looked up sharply, scalding water splattering over her hand.

But he was tapping the key against his chin, eyes left, starting to feel the high take full hold.

'You and Amos. Weird stuff. I don't want to tell you the state he's in. Scary. And I thought Mo was a mind fuck. Dilly, babies, DIY and gardening. That's my bag now. Just need the readies, y'know?'

'What did Amos say?' Diana demanded, but Pod wasn't listening.

'Need some cash to make life sweet for my new flower and buy a cosy cave for a little dragon.' He spun the key through his fingers, starting to talk hyperbole. 'Want to make things right.'

Diana squeezed the tea bag in the mug, watching the red stain of flavour seep into the hot water.

'There's a fortune hidden in the woods, Amos says. Poisoned money, he called it. Blood money. Y'know he doesn't want a penny of it? Stupid bastard. All he wants is you. He'd give up his life for you – his home, his children, his pride – what's filthy lucre compared to that? And just because the treasure didn't buy you and the boss happiness it doesn't mean I can't buy forgiveness, does it?'

'What did he say, Pod?'

But he wasn't listening. 'I guess those ghosts might get a bit upset if I take the lolly. But it's in a good cause. I'll be claiming it for all of us.'

Diana took the squeezed-out teabag and transferred it to the bin.

'I take it you want a share?' He watched her.

She added milk to the mug.

Pod twitched his lips impatiently. 'Of course, I knew you and I would have to negotiate this a little more.'

She looked up at the wall clock as she handed the mug to him. She had to leave soon.

'I'm not a greedy man. I just want a slice. You can buy my silence, you know?'

Diana slopped milk as she added it to the thermos, spilling sugar in equal measure as she spooned it in.

'After all, you did kill the old guy.'

She screwed the lid on very carefully.

'Did you bury the body yourself?'

Diana slotted the cup on to the thermos.

'Just tell me where it is. The booty not the body, I mean.' He laughed uproariously at his joke.

She thought about the horsebox driving towards Market Addington, full of chatter and excitement. The perfect family. Without her.

'Take it,' she whispered. 'Take it all, whatever's left. I don't want it.'

There was a long pause.

'You don't want it?'

She looked at the children's drawings, full of colour and happiness. Why had her world turned so black and white while theirs had jumped over the rainbow?

'I never wanted it. Not the money. He offered it all to me once and I refused to take it then. I haven't changed my mind. It's evil.'

'It's just money, Diana.'

'I don't want any of it. It's all yours. Just get out of my house. Out of my life.'

He pressed the mug to his red-stained cheeks, turning away to mouth 'Result!' to the wall in looped glee. Then he saw Mo's parka hanging there and almost cracked. He so nearly fell to his knees that he had to take a step back and lift his toes in his shoes as a counterbalance.

'Do you still love Mo?' Diana suddenly asked.

He didn't answer. Unable to turn back and face her, he stared at the parka and felt the severed heart-strings start to climb the rigging of his spine up to his head.

'If you're doing this for her, I have to warn you that Rory absolutely adores her and she adores him.'

'Bully for them,' he snapped. 'I want the cash, flower. Simple. Now . . . small matter of directions?' He held the key over his head. 'What does this open?'

Diana laughed bitterly. 'That, I won't tell you.'

He gaped at her over his shoulder. 'But you just said you don't want it . . .'

Diana saw the tears in his eyes and baulked. 'I don't think you want it either. You want Mo back.'

'Fuck off.' He marched past her, slopping tea. 'I want the cash. You don't. Now tell me how to find it.' His mouth spat at her ear.

'It can stay where it is and rot as far as I care.'

'So why did you get out the key?'

'I got out the tin, not the key.'

He laughed even more uproariously. 'Give us a clue, at least?'

Diana collected her tobacco tin from the table and carefully tucked the clovers and locks of hair back inside. 'Think like a ghost.'

Pod set his tea to one side and touched his mug-warmed fingers on her cheek where it had been laced with rose thorns. 'How d'you hurt yourself?'

She flinched. 'Ghosts keep pulling knives on me.'

He smiled, turning his head to examine the wound. 'I guess your barbed tongue is in your cheek so much, Diana, you're bound to cut right through occasionally.'

For a moment their eyes met and she remembered why she had felt such an affinity for him from the start. Even now, twisting around her life like a serpent, he had a passion she understood. And she knew it was a mutual empathy.

'I never stopped loving Amos,' she said urgently. 'Whatever happened between us, however sordid, we couldn't kill the love. My marriage was a farce as a result. Don't do the same thing to Dilly. If you still love Mo, walk away now. Leave them both in peace. The ghosts live in my head and they'll be in your head. They are the ones that bite the tongue in your cheek and cut your lips to shreds every time you fail to tell the truth.'

'Mo's the one with the ghosts, not me. I could never exorcise them, however hard I tried. I tried to haunt her more than they did, but it never worked.'

'Oh God.' Diana rubbed her hand on her face. 'You still love her so much.'

He looked at the children's pictures of Mo and Rory again. 'They say whoever wins the midnight steeplechase is forgiven their sins – by ghosts and mortals alike.'

Diana traced the tiny scars in her skin. 'That's just local hype.'

Pod pulled the bag of coke from his pocket and dabbed in his little finger before pressing it into each nostril in turn, snorting hard.

'I've been riding your stallion,' he told her, still sniffing. 'He's something else. Rode him all over those fucking woods, that parkland, the farms. Never saw a treasure chest.' He laughed quietly. 'I was mad at the old bat for selling him to Anke. I wanted to ride the steeplechase.'

Diana looked at him in disbelief.

'He's fast enough. Forget all that dressage crap. The horse can race.'

'I know. It's what he was bred for.'

'And trained for.' He cocked his head.

She groaned, realising what her aunt had been up to. 'Typical bloody Til. And she told me she just wanted him back to continue the breeding line. Just her luck to find a crooked jump jockey on her doorstep working as a forester. No wonder she couldn't resist.'

'So he really is the last of Firebrand's horses?'

'By a stallion called Passion, out of a mare called Lady.' Diana laughed hollowly.

'Bollocks. Tell me the real breeding.'

She bit her lip hard and winced as her broken tooth snagged her cheek.

'Rio's sire was directly related to Flint, the greatest ever Gunning hunter and the most prolific point-to-pointer in the country. Legend has it Flint was part Iberian cavalry horse, part wild, and part Pegasus. He jumped Look and Leap a dozen times and never fell. His progeny were fabled, but famously tricky to breed from.

'Flint's last grandson – Rio's sire – was born the spring Amos and I lived in the woods. He was the last foal Firebrand bred, a big near-black colt named Inferno, with chestnut tips to his mane and tail. He was an absolute beauty, hidden away from the world like his creator, destined for a life of leisure and pleasure. Firebrand planned to make him the sire of a whole new line. He told me that, when the time came, I would have the first Inferno foal. The first of the new line.'

'But you didn't hang around to see it?'

'After I – left, Aunt Til carried on the breeding programme Firebrand had mapped out.' Diana looked away and swallowed. 'When Inferno matured, Til put him to her best young mare – a mare she said she could trace straight back to the Godolphin Arab. But Inferno drove Til mad. He wouldn't cover the mare however much she flirted – then again, he wouldn't abide another mare near him. They became inseparable. Went demented if apart. They lived together like that for the rest of their lives, the odd couple. Then the year Inferno died, he sired his only foal from her.'

Pod clapped his hands together, elated that the love match had been so exclusive and elusive. 'The last of the Gunning line. Baron Areion.'

She nodded unhappily. 'Til always insisted I have him, however much I tried to dissuade her. She was fulfilling Firebrand's promise although it must have broken her heart to lose the last of his line. So one day, an unbroken two-year-old colt arrived at the Kensington Barracks kicking apart a ramshackle pony trailer driven by Reg Wyck. Everyone thought it was an IRA terrorism ploy. All hell broke loose. And Rio broke loose too, bolting all the way to Kensington High Street and past Stannard and Slingsby where I was having my hair done at the time. I knew who he was straightaway.'

Pod's eyes gleamed with the poetic justice of it all. 'Your stallion. Bred to race the midnight point.'

'Not my stallion any more.'

'But he *was* bred to race the point . . .'

'I wasn't.'

'Why d'you let him go?'

'He was always Til's.'

'So why did she sell him?'

She licked her dry lips, remembering the secret her aunt had let slip in a hailstorm. 'Maybe he just reminded her too much of the past?'

Pod put the key in his pocket and drained his tea.

'You didn't kill him, did you? The old geezer in the woods?'

She stared at her children's pictures again, today's task forgotten as she simply registered a great stab of love and regret that her past and present were at such loggerheads. 'Tell me about Amos?' she entreated one last time. 'Does he really hate me?'

Pod kissed her on the cheek, exactly where the indentation from the ring had been, making her start as if it was branded there once more, diamonds digging into her skin.

'He's going mad, queen. Just like you. Just like me. Wish me luck. I'm looking for buried treasure. You heading to the meet?'

She looked from the drawings to the thermos, and then studied her watch with a bleat of panic.

'Keep an eye out for Dilly,' Pod entreated as she grabbed her car keys and supplies. 'She's on that batty pink horse of hers. Don't trust the beast. My fault for getting him so fit. I should never have sat on him. Missed the stallion.'

'Mo's hunting too,' Diana said distractedly as she reached past him for her scarf.

Just for a moment, his eyes gave him away.

'She'll be safe. Rory's looking after her.'

His give-away eyes narrowed defensively. 'She's never safe. That's why I love her. That's why I'm looking out for her. Someone has to scare away her ghosts.'

'Rory can do that.'

'Rory's too much of a drunk.'

Diana couldn't argue with that and was in too much of a hurry to try. Instead, she blustered rather feebly, 'Leave them alone, Pod. I don't want my little brother getting hurt. He –'

'– adores her, yeah. So you say.' He headed for the door, spinning around as he went to fire back self-justification. 'Well, I'm not going to stand in her way. I'm not here to fight for her or race for her or die for her. I'd do all those things, but right now all I want is for her to have a house somewhere, far away from the cold night air, with one enormous chair and – bollocks. I'm out of here.'

Watching him spiral, Diana recognised her own Achilles' heel. She couldn't tell him to stay and fight for Mo. It wasn't fair on Rory. But she could help him challenge the ghosts.

As he headed outside, she sprang after him.

'Do you still want to ride the midnight point?'

He blinked, trying to shield the excitement in his eyes.

'Is this a challenge?'

She nodded, feeling sick.

He screwed up his forehead. 'Tell me, does Rory actually know about this yet? Only he might not be so keen.'

Diana stepped back in confusion. 'Who said anything about Rory?'

His brow continued furrowing. 'He wants to ride against me for Mo, right?'

She shook her head. 'Rory wouldn't be racing you.'

'So who would? Sharon?'

'Me.'

He howled with laughter. 'Thought you were too scared to trot these days?'

'Do you still want to ride the midnight point?' she repeated.

He looked down at the key, too much Class A in his veins to resist a dare. 'Yes.'

Diana looked as though she was about to faint. Before she could pull out, he was suggesting terms. 'Tell you what. If I don't find the treasure by New Year's Day, I'll race you for it.'

'I'm not racing for the Gunning cache.'

'I know that, queen. So if I win, you tell me where it is. I lose, it stays buried.'

She licked her lips. 'The treasure's the winning purse, then?'

'If you like.' He shrugged, knowing that it was more than that. His winning purse was also to have his sins absolved, like the legend said. Diana was after the same prize, without the cash bonus.

'That's agreed then.'

'What if the ghost wins?' He smiled wickedly as he turned to leave. 'I hear he always races the points.'

The blood thrummed in Diana's ears like a thousand runaway hooves. 'Then he keeps it.'

Whistling, he headed outside, stooping to bid farewell to the puppies.

Diana heard his trail bike starting up and ripping away along the track to Gunning. Pod would never work out what the key was for, she reassured herself. It was far too bloody obvious for a devious mind like his.

She hurriedly gathered her thermos and called for Hally to bring her puppies inside, then remembered something.

Til would be at the meet, waving her usual protest banner. She must open the worthy envelope so that she could thank her.

Upstairs, she retrieved the envelope and distractedly tucked it under her arm as she stooped to open her trunk.

She tried not to think about what she had just done. Pod had been full of cocaine and bravado when he accepted her challenge and was bound to change his mind. She had been full of compassion and self-loathing but was now just full of terror. He had been right – she was too frightened to trot these days. How could she ever gallop a five-mile point? It was madness.

She closed her trunk with a clunk, trying to shut away the bad memories of fear and flight. It was agreed. That was an end to it. By this time next week, she would either be free from the ghosts at last or dead in a ditch.

'Or possibly in traction.' She considered the options as she headed downstairs. 'Wheelchair-bound . . . minus a limb . . . missing all my teeth, ouch!' Her broken molar shot out a quick burst of pain.

Oh, Amos.

Oh, hell, the meet! She was so late.

She felt the pain transfer to her chest as she gathered up the thermos once more and held its cool metal side to her breastbone, feeling as though the brandy-fired liquid within was burning its way into her torn heart. One ventricle was pumping for her children, the other for her childhood love.

Oh, Amos.

Hugging a thermos flask was one of the sillier things that Diana had ever done in her life, but as she raced outside, for that split second it summed up her life – a cold, hard shell surrounding a piping hot core containing the comforting hot, sweet tea of motherhood and the fierce, dizzying brandy of true love.

Minutes later, unopened envelope pinned precariously to the roof of the car by a thermos flask and a digital camera, Diana felt around in her pockets for her keys and looked up suddenly.

He was here. Her heart hammered, her nerve-endings jangled. Every pore on her skin was pursing its lips and every hair on her body was standing to attention.

She knew he was here.

Oh, Amos.

She spun around, eyes searching the barns and manège and paddocks.

But there was nobody in sight.

Diana told herself not to be so dumb. She had to make the meet in time.

At last, she found her keys and hit the little button on the fob to unlock the car with a bleep

But before she could reach for the handle it locked itself again with another bleep.

She pressed the button. Bleep. The car unlocked.

Bleep. It locked again.

She looked up, eyes casting around in confusion. Nothing.

Bleep. She unlocked the car.

Bleep. It locked itself again.

Bloody electronics! Diana cussed under her breath, kicked the car door to make herself feel better in the light of her mechanical ignorance and tried the key on the door lock.

Bleep, bleep, bleep! It was locking itself non-stop now. She was going to take Audi to the cleaners over this.

Then she heard hooves.

Amos was leading two horses from the barn, her spare car keys trapped between his teeth.

Bleep. He locked the car again with a bite before spitting the keys out and leading the horses up to her. 'Can't run away in a German car. Bad luck.'

She let out a wail of laughter and tears.

'This time we run away properly.' He handed her a set of reins. 'This time we don't look back.'

'Amos, I . . .'

He shut her up with a kiss. A kiss that wiped away more than half a life. A kiss that made her eighteen again. A kiss that drew away the sorrow and filled her tongue and lips and mouth with the sweetest taste of happiness. It was a kiss so deeply infused with forgotten love that they had no past. They had no secrets, no responsibilities, no children, no lives outside one another's heartbeats.

Afterwards, suffocating with happiness, they twined into the tightest hug.

'We're running away,' Amos breathed.

'I know.' She laughed, caught between daydream believing and living happily ever after. This had to be happening. This *was* happening.

'It means giving everything up.'

'I know.' She was too giddy with love and excitement to register sacrifice. She had given up everything for him once and she would again. This was time travel at its best. Twenty years of her life had just been wiped out.

Something slapped her on the cheek.

For a senseless second, she thought he had hit her.

Then she saw Aunt Til's fat envelope dive-bombing between her and Amos in a gust of wind, making the horses start nervously.

It landed just a few feet away and she picked it up.

'What's that?' asked Amos, kissing her throat as she examined it, drunk with love.

'Leaving present,' she giggled, equally carefree as she ripped open the flap. 'We might be leaving one hell of a mess behind, but at least we know there's a donkey somewhere that's grateful.'

'What?' Amos watched over her shoulder as she attacked the fat envelope.

'Aunt Til – she always tries to save a soul on my behalf at this time of year with a charitable donation.' She raised her cheek to his and laughed. 'Our souls are being saved at last, so I guess it's only fair to pass on the favour.'

'I love you, Diana.' He kissed her ear.

'I love you too,' she shivered as his breath set off a seductive tickle from eardrum to throat to heart, belly and beyond in a long percussive downward thrum.

As she pulled out a wodge of paperwork, a postcard fell to the ground. Amos picked it up.

'It's Foxrush.' He stared at the picture. 'Christ, it was a beautiful house once.' He was so mesmerised, it took him a while to flip it over and study the message: *'Diana, this is yours,'* he read aloud. *'Fight the courts, fight the demons, fight the good fight. They cannot sell it against his will. He haunts us still. Til . . . Death Do Us Part.'*

Diana's hands shook as she flattened out the old, yellowing papers and tried to make sense of them.

'Oh, Christ.'

'Not saving a donkey's soul this year?' he suggested as he watched her blanched face.

'It's the deeds.'

Amos looked at her curiously. 'Good deeds?'

'It's the deeds to Foxrush – to Gunning,' she whispered, cold breath clouding between them.

Muscles catching anxiously in his jaw, Amos twisted the tangle of reins between his fingers.

'I don't understand,' she said shakily. 'Am I supposed to put these in a bank for safekeeping? Does she want me to give them to somebody?'

He looked at the postcard again. 'I rather get the impression she's just given them to you.'

'What for?'

'The estate's yours, Diana. Til has just given you Gunning.'

She shook her head frantically. 'It's not hers to give.'

'Who says? She had the deeds. Now you have the deeds. That makes it yours.'

'Ours,' she corrected in a whisper, staring blankly at the strange phrases, trying to take it in. 'It's ours.'

Amos nodded.

As Diana stood shaking, reading and re-reading the archaic words, he led the horses back into the barn and untacked them.

She was still frozen to the spot when he returned, trembling all over.

He took the thermos and poured her a cup of sweet tea laced with brandy.

She was shaking too much to drink. It spilled around her in a steamy cloud.

Amos leaned back against the car and looked up at the cold blue sky.

'Run away with me.'

'But . . .'

'No buts. Run away with me.'

'You put the horses back.'

'I thought we'd take the German car after all.'

Diana looked at his strong, broad-browed face with its broken nose and high cheeks. The eyes were darker than she had ever seen them, black with impatience.

'We have a chance to make things right here.'

'We'll never have that chance. You know that. We only have a chance to get away. We have to take it. Now.'

She swallowed, holding the deeds to her chest, her head suddenly swimming with muddled pictures of Amos as a young man, Amos now, the Pleasure Garden, their childlike joy. And her children – she saw her beautiful children in the Pleasure Garden that made everyone happy, good or bad. She was a hopeless mother, but she was their only mother. Amos was her only love.

She faltered and that was enough.

Seconds later he was out of sight. He was running too fast to catch.

The deeds to Gunning flew into the manure heap as Diana raced after him, down the Overlodes drive and into the deserted lane. 'No! No! Don't you DARE go away again! I love you, I love you, I love you! You BASTARD!'

He had already slipped away. Nobody could vanish into the countryside like Amos. He'd been taught by an expert.

'You only fell off twice,' Rory reassured Mo as they rattled back up the winding hill at dusk.

'The first time we were still in the market square.'

'That was Aunt Til's fault,' he reassured her. 'Her banners are always horrific. I don't blame Worzel for sitting down.'

'I didn't know horses *could* sit down.' Mo laughed at herself, remembering the indignity of sliding off backwards when faced with Til

Constantine and a bizarre banner that had read 'HUNT YOUR HEART NOT THE FOX'.

'I didn't fall off!' Mim crowed from the bench seat in the groom's compartment. 'I even kept up with Sharon when we cantered between coverts.'

Relegated to the back seat with the children, Sharon snarled. She hadn't been able to shake off the brat despite her best efforts. And she was very disappointed that Mo hadn't broken her neck, or at least broken her pelvis and written off any bed action for a few weeks.

Digby was snoring in her lap, having spent the day being led through gates at the back of the field by a kindly pensioner on a gypsy cob.

'Bloody bad show Diana not turning up,' Rory grumbled as he turned into the yard. 'I could have used that tea. Ah – looks like she had car trouble.'

The Audi was abandoned, the doors open and the thermos on its roof.

As Sharon swung down the ramp ready to unload the horses and Rory started hauling tack from the skirt lockers, Mo slithered stiffly from the cab and limped around to the groom's compartment steps to collect the sleeping Digby.

Mim was already racing towards the cottage to tell her mother all about their day, stopping off to gather a big fan of yellow paper from the lavender bushes. She looked at it curiously, decided it was boring and carried it into the house, dropping it among the puppy poop paper as she gathered up Goblin and shouted for attention.

A minute later, she met Mo carrying Digby along the path.

'Mummy's not here. The door was open, but she's definitely not here.'

'Maybe she's in the barn?'

As they went in search, they heard hooves coming up the drive.

Mo caught her breath. It was the girl from the photograph.

'Good God!' Rory laughed as he came out of the doors of the barn to be confronted by his sister in full hunting regalia, sitting on Ensign. Her face was spattered with mud, her cream breeches caked and her face high with colour, eyes gleaming with tears. She looked stunning. 'What on earth have you been doing?'

'Hunting.' She jumped off and pressed her face to her horse's old neck. 'I've been hunting.'

'Catch anything?'

'No. He got away. He always does. I'm never fast enough.'

31

Til could hear that wretched motorbike whining around the Gunning woods as she set out to visit Nanny at Lower Oddford nursing home, her basket crammed with pheasant and bilberry pâté, a new recipe she had been perfecting. Even if it proved too much for Nanny's teeth, she was certain Ingmar would appreciate it.

The little two-stroke engine droned and spluttered in the distance as she called Ratbag into the car and set off along the muddy track. She could see the tyre marks it had left in the mud, too. Some teenager had been given a Christmas present and wanted to try it out on truly rough terrain, she suspected. Whoever it was had been riding around Gunning land all week, upsetting her traps and making a nuisance of himself.

She stopped off at Amos's farmhouse to pass on some pâté and complain about the motorcyclist, but it was locked up – his dogs barking inside. She hadn't seen him all week. She left a jar on the doorstep and peered in through the windows. A macabre image of the poor man with a shotgun held to his mouth had flashed up in her head, but all she could see were a collie and a wire-haired terrier eating a cushion, feathers flying. Then she narrowed her eyes suspiciously as she spotted a fire burning in the grate, television flickering and a half-eaten sandwich on the table.

'Amos, are you there?' she called through the letter-box, making the dogs drop their cushion and bark like fury.

'Amos!?' Til shouted, swallowing a feather that came floating out through the letter flap.

He didn't answer, but she distinctly heard a muffled 'ouch' as the collie bounded over the back of the sofa.

'I do hope he's all right,' she told Nanny as they watched *Chitty Chitty Bang Bang* later in her room. Nanny was perched up in bed, groggy from a lunch-time nap. 'It's so unlike him to shut himself away. He's such an outdoors person. He was hiding behind the furniture.'

'Oh, he's a tough stick, he'll come through.' Nanny sniffed the pâté appreciatively. 'I shall ask Matron to serve me some of this on soft bread for supper. Ingmar has convinced most of the residents to stay up to toast in the New Year. I have just had my siesta so that I can stay awake later. And your lovely pâté will help me see in the dark. You are so clever.'

'Ah, yes – bilberries. They say pilots ate bilberry jam in the war to help with night vision, don't they? I should give some to Diana.' Til never took long to get to the point when she visited, which was one of the things Nanny loved about her.

'How so?'

'Reg says that she is planning to ride the midnight steeplechase tomorrow night.'

'My goodness!' Nanny almost dropped the pâté. 'Why ever would she want to do that?'

Til laughed and threw her arms wide. 'Whatever possesses Diana to do anything, Nanny? She's always been completely wilful.' She walked to the window and looked out across the formal gardens to the stream, spotting Oddlode spire swathed in mist in the distance. Another fog was rolling in. 'She's asked Pod Shannon to race her – Reg says he's been bragging about it in the pub all week. Rather an ambitious opponent, one would have thought. I might have aimed my sights somewhat lower.'

'Does Amos know about it?'

'Had he bothered to open the door, I could have told him. If he carries on like this he'll become a hermit – just like his father.'

'He must be warned – he can stop her.'

'I rather think not, Nanny,' Til sighed. 'Lord knows what she is planning to ride. Pod is on that dreadful flighty thing of Dilly's. I suppose I should offer Diana Areion, but I'm rather hoping there might be another late entry . . .'

'I thought you had sold him?'

'I have a retainer.'

Nanny's wise gaze studied Til's face, taking in the bright sparkle in those grey eyes, the smiling mouth, and the carefree mood of gay abandon. She looked like a young girl again. She looked like she had when she had first met William Delamere.

'Matilda Constantine,' she demanded in her sternest nursery voice, 'what *are* you up to?'

'Mmm?' Til smiled innocently.

'There is no point trying to pretend you don't know what I'm talking about,' Nanny thundered. She had known Til too many years to miss the signs. This carefree behaviour was typical when she had done something terribly wicked. 'You are plotting something. Poor Amos has locked himself in his house all week, turning into the shadow of his poor father.

Diana is planning to try to kill herself by riding that wretched, cursed race when she's too frightened to cross a field on horseback. And why? What have you said to them?'

'Nothing! I haven't said anything,' she pleaded, reluctantly adding, 'recently'. It was impossible to lie to Nanny.

'Well, in that case I think it's about time you said something pertinent again, don't you? This race has to be stopped.'

'No.' The smile had vanished and Til was the sad, frightened girl Nanny remembered packing off to school each term. 'I won't do anything to stop the race. They say the man who beats the ghosts across country saves his soul.'

'Or *her* soul.' Nanny shuddered and tightened the bow on her bedjacket as she took a firm hold of herself. 'We both know perfectly well that there are no ghosts, Matilda – just far too many secrets, some of which need to come out at last. You can never force a confession out of Diana, but you can at least let our little secret go.'

'I can't do that! I promised.'

'And I no longer hold you to that promise,' she insisted, thinking of her evening of champagne cocktails with Ingmar Olesen. It had been quite wonderful to talk. She should have done it years ago. 'It's time to put the record straight, Matilda. I gather that in this day and age it can even be rather fashionable to have such facts known about one.'

'You want to be *fashionable*?'

'Matilda, I am very old and very staid and rather dull nowadays. A little notoriety might spice up life. If I don't like it, I shall simply pretend that I cannot remember a thing. Like poor, dear Ingmar.'

Til perched on her bed and took her hands, at last becoming the kind, gentle child of nature that Nanny had secretly favoured over her sisters all these years. 'You do know what will happen if we spill the beans, Nanny?'

'I am well aware of the implications,' she said calmly. 'I have nothing to fear. I know that nobody can regret what happened more than I do. I have made peace with my ghost. I think it is time for the rest of you to do so before some fool child dies riding a race that's claimed more lives than I care to remember.'

There was a long pause as Til let go of Nanny's hands and started quilting the flowery bedspread between her fingers. 'And the estate?'

'What of it?'

'The trustees will have a field-day if they find out the truth.'

'My dear, I know that you refuse to accept this, but it is already sold. It really is.'

'Oh, I know. I sold it.'

Nanny almost spat out her false teeth. 'You did *what?*'

'Thought it's what he would have wanted. Already bought myself a little plot in Scotland so I have no use for the place.' She smiled. 'Hope to keep my cottage on, though. Rather like to come back to visit.'

'Til, it isn't yours to sell.'

'Actually, it is – or rather was – and I've given it away. Hate money being involved, making things messy. Had the deeds for years. No idea if they're still worth the paper they're printed on, but the trustees have always seemed powerless without them. Falstaff certainly thought they were legal when he gave them to me.'

'Firebrand gave them to you?'

She nodded. 'When I stood up Midwinter at the altar and came to live at Gunning. I think he was rather impressed.'

'But that was before . . .'

'Before the fire, yes. Before poor trollop wife died and he went into hiding – before the hell. It was our secret marriage certificate if you like. He wanted to show me that he trusted me with his life. He loved big gestures like that.

'He had a solicitor draw up all sorts of extra papers, so I think it was perfectly above-board, if totally hush-hush – got them all in the bank, too. I had a look at them last week when I collected the deeds, but couldn't make head or tail so just took out the pretty papers. The ones bound in red ribbon and sealed with wax. Already gift-wrapped, I thought. Never was any good at wrapping presents.'

'And who did you give this "present" to?'

'Diana, of course.'

'*Diana!*' This time a top set of dentures did fly out and landed on Til's lap.

Smiling, she handed them back. 'I didn't have thirty pieces of silver. Seemed the next best thing.'

'Fworghoorschluumpharty . . .' Nanny was struggling with her teeth.

'I thought she might come to see me this week,' Til speculated, turning her face away and watching Truly Scrumptious on the television, so that Nanny could slip her teeth back in without embarrassment. 'I could have explained about the papers in the bank and the bloody trustees and what-not, but she's definitely avoiding me. And now I hear from Reg of all people that she's riding the race.'

'Always was a selfish flibbertigibbet.' Nanny nodded, grateful to have her teeth back. Saying that was getting harder these days.

'Exactly.' Til cocked her head as Truly Scrumptious looked down at the windmill she was flying over. 'So, you see Nanny, spilling the beans on our little secret might not be very wise.'

Nanny bristled. 'What makes you say that? Surely she should know now more than ever? Stop her being so selfish.'

Til turned to stare at her, grey eyes sharper than ever. 'If we tell the truth, the deeds really will be worthless despite all that boring paper-work darling Falstaff had drawn up. The truth is it wasn't his to give away. Some distant Delamere cousin from Arkansas will probably roll up within a week announcing that he is the rightful heir to everything.'

'Good God, no!'

'Exactly.'

'But the race . . .' Nanny wrung her hands.

'Oh, Diana will never ride the steeplechase.'

Nanny tipped her head in grateful agreement. 'Her cowardice always was her undoing.'

'Pod will still ride, of course. Total maniac, that boy.'

Nanny squawked. 'Don't you even think about letting this go ahead, Matilda. The race can't run with one rider, thank goodness.'

'I know – lucky me.' Til started to chuckle. 'I have a retainer on the one horse in the county that could win it with his eyes shut – and no jockey to ride him . . . yet.'

'And just *who* were you hoping to come forward as a late entry?'

Til winked.

'Oh, for goodness sake, Matilda Constantine. The poor man is dead.'

'We'll see. Who knows? Maybe Diana will race after all and find herself alongside the man she murdered. Ouch!' Til leaped away as a pot of pâté was rapped on her knuckles.

Nanny settled back against her pillows and dismissed Til with her eyes, too exhausted by the gesture to speak. Sometimes old-fashioned discipline was the only way. Nanny always knew best.

32

Having spent the week being thrown off by her Christmas present, Faith was black and blue but still indefatigably in love with something truly four-legged once more. Peace had returned, as had her frizzy hair, springing back into its rightful place as soon as the wretched extensions were cut off.

'Much better.' Anke swept the stray cuttings from her daughter's shoulders and reached for a hand mirror to show her.

But Faith's vanity had vanished along with her crush on Oddlode's two baddest boys, and she barely glanced at her reflection as she bounded up to fetch an apple for Rio from the fruit bowl on the dresser.

Anke studied the lop-sided tresses fretfully. 'I still think we should take you to a salon next week to neaten it up for college.'

'It's fine.' Faith picked out the two biggest Braeburns, peeling away the labels with her teeth. 'I just want my helmet to fit better. See?' She hooked the crash hat back over her head. 'Perfect. Thanks! I'm going to bribe him into being good. Wish me luck!'

'Do you want me to sit on him again for you?' Anke offered.

'Nah – sooner or later he'll figure out I'm better on than off.' She bounded outside.

'Give me a shout if you need any . . . help.' Anke sighed.

Knowing how much Faith hated being watched during her battles with Rio, she joined Graham in the sitting-room, snuggling up in front of the fire and fretting. 'I am so afraid she'll get hurt. I had no idea he was so fit. I thought he was supposed to have been resting in a field for six months?'

'Maybe he secretly worked out at the gym?' Graham cast one of his Christmas books aside and kissed her on the nose.

'I think we should move him up to the Springlode stables so that she can be properly supervised.' Anke pulled his arm around her shoulders. 'We have no facilities here. Every time Faith comes off on to the frozen ground I think I can hear bones cracking. Better to travel to Springlodes to ride him than to watch him from her bedroom window here with her leg in plaster. I just wish she could see it that way.'

'Put your foot down, love. I'll back you up.'

'I am trying,' she sighed. 'But you should have heard her when I explained about Til Constantine's funny one-off full-moon clause. She refuses to accept it. She thinks Til is a witch.'

'She has a point.'

Anke pretended to smack his cheeks.

'Hang on!' Graham almost garrotted her as he checked his watch. 'Full moon tonight, isn't it?'

'Tomorrow. January the first.'

'You know what the horse is supposed to be doing yet?'

'I haven't heard from her at all.'

'Maybe she's forgotten about it,' Graham suggested hopefully. 'We should get him to Overlodes ASAP. The sooner we move that bugger away from our land the better. I don't want any more fires.'

'Oh, that poor horse has nothing to do with the talk of curses and fires,' sighed Anke, who had worked hard to secure Graham's approval to buy him, especially given the curious clause.

'I don't trust his bloody breeding,' he muttered. 'He's already cost me an arm and a leg – I don't want him costing me a new roof as well.'

'He's just a horse – a very classy horse.' Anke rolled on to her back, neck propped up on his thigh and ankles on Evig.

'We'll have a word with Rory tonight – see how soon he can take him. Bound to be at the party.'

'He and Mo are baby sitting at the stables,' she reminded him, looking up at his lovely cleft chin.

They had been invited to the New Year's Eve opening party at the renovated Springlodes pub, now proudly reinstated as the New Inn. Magnus had been helping the Sixsmiths day and night in the last-minute preparations.

'Has he decided which Disgrace he's in love with yet?' Graham asked.

'I think it changes daily.' She wriggled her shoulders tighter into the crook of his arm. 'I suppose he will have to look for a new job soon, now that the pub is finished. If you are really not re-opening Dulston's he will have nothing to do all day but make that dreadful noise in his studio.' Road Kill's band practices in the granny annexe were the cause of much unrest as the house shook under the onslaught.

'Ah – well I've been thinking about Dulston's.' He stroked the hair back from her cheek. 'I've got some ideas for the site.'

'Please don't tell me I am going to lose you to work again, *kaereste*?' she pleaded. 'I thought you said you were happy to take early retirement?'

'I am. But we both agree that sound-proofing the annexe is impossible, yes?'

'Yes.' She nodded cautiously.

'So why not suggest Magnus moves his studio a few miles away?'

Anke propped herself up on one elbow. 'Really?'

'Don't see why not. The buildings are still sound. I want to hang on to the plot – worth a small fortune if you could get residential planning permission up there one day. Makes sense to use it in the meantime.'

'But we have no insurance money to cover the repairs.'

'I think I can just about patch it together. Magnus has proved himself a pretty handy builder on the pub restoration, after all.'

'Won't it cost a fortune to set up a studio?'

'Not if we kit it out with second-hand stuff and recoup costs by hiring it out. Magnus can run it. Give him something to do.'

'Oh, Graham, you are so wonderful.' She kissed him all over his face.

'Steady, love – I'll be whisking you upstairs any minute and young Chad is entertaining his lady friend up there. Might give them ideas.'

'Which reminds me – Mo is picking them up at four.' She glanced at her watch. 'I must feed them.' Chad was staying at Horseshoe Farm Cottage that night, where Mo and Rory had offered to babysit while everyone partied at the pub. 'I promised Mo I'd give them high tea here.'

'Diana using all her friends for child-care again, I see?' Graham followed her into the kitchen, Evig at his heels.

'Not at all.' Anke was quick to defend her. Diana was on a knife-edge emotionally these days. She dropped her voice to a whisper in case Mim and Chad came downstairs. 'Tim – her ex-husband – was supposed to take the children for the whole of New Year; his family have a holiday cottage in the West Country, I think. Then, at the last minute, he said they couldn't come and that he would only be able to see them today and only for a few hours. He has done this so many times, and the children are terribly upset. Diana has driven Digby up to London specially to see him, but Mim wouldn't go.'

'Don't blame her. Selfish bastard.'

'His new girlfriend takes up all his time. Diana says that this woman likes the children, but they do not like her, and Tim won't make arrangements to see them on his own.'

'Prat.'

Anke stopped pulling the cling film from plastic containers and looked up at him, her big blue eyes and wise face saying it all.

'I know.' He held his arms wide and hung his head in recognition, mustering a grateful, abashed smile. 'New Year's Resolution. I will try to see my kids and make peace once and for all. God knows, Deirdre's now so chilled out she even put our move on her Christmas round robin this year.'

None of his grown-up children from his first marriage had made contact or sent a Christmas card, despite Anke carefully choosing presents to send them and making Graham write out their cards personally, with snippets of news and all the Wyck Farm contact details in case they hadn't received them the first time.

'A father is so important to his children.' She cupped his chin.

Hers was as impossible as ever. He now appeared to have organised some sort of pensioner rave at the nursing home to see in the New Year.

'I think he might be put on a formal warning soon. Your plans for Dulston's may have to be put into action straightaway if he needs the annexe.'

'Which reminds me,' he started cautiously. 'I've also been thinking about your father's shop . . .'

'You see, I *knew* you'd have to find yourself something to keep you from your family!' she teased, reaching up for a pan from the rack.

'Not me – you.'

'Me?'

'You always say that you feel stifled by being at home now that you no longer ride. Why not take over his business and build it up again?'

'I know nothing about it, *kaereste*. I don't have his clever mind. I would need to study for years.'

'You have a very, very clever mind. And you *are* studying, love. No need to stop.'

'So how can I hope to run a business as well?'

'I'll project manage the rebuilding work first. That will take a year at least, give me something to do close to home. You keep up your studies. Then we set up the business together and I can run the day-to-day stuff – mind the shop, do the tourist patter – while you fill up your clever head and fill up the shelves.'

She was so excited by the idea that she had filled the pan up until it was brimming over. 'We would have to ask Morfar.'

'Already had a chat about it. He's all for it, if you are.'

'He is?'

'You'd better ask him again yourself, mind you. Not sure he'll remember our chat or indeed who the hell I am in the first place.'

She allowed herself the freedom to laugh. 'You really mean this, *kaereste*?'

He held out his arms. 'No, I'm just kidding.'

She boofed his chin with her wet hand before slipping contentedly into the hug.

'How do we afford it all?'

'Your father gets his insurance pay-out, which pays for his new life. We take on the loss and secure a loan for the new business. Couldn't be simpler.'

She hugged him closer. 'So awful that there was no insurance for Dulston's. I hope they catch this dreadful man soon. I know that nobody has been hurt, but arson is such an evil thing, so wasteful and angry.'

She felt Graham tense, wrapping his arms more tightly around her.

'I am sorry, *kaereste*. I know. It's awful.'

Then he breathed in her ear, 'I burned it.'

She froze. 'You . . . did . . . what?'

'Dulston's, I burnt it.'

Anke felt sick. She tried to wriggle free, but was trapped. 'And our house? You tried to burn that, too? My father's shop? You –'

'Shhhh . . . shhhhhh, no! No, love, no. Christ.' He kept her gripped in his arms as he tipped back his head so that he could look in her eyes. 'I didn't start any other fires. I didn't even burn bloody Dulston's deliberately. I was trying to torch the camp.'

'The camp?' Anke looked at him, eyes darting around his honest blue stare, checking for flaws.

'Round the back of the office.'

'The arsonist's camp?' She groaned at the irony of it all. 'You were trying to *burn* that?'

'It wasn't an arsonist's camp. It was where I . . . it was where the girl and me – it was where I used to take –'

With her arms trapped, the only way to shut him up was with a kiss. Eyes clenched shut against tears, Anke pressed her lips to his and stopped him talking.

When they resurfaced, he looked as though he'd just been given the all-clear after a long illness.

'I thought I was such a prat, Anke. I just wanted to get rid of it, forget I had been such a fool and risked so much when all I ever wanted was you. The bloody thing reminded me of how much I'd risked. But I used too much petrol and the whole thing bloody spiralled. I hadn't accounted for the wind – it was like a ruddy gale that night. It was less than five minutes before the first of the buildings was up like an inferno. I was fannying around figuring out how to get to a pay phone to call the fire brigade with an "anonymous" tip-off because I was so freaked out I couldn't think straight, and the tractors were going up all around me – whoomp, whoomp. But all I could think of was you, and of having to tell you that I'd burned my bloody business down trying to destroy the evidence of an *affaire.*'

She shut him up with another kiss.

He emerged breathless, his eyes gleaming as though he had been led from Death Row to Millionaire's Row. 'I know it's bad, but I let the police think it was another arson. I was bricking it, but I couldn't admit the truth. It was so much more shameful to tell you why I had done it.'

'But I knew you were being unfaithful all along.'

'You did?'

'I guessed almost straightaway. I didn't know who it was at first – I thought it was Diana – but then –'

'Diana! God, no! It was –'

'I know.' She kissed him hard. 'Don't spoil this. I am being very noble and very Danish. You could learn a lot, Graham.'

'And you don't mind?' He squeezed her as tight as he could, utterly bewildered by love and remorse on a collision course.

She narrowed her eyes. 'Of *course* I mind. I mind so much that you had an affair, I mind that you were such an idiot that you burned down your entire business with no insurance, I mind that you broke the law and lied and deceived our family and betrayed me. I mind very, very much.'

'Oh.' His face fell. He was back on Death Row with the double whammy of a terminal illness. At last he released his grip and turned away, preparing to be given his marching orders.

'Don't you want me to forgive you?'

Her looked back incredulously.

'I forgive you. I know you did it for love. Now never do it again.'

'I love you, Anke Brakespear.' He shook his head in wonder.

'And I love you, Graham Brakespear,' she sighed, melting into his kiss.

Hovering in the conservatory, blood creeping from a cut on her chin and mud all over her breeches, Faith backed away and ran back to the stable where she had left Rio, sweaty and victorious from throwing her off again. He hated being ridden in the field, protesting with every fit, squirming muscle in his body.

'Right, you big bully.' She knotted the broken reins and led him out. 'We'll try something else. Let's go for a little walk around the block.' She picked up her high viz tabard from the mounting block and threw it over her head back to front and inside out in her haste to keep her nerve.

Faith wasn't the only one in a hurry.

As soon as she had her foot in the stirrup, they flew along the drive in a flurry of bucks, rears and spins, clattering out on to the tarmac in a shower of sparks and belting towards Oddlode. Faith only just clung on.

'Oh, heck,' she wailed, wondering in a brief, panic-stricken moment whether she should have mentioned to her mother and Graham what she was doing. She didn't even have her mobile phone with her. In her desperation to win over Rio, she hadn't thought this through at all.

The Wycks were lined up on their customary stools by the bar of the snug at the Lodes Inn, plying Pod with measures of scotch as they pursued the topic all the village was talking about.

'You really riding the midnight chase tomorrow?'

'Might be.' Pod cleared his throat and downed his drinks as fast as he could. The reality of doing the thing was starting to hit home.

Days of searching the Gunning Estate in the frosty fog had started to play with his head. The place frightened him for the first time. He kept getting lost, wandering in circles, chasing his tail.

To ride a horse from the derelict chapel through the woods to the parkland was not a tempting prospect, especially if the horse was not the brave stallion bred for the job, but his girlfriend's cowardly strawberry roan nutcase. When he had bragged one drunken night weeks earlier that he might give it a go, he had never really imagined it would happen, and certainly not that he would have been challenged to do it by Diana Lampeter.

'Can't ride it if the mist don't clear,' Saul pointed out. 'Need a clear night for the moon.'

'Can't have frost neither.' Alf rubbed his red nose with his sleeve.

The younger Wycks nudged one another as they saw the relief touch Pod's eyes.

'Thought you said they rode whatever the weather in the old days, pops?' asked young Tam.

'Yeah, and look how many died,' Alf tutted, shaking his head.

'Takes a brave man to ride them ditches and walls even on a clear night,' muttered Reg. 'And as for the hedges –' he sucked on his gums before whistling through his two remaining teeth '– they're grown men's fences, specially Look and Leap. Bloody big bastards, them thorns.'

'The girl will never do it,' Alf sniffed, beckoning for more whisky. 'Constantines are cowards.'

'All the village will be out to watch,' Saul told Pod, slapping his back.

'Everyone's been talking about it. I've started a book, but it's a one-horse race, innit? You're evens; Miss Toffee Nose is at five hundred to one and I still can't get a punter to take her.'

'You can always bet on me living or dying,' Pod joked.

'You never know,' Tam cackled. 'Old Firebrand might come out. Give you a run for your money.'

Pod downed the scotch that had just landed in front of him, feeling its heat burning his veins. He couldn't lose face.

'I'd rather race a ghost than a woman any day.' He slammed his glass down to rowdy cheers.

'If she thinks she can win her way back into this village by pulling a stunt like that, she's a fool.' Alf shook his head. 'Everyone knows she's a bad lot. Broke Amos's heart all over again, she has. Hardly been out of his house all week. You seen him, Pod?'

Pod shook his head. He was grateful for Amos's self-imposed exile. It had enabled his search, however fruitless. A guilty finger of compassion kept rapping him on the temples whenever he passed Gunning Farm, pitying such ferocity caged up in there, pacing the floors as Amos relived God knows what agony.

'She's got no such shame,' Saul pointed out as he slotted change into the jukebox. 'Seen her la-di-da-ing about all over the place in that big car of hers, I have.'

Suddenly, Reg Wyck clutched Pod's arm and cursed. 'You hear that?'

'All I can hear is that bloody awful music Saul's just put on,' Pod jeered.

'Hooves!' Reg cursed again, eyes wild. 'Them's hooves! The ghosts is out.'

'Shit!' Pod ran to the window.

The Wycks gathered beside him, wailing with gusto as a horse came galloping past through the fog, heading along the lane behind the Manor. It was moving so fast all they could see was a blur of black coat, glint of iron shoes and a rider with a bright yellow torso so garish that it could be aflame.

'Him's heading for the hills.' Reg said. 'I wouldn't go up to Springlode tonight if I was you.'

Pod laughed, feigning scorn to cover his apprehension. 'Miss a party with free booze? You must be kidding.'

'You've got a point. Need a few more for the journey, mind you. Another?'

Pod shook his head, fetching his coat from the hook. 'Have to pay a house call. Wish someone a Happy New Year.'

He had timed it perfectly. With predictable, quartz-set accuracy, Gladys Gates was trotting from the rear drive of the Manor and crossing the lane to Cider Court, a casserole in her arms. She paused and cocked her head as she caught the last faint drum of horse's hooves in the mist, facing Pod who was lurking behind a poop scoop bin and trying not to breathe. Then, tutting and shaking her head, she marched on, casserole aloft.

Pod had to stick close for fear of losing her in the fog. Just yards behind, feet as light as a cat's, he followed her past Ingmar's burned-out shop and through the narrow gate into the old Manor orchard. Together, they took the footpath over the wooden bridge that crossed the Odd and headed towards the railway.

The old Pullman was surrounded by dense firs and hollies, quite hidden from view. No wonder Pod had struggled to find it on an earlier recce. Shielded further by the fog, it was almost impossible to make out, overgrown with moss and ivy in its secret lair – a fat green crocodile – only the faint putter of a generator giving it away.

'Granville!' Gladys banged on his door and set the casserole on the breezeblock step, picking up an empty one that had been left there like a milk bottle for collection.

Pod darted into the shadows as she retraced her steps and then froze as she paused beside him with a curious sniff, a tilt of her head and her eyes sliding sideways thoughtfully.

'Happy New Year!' she called over her shoulder before trotting off.

Waiting until she was a safe distance away, Pod picked up the casserole and lifted the lid, giving it an appreciative sniff. Mmm. Beef stew. Tremendous.

The door of the carriage swung open and two mad mossy eyes widened in alarm.

'Room service!' Pod announced cheerfully, handing over the food.

'What'ya want?' Granville barked, backing inside.

'I want you to tell me what this opens?' Pod held up the key and then jumped back as a steaming casserole of beef stew was dropped at his feet.

It wasn't a flat-out gallop – more of a fast canter, and yet Faith had no way of stopping it. She had tried – boy, had she tried, pulling at the reins, bracing them against the saddle, trying to steer in a circle, sitting back, digging in – nothing worked. She was now almost too exhausted to hold on. She had no idea where they were heading, except that it was upwards. She could hardly see a thing in the fog and gathering gloom. They had raced past the River Folly, she knew that. And they had jumped two stiles, much to her surprise. They had loomed up in the whiteness and Rio had bounded over them without breaking his stride.

And yet she felt strangely safe – far safer than she had when trying to make the stallion simply trot a small circle in the Wyck Farm paddock. His ears were pricked and his sure-footed progress was determined and inevitable. He knew where he was going. She was certain he was taking her somewhere magical.

Mo laughed as Rory tried to pull her back into bed. 'I must go to collect the kids!' she complained. 'I'm late as it is.'

'But I like having you all to myself.'

'You'll have me all to yourself later, when they've gone to bed.'

'Good. Don't forget I'm cooking a special meal.'

'How could I?' She rolled her eyes. The kitchen had been out of bounds all day.

Indulgently, he watched her dress, loving the way her slim body disappeared into the tens of baggy, warm layers – his secret jewel.

'It's really bad fog out there – you will drive carefully, won't you? Do you want me to come too?'

'No – you stay and do feeds. It's not fair on Sharon otherwise.'

Rory waved her off in her tatty little car and, whistling cheerfully, headed into the barn to help Sharon.

'Looks like another cancelled hunt tomorrow with this weather.' He collected a pile of buckets.

'Reckon so. Might still run the race though.'

'What race?'

'Moonlit steeplechase.'

'They haven't run that in years. Everyone used to get killed.'

'Heard it was on this year. Thought you'd want to take part.'

'Not likely – who told you?'

'Pod Shannon.'

'That lunatic? No wonder. In that case I definitely don't want anything to do with it. Poor Mo has had enough torture from him already.'

She eyed him over the metal bins, scoop in hand. 'You cooking something special tonight for her, then?'

'Peppered steak in red wine sauce. Diana's given me the recipe – says it's foolproof.'

'Sounds delicious.' She remembered that Mo was a vegetarian and smirked. Foolproof but not Rory-proof.

'Are you going to the party at the pub, S?'

'Nah. Meeting some friends out Maddington way.'

He sat on an upturned bucket, watching her work, suddenly hit with a pang of conscience.

'Sharon, I know you realise that there was never anything between us – not a real relationship, y'know? But we had fun and I wouldn't want to hurt you in any way.'

'I know.' She threw scoops of oats into buckets as the horses started kicking at their doors.

'But I think it's only fair to warn you that I plan to marry Mo.'

'Fair enough.' She threw chaff on to the oats.

'You don't mind?'

'It's your decision.' She pulled open the lid on the steaming pan of sugar beet. 'You proposing tonight?'

'I might,' he shrugged. Having only just decided on the whole marriage thing, he was a bit vague. 'Depends how drunk I get.'

'Good luck,' she sniffed, straightening up to look at him, her face glistening with steam.

'Thanks, S.' He planted a kiss on her hot, damp cheek.

For a brief moment, she clasped his head with her chaff-covered hands, trapping his lips so tightly to her cheek that his nose bent sideways and he stopped breathing. Then she released him quickly and nodded.

The horses were banging frenziedly now.

'You go and start your big meal,' Sharon told him, turning away to the cupboard housing all the supplements. 'Let me finish off here. You always slow me up.'

'You're a star. As soon as Diana starts making us some money, I'll give you a pay-rise.'

'Paying me at all would be a start.' Sharon peeled open the lid on a container of Devil's Claw and listened as he bounced cheerfully along the aisle between his horses, kissing them all on the nose.

She slumped down on the bucket he had just vacated and stared vacantly in front of her. Normally, Rory could not resist a challenge. Tomorrow night, he was supposed to be riding the race for Mo's heart and losing it – not proposing tonight. This was all wrong.

Diana checked Digby was still asleep on the rear seat as she waited at the traffic lights in Market Addington, finally on her last leg back from London.

Her solicitor had kept his office open especially to see her that afternoon, but he hadn't minded at all. What she had shown him had been the most exciting thing he'd encountered in his entire professional career.

'Will it hold water?' she'd asked sceptically. She resisted the temptation to point out that it had narrowly missed being puppy toilet paper, saved only by Mo, who had whisked it off the kitchen floor, worried the puppies would choke on the wax seals, after the Boxing Day meet.

'I can try my damnedest to make sure it does,' he'd promised, already pulling books from shelves and plucking files from cabinets, unable to hide his glee.

Diana was surprised that he seemed to think it genuine.

The meeting had made her late to drop Digby with his father, and Tim's temper had not been improved by the fact that Mim was not with them.

'I have bent over backwards to make time for this, and you're late and one man down. We agreed fifteen hundred hours. Katie has gone on ahead to Somerset to make preparations for tonight. I can only spare an hour. I have to beat the traffic.'

Originally, Tim had been entitled to have the children for the entire week surrounding New Year. But that promised week had dwindled to two days, then one night and now just a few hours. And this short visit had only happened because Diana had demanded that he see his children for at least a few hours during their holidays – even if it meant bringing them to him. The expensive, belated Christmas gifts which had arrived by courier that week were no substitute for contact.

'And where is Mim?' he'd demanded when she ushered the reluctant Digby through the door to the old family home and into a hallway that had already been repainted from its familiar duck-egg blue to bright orange.

In the wake of his bad temper, Diana abandoned plans to make up a story about a head cold.

'She wouldn't come.'

'Sensible girl. Stupid to travel in this weather. One hour, all right?' He took poor Digby's paw and gathered him inside, shutting the door on her.

Diana had retreated to Hyde Park, sitting by the old sand school where she had ridden Ensign so often, wondering how she could have lived with Tim for so many years and not realised how vile he was.

That he was vile to her was understandable. It was all too easy for married love to curdle to sour loathing.

But to deny his children love was unforgivable. She still remembered the hollow promises from her own childhood, the gifts offered to make up for long absences. In one particularly bad year, when she was about fourteen, she had seen her father for ten minutes at Heathrow airport, and seen her mother for a few hours at Christmas. Tim came from the same selfish, prehistoric mould as her parents. She wanted to punch him. To have a lousy mother was bad enough, but they had been unlucky enough to suffer the double whammy, just as she had.

She had collected Digby after precisely one hour. Tim couldn't wait to bundle him out of the door, already shrugging on his coat and gathering his car keys for the drive to Somerset.

'Stupid to travel in this weather,' she'd muttered but he hadn't heard.

'Might have some leave again at Easter. I'll call.' He strode past them, leaving Diana on her old doorstep in front of her old house, wondering what had hit her.

She hugged Digby tightly to her. 'Was it nice to see Daddy again?'

'That man isn't my Daddy any more,' Digby said emphatically.

'Who is?'

'Uncle Rory.'

'Ah. Complicated.' She took his hand as she led him towards the Audi, only to be almost mown down by Tim racing past in his sports car.

'And Mo is my second Mummy – after you.'

'Glad I come first,' she laughed.

'You can share me.'

His brave face hadn't lasted long. Diana knew that the encounter with his father had devastated him and he cried himself to sleep in the back seat as they crawled along the A40 in New Year's Eve traffic, everyone escaping the city into the fog. He didn't want to talk about it, and Diana was lacerated with guilt for making him go. Perhaps she should have let Tim have his way and not see them. Perhaps they needed a clean break. At Horseshoe Farm Cottage, Digs was happy in his strange little family of second father and mothers. Mo had even coaxed him into eating food that wasn't orange – Diana having tried without success for five years. And Mo didn't even cook. All it had taken was a kiwi fruit and a game of dare. Now he ate orange food and kiwi fruits. Soon it would be sushi and black bean curries.

All the way to Market Addington, she had driven through the fog playing a dangerous game of 'what if'. What if she had run away with Amos at eighteen? What if she had run away with Amos at forty? What if they still could?

Now she reached for the ring on its chain and realised that she'd left it at the cottage – taking it off that morning when she had been feeding the puppies and they'd tried to eat it as it dangled from her neck.

She felt as though she'd left a part of her heart at home. She pressed the accelerator pedal.

'Eek!'

She slammed her foot on the brake, wishing she hadn't decided to drive in her heels.

Pulling up behind a suspiciously long line of tail-lights on the usually clear lane out of Maddington, Diana cursed under her breath.

Several cars behind her, blue lights flashed and an ambulance bumped by on the verge.

The fog had already claimed one poor victim that night. Diana hoped they were all right. It looked as though she was in for a long wait. She turned on Radio Four.

'It was a cold and heartless night,' cooed Anna Massey. 'The sort of night that sucked the marrow from bones –'

'Oh, do shut up.' Diana switched her off and banged her palms against the steering-wheel in frustration.

Still at Wyck Farm, Mo called Rory, waiting for him to pick up the Overlodes phone. He was lounging in the bath. 'There's a bit of a crisis here,' she announced when he eventually answered. 'Faith has disappeared, so has Rio. Everyone's been searching the fields and railway track. Anke thinks he's bolted. Of course now it's dark, they're starting to really panic. They've taken the cars out and I'm guarding the kids and the phones.'

'Christ, how bloody awful, especially in this fog. Do you need my help?'

'Better to stay put. I'll call if we need the lorry.'

'Sure.' He tried not to think about his romantic meal currently counting down at minus forty-five minutes according to Diana's schedule. She hadn't allowed for bolting horses when she'd told him when to put on the oven for the potatoes.

Rory replaced the receiver and heard an indulgent chomping behind him.

Cheeks bulging, Hally was polishing off two fat steaks, her puppies nipping greedily at her lips.

Rory groaned and looked at his watch. The shops would be closed by now. The Sixsmiths were laying on a huge feast that night. He was bound to be able to beg a few scraps. He called Mo back.

'I'm just popping out. I'll be on my mobile – call if there's any news. Love you.'

'You too.'

He went to warn Sharon to man the yard phone, but he couldn't find her. The horses were all bedded down for the night and her mobile home was in darkness. She must have left for Market Addington already. Scribbling a note and leaving it on her door just in case, he wandered down to the pub through the mist, his torch blasting white light straight back at him.

Such had been the density of cloud and haze all week, nobody had actually been able to see the finishing touches on the old building, the New Inn, now restored to its former glory and eighteenth-century identity. The bunting was invisible in the fog, the fairy lights dim. The windows glowed like soft Chinese lanterns.

And yet inside, it was a riot of cheer and activity. Drills buzzed, hammers banged, brushes slapped on paint and the Three Disgraces dangled prettily from ladders putting up streamers.

'Welcome!' Tony greeted Rory cheerfully from behind the bar, already well into the champagne and adoring his new role. He was wearing a T-shirt especially made for him by his daughters that said *Landed Here, Lording Over It.* 'Drinks are on the house as long as you help out.'

'Looks fantastic.' Rory couldn't help taking a jaw-dropping sweep around his old watering-hole. 'You haven't changed a thing.'

He had expected it to be opened out, the beams stripped, fashionable wrought-iron sconces everywhere to match the Cotswold trend for turning old pubs into rustic restaurant wine bars. Instead it was as though the fire had never happened. It was almost exactly as he remembered, and perfect for it. Only the name had changed.

'Beautiful, isn't it?' Tony Sixsmith said proudly, pouring Rory a glass.

'You're telling me. Thank God my sister never got her hands on it.'

'I'll drink to that.' Tony raised his glass. 'You bringing that gorgeous creature of yours here later?'

Rory pulled an apologetic face and explained his pilfered steaks dilemma.

'Sure – Dulcie can find you something delicious,' Tony promised and then winced as the sound of smashing pans and a torrent of furious Cuban Spanish came from the swing-doors nearby. 'Just give her a couple of minutes, huh? New kitchen staff aren't quite up to speed. We're expecting a couple of hundred tonight.'

'That many?' Rory whistled.

'Marquee out the back. Even got a band. Road Kill.'

'Oh, joy.' Rory grinned, checking his mobile reception and settling in by the bar. He could use a little Dutch courage to build up to tonight's task. He wasn't at all sure what Mo's reaction would be. He knew it was early days and he worried that she felt like a glorified nanny at times, yet she seemed to love life at Overlodes. She cheered the place up, brightened the place up and tidied the place up. He never wanted her to leave.

'Shit, shit, shit!' Pod burst in through the doors behind him, face bleached white from hearing the hooves again. They were chasing him. 'Shit,' he reiterated as he saw Rory sitting at the bar.

Rory gaped at him, having never really studied him close up in detail. He was smaller than he remembered – at least six inches shorter than Rory – and stouter. And right now, he had hollow cheeks, thick stubble, and scratches all over his face. But that face was still so good-looking that Rory felt sick with apprehension. He was a bloody dude. No wonder Dilly fancied him. No wonder Mo still cried out his name in her sleep.

'Hello, mate – you took your time.' Tony fetched a fresh glass and noticed blood on his forehead. 'You okay?'

Pod licked his lips, eyes darting. The heat and noise soothed him a little, but his heart still raced.

'Fell off me bike on the way up,' he muttered, reeking of whisky, Scouse accent thickened with fear and alcohol. 'I can't stay – got to be somewhere.' He reached into his leather jacket and drew out a fat envelope. 'It's all there. I'll see you later, eh?'

'Sure.' Tony took the envelope and placed it under a bar towel in front of Rory. 'Hey – are you *really* riding the old midnight point tomorrow?'

'Depends.' Pod turned to leave and then turned back to Rory. 'Your sister still up for it?'

He didn't trust his ears. 'Up for what?'

'She's riding the race, too. The moonlit steeplechase – from Foxrush to Oddlode. Haven't you heard?'

'No bloody way!' He laughed raucously, guessing this must be a wind-up. 'So far she hasn't made it into trot on that old pensioner she rides.'

Which made Pod feel a little better as he headed back out into the white blanket.

'What the hell was all that about . . . ?' Rory turned to Tony, who winked knowingly.

'I love being a landlord. You hear everything.'

'You're not even open yet.'

He winked again and drew the envelope from the towel, peeking inside happily before tucking it away.

Another loud crash came from behind, and this time Dulcie sounded close to murder.

'Better just check.'

Rory helped himself to more champagne from the bottle on the bar, letting it foam right over the rim – all over the bar towel.

'Butter fingers!' he chastised himself, checking to see if anyone was looking – but the local snagging team was still hammering and drilling away like mad behind him. He was too distracted to recognise Magnus amongst them.

He took the towel and mopped up the spillage, checking out the envelope. It really was fat. What was Pod up to, paying lump sums to Tony Sixsmith?

He peered inside.

It wasn't cash at all. It was a rare old book, full of neat hand-printed pages and glossy photographic plates. Unable to help himself, Rory took a look.

'Jesus.'

He was so absorbed that he didn't notice Tony reappearing from the kitchens, carrying a Tupperware container.

'Amazing, isn't it?'

Rory looked up guiltily, closing the book.

'No – have a browse. I wanted it for the pictures – going to have them copied and frame them around the place. There's lots of the village – and a piece about how the pub lost its old name. I'll frame that too.'

'Where did it come from?'

'Dunno. Pod said he found it.'

Rory studied the old book again, flipping through the musty pages, looking at the sketches and diagrams and photographs of Gunning in its heyday.

'Says the ghosts make people sinners, apparently. Nothing about fire at all. Something to do with a curse.'

Rory remembered hearing the same story from someone else. When had that been?

He looked at the first page. *Foxrush Hall – The Vault of Lost Souls* by Edward Quigley.

'Quigley,' he muttered, thinking back.

Ingmar Olesen had talked about Quigley. He'd had the book in his shop – the only copy in existence, he'd said. Everyone must have assumed it was lost in the fire.

'There's a chapter about the old race in there.' Tony nodded at it.

'Bloody terrifying cavalry charge by all accounts. Can't believe your sister wants to resurrect it.'

'There's no way she'll do it.' Rory leafed through to find the reference. 'You've been fed misinformation there, old chap.'

'Not what I heard. Pod's asked me to be starter. I said I'd no more step in that godforsaken place than let this place burn again, but he bribed me with the book. Midnight tomorrow. Soon as I lock up here, I'll be going there.'

Rory read the first few lines of the chapter about the steeplechase, cataloguing the number of lives it had claimed. Starting to feel seriously uneasy, he helped himself to more champagne.

Faith laughed as Rio finally clattered up the drive to Overlodes. The stallion was barely blowing, had hardly broken a sweat and was very, very pleased with himself. He let out a thunderous roar to announce their arrival, ears pricked, standing to attention by the doors of the barn so that she could slither off.

Knees buckling, she leaned against him and laughed with relief. 'For a moment I thought you were taking me to the haunted woods.'

The lights flickered on in the American barn.

'Been out for a hack?' Sharon appeared wearing one of Rory's fleeces and looking greyer than ever.

'You could say!' High on adrenaline and adventure, Faith couldn't wait to babble out the story. 'I was only going to take him up the road at home to calm him down, and when he took off I seriously thought I'd had it, but then he just bowled along and seemed to know exactly where he was going – and he jumped everything in his path. It was the most incredible –'

'You'd better wash him off and put him in the big box away from the mares.' Sharon cut her short. 'I'll call Wyck Farm. They're out looking for you.'

'Yes – sorry – of course.' Faith hung her head, loosening his girths. 'He was just so amazing.'

Sharon sidled up behind her and, in a rare moment of physical contact, patted Faith on the back. Unfortunately, such was Sharon's weight and power she winded Faith completely. 'Clever of you to bring him up here.'

'No choice,' Faith squeaked breathlessly.

Sharon touched the stallion's taut, hot neck with a sad smile. 'Shame I won't be here to see the race. Bet he'll win it.'

'What race?' Faith wheezed.

But Sharon was heading into the tack room to use the phone.

'Safe and sound,' she told Mo when the phone was picked up at Wyck Farm a moment later.

'Oh, thank goodness. They're still out looking. I'll call them, then I'll come straight up. Poor Rory's romantic dinner must be burned to a frazzle. Will you tell him I'm on my way?'

Face like thunder, Sharon made Faith a mug of instant hot chocolate with the tack room kettle and carried it out to her in the *Stroppy Mare* mug.

'You are like so fab, S.' Faith took it gratefully, starting to come down from her physical high with chattering teeth and weak limbs. Rio, by contrast, looked as though he had just enjoyed a light pipe-opener.

Finishing the job of rubbing down the stallion and putting on layers of wicking rugs, Sharon wiped her tears away on the rough blankets.

'Lost the Delilah look then?' she muttered, noticing Faith's cropped hair now that she had pulled off the crash helmet to sip her hot chocolate.

'Yeah – no point trying to make Rory fancy me now. I've gone off him anyway.'

'Reckons he's proposing to her tonight.'

'To Silly Toes?'

'Yeah. Told me earlier he wants to marry her.' Her voice stayed flat and emotionless, masking the car crash shock.

'How awful. Poor you.' Faith sought solace in her steaming mug of hot chocolate, her own heart barely bruised as she admired Rio's beautiful head bobbing behind the stallion bars. She felt this evening's escapade had bonded them, even though she had merely been a willing passenger.

'You really upset about it?' she remembered to ask Sharon eventually.

Hiding her face in Rio's flank, Sharon chewed the last of the tears from her lips. 'Nah.'

'Face it,' Faith giggled. 'You and I never stood a chance.'

Sharon said nothing, buckling up the last of the cross surcingles around the stallion's belly.

'Rory's like Rio – like all class stallions. He needs an alpha mare. Dilly was more of a My Little Pony and I was practically a companion goat.'

'What does that make me then?'

Faith mistook the shake in Sharon's voice for laughter.

'A lovely weight-carrying schoolmistress.'

'Thought Mo was the schoolmistress?'

'In bed as well, I think.' Still giggling, Faith snorted at her own daring. 'I guess you are like *so* out of a job now?'

'Yeah.' Sharon let out a dry cough of false laughter. 'Looks like it's time to move on.'

She adjusted the rugs slowly and patted the horse, letting herself out of the stable. 'We'd best leave him alone. I've got the keys to the cottage – we can wait there.'

When they got to the cottage, it was in darkness, the French doors to the kitchen wide open and puppies spilling in and out.

'Funny.' Sharon narrowed her eyes. 'I saw Rory go out. I'm sure he locked up.'

'Has anything been taken?' Faith asked nervously, waiting outside for her to check around.

'Hard to tell – place is such a tip. Could have been ransacked for all I know. Seems empty enough.'

While Faith played with the puppies and relived every second of her foggy adventure, Sharon checked out the debris Rory had already created in the kitchen. The engagement ring he'd bought wasn't hard to spot. It was on top of the bread bin.

Pretty.

Sharon turned it around in her fingers, wondering why it was attached to a chain.

'Hello, hello!' Mo burst in, pink-cheeked and relieved as she rushed up to Faith. 'You okay?'

'Fantastic!'

Mo grinned. 'Don't tell your mother that. She and Graham are stuck in a ditch halfway up the bridle-path to here, waiting for Bill Hudson to come and pull them out with his tractor. But they're seriously happy you're okay. They'll be here as soon as they can. Thanks, Sharon.' She straightened up.

'For what?' Sharon had hastily pocketed the ring, her grey slab cheeks glowing with two rare spots of colour.

'For looking after her.'

'She's not a little kid.'

'Unlike some others I could mention!' Mo laughed as Mim and Chad rushed inside from the foggy garden and raced upstairs. She gave a half-hearted chase. 'Don't lock yourselves in . . . the bedroom.' It was too late. From the giggling inside, love's young dream had found paradise on the top bunk.

'Where's Rory?'

Sharon shrugged.

'Wasn't here when I arrived,' Faith said helpfully.

'I thought he'd be . . . cooking.' Mo bit her lip as she noticed the state of the kitchen. It looked like a bomb-site as usual.

'Oh, yeah.' Sharon tapped her forehead at her forgetfulness. 'He went to check on the ponies in the top paddocks. Should have been back ages ago, now I think about it. I'll get the quad out and pop up there if you like, see if he's okay. Never sure in this fog.'

'I'll come with you – are you okay to keep an eye on Mim and Chad, Faith?'

'Yeah – whatever.' Faith wasn't listening as she cuddled a puppy to each cheek and relived every thrilling second of her dark ride. Forget the midnight point-to-point. She was certain that had been just as spine-tingling.

'Wait there – I'll fetch it out.' Sharon zipped up her fleece and left Mo by the barn doors as she headed into the dark corridor that ran behind the American barn and the old machinery barn, where Rory kept the quad bike parked out of sight.

Mo waited, hugging her sides and stamping her feet in the cold, wondering what was taking her so long.

'Can't you start it?' she called along the dark alley.

'Just getting the petrol. Rory left it empty. Probably why he couldn't be bothered to use it tonight.'

'Typical!'

New Year's resolution number one, she reminded herself. Don't try to change him.

She stamped her feet again, wishing she'd put on a few more layers. She missed Pod's old leather trench-coat that she used to steal during the winter.

She missed Pod.

She closed her eyes tightly. New Year's resolution number two. Stop missing Pod so much it hurts.

At last Sharon spluttered from the barn on the old quad in a haze of foggy fuel fumes, hood pulled up over a black woolly hat. At least someone knew about layering for warmth.

'Hop on and hold tight to the bars. Clutch is sticking so she's jumping a bit.' She kept her back to Mo so the tears pouring down her face weren't visible.

'Thanks.' She stepped up behind Sharon's comforting bulk and gripped the racks as they set off at a furious pelt along the bridle track that led to the Gunning Estate – a quick route to the back of the Overlodes land.

Pressed tightly into a hedge, sitting on a large trunk and catching his breath, Granville Gates ducked his head as they passed.

Further along the track, a trail bike lay twisted in a ditch, abandoned by its drunken rider. The quad flashed past without spotting it in the thickening fog.

Faith watched the puppies curled together in a big heap, snoozing contentedly.

The phone rang and a familiar gushy voice greeted her. Dilly Gently was already babbling nine to the dozen.

'Mo, I'm really sorry to call but I am so desperate. I'm ringing everyone. Mum's gone into labour. She won't budge out of the larder – that's where her waters broke. She's almost concussed a paramedic and has now taken Pixie hostage. You haven't seen Pod, have you? He's not answering his phone and we have no idea where he is.'

Faith started to giggle. She giggled too much to speak. Leaving the receiver dangling from the wall, she stomped on the ground and shrieked with glee.

What a night.

She couldn't help herself. She had to check on Rio.

At first, she thought the fog must have truly thickened to pea-soup proportions. It was like wading through an Ibiza foam party.

She could hear the horses stamping and crashing around in their stables long before she had even reached the end of the garden path, letting out great high-pitched whinnies and squeals. Some were banging furiously on their doors. Loudest of them all, Rio was blaring out a desperate foghorn warning.

Breaking into a run, she smelled the burning and realised it wasn't fog. It was smoke.

Taking a breath to scream, ash immediately hitting her lungs, Faith ran faster. She could hear the roar now, like a low engine, and an unmistakable crackling. It was exactly the same as the damp logs burning in the grate at home.

Headlights bounced up the drive as she rounded the corner to the front of the barn. Please let it be someone who can help get them out, she prayed as she hauled open the tall doors and smoke poured out, the horses trapped inside going frantic.

Faith stood glued to the spot with fear.

Parking at a safe distance, the driver leaped from her seat. 'Digby, stay in the car until Mummy says otherwise – and that's an order!'

'Oh god, oh no, oh god.' Faith started to howl, realising it was Diana Lampeter, a woman almost too frightened to catch her children's ponies let alone help rescue twenty huge panic-stricken horses. She stood hopelessly in the doorway, not knowing where to start. Blood pumped through her ears, deafening her. She couldn't breathe. She couldn't see straight.

Diana rushed up to her shoulder, already talking to emergency services on her mobile: 'Hard to tell how bad, but the horses are trapped inside and there's a lot of smoke. Okay. Thanks – yes, obviously we'll take great care. Please hurry.' She cut the call.

Faith howled some more as she saw Rio rearing up at his door, crashing his front hooves against the stallion bars.

Diana grabbed her shoulders. 'Okay, who's here? On site? Right now?'

'Just me and the kids,' she gibbered, crying frenziedly.

'They are in the house?'

'Waaaaaaahhhhhhhhh!' Faith wailed, witless with hysteria.

'Take Digby into the house and look after them all,' Diana told her as she looked up another number on her phone. 'You will be in no danger there, I promise. It's a long way from the barn – ah.' She pressed Dial.

'Caaaaaaan't leave the hooooooorses!' Faith sobbed as Diana dragged her to the car and handed her to Digby.

'Tony? Diana Lampeter. Emergency. I need a lot of bodies up here very quickly. The stables are on fire and the horses are trapped.' Thrusting her phone in her pocket and checking that Digby was sensibly leading the senseless Faith towards the cottage, Diana pulled her polo-neck up over her mouth and headed into the barn.

33

'Six . . . five . . . four . . . three . . . two . . .'

The whooping was too loud to hear the last counts as the old pub erupted into life.

'Happy New Year!'

'A New Innings!' came the toast as the Springlodes villagers welcomed back a long lost friend.

It had been one hell of a night.

The fire at the stables had postponed the pub party by hours as every villager and snagging helper raced across the Prattle to help fight the flames and lead horses to safety.

'I helped put on their halter-necks,' Fe Sixsmith told Tam Wyck proudly.

The fire had only really taken hold of the hay bales stacked in the pole barn behind the machinery shed. All the barns and the cottage were safe, but it had still been a frightening blaze, with smoke as thick as a velvet curtain amid the fog, making it a beast to fight. The horses had been terrified, although all had escaped completely unscathed. Alf Wyck had suffered the only injury of the night, having fallen over a bucket in the thick smoke and cracked his head on a standpipe. He was currently enjoying free brandy and heroic status at the bar as a result.

'I still think it's incredible the way Diana Lampeter had already got so many of them out by the time we arrived.' Magnus shook his head in awe. 'Talk about wonder woman.'

Sperry whistled in agreement. 'Must have been, what, two or three minutes from Dad ringing the bell to the first of us reaching the fire? And she'd moved half a dozen or more to the fields by then.'

'Including that wild beast of Faith's.'

'*And* she was wearing seriously high heels.' Sperry sighed. 'I don't care what Dad says. That makes her one cool chick.'

'Makes up for her useless brother,' muttered Tam Wyck. 'Rory was so off his face on all the champagne he'd drunk here, *he* had to be led to safety, too.' He cackled at the memory of poor, hapless Rory lurching about in the thick ash waving a head collar around long after all the horses were safely away.

'Heard the hooves tonight,' Reg Wyck was telling anyone who would listen. 'Knew Firebrand was up to no good.'

At the bar, Tony's eyes had started to glaze behind his wire-rimmed glasses as he helped himself to another glass of champagne and admired his new premises.

Propped on a bar stool beside him, stubbornly forfeiting free champagne in favour of bitter, Saul Wyck flipped through the Quigley book.

'Who d'you reckon's starting these fires then?' Tony asked him.

Setting Quigley aside, Saul drew a smaller and – as far as he was concerned – infinitely more precious book from his back pocket.

Leafing past odds for the Lodes Valley Blackhearts winning the Cotswolds League Cup, Pheely Gently's baby being fathered by Lord Lucan and Reg staying sober for more than ten days that year, he found the page marked 'Arsonist'.

'The posh bird – Diana – ten to one, Granville Gates fours, Ingmar Olesen twos, Pod Shannon hundred to thirty, schoolteacher nine to four,' he reeled off. 'My granddad evens, Til Constantine thirteen to two and Amos six to four against.'

'*Against?*'

Saul nodded, reaching for the pen behind his ear and making an amendment. 'Make that eight to eleven – Freddy Tyack just put on a monkey. And the schoolteacher's coming in at two to one on account of the fact she's disappeared tonight.'

'So's Ophelia Gently,' Tony pointed out. 'She was supposed to bring me one of her sculptures for the beer garden.'

'Having her baby,' Saul remembered, adjusting his odds. 'Which puts her out to a hundred to one, and Pod to twenties if he's boiling kettles and fetching towels. You're still at double carpets.'

'Ophelia's having her baby?' Tony reached for the bell to make the announcement and then stopped himself. 'How come I'm at sixty-six to one? I've never started a fire in my life.'

'You wanted this place, didn't you?' Saul put away his book and reached for his pint with a telling look.

Tony shrugged. 'In that case I'll have a tenner on myself. Each way.'

At Horseshoe Farm Cottages, Rory toasted in the New Year with another scotch to chase down the chewed fingernails which were lodged in his throat.

The fire brigade had left at last and the horses were safely housed in fields and amongst neighbouring yards. Diana was still talking to the police while Anke made tea and Graham made the sort of conversation Rory didn't want to hear.

'They reckon it must be Mo. All the evidence points there – that's why she targeted me and my family.'

Rory slammed down the scotch bottle. 'Never.'

'Poor girl. I knew she was a bit highly strung but I had no idea she was capable of such craziness. Makes you think.'

'It's not Mo.' Rory poured the dregs of the bottle into his glass, so drunk now that the neck slewed everywhere. 'I was going to propose tonight. I want to marry her.'

'They do lovely prison ceremonies these days.' Faith looked up from where she was curled up with the puppies, simmering unhappily because she had been so totally useless in a crisis.

'You can shut the fuck up,' he snapped.

'Rory!' Anke turned in shock.

'Sorry.' He held up his arms drunkenly.

'I think she knew you were going to propose.' Faith played with a velvet ear, made spiteful by her self-hatred. 'Sharon knew, so she must have told her when they went to look for you.'

Room spinning around him, Rory closed his eyes in defeat as Diana finally reappeared in the kitchen, looking drained.

'They're going to postpone the search until morning – no point in this fog, although all the road patrols know to keep an eye out. You guys might as well go home and get some sleep,' she told the Brakespears. 'We can't thank you enough. You've been wonderful.'

'I can't leave Rio here!' Faith protested.

'I'll bring him back tomorrow,' Diana promised. 'He'll be fine.'

'The witch might claim him!' Faith shrieked. 'The witch will sacrifice him to the moon, and he's only just been saved from death!'

Diana winced at the shrill outcry, wondering what on earth the teenager was ranting about.

'Just ignore her – delayed shock,' Anke reassured Diana with classic cool as she escorted her daughter outside with equally characteristic gentleness – the ultimate multi-tasker and perfect parent

Later, Diana saw Rory to bed, remembering him weeping the same way as a child told that Mummy wasn't coming home tonight . . . or the next night . . . or the night after that. The less than perfect parent.

'I love Mo and she ran away, Di – she ran away! Didshetrytoburn my horses you think?'

'Of course not.' She kissed his forehead. 'It'll all make sense in the morning – you'll see.' She wished he always wasn't quite so hopeless in an emergency.

In the kitchen, she found Rory's mobile announcing a text message. She quickly checked in case it was Mo. But it was from Dilly, so excited that she was texting everyone including her ex.

It's a boy! Born in the larder 11.59 New Year's Eve, weighing in eight pounds and three satsumas on old kitchen scales. Basil Gently. Mother and baby fine.

Attached was a photograph of something that looked like a large marrow. On closer inspection it *was* a large marrow. Dilly had yet to master her new picture phone.

Diana's phone was on the bread bin, out of charge as usual. She plugged it in and went out to check on the horses.

They all had settled surprisingly well after their ordeal, apart from Rio, confined to the stallion paddock in a thick rug looking highly put out as he charged around, nose in the air, bellowing.

Diana watched him over the gate, blasting her bright torch through the fog.

No wonder. There was someone running beyond the hedge to his field, feet thumping heavily on the hoggin bridleway from the direction of Gunning. The next moment, the figure spotted the torchlight and hurdled the short section of double post and rails beside the track to come sprinting through the field towards her.

She made to turn and flee, but he called out, splitting her heart.

'Diana! Wait!'

Emerging through the fog and darkness like a spectre was Amos.

She clutched the galvanised top bar, watching as Rio trotted up to him, whickering gratefully, nuzzling the familiar head as he followed him to the gate. Amos was almost speechless from running, his breath coming out in hard, croaking blasts sending dragon plumes of condensation through the cold air as he stooped to grab his knees and find an inch of spare breath between stitches to speak.

'Pod . . .' he gasped '. . . he took my Land Rover . . . I saw the little bastard driving off in it . . . fetched my gun and was hardly out of the gate when Granville turned up . . . started spouting off – waving a bloody knife about . . . saying it was his money and that we betrayed him.'

'Oh, God. The key.' Diana clapped her hand to her mouth.

He nodded. 'Granville said Pod made him tell him where the money was . . . he'd just seen Pod ram the big doors with my car . . . saw it from the lake road.'

She groaned. 'The Hall?'

'Foxrush . . .' He nodded, straightening up, his face twisted as the cramps in his side ripped at his lungs. 'He's in Foxrush Hall.'

The groan turned into a wail. 'He'll be destroyed in there.'

He nodded. 'Already is. I think I just saw Firebrand.'

Diana stared at him in horror.

As the cramps subsided, he leaped the gate and landed beside her, rubbing his face in his hands as he tried to make sense of what he'd seen.

'Granville was waving his knife around and screaming at me – the full number. He had a bloody trunk with him. We were on the farm track. I had my gun under my arm – wasn't about to point it at him, poor old fool. Then, out of nowhere, this quad bike appeared. No lights. Flying down from the beech ridge – straight through the trees as though it was the M40. You'd have trouble threading a mountain bike through those trees. Huge guy driving it – built like an ox. Couldn't see his face – wearing a great hooded coat and a balaclava. But I saw his eyes and –' He rubbed his face again. 'Jesus! They were his eyes, Diana. They were Firebrand's fucking eyes.

'He took the shotgun clean out from under my arm – reached out, grabbed it like a medieval jouster. I didn't have time to think. Next thing I know, he's driving like smoke through the oaks.'

'Towards the Hall?'

He nodded.

Diana closed her eyes and concentrated very hard. But when she opened them again, he was still there. Still wide-eyed and as stunned as she was.

She swallowed hard to find a squeaky voice around the lump in her throat.

'Why did you come here, Amos? Why not ring for help?'

'And tell them there's a ghost chasing some filthy Scouse cheapskate around his haunted house?' He laughed hollowly. 'I couldn't think straight. Granville fainted when he saw him – flat out on his trunk. It *was* Firebrand, Diana. I swear it was him. I didn't have a car to drive and your bloody phone is switched off, so I ran. Only you understand. It *was* him.'

'Then we'd better go and find him, hadn't we?'

They stared at one another for a long time.

'Are you sure?' Amos asked eventually.

'It's too late to run away. Pod's broken the bloody seal.'

As they headed to the cottage, Diana felt a strange, giddy panic take hold.

'A ghost on a quad bike.' She was close to hysterical laughter and suddenly understood how poor little Faith had felt earlier when confronted by the fire. 'Typical Firebrand. Why gallop around in flames on a horse when you can half-inch a Kawasaki from Graham Breakspear's yard before torching it? A motorised ghost. Oh God, that stupid bloody jockey.' A sob caught in her throat. 'Nobody damages the house. Nobody. I gave him the fucking key.'

'He didn't know it was for the door,' Amos pointed out as they rounded the midden to the barns. 'Jesus!'

'We had a fire,' Diana muttered, tears finally hitting her eyes. 'It seems Firebrand stopped off here first.'

He wrapped his arms around her and pressed his chin to the top of her head. 'I'm sorry, huntress. Oh, Christ, I'm sorry.'

'The police think it was started by Rory's deranged girlfriend, but I don't think she's capable. She can't light a cigarette without blistering her nose. I'm pretty sure the poor little creature just ran away in fright because she found out he was going to propose tonight.'

'Was anybody hurt?'

She shook her head, feeling the comforting weight of his chin stopping it from exploding in terror. 'Everybody's fine, from humans to horses to dogs to – shit!' She gasped, tearing away and running to the mobile home.

It was in darkness. She pressed her face to the glass and cupped her hands around it to check, heart hammering.

What was it that Faith had said? That Sharon must have told Mo that Rory was going to propose. Mo *and* Sharon. Mo and *Sharon* had gone to look for Rory? She hadn't taken it in properly, had caught it as a fragment when she was walking into the room. At the time, she had been too distracted by the sight of her brother about to pass out in his usual pissed-in-a-crisis stupor to care about Sharon. Nobody had thought much about Sharon. Nobody ever did. Poor Sharon.

She remembered Rory telling the police that his groom was in Market Addington for a New Year's Eve party. Diana herself had left a message on her mobile voice mail to prepare her for he shock of the fire when she got back pissed and jubilant in the early hours to find the horses in her care scattered around the fields and black ash everywhere.

Mo *and* Sharon.

'What is it?' Amos had followed her.

Diana raced towards the machinery barn, behind which the hay fire had started, scrabbling her way through the sodden black chars to search the long gap. Rory's quad was missing.

'How big did you say Firebrand looked?'

'Massive.'

'Did he have anyone with him? A small redhead maybe? A bit funny-looking? Like a pretty gnome?'

'Of course not.'

'But he was definitely wearing a balaclava and a hooded coat?' She had seen Sharon doing the early morning hay-run to the paddocks enough times to recognise the description.

'What is it, Diana?'

'Oh fuck, oh fuck, oh fuck, Amos.' She started to run. 'You didn't see a ghost. You saw a fucking arsonist.'

'It was *him*!' He gave chase.

'You can say that till you're blue in the face, but I still have to get there.' She ran towards the house to fetch her car keys. 'Oh fuck, oh fuck, oh fuck – the children!' She burst inside and grabbed the keys from the peg and her mobile from the bread bin, stooping to scribble a note, muttering as she did so: 'May God forgive me for being a worse mother than ever. I am going to leave my sleeping children with their unconscious uncle. It's either that or bring them with us. Even Rory is marginally better than Firebrand as a babysitter.'

Amos watched her bottom wiggle as she wrote the note and, in that curious way that thoughts have of crossing heads at the most inappropriate of moments, he remembered why he had always wanted to share every second of his life with her.

'Right.' Diana handed him her mobile phone as they leaped into the car. 'In a minute, you are going to tell me everything that happened tonight again very slowly so that I stand a chance of understanding it. Before that, I think you should call the police. Forget the ghost chasing scouse burglar through haunted house description. It's the early hours of New Year's Day and they get a lot of calls like that. Tell them the Lodes arsonist is at Foxrush and has one – possibly two – hostages this time.'

Nodding, he started to dial. 'I love you Diana. Even if you did kill him.'

'I love you too. And I didn't bloody kill him.'

Sharon peeled the gaffer tape from Mo's mouth with a force that almost took her lips off.

Her small, angry eyes loomed close, examining Mo's face like a specimen on a glass slide. 'Aren't you going to scream?'

'No.'

'Oh.'

Sharon pulled up her balaclava and drew out a small set of binoculars from her pocket to look across the lake at Foxrush Hall, a faint black monster in the mist.

Sucking her numb lips together to try to bring back some feeling, Mo inadvertently let out a series of popping kisses that hardly fitted the circumstances. She found herself battling giggles.

'Isn't this the point at which you're supposed to tell me why you're doing all this?'

Sharon ignored her.

'You started all the fires, didn't you?'

Professional pride loosened Sharon's tongue briefly. 'Not Dulston's. That was a bloody amateur job.'

Mo let out a few more popping kisses as she started to feel her lips again.

'What made you do it?'

Sharon ignored her, peering through the lenses, although it was too dark and foggy to see a thing.

Mo shifted, feeling the binder twine cutting into her wrists and ankles. The cold was starting to seep into her bones. She wished she'd put on some more layers.

Sharon jabbed the gun at her face. She liked doing that. She'd been doing it a lot since dumping Mo in the old icehouse with a lot of gaffer tape and binder twine to think about, roaring off into the woods and returning minutes later with a double-barrel and even more attitude.

'Get up.'

Mo looked at the barrels. 'Not until you tell me why you're doing this.'

The barrels waggled.

'I'm not budging.'

The barrels poked at her shoulder.

'Nup.'

Suddenly Sharon laughed. It wasn't a mad, baddy laugh but it wasn't particularly companionable either. It sounded like someone watching an old sitcom repeat they'd seen a hundred times, knowing the laughter cues by half-hearted auto-response, and then discovering to their surprise and slight dismay that they were still funny.

'Miss Stillitoe – silliest name I ever heard – you are such a bloody schoolteacher, aren't you? Is it time for show and tell, miss? Is that it?' Her small eyes gleamed.

'Yes, it is.' Mo pretended to be addressing an insolent eight year old, realising it might help hold back the scream that was bubbling up in her lungs. It did. 'I can tell you don't want to shoot me, and I figure it'll save us both time and energy if you tell me everything now so that you can concentrate on your dastardly revenge plot later – I'm guessing fire will be involved – and I can concentrate on struggling, trying to escape and begging for mercy, which believe me I will.'

Sharon looked impressed. 'I can see why he loves you.'

For a moment, heart leaping, Mo wondered who she meant. Then she stopped herself, addressing the eight year old again.

'I'm not normally like this I can assure you. Imminent death does funny things to the brain. So this is about Rory, yes?'

'I love him.'

'I know that. Why not let me go if I promise never to see him again?'

'Not as simple as that.'

'Yes, I had a nasty feeling that might be the case.'

'You've got to burn with your lover.'

'Christ.' For a moment Mo lost the glorious, steely self-control that had taken hold the moment that Sharon had raced past the Overlodes top paddocks, parked the quad in a disused barn on the edge of the Gunning woods, and lassoed her with brute force and binder twine.

'Why?' she asked in a small voice.

'Cos it's what my dad did.'

'Oh – right. Following the family tradition.' Phew. It was back.

'He burned his wife and her lover in these woods.'

Mo baulked. 'You father was Firebrand?'

'So my ma says.'

'And who is your ma?

'Peggy Wyck.'

Mo blinked. 'You're a Wyck?'

'I'm a Delamere!' she raged, waving the gun around. 'His heir. All this should be mine by rights.'

'Totally.' Mo nodded in agreement, suddenly remembering reading somewhere that a golden rule of surviving a kidnap situation was that a hostage should try to engage with their captor on an emotional level. 'So how did your parents – er – meet? Here in the woods?'

'No!' she scoffed, lowering the gun. 'The Fox Inn up at Badgecote.'

'Firebrand came out of the woods for the odd night out in the pub then?'

'Yes, as it happens!' The gun was raised once more. 'He used to ride a horse out and about, Mum says. Used the bridleways. She didn't know who he was then, of course. Called himself Bill Falstaff – that's what's on my birth certificate. They only did it the once.'

'In the back of his car in the pub car park? Oh, of course not. He had a horse.'

'Very funny, Miss Silly Toes. You'll be laughing on the other side of your –'

'Okay – sorry.' Mo hurriedly realised the golden rule didn't involve sarcasm. 'We haven't got time for all the threats and curses right now. So, let me get this straight. Firebrand is your dad and he liked to light fires, so you like to light fires, am I right?'

'Yeah.'

'And Firebrand killed his wife when he found out that she was being unfaithful to him, by setting light to the cottage she and her lover were sleeping in, right?

'Yeah.'

'So you plan to set light to a house with Rory and me sleeping in it in a sort of bound and gagged sleeping fashion, yes?'

'No! Not Rory, I love Rory.'

'But he's my lover.'

'No, he ain't. Pod is.'

'Pod?'

The golden rule turned out to be sham alchemy, after all. Why try to connect with her kidnapper on an emotional level when her kidnapper had already read the contents of her soul as background before the snatch? Sharon knew that Mo had never stopped loving Pod, that stopping loving Pod was like stopping breathing. There was no more emotional connection than that. Sharon had a better working knowledge of Mo's mind than she had herself. She tested her theory.

'Pod and I are through.'

'No, you're not.' It was as though her alter ego was talking back.

'I don't love him any more.'

'You do.'

'Don't.'

'Do.'

'Don't'

'Don't.'

'I bloody well do – I mean. Shit!' Mo had just been trapped more swiftly and seamlessly than when she was gagged and bound earlier.

Sharon smirked. 'Don't you deny it, Miss Silly Toes! You love Pod more than you love Rory. And he loves you too. That's why he came here tonight.'

Mo swallowed. 'Pod's here?'

'In the big house. Hunting for treasure.'

'And you're going to set light to it?'

'Any minute now. With you two in it.'

'Sharon.' Mo tried one last-ditch attempt at logic. 'You do realise that you've got the maths a bit wrong here, don't you?'

'Eh?'

'Your father – Firebrand – found out that his *wife* was being unfaithful with a *lover*. That is like you discovering *Rory* is being unfaithful with *me*. Which I'm sure you think he was. But the point is, Rory and I should die – not Pod. Pod has nothing to do with this.'

The gun barrels slammed into the soft hollow between Mo's collarbones. 'Don't you get clever with me, Miss Silly Toes. I've had enough of your nonsense. I can shoot you right now. Don't matter to me if I burn you dead or alive. I know I'll hear one of you scream. Now are you coming or what?'

Mo struggled upright. At least she would get to see Pod again before she died.

'I think I'll come along for the ride.'

Sharon pulled her penknife from her pocket to cut the twine around Mo's ankles so that she could get on the quad bike.

'Sharon?' she asked as she looked down on the balaclava, realising that she could kick out, probably knock her captor out – at least stall her – and run for her life at this juncture.

'Yeah?'

'Can I ask you a favour?'

'What?'

'You know you said you only had to hear *one* of us scream . . .'

Foxrush Hall breathed. That was the only way Pod could explain it. The house breathed Jack Frost cold, Jack the Ripper vicious, Jack in a Box jumpy breaths. It was alive, cryogenically frozen and gripping to its last live cells with long, gnarled nails.

It was evil.

And he was in its heart, surrounded by a slow, death-knell, crocodile heartbeat, his hands shaking so much that the little LED torch he was carrying would not stay focused on the lock, and the key kept falling from his fingers.

Pod had read the Quigley book. He knew about the blood stain on the cellar flags that could never be mopped up despite generations of terrified housemaids applying bleach with scrubbing brushes.

The stain was beneath his feet now. As the torch searched for the fallen key again and again it traced the bloody mark.

They'd hidden it well, he told himself, mustering bravado. He'd been all over the house. He'd been down here twice and hadn't seen it until now. It was as though the ghosts were moving it around to tease him. Well, he was taking it. This was less daunting than the midnight steeplechase. This was just myth and atmosphere. That was true danger. That bore no prize. This bore riches. Riches that could maybe even buy a heart back in time.

At last, his shaking hand held the key to the old trunk lock. He groaned in despair. It didn't even fit. The key was twice the size of the lock. Fucking Granville had lied to him.

But as he clicked the catches with fumbling hands ready to force the lock, his brows shot up. It was already open.

He lifted the lid, the torch shaking almost too much to see its contents.

As he finally prepared to set eyes on his booty, a pair of gun barrels settled snugly in the nape of his neck.

'Move and the last thing you see when you die are the contents of your throat on the wall opposite.'

'Mo?'

'Your one and only.'

Pod closed his eyes. If he was going out with a bang – and he had no doubt he was – he was going out with style.

'Hey, I knew I upset you, queen, but don't you think this is a bit of an over-reaction? I fucking came here for your sake.'

'For *me*?'

'I want to buy you the cottage. Our cottage.'

'With what?' The barrels poked tighter to the hairs that were standing up on the back of his neck.

He kept his eyes clamped shut. 'In the trunk. The treasure.'

She gave a low, throaty giggle that was barely more than a murmur. 'You take the copy of *A Horse for Emma* and I'll take the breeches.'

He opened his eyes again, torch wobbling. In the trunk at his feet was an old pony book, a few pairs of dog-eared breeches, a hacking jacket, a polo helmet and some rosettes.

'What the –'

'Shhh!' She rammed the gun harder against his neck, looking up at the ceiling from which dust was raining and heavy feet trampled above.

'Who's that?'

'The fucking ghost you kept banging on about,' she breathed. 'And she's setting fire to this place.'

'*She?*'

'Don't ask – just believe me when I tell you I am so glad I never tried to find out who *my* father was.'

He gulped. 'So why are you pointing that thing at me when you could be pointing it at her?'

'Because she took the cartridges out – it's unloaded.'

'What the fuck?' He swung it away and turned to face her.

She shrugged apologetically. 'I figured if we're both going to die, I might as well get my own back first.'

'You bitch.'

'I came down here to rescue you, didn't I?'

'Let's get out of here.' He gave the trunk one last angry glance and turned to run to the stairs.

Mo grabbed him and covered his mouth with her fingers as above them an empty jerrycan clattered to the floor.

'Not an option,' she breathed, glancing up. 'The only thing stopping a fireball coming down those stairs is the door at the top – it's metal-studded and half a foot thick. She's already set fire to the Hall. Threw a match in the tank of the quad bike she parked there, so I guess that rules out a quick getaway. I don't think *she*'s planning on leaving.'

'You mean we're already burning?' he yelped, pulling her hand away from his mouth.

'Shhh! She mustn't hear us. I promised we'd stay down here.'

'You *promised*?' he sneered in shock.

'If she hears us planning an escape she'll speed up to the bit where she gets to hear us screaming in agony as we die in flames.'

Whoomph! Another match was thrown into petrol above them.

'Jesus!' Pod cowered as drops of fire started falling through gaps in the floorboards like orange rain.

Mo winced and ducked. 'Only way out is an inferno. Everything else is boarded up, barred and padlocked, much as it has been for the past decade.'

He raced to the stairs, saw smoke pouring from beneath the door at the top and flames licking through its huge keyhole like a blowtorch, and hurried back to Mo. 'So how come you're so calm?'

She looked into his long-lost eyes and remembered what it was like to come home. 'I figured you'd be the one with the cunning plan.'

He ran his tongue around his dry mouth. 'I don't have one, queen.'

They heard another great whoomph of match hitting petrol over-head, and Mo burst into tears.

'I said call the police, not the pub!' Diana raged as she drove along the pitted tracks towards Foxrush Hall, followed by a cavalcade of drunken New Year revellers from the New Inn intent on a gawp.

The frost was lifting, along with the fog. It made for an eerie passage as a thick white ceiling hung just a few feet in the air and the white carpet melted away in front of them.

'We have emergency back-up right behind us,' Amos justified himself.

'We have a bunch of drunk drivers right behind us.'

'The Three Disgraces are looking after your two little monsters and big idiot of a brother at Overlodes now, thanks to Tony.'

'Oh, great – so we have emergency back-up and babysitters organised. Now let's go and save a couple of lives, is that it?'

'We have to keep the Gunning secrets.'

'I'm calling the police. Give me that mobile!' she demanded, swerving around on the track as she fought to grab it.

Amos hurled it out of the window.

'You might be a glorified gatekeeper to this wretched Estate, but I'm not!'

'And there's you owning all you survey.'

'I don't bloody want it.' Diana swerved around a tree. 'Not without you.'

'You made your decision on your birthday.'

'I did what?'

'We could have run away together.'

'And how far would we have got this time? Idcote-over-Foxrush Garden Centre?'

'I refuse to just be a passenger in your life, Diana!'

Diana gritted her teeth as she slalomed through the trees, noticing a few of the wacky racers behind her becoming grounded. 'Okay – a few truths. One – you *are* a passenger right now. Note the lack of a steering-wheel in front of you. Two – you didn't wait long enough for me to *make* a decision on my birthday. I'd like to run away with you right now, this second. Three – the house is on fire. Foxrush is on fire. Oh, Christ alive!'

'Emergency fire-fighters,' Amos groaned. 'One thing I forgot.'

Mo and Pod no longer needed the little LED torch. They could see perfectly well by firelight as the yellow fury burned overhead, licking through the floorboards.

'Why d'you come down here?' Pod screamed at her as he searched for an escape. 'Why not get out while you could?'

'Because you're a cockroach among men, Pod. And that means you'll get out.' Mo hugged herself tightly as she stood in the hot orange rain.

'I can't get out!' he yelled hoarsely. 'We can't get out. You stupid bitch. You didn't have to die here with me.'

'I did – I do. I can't live without you.'

'No!'

Suddenly he slammed against her, hurling her away from a timber that crashed down from above.

Knocked back on to the bloodstained flagstones by the weight of his body, feeling his lungs hammering her down further as he sobbed and gasped, Mo wrapped her arms around him.

'I can't live without you, Pod. It's no sort of life.'

'I can't live without you either.' He started to kiss her. 'And this is one hell of a death.' He kissed her eyes, her cheeks, her mouth, his shoulders taking the drops of scalding orange rain. He pulled up her skirt. 'You stupid bloody cow.'

'You stupid bastard.' She ripped at his fly buttons.

'I wanted you to live in a pretty thatched cottage and write poetry.' He kissed her lips angrily, starting to cry. 'I wanted you to feel safe and secure.'

'A cottage bought with a ghost's money?' She kissed him back.

'We all live on ghost money – earned before we live, spent after we die.'

'They'll be spending ours soon.' She felt the bare skin of her thighs connecting with his naked hips.

'We never had any.'

'I was happier poor with you than anywhere else, Pod.'

'Are you happy dying with me?'

'Never happier.' Laughing, she threaded her fingers through the hair she had missed touching for so long and drew him back into a kiss so deep they didn't hear the shouting at first.

'Hello!' screamed a voice outside. 'Hello!'

More voices outside. 'Get back!'

'There's no one in there.'

'Hello!'

'Can you hear me?'

Someone smashed a pane of glass behind a high, boarded window.

Pod gripped Mo tightly to the ground, his kisses rougher and faster. She could feel him hard against her, feel him pulling down her knickers.

'We either die fucking,' he breathed into her ear, 'or we don't fucking die. The choice is yours'

'Which means we can be together for ever?' Mo felt him between her legs, wriggled her hips further below her so that he was starting to be sucked inside her.

'For ever, queen. I love you.'

'I love you too.'

They looked into one another's eyes for a split second before rolling apart faster than Roman wrestlers at the end of a round and racing towards the voices shouting above.

'Hello! In here!' Pod yelled. 'Down here!'

More glass was smashed, hands hammered frantically against the boarding.

Mo hurriedly pulled *A Horse for Emma* from the trunk and tucked it into her waistband. She slid the trunk to the wall and stood on it, thumping her fist at a high metal grid encased in rotten wood. It gave. Seconds later, hands were reaching down from the tiny opening above to pull her out.

'Who's life's fucking cockroach?' Pod laughed as he lifted her from below until she was dragged to safety and then leaped after her.

He didn't fit. He had put on so much weight in recent weeks that he couldn't hope to wriggle through.

'No!' Mo screamed as she realised he was trapped. 'No! No! No! Let me back in!'

A pair of hands gripped her shoulders, stopping her from diving back through the gap.

More huge, burning beams were crashing down inside. The whole ceiling had started to cave in above the cellar.

'Tell Diana I'll ride that fucking race!' Pod screamed above the roar of falling timber. 'Tell her it starts at midnight tonight! I'll ride that fucking race and claim my treasure! And I'll marry my treasure. I'm going to marry you, queen, whether you like it or not. I love you Mopsa Stillitoe!'

'You'd better fucking live!' she screamed as the wails of sirens were heard in the distance.

Long afterwards, debate still raged at the New Inn as to whether Mo had screamed this because her one true love was facing death, or because he had publicly revealed her true name.

'You'd better fucking live!' she screamed again and again as the fire crew arrived, pulling her and her saviours away from the hell-hole.

★   ★   ★

'What are you doing?' Diana wailed as Amos dragged her away from the burning house. 'He might die in there!'

'Well, we sure as hell can't save him.' He pulled her across the old formal gardens and behind an overgrown yew hedge as police sirens joined the screech of more fire engines. Night was starting to turn into day as the fire took hold, a curious flickering sunset that seemed wholly inappropriate to Diana and Amos.

'We need to be there.' She tried to wrestle her hand free from his to run back.

He slumped breathlessly against the yew and looked over his shoulder. 'It'll burn for days. Shame we won't see the old bastard go.'

'We won't?'

He squeezed her hand. Just for a moment Diana stopped fighting and pressed her lips to it, her heart skipping, torn between lifetimes. Her life now, and her life with Amos. The two seemed impossible to connect. She couldn't glue them together.

'They'll have to drain the lake to put that out.'

And then it hit her. She realised why the glue had never stuck.

'Afraid they'll find his body in there? The one I dumped with the boulders tied to its ankles?'

His hand twitched.

'I didn't kill him, Amos.'

His eyes burned with love, brighter than Foxrush in flames. 'I don't care if you did.'

'Just so long as we run away together and keep running?'

'I'm trying to protect you.'

She looked at him for a long time, at that face which kept jumping decades, rewinding life twenty-two years and then propelling it forwards to today. That noble, angry, passionate face. It was a face that loved her. She could never doubt that. But now she realised that it was a face that no longer trusted her.

She wrestled her hand free. 'This is what it's all been about, hasn't it?' she gasped as it finally hit home. 'That's why you've stayed protecting this place like a lion at the gates all these years. You weren't protecting the woods. You weren't protecting the house or the parkland or the wildlife. You were protecting *me*. You think I killed him. You always have. And you think I'll be found out if they trample all over your woods – the developers and the tourists and the spook-hunters. You think they'll rumble my secret.'

'I love you, huntress,' he pleaded.

'And I love you.' She started to back away from him. 'With all my heart. But I won't run away from this one. I won't run away and hide.'

'I'll sacrifice everything! I'd do anything for you.'

She paused, fighting tears. 'Believe me.'

He stared at her in anguish.

'Believe *me*, Amos. That's all I ask. *Believe* me.'

Just for a moment his eyes ran to ground. It was too much for Diana. She started to walk towards the blue flashing lights and yellow flames.

'What are you doing?' he yelled after her.

'I'm giving myself up. Stick around if you want to hear my confession. I'll be making it tomorrow – just before I go to the gallows.'

'You don't have to confess! You never have to confess! Huntress!'

He watched her stumbling towards the police cars and fire engines, willing her to turn.

Diana didn't look around. She didn't want him to see her tears.

34

Amos took the photographs of his children from their frames and laid them carefully on the folded sweaters in his suitcase.

The house felt emptier than ever without the dogs for company. The television was doing its best to flicker companionably in the corner of the sitting-room, but he'd muted the sound now that the late local news bulletin had finished.

The footage from Gunning had been surprisingly short given the amount of time the television crew had spent filming the burning house, getting in the way of the fire-fighters, nosily asking everybody questions. None of the interviews they'd done had been shown, just a brief shot of Foxrush Hall pointing fiery tongues from every window in the mist, the reporter telling the camera that the arsonist was believed to have died in the blaze but that it would be many hours before fire-fighters could go in and look for a body. Then they'd swiftly moved on to a story about the first of the region's New Year's babies.

Amos closed the suitcase on the faces of his own babies and checked around the house, switching off the television and locking the back door. As he did so, a cold blast of air swept through the farmhouse from the front and he turned to see Til Constantine framed in his doorway.

'How are you going to run away without a car, Amos?'

He ducked his head and scratched his short hair in exasperation. 'I'll find a way.'

She nodded, sucking on her teeth. 'Shame to miss the race.'

'The race?'

'The riders will be at the start soon. The fire brigade won't let anyone near the house and chapel, of course, but Tony Sixsmith has decided that the old oak on Heaven Hill will count as it's the highest point on the estate. They'll set off at midnight. Ground's good, although the light's bloody awful despite the moon.'

Amos looked at her for a long time – incredulous, terrified, hardly daring to hope. 'Who's riding?'

'Ah. You'll have to come and see.'

⋆　　⋆　　⋆

At Wyck Farm, Anke checked on Diana's sleeping children and went downstairs to open more red wine to charge her nerves. Soon, they would set out for Oddlode church to join the crowd there, leaving Magnus in charge at home, much to his disgust at drawing the short straw. Graham was gathering torches and hip-flasks in anticipation of another sleepless night.

'They certainly know how to see in a New Year around here,' he yawned, rubbing Anke's neck with a warm hand as he passed. 'Do you think they stop drinking by February?'

Faith was sitting at the kitchen table, as white as a sheet, chewing at her knuckles.

'I hope he's safe. I so hope he's safe, Mum.'

'I am very proud of you. You did the right thing letting Diana ride him.'

'I wasn't talking about the horse.'

Anke gave her a curious look, but Faith was texting Carly on her new mobile to let her know that they would be setting off soon and that she would send video pictures as soon as she had them.

Diana twisted a hunk of mane through her shaking fingers as she rode along the bridleway from Springlode, trying to draw courage from the soft clank of the bit and the warmth seeping towards her from Rio's solid neck.

The woods beside her were alive with flashing blue lights and the glow of Foxrush Hall, still burning amid a gauze of smoke and mist. They said it would burn for days. It was hard to tell where the fog ended and the smoke started – and yet she knew that, once they were out in open country, galloping towards Oddlode, it would be clear. Everything would be clear then.

She could just make out torches dancing to the left, and the big black shadow of the old oak, standing alone in the park. Perhaps it was fitting that Oddlode's godless daughter would be riding the midnight point not from a chapel spire but from a tree as huge and old and twisted as her own family's.

Tony Sixsmith banged his hands together and shouted at his youngest daughter to get off her mobile to the Wycks on Oddlode green comparing the latest odds. Another daughter was trying to figure out how to work the night vision option on the video camera, and a third was doing great trade serving whisky macs to assembled Springlode villagers.

The fog had lingered above head height like a canopy all day. Nobody could remember weather like it. The full moon gave it an unnatural silver glimmer, like a daylight cloud left behind when night falls. Matched with the flashing blue beams and fire glow from the woods, the old parkland was alight.

'Here come the horses!' shouted an excited voice.

But there was just one lone rider jogging through the multicoloured mist and smoke. Diana Lampeter on a huge black stallion, the whites of her eyes luminous to the gathered crowd even a hundred yards away.

'Told you the young fella would never get out of hospital in time.' Tony shook his head. 'Not much of a race.'

'No – there's another horse – look!'

Galloping along the tree line to catch up came a steak of grey as a huge white thoroughbred drew level with the stallion and was reined back to a walk with a series of spins and rears. Both riders halted.

'Is it Pod?' asked Sperry Sixsmith, craning to see.

Tony pulled his binoculars to his face, but could only make out a dark figure dressed in black, helmet low over his eyes.

'Certainly riding as short as a jockey.' He adjusted the focus. 'Whoever it is, Diana don't seem very happy to see him here.'

In Lower Oddford nursing home, Nanny patted the counterpane on her bed and then settled back against her pillows as two of her former charges perched there.

'Isabel, Tallulah. Thank you for coming at such an unorthodox hour. I appreciate it is most demanding of me, but there is something rather important I have to tell you both tonight.'

'Yes, Nanny.' Hell's Bells glanced at her watch tetchily. 'Do get on with it.'

'I know it's uncommonly late at night to ask you here – Matron was most accommodating.'

'I was already here,' Truffle purred, having crept out of Ingmar's room to make Nanny's bizarre assignation. She let out a champagne hiccup.

'I'll pretend I didn't hear that, Truffle dear,' Nanny said sternly. 'The reason that I've asked you here –'

'You *do* know they're running the midnight chase tonight?' Hell's Bells interrupted, checking her watch again. 'I'm going to miss the finish if I don't leave soon. Diana's supposed to be entered.'

'My Diana?' Truffle quacked.

'I believe so.'

'Nonsense. She's far too spineless.' Truffle sensed her thunder being stolen after all these years and didn't like it at all.

'I have heard she's racing against the young jockey.'

'Never! Wasn't he hospitalised after the Foxrush fire last night?'

'These National Hunt types are terribly tough.'

'Diana isn't. Why in God's name is she doing it?'

'Rather dashing, I thought – touch of the old Constantine spirit.'

'She's a wimp.'

'Less so than you were.'

'I was known as the galloping goddess!'

'Only because you were so frightened you had the trots before every meet.'

'I galloped from Broken Back Wood to the River Folly one day.'

'Your horse bolted. It was hardly your choice.'

'WILL YOU GIRLS PLEASE BE QUIET OR I SHALL PUNISH YOU!' Nanny rasped, sinking back into her pillows once more in exhaustion from shouting.

They turned to her, chastened into silence.

Nanny smiled benignly at such obedience. She hadn't lost her touch.

'As I said, I have something very important to tell you tonight. And I would like you to hear it from me before you hear it from anyone else . . . It is rather scandalous, I'm afraid.'

'Oh, goodie.' Truffle laced her hands together. 'Will I be able to tell Ingmar?'

'My dear, after tonight you will be able to tell anyone – even those who might remember it afterwards. It is about to become public knowledge, after all . . .'

'Go back!' Diana howled at Rory. 'You don't need to do this.'

'I do!' Rory countered, his breath clouding in front of his face. 'You have to have someone to race.'

'I can do it alone.'

'No way! A horse is only brave enough to do a point if he has another at his side. White Lies has point-to-pointed all his life. He'll see us safe.'

'If this is some sort of misguided attempt to get one up on Pod, you're wasting your time.'

'I don't need to get one up on him. He practically died last night.'

'You won't win Mo back.'

'So we've both lost out on love, Diana. What have we got to lose – apart from the race?'

'No, Rory, no!' she wailed. 'This isn't some sort of kamikaze flight for the broken-hearted.'

'It isn't?'

'No!' she howled. 'You have no idea.'

'Afraid I might beat you, sis?'

'You'll never beat me.'

'This horse won the Devil's Marsh Cup for Spurs. He'll win any race.'

Diana tried to keep her eyes fixed on him as Rio danced beneath her, spinning pirouettes so that she turned her head again and again like a twirling ballet dancer.

'Rory, please don't do this.' For the first time that night she felt fear. Genuine, spine-tingling fear that stopped her blood, her breath and her logic. The only thing racing right now was her mind. She had to stop him doing this.

'Catch me if you can!' he hollered, cantering away to the torch-bearers.

Crossing from Oddlode village green to the church, a small figure lingered behind the group of rowdy Wycks, Gates and other locals who were making their way to the finishing post.

Swaddled in a vast tweed coat, tufty red hair hidden beneath a fake fur hat and a great scarf covering her face, she was well disguised.

Yet Anke recognised her immediately, as the Brakespears came along the lane from the opposite direction. She rushed forwards.

'How is he?'

Mo's huge eyes peered out from above the scarf, all cried out. 'Conscious. His face is so badly burned, he can hardly talk, but he was still screaming that he had to come here and ride. They've sedated him so he'll sleep.'

'I'm so sorry.' Anke hugged her tightly and Mo crash-landed in her warmth and softness.

'He'll never be beautiful again,' she whispered. 'Only to me.'

'You're taking him back, aren't you?'

Anke felt Mo's small head nodding against her shoulder. 'We're family. We always have been.'

'And Rory? You know he's riding the race to try to win your heart?'

Mo stifled a sob. 'He's not racing for me, Anke. He's racing for much more than that. He's racing for his family honour. It's time to put things right. He's doing it for Diana.'

Anke hugged her tighter, wishing she was right. 'Oh God, I hope they are both safe.'

'She's Emma from the book.' Mo's muffled voice laughed sadly. 'Diana is Emma from the book, don't you see? You always said it was a chapter short.'

Anke pressed her cheek to the fur hat and hid a worried smile.

So this was the chapter where Emma, living a happy but boring brother-and-sister life with Larch, looks across her fields one day and sees Suffolk riding Passion across the misty fens and realises that happy endings aren't always the easy option. This is the chapter where she jumps on Love and rides for her life, Larch chasing her on the ghostly Kindness.

'What happens to Larch?' she wondered aloud. 'I always said the poor man should die.'

Beside them, Faith was staring dreamily up at the dark, foggy sky, wondering where Orion would be if she could see him. 'He marries me.'

'I thought you preferred Passion?' Anke said distractedly.

'Not always. Kindness is its own reward.'

Til panted up towards the old oak ahead of Amos, the blood thrumming so hard in her ears from her exertions that at first, she didn't hear the chatter of the drunken punters ahead of her.

'Always was as mad as the Sarsdens, the Constantines. Them two are worse than all the rest. They say Spurs was a black sheep, but them cousins of his was brought up by wolves if you ask me.'

'They'll both break their necks.'

'Reckon they must have Sarsden blood in them, don't you? Old Firebrand knew the Constantine girls, didn't he? Their mother put it about a lot. At least one of them will be his. Probably both.'

'Cursed, they are. Poor bastards. Riding a madman's race that could kill them.'

'Good riddance.'

'*NO!*' Til roared breathlessly as she finally made it to the oak and leaned against it. 'They have no Sarsden blood in them, you fools.'

'Who's to say?' came a belligerent voice in the darkness.

'Firebrand wasn't either of those children's fathers,' she panted. 'And he had no more Sarsden blood in *him* than you or I. His mother was one of the house staff at Gunning.'

There was a shocked silence.

Realising she had gained her audience's hushed attention at last, Til gave herself a few moments to regain her wind and then, hoping that the old dear really had meant it when she said she wanted to be fashionably modern, she took a deep breath.

'Firebrand's mother was Constance Crump – Nanny Crump. She was unmarried and very young. She had no family to help her. She felt she simply couldn't keep the child. The Delameres were very rich and childless and absolutely desperate for an heir. He stood to gain all this.' She spread out her arms and looked around her, wincing as her eyes trailed past the burning house. 'Nanny thought she was doing the best by him. Her friend Rose Simmons helped her keep the pregnancy a secret and then the baby came here when he was just a few hours old to be passed off as the fifteenth Baron Sarsden.'

'So who fathered the mad bastard?'

As Amos caught up, Til looked across to Diana and Rory as they argued and shouted their way towards the group, horses spinning, unable to hear her. She lifted her walking staff and pointed it at them.

'Their grandfather. My father. The not very Honourable Francis Constantine, a man with three daughters but no son – at least none whom he knew of. Firebrand was a Constantine – the heir Daddy longed for but never knew existed. I only found out myself when we . . . when I . . .' She covered her mouth and turned away. 'He was my half-brother. He was Diana's uncle. And she killed him.'

Amos walked through the spellbound crowd as though it wasn't there. He walked up to Diana, not caring that the stallion stamped and turned and leaped at his side. He reached up and took the reins.

'I'm leaving tonight, Diana.'

She grabbed for his hand but he snatched it away, still hanging on to the reins close to the bit.

'Come with me.' He turned to look at the blazing house behind the woods. 'Your castle's burning down in front of your eyes. You don't need to make your confession now. You stand accused.' He turned back to look up at her. 'Come with me, Diana, before we lose each other for another twenty years. Please!'

Sensing his panic, Rio shied away, rising up on to his hind legs and spinning into the crowd, cannoning off terrified bystanders.

Yet when Diana started to talk, he dropped his front feet to the ground and stood still.

She raised her chin, raised her shaking voice and went for broke. It was time for the truth.

'He lived in the woods' – she told them all – 'in the Pleasure Garden there. It had once been a folly for the Barons, with an underground grotto. His father – his *Sarsden* father – had created a bunker from it during the war, reinforced and equipped to accommodate a whole house party of fascists for years on end. Firebrand turned it into a party playpen in the seventies, but it was still a solar-powered, petrol-generated subterranean world safe for a fugitive. He'd lived there for years when we turned up. He stole petrol from cars to power the generators – stashing it all in a great bowser by the chapel. It was the only time he used to come out of hiding. But he missed human contact. He'd started to take risks. He would have got caught sooner or later. Then we walked straight in and became the toys he was looking for.

'He kept us prisoner for weeks, but we didn't really complain. We had been trying to run away to paradise and it felt like paradise at first. He touched papers on our tongues like wafers at communion and he made the garden feel like Eden. He rolled our cigarettes and watched us laugh and dance and make love. He tried to join in and we laughed at him. He laughed, too, at first.

'But he started to change. He grew bored of watching. He touched me. He kept touching me. I couldn't stop him. He said he loved me. He talked about life without Amos. He sent him out to hunt, you see, and when we were alone he told me that I would be his wife. I tried to warn Amos but Firebrand was giving him so much acid that he couldn't take it in. And Amos wanted the money. He wanted to stick around until he could figure out a way for us to run away with the money. I couldn't get through to him. We stopped laughing and dancing and making love. We weren't allowed to make love any more. He started chaining him up. I tried to run away, but he chained me too.'

Til sobbed in horror, her head in her hands.

Rory let out a cry of outrage, eyes wide with horror.

Finding it unbearable to listen, Amos started to walk away.

'Til knew,' Diana went on. 'Til knew we were there, but she did nothing. She thought we were safe. She *trusted* him. She thought we were happy.'

'You could have got away,' Til screamed. 'You killed him! You stole the money.'

'There was a lot of money.' Diana nodded. 'He kept a fortune in a big metal trunk in his cave. He used to show it to us when he was really out of his head – count it, read through his deeds for the houses in Scotland and Italy, South Africa and Switzerland. None of which he could ever see or possess again. He offered me the money so many times, telling me it could me mine – ours – without Amos. I always just begged him to let us go.

'Then one day he unchained me, took the contents of the trunk to the lake and put it all in a boat – a rickety, leaky, old rowing boat that he set adrift as we watched from the banks. He reached into his knapsack and pulled out a petrol bomb and – as calm as calm could be – he lit the rag and threw the bottle into the boat. Then he told me to swim after it and that whatever I could save would be for Amos and me to keep and run away with. He said that he would give me a five-minute head start, and then he would go back to kill Amos. If, in that time, I saved enough of a future for us and brought it to him before he reached Amos, he'd spare his life. If not, Amos would die and I would have to live with him for ever.'

Amos stopped walking, eyes lit by the fire from the house as he listened.

'Amos was in chains in the cave – it was at least ten minutes from the lake. I didn't think. I just swam. I swam as fast as I could to that bloody boat. I pulled the burning papers from it with my bare hands – great piles of flames until everything that was alight was floating on the lake and the rest of the cargo was safe. My hands were so burned I could hardly swim back. I tied the rope from the boat around my waist and it almost drowned me. I never thought I'd make it.

'When I got to the banks I couldn't carry more than a few papers and bundles of money. I ran so fast towards the garden. I ran faster than if my life depended on it – because Amos's life depended on it and that was far more precious than my own. But as I ran I heard the gunshots. I heard the gunshots and I thought he'd killed Amos.' She stopped, her voice ripped from her throat by the tears that coursed through her body and streamed down her face.

Beneath her the stallion stamped before standing to attention once more.

Nobody dared breathe. In the distance, Oddlode church struck midnight. A mobile rang and was hastily silenced.

Diana looked across at Amos.

'I went back to the lake and thought about drowning myself. I sat there for hours waiting for him to come. I wanted him to come and claim me for ever only to see me die. I cried myself inside out, tearing up his wretched money.

'But he didn't come. It got dark. That's when I realised there was a fire in the house – in Foxrush. It wasn't boarded up then. No shutters. I could see the windows glowing across the lake – the house lit right up. Something took hold of me. Like a bloody justice. I can't explain. I decided I should burn his money before I died. I got in that rickety boat with his filthy, ripped-up cash and rowed it across the lake, my hands bleeding, their burned skin numb. Then I found some old sacks by the house and put it inside, dragging it in behind me.

'The doors were open. It was too smoky to see. I tied my wet shirt around my mouth and went in, not caring if I lived or died.

'Then I realised the house wasn't on fire. He'd lit every hearth. Each room had a great blaze in its rightful place, beneath the old clogged chimneys that were smoking like crazy. There were candles at all the windows, too. It was beautiful. Above the biggest fire – in the main hall – there was a great scrawl written across the wall. It said *Amos and Diana – together at last*. I just stared at it. Stared and stared.

'Then I left the sacks where I'd been standing and I ran.'

Amos slumped to the ground and groaned. 'You thought I'd killed him?'

She nodded. 'I thought you'd killed him. I thought you'd got free and killed him.'

'But I was still chained up when they found me!'

'I didn't know that. They never told me. I didn't know for years.'

'So who *did* fucking kill him?'

Diana shook her head and looked back towards the burning house. 'Maybe he *did* kill himself in the end.'

Amos stared too. 'And maybe he just fired some shots into the trees.'

Rory rode forwards. 'You mean he might still be alive?'

At that moment there was a huge roar from the burning house, making the horses rear up as the night sky turned yellow in the fireball that burst from the woods.

'The fuel bowser,' Til moaned. 'It should be empty.'

'He *is* still alive!' Rory gasped, but he couldn't say another word as, gripped with pure instincts that demanded full flight, his grey horse bolted towards Oddlode.

'Has the race started?' Tony Sixsmith asked in confusion, waving his flag.

'I think it must have,' Til sighed as Diana took off after her brother.

As furious calls were made to the Oddlode finishing post, Til walked up to Amos's hunched body.

'Still want to run away? Because if you do, I might tag a lift.'

Leaping up, Amos shot her a filthy look and ran in pursuit of the cavalcade of cars that was setting out to track the riders to Oddlode. As fast as an Olympic sprinter, he reached a pick-up and leapt into the back.

'Murderer!' he called out as they left.

'I didn't bloody kill him – I'm a pacifist!' Til wailed. 'And I bloody loved him. I was the only one who ever did . . .'

Hopping after them, Ratbag at her feet, Til cast a look across at the fireball. He'd always had balls. She had to hand that to him.

By Oddlode church, the mobiles were going frantic. Never a good spot for reception, villagers were clambering up yew trunks and on to gravestones in order to get better signals and hear the story.

'Never!'

'No!'

'You are kidding?'

'Still alive?'

The reactions were universally appalled wonder. Glad Tidings was squawking like a pricked chicken as she tried to keep up.

Anke collared Faith who had a hot line to one of the Sixsmiths.

'What's going on?'

'They're racing and the ghost man is still alive!' Faith shrieked excitedly, already dialling out on her mobile again. 'I must call Carly.'

Mo was leaning against a mossy stone seraph, shivering uncontrollably. 'Pod always said he was still alive. The fire-starter man.'

'But Sharon started the fires'?' Anke was confused. 'I thought she was obsessed with Rory?'

Mo looked up to the moon, which was starting to form a great white disc of pearl behind the lifting fog. 'Maybe they were working together? Sharon and the ghosts? She *was* Firebrand's daughter, after all.'

Diana had almost lost sight of Rory as he galloped ahead, whooping all the way.

And she whooped too. Despite every wretchedness, every memory that had been exhumed that night, every injustice and every broken heart-string, she cried out with sheer exhilaration as they galloped faster and faster. Fear gripped her every sinew, adrenaline coursed through her quicker than any illegal drug. She knew she could die. Even if she didn't fall to her death, perishing in the saddle from fright was seconds away. Facing such imminent mortality made her whoop all the louder to remind herself that she was still alive.

Rio didn't falter. He took the hedges like Pegasus. He saw the wire and the thorns and the potholes that she couldn't see, tucking his legs tightly to his chest as he leaped, ears pricked the whole way. He was claiming his birthright.

Any pain lifted out of her body and mind as she raced. Crouching tight over that stretched black neck, she urged him on.

They were flying. Truly flying. Her aching legs and frozen fingers couldn't contact her brain, however hard they tried. She didn't register pain as a soft curl of flesh became trapped between her gritted teeth, twisted tighter and tighter against her broken molar as she set the compass needle of Oddlode's illuminated spire between the stallion's ears and raced for her life.

'We have to win! We have to win! Amos's heart is down there!'

Up ahead of her, like two great black walls as high as her head, were the legendary hedges, Look and Leap. Rory had disappeared behind them. She could hear his hooves thundering ahead so she knew he was clear. As she felt Rio bunch up, preparing for take-off, she saw nothing but black in front of her, swallowing her into tomb-like shadow and she closed her eyes in terror.

'Weeeeeeeeeeh!' She was jumping over the moon, her heart stopping beating, her shaking hands slipping on the reins.

She opened her eyes as they landed between the hedges, deep in the sunken track known as the coffin, Rio already lifting his front hooves and shoulders to take the second hedge as his huge quarters reached the ground after the first jump and prepared to power them upwards. This was where the midnight chase had claimed its biggest losses. Backs had broken and skulls smashed where Rio's hooves had just landed. They were jumping through lost souls.

She knew she was going to fall. In that ephemeral, heart-stopping moment between jumps – like dropping briefly off the cliff of wakefulness, or reaching the lowest bounce point of a bungee, Diana's feet floundered, their stirrups lost. Her backside was no longer tucked into the saddle, her hands had dropped the reins and her face was plunging towards Rio's black shoulders.

Twisting as she fell, she looked up and saw another horse and jockey jumping right beside her, close enough to touch. And it wasn't Firebrand in flames. Nor was it Sharon waving a gun. It wasn't a headless horseman or a ghostly cavalier.

It was Pod, crouched high over Otto's roan neck, laughing from ear to ear, his big black baby eyes sparkling from his beautiful face. As his horse leaped beside Rio, he reached out an arm and plucked her back from death as easily as a huntsman plucking a fox mask from a hound's jaws.

Still laughing, he pushed her firmly into the saddle and gave her his customary wink.

Laughing too, Diana kept her eyes wide open as they rocketed over the second hedge and hollered even louder as Rio gave it a mile of black air to land beyond a terrified sheep and charge down the hill to try to catch Rory. She didn't dare look back, but she knew Pod had gone. He'd jumped out of the coffin and was safely tucked up in bed once more.

Ahead of her, Rory was getting away.

'C'mon!' She kicked Rio on. 'Let's get him.' The surge of speed beneath her took her breath away. The fear had disappeared. Only adrenaline and surging joy flowed through her veins.

Great thousand-watt torches swept across the two horses as they galloped, distant cheers and cries of encouragement filtering through the cold night, but Diana had no sense of anything in the valley apart from her brave horse – the last of the Gunning warriors, and his unlikely rival up ahead.

Rory would have beaten Diana. He would have galloped home thirty lengths ahead. But he'd already won his personal race when he leaped the old post and rails into the secluded grounds of empty Oddlode Manse and finally saw the floodlit spire of Oddlode church. He could take a pull at last, reining his big, tired grey gelding back to little more than a trot as he saw the crowd in the floodlit churchyard, almost veiled from sight behind the cedars and yews two hundred yards away. They hadn't seen him yet.

There were hundreds of them. Rory caught his breath and laughed, eyes shining.

The Constantines were entertaining the valley again. They had lived too long with the half-cocked spectacle of Hell's Bells' regimented charity gatherings, Truffle's love life and Til's eccentricity. This was full-blooded Constantine behaviour and they loved it.

He knew he'd had an unfair head-start. Rio was the faster horse. Had they started together, the black beast would have given his beloved Whitey a clean set of heels long ago. It wasn't his race to win. He had already won by taking part. Sacrificing a heroic finish was a small price to pay for his sister's happiness.

As Diana thundered past, her hopes between her stallion's ears, Rory dropped the reins and stooped to hug White Lie's sodden grey neck. He could hear them cheering now. Great raucous, wonder-struck cheers. Someone was ringing the church bells. It was a glorious reception.

Amos was standing on the church steps, arms stretched wide.

The love of his life had blood pouring from her mouth. She had half the valley stuck to her face and sweat trickling through her eyebrows. She was the most beautiful sight he had ever seen.

Diana fell from the saddle, her legs keeling so much that each step was a mountain to climb. But his arms were waiting and she would have galloped a hundred miles and scaled a thousand rock-faces to find them. She was still flying and he was her eagle soaring alongside. An eagle that suddenly swooped to gather her up when she thought her wings had broken.

And when his arms finally wrapped around her, Diana realised she wasn't ever going to land. She was up for life.

'You're bleeding, huntress.' He looked anxiously at the red staining her lips.

'I bit my tongue – or my cheek. I don't know which,' she laughed. 'One is usually firmly stuck in the other.'

'Not any more. It'll have to make way for mine from now on, and I'm a plain-speaking bugger.'

He kissed her – blood, sweat, mud and all. He kissed the beads of ruby from her lips and laced his cool, solid tongue against her bitten, broken, speechless one. He kissed the blood back into her veins and the breath into her lungs.

'Before this year is out,' Amos told the crowd between kisses. 'I would like to invite you all back here to witness me marrying this beautiful, amazing woman whom I loved first and most and for ever. We would die for each other but never kill for each other. I think that's a solid grounding for a relationship. Diana, will you marry me?'

She nodded furiously. 'Yes, please.'

The churchyard exploded with cheers.

Rory trotted up to Mo as the villagers clapped and roared. She was still perching by her stone seraph in its moss coat. They looked like they had compared outfit notes before setting out that night, two little angels wrapped in warm green tweed.

He slid from the saddle with considerably more dexterity than his sister had managed, standing up tall as he landed – a noble knight in mud-splattered black armour.

Anke took the grey horse and whisked him away without Rory noticing, joining Faith who was walking Rio around. They both watched worriedly as Rory dropped down on one knee at Mo's feet.

'Oh, poor man,' Anke breathed.

'He is so perfect.' Faith wanted to weep. 'She doesn't know what she's missing out on.' She took discreet text photo to send Carly.

But Rory was just trying the laces on his hunt boots as he gathered his breath. He looked up at her eventually, squinting through the lumps of mud trapped in his lashes.

'You win some, you lose some.'

Mo bit her lip hard as she smiled down at him through her tears. 'You'll find her. She's just not me.'

'I know. Can't help wishing she was. But if wishes were horses, I'd have even more of the buggers to feed.'

A couple of tears seeped out as Mo reached out a tiny hand and cupped his muddy cheek.

Then they both looked up in alarm.

Whoever was ringing the church bells was losing the beat big time. Crash, clank, boing, thump. The discords rang out like a maddened hunchback playing Hang Loose on the ropes.

Even the exhausted horses started back in alarm, looking up to the bell tower.

'Granville!' Gladys appeared from the crowd, waggling her brolly at the spire. 'Get down from there!'

'Good God.' Rory stepped back. 'Granville Gates is on the roof.'

Clambering out from the tiny opening between two gargoyles, Granville surveyed his audience, waiting for the bells to die down. It took quite some time. Five hundred kilos of swinging metal in various sizes didn't stop quickly. Every time he opened his mouth he was drowned out by a deafening peal.

It gave the crowd time to regroup, gathering around the base of the tower.

'It never bloody stops round here, does it?' Graham shook his head in astonishment.

Faith squeaked in surprise as she recognised Toad-eyes, the man who had saved her from being run over on the day of the wedding. She'd thought *he* was the ghost.

As the last bell finally came to rest, Granville could finally speak.

'Tonight,' he boomed. 'I have peace at last. They's back together, the young 'uns.' He peered at Diana and Amos while a small contingent of Oddlode youth giggled at the notion of the couple being young.

'I was shooting deer. The boy was useless at trapping them, so I used to shoot the beasts and put them in the traps for him. Shot a big stag that day – size of a racehorse he was. Took a few to take him down. One of them caught the Fireman. I din' mean to kill him. Stupid bugger was running through the woods right behind the steer. Running from the lake he was – he'd been there with the pretty one. I'd seen them. Thought he was taking her out in the boat. Don't know why he was running so fast. Ran straight into my gunshot. Caught him right in the head. Only wish I'd shot the venison as clean.

'I left them lying together. Din' seem right to take the big stag for the pot after that. He looked like he was guarding him. So I went and opened the big house up and made it pretty for the young 'uns. Thought it was only right. But the silly fools didn't want to live there. Ran away they did. I thought I'd made things right. Ungrateful beggars. Put the money in the cellar after that, locked it all up. Kept an eye. Nest egg for me and my Gladys. Some little bastard tried to steal it last night, but I saw him off, good and proper! Hid the pretty one's trunk in there. Thought it was funny. Then the girl came and ruined it all, setting light to everything. Like the Fireman had come back. Thought I'd lost my mind all over again. Saw her run away. Good job for her the police din' come 'til later, I thought. Big girl, she was. Couldn't run faster than an old woman. Took her ages to get up to Flint's Coppice.'

'The arsonist's still alive?' one of the Wycks gasped.

'No, the Fireman isn't alive,' Granville swung perilously from the stone crenellations, 'and he isn't a ghost neither, see. He's just a pile of old bones in the woods. Dead as the dodo maze,' he cackled. 'Never found him and the stag again, mind, but you can lose your soul in them woods. Lost so many traps there I can't remember.'

'That's all very well,' Gladys screeched up at him. 'But you must get down off that roof, Granville!'

'Straight away, my love!' he chortled happily. 'Tonight, I am coming home. All's put to rights and I can have my wife back in my bed at last.'

Turning pale, Gladys clutched a stone cross for support.

Amos and Diana laughed as they stole away across the graveyard and into the night.

'She'll wish she never said that.' He gripped her to his side as they crept past the yews.

'Like you'll wish you never invited the Wycks to our wedding.' She smiled up into his eyes.

Sitting on the family crypt, Til Constantine packed her pipe with home-grown dope and caught the eye of a snarling gargoyle above.

Every year, without fail, the oldest Gunning stag had visited her garden and wrecked her vegetable patch. She had threatened him with everything from scarecrows to fireworks with no success, amazed at his longevity. Next time he visited, he would find a candle-lit feast laid out. She might not move to Scotland after all. She should see the first of the new Flint bloodstock line born at Foxrush.

She winked at the gargoyle as she lit her pipe. He winked back.

Chuckling, Til poked out her tongue at his cheek.

Epilogue

The Manor flower-beds and borders were out of control. Eager to impress, the Bellings' new gardener had over-ordered late planting bulbs and had subsequently crammed them into every available corner. Now crocuses, daffodils, tulips, hyacinths and irises had burst out in happy, clashing, colourful clusters in the most unexpected of places. The Manor's grounds looked as though they had been used as a crash-landing pad for a vast flock of mutant parrots.

'I cut three hundred heads for the nursing home last week, and it still resembles a municipal park,' Hell's Bells told Truffle tetchily as she clipped tablecloths to trestle tables on the croquet lawn.

She and Sir St John were hosting a spectacular spring tea party to celebrate not only the restoration of the Manor and the River Folly, but the birth of their grandson, Garfield.

'He's a classic Constantine,' Truffle congratulated her sister as they paused to peer into an off-road three-wheeler parked on the terrace. 'Just look at that bone structure.'

Hell's Bells smiled indulgently and jiggled the buggy. 'And the grey eyes. Just like Daddy's.'

Two very blue and very suspicious eyes peered back from a face as square and chubby as a marshmallow, as two equally chubby legs kicked furiously in their stays, jettisoning hand-made felt booties designed to look like bumble-bees.

'I think he'll be a natural in the saddle.'

'Bound to break lots of hearts,' Truffle sighed.

'Little bugger needs changing.' Til loomed between them and hoisted Garfield on to her shoulder to go in search of nappies. 'I'll just hose him down and we'll be right back.'

'Not a natural mother.' Truffle wrinkled her nose.

'That's what comes of never having one of your own,' Hell's Bells agreed. 'I do hope Ellen gets back soon. Til's never changed a nappy in her life. She'll probably try to Velcro a dressage boot to his little rump.'

Both were livid that Ellen and Spurs had asked Til to mind Garfield for an hour.

'Jolly bad show sloping off on your big day,' Truffle sympathised. 'What is it they're doing?'

'Not quite sure,' Hell's Bells admitted through pursed lips. 'They said something about another garden party, although I'd know of any others locally. But they did promise they'd be back in plenty of time for the official River Folly opening.'

'Heartless, abandoning the little one here,' Truffle tutted with no sense of irony. 'Ah – here's my lovely Nord and our favourite sinner. Good lord, what *is* Nanny wearing?'

Both turned and smiled with fixed horror as Ingmar wheeled Nanny Crump on to the terrace.

Now that she was 'infamous', Nanny had taken to dressing the part. Today's ensemble involved a lot of frothy coral lace, a pair of white gloves and an ostrich-feather hat perched racily over her eyes.

'Let me see the little man,' she demanded, cataract-dimmed eyes peering through her hat plumes at the empty baby buggy. 'Is he underweight?'

Before the sisters could respond, Gladys Gates trotted out of the house waving a clipboard. 'We are all ready for a hundred guests at three-thirty, your ladyship.'

'Well done. Is St John still watching the racing?'

'I fear so.'

'Pull the plug on the aerial booster again will you, Gladys?'

'Certainly, your ladyship.'

'Never fails,' Hell's Bells told Truffle. 'He just thumps the television a few times and gives up. Total Luddite, bless him. How are you, Ingmar?'

Ingmar looked confused. 'Should I know you, madam?'

'Not at all. I am your sister-in-law. We hardly know one another. The same was true of all your predecessors.' Giving her sister a hard look, she marched into the house to check on Til and her precious grandson.

'Is she a friend of yours, my darling?' Ingmar asked Truffle.

'Vague acquaintance,' Truffle gurgled, patting his hand. 'Shall we take a tour of the flower-beds? They are rather splendid. Granville the new gardener did them. Bell thinks he's the next Dairmud Gavin.'

They left Nanny poking a suspicious finger into the buggy. 'You know I don't think there's a baby in here at all . . .'

'I thought we were going to the garden party at the Manor?' Graham asked Anke in confusion as they climbed the hill to Springlode in her new Mercedes.

'We are – but Diana called at the last minute and asked us to another little gathering beforehand. The children will be there too.'

'At the yard?'

'No, *kaereste*. We're not going to Upper Springlode. We are going somewhere you've never been. I think it's about time I took you there.'

Rory slipped his feet from the stirrups, hooked his legs over the saddle flaps and lolled back on White Lies' rump, staring at the very white clouds in the very blue sky as he lit a cigarette.

'I wish you wouldn't do that,' Faith grumbled as she bounced around beside them on Rio.

'What? Smoke?'

'No – lie back like that. It would only take a car backfiring or something and you could get killed.'

'Yeah – cars backfire around here all the time.' Rory admired a cloud shaped like a pair of giant breasts.

Scowling, Faith sat through a few spins and bunny hops as Rio let it be known that he recognised the turf beneath his feet and it was definitely for galloping.

They were on Gunning land, skirting Heaven Hill as they rode the horses beneath the outer canopy of the woods.

'What do you know about this hidden garden thing?'

'Not a lot – just that my sister and Amos want us all there.'

'I *am* invited, aren't I?'

'Sure. You're all invited. The Brakespear clan.'

She scowled some more, having wanted him to make her feel special and tell her that she, Faith, was specially invited because he said so – not just point out that she was a part of a general family invitation.

'Will Mo be there?'

He sat up again and shrugged. 'Maybe. Not sure.'

'What about Dilly?' she persisted with the theme, hating herself for feeling so jealous.

'Think so – Pheely and Pixie are certainly going to be there.'

'Do you think you two will ever get back together?'

'God, no.'

That, at least, cheered up Faith.

They rode on in silence for a bit, but she couldn't resist picking over hot coals. 'What about Sharon. Do you miss her?'

'S?' he snorted. 'She hardly lit up my life when she set light to my yard.'

'Is it really true that she got away from the Hall that night?'

'So they say.'

'So she could come back and set light to any of us while we sleep?'

'I think she might be keeping a low profile for a while, don't you?'

Faith mulled this over. 'We were quite close friends for a bit.'

'Mmm?' Rory was lying back on Whitey's rump once more, smoking his cigarette.

'We used to talk about you.'

'Oh, joy.'

She sat tight as a pheasant reared from just yards away, squawking furiously. Rio almost went into orbit, Whitey barely batted an eye.

I will marry you Rory Midwinter, she pledged silently. You might not know it yet, but you will love me one day and we will marry.

'So what did you and S used to say about me?' he asked eventually, his ego getting the better of him.

'That you were a jerk.'

He laughed so much he fell off.

Faith grinned as she watched him dust himself down and remount. It might take months – years even – to persuade him that she was his dream match. But she would get there eventually. He hardly even saw her as female right now. Well, just you wait, Rory. I will break you down a little at a time until one day you wake up and find yourself loving me as much as I love you.

Rory gazed thoughtfully up at his cloud as he relit his bent cigarette. He did secretly miss Sharon's breasts.

'I think I might develop a taste for buxom brunettes,' he mused out loud. 'Justine Jones is very pretty. I wonder if she's free for the hunt ball?'

Faith closed her eyes in horror. Dyeing her hair again was no obstacle to this new development, but breasts? Her stepfather would never pay for those.

Ellen and Spurs walked through the gateway in the copper beech hedge and stopped dead.

'I had no idea this place existed.'

'God, it's magical.'

The garden cast a spell over everyone. The Brakespears and their children, who were sitting on the wall that ran around a fountain full of naked nymphs tipping water over one another's nubile bodies, were no longer a wealthy stockbroker-belt family. They seemed to belong to the garden along with the statuary and climbing ivy. They were a family of beautiful, blonde amazons with golden skin and a natural, loving force creating a halo around the dancing nymphs. Anke and Graham were lacing their fingers together and sharing a private joke, Magnus and the Three Disgraces dipping their feet and sharing a spliff, Chad and Mim Lampeter pinching each other's upper arms and sharing a tube of Smarties.

Diana was playing hide and seek with Digby around the other fountains, pausing every time she passed Amos to kiss him as he looked anxiously through his notes. Black hair tousled, skin bronzed and eyes gleaming, she was a garden goddess worshipping her noble warrior.

'Is this some sort of engagement party for your sister and Amos?' Spurs asked Rory as he stepped into the garden behind him, a floppy-haired blonde knight in breeches and long boots.

'No idea – it's all bloody last minute. I hope there's something decent to drink. Your mother is only serving Lapsang Souchong at Oddlode Manor, by which time I hope to be lapsing into song if not unconsciousness. Jesus, this place is amazing.'

He looked around, too mesmerised by the sunken paradise of stone dryads, goblins, fairies and fountains to remember to grumble. It was a magical landscape of frolicking water-babies and carefree adults. Even Hally's puppies were here, gambolling around in a rosemary border with Ellen, who was wearing a floppy straw hat and a gypsy dress and looked like something from a 1970s' soft rock video.

'Have I died and gone to heaven?' he laughed when he spotted two magnums of champagne cooling in one of the fountains.

Faith bounced up behind the cousins. 'I've just put the horses out in that paddock and there's an old black mare in there – I'm sure she's in foal. Blimey!' She gasped as she saw Spurs, six foot of dishevelled and freckled testosterone in frayed jeans and a white shirt, and then she saw the garden for the first time. 'Blimey.'

'Is she your new girlfriend?' Spurs teased his cousin as she dashed shyly past him and raced towards her family, shrieking as the cupid squirted her.

'Christ, no – she's just some drippy kid that rides out at the yard. Oh, look – Dils *is* here, bless her.'

He went to kiss Dilly, who was bouncing half-brother Basil in her arms and showing him a naked bronze lady in the centre of one of the fountains with water streaming from her head.

'Hi, Roar,' she grinned. 'You okay?'

'Gorgeous as ever.' He kissed the baby on the head. 'Know what all this is in aid of?'

'No idea, but Mummy is convinced Amos and Diana are going to perform some sort of exorcism against Firebrand. She and Pixie are decked in crosses – look.'

It was true. Like Joan of Arc and a loyal acolyte, Pheely and her friend were stooped over with the weight of decorative crucifixes dangling from their necks as they nosed around furtively. They looked like two very nervous hippy nuns.

Finding herself sitting on a stone bench beside Spurs' wife Ellen, Faith cuddled a big, gangly puppy on her knee and eyed Dilly and Rory jealously.

'I knew we should have brought Garfield,' Ellen was saying as she watched Basil, a more mewly baby than her own gurgling newborn, enjoying the magical scene. 'But Spurs said we had to leave him at home in case any ghosts were wafting around.'

'There aren't really ghosts here, are there?' Faith shuddered.

'Course not.' Ellen patted her arm with a kind smile. 'Spurs is just hopelessly over-protective. Oh, look, something's happening.'

Amos was clearing his throat to get everyone's attention while Diana raced around handing out brightly coloured plastic flutes of champagne.

'Thank God.' Rory grabbed two and settled on the fountain wall beside the Three Disgraces.

'I know a couple of you have been here before, but most of you will be seeing it for the first time.' Amos' deep, growling voice was mesmerising. 'It's a very special place and we're very glad we can share it with you. We found out just this week that two good friends of ours sneaked off to get married without telling anyone – no, not your father, Anke. We all know that there's a lot of doubt about whether he and Truffle *did* marry on that cruise liner.'

Graham's big boom of laughter was quickly curtailed by a swift kick on the ankle.

'And no,' Amos went on, 'it wasn't Diana and I. Not yet.' His dark green eyes sparked as Diana joined him.

'This rotten pair weren't going to tell us at all.' Diana took up the tale cheerfully. 'But we think they deserve a lovely celebration, even though they are far too secretive for their own good. And so today we have invited all of you here without telling *them*.' She smiled wickedly, checking her watch. 'They should be here any minute – we know they'll be stopping by to look at the Pleasure Garden. We've seen them here every day this week. And so if you'd like to all come with me and hide in the dodo maze ready to surprise them . . .'

*　　*　　*

At the Manor, Hell's Bells was very agitated by the non-appearance of her son and daughter-in-law, and also of her nephew and niece. 'Where can they have got to? Have they no sense of family priorities? Sir St John will be speaking soon. He wants to make a reference to the ghastly Firebrand business and I really need Diana to help me dissuade him. Not the right occasion at all. Always could wind him round her little finger, that girl . . .' Still barking furiously, she marched across her croquet lawn to find her husband and brief him once more.

Left behind with Nanny, Til bounced Garfield on her knee and admired his round pink cheeks.

'Do you think he's dead or alive, Nanny?'

'Looks like a perfectly healthy baby to me.'

'I was talking about William.'

'Oh, Firebrand,' Nanny tutted. 'I rather think Granville must have shot him when he shot that stag, although thank heavens the police aren't pressing charges.'

'Are you sure he's dead?'

'Well, nobody can be absolutely sure, can they? But he would have tried to contact you if he were still alive, dear, I'm certain.'

'Yes, I rather think he would.' Til rubbed her nose against Garfield's to make him smile. 'And that girl? The one who claimed to be his daughter?'

'That wretched child,' Nanny shook her head. 'Causing such trouble. I have no doubt she will turn up again. Her sort always do. She is a Wyck after all.'

'Nanny!'

'Sorry, dear.'

Visiting the Pleasure Garden each day had become a ritual, as together they wandered between the dappled pools of light, stopping to kiss by every gargoyle, every carved stone and bronze statue.

'I love you.' He cupped her face in his hands and smiled. 'You make me good.'

'No, *you* make you good,' she laughed. 'I just make you happy. It's all I ever want to do.'

'*Touché.*'

They didn't hear the happy, sentimental sighs coming from the other side of the box hedge.

Mo looked up into his eyes – once black windows into his soul and later shuttered totally from her. Now they were bright and warm and open, dancing with desire and mirth. He had grown his hair longer so that it fell over his forehead and cheeks in wavy black curtains, but the red scarring on his face was impossible to hide, still set out in an angry relief pattern. The doctors said that it would always disfigure him, stealing the beauty that had once stolen hearts. Pod didn't mind the scars. He said they would always remind him how lucky he was to be alive and to be with Mo.

And she still found him more than beautiful. She could still sit up in bed hour after hour each night just to watch him sleeping.

Diana and Amos had let them have one of the Estate cottages. They had their fairytale thatched cottage, after all, although how long they could stay there was uncertain as legal ownership of the Estate was contested through the courts. For now, until it was settled, Diana remained its custodian as Til had once been, and Amos remained its guardian angel as *he* always had been. He guarded the gates and preserved the woods and parkland, and was now training Pod to do the same.

'Can we always come here to the garden?' she asked him now. 'Whatever happens?'

'Always,' he reassured her, starting to undress her.

She reached for his belt. 'We can make love here amongst the fountains even when we are very old?'

'Even if I have to install a stairlift.' He kissed her small pink nipple.

'You don't think making love here will wake Firebrand's ghost?'

'Never know until we try . . .'

Behind the box hedges, Diana had lined up the surprise wedding reception guests ready to leap out after Amos had checked that the time was right.

He turned back from the entrance to the dodo maze wearing a blush for the first time in his life.

'I think we might be rather late for your aunt's party,' he told Diana.

'What are you talking about?' She bustled past and then leaped back behind him with a squeak. 'Good God.'

Together, they hastily ushered their guests through the maze to its centre.

'Slight change of plan,' Diana told them, plonking her champagne magnums on the sundial. 'It seems the bride and groom are enjoying their conjugal rights.'

'What are conjugal rights, Mummy?' asked Mim.

'Something that one day, my darling, I hope you enjoy very, very much. Anyone want to see the revolving mirror chamber?'

★   ★   ★

When Hell's Bells errant guests finally joined the throng at the tea party, they were high on champagne and happily ran amok amid Gladys's lemon cakes, cream meringues and fruit loaf.

'Those woods have been up to their old tricks again.' Til shook her head in amusement and went to a quiet corner of the shrubbery to smoke her pipe. 'Dear Falstaff can still host a first-class party in his playpen when he wants to.

'Of course he's dead,' she told herself firmly, watching with a sad smile as a fox sneaked out from behind the camellias and trotted past her. 'Nanny is right. If he was still alive he would have let me know by now. Nanny is always right.'

As the Manor tea party headed towards the cocktail hour with the Lodes valley revellers showing no signs of tiring, nobody noticed the antique rug in the orangery starting to smoulder . . .